THE LOAN SHARK DUET

DUBIOUS (BOOK 1) & CONSENT (BOOK 2)

CHARMAINE PAULS

Published by Charmaine Pauls

Montpellier, 34090, France

www.charmainepauls.com

Published in France

This is a work of fiction. Names, characters, and incidents depicted in this book are products of the author's imagination or are used fictitiously. Any resemblance to actual events, locales, organizations, or persons, living or dead, is entirely coincidental and beyond the intent of the author or the publisher. No part of this book may be reproduced in any form or by any electronic or mechanical means, including photocopying, recording, information storage and retrieval systems, without written permission from the author, except for the use of brief quotations in a book review.

Copyright © 2017 by Charmaine Pauls

All rights reserved.

Cover design by Kellie Dennis (www.bookcoverbydesign.co.uk)

ISBN: 978-2-9561031-3-4 (e-Book)

ISBN: 979-8-6087353-1-8 (Print)

❦ Created with Vellum

DUBIOUS

THE LOAN SHARK DUET (BOOK 1)

1

Valentina

I never take the yellow glow of a light bulb or the blue staccato flicker of the television screen for granted. Looking for signs of life is an ingrained habit for people like me, people who live in fear. Already from the corner, I strain my neck to look at our floor. Then I stop dead. The rectangle of our window stares down at me. Black. Dark.

Oh, my God.

Charlie!

My palms turn clammy. I wipe them on my tunic and sprint up the remaining stairs to the second floor, almost tripping on the last step. A jerk on the handle confirms the door is locked. Thank God. Someone didn't break in, attack Charlie, and leave him for dead. I drop my keys twice before I fit them in the lock. From inside, Puff starts barking.

The damn lock mechanism resists. One of these days, the flimsy nickel is going to break off in the door. I force until the key turns. In my rush to get inside, I stumble over Puff who runs out to greet me. He scurries away with a yelp and his tail between his legs.

The darkness is menacing. Flicking on the lights doesn't expel the emptiness or the sick feeling pushing up in my throat. A hollowness settles in my chest as I take in the bowl of half eaten Rice Krispies and the glass of milk on the table.

"Charlie!"

Even if I know what I'll find, I run to the bathroom.

No one.

"Dammit."

Leaning on the wall, I cover my eyes and allow myself one second to gather strength. Something wet and warm touches my calf. Puff stares at me with his hopeful, sad eyes, his tail wagging in blissful ignorance.

"It's all right, baby." I pet his wiry hair, needing the reassurance of his warm little body more than he needs my caress.

Lightning rips through the sky, the sound lashing out a beat later. I close the curtains. Puff hates thunderstorms. After feeding him, I lock up and knock next door, but, like ours, Jerry's flat is dark.

Damn him. Jerry promised me.

It's a wild guess, but I'm betting on Napoli's being Jerry's favorite hangout. It's the only place he ever goes.

The rickety framework clangs under my trainers as I charge down the two flights of stairs. It's after eight. Having a car thief as a neighbor keeps me protected to an extent, but only from criminals lower in the hierarchy than Jerry. There are the drug dealers, mafia, and gangs to be reckoned with. I remain alert as I go, checking the abandoned houses, parked cars, and alleys. Staying under the streetlights, at least the ones not broken, I walk like my mom taught me––like I'm not a victim.

The brewing storm dissolves, taking with it the rain that would've washed away the neighborhood's stench and soot. It's summer, but the smoke from the cooking fires gives the

Johannesburg air a thick, wintry smell as I cross from Berea into Hillbrow. Most buildings in Hillbrow no longer have electricity. When crime took over, people who could afford municipal services moved to the suburbs, turning the city center into a ghost town. Shortly after, the homeless and others with more sinister goals invaded the deserted skyscrapers. The door and windowless buildings look like skulls with empty sockets and gaping mouths. Doors have long since been used for firewood. What is left is the carcass of a city. The vultures have picked the meat off the bones, and now there are only the scavengers who prey on each other, and if I'm lucky tonight, not on me.

The walk to Napoli's takes almost forty-five minutes. I'm scared, and my legs ache from standing in the veterinary clinic all day, but worry over my brother outweighs fear and exhaustion. By the time I get to the club, I'm close to collapsing. It's not the first time Charlie has disappeared. From experience, I know the police won't help. They have their hands full with murder cases and so many missing persons they don't have enough space on milk cartons to post everyone. Anyway, most of them are corrupt. I'll more likely get gang-raped by officials in a police cell than get assistance. I have to find my brother myself.

A group of teenagers in dirty vests sniffing glue at the corner shout insults.

The tallest climbs to his feet, his skin shiny with perspiration and the whites of his eyes like saucers. "Yo, white bitch. What ya doin' on my block?"

"Hey!" A meaty bouncer in a T-shirt with a Napoli's logo shuts them up with a look.

The bouncer doesn't stop me when I push through the entrance, but I feel his eyes burn at the back of my head as I walk down the black-painted corridor into the brightly lit interior. A song from a local rave-rock band blares from oversized speakers. The walls are covered in street art, the day-glo colors popping off the bricks under the fluorescent lights. The club smells of poppers and disco machine smoke. There's every kind of generalization inside, from the dark-suited Portuguese to the gold-chained Nigerians. Half-naked women do the rounds, most of them looking spaced out.

Please let them be here.

I run my gaze over the bar and the roulette tables at the back. On the left, raucous cheering is directed at the flat screen where a horse race is taking place. The spectators go quiet when they notice me. One of the men touches his buckle and widens his stance. A sign says the money lending office is upstairs. There's a queue outside the door. That's where gamblers and people who can't make the rent or pay off the mafia sign away their lives, pledging interest of up to a hundred and fifty percent on loans that will literally cost them an arm and a leg.

The men playing darts turn their heads as I pass. Shit. I'm getting increasingly anxious. As panic is about to seize me, I spot Jerry's orange afro in a circle of heads at one of the card tables. Charlie sits in the chair next to him. Almost crying with relief, I push people with plastic beer cups in their hands out of the way to reach my brother. Charlie's curls fall over his forehead, and his eyes are scrunched up in concentration. He's wearing a Spiderman T-shirt and his flannel pajama bottoms. The attire makes him look vulnerable despite his age and bulky frame. Anyone can see he doesn't belong here. How dare the sick son of a bitch who runs this cesspool allow my brother inside?

"How could you?" I say in Jerry's ear.

He jumps and gives me a startled look. "What are you doing here?"

Charlie is studying the cards in his hand. He hasn't noticed me, yet.

I press a hand to my forehead and count to five. "You said you'd watch him for me."

"I *am* watching him."

"He's not supposed to be here."

"He's a grown man."

"My brother is not accountable for his actions, and you know it."

Charlie looks up. "Va–Val! I'm wi–winning."

For now, my focus remains on Jerry. Alcohol and gambling are not his only addictions. "What did you give him?"

"Relax." He gives me an exasperated shrug. "Orange juice, that's all."

"Come, Charlie."

I take my brother's arm, but the croupier snatches my wrist.

"He's not going anywhere until his debt is paid."

My mouth drops open. How could Jerry let this happen? He knows I barely make ends meet. I jerk my arm from the dealer's grip. "How much?"

"Four hundred."

"Four hundred rand!" That's almost half of my weekly wage.

"Four hundred *thousand*."

The strength leaves my legs. Letting go of Charlie, I brace myself with my palms on the tabletop. We may as well carve dead on our foreheads.

"It's impossible." I can't process that amount. "In one night?"

The croupier regards me strangely. "Charlie's a regular. He's been running a tab, and his time's up."

"Jerry?" I look at him for an explanation, a solution, to tell me it's a joke, anything, but he gnaws on his bottom lip and looks away.

I slam down a fist, rattling the plastic chips. "Look at me!"

The table goes quiet, but not because of my outburst. The men's heads are turned toward the landing on the upper floor. When I follow their gazes, I can't miss the man who stands under the light, his hands gripping the rail. He wears a dark suit, like the Portuguese, but he's anything but a generalization. He's nothing short of a monster.

His body is muscular. Too big. There's not enough space in the room for him. He drowns everything in power and dominance. He's not young, but he isn't old, either. Rather than defining his age, his years give him the distinguished edge of men with experience. Thick, black hair falls messily over his forehead, the wisps brushing his ears. His features are rogue, wild, and uncompromising. The lines running from his nose to his mouth are deeply etched. They're the kind of lines men with hard, rough lives wear. A ghastly network of scars runs from his left eyebrow to his cheek. Under the disfigured patchwork, his complexion is tanned. The ruggedness of his skin gives the impression of being marred by bullets. A short-trimmed beard and moustache cover some of his imperfections, but the damage is too vast to hide. It's a face you don't want to see in the dark and definitely not in your dreams. It's a face that stares straight at me.

Heat of the scary kind crawls over my skin. When I look into his eyes, it's as if a bucket of ice is emptied down my shirt. An unwelcome shiver contracts my skin, and my fear turns from hot to cold. His irises are blue like the far-off glaziers I've only seen in pictures. Everything about him seems foreign. Out of place. Dangerous. He's the kind of bad that's even out of Napoli's league.

"Fucken fuck," Jerry mumbles when he finds his voice. "Gabriel Louw."

I've lived here long enough to recognize the name. His family runs Napoli's. If Hillbrow is the crime capital, Gabriel Louw is the king of the money lords. They call him The Breaker. He's a loan shark, and I've heard stories about him that make my blood freeze with their brutality.

The best time to run is when your opponent is distracted. If we have any chance of getting out of here alive, it's now, while Gabriel holds the attention of the room with unyielding demand. Taking Charlie against his will won't work. He weighs twice as much as me, and when he gets obstinate, he's an unmovable, dead weight.

"Let's get an ice cream," I whisper in his ear, "but you have to come quietly."

Charlie knows about being quiet. We practice it enough times when we hide from the mafia, pretending we're not home.

Charlie gets up like I silently prayed he would and allows me to lead him to the door. I pinch my eyes shut and wait for someone to shout, grab us, shoot, or all three, but when I glance back Gabriel lifts a palm, and the bouncer steps aside for us to exit.

Outside, I suck in a breath of polluted air. Clutching my brother's arm, I walk him back to our side of the tracks, which isn't much better, but it's all we have. He talks, and I let his voice soothe me, trying not to think. When we're home, I'll go over what happened. For now, I'm too preoccupied with lurking dangers.

At Three Sisters, I buy Charlie a cone with vanilla ice cream dunked in caramel, his favorite. It's not until we round the corner of our building that trouble strikes again. Tiny leans in the entrance, smoking a joint. When he sees us, he straightens, takes a last drag, and flicks the butt into the gutter.

"Well, well." He wipes his hands over his dreadlocks and saunters over. "Hello, sunshine. Tiny was looking for you." There's an edge to his voice. "Where were you?"

"Ice crea-cream," Charlie says.

"Is that so?" Tiny stops short of me. He's not Nigerian or Zimbabwean like most of the people on our block, but Zambian. His skinny frame towers over me, his black skin lost in the darkness of the night, except for the whites of his eyes and teeth. "You've got money to spoil your ol' brother here, but not for Tiny's tax?"

He calls himself the Tax Collector. He's not the landlord, but he gathers 'tax' on the rent from everyone who lives in our building. He's a mini-mafia within a bigger mafia, but dealing with him means I don't have to deal with the bigger mafia, and he's the lessor of two evils.

Putting his nose in my hair, he sniffs. "You smell like smoke. Club smoke. Who were you with?"

Tiny pretends he owns me. Mostly, he pretends I like him. In reality, he's a coward, but he still has the power to hurt me. I know this from a split lip and blue eye.

"You're dating now?"

"It's none of your business." Charlie's key is not on the cord around his neck. I'll have to ask Jerry about it later. I fish my key from my bag and hand it to Charlie. "Go up and lock the door."

Charlie takes the key, but doesn't move.

"Go on," I urge. "I'll be right up."

"O-okay." Charlie takes two steps and stops.

I give him an encouraging smile. "Quickly. I don't want you to catch a cold."

Tiny grabs hold of my hair. I close my eyes. *Please, Charlie. Obey.* I don't want him to see this. When I lift my lashes, my brother is climbing the stairs on the side of the building.

"Got the money?" Tiny pulls on my ponytail.

The bond on our flat is fully paid. My parents paid cash for the property years ago before anyone could predict how crime and dilapidation would render their investment worthless.

"We don't pay rent," I bit out. This means nothing to Tiny, but I have to try. God knows why, but I try every time.

"You still owe." He grins, flashing a row of straight teeth. "Tiny can't let you stay without paying tax. What example will that be for the others? Give it up, Valentina."

I freeze. "Don't you dare say my name."

He scoffs. "That's right, because you're my bitch." He yanks on my hair. "Ain't it so, *bitch*?"

"Go to hell."

"Now, now. That's no way to speak to Tiny." He clicks his tongue. "Who's gonna protect you if Tiny ain't around?" He tilts his head. "Won't ask you again. Where's Tiny's money?"

I swallow. "I'll have it by the end of the month."

"You know the rules. The fifteenth is payday."

"Please, Tiny." Tears burn at the back of my eyes. A cold weight presses on my heart.

In the middle of the dirty road, he pushes me down to my knees in the gravel, the stones digging into my skin. His eyes take on a feverish light as he unties the string of his sweatpants and lets them fall to his ankles.

"If you bite again, you'll walk away with more than a shiner. This time, I'll break your arm."

Taking the root of his dick in one hand, he grips my hair in the other and guides my mouth to his cock. Disgust wells in my throat.

He pushes against my lips. "Suck me, white bitch."

I don't do anything of the kind. I tune out of the moment and become an empty shell. It's a routine he knows well. He lets go of his penis to catch my jaw, squeezing painfully on the joints until my mouth opens of its own accord. Then he simply uses me, pumping and shoving until I gag. Tears roll over my cheeks. The saltiness slips into my mouth, mixing with the taste of sweat and filth. Mercifully, like always, Tiny comes fast. Not even a minute later, he ejaculates with a grunt and shoots his load into my mouth. When he pulls out, panting like a pig, I turn my head to the side and spit.

He chuckles. "One of these days, you're gonna swallow."

I wipe my mouth with the back of my hand. "When you're pretty and your parents are rich."

"Come on, baby." He pulls me up by the arm, his dick hanging limp between us. "Give Tiny a kiss. Let Tiny taste himself on that useless mouth of yours, because you sure as fuck don't know how to suck cock."

"Let go." I jerk free and snatch my bag up from where it has fallen on the ground.

His laugh follows me down the road as I run to our flat, hating myself as much as I hate him.

Jerry leans on our door as I come up the stairs. He looks away, avoiding my eyes. He must've left Napoli's shortly after us. That means he slipped past me in the street while Tiny got off in my mouth.

"You're a scumbag." I try to push him aside, but he doesn't budge.

"Val…"

"Did you get a kick out of watching?"

He shoves his hands into his pockets. "I'm sorry."

"For being a peeping Tom or dragging Charlie to Napoli's?"

"I couldn't resist the temptation. A Napoli's VIP pass doesn't happen every day."

"Four hundred thousand rand, Jerry."

"We'll sort it. Don't sweat."

"Right." The only way to *sort it* is to disappear, and we have nowhere to go. "How long has this been going on?"

He scratches his head and has the decency to look guilty. "A few months."

"You dragged Charlie out there at night, without my permission?"

"Come on, Val." Jerry braces his shoulder on the door. "I said I'm sorry."

I knock for Charlie to open. I'm physically and mentally too exhausted to fight now. "Whatever."

I cook and clean for Jerry to keep an eye on Charlie while I work, and although Jerry is a thief, he's not physically mean, at least not to Charlie.

After a while, when Charlie doesn't open, Jerry takes Charlie's key from his pocket and hands it to me. Puff barks as I unlock the door. He waits with a wagging tail.

"Good night, Jerry."

"Can I come in?"

"It's late. I need to study." I use the excuse even if I know there's no way I'll focus on a textbook tonight, but it's the quickest way to get rid of Jerry. Otherwise, he'll stay until four in the morning.

"Oh, come on. Just an hour."

I close and lock the door on his plea, waiting until his shoes shuffle down the landing. I brush my teeth three times before I fix

Charlie scrambled eggs and toast for dinner, put him to bed, and settle down on the sleeper couch with Puff.

Sleep doesn't come. I think of Charlie and the handsome fifteen year-old boy he'd been. He was one of those all-rounders who was good at sports and first in his class. He was my big brother. My hero. Two years younger than Charlie, I was in primary school when he went to high school. He fetched me when the bell went at the end of the day, carried my schoolbag, took my hand, and walked me to ballet practice. We didn't tell my parents he made a deal with Miss Paula to work in her garden so I could carry on dancing. If they knew, my father would've demanded he worked for money to buy *necessities*, those necessities being booze and cigarettes. Charlie helped me fit the ballet shoes Miss Paula lent me and waited the hour the dance practice lasted before walking me home to fix me a sandwich. He could've hung out with his friends, but he didn't. He took care of me.

If the accident hadn't happened, if I didn't want a stupid piece of chocolate cake that night, Charlie would've been Charles. My brother would've grown into the man he was born to be. Like every night, I weep into my pillow, shedding bitter tears that won't help one damn bit. Brain damage is irreparable.

PUFF CRIES AT THE DOOR, letting me know he needs to go. The sun is up, but it's barely five. I wait downstairs on the cracked concrete while he does his business against a dead tree and throw a stick for him to fetch a couple of times. Beside himself with joy, he trips over his paws to lay the broken branch at my feet. Puff is always a happy dog. One morning, yelping coming from a garden trashcan alerted me. I pulled out a starved, dirty, flea-ridden puppy. To this day, Puff is scared of trashcans.

He's not done playing, but I have to call Kris and tell her I won't make it to work today. I hate leaving her in the lurch, but I've got to figure out what to do. Four hundred thousand rand isn't going away. Maybe I can explain about Charlie's condition at Napoli's. Maybe if Jerry backs me up, we stand a chance. Napoli's is part of the big fish. They make mince of petty criminals like Jerry, but he's a regular, no less with a VIP pass. They feed on addicts like him. They need his business.

Back inside, Charlie is up. He offers me a smile that breaks my heart, because it's a smile that hasn't grown beyond fifteen years. Ruffling his hair, I turn to the kitchenette so he won't see the tears in my eyes. I call Kris, but her phone goes straight onto voicemail. Perhaps she's in the shower. I leave a quick message, telling her I won't be in and that I'll call back later to explain.

"Are you not going to wo–work?"

"Not today." I open the cupboards and scan the contents. There isn't much. Charlie eats like a horse.

"What's for brea–breakfast?"

I can't tell him how sorry I am. We can't have mature discussions about guilt and penance. "How about cookies?" The simple treats that make him happy are all I can offer.

"Cho–chocolate?"

There are flour, powdered milk, one egg, and cocoa. I can concoct something. If I could, I'd give him the world.

I heat the two-plate, portable oven, and let him mix the dough. While the cookies bake, I shower and dress before sending Charlie to do his morning grooming. At the same time the timer on my phone pings for the oven, there's a text message from Jerry.

Run.

A tremor rattles my bones. I shiver, even if it's hot inside from the oven. Hurrying to the window, I peer through. A black Mercedes is parked across the road. A woman sits in the front, but with the glare of the sun on the window I can't make out anything other than her black hair. A man in a suit gets out from the driver seat and another from the back. He holds the door. A third man folds his large frame double to exit, adjusting the sleeves of his jacket as he looks up and down the street before turning his head in the direction of our window.

Gabriel Louw.

My breath catches. I jump back before he sees me. Charlie comes out of the bathroom and starts making his bed like I taught him.

"The coo–cookies."

They're burning. I switch off the oven and use a dishcloth to dump the baking tray on a cork plate, trying not to panic.

There's no backdoor or window. The only way out is through the front. We're trapped. I lean on the wall, shaking and feeling sick.

Please, don't let him kill us. Scrap that. Rather let him kill us than torture us.

Everyone from Aucklandpark to Bez Valley knows what The Breaker does to debtors who don't pay. He has a reputation built on a trail of broken bodies and burnt houses. Puff, always sensing anxiety, licks my ankles.

Footsteps fall on the landing. It's too late. Fighting instinct flares in me. My need to protect my brother takes over.

I grab Charlie's hand. "Listen to me." My voice is urgent, but calm. "Can you be brave?"

"Bra–brave."

Puff barks once.

The knock on the door startles me, even if I expected it. I can't move. I should've taken Charlie and run last night. No, they would've found us. Then it would've been worse. You can't outrun The Breaker.

Another knock falls, harder this time. The sound is hollow on the false wood.

"Stand up straight." Don't show your fear, I want to say, but Charlie won't understand.

No third knock comes.

The door breaks inward, pressed wood splintering with a dry, brittle sound. Three men file through the frame to make my worst nightmare come true. They're carrying guns. Dark complexions, Portuguese, except for the one in the middle. He's South African. He moves with a limp, his right leg stiff. Gabriel is even uglier up close. In the daylight, the blue of his eyes look frozen. They hold the warmth of an iceberg as his gaze does a merry-go-round of the room, gauging the situation to the minutest details with a single glance.

He knows we're unprotected. He knows we're frightened, and he likes it. He feeds off it. His chest swells, stretching the jacket over his broad shoulders. He taps the gun against his thigh while his free hand closes and opens around empty air.

Tap, tap. Tap, tap.

Those hands. My God, they're enormous. The skin is dark and rough with strong veins and a light coat of black hair. Those are hands not afraid of getting dirty. They're hands that can wrap around a neck and crush a windpipe with a squeeze.

I swallow and lift my gaze to his face. He's no longer taking stock of the room. He's assessing me. His eyes run over my body as if he's looking for sins in my soul. It feels as if he cuts me open and lets my secrets pour out. He makes me feel exposed. Vulnerable. His presence is so intense, we're communicating with the energy alone that vibrates around us. His stare reaches deep inside of me and filters through my private thoughts to see the truth, that his cruel self-assurance stirs both hate and awe. It's the awe he takes, as if it's his right to explore my intimate feelings, but he does so probingly, tenderly almost, executing the invasive act with respect.

Then he loses interest. As soon as he's sucked me dry, I cease to exist. I'm the carpet he wipes his feet on. His expression turns bored as he fixes his attention on Charlie.

Taking back some power, I say, "What do you want?"

His lips twitch. He knows I'm bluffing. "You know why I'm here."

His voice is deep. The rasp of that dark tone resonates with authority and something more disturbing--sensuality. He speaks evenly, articulating every word. Somehow, the musical quality and controlled volume of his voice make the statement sound ten times more threatening than if he'd shouted it. Under different circumstances I would've been enchanted by the rich timbre. All I feel now is fear, and it's reflected on Charlie's face. I hate that I can't take it away for him.

"I'll only ask you once," Gabriel says, "and I want a simply yes or no answer." *Tap, tap. Tap, tap.* "Do you have my money?"

Spatters of words dribble from Charlie's lips. "I–I do–don't li–like them. Not ni–nice me–men."

The man on the left, the one with the lime green eyes, lifts his gun and aims at Charlie's feet. It happens too fast. Before I can charge, his finger tightens on the trigger. The silencer dampens the shot. I wait for the damage, blood to color the white of Charlie's tennis shoe, but instead there's a wail, and Puff falls over.

Oh, no. Please. No. Dear God. No, no, no.

It has to be a horror movie, but the hole between Puff's eyes is very real. So is the blood running onto the linoleum. The lifeless body on the floor unfurls a rage in me. He was only a defenseless animal. The unfairness, the cruelty, and my own helplessness are fuel on my shocked senses.

In a fit of blind fury, I storm the man with the gun. "You sorry excuse of a man!"

He ducks, easily grabbing both my wrists in one hand. When he aims the gun at my head, Gabriel says, his beautiful voice vibrating like a tight-pulled guitar string, "Let her go."

The man obliges, giving me a shove that makes me stumble. The minute I'm free, I go for Gabriel, punching my fists in his stomach and on his chest. The more he stands there and takes my hammering, my assault having no effect on him, the closer I come to tears.

Gabriel lets me carry on, to make a fool of myself, no doubt, but I can't help it. I go on until my energy is spent, and I have to stop in painful defeat. Going down on my knees, I feel Puff's tiny chest. His heartbeat is gone. I want to hug him to my body, but Charlie is huddled in the corner, ripping at his hair.

Ignoring the men, I straighten and cup Charlie's hands, pulling them away from his head. "Remember what I said about being brave?"

"Bra–brave."

So much hatred for Gabriel and his cronies fills me that my heart is as black as a burnt-out volcano. There's no space for anything good in there. I know I shouldn't give in to the darkness of the sensations coursing through my soul, but it's as if the blackness is an ink stain that bleeds over the edges of a page. I embrace the anger. If I don't, fear will consume me.

Gabriel gives me a strangely compassionate look. "You owe me an answer."

"Look around you." I motion at our flat. "Does it look like we can afford that kind of money? You're a twisted man for giving a mentally disabled person a loan."

His eyes narrow and crinkle in the corners. "You have no idea how twisted I'm willing to get." Gabriel grasps Charlie by the collar of his T-shirt, dragging him closer. "For the record, if you didn't want your brother to make debt, you should've declared him incompetent and revoked his financial signing power."

"Leave him alone!"

I grab Gabriel's arm and hang on it with my full weight, but it makes no difference. I'm dangling on him like a piece of washing on a line. He swats me away, sending me flying to the ground, and presses the barrel of his pistol against my brother's soft temple where a vein pulses with an innocent life not yet lived.

"Va–Val!"

He cocks the safety. "Yes or no?"

"Yes!" Using the wall at my back for support, I scramble to my feet. "I'll pay it."

Charlie cries softly. Gabriel looks at me as if he notices nothing else. His eyes pin me to the spot. Under his gaze, I'm a frog splayed and nailed to a board, and he holds the scalpel in his hand.

He doesn't lower the gun. "Do you know how much?"

"Yes." My voice doesn't waver.

"Say it."

"Four hundred thousand."

"Where's the money?"

The ghost of a smile is back on his face. Behind the scarred mask is a man who knows how to hurt people to get what he wants, but for now he's entertained. The bastard finds the situation amusing.

"I'll pay it off."

He tilts his head. "You'll pay it off." He makes it sound as if I'm mad.

"With interest."

"Miss Haynes, I assume." Despite his declared assumption, he says it like it's a fact. Everything about him shouts confidence and arrogance. "Tell me your name."

"You know my name." Men like him know the names of all the family members before they move in for the kill.

"I want to hear you say it."

I wet my dry lips. "Valentina."

He seems to digest the sound like a person would taste wine on his tongue. "How much do you earn, Valentina?"

I refuse to cower. "Sixty thousand."

He lowers the gun. It's a game to him now. "Per month?"

"Per year."

He laughs softly. "What do you do?"

"I'm an assistant." I don't offer more. It's enough that he already knows my name.

He regards me with his arms hanging loosely at his sides. "Nine years."

It sounds ridiculous, but the quick calculation I do in my head assures me it's not. That's almost five thousand per month, including thirty percent interest on the lump sum. I can't call him unfair. Loan sharks in this neighborhood ask anything between fifty to a hundred and fifty percent interest.

"Nine years if you pay it back with the lowest of interests," he continues, confirming my calculation.

Of course, I'm not planning on staying a vet assistant forever. It's only until I qualify as a vet in four more years. By then, I'll be earning more. "I'll pay it off faster when I get a better job."

He closes the two steps between us with an uneven gait. He's standing so near I can smell the detergent of his shirt and the faint, spicy fragrance of his skin.

"You misunderstood my offer." His eyes drill into mine. "You'll work for *me* for nine years."

My breath catches. "For you?"

He just looks at me.

"Doing what?" I ask on a whisper.

The intensity in those iced, blue depths sharpens. "Any duty I see fit. Think carefully, Valentina. If you accept, it'll be a live-in position."

I know what *any duty* implies. He's no different than Tiny. Loathing fills me.

Gabriel regards me as if he's making a bet with himself. "Either I shoot your brother and you walk away, or he's free, and you work off his debt."

"Give me whatever contract I need to sign, and I'll find my own way to pay you."

He chuckles. "It's my terms or none."

What choice do I have? My knees feel shaky, but it's hardly the time to be weak.

"I'll do it." As I say the words, a ball of ice sinks to my stomach.

For a moment, he looks surprised, but then his expression becomes closed-off. "You have five minutes to pack."

"I have a condition."

The amusement is back on his face. He taps the gun on his thigh and waits.

"I want my brother's safety guaranteed." If I'm not around, Charlie will need protection. I don't want a repeat of what got us into this mess.

"Fair enough. He'll have my protection."

"I need to call someone to fetch him. He can't stay alone."

He takes his phone from his pocket, punches in a code, and pushes it into my hand. "You'll use mine until we've ensured yours isn't compromised."

Turning my back on them, I type my only friend's number. While I'm dialing Kris, the man with the dark eyes searches my purse that hangs over a chair in the kitchen. I watch the men from the corner of my eye, my hand shaking as I wait for Kris to take the call.

"It's Valentina," I say when she answers.

Dogs bark in the background. "I didn't recognize this number. Do you have a new phone? I saw you called earlier, but I haven't listened to your message yet."

"Kris, listen to me. I need you to fetch Charlie. Can he stay with you for a while?"

"What happened?"

"Charlie made debt at Napoli's. I'm with the creditor."

"What?" she shrieks. "You're with a loan shark? Where?"

"My place. Things have changed. I'm going to work off Charlie's debt, but he can't stay alone." My cheeks grow hot as I add, "It's a live-in position."

"What about your job here?"

"I'm sorry. I know how much you need me."

It's always hectic at the clinic, and I feel bad for what I have to do. Kris is one of the best vets I know. She gave me a job when nobody else would, and I hate turning my back on her.

Gabriel checks his watch. "You have three minutes."

"I have to go. Will you call me when you've got Charlie?"

"I'm on my way."

"Thank you, Kris." I glance at Puff's body, forcing down my tears. "You'll have to--"

Gabriel takes the phone from my hand. "Hello, Kris." He keeps his piercing gaze trained on me. "The door to Valentina's flat is broken, but don't worry. I'll have it replaced." He cuts the call. "Two minutes. I suppose you'll pack light."

Stress drives me as I shove the few outfits and toiletries I own in our only travel bag. What will become of Charlie? For now, he's alive. I'm alive. That's what I need to focus on.

Gabriel's cronies help themselves to the cookies cooling on the table. Gabriel says nothing. Only his disturbing stare follows me as I move through the room.

I've barely zipped up my bag before he says, "Let's go."

Adrenalin from the shock makes me strong, strong enough to walk to my brother with confident steps and take his tear-streaked face in my hands.

I go on tiptoes and kiss his forehead. "Remember what I said about being brave. You can do it." I want to say I'll call him, but I don't want to lie. "Wait for Kris. She'll be here soon."

Gabriel takes my bag and steers me to the door, stopping in the frame to say to the man who shot Puff, "Stay with her brother until the woman arrives and bury the dog. Have the door fixed before you go."

The man nods. He's shorter than Gabriel, but not less muscled.

I look over my shoulder and take in everything I can--Charlie's haphazard hair, his soft hazel eyes, and the washed-out Spiderman T-shirt--because I don't know if I'll ever see him again.

2

Gabriel

The petite brunette stiffens when I take her elbow to steer her down the stairs. Her face is ghastly white, and her whole body trembles, but she walks with a straight back. I have dragged men three times her size kicking and screaming to a tamer fate than the one awaiting her. She has guts, but I already knew that from last night.

On the pavement, I take her hand to help her down the curb. Her delicate frame grows even more rigid, but she doesn't resist. Magda turns her head to the car window when we approach. She startles at the sight of the woman I have in the iron grip of my fingers, and then her expression turns stoic. My mother isn't happy. This isn't what she ordered. Tough luck. It's not going to happen the way she wants today, but I've got some explaining to do.

Madga gets out, her eyes shredding me to pieces.

"Put her in the back," I say to Quincy, handing Valentina over like a parcel.

Magda waits until Quincy shuts the door and walks to where we're out of earshot. "She was supposed to be dead."

"I made a deal."

"What deal?"

"Nine years for Charlie's debt."

She blinks. "You're *taking* her?"

I cross my arms. "Yes."

"You want to fuck her."

I don't deny it. There's no point.

"It's not that simple, Gabriel."

I saw her. I wanted her. I took her. Yeah, it's that simple.

"That wasn't the plan," Magda insists.

"The plan changed."

She throws her hands up in the air and starts pacing the sidewalk. "The price was death."

"Charlie has brain damage." That's a tougher price than death. To me, at least. "We shouldn't have granted him a loan."

"Well, we did. Retard or not, showing mercy is showing our enemies we're getting soft."

"Nine years are not exactly mercy." Not with what I'm planning for Valentina.

"She has to die."

"I never go back on my word. People in our business trust us because I keep my word. Rhett and Quincy heard me make the deal."

The charcoal lines around her eyes wrinkle. "What did you promise?"

"A live-in arrangement."

"Arrangement?"

"I said she could work back the debt."

Underneath Magda's controlled exterior she's simmering. A vein pops out on her temple. "Fine. You want to play doll? Have your fun, but we're setting her up to fail. When she does, she's dead and so is her brother."

A sharp pain jolts into my damaged hip. I make a conscious effort to relax my body, muscle by muscle.

"Come on." Magda is already on her way back to the car. "I'll figure it out on the way home."

For the first time, I regret never giving a fuck about professional relationship building. I don't care what people think or about anyone but my daughter, but Magda has always cast the net out wide, catching everyone she can put in her pocket. Her network and influence stretch much further than mine. She carries all the authority in this organization. Sometimes, I have the ugly suspicion the business is the only reason she married my father, so she could take it over. She makes a hell of a tougher loan shark than he ever did, and he was a scary bastard.

I get into the back with Valentina while Magda sits up front with Quincy.

"Drive," she tells my bodyguard.

Quincy and Magda are quiet, I guess because of the girl. An intense awareness of the woman next to me and my power over her spreads through my body, making me hard.

Fuck me. I own her.

She's mine.

The thought gives me a head rush. She's so small she looks like the doll Magda accused me of wanting to play with. Upright, Valentina barely reaches my chest. Her bones are fragile enough to crush under the lightest pressure. If I hug her too tight, her ribs may crack. I can wrap one hand around her slender neck. How hard I choose to close my fingers will be the discerning factor between life and death. Yet, she attacked me when Rhett shot her dog. She gave *me* an order when she told me to let Charlie Haynes go. She's strong and loyal.

I'm both fascinated and jealous of her love for her brother. No one has ever fought for me like that, and I doubt anyone ever will. Throwing *any duty I see fit* into the package was a test. I wanted to see how far she was willing to go for Charlie, not that her decision would've changed anything. I took ownership of her the minute I laid eyes on her. Last night, I already knew I was going to take her. Regardless.

When the club manager at Napoli's called to let me know my mother's target was in, the said target being Charlie, my plan was to go in, take Charlie out, and then his sister, who would've been home alone. Making examples of people who don't pay is standard procedure. Some people don't fear for themselves, but they always fear for their families. By Magda's design, Valentina would've been the sacrifice to serve as a reminder to our debtors as long as they owe, their families aren't safe.

Then I stepped out of the office, and there she was, all tits, ass, and legs. No woman, except for the prostitutes, goes into Napoli's willingly. A nerve pinches between my shoulder blades when I think of what could've happened to her had I not been there. She's either extremely naïve or stupidly brave. After this morning, I suspect the latter.

Come to think of it, I don't get how she survived here this long. According to Jerry, she's been residing in Berea for six years. The shithole she lived in is in drug valley. It's a surprise the drug and sex lords haven't kidnapped and sold her or a street gang hasn't raped and killed her yet. There are infinitely dark things that can happen to an unprotected, beautiful girl in this neighborhood.

I watch her from the corner of my eye. In the twenty minutes we've being driving, she hasn't said a word. Her brown hair is long and wavy, curling down her shoulders. A clean smell clings to her, like fragrance shampoo or body lotion. I like it. Complex perfumes give me a headache. In the white shorts and yellow tank top, her toned legs and rounded breasts are exposed to me. So is the vein that pulses under the golden skin of her neck. Her fear excites me. Her courage intrigues me. Long, dark lashes shutter the expression in her brown eyes from me. She's pretending to look through the window, but I know she's aware of me, and the gun resting in my lap.

The weapon is cool in my hand. I'm long since past the stage where my palms get sweaty before a job. I don't mind the killing. I live in a violent city. Only the toughest survive, and I'm a survivor. I won't hesitate to pull the trigger if anyone threatens or harms my family. Lay a finger on my property, and I'll break it off. I was the kind of kid who took pleasure in breaking other boys' toys. I still break. Mostly bones, these days. When it comes to hearts, I only break what's already broken. That way, I don't have to take responsibility for anyone's feelings. Now I've taken responsibility for a person on a whole different level. At least there's no risk of breaking Valentina's heart. She already hates me, and with what I'm planning for her body, she'll only hate me more, but she'll need me with equal intensity. Of that, I'll make sure.

Her gaze widens fractionally as we pull up to our property. It's a double-story mansion on big grounds surrounded by a six feet-wall fitted with electrified barbed wire and twenty-four hour, armed guards. In this city, only people with money are safe. She keeps her face perfectly blank as we clear the gates. The original Frank Emley design dates from the early 1900s and combines various styles with a strong Victorian influence, iron work, stone walls, and art nouveau stained glass windows. It's smack-bam in the heart of Parktown, in the middle of the homes of the bankers, diamond dealers, politicians, and everyone else who can be bought.

Quincy parks and opens the door for Magda first, then for me. While I'm stretching my stiff leg, he lets Valentina out and hovers with her purse and travel bag in front of the fountain.

"I'll take that." I grab her possessions and grip her arm to lead her up the porch steps. My fingers overlap the small diameter of her upper arm. This is the point where I expect her to kick in her heels and scream, but she remains eerily calm.

Magda overtakes us on the stairs. "One wrong move, one wrong word to anyone, and Charlie is dead. Get that?"

Valentina tilts her head away from my mother, a tremor running through her body.

Marie, our faithful old cook, opens the door. Her face freezes when her eyes land on the young woman.

"Prepare the maid's room," Magda says. "I'll brief you later." She enters ahead of us. "Gabriel, bring the girl to my study."

Before I can argue, Magda is gone. Marie's gaze remains fixed on the woman at my side. May as well get the introduction over with.

"This is Valentina," I say. "She's property."

Marie nods as if I bring *property* home every day, but she understands. She's been around the block. She scurries away without offering me my usual drink.

I steer Valentina to my mother's study and close the door. Whatever Magda is cooking up, I already don't like it. The sight of my mother's personal bodyguard, Scott, standing behind her chair with a pistol clutched in his hand makes me rest my hand on my own weapon tucked into my waistband. The threat is clear. Defy Magda and Valentina will end up like her dog––with a bullet between her soft, mud-brown eyes.

Magda addresses my tiny charge. "I understand you'll be *working* for us." She points at the chair facing her desk. "Sit."

I let Valentina go. She obeys, balancing on the edge of the seat. Mirroring Scott's stance, I remain standing, just in case.

"What are your skills?" Magda asks.

Valentina's lashes flutter as she lifts her eyes to me. They're big for her small face and hauntingly sad, but proud, also.

"Answer when you're being spoken to," Magda says in the headmistress voice she reserved for chastising me as a kid.

"I'm an assistant."

Magda's mouth pulls down. "That's it?"

"I also cook and clean for my neighbor."

Magda taps her fingernails on the desktop. After some time, she says, "You'll work for us as a maid and whatever else Gabriel expects from you." My mother gives me an acidic look, as if the sight of me gives her indigestion. "You'll work Monday to Friday until dinner's been served and the kitchen is clean. On Saturday, you're off from five in the afternoon. You're expected back by eight on Monday morning. If we have events at home, we expect you to work, regardless of afterhours."

The maid idea pisses me off, but the leisure time unleashes a rage in me, not that I have any ground to stand on. It's Magda's business and her debt to collect. I'm only the dealmaker. My new toy better not try to escape. I bet that's what Magda is bargaining on. It'll give her the reason she wants to eliminate Valentina and terminate my *idiotic* deal, as she put it.

"You'll keep the house tidy," Magda continues, "and with tidy I mean spotless. Everything on the inside of the building is your responsibility, except for the cooking. Marie takes care of that. If I need you to cook, I'll tell you. If you poison any one of us, you and your brother will die slow and painful deaths. Understand?"

Her throat moves as she swallows. "Yes."

"Yes, Mrs. Louw or ma'am."

Those dark eyes flash with defiance, but she averts them quickly. "Yes, ma'am."

"If you fail in any of your tasks, the deal's off, and you're dead." A sardonic light sparks in Magda's eyes. "Work well for…" She looks at me and waits.

"Nine years," I fill in.

"Work well for nine years," Magda continues, "and Charlie's debt will be paid off. We won't pay you a salary. The money we would've given you will go toward the settlement of your debt. I don't allow servants to eat from our table, but you may use the kitchen facilities to prepare your meals. Since you won't earn cash, my son will pay you an allowance for food and personal commodities. Any questions?"

"Is there a routine I need to follow? What do I do, exactly?"

Magda gets to her feet. "You'll figure it out. You start immediately."

Valentina follows Magda's lead, getting up from her chair with consternation on her face.

Before she goes, there's one thing she needs to understand. I grab her face in one hand, digging my fingers into her cheeks. "Run from me and you'll wish I shot you today."

Her body is close to mine, and I can smell her scent. I fill the olfactory gap I couldn't place in the car. Raspberry. She looks like a dove with her wings tied, but she doesn't falter under my stare.

"Are we clear?" I ask softly. I never raise my voice. I don't have to.

"Yes."

"Good." I let her go.

Her hand goes to her jaw, touching the imprint of my fingers.

"Marie will show you to your room," Magda says. "You'll find her in the kitchen."

I hand Valentina her travel bag, but hold onto the purse and remain standing since I haven't been dismissed.

The minute Valentina is gone, I say, "She doesn't know the way."

Magda goes to the wet bar and pours a tot of Vodka, which she dilutes with orange juice. "Letting her find her own way is her first test."

"Meaning?"

"The hidden cameras will record any traitorous acts she may conceive in her simpleton mind, and you'll use it to your advantage to break her." Magda takes a sip of her drink and walks back to her desk to pick up the internal phone that connects to the kitchen.

Marie answers on the first ring with a professional, "Mrs. Louw?" that comes over the speaker.

"Order maid uniforms for Valentina and linen for her room."

"Any preference, ma'am?"

"Black."

"The uniform or the linen?"

"The uniform. Make the linen…" she thinks for all of one second, giving me an over-easy smile, "…white." She hangs up and continues, "Black and white. Has a nice ring to it, doesn't it? It'll remind her of what she became––our servant and your plaything."

"She won't run," I say, a challenge in my voice. I just found Valentina. I'm not about to kill her on Sunday.

Magda smirks, swirling her glass. "That's not why I gave her Sundays off."

"Why did you?"

"To give her the illusion of freedom. Of fairness. For now, I'll let her believe she has a chance. People without hope can't be broken." My mother lifts the glass to her lips. "You see? I'm giving us both what we want. You get to break her, and I get to kill her."

Hatred laces Magda's words. The fact that I want this woman enough to defy my mother elicits Magda's scorn. I have no doubt she'll make Valentina pay for causing me to stray from the not so straight and narrow path cut out for me.

At my silence, Magda says, "You understand we can't let her meet her end of the bargain? That'll be weak."

"I promised her nine years."

"I have no intention of letting her live that long." Her smile grows until it invades all of her face. "She's bound to screw up sooner than later."

A sudden insight startles me. Magda is happy with the turn of events. She wants Valentina to suffer, and she's relying on my natural disposition to make it happen.

Valentina

My throat aches from pent-up tears as I leave Mrs. Louw's study. If I had any hope that Gabriel's mother would have compassion and help me, it's been eradicated in that room. She's worse than her son, her blackness far colder.

I'm sick to my stomach with worry over Charlie. I need to call Kris and check that he's all right, but Gabriel gave me my clothes and held onto my purse with my phone. I can't allow myself to think about this morning or Puff. Not yet. For now, I need to be strong.

With the imminent danger of death over, reality crashes down on me. Despair seeps into my pores. The calculation is harrowing. I'll be thirty-two before I walk free. *If* I ever walk free. There's no doubt in my mind Gabriel will kill me without blinking an eye. I know men like him. My father was one. The servant role isn't only to pay off a debt. It's a means of degrading me. I have no issue pulling the hair from Gabriel's shower or scrubbing his toilet. What's killing me is sleeping under his roof and eating food he pays for. I'm forced to allow my enemy to take care of me. It feels personal and wrong. The last thing I want from Gabriel is any kind of care. I'll talk to Kris and negotiate to work Sundays. That way I'll still be able to pay for my studies. No matter what, I'm not giving it up. It's my only hope, our ticket out of Berea. I'll just have to put my plans on the backburner for nine years.

After getting lost in corridors and too many rooms with sofas and chairs--How many lounges can one family need?--I finally locate the kitchen at the far east end of the mansion. The size of the house overwhelms me. It's going to be a hell of a job to keep the place spotless.

Marie waits for me in a sterile looking kitchen, a hostile expression on her face. "I better show you around."

Wordlessly, I fall in behind her. We go through the ground level with its reading, sitting, television, entertainment, and dining rooms, and up a flight of stairs. The bedrooms and bathrooms on the first level are luxurious and comfortable. As we move along, my heart sinks lower and lower. It's too much.

"Who's currently cleaning the house?"

Marie looks at me as if I asked her for a gold coin. "A cleaning service. I presume since you're here, they'll be fired."

Poor people. They're going to lose a big contract, but at least they're free.

At a wooden door with an intricate carving, she stops. "This is his bedroom. Next door is Miss Carly's. Mr. Louw's mother is at the opposite end."

She knocks on Miss Carly's door and opens it without waiting for a reply.

A girl of about sixteen lies on her stomach on the bed. The room is one of the prettiest I've seen. It's decorated in blue with whitewashed furniture.

"Carly," Marie says, "this is Valentina. She's the new live-in."

Carly lifts her head to look me up and down before burying her face in her iPad again.

"His daughter," Marie says, closing the door. She lowers her voice. "She sometimes lives with her mom, but she's mostly here."

So, Gabriel and Carly's mom are separated or divorced.

We explore the house until we end up back in the kitchen. Only the kitchen is surgical white. It's not a room the inhabitants of the house *live* in. There's no breakfast nook, books, or flowers, not a trace of warmth. It's a functional room equipped for the staff. This is where Marie pauses the longest to show me the adjoining scullery where they keep the household appliances and a fridge for the staff.

"You can keep your food here," Marie says. "The one in the pantry is only for the family."

Cleaning products are neatly stacked on the shelves on the wall. Everything is tidy and in its place. At least there are a state-of-the-art vacuum cleaner and washing machine to work with.

"Do you know how to operate these?" Marie points at the washing machine and tumble dryer.

I nod, even if I don't. I washed our clothes in the bathtub, but how difficult can it be to figure out a washing machine?

"The washing has to be sun-dried," Marie explains, "unless it rains. Mrs. Louw doesn't believe in wasting electricity."

From the scullery, a door leads to the maid quarters. This is where I'll be sleeping for the next nine years. I put my head around the frame. The room is small, the double bed taking up most of the space, but the cream-colored carpet is clean, and the mattress looks new. The paint is white, and there are no foul smells or damp to darken the walls. A connecting door gives access to a small bathtub with a shower nozzle fitted inside, a basin, and toilet. It's much better than what I'm used to. There are no linen or towels, and I didn't bring any, but I don't ask.

"Well," Marie dusts her hands, "I'll let you get on with it. Your uniforms will arrive later. For now, you'll have to work like this." She gives my legs a disapproving look.

"Can I have my phone?"

"You'll have to ask Mr. Louw about that."

The minute she's gone, I use the bathroom to splash water on my face. The enormity of the situation pushes down on my chest. I can't breathe. Needing air, I open the window, letting the breeze on my wet cheeks cool me. From here, I have a view over an enclosed courtyard. There's a circular clothesline in the center and a wheelbarrow pushed up against the wall. Through the open door giving access to the backyard, the blue water of a pool is visible.

Since I don't know how to go about my new job with the massive size of the house, I decide to dive into the deep end and swim. It's an approach that always works for me. For the next few hours, I work out a plan of action as I go, starting with laundry and dusting, then vacuuming and finally washing the floors and windows. My mind is filled with Charlie and Puff, and even if I can't fight my tears, I can hide them while I bend my head over the mop. As I mourn for Puff, I let my hate for Gabriel and the guy who shot him ripen. The only ray of hope in this nightmare is that today is Wednesday. On Sunday, I'll see Charlie.

IN THE LATE AFTERNOON, Gabriel summons me to the reading room. Stepping inside, I'm taken aback by the presence of an elderly man dressed in a Mandela style shirt and chinos.

Gabriel turns to me. "This is Dr. Samuel Engelbrecht. He's going to take a blood sample and examine you."

I look between the men. "What for?"

Gabriel ignores my question. "Are you on birth control?"

The wind is knocked out of me by the implication of the question, even if I expected it as an inevitable part of the deal I'd made. If the doctor recognizes the shock on my face, he doesn't acknowledge it.

"No," I force through dry lips.

The doctor offers me an impersonal smile. "Take off your clothes and lie down on the couch, my dear."

I can't move. I'm stuck to the carpet.

"How long do you need?" Gabriel asks.

"Twenty minutes."

"I'll be back for her."

On his way to the door, he stops in front of me. "If he hurts you, I'll kill him."

Dr. Engelbrecht chuckles over his open doctor's case. "It's not nice to make jokes like that."

"It's no joke."

Gabriel says it with a smile, but his words send a shiver down my spine. He walks from the room, shutting me inside with the doctor.

"Come now," the doctor says, "I don't have all day."

It's embarrassing to undress in front of a stranger who knows my employer is going to fuck me. My whole body blushes as I kick off my trainers, push down my shorts, and peel off my top.

He must see many patients at home, because he's well prepared. A disposable sheet is already spread out on the couch. I keep my eyes fixed on the ceiling as I lay down, trying to go someplace dark in my head.

He fits on a pair of surgical gloves. "Bend your knees."

"What are you going to do?"

"Don't worry, my dear, it's just a pap smear. You're supposed to do it every year. First time?"

I nod. It's not like I have money for doctors' visits.

He chats through the examination to put me at ease, but I'm tense, and when he takes the sample it hurts. He lets me get dressed before he takes my blood. He's just about done when Gabriel steps back into the room.

He walks to the couch where I'm sitting with my arm on the armrest while my blood runs into a vial. "How did it go?"

It's the doctor who answers. "Very well. I'll have the results tomorrow."

I guess Gabriel wants to be sure I'm clean. Can't blame him, seeing where I come from.

"Depending on the hormone level results," Dr. Engelbrecht continues, "I'll drop off an oral contraceptive." He removes the needle and gives me a cotton swab to press on the wound. After packing the samples in his bag, he removes the gloves, shakes Gabriel's hand, and takes his leave.

I stare at Gabriel when we're alone, heat burning under the neckline of my top. "You could've warned me."

"It would've stressed you unnecessarily."

"I'll be the judge of that," I say, jumping to my feet. "I may be working for you, but it's still my body."

"No, beautiful." He gives me a calculated look. "I beg to differ."

I don't have a reply. All I can do is rush past him, escaping the unsettling situation, and for now he lets me.

DUBIOUS

THE HARD PHYSICAL labor is an outlet for my anger, frustration, and even a bit of my fear. As I don't run into anyone while I'm cleaning, a false sense of calmness settles over me, but I start to stress again when I realize I can only manage the ground level in whatever time of the day is left. At least the house is immaculate. I can start with the first floor tomorrow. I won't manage unless I work on a rotation basis, deep cleaning some rooms only every second or third day.

I don't stop for lunch, and I never had breakfast. By the time I walk into the kitchen at sunset, I'm famished, sweaty, and tired, but everything downstairs is sparkling clean. Marie is stirring a pot on the stove. The delicious fragrance of tomato and beef stew fills my nostrils. My treacherous stomach gives a growl. My body doesn't understand pride or honor. It's ruled by the simple survival needs of hunger and thirst. Taking a glass from the cupboard, I fill it under the tap and drink deeply.

Marie wipes her hands on her apron. "I kept you a sandwich." She motions at a plate under a fly net on the counter with a white envelope next to it. "Mr. Louw left your food allowance. He said you won't leave the property before Saturday, but if you write down what you need, I'll order it for you. We have a delivery service that comes every day."

Of course they do.

Glancing at the wall clock, the housekeeper continues, "I'm off. The dinner is ready. Mrs. Louw is going out, tonight. Set the table for Mr. Louw and Miss Carly in the informal dining room. Make sure the kitchen is clean and the table set for breakfast before you go to bed. Mr. Louw usually sees to his own breakfast as he eats before I get on duty. I'll be in at eight."

A soft meow sounds from the door. I look down into a pair of yellow eyes flecked with green. A gray cat, his tail and paws tipped with white, runs inside and rubs against my leg.

I bend down to pet him. "Hello, you. What's your name?"

"That's Oscar," Marie replies.

From her tone, I gather she doesn't care much for him.

"He's Mr. Louw's late grandmother's cat."

Pleased with the attention, the tabby flops onto his side. He stretches when I scratch his chin.

"Nothing but a nuisance," Marie says with a click of her tongue.

This makes me like her even less. I don't trust people who don't like animals. "He seems quiet enough."

She snorts. "Pisses everywhere. You'll see how much you like him when you have to clean it."

"Has he been neutered?" I lift a back leg for a better look. Yep.

A puff of air escapes her lips. "Like I'd know." Marie takes her jacket and purse from a hook behind the door. "See you tomorrow at eight." She shuts the backdoor behind her with a firm click.

Curious, I tear open the envelope with my name on it and peer inside. I'm surprised to pull out eleven five hundred rand bills, five hundred more than my monthly wage. It's a lot more generous than I expected. I contemplate refusing the money on the principle, but I don't have a choice. Without an income, I can't take care of Charlie and pay for my studies. Or eat. Feeling my hunger with full-blown force, I refill my glass with water.

At the sound of the running tap, Oscar twitches his ears.

"Are you thirsty? Where's your bowl?"

When I move toward the door, he jumps to his feet and scoots past me to the scullery. There, next to the dishwasher, are two porcelain bowls, one filled with water and the other with kibbles. It doesn't take me long to locate the bag of pet food under the sink. It's a cheap brand, one with more fiber than nutritional value. Typically, it's manufactured to fill, but not to nourish. I top off the food, rinse the water bowl before refilling it with fresh water, and make myself at home on the floor next to Oscar where I feed him pieces of the ham and cheese I dig out of the sandwich. Not the healthiest meal for him, either, but at least it's tastier than the cardboard they're feeding him. The food makes Oscar my new best friend. As I set the table and bring the laundry in from outside, he stays by my side, stealing hopeful glances at me that I can only reward with caresses, at least until I have my own groceries.

It's late, but I'm worried I won't have time to catch up with all the outstanding work tomorrow, so I fold the clothes I can and put the shirts and dresses for ironing aside. As I wait for the iron to heat up in the scullery, I hear sounds in the kitchen. Immediately, my stomach tightens. How, I don't know, but I know it's *him*. It's as if the air thickens, making it difficult to breathe. I pinch my eyes shut and hold my breath, hoping he'll leave, but the iron hisses and spits, giving away my hiding place.

At the sound, Gabriel sticks his head around the corner. His eyes fix on me, and then on Oscar by my feet. It's difficult to read him. He's looking at me like he's appraising me or trying to find fault. I hate that he makes me fear. I hate even more that he makes me curious. I try not to stare, but the scars on his face have a magnetic pull on my gaze. What kind of weapon creates such scars? What kind of man survives it? I can't look away from the challenge in his stare.

Finally, the harsh lines of his mouth soften a fraction. "You better serve dinner while it's warm." Abruptly, he turns and leaves.

I let go of the breath I was holding, my chest deflating as his presence fades and the air decompresses again.

Carly sits at the table opposite her father, a smart phone in her hand, when I enter with a tray loaded with dishes. She doesn't look up from texting as I place everything in the center of the table. In contrast, Gabriel's eyes follow me around the room. I become intensely aware of my clothes and the state of my body. My skin is shiny with perspiration. I need a shower. To add to my discomfort, he inhales audibly as I sweep past him.

When the tray is offloaded, he nods at me. "Serve us, then leave."

I lift the lid on the bowl of rice and carry it to Carly. "Rice, miss?" I try to hide my discomfort as I'm forced to grovel and bow to my brother's enemy.

No reply. Her head remains bent over her phone, causing her wheat-colored hair to fall in a veil around her face. I hover until the slam of Gabriel's palm on the table make both Carly and I jump. The cutlery and glasses clatter from the force.

"Put away your phone, Carly. If I see it at the dinner table again, I'll confiscate it."

She glares at him with a cool, blue gaze. "Then I'll have dinner at Mom's."

A muscle twitches under one eye before he narrows both. "You're welcome to, but since *I* pay your allowance, your phone stays here."

She throws the phone down on the table, the mobile hitting the wood with a thud. "Fine."

"Valentina asked you a question."

She looks at me as if I'm the reason for their argument. "What?"

"Rice, miss?" I repeat, keeping my face void of emotion.

"For God's sake." She sighs with an exaggerated eye roll. "Call me Carly. I hate to be called miss."

"Rice, Carly?" I say flatly.

She steals a glance at her father and mumbles, "What the hell ever."

Gabriel's knuckles turn white around the stem of his glass. I can't get out of there fast enough. The atmosphere is so thick with tension I want to choke. I return to my ironing and listen, but there's nothing but the clanging of their cutlery and the clinking of their glasses as the meal progresses in silence.

By the time they're done, so am I. All the shirts are folded to perfection, a hated curse pressed into every, neat line. The dining room is empty when I clear the table. Loud music comes from upstairs. I don't want to contemplate the difficulties of Gabriel's relationship with his daughter. I don't care.

When I get to my room, there are towels and a heap of linen on the bed, together with my purse. In the cupboard, I find three black maid's dresses in my size. There's no key in the lock and no chair or other piece of furniture I can push against the door, not that it will do me any good. I made a deal with a monster, and the only way to survive is to honor it.

The first thing I do, is extract my phone and call Kris.

She answers immediately. "Tell me you're all right."

"I'm fine."

"Where are you?"

"At Gabriel Louw's house."

"Did he…?"

A flush works its way up my neck. He will, but I can't tell Kris. She's got enough on her plate. "No. How's Charlie?"

"He was upset when I fetched him, but he's calm, now. He's watching television."

"Thank you, Kris." I blink away the moisture in my eyes. "I didn't know who else to call."

"You did the right thing to call me. I was worried sick about you."

"I'm sorry."

"I tried your phone several times. Why didn't you answer?"

"I was working."

"Doing what?"

I clear my throat. "Maid."

"Maid or whore?"

"Kris, please."

"Val, you're worth more than that."

"I'm doing what I have to." A sudden wave of tiredness washes over me. "Can you please keep Charlie until the weekend? It's a lot to ask, but I've got no other options. I'll come visit on Saturday, and we can talk."

"Okay." She gives a relieved laugh. "I thought you're a prisoner or something."

"Can I say hello to Charlie?"

"Of course. Hold on."

She calls my brother's name. A second later his sweet voice comes onto the line.

"Va–Val?"

"Hey, how are you doing?"

"Bu–burgers."

"Kris made burgers?"

"Ye–yeah."

"You're going to stay with Kris for a while. I have a new job, and it requires that I stay in."

"Wi–will you vi–visit?"

"Every week."

"Whe–when?"

"Saturday."

"Sa–Saturday."

"Don't worry about a thing. I'm going to take care of you."

"Ta–take care."

"I'll see you on Saturday, okay?"

"Sa–Saturday."

"I love you, and remember to be brave."

"Lo–love you, to–too."

I hang up and stare at the phone for several seconds, battling to process how quickly our lives have changed. It's no use crying over things I can't change. I've gotten through bad situations before. I can get through this.

Exhausted, I make the bed and have a quick shower. I try not to think about the fact that it's *his* water or that I have to sleep in a bed that belongs to him, between his sheets, under his roof. Too weary to dry my hair, I pull on my nightgown and get into bed. My thoughts dwell on Charlie and Puff as my head hits the pillow. I want to say a prayer for them, but I'm so tired I fall asleep halfway into it, only to be jerked awake to a familiar and threatening presence in the room.

3

Gabriel

My new toy wakes with a soundless gasp. Purposefully, I let her fall asleep first. Disorientated, her defenses will be down. It makes it easier to see the truth. For the moment, the only truth is the fear in her eyes.

It's not so easy to see the truth in myself, because I don't know what I feel, except for the physical. Her intoxicating smell dominated my dining room and hardened my cock. I don't know what it is about her that brings out my lust. I only know I want her like I've never wanted a woman.

Straightening from the doorframe, I prowl to the edge of the bed. She watches me with her big, murky eyes, her chest rising and falling to the rhythm of my steps. Gripping the sheet, I pull it down slowly. She clings to the fabric, but after a second she lets go, surrendering to the inevitable.

It's the chase. That's what I want to tell myself. It's not that I need to lie to myself. It's just hard to find the truth in the fucked-up slush I call my heart. Maybe I simply want the things I glimpsed in her, the bravery and the love that made her strong enough to take this–– what's happening right now––and nine more years of it for the sake of her brother.

My mind tends to be overactive. It rarely shuts down, not even in sleep, but all of my logical thoughts still as I stare down at her body. She's laid out stiff and straight on the white sheet, her hair fanning over the pillow. I reach for the button of my collar. As it pops through the buttonhole, she gulps. Her fingers dig into the sheet. If her body tenses any more, she's going to snap like a twig.

I'm many things, including a killer. I know I'm a scary son of a bitch. I own mirrors, and I'm not afraid to look in them. I see what she sees in her eyes. They're wide and moist in the light that falls from the scullery. The room isn't cold, but she shivers in her nightgown. Inexplicably, this touches me. The women I usually fuck don't shiver. To soften it for her, I turn the scarred side of my face away when I switch on the light of her room.

With the sheet discarded at her feet, I take the hem of her nightgown and move it up over her body, exposing her thighs, cotton panties, and her full breasts that, like her eyes, are too big for her body. She's perfect. Her calves are toned and her ankles tapered. I can see her pubic bone beneath the humble fabric of her underwear, and even the sight of the simple cotton hardens my cock. Careful to tamper my lust down a notch, I take my time to study the swell of her stomach and the way her breasts slightly flattens to the sides. Her nipples are a dark pink, exactly like I prefer. For the moment, those peaks aren't contracted, but I know how to remedy that, despite her fear. I've had enough partners to accurately read a woman's body and give her what she needs.

To ease the tightness in my chest, I undo two more buttons, letting the cool air wash down my torso. When I climb onto the foot of the bed, the first sound leaves Valentina's lips. It's something between a sob and a gasp. I much rather prefer a moan. I fold my hands around her narrow feet. She jerks as if I shocked her with a stun gun. Slowly, I run my hands up her legs, over her hips, and up her ribs. Goosebumps break out over her skin. Careful not to touch any erogenous zones, I reverse the path, keeping the touch light. My cock twitches in the constraints of my pants, pushing painfully against my zipper, but this isn't about me. It's about setting her at ease and bringing her pleasure. After a long time of stroking her like this, she's still incompliant, but her muscles are less tense. With each caress, I move closer and closer to her breasts, until my fingertips skim inches away from her nipples. Even as they finally contract for me with the tips turning into little pebbles, she fights it, pursing her lips almost as hard as she's squeezing her knees together. She's holding back, watching my every action, trying to contemplate my next move instead of giving over to the feeling.

"Close your eyes, Valentina."

"Are you going to rape me?"

I chuckle. "No."

"Then what are you doing?"

"Getting to know your body."

"You're not going to fuck me?"

"Eventually, yes. When you beg me."

Her eyes glisten like cold tiger eye gemstones. "That will never happen."

"You talk too much. Close your eyes and shut your mouth, or I'll be forced to blindfold and gag you."

My words have the desired effect. She seals her lips and pinches her eyes shut. I retrace my movements, starting a slow rub from her feet to the underside of her arms. After a few minutes of stroking her like this, a flush spreads over her skin, marring her neck and the upper curve of her breasts. The erogenous zones of her body will be filling with blood, making her breasts heavy and her sex swollen, preparing her for penetration. This is the cue I've been waiting for. Drawing circles around her hardening breasts, I close the spiraling trace of my fingers until I'm outlying her areolas. I watch her nipples tighten more, extending into kissable pinnacles I ache to feel on my tongue. Ignoring the hunger that makes my balls draw tight, I roll her nipples between my thumbs and forefingers and am rewarded with a gasp that sounds very different now. There's a crescendo of pleasure and an undertone of shame. The mixture is an intoxicating sound, one I take perverse pleasure in. I want to own her feelings, her whimpers, her pleasure, and her breaths. Like a signal, her hips lift. I know what her body is asking for, and I know she'll fight it. I need total surrender.

Letting go of her pretty tits, I wrap one hand around her neck, applying gentle pressure. The touch is both dominating and protective, and the way she reacts to it will tell me everything I need to know about how to make her happy in bed. To my surprise, her head lifts slightly, pressing her neck harder into my palm. Valentina is a natural submissive. My favorite kind of conquest.

Keeping my hand in place, I reward her with a kiss on each nipple. Her lips part on a soundless moan, and her eyes fly open. She blinks at me in surprise. She either expected me to bite her, or she's battling to process the sensation. Holding her gaze, I flick my tongue over her right breast, sucking the delicious nipple deep into my mouth. Her back arches off the bed, and a soft cry falls from her lips. At the sound of it, she goes completely still. Instead of fighting her arousal, she lies back like a corpse, her eyes fixed somewhere on the ceiling. Her muscles unclench, going slack under my hands. This won't do. I won't let her hide from me in her mind.

"Look at me."

The command is at direct odds with my earlier one, but I'm learning to read and understand her reactions. Of course, she ignores me, wandering around in the void she has created in her head.

"If you don't look at me right now, we're going to start over. This time, we'll practice in front of the mirror."

Slowly, she turns her gaze back in my direction until she's watching me from under her lashes.

"Good girl. Keep on watching me and tell me what you feel. If you stop talking, we start from scratch."

"What?"

She furrows her eyebrows, but I don't give her time for another question. I resume the task of licking her nipple like it's my favorite candy. When a suppressed moan slips from her lips, I lift my head to give her a hard look.

"Valentina, I won't tell you again. How does it feel?"

She licks her lips, watching me as I lave her breast with my tongue.

"It feels ... hot." She flushes bright red. "Wet. I mean..."

"Good?"

She bites her bottom lip.

"Carry on." I move to her other breast.

"Uh... Soft. Ah! Hard."

She cries out as I nip her with my teeth. "Tell me."

"Sore. No. Different. I don't know!"

I suck her relentlessly, plumping up her breast in my fist and pinching the hard tip with my lips. "Be clearer."

"Good! Ah, God. It hurts...good."

She pants and squirms. It's good to have her in the moment with me. I need her to feel, because I get off on her pleasure. I kiss her breasts and fondle her nipples until she's close to hyperventilating, throwing incoherent words and phrases at me.

"I'm going to make you come," I say, "and you can't stop it."

She tenses again, her face a mask of agonized pleasure.

"Say it," I urge, pinching her nipple hard.

She yelps. "Can't...stop it."

"That's it." I suck on her nipple. "Let it go."

She wiggles. "I–I can't."

"I won't stop, Valentina. We'll go all night if we have to, but you're going to give it to me."

She grips my shoulders, her nails digging into my skin, and gives a frustrated sob. "I don't understand what you want from me."

"Just lie back and I'll show you."

Her grip on me tightens, and her neck strains up, fear dampening the arousal in her eyes.

"My cock will stay in my pants. Lie back."

Slowly, the muscles in her neck relax as she lays her head back on the pillow. Once more, her body goes soft beneath me, but this time she's present. There's no more holding back. Her legs go slack, her thighs parting an inch. The slow, raspy lick of my tongue over her nipple is another reward, strengthening her good behavior. When she lifts her shoulders off the mattress, I almost lose control. I suck her nipple to the back of my mouth, eating her breast like a piece of cake, and she throws the reward right back at me by pushing deeper, forcing me to take more and giving me what I've been waiting for. The sweetest whimpers fall on my ears.

So damn hot. My fingers tighten involuntarily around her neck, applying more pressure, showing us both who she belongs to. There's no intent to harm, and her subconscious mind knows this. I lave her other breast with the wet strokes of my tongue, giving the plump curve the same meticulous attention as its twin until she squirms in my hold. Loosening my grip on her neck, I let my palm slide down her throat, between her breasts, and over her stomach. Her skin is slick from my kisses, and the wet trail makes her tummy quiver. Keeping my hand on her stomach, I kiss a path to her pubic bone, nuzzling her skin with my nose. The smell of her desire drives me crazy. She's wet, and the possessive side of me revels in the knowledge that I'm the cause. I'm the master of her desire. I brought her this far. I'll take her over the edge.

She seems barely coherent as I hook my fingers in the elastic of her underwear and pull it over her hips and down her legs. I free her ankles and discard the piece of clothing on the floor. She's turned on enough to take it a level rougher. I push her legs wide open, giving all of my senses access to her deepest core.

It's no secret that I love fucking. This is the part of women I love with reverence. I love their delicate folds, their taste, their smell, and the sounds they make when I invade their bodies. Valentina's cunt is beautiful. Her pussy lips are pink and plump, glistening with arousal. Her clit peeks from between her swollen labia like a pearl. The pucker of her asshole is a rosebud, and the tightness tells me no man has claimed her there. I don't mind her dark, silky pubic hair, but it has to go. I want to see her bare skin when I part her with my cock. I want to see her peachy lips stretch as wide as they can go when I take her deep, but thinking ahead only fucks with my head and torments my aching dick. I close my eyes and focus on her taste, instead. My tongue sweeps over her slit to the tip of her clit. She jerks violently, a sweet cry bouncing off the walls. Her hands dig into my shoulders, shoving and pulling simultaneously. She stopped talking. The only sounds coming from her lips are the moans I was chasing after.

"Just feel," I whisper over her skin. "You have no control, no choice."

She relaxes and opens wider, giving me better access. I spear my tongue into her pussy, and groan as her thighs hug my face in a soft vice. Her honey coats my tongue, the taste a powerful aphrodisiac. I could stay with my head buried between her legs forever, but even my patience, the resolve and control I'm so proud of, has limits. I eat her like a starving man, my teeth grazing and nibbling while my lips pinch and suck. Her nails dig into my skin and her heels kick into the mattress. When I lift my eyes, I'm shocked to see she's staring at me, her brown pools drowsed in desire. Soft, feminine pants and moans lash at me as I suck her harder, feeding my addiction for this, for everything she's giving me.

A little surprised cry fills the air, and her hips lock. I know what this means. I push down with my palm on her stomach to measure her body's reaction, but it's not necessary. I know exactly at which point she comes. She utters a high note and contracts around my tongue with a tangy explosion of moisture. I want to use her orgasm to drench my cock, to make it slick so I can sink it deep into her body, as deep as she can take me, but for now I only kiss and lick her clit, prolonging the shockwaves and reveling in her release. Despite my earlier resolution, I'm more than ready to fuck her, but something is holding me back. For some reason, I feel like it's her first time coming. A hot wave of satisfaction and immense anticipation washes over me as I consider the impossible.

Valentina is a virgin.

And it fucking crushes me.

I can't break something that is whole *and* pure.

Valentina

I'M INEXPERIENCED, not stupid. I know I had an orgasm, but it was my first and I'm devastatingly sad. Ashamed. I gave in to the man who was going to kill my brother, but those hands on my body… I expected force and roughness. Instead, he gave me gentle. It confused the hell out of me. The way his fingers explored my skin soothed me, and when I gave up on my fear, he set me on fire. He knew exactly what to do. There's no doubt he's a skilled and intuitive lover. He touched me like no man ever has, in a way that made my skin come alive. He twisted and primed my body, playing it like an instrument until it gave him the tune he wanted. I thought he was going to rape me. In a way, he did. In a way, this is worse. He raped my senses, took my defenses, and left me vulnerable, but not yet cold. His arms fold around me, pulling my naked back to his clothed chest. Hot, unwanted tears drip on the pillow.

I gave in.

I lost.

My body betrayed me.

Big, hard hands, hands that tortured my nipples into aching points of need, brush over my hip. One arm curls under me, strong fingers locking on my breast, while the other strokes my thigh gently as I battle to get my sobbing under control.

"Shh," he whispers against my ear. Repeating the same mantra from earlier, he gives me absolution. "You didn't have a choice."

There are many things I can take, but not his gentleness. I need to hate him. Prying his fingers open, I roll to the edge of the bed and jump to my feet.

"Get away from me." I jerk my nightgown down my body.

His eyes harden, but he doesn't reach for me. With his dark expression on top of the scars, he looks scarier than any man I've seen.

Lifting up on one elbow, he says, "You should've told me it was your first time."

Why can't I feel indifferent? Indifference won't hurt or cut so deep. The ache and betrayal won't let me go. Using that pain, I mold it into a shield of hatred.

Loathing infuses my tone. "What difference would it have made?"

There's a warning in his voice. "Valentina, I took nothing you didn't promise to give."

"Exactly," I snap. "I promised to give, not to take."

His lips lift in one corner, giving him the same amused expression from this morning when he threatened Charlie's life. "Give and take, now that's a debatable subject. The way I look at it, this was all give on your part. I did all the taking."

I'm fuming. I expected him to use me, but to do it like Tiny. Instead, he somehow managed to make me a partner in whatever he executed.

"Are you angry that I made you come or that you enjoyed it?" he asks, hitting the hammer on the nail.

Shivering with fury, mostly at myself, I wrap my arms around my body. "Is there something else you want? Any other *service* you require?"

He smirks. "All in good time." A wince replaces his cocky smile as he gets to his feet. "I'll have my breakfast at five. Grapefruit, orange juice, coffee, and omelette with chili. Make sure it's ready."

Adjusting his pants over a hard-on impossible to miss, he limps from the room. I wait a good five minutes after the clack of his heels on the kitchen tiles has disappeared before I shut the door, leaning against it with wobbly legs. My shoulders shake with more unwelcome sobs, but I can't stop them. It takes me a few minutes to find my control. I want to have another shower to wash away the remnants of Gabriel's touch, but a glimpse at my phone tells me it's past midnight. I have to wake in four hours, so I slip into bed and give myself over to the escape of a shallow and fitful sleep.

It's torture when my alarm goes off at four. Oscar is stretched out on the foot of the bed, purring like an engine. He must've jumped through the window during the night. I can only spare him a quick cuddle, or I'll be late. I put last night out of my mind, making a conscious decision to not dwell on the shameful memory. Torturing myself with the details won't change anything. I'll only make it harder on myself.

After a shower, I dress in the morbid, black dress and tie my hair into a ponytail. Knowing I'll be on my feet all day, I slip on my trainers. Half an hour later, I'm in the kitchen, chopping chili for Gabriel's omelette while the coffee percolates. Cooking comes easy for me. I've fed Charlie and myself since I was fourteen. I miss my brother so much. We've never been apart. It feels as if my anchor has been dislodged, and I'm floating aimlessly in a dark and treacherous sea.

My back is turned to the door, but I know the minute Gabriel walks into the kitchen. I first feel and then smell him. Heat creeps up my spine, making me break out in a cold sweat. The air becomes thick like smoke hard to breathe. My body registers his scent from where I've categorized it in my brain, connecting the dots to the sensual experience from last night, an experience I'd rather forget, but I can't help the powerful association. The clean, spicy fragrance of his skin triggers an unwanted reaction in my belly, contracting my womb with a fluttering echo of my first orgasm. My cheeks flame at the thought. I hope he'll think it's from the hot stove plate.

"Good morning, Valentina."

That voice again. Now that I'm less frightened, it leaves a complex mixture of sensory impressions on me--dark, smooth, bittersweet, and deep. Like burnt sugar. I glance over my shoulder. He's dressed in a dark suit with a white shirt and red tie. His hair is damp and his beard trimmed.

I fold his omelette, doing my best not to let my nerves show. "Good morning."

He comes to stand next to me, so close that our hips almost touch, and reaches for two mugs in the cupboard above. As he pours the coffee with a steady hand, mine holding the spatula starts shaking.

"Sleep well?" He pushes one of the mugs toward me, angling the scarred side of his face away.

Of course not. "Yes, thank you."

"Have you eaten?"

"Later."

"We can share the omelette."

"I can't eat this early."

I'd rather die of hunger than share his omelette. It's an illogical thought, since he gives me the allowance that pays for my food, but I have to hold on to whatever pride I can salvage.

"The doctor emailed your blood test results. You're clean."

Our eyes lock when I involuntarily jerk my head in his

direction. We both know what this means. As soon as the birth control takes, he'll fuck me. Unless he uses a condom to do it sooner. Before he can say anything else, I serve his omelette on the plate I heated in the warmer drawer and carry it to the dining room. Then I disappear to start my duties for the day, trying not to think about what he said in the kitchen or that I'd become a maid with benefits. A whore.

I QUICKLY GET a handle on the house routine. Carly gets up at six and leaves the house at seven without breakfast. Marie comes in at eight, places the grocery orders for the day, and starts preparing lunch. I give her my habitual shopping list. My staple diet consists of instant noodles and apples. Apples are cheap, filling, and nutritious. The noodles give me a boost of energy when my blood sugar levels drop too low. I need the bulk of the money I save for Charlie and my studies.

As I make the bed in Gabriel's room, I try not to gawk at his private space, but my curiosity outweighs my manners. Like him, the room is overly masculine. Heavy, silver-gray curtains drape the windows, and his furniture is bulky, modern, and square. The bed is bigger and longer than a king size. The monogramed initials on the sheets indicate they're custom made. The fabric is soft between my fingers. A glance at the label tells me it's a high-thread Egyptian cotton. There are many black and white photos of landscapes and buildings on the wall. The pictures are of foreign places and cities, maybe places he's visited.

A walk-in closet connects his bedroom to his private bathroom. The closet is bigger than my room with suits organized by color and shelves for shoes and ties. Gabriel is painstakingly neat. There are no dirty clothes or towels on the floor. Whatever toiletries he uses are stored in the cupboards. Nothing stands on the shelves, not even a toothbrush. His bathroom tiles are black and white with a gray border running above the twin basins. The taps and fittings are brass, and it's a bitch to polish them to a shine. I scrub until my nails are chipped, but that's the easy part. The not-so-easy part is trying not to feel the shame of my reaction to him as, even in his physical absence, his lingering presence taunts and torments me, forcing me to remember.

Oscar follows me around, keeping me company. By the time the morning deliveries arrive, I'm shaky with hunger. After wolfing down a bowl of noodles and an apple for breakfast, I feel better. Walking into my room for a quick bathroom break, my gaze falls on a box on the edge of the basin. I pick it up to read the label. Birth control pills. My face is ablaze with heat, even as my stomach turns to ice. I've never used birth control. Never needed it. With a shaky hand, I take out the leaflet and read the instructions. It feels like I'm crossing the last line by accepting the pills, but falling pregnant will be a disaster, and as crazy as it sounds to appreciate any gesture from my captor, I'm thankful to Gabriel for his consideration in this regard.

I'M HANGING out the laundry when a whistle catches my attention. The driver from yesterday enters through the courtyard door.

"Morning." He offers me an uncertain smile, eyeing my uniform. "How are you?"

I don't know what to make of his greeting, so I simply say, "Fine, thank you."

"I'm Quincy."

I tug a stray strand of hair behind my ear. "Hi."

When I resume hanging the washing, he cuts the small talk. "I came to warn you not to come outside before clearing it with the guard house."

"The guard house?"

"We live in a staff house at the back of the estate. There's a phone in the kitchen. If you dial the button marked guard house, one of us will pick up."

"Oh."

"Next time, if the door is open," he motions at the garden access, "call before you come outside."

"Why?"

"Gabriel keeps a guard dog. He patrols the garden, and we've had an accident before."

"Okay."

"Well then, have a nice day." He must realize what a stupid thing that is to say, because his cheekbones turn a shade darker. "See you later." With an awkward salute, he hurries away.

Picking up the empty basket, I notice Marie in front of the kitchen window, watching me.

S<small>OMETIME DURING THE DAY</small>, Gabriel and Magda must've left, because they're gone when Carly comes home at five. Judging by her casual clothes and the late hour of her return, she attends a private school. Public schools require uniforms and are out before lunchtime. Marie has already left when Carly finds me ironing in the scullery.

"Valentina, right?" She leans on the wall and bites into a peach.

"That's right."

"My dad didn't say he was hiring a maid." She regards me from under her lashes. "Can you bake?"

"Yes."

"Will you bake me a cake for dessert? Marie made flan. I hate flan."

I crane my neck to check the time on the wall clock in the kitchen. I need to finish earlier tonight so I can do my homework, but I can fit something in if it's not too complicated.

"What do you like?"

She swings the fruit by the stalk. "Anything with coconut."

I know a simple recipe for honey and coconut cake that doesn't take long. The ingredients are common enough. The chances are good I'll find everything I need in the pantry. I switch off the iron. "All right."

When the base cake comes out of the oven, I pour the melted butter, honey, and shredded coconut over the top, and caramelize it to a crispy brown under the grill. Carly leans on the kitchen counter as I remove the cake, her blonde hair hanging in a braid down her back. She's a stunning girl. She doesn't take after her father. Her mom must be gorgeous.

Carly sniffs appreciatively. "That smells good. I'll have a slice now."

She's not a child, but I say what I'd say to Charlie. "You'll spoil your appetite for dinner."

"Come on, Valentina." She pouts. "My mom never lets me have sweets. It's bad for my figure." She motions at her body on which there isn't an ounce of fat. "Daddy will be home any minute now, and I don't want him to know I'm snacking before meals. I'll never hear the end of it."

"You're a big girl." I push the cake toward her. "Don't say it's my fault if you're not hungry for proper food later."

"Oh," she winks, "I won't." She cuts a generous slice and bites into the warm cake, humming her approval. "Oh, my God, this is so good."

"I'm glad you like it." I return to my work, happy that I pleased her. Instinct tells me getting on with Carly won't be smooth sailing.

Twenty minutes later, I'm folding the last of the ironed shirts when Gabriel's thunderous voice bursts through the house.

"Valentina!"

Oscar scoots off the top of the tumble dryer where he's been sleeping and escapes to my room. I jump, burning my arm on the still-hot iron. A second later, Gabriel storms into the kitchen, almost knocking me off my feet as I exit through the scullery door.

He grabs my arm, his fingers digging into my flesh. His face is pale, making the red scars stand out more. "There's a first aid kit in the pantry. Top shelf on the left. Get it and bring it to the television room."

4

Valentina

I jump to execute the command, running through every lounge on the ground floor with a big screen in it until I find Gabriel on his knees in front of the couch in what must be the television room. Carly is lying on the couch, panting through an open mouth. Her skin is blotchy and puffy, and the glands in her neck are swollen. The sight shocks me to a standstill, but Gabriel's calm, strong voice commands me.

"Give me the epinephrine auto-injector. It's a yellow and white box." He loosens his tie and pushes a cushion under Carly's head.

I find the box and hand it to him with shaky fingers. Contrary to my trembling hands, his are steady as he opens the box and retrieves the injector. He removes the gray cap and pushes the red tip against Carly's thigh, then counts out loud to ten. When he's done, he checks that the needle has extended and caps it with the protective cover. I'm a vet student, not a doctor, but I know what epinephrine is for, and I know a severe allergic reaction when I see one.

There's underlying panic in Gabriel's steady voice. "The ambulance is on its way, honey."

"Allergy?" I force from a tight throat.

The only answer I get is his cold, frightening glare. I want to ask what she's allergic to, but the ringtone of a phone cuts me short. A mobile vibrates on the coffee table. Gabriel holds out his palm in silent instruction, his eyes back on his daughter.

When I place the phone in his hand, he glances at the screen, and answers in a flat tone. "The ambulance is on its way." His expression turns hard as he listens to a reply. "Yes, I take full responsibility if anything happens to her, and no, now's not the time to threaten me with sole custody. Come over if you want to see for yourself how she is or wait for us at the hospital, but stop calling every two minutes. It's not going to change a damn thing." He cuts the call and dumps the phone on the couch.

Before I can get my bearings, the doorbell rings. I run to get it, but the door opens to reveal one of the men from yesterday, the one who shot Puff. He leads two paramedics pushing a stretcher inside. A private ambulance is parked in the circular driveway.

"Where?" one of the men asks tersely.

"Follow me."

I lead them to the television room. The medics go inside and shut the door on me. Puff's killer gives me a hard look before he exits the house. While I'm pacing the corridor, a model-pretty woman rounds the corner and stalks my way. Her blonde hair is twisted into a French roll. A white two-piece suit clings to her body, defining her curves. There's a striking resemblance between her and Carly.

"Where are they?" she asks with regal calmness.

I indicate the door. "Through here."

She opens and slams the door, causing it to shake in the frame. Through the door, I hear the heated tones of an argument, but I can't make out the words. Carly's mom must live close by to be able to get here so fast.

Not sure if I should wait or leave, I decide to stick around in case they need me. Why didn't Carly call for me? Maybe she did, and I didn't hear. It can't be the cake. Carly would've told me if she's allergic to eggs or honey. It can be a bee sting. The sliding doors to the pool deck are open.

Seconds later, the paramedics exit, pushing Carly on the stretcher. Gabriel and the blonde woman walk next to the stretcher, Gabriel's face tense.

At the front door, the paramedics stop.

"Only one of you can accompany us in the ambulance," the older man says.

"You go." Gabriel drags a hand through his hair. "I'll meet you at the hospital."

When Gabriel's guard helps the men to lift the stretcher down the stairs, the woman I presume to be Carly's mom turns to Gabriel. "I expect you to deal with this."

"I will," he says tightly.

She looks down her nose at me before clacking a path down the stairs to the waiting ambulance. At the bottom, she throws her keys to Puff's killer. "Rhett, bring my car to the hospital."

Rhett glances at Gabriel, who gives a small nod. Carly's mom gets into the back of the ambulance, and the door is pulled closed from the inside. As the vehicle pulls off with blaring sirens, Rhett gets into a Mercedes sports model and follows.

We are alone in the entrance now, Gabriel and I, and fury replaces the coldness in his eyes.

"You have a lot to explain."

Panic speeds up my breathing. "What?"

"The cake."

To say I'm shivering in my shoes is an understatement. "Oh, no, Gabriel." This can't be happening. "I'm so sorry."

His eyes drill into mine. "Why did you do it?"

"I just wanted to make something nice for dessert."

"*Nice* could've gotten her killed. Or did you know all along? How did you find out?"

"I swear I didn't know. I still don't know! Was it the honey? The eggs?"

"Carly is allergic to coconut."

"What?" My mind is reeling. "She specifically asked for it."

He looks at me with an expression that stops my heart before sending it into overdrive, the beat pounding in my ears.

"If you're lying, you'll pay dearly." He grabs my arm with such a strong grip it hurts to the bone. "You don't want to know what I do with people who threaten my family, let alone try to kill them." He shakes me hard. "Next time, stick to what's expected of you and leave the menu planning to Marie." He shoves me away and takes his phone from his pocket.

I'm hugging myself while he barks out a command into the phone.

There's a dark threat in his words. "Stay with Valentina until I return." After putting away his phone, he hisses, "Be very glad she's not dead and be even gladder Magda is at a dinner party tonight."

A guard comes jogging up the path, an automatic rifle in his hands.

When he reaches the porch, Gabriel says, "Don't let her out, and if Magda returns, don't let her near Valentina."

The guard nods, taking up a position by the door.

I try to calm my breathing as I meet Gabriel's livid stare. He has all the reason in the world to be angry, and the fact that he doesn't hit me makes me fear him more. It means he has control, and men with control are the most dangerous.

"Go inside." The words sound like an ice lake cracking. "Don't even think about running. The windows and doors are protected with an alarm."

I bite my cheek to still my chattering teeth and do as I've been told. I'm scarcely inside when I hear the tires of a car shooting up gravel. Through the lounge window, I see a Jaguar convertible clear the gates.

I'm shaking all over when I get to my room. Oscar is my consolation, offering me affection as I sink down on the bed and sit in the dark until my breathing is more normal. As the minutes roll into hours, I try to calm my mind by studying, but I can't concentrate on what I read. One hour becomes two, then three, four, and five. I don't have the courage to shower or change. All I can do is wait for Gabriel and Carly's return. Not able to stand the tension any longer, I take up a post in front of the window in the dining room that overlooks the street-side of the property.

It's almost eleven before the headlights of a car illuminates the gates. It can be Magda, returning from her dinner party. Relief washes over me when the Jaguar pulls up to the door. A haggard-looking Gabriel gets out and limps around the car to help Carly from the passenger side. With his arm around her shoulders, he leads her up the steps.

I rush to meet them in the entrance. "Carly! Are you all right?"

"She will be," Gabriel says, moving past me.

"I kept the dinner warm."

"I'm not hungry," Carly says.

"You need your strength, honey. Bring it up to Carly's room."

He doesn't spare me a glance as they make their way upstairs. I prepare a tray and knock on Carly's door before I enter.

Gabriel sits in a chair next to the bed, Carly's hand clasped in his. He turns his scars away from me. "Leave it on the table. We'll serve ourselves."

I obey and escape to the false safety of my room. I'm petrified Gabriel won't believe me, but even more terrified that my mistake will cost Charlie's life. 'One wrong move,' Magda said. I don't get why Carly would do something like this.

For another hour, nothing happens. Eventually, my tiredness wins over my anxiety. I have a quick shower and get into bed.

Gabriel

IN THE SOLITUDE of my study, I sit down at my desk to contemplate my options. It's a difficult decision. I watched a playback of the security feed from the cameras in the kitchen. Carly's voice was clear when she asked for a cake with coconut. Valentina told the truth. With a sigh I feel all the way to my bones, I pour a shot of whisky and down it in one go.

I don't understand my daughter. I failed her. There's a gorge so wide between us I'm afraid I'll never bridge it. When the crack started, I can't say. Was it during Carly's toddler years, when I was always absent from home, the family business taking up my days and nights? Is it because Sylvia and I couldn't make things work? If I can pinpoint when it started, maybe I'll find the reason. Carly and I both know there's a problem. We don't acknowledge it, because it's easier to skip the drama. If I believed Carly has a better relationship with her mother, I'd encourage her to stay with Sylvia, but she's old enough to choose, and the fact that she lives here tells me enough.

Despite being scum, I try to be fair. It's the only shred of humanity that stands between the man and the monster, but in my business, fair only applies to family. Putting any staff member above family, right or wrong, won't be tolerated. Such an act could get said staff member killed. Innocent or not, actions have consequences, and Valentina can't escape taking responsibility for hers. Sylvia expects me to inflict suitable retribution. She's not going to forget or let it go. If I don't do it before Magda comes home, Valentina will die for what happened tonight. I don't feel like punishing Valentina for something Carly should pay for, but I don't have a choice.

I refill my glass and shoot back another shot before I pick up my phone and dial Rhett. "Come to my study," I say when he answers.

The fact that something ignites in me, making me hard, when I think about what I'm about to do is proof of how far gone I am. It could be that the alcohol is fuel on my rusty inhibitions. Maybe it's heredity, and it's in my genes. I'm not a made monster. I was born one.

The door opens, and Rhett enters. "You called for me, boss?"

"Take Valentina to the gym."

The twitch that wrings his lips into a smile makes me want to break his nose. I add it to the mistake he made of shooting the dog. Deep down, I know it's not Rhett's fault. He never expected me to let the Haynes' live. He did what he believed was right, but he caused Valentina suffering, and he'll have to pay. Lucky for him, he leaves without question. I could do with another drink, but I won't risk it. I have to be sober. I'll need utter control.

The house is dark and quiet as I make my way downstairs to the basement. It's a windowless room where my guards and I work out, but it also serves as interrogation room when the need arises. For this reason, it's soundproof. Carly can never know what happens in the depths of the house when she's fast asleep upstairs.

5

Gabriel

I flick on the lights and walk around the room, trying to still the upsurge of regret that's not powerful enough to wash out my excitement. The exercise mat absorbs my steps, not giving sound to the unequal harshness of my soles.

Regret makes me weak. Excitement makes me cruel. Anger makes me dangerous. I assess my state carefully. Anger is not part of my repertoire tonight. That's a good thing, or I wouldn't be able to do this. It would be much too hazardous.

Rhett enters the room with Valentina, his hand folded around her upper arm. She's wearing her nightgown, which exposes her toned legs. Rhett's fingers leave white indents on her skin. It shakes up all kinds of sentiments in me, but they're like shredded pieces of paper. I can't make sense of anything, except that I want to chop off his hand and poke out his eyes.

With a flick of my head, I direct him to the back wall. He knows what to do. Her eyes hold mine as he drags her past. The quiet kind of anger I often recognize in myself makes the brown of her irises sizzle with sparks. Within seconds, Valentina is strung up by her arms on a rope knotted to her tied wrists, facing the wall.

"Go," I say to Rhett.

He gives me a questioning look. The surprise and disappointment on his face threaten to unleash my rage. I've never dismissed him when punishment or interrogations are executed, but this isn't a goddamn show for his entertainment. Rhett knows me well enough to read the signs. With a last, confused glance in Valentina's direction, he walks from the room, shutting the door behind him.

When there are just the two of us, I breathe easier. The violence dissipates. It becomes something different, something that turns my already erect cock into a raging hard steel rod. I adjust the rope, stretching it gently through the eye in the ceiling until she's barely touching the mat with her toes, and secure the cord to the hook on the wall. I don't want her to struggle or move. It's safer this way.

She peeks at me from over her shoulder, her eyes big and her cheeks pale. "What are you doing?"

It's not an easy question. There are many layers to it. I unbutton first one, then the other shirt cuff, rolling the sleeves back as I contemplate the answer. I don't lie if I can prevent it. I decide to give her the simple truth.

"Punishment, Valentina." I let her name roll over my tongue, loving the sound of it. Such a pretty name. *Valens*. Strong. It suits her.

She twists in her constraints. "I didn't do it on purpose."

I reach up from behind, grabbing her arms to still her. "I know."

She stops struggling, and her body freezes. "Then why are you doing it?"

I sweep her silky hair over her shoulder and brush my lips down the curve of her neck. "Because I get off on this." Another layer of truth.

A sob tears from her throat. "Please."

My cock twitches. There's begging in that word, but also acceptance. She knows there's no turning back. Even if there weren't Sylvia's expectations or my mother's threat, I can't stop myself. Not anymore.

I kiss the shell of her ear.

"Gabriel…"

She should call me sir or Mr. Louw, but the sound of my name on her lips is a treat I'm not going to deny myself. Already battling to carry her weight, she tips back. I catch her around her waist. My hands dip under the hem of her nightgown, gliding up her soft thighs. Hooking my thumbs into the elastic of her underwear, I pull it down over her hips and calves, leaving it around her ankles.

She shivers under my palms, but wisely doesn't speak. There's nothing she can say to stop this. When I step away, her body sways backward. Like a ballerina, she dances on her toes to regain her balance. A cry leaves her lips when I grip the collar of the nightgown and rip it down the middle. The fabric hangs loosely down her body, giving me a glimpse of her smooth back and the curve of her ass, but I'm greedy. To save time, I use one of the combat knives from the weapon counter, cutting open the arms to free her from the constraining clothing.

I step back to admire the view. Fucking hell. Restrained, with only her panties around her ankles, she's an erotic image that will haunt my dreams. Her frame is a flowing portrait of S-lines, from the slender curve of her neck to the sides of her plump breasts and the narrow diameter of her waist to the swell of her hips and the rise of her firm ass. My eyes follow the trail of her legs from her quivering thighs to the dip of her knees and from the gentle expand of her calves to where they taper to her delicate ankles. My fingers ache to bury themselves in the cheeks of her buttocks and in the warm, wet depth of her cunt. I expel those thoughts almost violently, knowing I can't enter her there. For now, I'm content to have her naked and bound, and if I'm honest, I'll admit this isn't about retribution or proving to my mother I'm not weak. This isn't even about saving Valentina's life. This is all for me.

I cup her breasts from behind and search the soft sweetness of her skin, dragging my lips down the elegant curve of her neck. "If I don't do this, Magda will kill you."

She turns her head to the side, away from my caress and voice.

So be it. She won't defy me much longer. I can never have my fill of looking at her like this, but her arms can only hold her weight so much longer before I risk tearing them from their sockets. I shake my fingers to loosen them and breathe in and out a couple of times to find my control. It'll be easy to go over the edge with her. Too easy. There's something about her that shatters every ounce of willpower I possess, a new experience I'm not sure I like.

I loosen my buckle and pull the belt from the loops of my waistband. Only then does she look at me again. Finally, she understands my intention. Her eyes grow large, and her lips part.

"Eyes in front." I don't mind seeing her tears or hate, but I don't want her to see the lust in mine, the darkness that makes me the monster.

Stepping so close I can smell the raspberry fragrance of her skin, I smooth my hand over her ass. When she clenches her muscles, my cock pushes painfully against my zipper. I knead her ass cheeks, playing with the firm softness of her flesh. Parting them, I can glimpse the pretty pucker of her ass. I draw a finger down her crack, teasing the dark entrance before running the tip down to test her pussy. She's dry. Good. I love the challenge.

I take a step away, widen my feet and find my stance. Drawing my arm back, I practice careful control with my strength, letting the leather collide with her ass hard enough to sting, but not forceful enough to bruise.

Whack.

The red line that welts over her golden skin makes my cock twitch. A drop of pre-cum heats the tip of my shaft.

Whack.

She cries out softly and jerks in her restraints. She's holding back.

Whack.

"Let me hear you, Valentina."

Fire simmers with tears in her brown eyes as she glances back at me. "Fuck you."

"Very well."

The next lash falls over her thighs, just under the curve of her ass. She squirms and whimpers, grinding her teeth so hard I can hear it. The next smack is gentler, aimed higher to heat her pussy.

Her cry comes involuntarily. She tenses up as the sound escapes. I let the lashes go higher, leaving a crisscross pattern over her back and shoulders. Allowing the tip of the leather to fold around the sides of her breasts, I keep well away from her nipples. My lashes are not hard enough to draw blood or break skin, but before long she's grappling for air, moving as far away as the position allows, which isn't much. I let the belt curl around her waist, letting her feel the bite on her stomach, and move back down to her ass and thighs.

I give her a break to catch her breath, using the time to free her underwear, spread her legs, and tie each ankle to a cuff on a chain extending from the wall. She can move her legs forward or backward, but she can't close them.

I walk around to face her. Grabbing her jaw, I kiss her hard. She's crying into my mouth, her lips defenseless as I sweep my tongue over hers, devouring her like a starving man. Forcing myself to pull away, I steal a last, chaste kiss before taking my place behind her again.

"Ready?"

I test my strength by swinging the leather under the curve of her ass. When her golden skin is left unmarred, I twist the belt one more time around my hand, leaving a shorter bit at the end, and let a succession of soft but fast swats rain between her legs, aiming the leather to heat both her labia and clit. She fights it at first, flinging her head back, and pushing her breasts forward.

"Let me hear you."

I don't stop until she finally breaks for me with a scream. The breath she's been holding escapes, allowing her shoulders to rise and fall with violent sobs. At her surrender, I cast the belt aside and grab her to my body.

I want her. I want her so fucking bad I can't think. For all of my intentions to be gentle, I can't help the rough way my fingers feel between her legs. A groan is trapped in my chest when I find her wet. I need to be inside her. Now.

My hands shake as I undo my pants and let them fall to my ankles to free my cock. My shaft aches with need, the root pulsing as I grab it in my fist and guide it to Valentina's wet pussy. Bending my knees, I spear through her thighs and drag the head of my cock through her folds. I shiver in anticipation as her moisture slickens me, and the heat emanating from her core invites me deeper. Driven by primal hunger, I place the sensitive head against her opening. My only instinct is to impale her, to take her as deep as I can, but it's her frightened whimper that pulls me back from my dark lust.

Barely holding onto reason, I coat my dick in more of her arousal before slipping free from between her legs. I'm too far gone to back off completely, and as much for my sanity as her chastity, I carefully open her ass cheeks, and wedge my slick cock between them.

"Please," she begs, arching her back away from me.

My voice is guttural. I don't recognize the sound. "Relax. I won't fuck you."

She stills at that, but only until I start gliding up and down, folding her ass cheeks around my cock with my palms. I have to push her body against the wall in front for leverage. When I move faster, she starts squirming in all earnest, twisting to the left and right.

"Keep still," I hiss, "or I'll accidently penetrate your asshole."

Again, she goes slack, allowing me to find my release by grinding my cock up and down the crack of her welted ass. I find her breasts and hold her to me as I come, shooting my seed up her spine, the hotness of my release dripping down between our bodies. When there's nothing left to give, I let go, stumbling back a step to look at her. She's marked with the imprint of my belt, and my sperm running between her ass cheeks over her pussy and down her thighs. Intense satisfaction surges inside of me, overriding even the physical high of ejaculating on her skin. It's the most beautiful thing I've seen, and that fucking scares me.

Coming to my senses, I pull up my pants and unlock the cuffs around her ankles. I loosen the rope from the hook on the wall, releasing her arms. Valentina falls backward, but before she hits the floor, I catch her around the waist and use the same knife I used to cut off her clothes to cut through the rope around her wrists. She's crying and shaking, her body limp in my arms. I use her nightgown to wipe her back and between her legs, getting rid of most of the semen, and then I pick her up in my arms and carry her to her room.

Placing her inside the bath, I run a cool shower and sponge her down. She doesn't object to anything. Her pretty eyes are closed, but tears are leaking from under her long lashes, and I have to look away. I find them way too appealing. She's like a ragdoll in my arms when I towel her dry, taking care not to press on the marks of my belt. They'll be gone in a day, but she'll hate me much longer. No marks will be left on her body, but not everyone carries their scars on the outside.

I put her to bed on her stomach, naked, and don't pull the sheet over her. She'll want nothing to touch her skin for a while. Going down on my knees between her legs, I make her come with my mouth until she begs me to stop. Through her begging, I wring one more orgasm from her before I'm satisfied. Then I get onto the bed next to her and pull her onto my chest so that she's stretched out on top of me. I kiss her head and stroke her hair, holding her until her breathing takes on the even rhythm of sleep.

It's after midnight. Magda will be home any minute. Valentina doesn't wake up when I ease out from under her. Looking down at her slender back marred with red welts, I'm filled with the devastating affirmation that I can't play with a perfect, new toy without breaking it.

I WAIT in my study for Magda to return. I prefer to relay tonight's events to her myself, before she hears the news from Sylvia or Carly. I can still taste Valentina on my lips. Her arousal is a powerful aphrodisiac that twists my balls into rock hard knots and feeds my lust. There's peace in knowing I own her pleasure and discord in not being able to take her. Until she's no longer a virgin, I can't bury my cock in her soft body, and I want nothing more than to train her to come with my dick until she gets wet from the mere sight of me. It takes everything I have not to go back to her room and fuck her raw. I drag my tongue over my bottom lip. Savoring Valentina's womanly scent one last time, I pour a drink and down the liquor, drowning the perfume of her skin in alcohol.

Magda is pissed as hell when I give her a brief summary of how the night turned out. It's when I assure her Valentina's been punished, and she watches the video feed of Carly asking for a coconut cake that she calms.

"You have work with Carly," she says. "That girl has issues."

"I know." I rub my eyes.

"Do something about it, before it becomes a disaster we can't fix." She walks from my study without saying goodnight.

I touch the photo of Carly on my desk, having plenty of questions and no answers.

Valentina

It feels like Gabriel took something from me. I knew he was dangerous, but I had no idea how dark he is. What Tiny did to me was almost more bearable, because it never turned me on. What Gabriel did to me last night made me wet, and that makes me sick. I, of all people, should be disgusted by the violence. It wasn't the lashes on my back. It was the intense rhythm of the leather between my legs. I both resented and appreciated that he took care of me--both emotionally and sexually--afterward. It was something I needed desperately, and I hate myself for it.

Wanting to hear a kind, safe voice, I call Kris before she's due at the practice, and speak to Charlie, who sounds as happy as only Charlie can be. It soothes me enough to get me through my Friday morning chores. My body is sensitive from Gabriel's lashing, and each brush of the rough linen of my dress is abrasive on my skin. Carly is at home today, skipping school to recover, and I do my best not to run into her. I only clean her room when she's outside by the pool.

Marie avoids my eyes. If she knows about last night, she doesn't say so. She comes looking for me in the entrance where I'm mopping and fixes her gaze on a spot behind me. "Mr. Louw says the towels in the gym needs washing."

"Okay." I mop past her feet.

"You must take clean ones. Now."

She leaves stiffly, hiding her discomfort behind her brusque manner.

I fetch a clean pile of towels from the linen closet and make my way down the hallway. As I descend the stairs to the gym, my stomach clenches, and my throat closes up. Forcing my feet to move forward, I stop abruptly when the door opens, and Rhett exits, blood all over his naked chest. He's pressing his palm to his nose, his head turned up, and almost bumps into me before I have time to jump out of the way. The reason for the blood seems to be a broken nose. The bridge is swollen and the cartilage askew. His right eye sports a shiner, and the skin on his cheekbone is split. When he notices me, he glares and pushes past, making for the stairs. I'm still staring after him when Gabriel walks through the door dressed only in sweatpants and clutching the ends of a towel draped around his neck. His face and chest glistens with perspiration.

My face flushes at the memory of last night, and my mouth goes dry. Where I come from, I've seen a lot of gangsters who pump iron in the gym all day, but no one as hard or perfectly cut as Gabriel. His upper arms are the size of my waist. Deep lines define his pecs and abs. A trail of dark hair starts beneath his navel and disappears under the pants, the V of his hips cutting sharply down to his groin. It's not the beauty of his body that renders me speechless, but the power of it. Even with his disability, he stuffed Rhett up badly, and Rhett is a hulk. As he advances, I stand there like an idiot with the towels in my arms, not having words.

A smile flirts with his lips. "Training," he says with a shrug, grabbing one of the clean towels off the pile to wipe his face. He gives me his intense stare, searching my face. "How are you?"

"Fine."

"Good." Dumping the towel in the basket by the door, he limps away.

It's the first time I see him in anything but a dress shirt and suit pants. The broadness of his shoulders and the tightness of his ass don't surprise me as much as the way the sight of him, half naked, makes my womb flutter. I can't feel desire for a man who tortured me. It will make me as twisted as him. It will drag me down to a place I won't be able to come back from.

Angry at my unwelcome reaction, I enter the gym and pack the clean towels on the shelf before picking the dirty ones off the floor. I take my time to do what I haven't done last night––take stock of the room. There's a section with free weights in the corner and a small bathroom off to one side. Judging by the metal rings bolted to the ceiling and the hooks fitted on the walls, this is where Gabriel tortures his enemies. A chill fills my veins, and I'm not able to look any longer.

I rush back upstairs, banishing my memories of last night to the depths of the gym. In the lounge, I run into Carly.

She props a hand on her hip. "Hey, Valentina."

I can't ignore her without being rude. "How are you feeling?"

She cocks a shoulder. "I'll be fine."

"Why did you do it?"

"To get you fired."

I don't know if she knows what her dad does for a living, but if she doesn't, it's not my place to disillusion her. I can't tell her I'm here against my will, especially not after Magda's threat to kill Charlie and me for one wrong word. All I can ask is, "Why?"

"I saw the way my father looked at you at dinner."

"What way?"

"A way he never looked at my mom. It's the money, isn't it?" She gives me a wry smile. "It's always the money. Well, plenty of others before you tried, and it always ends the same way. He won't marry you, and you won't get a cent, so save us all the trouble and pack your bags now."

"Yes, it's the money, but not how you think. I can't give up this job, even if I want to."

"You don't belong here. I want you gone."

"So badly that you'll endanger your life?" I ask with a note of anger.

"Oh, come on. Why are you so upset? It didn't work, did it? You're still here."

"I have every reason to be upset. What you did was foolish and irresponsible."

"What's your problem? You're acting like you're the one who almost died."

"My problem is that if you *had* died, I would've carried your death on my conscience for the rest of my life. Have you considered that?"

"Who do you think you are to speak to me like this?"

"Is it the attention? Is that the only way you can get your parents to show you they care?"

She draws back her arm and lashes out. Her palm connects with my cheek, leaving a burning sting. "You know nothing about me."

In that moment, her guard is down, and a vulnerable part peeks out from under her bitchy veneer.

I cup my cheek, pressing a cool palm on my heated skin. The fight goes out of me as I only feel pity for the poor, rich girl who, underneath it all, is just a girl.

I sigh. "Listen to me, Carly. You're young, beautiful, privileged, and healthy. You have your whole future ahead of you. You can have anything you want. It's more than most people get. Don't waste it. Even if you don't see it now, your parents would've been devastated if anything happened to you, and I would never have forgiven myself."

"Yeah?" Tears glisten in her eyes. "Like you know me or my family. Don't you dare preach to me. Maybe you would've liked to be a psychologist, but you're not. You're a *maid*, so stick to your trade." Her eyes turn hard. "I'll be outside. Bring me a turkey sandwich and lemonade. Plenty of ice. When you're done, you can clean my bathroom again. You missed a spot. Then you can iron my new blue dress. I want to wear it to school tomorrow."

I want to say I don't answer to her, but that's not true. By the rules of our kind, I'm lower on the hierarchy than the cat.

THAT AFTERNOON, Carly doesn't touch her lunch. It's a delicious looking lasagna, but she's not to be persuaded to take a bite. Magda and Gabriel treat her with kid gloves. Gabriel goes out of his way to drag a conversation out of her but gives up after a while.

After clearing the table, I salvage the portion from Carly's plate and set it aside to eat later. The rest I scrape into a plastic container I store in the staff fridge for the street dogs. I hate wasting, and I'm famished, hungry for something other than apples and noodles. I'm sure no one will mind if I eat a leftover portion destined for the trashcan.

During my lunch break, I put a cushion from a patio chair on the deck steps and make myself as comfortable as I can on my bruised butt. Then I dig in. The lasagna is rich with white sauce and cheese, the meat dripping with fresh tomato and oregano. I close my eyes as I chew, savoring every bite. Marie knows how to cook.

I'm almost finished when barking draws my attention. Quincy stands at the edge of the pool with a vicious looking Boerboel. The beast is straining on the leash, baring his teeth.

Quincy jerks on the chain. "Quiet!"

The barking stops, but the dog still growls at me, his lips pulled back over his teeth.

"What the hell are you doing outside? I told you to call. You shouldn't be in the garden when the dog is out." Quincy takes a few steps toward me, but stops a safe distance away. "I told Marie I was taking him for a walk."

"I guess she forgot to tell me."

"I'll have a word with her." With a tight nod, he continues on his way, the dog hopping along on three legs.

"What's wrong with his paw?" I call after them.

He pauses. "Don't know. I'm taking him to the vet tomorrow."

It looks painful. I leave the plate on the step and get to my feet.

Quincy looks mildly surprised when I approach, but when I'm almost within reach of the leash, he holds up a palm. "Don't come closer."

The dog goes ballistic, barking and straining toward me.

"Down, boy," I say in a stern voice.

The dog reacts immediately. He stops barking and sits down.

"That's better."

As I reach for the dog, Quincy looks like he's going to have a heart attack. "Valentina! Stay——"

His words are cut short when the beast flops down on his side and turns on his back, all four legs in the air.

I go down on my haunches to stroke his belly. "That's a good boy. It's not polite to make so much noise for nothing."

Quincy stares at me, his mouth agape. "How did you do that? No one is able to touch him but me, and I've trained with him for a year."

"I have a thing with animals."

"You don't say."

Smiling at the surprise in his tone, I look up at him. "What's his name?"

"Bruno."

"Of course it is. Can I have a look at his paw?"

He squints at me. "If he'll let you."

Taking the injured paw in my hand, I study the pad. A broken thorn is lodged in the flesh. The poor baby must be suffering.

"It's a thorn." I point it out to Quincy. "Do you have a pair of tweezers?"

"No." He thinks for a bit. "Wait. Maybe this'll do." He pulls a Swiss Army knife from his pocket and unfolds a small pair of tweezers.

"Perfect." Taking the knife, I scratch Bruno's ear. "I'm going to make it better."

It takes a second to extract the thorn. The area around the wound is inflamed. Handing the knife back to Quincy, I ask, "How long has he been like this?"

"He's been limping all week. I couldn't get an appointment at the vet sooner."

"You'll still have to take him." I straighten. "He needs an anti-bacterial and anti-inflammatory cream."

He tilts his head. "How come you know all this stuff?"

"An interest."

Bruno rolls back onto his paws and licks my toes.

"No shit." Quincy shoots me a smile. "Thanks for your help. He wouldn't let me touch that paw."

"Don't mention it."

"I'm not sure Gabriel is going to be happy when he learns you turned his guard dog into a drooling puppy."

"It'll be our secret. As far as the rest of the world is concerned, Bruno is a vicious guardian."

He whistles through his teeth. "Come on, Bruno. Time to finish your walk." He salutes, and walks off with Bruno in the direction of the orchard.

MY HOMEWORK IS FALLING BEHIND. I have an essay to finish before Friday next week, but I'm too exhausted to read further than one page. With what happened last night, I didn't get much sleep. I *have* to meet my study deadlines. I won't give up. I can't. It's not only my dream that keeps me motivated, it's knowing that I'll have something to fall back onto when I'm free. Charlie and I will need an income. We're not going back to Berea. I have to build a better future for us, and Gabriel Louw isn't taking that away.

I take a cool shower, still feeling the sting of the water on my back and butt. Since the only nightgown I owned is destroyed, I pull on a T-shirt and a pair of panties before slipping into bed.

Like the first night, Gabriel comes to me when I'm sleeping. I'm not sure if it's the way he softly cups my breasts or the sound of my moan that wakes me, but I'm too tired to fight it. I simply let him hear what his touch does to me. I'm rewarded with a kiss on the mouth, startling me to a fully awake state. It's nothing more than a brush of his lips over mine, but the intensity burns like a fire, and I find it…pleasurable. His mouth is cool and dry, and his breath smells of mint and alcohol, like whiskey.

Warm air blows over my ear as his lips graze the shell. "Turn over for me, Valentina."

He lifts the sheet for me to make it easier, but my feet get tangled in the duvet at the foot. Carefully, he frees each foot, stopping to caress the bridge before planting a kiss on the sole. The tender act confuses me. I expected him to hurt me like last night, not to trail his hands gently up my body and twist my hair into a ponytail before arranging it on the pillow next to me. Maybe he will. My body tenses. Gabriel is anything but predictable. He lifts my arms and, bending them by the elbows, puts my hands above my head. A tap on my inner thigh makes me lift my head to look at him, but he cups my neck and, with the slightest pressure, pushes my face back into the pillow. He taps on my thigh again. Understanding the cue, I open my legs. The mattress dips as he gets onto the bed behind me. He doesn't undress me, but pushes the T-shirt up to my shoulders and pulls the panties down to the under-curve of my butt.

Heat drenches my skin as he stretches out on top of me without touching our bodies together. Keeping his weight on his arms, he flicks his tongue over a welt on my shoulder, making my nerve endings pop with electricity. Goose bumps break out on my skin when he blows air over the wet trail of his tongue. He continues down my body, treating each lash with the same care, until he reaches the dimples of my ass. As he licks and blows over my ass cheeks, moisture gathers between my legs. This goes on for a long time, until my clit is swollen and pulsing in need.

The first time he lays his hands on me after kissing my bruises is to remove my underwear. Gripping my hips, he lifts my ass. He takes his time to position me like he wants, kneeling with my legs spread and my forehead resting on the pillow. With my ass and sex exposed to him, he sits back and watches. I can't see, but I feel his eyes on my body, burning on my naked parts. His palms glide over my buttocks before he takes a cheek in each hand, parting me like fruit while running his nose from my coccyx to my opening. A shiver runs through my organs. My depraved body knows what's coming and wants it. His tongue flattens on my clit, warm and wet. I cry out as the raspy, hot surface draws over my slit, all the way to my asshole. Somewhere in the back of my mind there's a cry of embarrassment, but it's no use giving rein to the sentiment. Gabriel will do what he wants.

He continues to lap me like this until I'm desperate to come. Unable to stand the slow torture any longer, I moan loudly into the pillow. He hums his approval and finally gives me what I want. Catching my clit gently between his teeth, he flicks his tongue over the nub––fast, but too light.

My hands fist into the sheets. "Ah, God. Please."

"Please what?"

"Please make me come."

As soon as I verbally express my need, he opens me wider with his hands and nips at my folds, alternating the gentle bites with sucking on my clit. It takes me seconds to come with a violent spasm of my womb. Pins and needles prick my genitals. My toes curl. I can't take more.

"Stop. Please."

Begging doesn't help. He milks me dry until I'm a quivering mess, and only then does he push on my back to lower my pelvis to the bed. I'm shaking and boneless. I never thought it could be like this. He lowers over me, at last pressing our bodies together, until my trembling stops. With a kiss on my neck, he lifts from the bed. I turn on my side to look at him, some part of me needing to see his expression, but he turns his face away.

He taps his fingers on my lower back. "Go back to sleep."

Then he's gone.

For a long time, I lie in the dark, trying to understand Gabriel. I don't get it. What is he doing to me?

Gabriel

IT DOESN'T HELP that Valentina is around every hour of every day. I'm a walking hard-on, suffering from constant blue balls. No amount of wanking is enough to relieve my ache. I want inside her. Deep. Deep enough to hurt. The only niggle is her virginity. It's a barrier to me, literally and psychologically. I don't want to be the one to break her that way. Her first time needs to be special, not monstrous. Even I am not that cruel. She deserves a pretty face and gentle kisses, not a scarface who loves to fuck rough.

In this lies the problem. I can't take her virginity, and I can't stomach the thought of someone else taking it, either. I won't last much longer without relief. I consider calling Helga, but when I think of another woman, I can't get it up. The image of Valentina's strung-up body with her underwear around her ankles haunts my nights. I wish I'd taken a photo so I'd have something concrete to jackoff to.

The emergency with Carly is further fuel on my nerves. I'm not sure if I should punish her or call in professional help. I'm not a great moral example. I have no ground to judge or discipline her. If there's one thing I'm sure of, it's that Carly won't live the life I lead. My mother never gave me the choice. She put a gun in my hand when I was twelve and told me to pull the trigger. When I couldn't, she shot me in the foot.

There's no point in talking to Sylvia. Sylvia is way too much like Magda. God knows why I ever thought we had a chance. I loved her. I truly did. I believed she'd learn to love me with time, but the only thing that became clear with time was her ambition. What she wanted was my money and protection, not my love. She married me on her father's orders and got out as fast as she could, as soon as she produced the heir expected of her. Her sacrifice got her what she wanted. As the mother of my child, she'll always have my money and protection. After Carly, she insisted on a hysterectomy, ensuring she wouldn't bear me any more children. Sylvia hated every minute of being pregnant. She was devastated when the doctor confirmed the results of the pregnancy test. Carly stretched and scarred her body. Sylvia never forgave me for that. The minute Carly was born, Sylvia went on a diet and a binge of plastic surgery, letting the nanny take care of our child. Maybe Carly subconsciously felt the rejection. She was a colicky baby. She's never been an easy child, but she's my daughter, and the only human being I love in this world. I wish I knew how to fix this.

Magda's high-pitched voice and fast-slapping heels on the marble floor in the foyer pulls me from my troubles. An itch works its way down my shoulder blades.

"That's it! I've had it."

I pull the door open to see Magda charge down the hallway with Oscar. She's got him by the skin of his neck.

"What's going on?" I barely hide the irritation in my voice.

She doesn't stop in her stride, but calls over her shoulder, "He peed on my Louis Vuitton sofa. Quincy! Get your ass over here."

Quincy rounds the corner, a question on his face.

"Here." Magda pushes the clawing cat into his arms. "Take him to the vet and have him euthanized."

I'm about to tell my mother she's overreacting when Valentina flies from the lounge, a cloth and spray bottle in her hands.

"Oh, no, please, Mrs. Louw, you don't have to do that. It's not his fault. It may be a urinary infection. I'm sure antibiotics will fix the problem in no time."

Magda turns on Valentina. "What makes you the goddamn expert?"

"She's got a point," Quincy says.

The fact that he puts himself between Valentina and my mother isn't lost on me. I don't like it. Not one fucking bit.

"I'm heading out to the vet with Bruno, anyway," Quincy continues. "I can take Oscar."

"I'm not spending another cent on this fur pollution. He's just signed his death warrant."

That figures. My mother never harbored any love for my late grandmother's overweight cat. If it was up to her, she would've abandoned him at my grandmother's house after the funeral, but Carly insisted we bring him here.

"I'll take him," Valentina says quickly. "I mean to the vet. You don't have to pay anything, I promise."

I lean in the doorframe, enjoying Magda's irritation. "It was Grandma's cat, after all," I drawl.

My mother shoots me a dirty look. "Fine," she says to Valentina. "If you've got money to waste, do as you please, but if he pees in the house one more time, he's dead."

"I can take him on Sunday when it's my day off."

"Today or never," Magda says, marching to her study and slamming the door.

Valentina looks at me. There's a plea on her face. I haven't missed how Oscar follows her around or that he sleeps in her bed. She's fond of the shedding fluff ball.

"You can take an hour this afternoon," I say.

Her face lights up, and a smile transforms her features into something angelic, something too good for me. I take it anyway, enjoying the knowledge that I put that expression on her face, giving her something more than physical pleasure.

"I'll drive you," Quincy says.

Immediately, my good mood evaporates. Dark, suffocating jealousy smothers my reason. My bodyguard may mean the gesture in the most platonic way possible, but I want to break every single one of his ribs. The only thing that prevents me from kicking the life out of him is that Valentina doesn't see the way his eyes soften as he drags them over her, because she's looking at me. She's looking at me for permission. The submissive act somewhat calms me. I don't manage more than a nod.

"Thank you," she says, her gaze wary, as if she's reading the change in my temper.

I'll be watching Quincy from now on.

Valentina

THE VET BILL eats a hole into my allowance, money I was going to use for my studies, but the tests are done, and Oscar has medicine. It's a urinary infection as I thought. The vet assures me he'll be back to normal in a couple of days. It was my plan to take him to Kris on the weekend. She would've treated him for free, but I couldn't risk his life, and I don't doubt for a second Magda would've had him put down. To play it safe, I lock him in my room with his litter tray and food, waiting for the frequent urination to stop.

When I get to my room that night, there's a bundle of colorful silk tied with a ribbon on my bed, and a note tucked underneath. Curious, I pick up the piece of paper. The handwriting is neat and square.

Shave your pussy.

Gabriel is the most warped man I know. Flinging the note aside, I pull the ribbon off to reveal seven nightgowns in red, navy, white, pink, baby blue, black, and cherry plum, all with lace and ribbon trimmings. Did he get me new nightgowns because he destroyed mine, or are the sinfully sexy sleepwear something that turns him on?

I should be studying, but I can't stop thinking about the note. There will be repercussions if I disobey. In the shower, I trim and shave my pubic hair. It's a surprisingly lengthy task. After moisturizing my body, I pull on the navy nightgown, which is the least revealing, and sit down on the bed to wait.

It doesn't take long before I hear footsteps in the kitchen.

Oscar, who sleeps on my bed, twitches his ears, but he doesn't move. Gabriel's tall frame appears in the doorway. With the backlight from the scullery, his face is in the dark. I can't make out his expression. He flicks on the light and enters the room with slow but purposeful steps. He's a man who always knows what he's doing and who always has a reason for his actions. His gaze slides over me from top to bottom, but there's nothing of Tiny's lustful need for a quick fix in his eyes. They're filled with questions as he runs his fingertips down my arm from my shoulder to my hand. There's a crazy moment when I almost trust him with my body, that I almost surrender my mind. It's like being in a car with a good driver, knowing you'll end up safely at your destination. I must be going nuts. It's the endorphins my body releases when he touches me. Purely hormonal. Biological. Gabriel is a sadist, and he made me a whore. I can never trust him.

He slides a finger under the strap of the nightgown. "It looks good on you."

"Thank you," I say awkwardly. "You didn't have to."

"Yes, I did." He lifts Oscar from the covers and puts him in his cat bed in the corner. "He doesn't need to see this."

I'm not sure if he's joking or serious, but the insinuation behind his words makes my underwear damp. I don't want this reaction, but I'm helpless to stop my body from wanting what he gives.

He drums his fingers on my wrist. Whatever is going through his mind, he's giving it deep thought. Finally, he breaks the silence with a single command.

"Undress."

I can fight and argue, cry and plead, but it won't make a difference. It never does to men like him. Sitting up, I take the hem of the nightgown and pull it over my head. My underwear follows next. I don't want to drag it out. The quicker we get this over with, the quicker I can go back to pretending I don't want him to touch me like this.

Gabriel doesn't hide his arousal from me. He's comfortable

with it, like he is with his body and clothes. His erection strains under the fabric of his pants, but he doesn't touch it or go for his zipper. He tucks my hair over my shoulders with a gentle brush and continues with his orders.

"On your knees and open your legs."

Heat creeps up my neck as I take the posture that opens me up for his gaze, but I lift my chin and face him squarely. I won't surrender to my shame, not with him in the room. For a long moment, his eyes fix between my thighs, seemingly pleased that I obeyed his order to shave.

He tests the weight of my breasts, sending an uncontainable shiver over my skin. I can't prevent my nipples from hardening.

"Shoulders back, tits forward."

I give him what he wants and wait.

A rare smile tugs at his lips. "You're so brave, Valentina." Without warning, his hand slips between my legs. He cups a broad palm over my sex. "I love your cunt bare. Do you know what I want to do to you?"

He doesn't wait for my answer, but flicks the forefinger of his free hand left and right over the tip of my breast. The movement is firm and fast, and it makes my already heavy breast turn even more swollen. While he's toying with my nipple, he pushes his middle finger against the opening of my vagina. He doesn't penetrate me, but runs the tip of his finger up and down my slit. The rasp of the rough skin of his pad feels more intense on my shaved skin. Strangely, his touch on my breast echoes in my clit. The nub between my folds swells and throbs with aching need. Wetness coats his finger. I can feel the moisture as he slickens the outer walls of my opening with my arousal. Determined not to give him a sound, I gasp nevertheless when he grips my nipple between his thumb and forefinger with a pinch.

Satisfaction bleeds into his expression. For some reason, he's happy with my reaction. He's happy that he has this effect on me. Another cry leaves my lips as he rolls my nipple.

"Valentina," he says with a moan, "you're everything I want."

Alternating between pinching and rolling my nipple, he works my body into a state of desperate need. The bite of pain followed by the softer caress is too much to bear. No man has ever touched me like this. There's so much wetness, his hand is covered. It takes everything I have not to grind into his palm. I don't have to. He presses the pad of his thumb down on my clit, massaging in circular movements. His deft fingers abandon my tormented breast to start working on the other one. When he gives the curve a soft smack on the side, making it bounce, a gush of liquid heat spills from my body and coats his fingers.

His eyes widen, and his pupils dilate. "You like that."

My lips part, and sounds I don't want to make tumble from my mouth. Nerve endings in my lower body spark with electricity, and an invisible band of fire draws tight around my womb. It implodes, drawing all my feminine parts tight in my core before it snaps and explodes from my clit outward. All the while, I watch his face. I hold his eyes as much as he holds mine. For the briefest of moments, he's exposed, and I understand why he's enjoying this. My pleasure gives him power.

With a hand on my back, he presses my upper body to his chest while he holds my sex in hand, applying gentle but unyielding pressure to my clit while aftershocks from my orgasm wrack my body. I shake in his hold, my energy spent, and my pleasure his. Only when my body turns quiet does he stop his assault on my clit. He keeps his hand between my legs still while he brushes a broad palm over my hair and down my back. His lips are warm and dry as he plants kisses from the arch of my neck down to my shoulder. His breath is a mist of heat on my skin. His erection is a steel rod that presses against my stomach from the difference in height with him standing and me on my knees, but he doesn't pay it any attention. Slowly, he pushes me back on the mattress and straightens my legs. Kneeling on the floor between my legs, he kisses first my clit and then my folds, running his tongue over the wetness and lapping it up until I'm only wet from his tongue, but no longer slick.

When he finally gets back on his feet, he wipes his mouth on the back of his hand. A flush burns on my cheeks.

He smirks and bends over me to plant a firm kiss on the corner of my mouth. My scent is musky on him. He continues to plant kisses down my body, turning rougher. I'm still soaring from my orgasm when he starts nipping my nipples and pinching my clit. It takes him a long time to bring my body to a quick, but intense, second orgasm. His roughness, in contrast to the first orgasm, feels like punishment, but I can't think of a single reason why. His house is spotless, and I stay away from the kitchen. By the time he's done with me, he's panting as hard as I am. He doesn't angle his face away from me like I'm used to, but pulls me into a sitting position on the edge of the bed while his hands go for his pants.

The air squeezes out of my lungs.

He's going to fuck my mouth.

6

Valentina

Visions of me on my knees in the middle of the road for anyone to see make my throat tight. I close my eyes, trying to visualize a black hole in space, anything so I can escape into a dark corner of my mind.

"Open your eyes," Gabriel commands.

I obey. I don't have a choice.

"Unzip me."

He has undone the button of his pants. A trail of hair peaks out from under the open flaps. My hands shake as I pull down the zipper. I'm on eye level with his crotch, and he's towering over me. The difference in strength between us chokes me. He can easily make me swallow him, and there will be nothing I can do.

"Take me out." His voice is quiet and calm. There's nothing threatening about it.

Slowly, I push the elastic of his briefs down his hips to free his erection. He's impossibly big. Free from its constraints, his cock twitches and hardens more. The crest is broad and smooth. Manly veins run over the thick shaft to where the root is cushioned by heavy balls.

He doesn't grab my hair and force himself into my mouth, but simply stands there, watching me as I study his cock. I've never seen one from close-up. I've had Tiny's down my throat, but I deliberately never looked at it. Gabriel's is beautiful, a work of art.

He doesn't object when I slide a finger over his length from the bottom to the top, so I carry on with my exploration, caressing the velvety head. I'm rewarded with a drop of moisture that spills from the slit. In response, liquid heat gathers between my legs, even if I've just had two orgasms. When I wrap my fingers around him, he groans. Loudly. He's not afraid to let me see the power I have. The deep lines that cut from his hips to his groin fascinate me. I abandon his cock to trace them with my fingers, surprised at how hard the muscle is underneath. A white scar runs across his hip, covering bone and flesh. He grits his teeth when I trace it, but doesn't say anything. His cock jerks when I run my hands down to his inner thighs and cup his balls. They're soft and heavy, contracting in my palm.

"Valentina," he moans, "suck me already or zip me up."

He's giving me a choice? Emotion clogs up my chest. I swallow and look up to catch his expression. He's looking down at me with something like hope and acceptance. He'll take whatever I'm prepared to give.

He strokes my hair, his big hand cupping the back of my head. "Take only what you want."

At the verbal confirmation, my fear vanishes. He'll let me stop. He won't hold it against me. I lick my lips to moisten them, uncertain how to proceed. I've never done this without force.

"However you want," he whispers. "There's no right or wrong way."

I inch to the edge of the bed, taking his cock in both hands. Holding him close to my mouth, I flick out my tongue to taste him. A strangled grunt escapes when I lick over the crest. He tastes of earth and sea, a mixture of fertile soil and salty air, and I love it. I lick down to the base to see if it's the same, and when I suck a testicle into my mouth the heady taste intensifies.

"Fuck. Goddammit."

He threads his fingers through my hair, but he doesn't pull. He's holding onto me for support as I take his control. The knowledge gives me more power, and it makes me brave. I slicken the whole shaft with my tongue, using my saliva as a lubricant for my hands. I grip his girth firmly, one hand above the other, and move my fists down while pushing my lips over him.

"Ah, fuck." Air wheezes through his teeth. "Yes."

I suck him into my mouth, hollowing my cheeks, and running my tongue over the head.

He buries his fingers deeper in my hair. "Yes, beautiful, just like that."

When I glide my hands up and down his length where my mouth doesn't reach, he grows even thicker in my mouth. His hold on my hair tightens, and his ass clenches. "Pull out if you don't want to swallow."

I don't want to give my power away, yet. He's letting me do what I want with him, and his cock is jerking in my mouth. He's close. I want to take him all the way. There's agony in his eyes. I recognize the look, know the depth of that kind of pleasure. I felt it at his hands, lips, tongue, and teeth. I open my throat and take him deep, breathing through my nose.

His jaw clenches as he grunts out his pleasure while warm jets coat my tongue. He holds my head in the gentle vice of his palms as he empties himself. Keeping his hips still, he lets me suck him dry rather than moving between my lips. I take every drop like I earned it, drinking down the dizzying cocktail of male ecstasy and feminine power.

Looking spent, he bends over and leans our foreheads together while he catches his breath. I'm still floating on a cloud of warm satisfaction knowing I pleased a man like him, when he tilts my head and crushes our lips together. He kisses me fiercely, tangling our tongues, and sucking my bottom lip into his mouth. When he finally lets go, I'm breathless.

His eyes crinkle in the corners. "You taste good with my cum on your tongue."

A wave of heat creeps up my neck and spreads to my cheeks.

He chuckles and kisses my forehead. "Zip me up."

I bend to pull up his underpants and pants. There are more scars on his leg, but I don't linger there. For now, I'm concentrating on adjusting the clothes over his cock. He's still semi-hard. The velvet feel of his warm skin is pleasantly erotic. He catches my hand and moves it away, finishing the task of zipping his pants up himself. He plants a warm, wet kiss on my mouth and pushes me down to the mattress with a hand wrapped around my neck. For a second he stays like that, watching me, and then he lets go.

"Not yet," he says, as if to himself. "Good night, Valentina."

Then, like last night, he's gone.

It's ten when I go up to Gabriel's room to make his bed. By now, he'd have finished his morning workout and shower. He'd be working in his study. As I'm pulling the sheets over the mattress, the bathroom door opens, and he steps out with a towel tied around his waist, his hair wet and droplets running down his chest.

I gulp and almost choke on my saliva. Heat gathers in my underwear as my imagination completes the picture hidden under the towel. A slow smile spreads over his face. He twists his head, hiding the scars from me, and walks to the dressing room.

"Shall I make the bed?" I ask in a small voice.

He turns to watch me, letting his eyes slide over my dress, making me feel naked. "Unless you have other ideas?"

His smile broadens as a flush heats my cheeks.

I clear my throat. "I meant I could come back later."

He drops the towel, flashing me with a full frontal of his glorious, naked body.

"There's nothing you haven't seen," he says, "so don't let me keep you from your work."

He's wrong. The white, embossed line running diagonally across his knee is new to me. So is the circular mark surrounded by finer lines, like a spider's web, on his foot. He looks like a perfect Frankenstein specimen, angrily stitched together and magnificently hard. There's not an inch of him that's not one hundred percent man, in every right and every wrong way possible.

For an utterly embarrassing moment, I'm frozen to the spot, staring at him like an idiot. It's Gabriel who breaks the spell by walking to a rack of shirts. His ass looks like it's chiseled from marble.

My breath flutters as I force my eyes away and continue the task of making his bed. All the while, I'm aware of him. He pulls on a white shirt and buttons it up. Next follow briefs, black slacks, and silver tie. He sits down on a stool to pull on socks and expensive looking shoes. He opens a drawer and selects a pair of cufflinks, which he fits without difficulty.

I've never watched a man's grooming. There's something intimate about it. It's like a privilege he's given me, allowing me to watch. All dressed up, he leaves the room, trailing his palm over my backside on his way out. The caress is so light, maybe I imagined it. Alone, with no one to see, I fluff out his pillow and push my face into it. I inhale his scent, remembering the taste of him in my mouth. What is it like to be a woman from his world, treasured and respected, and not a maid or sex toy? We're worlds apart, and our worlds don't mix.

For the remainder of the day, I keep a watchful eye on Oscar. His frequent urination stops in the late afternoon. It's safe to let him out of my room. Besides, he can't stay here all weekend when I leave.

Gabriel is out when my weekly shift comes to an end. I'm nervous to leave the grounds even if Magda was clear on the rules, but I'm also anxious to see Charlie and Kris. I shove a change of clothes and the container of food remains into a grocery bag and check that Oscar has enough food before I go. Outside, I find Rhett on the porch.

"Hi." I clutch the bag in my hands. "I'm off until Monday."

"I know."

"I'll need the new key to my flat."

"You're going back there?"

"I need to tie up loose ends."

"Wait here." He disappears inside and exits a short while later with a set of keys he places in my hand. "The big one's for the main lock, and the two small ones for the top and bottom deadlocks."

"Thank you."

"Are you going there now?"

"Probably tomorrow. I'm first going to see my brother." I also want to visit Puff's grave. "Where did you bury Puff?"

"You don't want to know."

"I want to put flowers on his grave."

"You don't want to put shit out there. In fact, I'm not sure you should go anywhere near that neighborhood."

From the look he gives me, I'm scared he's going to prevent me from leaving, so I say quickly, "See you Monday."

He doesn't reply, but doesn't stop me either. When he presses a code on his phone that opens the gate, I rush through with relief. There are no public busses in this area, but if I walk far enough, I'll eventually hit the off-ramp to the highway where I can catch a minivan taxi. I flag one down after a fifty-minute walk. I'm the only white girl in the van and receive nasty remarks about the color of my skin from the other passengers, but the driver is kind and lets me sit up front until he drops me off in Orange Grove.

A Jewish community mostly populates the area because of the synagogue. In Rocky Street, I pause to feed the food remains to the street dogs before hurrying the last two blocks to Kris' house. I enter through the adjoining clinic. A few clients are waiting in the reception area. Kris runs an honest to God good practice for the love of it. She charges way less than what she should, and I know she treats a lot of animals for free when the clients can't afford the medicine or consultations. She barely makes ends meet, and I feel bad for saddling her with my problems, but I have no one else.

There's no assistant. She hasn't replaced me yet. I knock on the consultation room door and push it open.

Kris lifts her gaze from a Yorkshire Terrier and shoots me a smile. "Get me a vaccine shot while you're here, will you?"

I scrub my hands in the basin and enter the small backroom where she keeps the vaccines. She's in over her head, so I stick around and help out where I can.

After seven, she pats my shoulder and jerks her head toward the door. "Go on. Charlie's in the house. I know you're anxious to see him."

"Thank you." I offer her a grateful smile and hurry through the back to the house.

Charlie sits in front of the television in the lounge, wearing a Superman T-shirt and shorts, his fringe falling into his eyes.

When he sees me, his eyes light up. "Va–Val!"

He jumps up and grabs me into a hug, almost crushing my ribs. Sometimes, he forgets his strength.

"Hey." I brush the hair from his face. "How are you? Is Kris taking good care of you?"

"Loo–look." He points at a stack of comic books on the coffee table. "Kri–Kris gave me money to ex–exchange th–them."

"That's great," I say, even if I worry. The comic store is across the road. Charlie has to cross a very busy street to get there. "Have you eaten?"

"Kris is a good coo-cook. She's making ma-macaroni and chee-cheese to-tonight."

"Sounds good." I tie an apron around my waist, and set to work cooking dinner and cleaning the kitchen. Dirty dishes are stacked on every surface. The trashcan needs a good scrub and the floors a wash. Kris has never been tidy, but she spends every free second in the practice. An hour later, the kitchen is spotless, and the lounge and bedrooms vacuumed. I'm busy putting clean linen on the beds when Kris enters, looking shattered.

"Dinner's ready." I pull out a chair by the small table in the kitchen where Charlie is already seated.

She looks around and shakes her head. "You didn't have to."

"Are you kidding? After what you're doing for Charlie?"

"Yeah." Her eyes are probing. "We need to talk about that."

I glance at my brother and give her a pointed stare. "After dinner."

"Okay."

Later, when I've tucked Charlie into bed, I take the clean laundry from the dryer and start folding it. Kris takes two beers from the fridge, cracks the cans, and hands me one.

She leans on the counter and props a foot on the cupboard door. "So, care to tell me about this new job of yours?"

I take a long swig from the beer before I face her. "There's nothing more to tell."

Her eyes narrow on me. "How long?"

"Nine."

"Nine months?"

"Years," I say from behind the beer can.

She sprays the swallow of beer she's just taken over the clean floor. "Jesus, Val." She shoves a hand into the pocket of her jeans and stares at me with an open mouth.

"I know. It's not like I have a choice." I don't go into the gritty details.

"Hold on. Are you telling me you're his live-in maid for the next nine years?"

"Yes." I dab up the spilled beer with a paper towel.

She starts pacing the floor. "What about your studies?"

"I'll still carry on."

She stops. "Will you manage?"

"I'll have to."

"It's a lot of studying. A fucking lot of studying."

"I know."

"Did you sign a contract?"

"I don't need a contract. Paper is worthless to men like him. His word is enough."

"How does this agreement work?"

"The salary he would've paid me goes to settling the debt."

"How could he approve a loan for Charlie? I mean, Charlie. Of all people. There must be a law that prevents institutions from granting loans to disabled people."

"I never declared Charlie incompetent. A big oversight on my part. In any event, fighting him with the legal system won't work. You know every judge in this country is corrupt. The man with the most money always wins."

"Fuck, Val, there must be something we can do."

"Look, I can't change it. I have to make the best of it."

"If you're working for him for nothing, how will you afford your studies?"

"He's giving me an allowance. It'll be enough to pay the portion the bursary doesn't cover, and I was kind of hoping you'll keep me on for Sundays."

"You're going to burn yourself out."

"That's rich coming from you, Miss Workaholic."

She smiles. "You know I'll do whatever to help."

"I'll pay for Charlie's food and expenses. I don't expect you to put him up for nothing."

"Forget about it."

"It's not up for negotiation." I hesitate. "Nine years is a long time."

"Don't worry about Charlie. He's welcome here for however long it takes."

"Thank you, Kris." A heavy weight lifts off my shoulders. "I don't know what I would've done without you."

"What about your flat?"

"I'm selling it. There's no point in keeping it if it's going to stand empty."

"Good luck. You'll battle to give it away for free."

I sigh. "I know. Listen, about Charlie." I twist the tip of my trainer on the floor. "He told me about the comic store. It's a busy road, Kris."

"I taught him to wait for the green light. We did a few practice rounds together. You've got to let go a little, give him some freedom. I know you feel protective, and it's understandable, but you have to push him to be as autonomous as possible."

"I just…" I swallow. "I just don't know. I feel responsible."

She leaves her beer on the table and takes my shoulders. "It's not your fault. It was an accident. You have to let it go."

I wipe at the unwelcome tears in my eyes and look away. "I know."

"Hey." She wipes my face with her palms. "Everything's going to be all right. It'll work out. You'll see."

"Sure." I only say it to placate Kris, because once she's on a roll, she won't stop until she believes she has me convinced. Kris is the queen of positive thinking, and for that I'm as grateful as I am for her giving me a job and taking Charlie in.

"Come on." She hooks her arm around mine and drags me to the lounge. "Let's watch a stupid sitcom and laugh ourselves silly."

"I don't know." I pull back. "I have to get to the flat."

"What, *now?*" She points at the window. "It's pitch black dark outside. How will you get there? I'm not letting you out of this house tonight. You can bum on the couch. By the way, I cleaned up your place and emptied out the fridge."

Tears of gratitude stream over my face. I really need to put a cork in it, but it's as if the dam wall has broken.

"Now, now." She hugs me tightly. "Tomorrow is another day."

I WORK all Sunday in the practice, and after buying a few groceries to stock up Kris' cupboards, I head out to Berea in a minivan taxi before it gets dark. The agent I called that morning is waiting for me in front of the building when I arrive. I wonder about Jerry, but I already see from the street his windows are dark. When we exit the stairs on my floor, my heart lurches. The door stands ajar.

"Wait," the elderly gentleman says, pushing me aside.

He takes a pistol from the waistband of his pants and nudges the door open with his shoe.

Chaos greets us. Every single cupboard is open. Broken crockery is scattered over the floor. The mattress is shredded, foam peeling from cuts in the fabric. The cushions have been destroyed, too.

He lowers the gun. "Is anything valuable gone?"

I shake my head. There was nothing, except for our kitchen utensils. "Why would anyone do this?"

"Destruction. They don't need any other reason."

We study the door together. It's not broken.

"The bastards picked the locks," he says, confirming my deduction.

As I start sweeping up broken glass and porcelain, the agent inspects the ruined space. He ums and ahs, testing the taps and the button to flush the toilet.

"Everything looks clean," he finally says, "but it's tough selling in Berea these days."

My heart sinks, even if I know no one in their right mind will buy a place in the heart of drug valley, and those who'll risk it here don't pay rent. They simply take or vandalize.

"Can you try? I really need the money."

"Don't we all? What about the furniture?"

"I'm having it picked up by a pawn shop." Kris gave me the contact. They offered me a few bucks for our belongings.

"I'll keep in touch."

After he's gone, I ensure the fridge is empty and have a shower before I switch off the geyser. Tomorrow, I'll have the electricity and water cut. It's additional bills I don't have to worry about. The money will go to Kris to help pay for Charlie's part of the living expenses. Tonight is the last night I plan on spending here. I never want to come back. When I'm done paying Charlie's debt, I'll join Kris in her practice and get Charlie and me a place of our own. Kris promised me a full partnership when I graduate from vet school.

It takes a good couple of hours to clean up the flat, after which my grumbling tummy reminds me I haven't eaten since lunch. I drink a glass of water, but the hunger pains won't go away. There's nothing in the cupboards. The thieves took all the tinned and dry food that was left. There's ten bucks in my bag from the allowance Gabriel paid me, but I'll need it for taxi fare. I turn the broken side of the mattress onto the bedframe and make the bed, trying not to think about food. I double-check that the door is locked. The new door is sturdy and comes with a deadbolt on the inside, which I slide into place. It gives me a small amount of added security.

Sometime during the night, there's a thunderstorm. I lie awake, watching the lightning run across the sky and listening to the drops falling on the roof. I long for Charlie and Puff. A selfish part of me wishes they were here so I could hold them in my arms, while the logical part of me is happy that they're free from this hell. It's a miracle that I'm here, unbound, that despite my debt, I have a measure of freedom. It gives me hope. Maybe Magda has some fairness inside of her. My thoughts drift to Gabriel as I fall asleep, and my dreams are filled with disturbingly erotic images of his scarred body.

WHEN THE ALARM on my phone goes off at five, I haven't slept much, but I can't risk being late for work. The gangs and criminals are mostly active at night. At this time, most of them will be passed out from alcohol or drug abuse. There's little chance I'll run into any unfavorable elements on the street. After brushing my teeth and washing my face, I pull on my clean dress. I lock the door, drag the trash bags with our broken crockery downstairs, and hit the streets.

My trainers fall quietly on the pavement as I dodge the potholes filled with water. The air is fresh after the rain with steam coming off the tar. There's a quiet after the storm, leaving me peaceful and calm, but my tranquility doesn't last long.

A little way down the street, a tall, slender figure emerges from between two buildings.

7

Valentina

My heart lurches in my chest. Maybe he hasn't seen me. I clutch the bag to my body, searching for a side road to slip into, but it's too late. The man heads straight for me. I know that step. There's a slight bend to his knees, and his arms are spread wide. My breathing quickens, and my body breaks out in a sweat, but I lift my chin and give him a defiant stare when he stops in front of me.

"Well, now," Tiny says, "if it ain't Little Red Riding Hood."

"I don't have time for your games."

I try to move past him, but he grabs my arm.

"No time for Tiny? My, my, are you an uppity-ass, now?"

"Unlike you, I work. Let me go or I'll be late."

"High and mighty, huh? Tiny heard you left. Tiny was watching your flat, waiting for you."

His words shake me. I didn't run into him by chance. He *waited* for me.

"Tiny…" I want it to sound like a warning, but there's a wheeze in my voice.

"You still owe Tiny. You'll always owe Tiny. Tiny has waited long enough."

He starts dragging me by my arm toward an alley. I kick in my heels and try to pry his fingers open, but his grip is like steel. Panic gets the better of me. This time is different. If he was going to fuck my mouth he would've done it in the street, as always.

"Tiny, no!"

"You can scream all you like. Nobody gives a fuck."

He shoves me down the foul-smelling alley all the way to the end where the exit is blocked by overflowing trashcans and rips the plastic bag from my hands. Peering inside, he takes out my purse, drops it on the ground by his feet, and throws the rest onto the heap of garbage.

"Come here, white bitch." He takes a wide stance and feels his way up under my dress, dragging his sweaty palms over my hip and stomach.

Oh, God, I'm going to be sick. "Don't."

"Or what?"

My defenselessness infuriates me. The anger boils over. I pull back and punch him on the jaw as hard as I can. For all of one second he's off balance, but before I'm one step away, he grabs my arm and throws me against the wall. My back hits the bricks with a thud. He slaps me so hard my ears ring.

"Fucking bitch."

I scream and scratch, my fingers going for his eyes while my knee aims for his crotch, but he catches my wrists above my head and presses my body to the wall with his weight.

"Wanna fight?" he hisses, the repugnant air from his mouth fanning my face.

"Let me go!"

He laughs and shifts, holding me secure with one hand to stick the other down the front of my panties. "What have you been doing with this cunt, huh?" His fingers drag over my clit, parting my folds.

I press my knees together, but it's no use. He wiggles his fist until it's lodged between my legs, forcing my thighs open.

He licks my neck, inviting a shiver of repulse.

"Tiny's gonna fuck you so hard, you're gonna forget your name."

His upper body crushes me. I almost sigh in relief when he pulls his hand from my underwear, only to cry out in despair when he shoves his pants down over his hips.

Please, no. Not this.

He knocks my knuckles into the wall, but I hardly feel the pain. I need to fight. I struggle like mad person, which only makes him laugh. By the time he has his dick out of his underwear and my dress hitched up to my waist, I'm already panting from the exertion of fighting him while he hasn't even broken into a sweat.

"Tiny." The plea falls from my lips while tears stream down my cheeks.

"Yeah, say my name, bitch."

When he rubs up against me, I bite my lip so hard I taste blood. The fear I've fought against my whole life finally gets to me, making my throat constrict and my heart pump with furious beats. It's difficult to breathe. It happens all over again, the man who raped me. I fight the images that play over in my mind, but I'm back in the bar where the men dragged me, on my back on the pool table while the one with the deep voice unzips his fly, and the rest watch. I'm in a zone where I don't want to be, but I can't come back. Tiny's hand is around his flaccid cock, pumping it to life, but I already feel the tear in my body and the dribble of blood running down my legs.

"Get your hands off her."

The voice that spoke isn't part of the memory. The men cheered him on. They didn't tell him to remove his hands. They were filming it, laughing as I cried.

"Now."

The deadly calm in the baritone voice is dangerous. It's like this morning's quiet before the storm. Tiny freezes, bringing my attention back to him, to the present. He drops his penis and lifts his hands, glancing over his shoulder as he takes a step back.

"Easy, man," he says in a thin voice. "You're interrupting our fun."

"Fun?" The tall, broad figure in the dark steps forward, a gun aimed at Tiny.

His face is in the shadows, but I know it's him. I know his voice, his shape, his smell, his very presence.

"Doesn't look like she's having fun," Gabriel says.

"Whoa." Tiny laughs nervously. "You've got it all wrong, here. Tiny ain't doing nothing wrong. She's Tiny's bitch. Ain't you, honey? Come on, love." He jerks his head in Gabriel's direction. "Tell the man."

Gabriel moves so fast, I don't see it coming. The one minute he's standing at the entrance of the alley and the next he's in front of Tiny, hitting him in the stomach with a punch that sends him flying through the air and falling in the gutter water. Gabriel steps over him, pointing the gun at his head.

"Oh, fuck." Tiny lifts his hands. "I'm sorry, bro. I didn't recognize you."

Gabriel cocks his neck, cracking a bone. "Apologize."

"I'm sorry, Mr. Louw, really I am."

"To her, not to me, you prick."

Tiny licks his lips and glances at me briefly before returning his gaze to the gun. "Sorry. Tiny didn't know you and Mr. Louw are friends."

"Friends?" Gabriel utters a cold laugh that vanishes as quickly as it started. "She's property."

Tiny gulps and starts crying. "Fuck, man."

I'm shivering in my dress, feeling like I'm stuck in a very bad dream.

"Valentina." The firm way in which Gabriel says my name commands my attention. "Walk to the street and wait on the corner."

"No," Tiny says, shaking his dreadlocks, snot running from his nose. "Please, fuck. No."

Gabriel is going to shoot him.

"Gabriel, please…" I take a step toward him. I need to find a connection with him, to reason with him. "Please, look at me."

He doesn't look away from Tiny. "I won't tell you again. Leave the alley and wait at the corner."

I start crying myself, touching Gabriel's arm. "He's not worth it. Don't."

I can't live with myself knowing I'm the reason for another man's death. My father is enough.

Gabriel cups my nape, and drags me closer, pressing me hard against his body without moving his aim from Tiny. He kisses my temple with his gaze fixed on the man on the ground and speaks softly against my ear.

"Go. Now."

In Gabriel's world, there's vengeance and violence. Violence can be dissuaded, but never vengeance. I know how it works. If he doesn't shoot Tiny, Tiny will have to kill him or look over his shoulder forever. I don't want this for Gabriel. I don't want him to carry another life on his conscience, especially not because of me.

"Gabriel––"

Quincy comes running down the alley. He brakes in his tracks when he takes in the scene.

Roughly, Gabriel shoves me toward Quincy. "Take her to the car."

Quincy doesn't hesitate. He drags me kicking and screaming down the alley, all the way to the car where Rhett waits. He bundles me into the back and wipes a hand over his face. Rhett gives me a grim look in the rearview mirror. I huddle in the corner, unable to control my shaking. I wait for a shot to go off, but hear nothing. Gabriel would use a silencer. A few seconds later, he exists the alley, adjusting his cuffs and walking with brisk strides to the car, my purse in his hands.

Once he's in, Rhett pulls off. No one says a word on the way home. Gabriel puts his arm around me, holding me tight, and I close my eyes and cry quietly for the terrible act he committed for me.

Gabriel

AT THAT HOUR, everyone at home is asleep. We park at the back so I can carry Valentina to her room without having to traverse the whole house. She objects when I lift her into my arms, but I don't heed her. Rhett and Quincy will go back to deal with the body. They know the drill. Since that scumbag fucker son of a bitch Tiny wasn't connected to any gang, there are no logistics or payoff to iron out. My priority is Valentina.

Oscar jumps from the tumble drier and runs ahead of me into Valentina's room to keep guard in the windowsill. I lay her down on the bed and remove her trainers before stripping the dress. It's going to the trashcan. I don't want anything that filthy Zambian touched on her skin. Anyway, the dress is threadbare.

Going through the shelves of her closet, I find one T-shirt, a tank top, a pair of jeans that has seen better days, and a pair of shorts. These are all the clothes she owns? I make a mental note to go through her belongings later and grab the T-shirt.

Helping her to sit up, I dress her. After what happened, I don't want her to feel vulnerable, and nakedness will do that.

"What time is it?" she asks.

"Almost six."

"I need to get ready for work."

She tries to get up, but I push her down.

"Stay."

"I'm fine." She looks up at me through her wet lashes, her lips quivering.

Yeah. She looks anything but fine, but she's obstinate and worried that she'll fail in her job and therefore get shot.

"Don't move," I say with enough authority to make her obey as I leave the room.

In the kitchen, I pour a stiff shot of whiskey and take a mild sedative from the medicine kit. The remedy is natural and won't have adverse effects with the alcohol.

Sitting down on the edge of Valentina's bed, I lift her head, slip the pill into her mouth, and hold the glass to her lips. "Drink up."

She doesn't argue. Her blind obedience heats my insides. It's a huge step, and I don't think she realizes how much trust she's showing me.

Depositing the empty glass on the floor, I take her hand in mine. Her bones are delicate and thin in my palm––breakable. There are scratches on her knuckles, but they're not deep. We can worry about that later. The sight of those marks unleashes the monster in me, though, and it takes some effort to calm myself enough to ask, "Do you want to talk about it?" I do, but I'm not going to push. Not now, at least.

She puts a hand on her forehead. "I–I don't feel so good."

My body tenses, every muscle going taught. "What's wrong?"

"I don't know. I just feel weird."

"Tell me what you feel."

"Dizzy. The world is turning."

The effect of the alcohol is kicking in, but instead of relaxing her, it's making her drunk.

"When was the last time you ate?" I ask with caution.

She lifts her eyes to the ceiling while she thinks. "Lunch."

I try to keep my voice normal. "Yesterday?"

She clutches my hand like a riptide is about to pull us apart. "Gabriel?"

"It's just the whiskey I gave you to relax. You need food. I'll get you something to eat."

"You don't have to. I can." There's a slight thickness to her speech.

"I know you can, beautiful."

I pry her fingers open gently and go back to the kitchen to rummage through the fridge. Going for as much carbs, fat, and protein as I can find, I pile a plate high with leftover Bacon Carbonara and add lots of cheese. While the food is heating in the microwave, I grab a fork and paper napkin. Back in her room, I prop her back up against the pillows and twist the pasta around the fork. When I bring it to her mouth, she utters a weak protest.

"Open," I say.

Again, she obeys.

I feed her until the plate is empty before I pull her into my lap. "You should sleep now."

She shakes her head, brushing her cheek over my chest. "Can't. Have work to do."

"It's an order, not a request."

Her eyelids are already heavy. "Thank you for saving me."

"You're welcome."

"Why were you there?"

I run my gaze over her face, drinking in her pretty features as the truth registers in her expression.

"You followed me?" she asks with disbelief, a tinge of hurt thrown into the mix.

"Your phone," I replied flatly. "I planted a tracker in it before I gave it back to you."

"Why? Don't you trust me? Do you think I'll run?"

If she knows the intensity of my obsession, it'll expose the one weakness I can't afford. I'll lose my power over her, and that's not something I'm willing to let go, ever, so I give her a warped version.

"You're worth a lot of money to me, Valentina. I'm protecting my interests."

Hurt shimmers in her eyes and creeps into the tremulous smile she gives me. "Of course. How could I forget? Four hundred thousand rand."

I let a note of warning infuse my tone. "You chose. I never forced you."

"You're right." A single tear slips free and runs over her cheek. "I'm sorry."

Her apology catches me off-guard. "About what?"

"That this morning happened."

I catch the drop on my thumb and stick it in my mouth, tasting her sorrow. "It wasn't your fault." I hesitate, choosing my words carefully. I don't want to contradict what I just said by making her feel responsible for what happened. "What were you doing back at your flat?"

"Trying to sell it."

There can only be one reason she would risk it out there to make a sale. The state of her almost bare closet gives me a hint. "You need the money that bad?"

She looks away. "It doesn't make sense hanging onto the place if neither me nor Charlie is going to live there."

That's not the point. The point is that no one is going to buy a bachelor flat in Berea. Homeless people and thugs may move in, but they're not going to pay a cent. I get it, though. She's proud. She doesn't want to tell me why she wants the measly money that shithole is worth. I give her more than enough money to feed and clothe her, with plenty left to take care of her brother. It's not that she owes anyone. I checked with the money lords. There's something else.

"How much are you hoping to get?" I ask.

"Ten, twenty thousand, maybe?"

If this is part of a scheme to pay me back quicker, I'll play along for now. In time, she'll understand I'm not letting her go. Anyway, she won't get a lousy buck for the place. If she wants twenty grand, I'll give it to her.

"I'll handle the sale for you." She doesn't have to know I'll be the one to buy it. "You're never going back to that area. Do you understand?"

"Oh, no." Her eyes grow large. "I'm not making my problem yours. I can do it."

"I know you can do it, but I said I'll deal with the agent. End of discussion. There are too many others like Tiny out there."

She goes quiet at the mention of the fucker's name. *Way to go, Louw. Why don't you rub her face in it?*

"You shot him, didn't you?" she asks in a small voice.

I hug her tighter. "He'll never bother you again." I'm afraid to ask, but I need to know if I should call out a doctor. "Did he hurt you?"

"Some."

I go cold, the fury from earlier reviving in my veins. "How?"

"When he slapped me. My hands."

That explains the bruises on her knuckles. "Anything else?"

"Not like *that*."

Relief has me close my eyes briefly. "It wasn't the first time he bothered you." I of all people know when a man is proprietorial, and Tiny acted like she was territory.

"He collected levies for our building. It doesn't matter now."

It does. I can only imagine how he made her pay. The thought has a nerve twitch in the back of my eye, making my eyeball jump in the socket.

"What did he do to you?"

"Nothing."

"It didn't look like nothing."

"It wasn't always like this. Today was different."

The light bulb goes on in my head. "He made you give him head," I state matter-of-factly, keeping the agonizing rage from my voice, because I need to know.

"I gave nothing," she bits out. "He used my mouth, but I didn't give him a single damn thing."

That lowlife fucking son of a bitch. I wish I had more control back in that alley, enough to hold back from shooting him straight away. I should've tortured him to death, starting by cutting off his dick. The irony of the situation isn't lost on me. I'm condemning an already dead man to a slow, painful death for something I'm guilty of myself. I took her and decided to keep her. I eat her pussy every night and get off on her climaxes. I stuck my dick in her mouth and shot my load down her throat. Yes, I'm no goddamn better than the man I killed for her today, but she's *mine*. Tiny had no right to lay his hands on her.

Turning my scars toward the shadows, I bring my head down and brush our lips together. I want to wipe the imprint of every other man's dick on her lips away. I press my lips on the mouth that cocksucker Tiny abused God knows how many times.

"There." Despite my dark mood, I try to keep things light. "All kissed better."

A smile curves her lips. She looks so damn innocent looking at me like this. After what happened to her, the enormity of the oral sex weighs heavy on my shoulders. She's mine like no other person has been, not even my ex-wife. When I took possession of her body, I also committed myself to take care of her feelings. I'm training her body to want me, because God knows I'm too ugly to inspire spontaneous desire in a woman, let alone love, but she needs to understand sucking my cock isn't mandatory.

I smooth my hand over her hair. "You never have to do that again. Not for anyone. Not even me."

She lifts her head to look at me, her brown eyes soft and wide. "It wasn't the same. With you, I wanted to."

The alcohol loosens her tongue, but it also makes her speak the truth. A foreign feeling crushes my chest. Gratitude. It's the first time in my life I feel gratitude toward anyone.

Not knowing what to do with the emotion, I rock her in my

arms until she drifts off. For a long time I hold her, until Marie is about to arrive. Easing her limp body down on the mattress, I cover her with the duvet and put Oscar on the bed to keep her company. I go straight to my study to call my PI. I prefer to conduct sensitive calls in a room swept for bugs every day.

Anton answers on the first ring. "Gabriel," he says jovially, "what can I do for you?"

"I need a detailed report on the financial activity of Valentina Haynes and anything you can get on her history."

"Marvin Haynes' daughter?"

"The one and only."

"I'm on it. By when do you need it?"

"Yesterday."

"I don't know why I still ask."

I'm about to head for a shower when Rhett returns.

"The flat was broken into," he says. "I spoke to the agent Valentina met there. Apparently, the place was turned upside down."

Why the fuck would someone burglar her place when it's under our protection? It's a stupid act only an idiot on a suicide mission would risk.

"Any leads?" I ask tightly.

"No. Must be a random break-in, maybe a thief who's new to the neighborhood and doesn't know shit about the hierarchy."

True. There are thousands of murderers and thieves out there. Not everyone is familiar with the families or how we operate. Still, I smell a rat, and I don't like it.

I give him a pat on the shoulder. "Get some rest."

He's been up with me all night. If the business meeting on Saturday hadn't run overtime, I would've been home before Valentina left for the weekend. I was irritated for not being able to see her before she was off for two nights and a day. I tracked her via her phone to Orange Grove, and when she went back to Berea, we spent the night outside her flat, parked in a nearby street. I was lucky I checked the tracker when I did, or I wouldn't have noticed she was on the move, being attacked in a dirty alley by that filthy Zambian. I didn't expect her to leave that early. My bodyguards must think I'm crazy, but they're wiser than to comment. I could've broken down her new door again and dragged her home to safety, but I want Valentina to have an illusion of freedom. Magda wants her to have hope, but I want her to be happy. Suddenly and inexplicably, it's important to me.

Valentina

IT'S after noon when I wake with a start. Ice fills my veins when the memory of this morning floods my mind. Gabriel shot a man because of me. I know it's not the first man he's killed, and it won't be the last, but I didn't want to be responsible. If I'm to function today, I can't think about it. Pushing the dark memory from my mind, I pull on a uniform and braid my hair.

Marie looks up when I enter the kitchen, her face pulled into a scowl. "Mr. Louw said you're sick. Apparently, so is Carly. Must be a bug going through the house. I made the beds, but you better see to the laundry."

I grab the washing basket and brush past her to fetch the dirty clothes from the bedrooms. Before I reach Carly's room, heated voices coming through the open door stop me in my tracks.

"Dad, come on, I'm old enough to go on a date."

"Not with a boy I don't know from Adam."

"You want to *know* every boy who asks me out on a date? Jesus, Dad, they're too scared of you to come to our house. I may as well become a nun now and get it over with."

"Watch your tongue, young lady."

"All the girls in my class are going with dates. It's only a movie."

"I said no."

"I'll look like an idiot if I go alone. Everyone will think I couldn't get a date."

"If that's your only motivation for wanting to go with him, you're not doing it for the right reason."

"Dad!"

"If it's really such a big deal, I'll get the Hills' boy to go with you."

"You're mean and cruel! I don't like Anthony Hill. I like Sebastian."

"I don't give a damn. I don't trust a man I don't know, and I don't know Sebastian."

"You're ruining my life!" Carly storms from the room, her eyes brimming with tears. "I hate you!"

She runs down the stairs, her sobs audible until the front door slams behind her. When I look around the door, Gabriel stands in the middle of the room, his eyes closed and his head turned up to the ceiling.

"What are you doing?" Magda says behind me, making me jump. "Eavesdropping?"

"Laundry." I lift the basket.

"Get on with it then."

I get out of her way and load the washing machine, but I can't stop thinking about Carly. In some regards she's a brat, but I feel for her. I remember what is was like when my father told me who I'd marry and that I'd never be allowed to go out with other boys. At the time, it felt like my world had come to an end.

Later, when I wash the windows, I see Carly sitting outside by the pool, her cheeks streaked with tears. I pour a glass of lemonade and carry it outside.

Leaving it on the table next to her, I say, "I'm sorry you're upset."

She crosses her arms. "I'm sure you are."

"He's just being protective."

"He's a pain in the ass."

My mom always paved the way for me with my dad. "Why don't you ask your mom to speak to him?"

She snorts. "Like *that* will help. She's ten times worse."

"When is this big night?"

"Friday."

"Maybe he'll come around."

"If that's what you think, you don't know my father."

I stare down into her unhappy face, seeing myself at a younger age when I already knew I'd never have love, not the kind people marry for, anyway. Maybe it's the futility of my life, of my own unhappy existence that makes me blurt out, "Do you want me to speak to him?"

She jerks her head up, her lips parted. "Will you?"

"I can't guarantee he'll listen, but I can try."

She turns her face toward the pool, staring at the blue water with empty eyes. "I guess you're my only shot. No one else will try."

"All right. Now cheer up. Sulking gives you wrinkles."

A smile almost curves her lips.

Gabriel

I'M PORING over the information Anton sent about Valentina––the general stuff that's easy to come by––when the object of my research walks into my study.

"Excuse me, do you have a minute?"

Lowering the report, I scrutinize her. She looks pale. "Feeling better?"

"Yes." She fixes her gaze on the carpet and shuffles her feet. "Thank you."

She's nervous. "What is it, Valentina?"

"Earlier on, back there," she throws a thumb in a general direction, "I couldn't help but overhear the argument."

I lean back in my chair and narrow my gaze. "With Carly?"

"It's none of my business, but––"

"Damn right, it's not." Carly is *my* daughter, and whatever issues I have as a father are private.

At my tone, her eyes grow large. I can practically see the fear bleeding into them. Making a conscious effort to soften my tone, I say, "Whatever you want to say, I'm sure you mean well, but your opinion is unwanted." I turn my face to the computer screen, not dismissing her, but showing her she no longer has my undivided attention.

For a moment, she says nothing. I believe she's going to bolt, but then she lifts her chin and looks down at me from her meager height.

"Gabriel."

All I want is to throw her over the desk and fuck her, but in this, I have to show her her place.

"It's sir when I'm not going down on you."

Her cheeks turn pink, but she stands her ground, her gorgeous courage making me hot around my collar and hard in my pants.

"*Sir*, I promised Carly I'd speak to you. You can do to me whatever you want, listen or not listen, but I won't break my promise."

The chair scrapes over the floor as I push it back and get to my feet. "I won't tell you again, keep your nose out of my business."

The hem of her dress trembles––her knees must be shaking––but she doesn't back down. "You're making a mistake."

I round the desk and stop in front of her. "Am I, now?"

"You should let Carly decide who she wants to go out with."

"You would know."

"Yes."

"You're not a parent. Until you are, keep your opinion to yourself."

She cranes her neck to look me in the eyes. "No, I'm not a parent, but I've been there. I know what it feels like."

The angry part of me stills as I picture her as a young woman asking her father's permission to go out on a date. From the report I just read, I know she was only thirteen when he died, way too young to date, but I'm curious.

"My father already decided who I was going to marry when I turned ten. It didn't matter what I wanted or how I felt. My mother was already gathering a trousseau for the day I'd turn eighteen. My father passed away early, saving me from that fate, but if he'd still been alive, I would've been far, far away from here."

There's nowhere far enough she could've run. Marvin would've found her. He was a small fish in a big pond, but he was part of the mob. Every single man in the business would've been looking for her. My curiosity piqued further, I ask, "Who were you supposed to marry?"

"Lambert Roos."

It makes sense. It would've strengthened Marvin's connections, but hearing her say it doesn't sit right with me. Lambert is an old fart. I feel like killing him now just because he once upon a time considered marrying her. Which raises the questions I've been mulling over for the last hour. Why didn't anyone in the family take the Haynes orphans in? Now I want to know, why didn't the Roos family take Valentina and Charles when their mother died? Lambert's family should've claimed them and raised Valentina until she turned a marriageable age. Too many things about Valentina don't add up.

She watches me with her big eyes. "Don't push her away. Give her reason to confide in you, not to do things behind your back. Carly is her own person. She deserves to make her own choices, even if they're mistakes."

Everything she says is true, but the protective side of me is too fierce.

"It's just a date," she continues. "You can't lock her in a glass cage forever. She has to find her way in life."

"I'm not sure I can."

"Of course you can. At least meet the kid before you cast judgment. Invite him over. That way you can decide if she's safe with him."

I consider her words. I'm not the world's greatest father, but I want what's best for Carly.

"You can always kill him if he misbehaves," she says with a hint of a smile.

It's her way of telling me she accepted what happened this morning, not that I need her acceptance. I'm not worried about her ratting on me, either, because I know how desperately she wants to keep her brother alive. Anyway, it won't do her any good. Magda practically owns the police force.

I sigh and wipe a hand over my face. "I have to discuss it with her mother."

Hope lights up the somber depths of her eyes. "Can I tell her you'll think about it?"

"Fine." I shove my hands into my pockets. "I'll think about it, and I'll tell her myself."

"Thank you," she says, as if I just granted *her* freedom to date, which brings another nagging issue to my mind--Valentina's virginity.

I won't be able to hold off much longer. At some point, my control is going to snap. It tears me apart to even think about it, but soon I'll have to face the decision I've been putting off for far too long.

When Valentina is cleaning upstairs, I send Marie out on a shopping errand with Quincy, and go through Valentina's room. Except for a few pieces of clothing, a pair of flip-flops, and a change of plain, white underwear, there are raspberry-scented shampoo, body lotion, deodorant, and tampons in her closet. There are no cosmetics, jewelry, or shoes, not even a hairclip.

On the bottom shelf, I find a stack of text and notebooks. From the titles, I deduce they're on veterinary science. Could it be that Valentina is a university student? It should've occurred to me earlier. She's clever, driven, and ambitious. It makes sense that she'd want to further her education. As I'm staring at her neat handwriting, I'm struck by another foreign emotion.

Pride.

The pride I feel for Carly is her birthright, but this is different. This pride is *earned*. A piece of the ever-present coldness in me makes way for a pleasant rush of heat. Valentina wants to be a vet. She'll make a brilliant, gorgeous animal doctor. This is why she needs the money. I finished an MBA after high school, and I know how much hard work it is. She won't keep up this job and her studies. Not for long. The part of me that wants her to be happy wants her to have this, but I'll have to find a way around Magda.

I'm enjoying the sensation of warmth in my chest too much to let it go, but when my gaze sweeps over her belongings, a new feeling dampens my pride. It takes me a while to place it.

Fuck me. I feel compassion. Big, empathic compassion. I always knew Valentina was going to play havoc with my body, but what the hell is she doing to my heart?

Valentina

"Which one?" Carly holds up a pink strapless dress and a blue one with a tight-fitting bodice.

I stop ironing to consider the options. "The pink one." Gabriel will definitely object if she shows off too much of her figure.

She puts the pink one on the ironing pile and lifts her hair on top of her head. "Up or down?"

"You have a pretty neck. I'd say up."

She all but skips from the scullery, leaving me with a smile. I'm glad Gabriel finally agreed to let her go out after meeting Sebastian and his parents. It didn't take a brain surgeon to see Carly was smitten with the boy. He has all the qualities to make a schoolgirl's knees weak, including playing for the school rugby team.

I finish pressing the tablecloth, hiding a yawn behind my hand. I'm exhausted. It's a battle to keep my eyes open past eleven. Every night, Gabriel comes to me. My body has learned not only to respond to him, but also to need the pleasure he gives me like I need food and water. When my body hits the mattress, it starts craving him. I'm wet and aching before he even walks through my door. By the time he fondles and kisses me, I'm begging for release. Sometimes, he lets me return the favor. It's always the same routine. When it's me making him come, he leaves everything up to me. I find comfort and power in this, and I also find I need more. I'm ashamed to admit I want more from Gabriel than oral sex. I'm fantasizing about having him inside my body, feeling him rock a rhythm into me with his cock. I shouldn't want this, not from him of all people. I crave what he does to my body, but I hate him for having this effect on me. I never wanted a man before or had erotic dreams, but now I wake up soaked and needy every morning, my senses super aware of him as he moves around the house. Last night, I was on the verge of asking him to fuck me, but my pride won't let me. Maybe controlling me with powerful orgasms is enough for him, but it's not enough for me. Not only did he make me a whore, he made me a greedy one.

"Meeting in the kitchen," Marie says, breaking my train of thought.

I let my hair fall around my face to hide my flustered cheeks. "Coming."

Magda is waiting for us with a clipboard in her hand. As usual, she jumps straight into business. "It's my son's birthday in four months, and we're hosting a party at the house. I'm hiring caterers and servers, but everyone's help is needed. Make sure you're available on Saturday and Sunday the tenth and eleventh of March. It'll finish late, so, Marie, you'll have to sleep over. You can share Valentina's room. Any questions?"

Both Marie and I shake our heads.

"Good. I'll give you more details closer to the time."

When she's gone, trying to sound casual, I ask, "How old is he?"

"Thirty-six."

"He had Carly young."

"He married Mrs. Louw when they were both only nineteen. They had Carly the following year."

"Was it an arranged marriage?"

Marie pulls her back straight. "You shouldn't ask questions about affairs that don't concern you."

She's right, but I have an insatiable curiosity about my keeper. I'm devastated to admit I want to know everything there is to know about him.

"The table needs to be cleared," she says harshly.

I tidy the dining room and smuggle the untouched food to my room. On my break, I carry the Shepard's Pie outside and make myself comfortable on the low wall separating the garden from the pool.

Gabriel

BEFORE VALENTINA'S ARRIVAL, I never spent time in the kitchen. I never had reason to. Now, I gravitate to that part of the house with increasing frequency. An urge to see Valentina drives me there, but she's nowhere to be seen. Marie can't hide her shock at my presence, more so when I switch on the kettle and take a mug from the cupboard.

"Anything I can do, Mr. Louw?"

"I've got this."

She eyes me warily as I drop a teabag into the mug.

"I can prepare you a tray," she says, "or get Valentina to bring it to your study."

"Where *is* Valentina?"

"Lunch break." The way she wrinkles her nose tells me our maid isn't one of her favorites. Any resentment she has should be directed at me. The little maid came voluntarily, but only because I made sure there was no other choice.

"Shall I call her?" Marie asks, watching me with hawk eyes.

"No." Valentina needs her rest. Her back is breaking under the burdens Magda piles on her.

"As you wish." Her dismay is laughable. If she weren't a loyal employee, I would've kicked her ass out on the spot.

As if sensing my discord, she moves away quickly, busying herself with chopping vegetables. I don't really want the damn tea, but if I abandon the task, Marie will know my ulterior motive for gatecrashing in the kitchen.

I walk to the window while I wait for the water the boil and jolt to a standstill. Valentina sits on the wall with a plate in her hands.

I go colder than the morgue.

Bruno is out. Quincy told me ten minutes earlier he's letting him run free for exercise.

"Valentina!" My voice carries through the window, because she lifts her head with a frown.

Jumping to action, I sprint as fast as my limp allows to the backdoor, my body in fight mode. I clear the house in record speed, but my voice didn't only attract Valentina's attention. The Boerboel rounds the corner, his ears drawn back in alert. My heart stops. My lungs collapse, making it impossible to draw in a breath.

"Quincy!" Where the fuck is he? "Valentina!"

I don't have time to elaborate on my warning. The dog spots her and charges.

8

Gabriel

The chances are in Bruno's favor of making it to Valentina before I do, and I don't have my gun on me. I throw my weight behind my effort, but my disability makes me too slow.

One more second and Bruno is next to the wall. Horrible visions play off in my mind. I reach for Valentina with an outstretched arm, trying to throw myself between her and the dog, but Bruno is at her feet, his enormous jaw going straight for her delicate ankle. I'm about to tackle and strangle the animal when the fact that he's licking her leg instead of tearing her apart registers in my frantic mind. I barely stop myself from crashing head-on into both of them. My hands are shaking, and my skin is clammy. The powerful rush of adrenalin drops as quickly as it has flared, making me feel physically ill. I swallow several times to suppress the urge to puke. While I'm battling to settle my guts, Bruno slobbers all over her.

Valentina gives me a confused look, uncertainty creeping into her eyes. She puts a plate with a half-eaten serving of Shepard's Pie on the wall and pushes it away from her, as if the food is the cause of my reaction. Bruno puts his forepaws on the wall and stretches. When she scratches behind his ear, he closes his eyes, and tilts his head to her touch.

"Is everything all right?" she asks in a small voice.

I must look like I feel--a fucking madman.

Quincy comes running from the back, jogging up when he spots me. He stops with his hands on his hips, looking between Valentina and me. "What's going on?"

I can't look at him right now. The chances are too big that I'll rip his head from his body. Instead, I lock gazes with Valentina. "What the fuck are you doing outside when the dog is loose?"

She stops petting Bruno and drops her hand. "He doesn't mind me."

"He's a guard dog, not a lapdog."

The vixen dares to challenge me. "He seems friendly enough to me."

"She's right," Quincy adds quickly. "Bruno likes her. He won't attack."

"You," I turn to him with ice in my tone, "are supposed to check that nobody is out before you let him loose."

"It's not Quincy's fault," she says. "I didn't tell him I was coming outside."

She's covering for Quincy? With the aftermath of the adrenalin still burning in my veins and my leg aching like a bitch from the overexertion, this is as much as I can take.

I grab her arm and pull her from the wall, catching her around the waist before she falls. "Inside."

Her face pales at my tone, even if the command was no louder than a whisper.

Quincy lifts his palms. "Gabriel, take it easy."

"Are you giving me an order?"

He backs down. "Of course not."

"Next time, follow instructions," I snarl.

I don't care that Marie stops to look at us as I drag Valentina behind me through the kitchen. I don't stop until I get to the gym. Shoving her inside, I lock the door and turn to face her. She wraps her arms around herself, regarding me calmly, but there's wariness in her eyes.

For a moment, I just look at her. The thought of anything happening to her leaves an acidic, bitter, fucking horrible taste in my mouth. The intensity of the notion shocks me to my core. I hate her for it. I hate her for the crippling anguish I suffered on her behalf. It's a goddamn sick feeling, and it makes me fucking weak. I like my sex wild, and I love a woman's tears, which is why I sleep with women who crave my money enough to take what comes with having sex with me. But Valentina? I never wanted to hurt her up to this moment. When I belted her, it was to prevent Magda from killing her. Yes, it turned me on, but I regretted it. Now, I want to paddle her ass until she screams. I want to punish her for what I feel.

I undo the buttons of my shirt cuffs and fold them back twice. Her eyes follow the movement, but she says nothing. It's only when I walk to the weight bench and sit down that she finds her voice.

"Gabriel, please."

"Come here."

She doesn't move.

"If I have to come get you, you're going to suffer double as much as what I've got planned for you."

Slowly, she moves to me, her eyes flittering between my face and lap.

I point at my knees. "Bend over."

"Gabriel..." Her lip starts to tremble.

"You endangered your life, and your life is mine, which means you put my property at risk."

"Nothing happened."

"Don't make me tell you again."

She shuffles closer until her knees brush my thighs.

"Bend over my lap and press your palms and feet flat on the floor. Keep your legs spread."

She lowers herself across my lap so that her head hangs down one side of my thighs and her legs down the other. The bench is low enough for her hands and feet to touch the ground.

I pull her dress up to her waist and move her panties down to her thighs. "If you move, your punishment will be tripled."

Her smooth, golden ass and plump, pink pussy are exposed to me. I take my time to admire her perfect body, her unmarred beauty and unsoiled innocence. My cock stirs and grows impossibly hard. I lift my hand and take aim.

Smack.

My palm lands on the tight curve of her left ass cheek. She jerks in my lap, driving her belly into my hard cock.

Smack.

The second marks her other cheek. She sucks in a breath, but she doesn't give in to me. Her silence is her defiance. Not giving her time to draw another breath, I land a succession of firm blows over her ass until I find my rhythm. I keep it light enough not to bruise, but hard enough to turn her skin pink. She squirms and whimpers, but she doesn't break her stance. Her ass clenches with each slap. I keep going until not a patch of her skin is left unmarked. When I start to repeat the pattern on her inflamed skin, she finally breaks. A loud cry escapes her throat. I keep at it mercilessly, not giving her reprieve until her body goes slack.

As she relaxes under my touch, her cries become different. The whimpers turn to moans. She mumbles my name and grinds her body down on my cock. I reward her by stopping the blows and reaching between her legs to cup her sex. She's soaked. My cock rises against the constraint of my zipper in satisfaction. I didn't plan on taking it here, but I can't help myself. The fight has gone completely out of me. All that's left is the gnawing lust. I pet her folds for a while, reveling in how they swell to my touch, before I rub my middle finger in circular movements over her clit. I like the vantage point I have on the view. When I bend my head, her pussy is so close I can smell her arousal. It drives me insane. Her beautiful female parts clench, and her lower body shakes. Her thighs and arms quiver as she screams out her orgasm. I let her have it and more. I carry on rubbing and pinching her clit until she begs me to stop, but I don't let up until I'm certain she can't take any more. Only then do I adjust her clothes, help her up, and pull her into my arms with her head cradled against my chest. While she's sobbing it out, I caress her cheek, wiping the tears away as they fall. Every molecule in my body is aware of her. I'm intoxicated with the woman I hold in my arms, the woman I'll eventually have to kill. It's then that I acknowledge the truth. I'm not going to kill her. I was never going to. She's meant to be mine.

When she stops crying, I dry her tears with my palms. "Don't ever do that to me again."

She blinks. She's confused. Hell, so am I. Spanking her makes me hot. Holding her makes me forget why I spanked her in the first place. With her arms wrapped around my neck and her ass cushioning my dick, I can't think straight. All I know, is that I can't lose her.

"From now on, I want Quincy to train you with Bruno."

She lifts her head to look at me.

"You're not allowed outside if he's loose, unless you give me a demonstration that proves you can handle him."

"He won't attack me."

"He's bitten a trespasser before. Fuck, Valentina." I drag a hand through my hair. "Not even Magda risks it out unless he's closed in the back."

"Why do you keep a dog if he's so dangerous, even to your own family?"

"Protection. People who want to break in badly enough will eventually find a way."

"Bad people will also poison a dog."

"He's trained not to take food from anyone but Quincy." I study her tear-streaked eyes. "What did you do to him? How did you get him to heel?"

"I removed a thorn from his paw."

"That's it?"

"It's not hard at all. You just have to show him who has the authority. You can't be frightened. Animals sense fear."

It sounds a lot like me. No surprises there. I'm an animal, at best. I brush my lips over her hair, inhaling her sweet, raspberry scent. "Was my lesson clear enough for you, or will you need a repeat?"

"No," she says quickly. "I get it."

"Do you fear *me*?"

"Why? Do you sense it?"

"Yes," I say gravely. I do, and I'll encourage it, even if it's only to use her fear like a leash, holding her close to me.

I lift her to her feet. "I'll tell Quincy to set aside some time later today."

She brushes her hair behind her ear.

"Do you need a moment?'

She gives a grateful nod. "Please."

I give her the privacy she needs to gather herself. After arranging for dog training with Quincy, I distract myself by catching up on business, and then I access the financial records Anton emailed me. Valentina earned a salary from Rocky Street Veterinary Clinic. When she said she was an assistant, I assumed it was the secretarial type. That explains the white tunic the first night in Napoli's. Debit orders went off from her account for water and electricity, which she stopped yesterday. Her credit card statements show the usual expenses for food and essentials. Other than that, Valentina isn't a spender. Not that she had the means. There are no luxuries, nothing of the things women like, not even a tube of lipstick. Every month, she withdraws a substantial amount of cash, and it's always the same amount, to the last cent.

I call my private banker and arrange for twenty grand to be transferred to her account. Next, I get the agent on the line and offer him a five grand commission to transfer the Berea property to my name. He's happy to oblige. Firstly, he knows who I am. Secondly, he knows he'll otherwise not get a cent for the flat. I arrange for the necessary transfer of ownership documents to be delivered. For Valentina's sake, the sale must look authentic.

With the finances in place, I call the club manager at Napoli's. I'd like to have a word with Valentina's ex-neighbor about the burglary, and Jerry hasn't been home since we took her and her brother. The manager assures me Jerry hasn't been back, so I put word out that I'm looking for him. Whoever wrecked Valentina's flat will pay. I leave the most unpleasant task for last, dialing Lambert Roos. The phone rings for a long time without going onto voicemail. Looks like I'll have to pay Lambert a visit.

It's only when I grow more settled again and reflect on this afternoon's episode that I recall the lunch Valentina never finished. On strict order from Magda, Marie won't serve the food she prepares to the staff. Is Valentina eating our leftovers? Goddamn. An uncomfortable emotion lances into my heart. The pinch in my chest won't let up. I pull our grocery order records. Valentina is living on Granny Smith apples and cheap Chinese noodles. I feel too many things to distinguish one from the other. There are pity, concern, and anger at myself for not discovering the truth earlier. She's starving right under my nose.

This won't do. I need her healthy. I adjust the order and send Marie a note. From now on, Valentina will eat what *I* decide.

Valentina

THERE'S a box with my name on it in the kitchen when I come in from washing the patio.

"That's for you," Marie says, drying her hands on a dishcloth.

"For me?" I lift the flaps to peer inside.

There are meat, cheese, eggs, veggies, fruit, bottled water, and juice. In a smaller box, I find a variety of delicatessens, including olives, nuts, cold pressed cooking oil, and dark chocolate. There must be a mistake.

"I didn't order these."

"It's from Mr. Louw." She scrutinizes me. "Whatever you did, it made him very happy."

I shouldn't feel guilty, but a flush warms my cheeks. I'm ashamed of my poverty. Always have been. Gabriel's gesture only reminds me of the gap between us. The kindness makes me irrationally sad and inexplicably angry. I'm nobody's charity case. I'll return everything, but for now I unpack it in the fridge to prevent the expensive food from spoiling.

When Gabriel comes to my room, I fight the orgasm he forces on me, doing everything in my power not to come, but it's a losing battle. Eventually, the pleasure takes over. My body gives in and delivers what he wants. His power over the physical part of me is complete. He stripped me of my defenses. I can't allow him to strip me of my pride.

Afterward, he pulls me into his arms. His voice is gentle, but stern. "What's wrong?"

"Nothing."

"The harder you fight me, the harder I'll push."

I lower my eyes. "The food... I don't appreciate the gesture."

"Ah." He says it as if he suddenly understands everything that's going on in my head. "Look at me."

I oblige. Grudgingly.

"What are you to me, Valentina?"

"An investment," I bit out.

"What do I do with my investments?"

"Take care of them."

He brushes a thumb over my cheek. "I *like* to take care of you. Is that so bad?"

Yes, dammit. I want to be more than someone's investment. "You can't force food on me."

"Yes, I can. You can eat what I tell you or be force-fed. It's your choice, but it'll please me if you accept it without arguing."

It shocks me how badly I want to please him. What the hell is wrong with me?

"Whatever you need," he continues, "I want you to tell me."

I can only stare at him, not sure what is changing between us, but the balance is shifting.

He runs a forefinger over my lips. "Is there anything you'd like to tell me now?" The air of anticipation that hangs around him makes him seem vulnerable, as if he has more to lose than me in this strange game playing off between us.

"No," I croak, not sure what he wants from me.

As I expected, my answer disappoints him, but he doesn't pursue the matter. He simply kisses me until my desire spikes again before he gets to his feet and unbuckles his belt.

Gabriel

WHAT DID I expect from Valentina? To open up to me? Why is it important to me that she tells me about her studies out of her own, free will? I don't have an answer. I only know I want to hear it from her. Until she admits it, I won't tell her I discovered the truth.

Besides keeping an eye on Valentina's eating habits, worry about Carly's date dominates the rest of my week. On Friday night, I have men placed around the movie theatre. Discreetly, of course. Still, I don't relax until my daughter is home safe and sound, bubblier than ever. If Sebastian put as much as a finger on her, my men would've acted, and I'm glad it didn't come to that.

Carly comes to my study to say goodnight. She surprises me with an uncharacteristic kiss on my cheek and a hug.

When the house is quiet, I make my way to Valentina's room. It's a routine I look forward to, a fix to which I'm already addicted. My steps fall unevenly on the kitchen floor. My limp is heavier, tonight. There's rain in the air. The humidity makes my joints ache.

My breath catches when I open her door. She's spread out on the bed, naked. Her golden skin is flawless, except for the tiny beauty spot under her left breast. The small mark of imperfection only adds to her allure. In her sleep, she looks more vulnerable and innocent than when she watches me with her big, frightened eyes. Her folds already glisten with the arousal I conditioned her to have. Walking to the bed, I stare down at her. Usually, my presence is enough to wake her, but she's been tired, lately. Too tired. It doesn't help that I steal an hour of her sleep time, but I have very little control where Valentina is concerned. I take another moment to study her body. I like looking at her when she's sleeping. The voyeuristic act is invasive, but it turns me on and feeds a dark part of me.

After a few seconds, she starts to stir. Her eyelids flutter, and her lashes lift. I read her expression as she rises from her sleep. First, there's recognition and then desire. There's no more fear or resistance. She's ready for the next step.

Keeping my clothes on, I stretch out next to her on the bed, lifting myself up on my elbow. Immediately, she spreads her legs. The submissive act makes me dizzy with desire. If I'd remained standing, she would've sat up on her knees for me, legs wide, just like I taught her. I reward her with a soft kiss, my tongue spearing through her lips and stroking hers while I'm playing with her breasts. I can get drunk on her moans. I want to drown in her arousal, but I have other plans for her pussy tonight.

I run my hand down her stomach to her sex. I stroke the pad of my middle finger up and down her slit, working moisture to her clit. When she's drenched in her own wetness, I clamp my mouth over hers and drive the first digit of my finger into her soaked channel. She's soft like velvet and so fucking wet. So hot. Her eyes fly open, and she gasps into my mouth. I eat the sound like an addict, greedily swallowing the whimpers that follow when I twist my finger a few times. When Engelbrecht examined her he told me there's no membrane--not an uncommon occurrence with virgins--so there shouldn't be any bleeding, but goddammit she's tight. Sucking her lips into my mouth, I drive home, burying my finger all the way inside, and then hold still while I stretch her. This time, she moans loudly into my mouth. I don't mind if she screams. Her room is too far for anyone in the house to hear, but I want to eat her sounds of pleasure like I eat her orgasms. I want to swallow her essence in every sensory way possible to carry it inside of me. I want her to be a part of me in the most literal sense.

She's panting in my mouth, sucking the oxygen from my lungs, and fueling me with rapid breaths of ecstasy. I take as much as I give, drinking her air like a vampire. It becomes a battle of breaths, a sucking and exhaling, a give and take. Putting my free hand on her forehead, I smooth back her hair in a soothing caress, preparing her for what's to come. As she starts breathing more easily from my mouth, accepting only the air I choose to give her, I pull out my finger and push back in. Her internal walls quiver around me. I drive in and out, finding a rhythm that matches the rise and fall of her chest. My thumb finds her clit, pressing down while I curl the finger inside to caress the soft spot under her pubic bone. Her hips lift toward me, chasing my touch, so I give her more, a bit harder, a bit faster.

Her lower body trembles. I want to make her fly so fucking high. The thought has my balls climb up into my body. When the first flutter of a spasm strokes my finger, I glide my palm from her forehead over her eyes to pinch her nose shut with my thumb and forefinger. Before she has time to register my intention, I start fucking her with my finger in all earnest, slapping her pussy hard enough with the heel of my palm to turn her clit pink.

I suck the life from her body with my mouth while I give back with my hand. Her legs scissor. Her ass lifts off the bed, and her toes curl inward. Then she begins to fight. She tries to twist her head in my hold while shoving at my shoulders. Realizing she's no match for my strength, she scratches. My skin burns deliciously hot where her nails leave long gashes in my neck. She bites my tongue. The metallic taste of blood coats my lips and drives me wild. One more second and her body jerks as if she's taken a thousand volts. I can own her life for several more seconds before she'll pass out, but I don't want it to go that far. I only want her to have the pleasure. Two more seconds and she falls limp, taking the relentless fucking of my finger in and on her pussy without fighting it any longer. She does nothing but ride the pleasure I force out of her, allowing me to control her breathing.

Total surrender.

I ease my hold on her nose and mouth, keeping our lips a hairbreadth apart. She sucks in the cool night air with a hoarse gasp, her neck arching from the intensity of the action. Shockwaves ripple through her abdomen, dissipating in her pussy. I keep her pussy in the vice of my middle finger, which is still inside her, and my thumb, which is pressing on her clit, until the tremors pass. Her vagina feels plump and ripe from my workout. I kiss her lips one last time, tracing my tongue over a spot where she bit herself during the struggling, and move down her body until my tongue finds her folds.

She shivers when I push inside to taste her climax. It's uniquely Valentina. She tastes raw and well loved, and I have a shocking desire to taste her with my cum in her body. I'm beyond myself with need. She protests with a meek whimper when I shove her thighs wide and push my hands under her ass, digging my fingers into the fleshy globes to pull her open. I stare at her cunt. She's more than a treat. She's the food I need to survive. I bury my head between her legs and devour her flesh. I eat her like I need her, with no excuses and no mercy.

"Gabriel, no more. Please."

I ignore her begging. The business about finding her a man, a pretty man, to take her virginity has me on edge. I'll give her a handsome man only this once, even if it feels like carving my heart out with a blunt knife, but fuck it, I own her. I need to show us both after all that will happen, she'll still be mine. Her pleasure is mine. Getting her off is my addiction.

I make her come once more with my mouth and twice with my hand. When I'm done, she's boneless. I'm not even sure she's conscious. I settle down beside her and drag her against my body. Folding my arms around her, I hold her until I drift into a haunted sleep.

Valentina

I WAKE up with a weight on my stomach and chest. Gabriel is draped around me, fully dressed, except for his shoes. It's the first time he stayed after making me come. A full-body flush heats my skin when I remember what he did last night. My breasts grow heavy, and my clit starts to throb. It was carnal. Deadly. Somewhere between the last orgasm and Gabriel petting me, I passed out, too tired to lift an eye. Careful not to move, I revel in the comfort of being in his warm arms. The sun is barely up, tainting the curtains with a golden glow. I don't have to face the reality yet, that he's the man who holds the power over my life. Charlie's life. I bite my lip as I acknowledged the painful truth. I liked what he did. Very much. Once I got over my initial panic, I gave over to him, trusting him to keep me safe, and he did.

Gabriel moves, his hold on me tightening. His breathing doesn't change, but he drags his chin over my jaw and kisses my ear. His beard grates my skin, making me aware of his masculinity in a rough, pleasant way.

"Morning, beautiful." He nibbles on my earlobe and sweeps his palm over the goose bumps that break out on my skin. "Coffee?"

Gabriel is offering me coffee? I turn to face him, trying to read his expression, but his face is blank.

Without waiting for a reply, he swings his legs off the bed and gets to his feet. I don't miss the flinch he tries to hide as he puts his weight on his damaged leg. His white shirt is crumpled, and his black hair sleep-messy. He looks gorgeous. I want to tell him how grateful I am that he didn't leave me last night, how much I needed his arms around me after the intense way he treated my body, but he limps to the door and disappears before I can formulate the words.

I have another ten minutes before my alarm goes. Cuddling under the covers, I feel replete and strangely happy. A short while later, Gabriel returns with a cup of steaming coffee, the welcome aroma filling my room.

I prop myself up on the pillows to take it from him. "Thank you." I'm not sure what else to say. It's such an unexpected act.

"Milk, two sugars," he says.

He knows how I drink my coffee? I blink at him, not sure if I should ask, but he doesn't give me a chance. He wipes a thumb over my bottom lip, over the mark where I bit myself, and drags his heated eyes up to mine. From the way his cock hardens, he's thinking about last night.

He checks his watch and angles his head away from me. "I'll be out tonight. Don't leave tomorrow without saying goodbye."

The minute he walks out of my room, the air changes. A cold emptiness expands in my chest. Needing some warmth, I cradle the cup between my hands. I allow his act of kindness to warm my heart and fill my empty spaces. He's a contradiction of sensations, a very bad kind of good.

Gabriel

When I walk into my study after lunch, Helga sits in my chair. How the hell did she get past security?

I click the door shut. "How did you get in?"

"Hi to you, too." She leans back in my chair and crosses her ankles on my desk. Her dress rides up to her thighs, exposing black garter stockings. "Chill. Your mother let me in."

I'll have to have a word with Magda. For Carly's sake, I don't invite my bed partners home. Seeing her reminds me that I haven't fucked a woman in a very long time, not since I took Valentina.

"Why did you come?" I approach the desk, irritated with her presence. "You know the rules."

She pouts. "I miss you."

"Carly's home, for fuck's sake."

"You haven't called. It's not like you."

I cross my arms and stare at her. I don't owe her explanations. We fuck when we're both in the mood, and that's that.

"I need you, lover boy."

"I've told you before, don't call me that."

She uncrosses her legs and plants a heel on each side of my desk. No panties. Her fanny is bare, shaved like I prefer. The wide posture gives me a prime view of the goods on offer.

"Tell me what to call you, ugly boy."

Normally, Helga would have my balls in a knot with the act. By now, I would've had her bent over my desk. I would've spanked her pink before fucking her smart mouth, but not today. My cock doesn't stir. Not even a twitch.

"I'm busy."

"It'll only take five minutes."

I smirk. "You know me better than that."

"Okay," she gives me a sly grin, "thirty if you make it a quickie."

"You have to leave."

"Throwing me out?"

"Don't make me. It won't be pleasant for either of us."

She narrows her eyes. "Who are you fucking?"

"No one."

"Come on. I know you. You can't go a day without sex, let alone weeks."

I don't have time for this shit. I round the desk and stop next to the chair, intimidating her with my size and height. "I'll ask you nicely one last time."

She grabs my tie and pulls me down to her level. "You don't scare me. Whatever you want to give, I can take it."

A knock on the door interrupts us, but she doesn't let go or break the stare. I'm going to be a first-class jerk. I give her a calculated smile.

"You won't."

"Watch me," I whisper.

"It can be your daughter."

Carly never knocks. It's probably Quincy or Rhett. "Come in," I call in a loud voice.

Helga's eyes grow large. By now, she should know I never bluff. She brings her knees together and pulls down her dress, but not before the visitor who opens the door gets a full glimpse of her pussy.

Triumphantly, I turn my head to see who the lucky spectator is and freeze. Valentina stands in the doorframe, a stack of white envelopes in her hand and shock in her eyes.

9

Gabriel

"I'm sorry," Valentina says. "I didn't know you were busy."

I free my tie from Helga's grip and straighten, not missing Helga's curious expression. I have to be careful. Helga is perceptive. Raising a brow at Valentina, I encourage her to continue.

She swallows and holds up the envelopes. "Your mother sent me to bring you these."

"Leave it on my desk."

She approaches with averted eyes and puts the stack on the corner. With a small nod, she hurries out of the room.

"New staff?" Helga asks. "You never told me you have a maid. I thought you used a cleaning service."

I grip her arm and drag her to her feet.

"What are you doing?"

"Tell me why you're really here."

She licks her lips. The facade finally drops. "I need money."

I always leave money after fucking Helga, and she'd feel two weeks without a bonus. Letting go of her arm, I take out my wallet and press a couple of thousand in her hand. She bats her eyelashes when I take her wrist and pull her around the desk.

"Does this mean we're fucking?"

"It means I'm walking you out." I all but drag her to the front door where Rhett stands guard. "See to it that she leaves the grounds."

"Gabriel!"

The last thing I see before shutting the door in her face is her disgruntled expression. It's over. I never want to see her again.

Valentina

GABRIEL LOUW HAS A REPUTATION. He's dangerous, and the women who have first-hand experience say he fucks like a horse. Why seeing it with my own eyes hurt so much I can't fathom. It's not like I found out today. What did I expect? Exclusivity? Last night was sweet. The dull ache between my legs reminds me of how Gabriel fucked me with his finger. It's the kind of hurt that feels good, until a few moments ago, before I walked in on a pretty blonde with her naked parts splayed on his desk. It's a game to him. I'm his toy. When he tires of me, he'll cast me aside. The only thing he values is the debt I owe. When I walk free, I don't want to leave a piece of my heart here. That will be too ironic. It's a good thing I walked in on them. No, it's a good thing he *allowed* me to walk in on them. I guess he wanted me to see that, to remind me I'm not special. I'm one of many, and for the moment, I'm convenient.

I get through the day by working myself to a standstill. Even my brain is too tired to think. That night, for the first time, he doesn't come to me. I'm a heap of shivering and aching need when morning comes, cursing him and my body. Visions of him in the blonde woman's bed drive me to maddened tears. He's ruined me for other men. He's ruined me for even myself.

I'm busy with the vacuuming the following morning when he stumbles through the door, Rhett and Quincy in tow. His hair is disheveled, and there's blood on his shirt. His knuckles are bleeding. My heart squeezes, and my pulse quickens. He glances at me, but limps down the hallway without a greeting. I contemplate the reason for his state the whole day, refusing to acknowledge the worry that gnaws on my gut. Worrying means caring, and I don't care.

At five, I have a shower and change into my shorts and T-shirt. I throw my tank top into my bag together with the food for the homeless dogs. I'm not in the mood to face Gabriel, but I'm not so stupid as to ignore his order to say goodbye before I leave.

Like yesterday, he calls me in when I knock on his study door. I don't enter, but only pop my head around the frame.

"Have a good weekend. I'm off." I retract my head, hoping to get away with a quick greeting, but I'm not that lucky.

"Valentina."

I close my eyes and take a deep breath before facing him again.

He gets up from behind his desk. He's wearing a blue shirt with navy pants and a striped tie, looking as hot as ever. "I'll take you."

All I can do is stare at him in confusion. "What?"

"I'll drop you off."

Gabriel is offering me a lift? I'm not sure how I feel about that. I don't want him to be kind to me. "That's not necessary. I can find my own way."

"Like you did last week?"

"Um, yes."

"In a minivan?"

"Yes."

He crosses the floor with menacing steps. "If you ever get into a minivan again, I'll tan your ass so hard, you won't sit for a week."

I blink up at him.

"Do you have *any* idea how dangerous that is?" he asks.

For a white girl, he means. Other people have cars. Nobody dares walking in the street alone. The chances are too good of getting raped, tortured, and murdered. Life carries no value in this city, but in my world, if you don't have a choice, you just have to take your chances.

"You're worth a lot to me, Valentina. I own you, and I protect what's mine."

He returns to the chair and lifts his jacket off the back. Picking up his keys from the desk, he takes my hand and leads me to the garage.

I feel small next to him in the luxurious interior of his car. He says nothing as he steers the sleek Jaguar down the driveway and into the traffic. Instead of heading east, he goes north. He doesn't ask where I'm going, so I keep my mouth shut until he pulls up in front of an exclusive store in Sandton. I get out when he comes around to open the door for me, clutching my bag to my chest as he guides me inside the luxurious shop. It's not like any department store I know. There are no items on display. There's only a leather sofa and a glass desk stacked with clothes, purses, and shoes. A pretty, young lady greets us by the door and waves an arm to the desk.

"Everything's ready for you, Mr. Louw."

He acknowledges her with a curt nod and ushers me forward. "Go ahead. Choose whatever you like."

Dumbfounded, I gape at him.

"What's your color, darling?" the woman asks. "Red will look good with your complexion. White, too. Silver for the evening." She starts pulling dresses from the heap and drapes them over the sofa.

"Um, excuse me." I clear my throat. "May I please have a moment with…" What do I call him in front of her? "…Mr. Louw."

"Gabriel," he corrects.

The woman looks from me to Gabriel. There's judgment in her

eyes, even if she tries to hide it. "I'll fetch refreshments. Take your time."

When she disappears into a backroom, I turn to Gabriel. "What are you doing?"

"I'm getting you clothes."

"Why?"

"I threw your blue dress in the trash."

"I don't expect you to replace it."

"I told you I like to take care of you."

Wringing my hands together, I close the distance between us. "I can't take your money."

His eyes darken, the chipped blue turning stormy. "It's legal money."

"It's not that. It just doesn't feel right."

"Feels pretty damn good to me. Are you saying making me feel good isn't right?"

"Don't twist my words."

He grabs me to him so suddenly my breath catches. Holding me around the waist with one arm, he cups my breast and gives my nipple a soft pinch. "Don't test my patience."

Immediately, heat floods my body. It bubbles in my veins and sends blood to my clit. My nipples are as hard as pebbles. I want to hate the feelings coursing through me, but I can't. As my body puts my arousal on display, the same heat I feel reflects in his eyes.

The shopkeeper returns with a pitcher of ice tea and glasses, but Gabriel doesn't let go of me.

She measures our stance. Depositing the tray on the table, she says in a professional tone, "Have you chosen anything yet?"

An hour later, I walk out with a new dress, designer jeans, two T-shirts, a casual trench coat, a pair of ballerina flats, five sets of pretty underwear, and a cute off-shoulder sweater. Gabriel pushed me to take more, but this is already more than I need.

He loads my parcels in the back of his car, and when we're seated, he turns to me. "Where to, beautiful?"

I'm sure he already knows, but I give him Kris' address. On the way there, I try to figure out what just happened. By the time we pull up in front of the practice, I'm still nowhere near understanding Gabriel.

He switches off the engine. "Your flat has been sold."

"Wow, that quickly?"

"I arranged for the money to be paid into your bank account. I hope that's in order."

"Gabriel..." I'm at a loss for words. "Thank you." The words don't express my gratitude, but they're all I can muster.

"No need to thank me. I said I'd handle it."

He reaches over me and opens my door, his arm brushing against my breasts. Before I can object, he gets my parcels and carries them to Kris' house. Charlie meets us by the door, taking me into a bear hug.

"Va–Val!"

"Hey, big brother."

Gabriel holds out his hand for Charlie to shake. "Hi, remember me?"

"You're the ba–bad ma–man."

Gabriel chuckles. "I guess you can say that, but I prefer Gabriel."

Charlie takes a step back and looks at me with big eyes.

"It's okay, Charlie. Gabriel isn't going to hurt us. I work for him, remember?"

After contemplating my response, Charlie's good manners finally win. "Want a jui–juice?"

"Sure." Gabriel flashes me a smile and makes himself right at home in Kris' kitchen.

I'm wary of having him around my brother. I watch him like a hawk while he makes small talk with Charlie, but Charlie quickly warms up to Gabriel. When he leaves an hour later, you'd swear they're best buddies. What game is Gabriel playing? He can toy with me if that's the price I have to pay for Charlie's freedom, but I won't let him disrupt my brother's life.

Gabriel

SINCE CARLY IS at her mother's this weekend, I have the evening and tomorrow to myself. Magda is out with friends. I ensured that no business meetings were scheduled and gave Rhett and Quincy the weekend off. I pour a whiskey and settle into an armchair in the reading room with Valentina's file in my lap. There's not much in her history I don't already know. Her father, Marvin, was involved in a car cloning syndicate. Her mother, Julietta, was a housewife. Valentina grew up in Rosettenville, in the south. When she was thirteen, their Chevrolet went off a bridge. Marvin was killed on impact. Valentina survived, and Charlie incurred serious injuries resulting in brain damage. One year later, her mother was killed during an armed bank robbery. An aunt took care of Valentina and Charles, moving into the flat her parents owned in Berea when their house was auctioned to cover the outstanding accounts and funeral costs. The aunt died after Valentina's nineteenth birthday, leaving her to take care of Charlie alone.

My earlier question remains. Why did no one take care of Julietta and her kids? In our business, family is everything. We take care of our own. Marvin wasn't at the top of the hierarchy, but he wasn't a petty thief, either. He had enough influence and support to guarantee his widow and children protection, a roof over their heads, and food. Instead, they lived from hand to mouth after his death.

I put the file aside and wipe a hand over my face. The second folder contains Valentina's bank activity of the day. Half of the money I paid her for her flat was transferred to Kris' account. The other half, she paid into an account registered to UNISA.

Following up the lead on the University of South Africa, I confirm my assumption. Valentina is enrolled in a correspondence degree in veterinary science. Using my contacts, I have a number for Valentina's mentor at the university within minutes. Even if it's late, I dial the number. It doesn't take me long to convince Mrs. Cavendish to have breakfast with me tomorrow.

I sit at a table tucked away in a private corner on the Rosebank Hotel rooftop when Aletta Cavendish arrives. She's not the old prude her voice made me imagine. The only reason I know it's her is because she walks onto the rooftop at the exact time we agreed. The tall platinum blonde is in her late thirties. Wedding ring. Big diamond. The husband must have a cozy job, because university professors don't earn that much. Her hair is loose around her shoulders, and there's not a trace of makeup on her face. Even without the help of cosmetics, she's attractive. She wears a white T-shirt and flowing, Indian-print skirt with leather sandals. There must be twenty bangles on her arm. The flower-child type. From her straight back and square shoulders, I gather she has confidence. Her walk is easy and light. Clearly the type who sleeps well at night.

She gives her name to the waiter, and when he motions in my direction, she meets my eyes with a level and friendly stare. For a moment, there's shock on her face when she takes in my features, but her smile doesn't unravel. Her earrings dangle as she approaches my corner. I'm on my feet before she reaches the table.

She greets me with a firm handshake. "Mr. Louw."

"Gabriel, please." I pull out her chair and seat her. "Thank you for meeting me."

Dropping an oversized bag next to her chair, she gives me a scrutinizing look. "I have to admit, if the student concerned wasn't Valentina, I wouldn't be here."

"I appreciate your time." I nod at the waiter. "Shall we order?"

As she studies the menu, I observe her. Aletta is intelligent and doesn't beat around the bush. I like her. She's passionate and dedicated. Must make a good teacher.

We both order coffee and eggs benedict. When the waiter's gone, she says, "You said on the phone you're Valentina's new employer. I didn't know she'd changed jobs."

"It's very recent."

"What does she do for you, exactly?"

"House management."

She tilts her head. "Like a maid?"

I smile, keeping my expression even.

"I'm surprised," Aletta continues. "She loved the job at the vet practice, and it was good experience."

"I made her an offer she couldn't refuse." No lies there.

The waiter returns to serve our coffee. Aletta stirs in one sugar and milk. "In that case, it must be for better money. God knows, she can do with every extra cent."

"I'm concerned about her financial welfare, which is why I wanted to meet. Valentina doesn't know about it, of course. She's proud. I'd appreciate it if we can keep this discussion between us."

She blows on the coffee, watching me from over the rim. "What are you asking me?"

"How much does she owe?"

"Isn't that a question you should ask her?"

"All right. I'll rephrase that. How much does a veterinary degree cost these days?"

"You're looking at roughly fifty thousand a year, excluding books and material."

"I know how much she earned before she started working for me. How did she manage?"

"She has a partial bursary, but it's not enough to cover everything."

"Is she a good student?"

"Honestly? She's hands-down the best I've ever had. Her grades are top, but that girl has a natural vet in her. I've never seen animals react to anyone like they behave toward her."

You bet. "Then how come she secured only a partial bursary?"

"With the financial collapse and political unrest there's very little left in the university coffers. There are no full-time bursaries for vet students. I'm donating her books, but as you said, she's proud. Luckily, Valentina is also strong. Becoming a vet is her dream. She'll find a way."

The food arrives. The waiter arranges the salt and juice, shifting it around several times before he can fit the plates.

I've never had to worry about money. If I want something, I go out and buy it. I can't imagine what it's like to work your fingers to the bone and worry about covering your bills, which is ironic coming from a man who makes money from other people's financial troubles.

I lean back in my chair. "If I'm to create a bursary, can I choose to who it'll go?"

The knife stills in her hand. "Yes." She looks at me with mild surprise. "You can name the beneficiary."

"The beneficiary doesn't need to know who the sponsor is?"

A smile warms her eyes. "You can call the bursary whatever you want. It doesn't have to carry your name, and it can certainly be anonymous."

I lean my elbows on the table and tip my fingers together. "In that case, I'd like to offer a full bursary, all expenses paid."

Her smile turns ten degrees warmer. "I'll put you in touch with the right person in finance."

"Monday." I want to pave this road for Valentina as soon as possible.

"Gotcha." She takes a bite, chews slowly, and swallows. "You know, I had my doubts about you."

"Yes?"

"I thought you were going to tell me Valentina's studies are interfering with her job."

"Oh, no. Nothing like that."

"I'm glad I was wrong."

She has no idea.

AFTER BREAKFAST, I text my private banker and give instruction for the bursary to be set up. Then I head to Rosettenville. I drive past the address in my file, the house in which Valentina grew up. It's a humble miner's house, the cheap, cookie-cutter type the gold mines constructed for their workers and later sold to private owners. In this street, everything looks the same. It's hard to imagine someone like Valentina walking the streets of this average and dull neighborhood. She belongs someplace exotic, someplace beautiful. The main street that houses most of the commercial businesses is quiet. The shops are closed on the weekend. At the mechanic workshop, I park my car and tuck the gun into the back of my waistband. Lambert Roos lives in a house adjoining the workshop. The simple dwelling has a low wall in front, an easy target for thieves. With the fall of Hillbrow and downtown, Rosettenville became a dangerous neighborhood. The fact that he hasn't raised the wall and fitted it with electrified barbwire tells me one of two things. Either he's too poor or he's powerful enough for criminals not to fuck with him. Judging from the peeled paint on the walls and the missing roof tiles, I'm putting my money on the first option.

I jump over the wall and bang on the door. Footsteps shuffle inside.

"Who is it?" a male voice calls.

"Gabriel Louw."

There's a moment's hesitation before the door swings open on a crack. A short, bald man dressed in a vest and a pair of boxer shorts regards me with skepticism. He shoots a look over my shoulder, his gaze traveling up and down the street.

"I'm alone," I say with a cold smile.

"Well, well, if it ain't Owen's ugly duckling. Howzit?"

I should kill him for that remark, but I need information. Shoving past him, I make my way into his house. The place smells like old socks and stale cabbage. The carpets are worn, and the furniture has seen better days. Business must be slow. Or maybe not. On the table, there are several bags filled with white powder. Coke or maybe cat.

His eyes follow mine. A thin layer of perspiration shines on his forehead. "What can I do you for?" he asks with humorless slang. "Want a beer?" He shifts his weight.

He's hospitable enough, but he wants me gone.

"Remember Marvin Haynes?"

Cocking his neck, he blinks twice. "Yeah. Who doesn't?"

"You must've known him well, seeing that you were supposed to marry his daughter."

His puffy eyes narrow, and he utters a forced chuckle. "He lived down the road, but we weren't thick with each other. Saw his missus from time to time in the pharmacy. Why do you ask?"

"If Valentina Haynes was promised to you, why didn't your family take her and her brother in after her mother died?"

He scratches the back of his neck. "With her daddy gone, the deal was off."

"You didn't want to honor the agreement?"

"She's not my type."

Bull fucking shit. "She's a very pretty woman, isn't she?"

"Yeah."

"You don't like pretty? Or you don't like women?"

"Look, she didn't do it for me."

"You backed out because she didn't do it for you?"

"Yeah."

He's lying through his crooked, yellow teeth.

"Why do you want know?" he asks, trying to look nonchalant, but his voice breaks on the last word.

I shrug. "Curiosity."

With a nod, I go back to my car. Before I'm inside, the idiot has his cellphone in his hand, looking at me through the tattered lace curtains as he makes a call. I should've tapped his phone before my visit. It doesn't matter. I'll find out. I text Anton with Lambert's name and address, as well as the date and time, instructing him to get a recording of the conversation and send it as an encrypted message to my private email account.

Valentina

WHEN I STEP OUTSIDE KRIS' house on late Sunday afternoon, Rhett is waiting across the road next to the Mercedes. He opens the backdoor in silent instruction for me to get in. Not a word passes between us during the drive to Parktown. My heart is sad to leave Charlie. I feel guilty for not being able to take care of him, but more than that, I miss his presence. His joy is innocent and genuine. He's the only piece of uncomplicated truthfulness in the twisted emotions of my life.

Despite my sadness, my body starts humming when we get nearer to the house. Like a conditioned animal, my body becomes aroused at the knowledge that it will soon be with my captor, while my brain condemns the reaction. I hate this division between my thoughts and physical reactions. I'm at constant war with myself.

Gabriel himself waits on the porch. My heart gives an unwelcome lurch at the sight of his muscular shape. He gets the door and my parcels, the new clothes still unpacked and the price tags intact. Rhett disappears to wherever. The minute he's gone, Gabriel brushes his lips over the shell of my ear.

"Welcome home."

The words grate on me. This isn't my home. My home is with Charlie. What Gabriel is doing to us as a family is wrong. I hurry inside and make my way to my room. A minute later, Gabriel steps inside, standing like a menacing, dark energy at the foot of the bed.

"What's wrong?"

"Nothing."

"Aren't you happy you got to spend time with your brother?"

I give him a hard look. "Of course I am."

I start unpacking the clothes, taking my time to fold each item meticulously.

He lets me carry on like this for a while before taking the pile from my hands and leaving it on the bed. "Let's go for a swim."

My jaw drops. He's inviting a house servant for a dip in his pool?

"What do you say, Valentina?"

"I don't have a bathing suit."

"You don't need one."

Without waiting for a response, he takes my wrist, pulls me through the kitchen and out the backdoor. On the deck, he starts stripping his clothes.

I glance around to make sure we're alone. "What are you doing?"

"Swimming naked with you."

"Are you crazy?"

"We're alone. Magda's out, and Carly won't be back before tomorrow."

Gabriel stands stark naked and hard in front of me. His scarred body is terrifying in its brutal beauty. The marks on his foot and knee don't diminish his physical perfection. To me, they add to his appeal, making him breathtakingly perfect in a broken kind of way. Is it the warped attractiveness of imperfection, or is a part of me is just attracted to everything that's dark and destructive?

Flashing me his rock-hard ass, he walks to the deep end and

dives. Water splashes onto the side, the sound reminding me of holidays and stress-free times long gone.

"Come on," he calls. "The water's good."

It's tempting. It's been a hot as hell day, and my body feels sticky. I can't remember the last time I swam.

My gaze travels in the direction of the staff quarters. "Rhett--"

"Rhett won't come near the house unless I give him an order. Now I'm giving you one. Get in."

"All right."

Pulling off my trainers and clothes, I walk to the edge of the pool. The minute our gazes lock, there's a shift in his. The ice in his eyes makes way for a molten look of heat. Unashamedly, he ogles my breasts and lower. His cock grows enormous under the water. I wish I wasn't tingling between my legs or that my nipples hadn't hardened, but I'm as helpless to my reaction as I am to his wordless command when he curls a finger at me. Stepping into the cool water at the shallow end, I leave my guilt and judgment behind. No matter how hard I protest, Gabriel will do whatever he wants. The crazy, unequal power play gives me a measure of absolution.

When I'm up to my waist in the water, he swims to me and grabs a fistful of hair. Pulling my head back to arch my upper body, he latches onto a nipple, and sucks my breast deep into his mouth. I cry out as pain assaults the sensitive tip. Immediately, he pulls back to look at me.

"You usually like that."

I cup the sore curve. "It's almost that time of the month. They get overly sensitive."

He studies my breasts with new interest, taking both into his hands. "They're bigger." He jiggles them, making me groan with the discomfort. "And heavier." His hands move down my sides to my hips, and over my swollen stomach. "When's your period due?"

"Tomorrow." I shake a little when I say it. After that, the birth control will be effective, and nothing will prevent him from taking the final step.

He eases up then, setting my body free. "Maybe the water will do you good."

It does. We swim a few laps and just drift around without talking. By the time we get out, my skin is wrinkled. Gabriel fetches towels from the pool house and covers me with one on a deckchair. For a few blissful moments, I forget my circumstances and simply enjoy the rays of the setting sun on my face. I've never been alone with him in the house. There's less tension when no one else is around.

When it starts to get cool, he carries me inside and lies me down on my bed. Like every night he came to my room, he makes me come. He's gentle, avoiding my sore breasts and swollen abdomen. Afterward, he lets me take him in my mouth and stays with me for another hour.

Does he hold other women like this? Does he go out to fuck someone after he's been with me? I've never seen another female in the house except for the woman in his study, but that doesn't mean he's celibate. Maybe he entertains his women elsewhere to protect Carly. For all I know, he has a girlfriend. Maybe it's the woman I saw. Maybe he's fucking her brains out every night after he leaves my room. Our silence is no longer amiable.

I can't help myself from asking, "Are you sleeping with someone?"

His chest vibrates against my back with a chuckle. "Does it matter?"

If the ache in my ribs is anything to go by, yes, it does, but I'd die before admitting it. "Just wondering." Hell, I don't even sound convincing to myself.

"Her name is Helga."

Humph. It's like he punches the wind out of me with a fist in the stomach. I wanted to know, and now I regret asking. I especially don't want to know her name. Pain lances at me from all directions, rendering me vulnerable. Jealousy mounts in my chest.

"She's the woman you saw in my study. That's what you're really asking, isn't it?"

Now that it's out, I may as well go the full nine yards and let myself hurt thoroughly. Maybe the ache will dampen my need for Gabriel. "Did you sleep with her?"

"Yes." After a moment, he continues, "But I haven't fucked her since you arrived."

Something gives in my torso, like an elastic band that snaps. Stupidly, I feel like crying. Correction, I feel like bawling. Damn PMS. "It doesn't matter."

His laugh is knowing. "Of course not."

"Why haven't you slept with her?" I hold my breath for something I can't name.

"I don't want to."

But he may. Gabriel is the kind of man who takes what he wants, not by force, but by making your own body betray you, by stealing your will and breaking every one of your good intentions, leaving you with a hole only he can fill. Where I'm aching now, only his cock can fill the empty feeling. It's twisted. He made me want him––need him––like I need water, while he can walk away on a whim, whenever he doesn't want me. There'll come a day I'll be the next Helga, a day he won't come to my room to make me come, just because he doesn't *want to* any longer. He's an asshole, and I hate myself for being affected.

"You're quiet," he muses. "If you're tired, I'll let you sleep."

Longing for solitude so I can curl into a ball, I let the lie spill from my lips. "That'll be kind."

My heart drops when his weight lifts from the mattress. With a chaste kiss on my forehead, he walks from my room. Finally, I have the solitude I demanded, but I'm utterly and miserably lonely.

On Monday morning, Magda awaits me in the kitchen with shocking news. Marie had a stroke.

"You'll take over the menu planning," she says, "and the cooking. Run it past me to approve." She points at the computer in the corner. "You'll find the budget and supermarkets that deliver on the system."

"Will she be all right?"

"I don't know. Her daughter will let me know. It's mighty inconvenient, though, seeing we have a formal business dinner at the house on Friday. Oh, you'll have to see to the catering and serving. I'll email the menu to the kitchen computer. I'm only expecting two or three guests." She writes a code on the message pad. "Here's the password."

She's halfway to the door before I find the courage to speak. "I'm not sure I can manage."

She twirls around to narrow her eyes at me. "Do you have a problem?"

"The cleaning and cooking…it's a lot for one person. It's not that I'm not willing, but it's a big house. I don't want to neglect one or the other."

"Then make sure you don't." Her lips thin into a smile. "Your life depends on it."

I stare at her back as she leaves the kitchen. I hate the haughty clack of her heels as much as I detest the traffic cone color of her lipstick. She may look down on me because I'm poor and treat me like a slave because she owns nine years of my life, but when those nine years are over, I'll never take an order from her again. I'll take Charlie and move to another town, a city where the Louws don't rule. Allowing the intention to strengthen my resolve, I switch on the computer and wait for it to boot up so I can place the grocery order for the day.

Monday and Tuesday pass in a blur. I wangle some sort of schedule, vacuuming only every second day and ironing later at night. By Tuesday evening, we get an update from Marie's daughter, stating that she won't be back at work for at least six months. Since I don't know Marie's recipes, I don't have a choice but to change the menu. What I know is more my late mother's Mediterranean style. I find a small, local producer of fresh produce, which turns out not only to be organic, but also cheaper. The fruit and vegetables aren't pretty, but they're tasty. I also order less cleaning products. I can wash a floor just as well with a bit of vinegar in water than with an expensive product that smells like a summer orchard, but has been tested on animals. The result is a thirty-percent saving on the weekly grocery bill.

The new work pace is strenuous. On top of that, my period arrived right on time. I've always suffered from a heavy flow that leaves me feeling weak. I order an iron supplement with my personal deliveries to boost me for the big night on Friday. The last thing I want is to fail my first dinner party test when my life depends on it.

Despite my period, Gabriel still comes to me at night, but instead of bringing me to the earthshattering climaxes I got used to, he fondles my body with backrubs and massages. It's strange and out of character for him, not that he's predictable. The more Magda pushes me, the kinder Gabriel acts toward me, which infuriates Magda. It's a vicious circle between the two of them, and I'm caught in the middle.

Carly is cool but not completely unfriendly since she got to go out on her date. Sebastian is allowed to visit her at home with her grandmother or father's supervision, but as Gabriel is always out during the day, it's mostly Magda who keeps an eye on the lovebirds.

On Wednesday, Carly is alone by the pool. When I pick up her towel to put it in the wash, I notice she left her iPad outside again, something she does often. I take it with the intention to put it away in the house, but as I reach the sliding doors, Quincy's voice stops me.

"Hey, Val. Look, Bruno's all better."

Bruno runs on a leash with Quincy, the limp gone. The dog barks and wags his tail furiously when I approach. Leaving the iPad on the wall, I go down on my haunches and get a sloppy dog kiss.

I laugh, wiping my face with the back of my hand. "Glad to see you're back in shape, boy."

"Thanks, again."

"I'm glad I could help." I straighten and glance over my shoulder at the house. "I better get back. Lots to do."

"Yeah." He looks uncomfortable. "Are you coping?"

"Sure."

"Valentina," Magda says from the door, her condescending stare resting on Quincy and me as if she caught us making out or something, "if you've finished socializing, we need to talk about Friday's menu."

"Bye, Bruno." I stroke his back and smile at Quincy in greeting.

His eyes are hard as he directs them to the door where Magda waits with her hands on her hips, but I don't give it further thought as I hurry inside.

It's not until the following morning when Carly makes a ruckus at breakfast about her missing iPad that I remember leaving it outside.

Magda summons me to the dining room. At first, I'm in the dark when Carly points a finger at me and exclaims, "She took it. It was there last night, and now it's gone."

"Did you take Carly's iPad?" Magda asks. "Don't bother lying, because I'll be going through your room myself."

My insides freeze, remembering where I left it. They go even colder when I look at Gabriel. He's regarding me with a frown. He believes I stole it? Hurt lances into my heart. Why does it matter what he thinks?

"Well?" Magda asks with a flick of her penciled eyebrow.

"I meant to bring it in last night, but I got distracted and forgot it on the wall."

"Distracted with Quincy," Magda says snidely.

A thunderous expression darkens Gabriel's face. Of the three people in the room, right now, I'm most scared of him.

"I'll go get it," I offer quickly, but Carly's already on her feet, heading for the door.

Magda folds her hands on the table and gives me a single instruction. "Stay."

I stand quietly in the uncomfortable silence until Carly's screaming filters through the backdoor. Everything inside of me tightens further.

"It's ruined!" Carly shouts, running into the room with the iPad. It's dripping with water.

Gabriel's tone is flat. "On which wall did you leave it, Valentina?"

"The one by the pool!" Carly shoots daggers at me with her eyes.

"The sprinklers reach there at night," Gabriel says almost distantly.

"This is your fault," Carly continues in hysterics. "Do you realize how many photos I had on here? Not to mention my homework!"

"Carly." Gabriel's quiet but hard voice instantly shuts her up. "Let that be a lesson well learned for leaving your iPad outside. It's not the first time. It was bound to happen."

"Dad!"

He holds up a hand, giving her a dark look. "Let me finish. You can recover your homework and photos from iCloud."

"I didn't activate it!"

Gabriel's tone is uncompromising. Not a flicker of sympathy warms his eyes. "Lesson number two, well learned. From now on, you'll make a backup like I told you." He turns to me, suddenly looking tired. "I'll deal with you after breakfast."

"You'll replace Carly's iPad," Magda says. "It'll teach you to be less forgetful in future." She shakes her napkin out on her lap. "Now, I want to eat in peace. Quiet all of you."

Carly flops down in her seat, her face red.

I'm shaky as I return to the kitchen, cursing myself for my negligence. I can't afford to replace the iPad, not without making more debt.

It doesn't take long for Gabriel to come find me. The words I dreaded most leave his lips. "Go to the gym after you've cleared the table."

Going down to the basement is like a walk to the gallows. He's already waiting inside, his tie removed and his shirtsleeves rolled back.

"Close the door," he says quietly.

I push until I hear the click, but I don't have the courage to turn and face him.

"Come here."

I bite my nail as I gather enough strength to obey, one step at a time.

When I stop in front of him, he pulls my hand from my mouth. "Undress."

My eyes lift to his. I don't mean to beg, but it slips out anyway. "Please."

He doesn't bat an eye. There's no compassion, no mercy. "Undress."

As I pull off my shoes, dress, and underwear, he watches me like a hawk. By now, I'm used to his scrutinizing stare, and it's less embarrassing than during those first few times, but not less frightening. Once I'm naked, he taps a finger on his lips, studying my face. Finally, he drops his arm, as if he's made his decision, and points at the floor. "On your back."

I swallow as I lie down on my back, watching him fetch a bar with a set of handcuffs secured on each end.

"What are you doing?" I ask as he locks my wrists on either end.

He gathers my panties and bundles them into my mouth. "Sorry, beautiful, but I'm not in the mood for dialogue right now."

I mumble a protest when he locks my ankles to my wrists, spreading me open on the bar. He pushes the bar back until it touches the mat, raising my arms above my head and my legs with them. Flat on my back, my ass and pussy are exposed in the most vulnerable way. My hamstrings are on fire. I shift in an effort to relieve the uncomfortable stretch when he fetches an object from the torture shelf.

He returns with a wooden paddle. I shake my head, pleading with my eyes, but he grips the bar and lifts a few times, giving me brief reprieve from the position before he pushes down flat and starts paddling my ass. The first whack on my ass cheek comes as a shock. I scream behind the bundle of fabric in my mouth, even if the sting heats my skin without hurting. The second lash makes me jerk, but when I realize he's caressing my skin rather than inflicting pain, I almost relax. He works his way from left to right on the fleshy part of my ass until my nerve endings are on fire and my clit is a pulsing nub of ache. My vagina feels swollen. The need for release is severe. When I'm no longer begging with my eyes for him to stop, I'm begging him to let me feel the paddle where I crave it most. Only after every inch of my skin is humming with electric sparks does he finally bring the paddle down right in the middle of my pussy, covering my opening and clit. With the tampon inside me, it feels full. And good. I grind up, desperate for more, but he changes to a slower and gentler rhythm, teasing me mercilessly with a few too-soft taps on my swollen parts.

Just when I think I can't take more, he pulls the underwear from my mouth and says, "Beg."

I don't hesitate. "Please, Gabriel."

"Please what?"

"Please, please fuck me."

He goes still. There's a mixture of shock and disbelief on his face, which is slowly replaced with satisfaction. Heat darkens his eyes. His jaw tightens as he looks down at my sex.

"Please."

His chest is rising and falling rapidly, his breathing as harsh as mine. There's only the sound of our pants in the room. Then he exhales with a long, shaky breath. He pushes the paddle down on my clit and starts massaging with circular movements. Everything clenches as I come violent with a spasm that shatters my respiration. I'm out of air by the time he frees the constraints and drags me to my knees. In his haste to undo his pants, his fingers fumble with the button. I grab the waistband and pull it down his hips to help, not bothering with the zip. His cock juts at me, the tip close to my lips. I devour him like a crazy, starving woman, sucking and licking until he grabs my hair for leverage. He clenches his ass with a primal roar and a curse as he empties himself in my mouth. I swallow as best as I can, trying to breathe through my nose. I don't want him to pull out. I want him in me forever.

After a moment, he grips my face in the vice of his giant hands and eases out of my mouth. He uses my hair to wipe himself clean, an act I find strangely and savagely satisfying. Pulling me to my feet, he shoves his tongue between my lips, tasting himself on my mouth. He nips and sucks, bites and laves. I'm aware of nothing but the heated skin of my ass and the wetness of his mouth as he steals my reason. His taste is addictive. I don't know for how long he kisses me before he pushes me away with a gentle shove.

"Get dressed," he says in a hoarse voice. "And leave."

Confused by the change in his behavior, I obey wordlessly,

empty and dissatisfied despite the orgasm I just had. At the door, his words make me pause.

He grits out every syllable like he has to push it from his throat. "Put on a pretty dress, tonight. You're going on a date."

Gabriel

WHEN I ASKED her to beg, I expected her to beg for release. Instead, she begged me to fuck her.

She's ready.

I both rejoice and shiver in dread, because the first time won't be with me. No matter how much I want to take her virginity, I made a promise to myself, and I never break my promises. This time I may be pushed to my limits to keep this promise, but I already have a plan.

Magda waits in my study when I get back from the gym. I grit my teeth as I stroll past her.

"Did you do it?"

I know what she means, but I ask anyway, "Do what?"

"Punish her."

"Yes." I sit down and open my laptop.

"How?"

"Appropriately."

Carly learned a valuable lesson. There was nothing to punish Valentina for. I'm a sick bastard for using the situation to feed my own lust.

Magda doesn't budge. "How?"

I shoot her an incredulous look. "You want the juicy details?"

"What is it about her that's got you thinking with your dick instead of your head?"

"Don't insult me, and your reference to my dick is highly inappropriate."

Her eyes, the same watery blue as mine, turn dark with anger. She slaps her palms on my desk, bringing us at eye level. "You're just like your goddamn father."

Keeping my voice calm and my gaze indifferent, I say, "If you can't speak without repeating yourself, and you have nothing new to say, please get out of my office so I can focus on the business of running your business."

Her nostrils flare. The thick layer of foundation around her nose cracks with thin lines. The pores are big with white hairs standing erect in each follicle. Every minute detail of her age catches my attention.

"You won't live forever, Magda."

She straightens and adjusts her jacket. "Neither will you." A superior smile curves her lips. "Who knows? You may die before me." She turns, making it clear she's leaving my office on *her* terms.

There's no love lost between my mother and I, and no amount of introspection to figure out where it went wrong will change that. We are who we are.

I pick up the phone and set out to do what I've been meaning to when I walked through the door.

Quincy answers with a bright, "Yes, boss?"

"Come to my study."

I take a deep breath, and steel myself. A short while later, he enters. I want to break his face, but it's not his fault he's fallen for Valentina. As little as it's hers. She's a gorgeous woman with a courageous heart and a soft spot for animals. How could he not be under her spell?

"Sit." I point at the chair facing my desk.

He takes the seat, his posture at ease.

"I have a mission for you tonight."

He waits quietly for me to continue.

"You're going to fuck Valentina."

10

Gabriel

I may as well have drenched Quincy with a bucket of ice water. He coughs. "Excuse me?"

"Take her out on a date. Someplace nice. Romantic. Dinner by candlelight, that kind of thing." I flip my credit card at him. "All expenses paid. Take two guards to make sure you're safe."

His eyes grow larger by the second.

The next part is hard for me to get out. I swallow the bitter taste in my mouth. "Then get a room at the Westcliff Hotel and fuck her."

His skin is as pale as the whites of his eyes. "I don't understand."

"There's nothing to understand. Wear a condom and be gentle. It's her first time. Oh, and she's having her period. That kind of thing doesn't put you off, does it?"

"Of course not, but––"

Not able to stomach the conversation any longer, I say gruffly, "You're dismissed."

He jumps to his feet, obviously eager to escape my presence.

"One more thing," I say as he gets to the door, "I don't want to see you until tomorrow morning. Make sure you stay the hell away from me until sunrise, and then I expect a full report."

He all but jumps through the door, leaving me alone with a kind of agony no human being can understand.

IN THE AFTERNOON, a visit from Sylvia puts me further on edge. I meet her in my study. It keeps things professional. She declines my offer for a drink and sits down on the corner of my desk, the slit of her skirt riding up her thigh. At some point in time, I would've kneeled at her feet and kissed my way down that leg, all the way to her toes. Now, there's no desire for the woman who married me in a pretty white dress with a fake smile on her face.

"What's with Carly's new diet?" she asks. "We already discussed this. You're not supposed to change her meal plan without consulting me."

I fight to control my irritability. "I'm not aware of any diet."

"She's wheat intolerant, for God's sake. She's not supposed to eat pasta. What's wrong with Marie? Is she going senile?"

"Marie had a stroke. Valentina's taking care of the cooking."

"The maid who tried to kill our daughter?" she shrieks.

"She didn't do it on purpose. It was another one of Carly's attention-seeking, self-destructive actions."

"Don't you dare take that maid's side over our daughter's."

I sigh deeply. "Relax. Valentina has been punished. It won't happen again."

"I won't relax where Carly is concerned. She has a modeling audition in a month. She can't afford to pick up weight with carbs and creamy pasta sauces."

"She's *not* doing a modeling audition."

"It's not up for discussion."

"Have you called the therapist?"

She stiffens. "Carly doesn't need a therapist. It's hormones. Normal teenager issues."

"Sylvia." I say her name warningly. "Carly never got over our divorce. It's time to face the fact that she may have issues we're not equipped to deal with."

She snickers. "That's rich coming from *The Breaker*."

"Keep the business out of this."

"How can I? It's all that matters in your life."

"Yet, that's why you married me. Security and money, don't you remember?"

"Don't be so dramatic. Why do you always have to bring up the same old accusations? It's boring." She gets to her feet. "Shall I speak to your maid?"

"You lost the right to address my staff when you walked out."

She rolls her shoulders. "Dear God, Gabriel, get over me and move on."

"I am, Sylvia. You have no idea."

"Good. It'll make you easier to get on with." She walks to the door with a straight back. "Tell Carly I dropped in."

"Why don't you call her tonight and tell her yourself?"

She narrows her eyes. "Fuck you, Gabriel. I love my daughter, and she knows it."

"Does she?"

She yanks the door open and slams it hard enough to shake the frame. Dragging a hand over my face, I take a moment to calm myself before I go out for the business of the day that requires the end of another scumbag's life.

When I get home, I shower and spend time with Carly, helping her with her math homework. I don't go down for dinner. I can't bear to look at Valentina. I'm too terrified I'll change my mind.

After a whiskey too many, I call Rhett and tell him to meet me in the gym.

He enters cautiously, probably thinking of the last time we wrestled because he shot Valentina's dog.

Dragging a bench from the free weights section to the metal chains attached to the wall, I sit down. "Cuff me."

It takes him a moment to find his voice. "What?"

"You heard me."

Not stupid enough to defy me, he approaches slowly. I hold out my wrists. He secures first the one, then the other in the metal cuffs.

"Take the key with you," I say, "and don't give it to anyone, no matter what."

"The key for the cuffs or for the door?"

"Both."

His head bobs up and down, like a toy dog on a car dashboard. "When must I come back?"

"At six tomorrow morning and not a second before. Got that?"

He gulps. "Yes."

"Go."

His eyes say I've finally lost it, but he doesn't argue. The key scrapes in the lock after he has closed the door, making me a prisoner of free will.

Valentina

WEARING the new dress Gabriel bought, I bite my nails while I wait in the kitchen. I've never been on a date. I should be studying, but I'm curious about what Gabriel has planned. The door opens just after eight, but it's not Gabriel who steps inside. It's Quincy.

"Hi," I say with an easy smile, half-relieved and half-stressed, because now I'll have to go through the waiting anxiety again.

There's a flush on his cheeks as he takes in the red dress. "You look nice."

This is so uncomfortable. "Thanks."

"Ready?"

I blink. Maybe he's driving me somewhere to meet Gabriel. "Um, yes."

"Let's go." He looks me over. "Take a jacket. It'll get fresh later."

I grab my black trench coat and follow Quincy to the car. He drives. Another car follows at a distance. I peer at the headlights in the side mirror.

"Are they going to follow us all night?"

"Protection," he mumbles, his forehead pleated in a frown.

"Where are we going?"

"I was thinking the Thai Hut. It's got five-star reviews for its curry dishes, and it's fancy without being uptight. What do you think?"

I have no idea where or what the Thai Hut is, but my brain is stuck on something else. "Wait, you mean you and I decide? Gabriel's not coming?"

He shoots me a quick look. "Ah, fuck. He didn't tell you."

"Tell me what?"

He clenches the wheel and faces straight ahead. "This is—How do I put it? He set us up on a date."

"Me and *you*?"

"Hey." He utters a wry chuckle. "I know I'm not the world's greatest hunk, but there's no need to say it like you won't go out with me if I'm the last man on earth, which you probably wouldn't, even if it was true."

I'm so gob smacked I have to remind myself to shut my mouth. "I don't understand."

"Neither do I." He shifts in his seat. "Look, I'll be honest with you. All I know is Gabriel ordered me to show you a good time tonight."

"He *ordered* you?" Who the hell orders anyone to go on a date?

What am I? A piece of meat up for auction? I narrow my eyes. "What else?"

He steals another glance at me. "What do you mean what else?"

"A good time and what else?"

He wipes a hand over his face. "Dinner, candles, and..."

"And what?"

"He wants me to sleep with you."

"Stop the car."

"Valentina--"

"Now!" I'm already jerking on the door handle.

He brings the car to a screeching halt on the side of the road and grabs my arm. "Please, calm down. We've got his guards watching us."

I still at his words. I can't believe Gabriel set me up with Quincy. For sex. I cover my face with my hands. "I'm so embarrassed."

He pulls my hands away. "It's not your fault. You have nothing to be ashamed of. I don't know what Gabriel's idea with the whole thing is, but we may as well go out and have a good time since he's paying." He adds quickly, "I'm not saying you have to sleep with me. We'll just say it didn't work out that way. I know you don't feel for me like that, and I'm not in the habit of forcing women."

"Thanks." I drag in a shaky breath. "I guess you're right. We'll just go on our make-believe date and order the most expensive dishes on the menu."

"Good." He pats my hand. "Now I can relax. Man, this was eating me. You have no idea."

I can't help but laugh. "Sorry. I didn't want you to stress over sex with me. Must be a terrifying thought."

He gives me another wry smile. "Don't put words in my mouth, now."

The tightness in my chest vanishes a bit, but not the hurt that Gabriel would rather send me off to be serviced like a cow or horse than deal with me himself. I need to change the uncomfortable subject.

"How come you got to train with Bruno?" I ask.

"I was the only one more or less not scared of him."

"You should treat him better. I saw what you're feeding him. May as well give him sawdust."

He chortles. "Yeah? What do you recommend?"

"I'll give you the name of a good brand, but you'll have to order it from the vet."

"Is this an order or a request?" he asks mockingly.

"It's not like Gabriel can't afford the best."

"You're right." His smile is bright. "We'll give it a try."

The Thai Hut is a small wooden house on stilts with colorful fairy lights draped over the porch. The interior smells of curry, and the ambience is warm. Despite myself, I relax with Quincy's easy banter. We polish off a bottle of wine, and by the time we ask for the bill, there are no other diners left. Since Quincy is over the limit, one of the guards drives us back. At home, he kisses me on the cheek and saunters off to the staff quarters.

The night guard lets me in. After a second's hesitation, I take the stairs to Gabriel's room. I want some answers, and I want them now. I push the door open, anger making me brave, but the room is dark and empty. Maybe he's out himself, doing what he wanted me to do with Quincy. Banishing the thought from my mind, I go to my room and try not to think about him as I fall asleep.

Gabriel

THE OVERHEAD TUNGSTEN bulbs buzz with a constant noise. Their blue-white light washes out the shadows with an overly bright intensity. It's been an hour since Rhett left me in the gym. I'm going through the week's business in my mind, trying to focus on planning and figures, but my thoughts keep on drifting to Valentina and Quincy. Where are they? What are they doing? What is she wearing? Is her hair hanging loose down her back, or did she take it up in the messy bun she does on a Sunday? Maybe it's tied in the ponytail she wears for work, and my guard is pulling the elastic from the silky strands right now, letting is spill over her full breasts. Is he pressing his lips against the soft, plump curve of her mouth? Is his hand between her legs?

I jerk on the cuffs, rattling the chains like a beast in a cage. A cry of outrage fills the space. It takes me several long breaths to find some resemblance of calm, forcing my brain to function rationally. I made a promise. This is for Valentina. It shreds my heart to bleeding pieces, but I've seen the way they look at each other. Quincy is smitten with my woman, and she likes him more than she'll ever admit. Daily, I'm forced to witness the way her eyes light up when they run into each other in the garden. His gentleness toward her is shoved down my throat. It's a reminder that I'll never have her like another man can have her, a man with a handsome face and an easy smile. A man without darkness and a need to hurt and own her. She'll never be mine like that--freely--but it doesn't matter. I'll never let her go. In exchange for forever, I'm giving her this one night. She deserves it pretty with a gentle man on top, offering her a handsome face to stare up at and an unbroken body to hold onto.

Does he find her wet?

"No!"

I strain against the chains. My roar sounds animalistic, even to my own ears. I can't do it. I can't stand it. Fuck my promise.

"Rhett!" My voice carries through the room, lifting the roof. "Let me the fuck out! Open the door!"

I shout profanities and utter threats even Magda will be ashamed of, jerking on the cuffs until my skin is chaffed raw and I'm running the risk of pulling my arms out of their sockets. I scream until my voice is hoarse, but the sounds are trapped in the room designed for exactly that purpose.

"Valentina!"

I struggle in a rage so dark that reason flees my mind. I grapple with thoughts that slice my heart open and blind me in the red fury of my possessive jealousy. I wrestle with nothing but the air, as if I can strangle those images torturing my mind and lay them to rest. Clawing and kicking, I twist my body until the bench falls from under me. I kick at the wood with my boots, the splintering crunch as it breaks a satisfying sound that feeds my need for violence. Pain shoots up my injured leg, a sharp stab lancing in my knee. I fight until every part of me is hurting as much as my heart, until I have no more energy left.

Sweat-drenched and battered, I sag in my chains, hanging by the threads of sanity. The irony of where I find myself isn't lost on me. I'm chained in my own torture chamber, suffering a self-inflicted torture far worse than anything I've done to any enemy who's ever had the displeasure of crossing this doorstep.

"Valentina."

Her name is a croak. My throat burns. I can no longer scream. I can only sob and give in to the cruelty of my imagination as it leads me on a graphic tour of Valentina's first time.

SOMETIME DURING THE EARLY HOURS, I wake. I found a position on my knees, my arms pulled up and my head hanging between my shoulders. I must've passed out from physical exhaustion. My throat and eyes are dehydrated. Scratchy. Everything inside of me is raw. I did her a favor, but the selfish part of me is too great, the possessive part of me too complete to accept it gracefully. I glance at the wall clock. It's done.

Too late.

The key turns in the lock, and the door opens. Rhett pauses when he takes in the scene.

"Come get me," I grate out.

He hesitates, but finally approaches with quick steps. As he unlocks me, he avoids my eyes. The minute I'm free he retreats to the far end of the room.

"Leave," I growl, frightened that I'll take it out on him.

He doesn't let me tell him twice. Like an arrow from a bow, he shoots through the door, his steps falling in a fast jog down the hallway.

I wipe a hand over my face, the stubble where there's no beard a reminder that I need a shower and a shave. Every ounce of my body is pulled tight. More than anything, I want to hunt Quincy down and kill him. In less than an hour, I'll face him and listen to his account. I want every fucking detail so I can pretend I've been there, part of it all. I'm too damn jealous to even spare myself the pain.

Walking to the wet bar that's always stocked with bottled water and drinks--torturing people is thirsty work--I pour a whiskey and shoot it back neat. Then another. And another. I need the alcohol if I'm not to crush Quincy's windpipe and rip off his dick. For good measure, I have a fourth. The alcohol burns my stomach and relieves the worst of the rawness in my throat from the vile curses I uttered all night. My skin heats, and my brain blurs enough to dull my emotions, enough to get through the hour that awaits without committing a murder in my own house.

Valentina

AT FIVE, I'm up as usual, but Gabriel doesn't come to the kitchen for his coffee. I leave his breakfast on the hot tray and shrug inwardly. If he had a rough night, I hope he wakes up with a hell of a hangover. It will serve him right for the stunt he tried to pull on me. Still seething with annoyance, I take the washing basket and set out to collect the dirty laundry. In the hallway, my step slows as none other than Gabriel turns the corner, heading my way.

He looks like shit. His hair is disheveled, standing in every direction, and stubble blurs the neatly shaved line of his beard. His eyes are bloodshot and his clothes--the same clothes from last night--are creased. Wherever he's been, it looks like he slithered out of some woman's bed a second ago.

His eyes fix on me with the kind of intensity that isolates us in this moment. Everything else fades away as he nails me with his glacier stare, making me shiver inside. He holds me locked in invisible constraints until he's almost on top of me. Even if I want to, I can't move. I'm frozen to the spot.

He leans an arm above his head on the wall and crosses one ankle over the other, his stance both relaxed and intimidating as he stares down at me.

"So," his eyes run over me from top to bottom, "how was last night?"

There's a bite in his words that's contradictory to the flash of hurt in his eyes. The whiskey that laces his breath drifts to me on the air. He's been out drinking?

I want to tell him he's an asshole, but his masculinity folds around me like a cloak, the power he has over me both frightening and exciting.

"Did he kiss you?" he asks on a drawl, cool amusement masking something else I can't place.

"On a first date?" I say sarcastically. "Some men are gentlemen, you know."

First, he looks surprised, then relieved, and then angry. "Are you telling me nothing happened?"

"Like I said, Quincy is a gentleman."

Predator intent fills his eyes. He moves so close to me, I can see his pupils dilate. "Then it seems it's not a gentleman you need."

I pull myself to my full height, my breasts brushing over his chest in the process, but I don't care. "Why, Gabriel, you look disappointed." I bat my eyelashes in mock innocence. "What were you hoping for?"

He reaches out so fast I jump in fright and drop the basket when he grabs my wrist.

"I offered you a chance to have it pretty." His lips thin. "I offered you beautiful. You blew that chance, and now you're left with hard and ugly." He squeezes to the point of pain. "You're left with *me*."

There's so much meaning in those words, I can't stop the shiver that crawls up my spine.

He releases me with a soft shove and says in a quiet, threatening voice, "Remember, you begged for it."

Picking up the basket, he pushes it into my arms and walks around me like I'm nothing but an irritating obstacle in his way. If I was infuriated last night, I'm ten times more so now.

"You can't pass me around like a toy for your men," I say to his back, "and you can't decide who I sleep with."

He stops and takes two steps back to me. His smile is cold and cruel. "That's where you're wrong. You're *property*, Valentina. You agreed to *any duty* I see fit. I can share you however I want, but you don't have to worry about being a toy for my men. I don't like to share my toys. Last night was a big fucking gift. Not for Quincy. For *you*." Heat and possessive intent darken his eyes, making him look more dangerous than ever. "And it'll never happen again."

He stalks away with a heavy limp, leaving me trembling with something other than anger. Understanding blooms in me. Gabriel wanted my first experience to be with someone normal. He wanted me to have a taste of how sweet it can be before he submits me to the dark lust I sense in him. I brace my back against the wall and take a few deep breaths. I'm not sure what's worse, that I find his intention sweet or that I crave the darkness he's withholding from me.

11

Valentina

That afternoon, Gabriel goes out on a job and doesn't return for dinner. I'm already in bed when I hear his uneven gait in the kitchen. Rummaging sounds come from the pantry. If he's hungry, I left his food in the oven. I'm not ready to face him, but I can't put it off indefinitely. Rather now, than later.

Entering the scullery, I forget my apprehension. Gabriel is removing a bloody shirt over the basin, the medicine kit balanced on the edge.

"Gabriel!"

I run to him, my eyes doing a quick evaluation of his state. There's a cut in his shoulder through which blood is oozing and several scrapes on his stomach and ribs.

He presses the shirt to the wound and opens the tap. "Shh. Where's Carly?"

"She went to bed after dinner. What happened?" I take the shirt from him and dump it in the trashcan. It's torn and stained beyond saving.

"Business."

He flinches when I touch the wound to assess how deep the cut is.

"This needs stitches. Where are Rhett and Quincy?"

"I sent them to bed. It's not that serious." He flashes me an amused smile. "But your concern is flattering."

"This is no time for jokes." Taking disinfectant and sterile gauzes from the medicine kit, I start cleaning the wound.

"Good thing blood doesn't make you queasy."

I don't return his smile. I don't even want to think what sinister activity earned him these injuries.

"Give me a needle and thread," he orders.

Only Gabriel will keep sterile needles and surgical thread in his medicine kit. I locate the items and hold them out to him. He takes a vanity mirror from the shelf and balances it on the counter. I watch as he pulls the thread through the eye of the needle, but when he angles himself toward the mirror and pushes the needle through the skin at the top of the cut, I take over. He lets me, studying me as I work to sew him back together. I'm no nurse. I'm not even a vet, but I've watched Kris stitch up cuts plenty of times. He winces, but he doesn't say a word until the cut is closed and dressed.

"Thank you."

"You're welcome."

I dispose of the used materials and scrub the basin and my hands with disinfectant. When I'm done, I give him a painkiller and anti-inflammatory with a glass of water. He drinks the pills without protest. Fine lines of fatigue mark his eyes and the corners of his mouth. His permanent frown lines run deeper than usual. Taking his hand, I lead him to my bathroom.

"What are you doing?" he asks.

"Getting the blood off you. You should be worried about catching AIDS."

He grins. "Next time, I'll wear surgical gloves."

I snort. He lets me undress him while the water runs warm. I have to undress as well so my clothes don't get wet, but the shower in my bath is too small for both of us to stand comfortably. When I'm with him in the shower, he has to drape me over his body or hold me in his arms. I angle the water away from his wound, and wash the rest of his body, trying to be gentle on his abdomen where he's bruised. When he's clean, I wrap a towel around his waist and take another to pat him dry. I have to stand on the toilet to reach his hair. Judging by the teeth he flashes me, he finds my care amusing, but he doesn't interfere or take over. I dry his back, chest, and arms, and then I go down on my knees to rub the towel up his legs. There are so many muscles on these legs. They knit together in rigid lines, defining the man's hard exterior with an accurate mirror image of what lies inside his soul.

As I'm pushing to my feet, he prevents me with his hands on my shoulders. I look up. He's devouring me with his eyes, his cock tenting the towel at my eye level.

"Valentina."

There's a plea in the way he says my name. I can't help but want to please him. My reply to his unspoken question is to tug on the towel and let it fall to the floor. I take him in my mouth, and like always, he lets me do whatever I want. I suck him as deep as I can take, eating him hungrily. He groans and dips his knees, giving himself over to me. I take his pleasure like I own it, like it's his duty to give it up to me. He's breathing hard when I'm done, but so am I. He hooks his hands under my arms to help me to my feet, pressing our lips together, and dipping his tongue into my mouth like he always does when I've swallowed his seed. He growls deep from his chest as he sucks on my tongue. The primal sound makes liquid heat gather between my thighs. I'm impossibly slick, my body preparing itself for his invasion, an invasion that's yet to come.

After drying the water that splashed on me while I washed Gabriel, I take him to my bed, and make him lie down on his back to avoid putting pressure on his shoulder. I curl up against his side with my head on the uninjured side of his chest.

"Why did you do it?" he asks.

"Do what?"

"Take care of me."

"I don't know." Deep inside, I wanted to. It frightened me to see him hurt.

"It doesn't matter." He cups my sex, stroking a thumb over my clit. "It was sweet."

He delves a finger into my wetness, teasing and torturing me until he drags a long and slowly detonating orgasm from my body.

Later, as he holds me in his arms, I say, "Gabriel?"

"Mm?"

"Are you ever afraid of dying?"

He answers without hesitation. "Every day."

The big, strong man next to me suddenly seems too vulnerable for my liking. "The scars, are they from fights like today?"

He gives a low chuckle. "You didn't think I was born *all* ugly, did you?"

I cup his cheek. "That's not what I said. I just tend to think of you as indestructible. Untouchable."

He places his hand over mine and rubs his cheek against my palm. "I'm not untouchable, Valentina. I'm far from it." He moves my hand to his chest. "I do have a heart."

I kiss the flat disk of his nipple and put my ear on his chest, just for good measure. The beat is strong and rhythmic. It sounds sure and secure. I have to believe nothing will happen to him. If he's gone, our nine-year deal is off, and I'm dead. Magda won't honor the agreement. Of that, I'm certain.

I push up on one elbow to trace the embossed lines on his face. "Tell me how it happened."

He catches my hand. "Not tonight."

"Nothing?" I ask with a tinge of disappointment. I want to know his history. I want to understand the man inside the sadist.

"All you need to know is that I regret them." He moves my palm to the bandage strip covering the cut on his shoulder. "For this scar, on the other hand, I'm eternally grateful. I hope it never fades."

"Why?"

"Now it's a reminder of you." He kisses my temple. "Go to sleep. It's late."

The balance that started shifting between us from the day he bought me food tips to the one side of the scale, the side where affection surpasses the physical. There's no denying it, any longer. I'm starting to care for my jailer. Maybe I'm suffering from Stockholm syndrome. Not that it matters how or why it happened. Whatever sparked my feelings, they're real.

When I wake up sometime in the middle of the night, he's gone. I don't even have a scar to run my finger over, no raised tissue on the surface of my skin that can make me feel closer to him. All I have are the marks he's leaving on my heart.

My period is over. My breasts and womb are no longer sensitive, but my body is primed with a powerful arousal that won't grant me relief. The orgasms Gabriel gives me are no longer enough. He made me like this, a pathetic addict who needs, craves, and aches, and still he denies me the remedy, even when I beg. I lie in the dark for a long time, trying to make myself come. It's not my fingers, my touch, I need. It's not even Gabriel's touch. I want him *inside* me. I don't care that he's ruined me or that he still holds my life in his hands. He's conditioned me, and I'm at the end of how far I can go. I'm at the edge of a dark abyss, and even if I fear the plunge, I can't turn back. Getting out of bed, I pad barefoot through the dark house.

He won.

Again.

Gabriel

Leaving Valentina in her bed is becoming harder. I want her next to me all night. It's an impractical and dangerous notion. If Carly sees us or Magda suspects I'm taking it further than the game I claim, I stand losing both my daughter and the woman who dominates every minute of my waking hours and even my dreams. The alarm beeps, pulling me from my thoughts.

The red dot on the bedside monitor warns me of movement in the house. Our security is top-notch, but even the best systems are breached. I check the doors and windows on the monitor. No entrances have been compromised. It can be Carly or Magda. Still, I'm not taking any chances. Whoever is moving through my house is at my door. The creak of a floorboard confirms the information on the screen.

I reach for the gun on the nightstand. When the door opens with a soundless swing, I take aim. My finger freezes on the trigger. It's Valentina's slender form that fills the doorframe. A bolt of shock runs through me for how easily I could've shot her. I lower the weapon. The fight leaves my body, but my muscles don't relax. They're tense with a different kind of anticipation. Her white negligee glows pearly in the moonlight. She's staring at me, biting her lip. Putting the pistol back on the nightstand, I flick on the lamp for a better view.

I know what she wants. We both know why she's here.

I told myself I couldn't do it, and yet, I've never wanted anything more. I've belted and spanked her without breaking a molecule on her skin, but if I take her tonight, I won't only break her virgin body, but also my promise. Call me a weak man, but I already lost the battle the night Rhett locked me in the gym. It was only a matter of time. Tonight is a night for broken promises.

I hold out my hand. "Come here."

She walks to the bed and crawls over me. Every inch of my skin catches fire. By the time her pussy is resting on my crotch, I'm a live wire, ready to explode, but I hold back, giving her control, because she came to me and it's the sweetest moment of my entire fucked up life.

I'm not a man to make small talk or beat around the bush. Especially not when something as serious as this is about to happen. When she doesn't move for several beats, seeming uncertain of where to go from here, I roll us over, pinning her underneath me.

"Get rid of the clothes." I give her just enough space to pull the negligee over her head.

Impatient, I pull the panties down for her, and she kicks them free. She wiggles my pajama bottoms over my hips to my knees. I have to lift first one and then the other leg to get rid of them. Stretched out on top of her, naked, static sparks detonate in every cell of my body. My cock is heavy and painfully hard, cushioned between her soft thighs. My balls ache from too many weeks of celibacy and not enough hand and blowjobs. The need to drive into her is so fierce that I have to grit my teeth.

I slip my hand down our bodies and dip my fingers between her legs. She doesn't need foreplay. She's dripping wet. For *me*. The nights of training her body to want and need me are like one long endless stretch of foreplay, and finally, it's about to explode. I've sucked and tweaked her tits, eaten her pussy, and played with her clit for weeks. What's left is to give her every inch of my cock. Once I'm inside her, there's no turning back. Her body belongs to me, but when I'm done fucking her, her soul will be mine. Once my seed spills in her womb, no other man will touch her again. Not tomorrow. Not when her nine years are up. Never.

Spreading her pussy lips with my fingers, I push the head of my cock against her entrance. My head spins as if I'm on a high. I keep my eyes open. I want to see her face the moment I sink into her. I want to remember her expression. I want to know what she looks like when she comes on my dick, and what she feels when I mark her inside with my cum.

She meets my stare head-on, as bravely as I thought she would, and takes my face between her hands.

"Gabriel…" She inhales deeply.

There's hesitation in her voice. I'm ready. So is she, or she wouldn't be here. The only thing preventing me from tearing into her is the air trapped in her lungs along with her unspoken words.

"Say it," I grit out, my need painful.

Placating my libido, I grind down on her pubic bone. The tip of my shaft edges forward, dipping into the slick heat that waits. Almost violently, I jerk back before I lose all reason and fuck her before she's spoken.

"I know you think I'm a virgin," she says softly, "but I'm not."

For a moment, I'm shocked to a pause. How could I have been so wrong? My judgment concerning a woman's body is always on the mark. All this time, I punished myself, withholding from her, making promises I couldn't keep. To think I almost let Quincy have her. I shake the thought. It's not where I want to take my mind, right now. Whoever her lover was, the asshole didn't know how to get her off. In that regard, I'm definitely her first. Anyway, I don't care who her first was. It doesn't matter, because I'll be her last. It makes no difference to me if she's a holy virgin or a whore.

"I don't care," I say gruffly, grabbing my shaft and directing it to the place that will give me access to her soul. It's when you take a woman, when you make her fall apart in your arms, that you see the nakedness of her heart, and all the truths she hides from the world.

"It doesn't matter to you?" she asks with a tinge of disbelief.

"Of course not." I nip at her ear. "Why would it? I'm no virgin, either."

"I just don't want you to be disappointed."

Disappointed? Is she crazy? "Believe me, nothing about this," I rub my dick over her slick folds, "can be disappointing."

A sob tears from her throat. It catches me so off-guard I almost miss the flash of terror that sparks in her eyes.

"Valentina." I pull back an inch. "If you're not ready, you have to tell me now." I used seduction as my weapon to lure her into my bed with good reason. There's no pleasure in it for me if it's by force.

"Is that why you waited? You thought I'm not ready?"

"You know why I waited. What are you really asking?"

"Do you...?" She bites her lip. "Do you want me? I mean, do you want me like *this*?"

"Goddamn, Valentina. This isn't an act of kindness or a favor. The reason you're here is because I wanted you from the moment I first saw you, and a second from now I'm going to fuck you like I've been wanting to for a very long time, so you better tell me if you're having second thoughts."

"It's not that." She sounds ashamed. "I don't know what to do."

"Wait..." If she's not a virgin, but she doesn't know what to do? A cold feeling of rage unfurls in my gut. Bitterness fills my mouth. The truth lodges like a stake in my heart. "You were raped."

"Yes," she whispers, "but it was a long time ago."

The pace of my breathing quickens, changing direction. I go from turned on to raving mad. Fucking furious. I'll kill the son of a bitch with my bare hands, peel his skin from his body, and cut his muscles from his bones. Forcing back my emotions, I let go of my cock, easing up to cup her cheek.

Calmly, so as not to frighten her with the force of my anger, I ask, "Only once?" while holding my breath for the answer.

"Only once."

"When?"

She turns her head to the side.

I won't let it go. I need to know. "Look at me."

She obeys, her eyes begging me not to push, but the more she holds back, the more uneasy I get.

I brush my thumb over her cheek. "When?"

She purses her lips and stares at me with big eyes, as if I'm going to judge her. "I was thirteen."

When I lay my hands on that motherfucker he's going to suffer. There's only one question left to ask. "Who?"

"I don't know."

She's not lying. She doesn't blink or look away, and her pupils don't dilate. She was a random victim. I'll find and kill him for her. If she wants to, I'll give her the gun and let her shoot him herself. If it's the last thing I do, I'll make the bastard pay.

I kiss her lips. "It wasn't your fault."

"I know."

I'm glad she told me. This will require a different skill and attitude. Technically, she may not be a virgin, but physically, emotionally, and mentally she's the virgin I took her for.

Easing over her body, I cup her jaw and hold her in place for my kiss, bruising our lips together. She gasps into my mouth, but lets me take control. As she can't move her jaw, I'm the one nipping, sucking, and molding my lips around hers, taking and giving and making the moment mine. After a while, she starts fighting me, wrapping her arms around my neck and pulling me down for a deeper kiss, her tongue tangling with mine in an urgency that sets me ablaze. I shift my palm from her jaw to her neck, squeezing with dominant control. She embraces the touch, arching up into my hand. I pin her to the mattress with that commanding hold while I shift to her nipples, starting a slow seduction of tongue and teeth on every erogenous zone of her body. I nip the insides of her elbows and bite into the flesh where her pussy meets her thigh. I drag my tongue over the insides of her legs and dig my fingers into her ass, pulling the curvy flesh apart so I can lick down her crack to her pussy. By the time I've kissed my way from her feet to her mound, her legs are wrapped around me, and she's sliding her wet sex over my cock, seeking the friction that will bring her release.

"I want you," she whispers, breathing beauty into my room. "I want you, Gabriel. Please."

A low groan vibrates in my chest. She's begging *me*. She wants me like no other woman has wanted me before--not for my money or protection, but to ease the need I so carefully planted and nurtured inside of her. Her pleasure is mine, and I'm keeping it forever.

"Oh, God, please." She digs her nails into my back. "Fuck me, already."

We're both out of control. I need to be lucid, or I risk hurting her, but she has me by the balls--literally--dragging her sharp nails from my sac up my ass and sending me way beyond sanity.

I grip my shaft and squeeze the root hard, praying the bite of pain will keep me within reason. Pushing up on one arm, I pull myself from the vice of her thighs and part her legs with my knee. When she's wide and open, I take only a second to enjoy the sight before I lodge the head of my cock in her pussy. Her lips spread wide around my girth, stretching to accommodate all of me. I have precious little control left.

"Look at me," I demand.

She opens her eyes. They're hazy with desire and smoky with need, but they're focused on me. I rest my elbows on the mattress so I can cup her face between my hands, needing to catch her expressions like a prayer between my palms. The movement shoves me another inch into her. She gasps, and her eyes widen. She's tight and hot, her unused channel already pushing to expel the foreign object lodged in her entrance. I push deeper, feeling her like a velvet fist around me. I'm big, and she's fragile, small. Her slickness helps, but it's like pushing into a narrow chamber of hot, melting lava. The deeper I go, the more she squirms. I see it all in her face--the shock, pain, trust, and all-consuming need.

Sweat beads on my brow and torso. My skin is on fire. Her breaths explode from her chest.

"Gabriel..."

It's a plea for mercy. It's moving too slow. I can drag out the discomfort or make it hurt hard and quick before fucking it all better. Pulling back until only the head of my cock is held in place by the stretching muscle in her opening, I hold on to her face tightly and drive home. Tearing through feminine tissue, I bury myself inside her body as far as I can go. It's the moment I've been dreaming of, of hearing her sounds, seeing her surrender, inhaling the scent of our sex, and feeling her body stretch for my cock. She's shaking, her fingers digging into my hips.

"It's almost over, beautiful. It won't hurt for long." I kiss her jaw and move, taking her with long, careful strokes until her body surrenders just like her mind, her tight channel embracing my dick rather than pushing it out.

Her moans turn to panting. It's music to my ears. When she throws her head back, I let go of her face, holding only her eyes. I play with her body, petting her breasts and clit as I stroke deeper and faster, taking everything she can give, everything that makes Valentina a woman. I knead and massage until she's soft and pliant in my arms. She molds like wet, earthy clay under my touch, until her hips start moving to the rhythm of my fingers on her clit.

And then it's over.

She breaks.

Her body sucks me deeper, catching my cock in a trap of painful ecstasy. Her pupils dilate like shooting stars, and her gaze flies away from me like a comet as she comes and leaves a burning trail in my soul. In this moment, she can ask me anything, and I will bust my balls to give it. I'll fetch her the moon and the stars, if that's what she wants, but she only says, "Hold me," and I give her what she desires.

Valentina

GABRIEL'S ARMS are safe around me. He's given me uncountable orgasms, but this one was different. This one was deeper and more intense, stirring the buried emotions I haven't had the courage to look at for so long. After my assault, I shied away from men. The event prevented me from exploring my sexuality. I was afraid to go down that road in the fear of uprooting everything I experienced that awful night, but what I shared with Gabriel was nothing like that. It was a carnal, guilt-free, and necessary need. He took my freedom and made my body a slave to his, but right now, there's nowhere else I'd rather be. This is where I belong. This is where *he* belongs. As much as he took me, I took a part of him, too. I took something of him for myself, and I'll always keep it in my heart. I feel connected to him as I lie in his embrace, enjoying the afterglow of my orgasm. Now that I've had him inside me, I'm hungrier than ever for more. I'm starving for information that goes beyond the sex we share. I want to know why his beautiful physique is broken. I want to know everything about him.

I slide my hand down his body to trace the scar on his knee. Maybe he'll tell me tonight. "How did this happen?"

"Got my kneecap shot away by one of our rivals," he says matter-of-factly.

"And this?" I stroke his hip.

"Baseball bat."

"And this?" As I'm about to cup his cheek, he catches my hand.

"Shrapnel. Explosion. A debtor tried to blow us up with the building where he was laundering the money he stole from us."

"Did he survive?"

He gives me a forced smile. "What do you think?"

"Have you ever considered having it fixed?" I ask as gently as I can.

He replies in a cold voice. "This *is* fixed."

Horror, not because of the ugliness, but because of the sadness, invades me. How did he look before, if this is *after*?

He utters a small sigh. "My bones were crushed. Underneath the skin, there's mostly metal. The risk of the muscles collapsing with more plastic surgery is too high."

I wrap my arms around his waist, holding him tight to me.

Saying his mask of pain doesn't bother me will only sound frivolous, even if it's true.

I rest my cheek on his chest. "Your foot?"

All of his muscles go tense. It takes him several seconds before he relaxes under me again. Just when I thought he wasn't going to tell me, he says, "My mother shot me."

I barely manage to swallow my gasp. "Why?"

His tone is flat. "When I turned twelve, she gave me a gun and told me to shoot a man. I couldn't."

A lump in my throat restricts my speaking. I can't imagine the kind of childhood he had. A part of me relates to that and understands. There's quiet accord between us as we hold and comfort each other, two damaged people with different scars.

IT'S STILL DARK when Gabriel wakes me with a kiss on the mouth. I stretch, feeling the roughness of his loving in the tenderness between my legs, even if he's been as gentle as I guess he can be.

"Good morning." He nips my bottom lip.

His cock is hard against my hip, a reminder of last night and of what I can have again.

"Gabriel." My voice is breathy.

He chuckles. "If I weren't so concerned about not letting you sleep enough, I would've been buried between your thighs an hour ago."

I shiver at the thought, desire making me wet.

A shadow creeps into his eyes. "You have to go. Carly will be up soon."

It's a logical comment, but it hurts, and that's a surprise. Maybe it's because creeping down the dark hallway like I have something to hide, like what I did with Gabriel belongs to the shadows, kills the emotional upsurge of last night.

"You're right." I sit up, clutching the sheet to my breasts.

Groping around under the sheets, I find my nightgown and underwear and pull them on. As I swing my feet off the bed, he grabs my arm. I pause, but I don't look back at him. I'm scared he'll see what I feel in my eyes. That I care.

He kisses my shoulder and brushes his lips up the curve of my neck to my ear. When he releases me, I take it as my cue to leave. I close his bedroom door quietly behind me and glance down the hallway to make sure it's clear before I sneak back to my room. The room looks empty and cold. Out of nowhere, I have an attack of inexplicable loneliness, followed by a bout of guilt because Oscar is sleeping alone on my pillow.

I pick him up and hug him to my chest. "Poor baby. I'm sorry I left you all alone last night."

He purrs and rubs his face against my jaw, not halfway as unsettled as I am.

Gabriel

THERE'S NOT much information in the country Anton can't lay his hands on, so when he tells me Lambert Roos' phone records have been wiped, I know the rat I smelled is real. I order Anton to dig into Lambert's history, present and past, and to flag anything suspicious that comes up, especially pertaining to the Haynes family. Lambert did business with Marvin. I want to know why he stopped brokering the car cloning business after Marvin's accident. I also want to know who Valentina's rapist is, but I'll have to get more information from her, a delicate situation I don't look forward to. I already checked the police records. The family didn't report her rape. My own research produced nothing helpful.

The remainder of my time is dedicated to preparing for tonight's dinner meeting. Despite her protests, I ship Carly off to Sylvia for the weekend. I don't want her around for the dinner party, not with the guests Magda invited. We'll be catering for the Ferreira drug cartel men, Jeremy, the owner, and his son and future heir, Diogo. It's tough enough stomaching the political pawns Magda likes to entertain. I don't like hosting drug thugs in our home, but Magda is wheeling a deal to open a new financing franchise in Westdene, the heart of Jeremy's territory.

From the minute they walk through the door, I dislike them. Jeremy has the close-set eyes of a crocodile who acts asleep to snatch his non-suspecting prey. He grabs my hand in a jovial shake, treating me like his long-lost son, while Diogo, a smooth, handsome man in his late twenties, gives me a measuring look that tells me he finds me too short, not in the literal sense, of course. He may be ten years younger than me and blessed with a whole body, but I have years of experience over him and a darkness he can't begin to understand.

They kiss Magda's hand and accept the cocktails and hors d'oeuvres she offers in the lounge. Their chitchat and pretense at civility irritate me. If it was up to me, I would've cut through the bullshit and gotten to the point. We want exclusivity in their area. They want our money. Simple. We pay a kickback, and no other loan sharks get in. A deal also guarantees that we don't fuck with them, and they don't kill our men.

Magda navigates through a whole family tree of questions about their wives, kids, grandmothers, and whatnot before she finally announces dinner is served. The tux I'm wearing for the occasion, these affairs being sordidly formal, is too hot. I hook a finger between my neck and the collar of my evening shirt and tug. The bowtie gives marginally, but I only breathe easier when Valentina walks into the room in her somber black dress and hair pulled back in a neat bun in the nape of her neck.

I watch her unabashedly as she serves our starters. The curve of her neck is long and elegant. Her fingers are slender, but they serve with efficient and sure movements, not spilling a drop of the gazpacho soup. A smell of raspberry fills my nostrils as she brushes past me, the fabric of her dress touching my chair. She's present in all of my senses, even in my thoughts with a memory of how her body surrendered to mine last night. My cock hardens. It's a good thing we're seated.

It's hard to tear my attention away from her, but I need to concentrate on the negotiation and the subtle nuances of the conversation. I'm good at reading body language. I may not say much, but if our partners try to fuck us over, I'm always the first to get the hunch. With difficulty, I return my attention to the people seated at the opposite side of the table, but as I lift my eyes, I notice the way Diogo stares at Valentina. Anger explodes in my body and courses through my veins. The only thing that prevents me from reaching over the table and drowning him in his bowl of soup is that Valentina leaves the room, cutting his ogling short. I can't wait for this night to be over.

Halfway through the main meal, we come to an agreement. The minute we shake hands on the deal, Magda's tenseness evaporates. She becomes the engaging hostess she's known for, drawing Jeremy into a friendly argument about the opposing rugby teams they support. Diogo asks for directions to the bathroom and excuses himself.

The skin between my shoulder blades pinches. I push back my chair. "Excuse me. I'm going to check on dessert."

Magda shoots me a look, but I'm blind to the annoyance in her eyes. My soles are quiet in the carpeted hallway. In the entrance to the kitchen, I come to an abrupt halt. Valentina has her back pushed against the wall and a kitchen knife aimed at Diogo.

12

Gabriel

The knife in Valentina's hand makes me see images that will haunt me forever. A million scenarios pop into my head. The thought of Valentina hurt or Diogo's hands on her, pulls me from reason into a state of madness. In a flash, I pounce on Diogo, throwing him on the floor. I slam his face into the tiles and pin him down with my knees, my fists pounding into his ribs. The sounds of his strangled grunts and bone cracking aren't enough. I want him to cough up blood until his lungs drown in it.

"Gabriel!"

Valentina's voice pierces the ugly bubble of my rage. The piece of shit under me is struggling for his life. Slowly, I return to the distant part of humanity inside me, the little that's left in my soul. Magda and Jeremy come running into the room, probably alarmed by Valentina's scream.

"What in God's name?" Magda grabs my arm and tries to pull me off the man sprawled out on the floor.

I shake her off, but it's Valentina's round, fearful eyes that beckon me to let the scumbag go.

Getting to my feet, I adjust my jacket. "Get up, you son of a bitch."

"What the hell's going on?" Jeremy takes Diogo by his shoulders to help him to his feet.

Pulling him up is a struggle. It looks like he has trouble breathing. I must've knocked the wind out of him and broken a few ribs. His nose is bleeding from the blow on the tiles.

Magda flutters around him like a hen. "Gabriel! Are you out of your mind?"

I jab a finger at Diogo. "If you put a finger on her, asshole, you're dead."

Magda and Jeremy turn their heads toward Valentina. She's still standing with her back against the wall, her body trembling and her eyes fixed on Diogo.

I take the knife from her hand and leave it on the counter. Lowering my head, I put us on eye level. "Look at me." Once I have her undivided attention, I ask, "Did he touch you?"

"No," she whispers.

Magda starts speaking, but I cut her short. "What did he do?"

"He wanted to–to…"

She doesn't have to say it. I know men like Diogo. I know the things they want to do. I turn to Diogo with cold calculation. "If I didn't walk in here, what were you going to do?"

He spits blood from a split lip on the floor. "Have myself some fun. She's only a maid, for Christ's sake."

My voice is soft, but my anger carries in my tone. "That gives you the right to assault the people living under my roof, the people I protect?"

"Hold on, son." Jeremy steps between us, his palms raised. "You're not going to risk our newly forged relationship over a maid, are you?"

I turn my vengeance on the old man. "She's not just a maid. She's property."

Jeremy knows what that means. In his and my world, property is more untouchable than a man's wife. You may fuck someone else's wife and pray you don't get caught, but you don't lay a finger on another man's property without accepting that you're going to get your hand chopped off.

"Whoa." He utters a nervous laugh. "Honest mistake. Diogo didn't know. We're used to helping ourselves, if you know what I mean."

"Are you insulting me by insinuating my house is a brothel?"

"Jeremy," Magda takes his arm, "your son needs medical attention. I'll cover all the costs, of course. I do apologize for this unfortunate misunderstanding."

It's a subtle way of telling him to leave. Magda knows me too well. I'm a lunatic, and right now, I'm about as stable as an active volcano.

Jeremy frees his arm. "Let's go, Diogo."

Diogo sneers at me as he passes, clutching his side. He should've just carried on walking, but the mistake he makes is to turn back in the doorway.

"You know what your problem is, honey?" he says to Valentina. "You're too damn pretty. It's a shame you're also a prude. I think you would've enjoyed it if I'd jumped you against the wall."

Just like that, my frayed control unravels. Magda grabs for the hem of my jacket as I lurch forward and catch the cocksucker around the neck. Jeremy is cussing and trying to pull my arms away from his son, but not a hundred horses are enough to tear me away. I drag him by his scrawny neck to Valentina and force him down on his knees at her feet. I grab a fistful of his perfectly styled hair and jerk his head back. Reaching for the same knife Valentina used to defend herself, I push the tip against his lilywhite, pretty-boy neck.

"Apologize."

"Diogo," Jeremy says from behind me, a tremor in his voice, "do as he says."

"Gabriel." There's consternation in Magda's tone, but she doesn't touch me. The situation is too volatile. I'm too unpredictable. A flick of my wrist and Diogo's life will bleed out at Valentina's feet. Only, I don't want another man's blood on her conscience. She already feels responsible for Tiny's death. Diogo doesn't deserve the guilt she'll suffer over him.

"I'm sorry," Diogo grits out.

I jerk harder on his hair, making him cry out in pain. "Say it like you mean it."

"I'm really fucking sorry."

I lodge the tip of the knife under his skin. "Beg." A thin trickle of blood runs down his neck under his collar.

"Forgive me," he says. "I beg you."

I look at Valentina. "Do you forgive him?"

She looks at me with owl eyes. "Yes."

"You're more compassionate than me." I yank him up by his hair until he finds his feet. "Get the fuck out of my house. The deal's off, and you better pray I don't run into you on the street. You better stay very far away from me."

When I let go, Diogo stumbles to his father. Magda is paler than the white tiles on the floor, quiet for once. Jeremy gives me a narrowed glare, but he takes Diogo's arm and escorts him from the room. You don't insult a man in his own house. Jeremy knows this. He knows I can cut Diogo's throat for that, and none of his business associates will retaliate.

Magda rubs the back of her neck. "I'll see you out." She turns to Valentina. "You better go to your room and not come out until morning. If I see your face before, I may not be able to suppress the urge to kill you."

When it's just the two of us in the kitchen, I take her in my arms and give her a hug. "You okay?"

She nods. "I didn't want to cause trouble."

"You did the right thing." I kiss her nose. "I'm proud of you."

"You put your life at risk. They're going to kill you."

"They'll try, but so is every other criminal and cop in the country. You're mine, Valentina, and nobody touches you."

The clicking of Magda's heels down the hallway makes me go rigid. "Go to bed."

"The kitchen––"

"Can wait for tomorrow. Go."

She obeys wordlessly. By the time Magda reenters the room, Valentina is out of sight.

"In my study." Magda stalks from the room, not waiting to see if I'm following.

She holds the door for me and slams it when I step over the threshold.

"Are you out of your goddamn mind?"

"You know I am, Magda."

"Do you have any idea how hard I worked to secure that deal?" She pushes her finger in my face. "What gave you the right to blow it away? Over a fucking maid!"

I grab her finger and move it away with force. The act catches her off-guard. She stumbles a step back and gapes at me with a mixture of disbelief and fear.

"If you ever push your finger in my face again, I'll break it."

"Gabriel," she exclaims on a gasp, "I'm your mother."

"You've never been a mother to me. Don't claim the designation now."

"What's gotten into you? You blew a multi-million-rand deal, for God's sake!" She straightens her back, her fear suddenly gone. "Don't think you're above my punishment because you're my son. You're taking this game you're playing with the girl too far. You've had your fun. Let her slip up and kill her so we can all go back to our lives."

"I'll decide when the fun's up."

"Is part of the fun buying her fancy clothes? Playing with a doll isn't enough for you? You have to dress her, too?"

"Are you checking my bank statements?"

"I know the owner of the boutique where you took your slave on a shopping spree."

"That's none of your business."

"You're fucked in the head, you know that? Just like your father."

"How can I forget when you're doing such a great job of reminding me?"

She wipes a hand over her face. "I need a drink." Propping her hands on her hips, she regards me from under her lashes. "Get her out of your system, Gabriel. Do whatever it takes. Eventually, you're going to have to kill her."

"Good night, *Mother*."

I leave her alone in her study, going to my own for a stiff drink and to mull over the evening. I should've broken Diogo's nose the minute he stepped over my doorstep. That way, I would've saved myself a whole evening of his unpleasant presence. My thoughts don't dwell on the cocksucker for long. As always, my attention is reserved for Valentina. I'm not sure in what emotional state she'll be when I go to her room, but I'll be there for her, regardless. She should feel safe under my roof, knowing I won't let anyone harm her. The kind of hurt I want to give her, that's something entirely different. The kind of pain I like to inflict is as much for her pleasure as mine.

When I walk through her door, I don't find her curled up in bed or huddled in a corner. She's spread out on the bed, naked, waiting for me. My balls draw tight. My cock swells.

I can't look away from her fingers where they rest between her legs. "You played with yourself?"

"Yes."

"Did you come?"

"No, I was saving that for you."

"Good, because otherwise I would've had to punish you. I own your orgasms. Say it."

"You own me, Gabriel. All of my orgasms."

I swallow away the hoarseness in my throat. "Show me. Play with yourself."

"Later." She wiggles her hips. "I want *you* inside me."

Holy fuck. What she does to me. I strip my clothes and climb between her legs. Even if she's offering herself, I want to hunt her. I want to catch her in the wild, wild, darkest woods of our desires and conquer her body. I want to tame her soul. I've got her, but I'm terrified I'll lose her. I need to pin her down and constrain her, keep her in the cage of lust I so carefully constructed to trap her.

I flatten my palm on her pelvis, keeping her lower body in place as I push two fingers inside her pussy. She's wet. The suction of her inner muscles welcomes me. I can't wait. I grip the root of my shaft and place it at her entrance, but she shakes her head. It takes every ounce of willpower I possess not to give in to the urge to tie her up and make her have it my way. It takes strength to lift my hand from her abdomen and allow her to escape, but she doesn't run away from the monster in her bed. She embraces the need that's chasing us both by turning over on her hands and knees. She looks back at me from over her shoulder, putting her beautiful cunt on display.

"Take me like this," she whispers.

The animal in me rises to the occasion. I open her pussy with my thumbs, align my cock with her slick folds, and drive home. Her back arches from the fast and hard intrusion, but she slams back, meeting my force with an urgency of her own. I'm giving her my all, thrusting our groins together with enough force to bruise her skin.

"More," she pants. "You're holding back."

I'm fucking the air from her lungs, and she's begging for more.

"Harder, Gabriel. Please. Please, God. Let it go. Make me forget. Make me forget what happened tonight."

I do. The walls of my constraint break, crumbling around her, and I take her like I've never taken a woman before.

Valentina

GABRIEL IS POUNDING INTO ME, hurting me inside, but I need more. With him, I'll always need more. He steals my breath, takes my pleasure, and owns my desires. I am so filled with him, I can't take more, and, yet I want him in every crevice and corner of my body.

Reaching between my legs, I caress his testicles, feeling their charged sway as he slams his groin against my ass.

"More," I moan. "Please."

"If I fuck you harder, I'll break you."

I want him to bleed into my cells until we are inseparable, until our DNA is entangled and my life is grafted with his. Together, we're invincible. As long as he's with me, no one else can touch me. Like this, there's no ugly. No Diogo. No men like Tiny. Only Gabriel who makes me forget everything, even that he owns me.

"Fill me, Gabriel. Fill me more."

"Goddammit, Valentina. You kill me."

I look back at him from over my shoulder. His face is scrunched up with pent-up desire, his cool eyes dark with lust, and his jaw tense with control. Without breaking his pace, he lets go of my hip to stick his forefinger in his mouth. He opens my ass with his free hand and sticks his wet finger into my dark entrance. I fall forward and catch my weight on my arms. With the intrusion in my ass, the pressure in my pussy increases two-fold.

"Yes," I whimper. "Like that."

I brace myself for the impact. His hands being otherwise occupied, he can no longer support my hips. The force is too much. My body is helpless under his brutal hammering. Every thrust shifts me higher up the mattress. He follows me, pulling out and pushing back in, his cock and finger working in synchrony.

One hand moves around to the front of my body, finding my clit. A few fast strokes and I come, yelling his name. I expect him to come with me, but he doesn't. While I'm riding the incredible wave of my release, he stretches me by adding a second finger to the first in my backside. I'm overfull, but I don't care. I'm contracting and sizzling, my body a canvas of receptors for pleasure. I'm floating in a space of euphoric bliss. I don't care what he does with my body.

After a while, he pulls his cock free. Only his fingers are punishing my ass. This, too, stops. His touch disappears.

"Don't move."

Exhausted, I melt into the sheets. I'm not going anywhere. The bed dips, and then he's gone. Cupboards open and close in the kitchen. What is he doing? I have my answer when he returns with a bottle of cooking oil. He places it on the floor and continues right where he left off, working two fingers into my ass. The sensation is wrong and thrilling. A forbidden kind of pleasure runs up my spine. After a moment, he withdraws his fingers and opens my crack. Cold liquid squirts into my ass. After the heat, the cold comes as a shock. I squirm to escape the onslaught, but he grabs me between the legs and holds me still while more of that slippery liquid fills me up. The oil. It feels like when he comes inside of me, only colder. He smears the substance around the tight ring of muscle, and when he pushes his finger back, it slips right in. I arch my back in response, needing more of the friction. The second finger joins the first, and soon a third finger stretches me. It doesn't hurt, but it's too full. I'm about to say so when his hand disappears and a hot, smooth surface pushes against my dark entrance. I look over my shoulder to see him positioning his cock where his fingers have been.

I try to lift my upper body, but he pushes me down with a hand on my lower back, working himself into me an inch. It burns like hell. I moan and squirm and try to push him out, but the harder I clench my backside, the harder he pushes.

"Relax," he says in a tight voice. "I'll take your ass regardless."

I know he will, and I want him to. I take a deep breath and try to let the tension go, but when he moves deeper, I cry out and bite into the pillow to muffle the sound.

"Almost there," he says, rubbing his palms over my ass cheeks.

God, it hurts. I'm not sure I can take it. "Gabriel."

"Hush, beautiful." He bends down and kisses my spine. "Take a deep breath."

He talks me through it, making me breathe in and out until he has buried all of him inside me. The last inch is the worst. I gasp and swallow air. When he moves, I scream, grinding my pelvis to the mattress to escape the touch, but he chases after me, fucking me deeper. With every thrust he pounds the breath out of me until my voice is raw, and then he stills, keeping his cock in my body. I'm barely aware of anything but the invasive hardness. Carefully, he slips two fingers into my pussy. The pad of his thumb rests on my clit, stimulating my need. As my desire starts climbing again and my muscles contract around him, he moves again. He takes me to a place I didn't know existed, where pleasure and pain are one, and the effect of having both sensations simultaneously on my body makes it impossible to discern where the one starts and the other stops. He's kindling the biggest need in me yet. I'm full and fulfilled. I'm aching, but he's soothing me. I'm hovering on the edge. If I tumble over, I may not stop falling, but I'm powerless to prevent it.

My body tightens. As the wave starts rolling, he drags his wet fingers from my pussy. His hands fold around my neck, squeezing just enough to cut my airflow. I need to fight, but I'm too weak. I don't have enough energy left. I can only lie there with electric shivers running through my clit, and Gabriel's cock ramming into my ass while white spots start to dance in my vision, and my pulse hammers in my ears. The minute he gives me back the gift of oxygen, of life, I come with a force that shatters my body and mind. Thousands of volts of pleasure course through me, pulling every muscle, finger, and toe so tight my body is one, great spasm. I must've fallen over that edge, because I'm drifting like a feather, and everything around me turns into a comfortable darkness where the brutal pleasure mercifully stops.

Gabriel

FUCK. Shit. It's the first time I fucked a woman unconscious. I turn Valentina's limp body on her back and slap her cheeks.

"Wake up, baby."

She doesn't move. Not even her eyelashes flutter. The euphoria of my climax evaporates. Fuck, fuck, fuck. I pick her up in my arms and carry her to the shower. I can barely squeeze inside with her draped over me. I adjust the water to a lukewarm setting and, tipping her head back, let it run over her face and hair.

She frowns and stirs.

"That's my girl. Come on, Valentina."

She gasps and coughs. Her eyelids lift to reveal tiger-eye gemstones staring at me. "Gabriel."

Relief washes over me, and the tightness in my chest expands marginally. "I'm here, beautiful."

I hold her to me, letting her find her feet without releasing my grip on her waist. Allowing her to pass out wasn't part of my plan. I'm furious with myself. She deserves better than a sadist who pushes her to the limits of pleasure, all the way into fucking fainting. The only way I know to make it right is to give her comfort. Like she took care of me the night I was stabbed, I take care of her, washing her hair and her body from the top of her head to the tip of her toes as best as I can in the confined space. I'm careful with the tender part between her legs and especially her ass. After drying and dressing her, I put her to bed. It tears me up, but I have to go to my own. I'm too exhausted to risk staying with her. If I fall asleep, I may not wake up before Carly. I don't want to leave her like this, but I must. For how much longer can I keep up the pretense?

AFTER MY MORNING workout with Quincy and Rhett, I meet Sonny and Lance, two of my franchise owners, about a dispute over territory. Lance has been casting his nets in Sonny's reservoir, and as much as I hate playing ombudsman, I prefer to step in before we have a war on our hands. It's a glorious day, and we're having our discussion by the pool. My leg has been bothering me more than usual after last night's sexual marathon, and the exercise in the water does me good. I swim a few laps before stretching out on a deckchair in the sun, listening to the squabble between the grown men. When it gets close to one o'clock, I interrupt their bickering.

"No eyes on the housekeeper."

Sonny and Lance exchange a glance, but comprehension dawns on their faces when Valentina exits from the kitchen, a tray loaded with food in her hands, and walks our way. Sonny looks up at the sky while Lance fixes his gaze on his toes.

Her figure is slender in the dark dress. With tendrils that escaped her ponytail, she looks feminine and vulnerable. I want her next to me, in my arms, not at a distance acceptable for a servant, not with a barrier between us that lets me enjoy the sunshine while she's standing there in her black garb, sweating in the sun.

There's not a stitch of resentment in the brilliant smile she gives me. "Can I get you anything to drink?"

"Lemonade." I turn to Sonny and Lance, who are looking anywhere but at Valentina. "Beer?"

"Please," they say in unison.

"Anything else?"

I'm suddenly bothered that she has to serve men not worthy of kissing her feet. "No."

Her smile is genuine and pure, a ray of beautiful that doesn't fit in the filth of my world. "Just shout if you need me."

As she walks back to the kitchen, I can't help but stare after the frail set of her narrow shoulders with an emotion that, this time, isn't foreign to me.

Longing.

I'm consumed by longing.

Valentina

NOTHING IS WORSE than the helplessness I felt at the hands of men who bullied and assaulted me. Tiny lifted the tightly sealed lid on those emotions. What Diogo tried to do made me relive those feelings. Those forbidden sentiments, the ones I banished to the depths of my mind, make me shaky with shame and anger. I hate not being able to defend myself. Then there's Gabriel. The things I feel when I'm with him are too complicated to examine, and I'm too scared of what I'll find. What I need is not to analyze what's happening between me and my keeper--I can't change it, anyway--but to learn to protect myself from people stronger than me. Maybe I could get a weapon and learn how to use it.

I'm sweeping up the leaves on the pavement, fantasizing about my options, when Magda walks up.

"I want all the leather sofas treated with beeswax and polished to a shine today. Carly is complaining her cupboards are full of dust. Unpack everything and wipe down the shelves. Her closet can do with a good reorganization."

"Yes, ma'am."

"I want dinner to be served an hour earlier, tonight. I have an appointment after."

"I'll make sure it's ready."

"Tomorrow you need to start taking down the curtains and wash them. Start with the bedrooms. You can do one room every day."

"Yes, ma'am."

She checks her watch. "Don't wait for the afternoon to sweep the pavement. It has to be done every morning at eight. The neighbors must think we're pigs living in a pigsty."

"I'll do it at eight."

"Are you any good with a sewing machine?"

"I've never used one."

"Better learn. You can adjust the hems of the new curtains I bought for the lounge."

The delivery van pulls up, thankfully saving me from more tasks she can think up, as I have to check and sign for the produce.

For the rest of the day, I race through my chores, skipping lunch and teatime. It's hard not to stress over screwing up a task or failing to execute it when your life's in the balance. I haven't slept enough in weeks, and I haven't studied in days. I missed deadlines for two assignments and only got extensions because of my good grades, but no matter how fast I work, there's always more work and too little time. My mentor warned me if I miss another deadline, I'd get a zero for the assignment. She can't keep on making exceptions for me.

DURING THE NEXT TWO WEEKS, Gabriel is hardly home. When he comes to me at night, there are lines of strain on his face. I don't ask about his business, but from the way he takes me, hard and relentless, I know in his own way, he's as stressed as I am, so I don't complain. When I'm at Kris' house, I cook, clean, help in the clinic, and spend as much time with Charlie as I can. At night, I try to catch up with my outstanding projects, but I'm several weeks behind. I sleep between four and five hours per night, returning to my studies when Gabriel leaves me to go back to his own room. I don't dare confess to him in the fear that he'll take it away from me, and I can't lose my dream. Despite the explosive sex, I'm still property. Nothing but an amusing toy. Gabriel takes care of me like one would maintain an expensive car or look after a cute pet. Copious amounts of coffee keep me awake and jittery during the day. It's only by sheer willpower that I finish the tasks Magda doles out. The harder she pushes me, the harder I try. The more she demands, the more I deliver.

It's a bright December morning when half a kudu carcass is dropped off in the kitchen.

"A gift from business colleagues who went hunting," she says, regarding the piece of meat with her hands on her hips.

It's not hunting season. "Where does it come from?"

"A friend did some culling on a game farm up north."

"What shall I do with it, ma'am?"

"Marie used to process the meat. The leg is good for biltong. You can use the offcuts for sausage."

I've never chopped up half an antelope, but I'm not going to admit it. When she's gone, I do an internet search and come up with page that gives detailed illustrations on how to process a carcass. It's too heavy for me to handle alone, so when Quincy walks past the kitchen with Bruno, I ask him to help. Together, we use the meat axe to chop the meat into smaller, more manageable pieces. He helps me to set up the electric meat saw and grinder on the island counter. While he's cleaning the blades for me, I order the intestines for the sausage from a local butcher.

"All ready," he says. "Need some help with the grinding?"

"I'm good, thank you." I'm proud that I figured it out.

"Just shout." With a wave, he's off.

For the next hour, I cut the bigger pieces into smaller parts, keeping the strips for the biltong aside, while soaking the offcuts in a solution of vinegar and salt for the sausage. It's a long and time-consuming process. I'm stressed about preparing dinner, but

I can't cook in the dirty kitchen. I'll have to disinfect the countertops, first.

My phone beeps while I'm pushing the meat through the blades to make sirloin steaks. Normally, I won't interrupt my work to check my messages, but the beep tone tells me it's from my mentor, Aletta. I flick the switch on the saw and gingerly fish the phone from my apron pocket between my thumb and forefinger. The message hits me like a hammer between the eyes.

Come see me. You failed your cell biology test.

My hand trembles as I leave the phone on the counter, reading the text over and over. The repercussions are enormous. The test scores are taken into consideration at the end of the year. If I fail one subject, my partial bursary will be revoked. I'd have to drop out. Devastation crashes over me. I want to remain positive, but the realistic side of me brings my mind to a standstill to evaluate the facts and face the truth.

I'm not going to make it.

There's a terrible finality in the notion. It's as if an anchor has been cut from my life, and now that I'm no longer grounded to a dream, I'm floating meaninglessly in a life which only purpose is to keep Charlie alive. Swatting at the moisture building in my eyes, I try to let my pride keep me strong. I won't cry over this, but my heart is not on par with my mind. Fresh tears blur my vision as I switch the saw back on and start feeding the meat through the blades. I work on autopilot, letting the rhythm of my hands and the noise of the machine dull me to a state of unfeeling, automated movements. It liberates my mind to think. Not making my dream come true will hurt my heart, but failing my brother will destroy me, so I make peace with giving up the dream.

The very moment I make the decision, a hot sensation explodes in my right hand and travels up my arm. I look at the slicer and the meat I clutch in my hands, but I don't make immediate sense of the scene. My brain registers the blood squirting from my thumb long before it does the pain.

13

Valentina

The first digit of my thumb is gone. I cut it just above the metacarpal bone. My mind switches down, and my body goes into automatic functioning mode. I open the cold-water tap and hold my hand under the stream. Water-diluted blood swirls down the drain. The first thing in reach is a clean drying cloth. I turn off the tap and wrap the cloth tightly around my hand to stop the bleeding. I switch off the slicer by the wall and, careful of the blades, go through the reservoir until I find my severed thumb. I feel sick and dizzy, like I'm about to vomit and pass out, but adrenalin keeps me going. After putting the top of my thumb in the mini icebox, I retrieve an icepack from the freezer for my right hand. I grab my purse with my identity card and walk through the house, looking for someone, but only Carly is in her room.

"My dad's out," she says without looking up from her book.

I can't afford an ambulance, and I don't have medical insurance. Private insurance costs a fortune in this country. I'll take my chances with the public hospital, but I need a ride.

I go out the front and find Rhett by the door. "I need a lift to the hospital. Can you please drive me?"

He takes one look at the bloodstained cloth around my hand, and takes the car keys from his pocket. He opens the door for me and helps me into the Mercedes.

"Joburg Gen is the nearest," I say.

He nods and steers the car down the road with a speed that will most likely get us killed before we arrive at the hospital. On the way, he dials Gabriel on voice commands via the hands-free kit and is directed to his voicemail.

"It's Rhett. I'm driving Valentina to the Joburg Gen. She..." He looks at me.

"Cut my finger," I fill in for him.

"I'll keep you posted." He disconnects and dials another number to instruct a guard to take up his post by the Louw residence front door.

When he hangs up, he shoots me a sidelong glance. "You okay?"

"Yes." As if on cue, the pain intensifies. I lean back and purse my lips. My hand is throbbing like a giant heart.

The emergency entrance drive is blocked with vehicles, so we go to the underground parking. The state of the place comes as a shock. Garbage litters the surface up to my ankles. We take the lift to the emergency floor, and when we exit, I'm halted by the rows of people sitting on the floor in the hallway, all looking ten times worse than me. Some of them have gaping wounds, and others have invisible ailments that seem no less fatal judging by the lifeless shine of their eyes. The corridor stinks of vomit and urine. I haven't seen the inside of a hospital since the age of ten when I fell and needed stitches on my head. This makes me never want to come back. We walk past a man with a fracture, the bone sticking through his skin. Another one has a gush in his arm so deep, I can see the tendons. The woman next to him has a broken beer bottle still lodged in her cheek. Violence screams at us as far as we go.

I feel for Rhett's hand with my good one, clutching his fingers as we make our way through misery and despair to a front desk where a bored-looking nurse looks up.

"What's your problem, love?"

When I sway, Rhett catches me. "I cut my finger."

She pushes a clipboard with a form across the counter. "Fill that out." She scratches her head with a pencil and points at an area at the far back. "Waiting area's over there."

We pass an examination room. A naked man lies on a bare mattress. He's handcuffed to the iron bedpost. A nurse is washing blood from his legs. The floors are dirty, and the walls are stained. There are no pillows, sheets, or dividers. Our eyes connect. I avert mine quickly, but feel his follow me until we're out of sight.

All the seats are taken, but I don't want to risk sitting on the germ-infected floor. Rhett takes the pencil from me and calls out the questions while I tell him what to write.

From the way the cloth is soaking up the blood, the bleeding hasn't stopped. I'm starting to feel the effect of the blood loss, or maybe it's delayed shock that's making me feel like fainting.

"Come on," Rhett says gently, taking my arm to lead me back to the reception desk when the questionnaire is completed.

The nurse takes the form, but is in conversation with a colleague and doesn't look up to acknowledge us.

"How long does she have to wait?" Rhett asks tightly.

"What's that, love?"

He jerks his head toward the long line of people. "How long?"

She chuckles. "See that man over there?" She points at the one with the gash in his arm. "He's been waiting for twelve hours."

He opens his mouth to argue, but there's no point. These people are in as much need, if not more, than me.

I touch his arm and say softly, "I think we should do it at home." I won't be able to hold the severed piece in place and stitch. "Can you help me?"

The nurse's attention is already on her colleague again. They're laughing together, sharing a joke.

He nods at my hand. "Show me."

I unwrap the cloth slowly to reveal my thumb. Blood pumps from the digit as if bubbling from an underground fountain.

Rhett blanches. "Jesus Christ." He sweeps me up in his arms and starts walking with long strides back in the direction from where we came.

"Rhett! What are you doing?"

"There's a private clinic in Brixton. It's only seven kilometers from here."

"I don't have medical aid. I can't afford a private clinic."

"I'll pay." He shifts my weight in his arms. "Don't worry about the money, okay? I'm not leaving you in this dump for one second longer."

"We can do it at home," I insist.

He doesn't say anything, but the hard set of his jaw tells me he disagrees.

Twenty minutes later, we're going through the same procedure at the Garden Clinic, but the change is remarkable. The building is clean and sterile. A nurse takes charge of me the minute we enter, and no less than ten minutes after Rhett put down the cash for my treatment—which was required upfront—I'm wearing a hospital robe, lying on a gurney outside the operating room. Rhett is pacing the hallway, his figure passing from left to right and back in front of the door window, his phone stuck to his ear. The doctor who introduces himself as the surgeon tells me the good news is that he can try to save my thumb, thanks to my foresight to recover and bring the missing piece. As they start pushing me toward the operating room, the door slams into the wall, and Gabriel rushes into the corridor, his limp heavy and his short hair messy.

"Excuse me," the doctor exclaims. "You can't barge in here."

He doesn't look at the doctor. He finds my eyes and holds them. "She's with me."

"I don't care if she's with the queen of England."

Gabriel's blue eyes grow hard. His face sets into a frightening mask, and when he turns it on the doctor he says in a cold voice, "I'm staying with her."

Gabriel reaches for my uninjured hand, but the doctor cuts him short.

"Get out or I'll have you removed."

His gaze fixes on my covered wound, and like Rhett, he pales.

"Good thing you're not squeamish, huh?" I smile at him, feeling a little high from whatever they injected me with to kill the pain.

"Call security," the doctor tells the nurse.

Gabriel lifts his palms. "Calm the fuck down. I'm leaving."

"I guess no one is eating meat tonight." The thought sends a sudden rush of hysteria through me. "Oh, my God, Gabriel. The dinner." I trip over my own words, trying to get them out. "It was a stupid accident. I didn't pay attention. I'm so sorry. Please don't let Magda kill me."

"Forget about the goddamn dinner," he says harshly. When the doctor shoots him a warning look, he continues in a softer tone, "I'm taking care of everything."

He holds my gaze as the medical staff rush me toward the swinging doors. As I look back at him, standing there by himself, I have this weird notion that he's alone in the world. Suddenly, I long for him, inexplicably and completely. In this scary moment, it's him I want by my side. I reach for him, recognizing the helpless expression on his face, and then the doors shut out his image. Coldness washes over my body and invades my soul as the doctor pushes a mask on my face and tells me to count to ten. I get to three before the memory of Gabriel's face fades.

THE DOCTOR KEEPS me overnight and discharges me the following day at noon. He tells me the operation went well, and that he gave me a tetanus shot. A tense and tired-looking Gabriel enters my room with a huge bunch of white lilies when the doctor leaves after examining me.

"Hey, beautiful." He kisses my lips. "How do you feel?"

"I'm fine, thanks."

"Come on." He helps me to get dressed, and even if I protest when a nurse pushes a wheelchair into the room, he lowers me into the chair. "It's the chair or my arms." He gives me a smile, but it's weak. The expression in his eyes is shuttered, making it hard for me to read him.

"I have your prescription from the doctor," he says. "We'll stop at the pharmacy before we go."

We leave armed with antibiotics and painkillers from the hospital pharmacy. On the way home, Gabriel clutches my fingers, and when he shifts gears, he places my bandaged hand on his thigh.

It's only when we take the off-ramp to Parktown that he speaks. "Don't ever do that to me again."

His anger sparks annoyance in me. It's with difficulty that I keep my temper in check. "It was an accident."

"You have no idea what you put me through."

"I can guess. You were worried about your investment."

He swerves and brings the car to such a quick stop on the shoulder of the road that my body is thrown forward, and the seatbelt cuts into my chest. I utter a shocked cry, but it's lost in his mouth when he grabs my shoulders and presses our lips together. His kiss is frantic and brutal. His teeth cut my tongue, and the force of his caress bruises my lips. My jaw aches when he finally lets me go. We're both breathing hard, our chests rising and falling rapidly. I can only stare at him, both turned on and frightened.

"Valentina…" A flash of something tightens his eyes and makes his nostrils flare. "You have no idea…" He drags a hand through his hair, messing it up more.

I swallow away the constriction in my throat that makes it hard to speak. "I said I was sorry."

He cups my cheek and brushes a thumb under my eye. "Not as sorry as I am."

In that moment, he lets me see his anguish. I remember what he said about having a heart the night I asked him about his scars. Compassion replaces my irritation.

I place my hand over his. "It's going to be all right."

A flicker of a smile plucks at his lips. "I'm supposed to say that, dammit."

"Then say it." I dare him with my eyes, urging him to let go of whatever darkness took hold of him.

"It's going to be fine, Valentina."

"That's better." I bring his palm to my mouth and plant a kiss on it.

"I'm supposed to do that, too," he says with a hint of sadness.

I wordlessly offer him my palm, but he doesn't kiss the inside. He draws my hand to his lips and sucks my forefinger into the warm depth of his mouth, biting down gently on the tip. Heat floods my underwear as he swirls his tongue around the digit. Then he pulls my wet finger from his mouth and dries it on his shirt. The kiss he leaves on the top of my hand is the opposite of what he did to my mouth. It's sweet, tender, and careful. After holding my eyes for another second, he puts my hand in the same position as earlier on his thigh and steers the car back into the traffic. When he's not shifting gears, he plays with my fingers, rubbing his thumb over my knuckles.

At home, Rhett opens the door and helps me from the car. "If you need help with anything, you only have to say."

"Thanks for driving me, yesterday."

Gabriel's dark expression stills Rhett. I'm not sure what Gabriel's problem with Rhett is, but the guard immediately excuses himself and leaves.

Inside, Quincy and Carly rush to greet us.

"Show me your hand," Carly exclaims. "You could've told me."

I hold up my bandaged thumb. "It's not so bad."

"Lunch is in the oven," Quincy says. "We had to improvise, but it's edible." He turns to me, looking guilty. "I shouldn't have left, yesterday. I should've stayed and helped."

"It's not your fault."

"Come on, Dad," Carly hooks her arm around Gabriel's. "I'm starving."

He hesitates for a second before he follows her to the dining room, his eyes finding mine over his shoulder.

To be honest, I'm happy for the time alone. I haven't dealt with the shock, yet, and I want solitude to process what happened. Oscar greets me by the entrance to the kitchen, rubbing his soft body against my legs.

"Hey, baby." I take a moment to pet him and check that he has food.

There's no place to put the enormous bouquet of flowers in my room, so I borrow a vase from the crystal cupboard and leave them on the counter in the kitchen. Thankfully, Quincy left the kitchen tidy. I'm prohibited from using my hand or working for a week, but I won't allow that to give Magda a reason to kill me. Or Charlie. She's only biding her time, waiting for the right excuse. Packing the dishwasher and doing a few minor chores, I find that I cope well enough with one hand, but Magda grudgingly tells me to take the rest of the day off. I use that time to rest, catching up on sleep.

Much later, Gabriel comes to my room. He covers every inch of my skin in kisses and makes love to me gently. When he holds me afterward, I allow the warmth of his arms to soothe me. Uninvited tears flow over my cheeks. The grief of giving up my studies and the shock of the accident come tumbling down on me, pushing me under a wave of sorrow that makes it hard to breathe. Sobs wrack my shoulders as I cling to him, holding onto the man who took my freedom. In what feels like my darkest hour, he's all I have. It's so damn screwed up. How much more can I handle before Gabriel completely destroys me?

He pulls me into his lap and kisses the top of my head. "Hush, beautiful."

"Gabriel." I bury my face in his neck, inhaling the spicy fragrance of his skin. "Set me free, I beg you."

He rests his chin on my head and inhales slowly. "You may as well ask me to cut off my arm."

When I fall asleep a long time later, I dream that I'm standing on one end of a hospital corridor and Gabriel on the other. Between us, there are rows of people with horrendous injuries, the number of patients too big to count. I'm pushing my way through the bodies, trying to reach him, but when I get to the other side, he's gone. I wake up in a fit of pain, sweating, and alone in my bed. I take a painkiller and count a hundred sheep ten times before I drift off again.

Gabriel

THE FIRST THING I do the following morning, is have the meat saw driven to the dump. The second is to take out medical insurance for Valentina. As long as I'm alive, I'll cover her bills, but I may not live as long as I'd like, especially not with my kind of business. I almost fired Rhett for his stupidity of taking her to the goddamn Joburg Gen. The only thing that saved his skin is that I couldn't punish him for my negligence. I should've thought about Valentina's health the minute she crossed my doorstep. I should've informed my staff in the case of an emergency, she's to be treated like any member of the family. All sorts of bad things could've happened. She could've bled to death. She could've caught an infection. With all the filth and blood around the Joburg Gen, she could've contracted AIDS. To think she considered sewing back her own thumb. That she didn't panic gives me a new level of respect for her. It's one thing to stitch me back together, but quite another to pick your thumb off the floor and not raise the roof in hysterics.

She's managing with one hand, like she always does, but this isn't what I want for her. She's been in my house for less than a quarter of a year, and my perfect doll is already broken. I threatened her with the whip if she doesn't rest. Magda isn't happy with the turn of events, but she only raises the issue when we're alone in the car on our way to one of the loan offices.

"Why did you do it?"

I glance at her from over the rim of my sunglasses. "Do what?"

"Pay Valentina's hospital bill."

"Jesus, Magda, did you expect me to sit back and let her lose her thumb? Anyway, Rhett paid for it. I only reimbursed him."

"You're investing in dead meat."

"We've been through this enough times already."

"When are you going to let go?"

"When I'm ready."

"When will that be?"

I gave her a hard look. "When I'm damn well ready and not a second before."

"I've been lenient with you, but my patience is wearing thin. Don't make me choose a date."

"I'll choose a date," I say evasively, placating her for now. Maneuvering the car down the steep hill into Braamfontein, I ask the question that, for the last few weeks, has been foremost on my mind. "Why do you want her dead?"

She blinks and looks away. "I told you, to make an example out of her."

"Why her?"

"Why not?"

"If it's just about the money, I'll settle her debt."

She turns in her seat. "You're willing to buy that little slut?"

Anger spurts into my veins, setting my heart off at a dangerous beat. "She's anything but a slut."

She gives a cynical snort. "Maybe you prefer a different term, but she's your fuck toy, and in my opinion that makes her a slut."

"Easy, Magda," I say evenly. "You're pushing me too far."

"Gabriel," her voice takes on a softer tone, "you can never trust her. If you lower your guard, she'll stab a knife in your back or steal you blind."

I can't say for sure about the knife in my back. I'm sure Valentina has wished me dead plenty of times. What I do know is that she's not a thief.

"She's been managing the food budget since Marie's stroke, and she's saving us a lot of money."

"That doesn't say anything."

"It says she's trustworthy where money's concerned. Don't think I'm unaware of the money Marie pocketed for herself with the kickback she got from the suppliers."

"It's small money."

"Doesn't change the principle. Stealing is stealing, which makes Marie a thief. Yet, you never lashed out at her."

"That's different. Marie is practically part of the family. Her mother worked for my mother. Your fuck doll is neither family nor loyal. I don't care how much money she's saving us, her time's running out."

"*Let it go.*"

At the cold deliberation in my tone, she turns her head to look through the window. "Anyway, I'm not interested in selling her. You won't settle her debt."

I let it slide, making an effort to calm myself. "I called our old cleaning service company. They'll stand in until next week."

My mother scoots up straighter. "You did what?"

"Valentina is booked off. You know that."

"This is the perfect opportunity to let her fail."

I clench my jaw. "Don't make me repeat myself."

"Fine." She waves a hand in the air. "Treat her like a princess and wrap her in cotton wool. It'll make her fall so much harder."

My fingers tighten on the wheel. I feel like leaning over my mother, opening her door, and shoving her out of my car and my life. We keep on clashing heads over this, and if she can't accept that Valentina is a part of our lives for good, it's going to get ugly.

THE WEEK DRAGS on with Valentina being withdrawn and quiet, keeping to her room. At least she has time to rest and maybe study. She still hasn't told me about her studies. I'm not sure if she's hiding something else from me, or if it's the after-effect of the anesthesia that's giving her the blues, but she's not herself. I suppose it's normal, given what she's been through. All I can do is give her my support and care until she's back in the kitchen in her black dress. I'm not happy about it, but I haven't found a solution to the dilemma, yet, and Magda won't budge.

On top of my worry about Valentina, I need to raise a difficult issue with Carly. Carly doesn't normally eat in the morning, but since Magda isn't present today, I ask my daughter to have breakfast with me so we can speak in private.

I wait until Valentina has left us after serving bran muffins before I say, "I know you love your mother and our divorce was tough on you. We didn't discuss it much when the breakup happened. I think it's important that you have someone neutral to talk to."

She stares at me with wide eyes. "It's a bit late for that."

"It's never too late."

"It won't help." She hides her face behind her hair.

"You can't say unless you've tried."

She pushes the fruit around on her plate.

"Stop hiding behind your hair and look at me."

She lifts her head, her eyes throwing daggers at me. "There's only one thing that'll help, and that's if you and mom get back together."

I sigh deeply. "It's not going to happen. You have to accept it."

She bangs her fork down on her plate. "Why not? Why can't you live together like a normal couple?"

"Your mother and I, we don't love each other any more. That doesn't mean we don't love you."

"Bullshit." She pushes her chair back and jumps to her feet. "You don't know the meaning of the word."

Grabbing her bag, she sprints for the door.

"Carly!"

I want to order her to come back and finish her breakfast, but my common sense tells me to give her space until she has cooled down. Dwelling on my parental problems, I finish my breakfast alone, even if I no longer have an appetite.

Valentina's voice pulls me to the present. "Can I clear the plates?"

The new melancholy that has invaded her makes her big, sad eyes more haunting than ever. I gather my plate and glass to carry it to the kitchen, and return with the tray while Valentina takes the rest. Knowing how proud she is, I try to make things easier for her without making it obvious. While I'm loading my plate in the dishwasher, I notice that she scoops Carly's untouched muffin from the plate, carefully wrapping it in a paper napkin. The rest of my half-eaten muffin she packs into an ice cream container half-full with bones, bits of meat, and cooked vegetables, which she keeps in the staff fridge. I've never seen her clear the table before, but it's obvious she's in the habit of collecting the left overs. What does she do with the food that's meant for the compost bin? My morning conference call is due, so I don't give it further thought, but leave the kitchen with a feeling I can't place. It's as if my time with both Carly and Valentina is running out. I don't like it. The last time I felt like this was right before I tripped a wire and was left for dead with half of my face blown to pieces.

I TIME my meetings so that I'm free during Valentina's lunch breaks to check on her. Before going outside, I spend a few undisturbed minutes observing her through the kitchen window. I love looking at her like this, when her guard is down. The perverseness in me likes to invade her privacy, stealing a part of her I'll otherwise never have. I came to accept that Valentina will never be one hundred percent open with me. Our forced relationship isn't the kind that nurtures an unconditional sharing of the soul.

As always, she's sitting on the low wall by the pool. Bruno is lying next to her on the grass, his head on his paws, staring up at her with doting eyes. Her hands are cupped around an object, like the petals that protect the stigma of a flower. She opens them to reveal something round and white. What is she holding? It looks like a paper napkin. Folding the napkin open carefully, she breaks the muffin that's inside in two, and feeds one half to Bruno while she eats the other. The dog gobbles it up in one gulp, and wags his tail optimistically, watching to see if more is coming. She eats slowly, like a person who tastes every bite.

Everything inside of me slams to a standstill. What I'm witnessing is an ordinary scene of a woman nourishing her body, but it shatters me. I've seen many atrocious deeds and tortures that will make most grown men crumble, but *this*--Valentina eating our leftover food--this does something to me not even a killing does. I'll double her allowance and buy her more food. I'll put her brother in a fancy institute. I'll do anything it takes for her to never have to eat the crumbs from someone else's table again. That bursary better come through soon. I go back to my study and call my CFO, who ensures me it's a matter of days now. Some red tape at the university is slowing down the process.

When I go to her that night, I decide to broach the subject. I strip her naked and drive my cock into her, keeping us both on a precipice of pleasure. I drag it out until neither of us can tolerate it any longer.

Her nails dig into my shoulders. "Gabriel, please." She rocks her hips against mine, trying to create more friction.

I pull out almost completely and still my movements. "Who do you belong to?"

She shivers when I press my thumb on her clit. "You."

"Who takes care of you?"

"You."

"How do I take care of you?"

"However you like."

"Damn right. How the hell ever I like." Her back arches when I pinch her nipple. "Who makes you come?" I shove back into her.

"You," she cries on a gasp.

"Who dresses you?"

"You."

I move again in all earnest. "Who feeds you?"

"Ah, God, Gabriel! You."

"That's right, beautiful." I kiss her lips. "Me."

I slam our bodies together so hard I have to cup her head to prevent it from hitting the wall. She cries my name as she comes with a violent spasm, her pussy sucking me deeper and milking me dry. There's nothing more satisfying than coming inside her. I empty my body in hers, making her take every drop, but I don't pull out. Her cheeks are flushed, and her hair sticks to her damp forehead.

I frame her face between my hands. "Anything you need, you've got it. You only have to say the word. Understand?"

She closes her eyes.

"Look at me, Valentina."

When she opens them again, they're moist with tears. "Why are you doing this? It's not part of our deal."

I kiss each eyelid and then her nose. "Because I'm everything you need."

The sadness in her gaze intensifies, fueling my fear, which in terms spurs my anger. "Say it."

She licks her lips, but doesn't reply.

I wrap my fingers around her neck and squeeze. "Say it, damn you."

Her body tenses, but she doesn't fight my hold. Instead, her shoulders sag as she slowly lets out a breath. "Yes, Gabriel. You are my everything."

Heated satisfaction warms my balls, spreading all the way up my spine. My cock grows hard inside her again. I have her in every way I want, but I still need her in so many ways. Rising on my knees, I hook her legs over my shoulders and use my cum to lubricate her ass. She screams when I enter her there, but with my fingers in her pussy and on her clit, she quickly gives me the moans of ecstasy I'm after. Long after she had her second orgasm, I'm still punishing myself with new pleasure. It takes a long time before my second release. With her, I can go all night, but she needs her rest, so I gather her body against mine and hold her until she falls asleep.

Valentina

MY MOTHER USED to say if something bad happens, celebrate something positive. That way, you'll never become depressed. Maybe that's how she survived when my dad died and we lost everything. She never left the house without red Estee Lauder lipstick.

"If you're sad, Valentina," she used to say, "put on your red lipstick."

I fish the tube I ordered with my supplies from my bag and apply the lipstick in the mirror. The red stands out on my tanned skin. I scrunch my curls around my face, letting their natural glossiness stand out. I'm wearing the pink T-shirt, jeans, and flats from the Sandton boutique. On the outside, I look pretty. No one will know how broken I am on the inside. Maybe, one day, I'll be able to just look at the pretty and forget that I've been a whore to the most dangerous killer in the city.

When I say goodbye to Gabriel for the weekend, he looks at me like he may object to me leaving the house with the makeup on my face, but I'm not his daughter, and this is *my* time.

He swallows as he studies me, jiggling the keys in his pocket. "I'll drive you."

I don't argue anymore. It's pointless. On the way, I ask him to stop at the corner bakery to pick up a Black Forest Cake. I could've baked it for half the price, but that's not the point. I've never purchased a cake in my life. I hold the fancy shop cake in its plastic container on my lap, the black cherries shiny with sugary syrup on top of the whipped cream.

Gabriel glances at the cake and then at me. "Whose birthday is it? I know it's not yours."

"No one." I look from the window at the passing cars.

"What's the occasion?"

"Nothing."

He purses his lips, but doesn't continue the interrogation. Near Rocky Street, I ask him to stop again so I can feed the hungry dogs. The minute they see me, they come running. Gabriel leans against the car with his ankles crossed, watching me as I distribute the food between them. I wipe the plastic container out with a paper towel, and wrap it in a plastic bag to wash later. A shadow of a smile plays on his lips as I get back to the car.

"What?"

He tucks a strand of hair behind my ear. "You're every kind of good."

"No, I'm not."

"To me, you are."

He doesn't give me a chance to reply. He opens the door and helps me inside.

When he drops me off across the road from Kris' place, I wait until his car turns the corner before I head over to the house. Charlie nearly knocks me off my feet as I enter through the kitchen door.

"Hey." I laugh and deposit the cake on the counter. "How are you?" I take him into a big hug. There's more meat on his bones and a tube around his middle.

"Ca–cake!"

"It's for after dinner." I squeeze his shoulders and sit down next to him on the couch, switching off the television.

We play Chinese Checkers until Kris locks up the practice. As habitual, I cook, and she gets to take a much-needed break after she spends the first ten minutes freaking out about my thumb. When Charlie is seated with a big slice of cake in front of his favorite cartoon, she takes the chair opposite me at the kitchen table.

"What's with the cake?" she asks through the motion of chewing.

"We're celebrating."

"We are?"

"Yep." I lick the chocolate filling off my spoon.

"Can you be a little less secretive?"

I shrug. "We're celebrating that I have more free time and money. I can now pay you proper board for Charlie."

She makes big eyes at me. "Did he give you a pay rise? More off-time?"

I take a big bite. My mouth is too full to answer.

"Well?"

I wipe the cream from the corner of my mouth with my good thumb and lick it clean. "Not exactly."

"Val." Kris pushes her plate away and folds her arms on the table. "What's going on?"

"I dropped out of uni."

I'm saying it like I just told her it's hot today, hoping she'll let it go, but I already know better.

"Like in, quit your studies?" she exclaims.

Charlie looks up from the television.

"Shh." I give her my best angry frown. "You'll make him think something's wrong."

"Something *is* wrong."

"Kris."

"Why?"

"Look at it this way, I don't have the burden of paying a huge school bill any longer, or worries about exams, and spending late nights studying anatomy."

She dips her head, searching for my eyes. "Why?"

I sigh. "The cook had a stroke. I took over her duties."

"They're going to hire another cook, right? You can't give up. Val, you've completed more than half of the course!"

"I can't keep up the job and the studies. It's too much."

Her lips thin. "You're letting them win."

"I don't have a choice," I say through gritted teeth. "I work until dinner is served and the kitchen is clean, which means I'm lucky if I get off at ten. God, I'm lucky if I go to bed by midnight, and I'm up at four every morning." I don't say that Gabriel occupies another hour or more of my day, fucking me senseless and giving me orgasms until I pass out.

Emotions play on her face. Thank God she doesn't say something meaningless like she's sorry.

"It's for Charlie." I lower my voice. "Nothing will matter anyway if he's dead. He's all I've got."

She covers my hand with hers. It is a big, strong hand with cat scratches and dog bite marks, and a calloused skin that tells its own story. "You've got me, babes."

Warmth spreads through my chest, making tears build at the back of my eyes. "Thank you."

"You can still work here. I mean, after…"

"I know." After nine years, I'm not sure I'll still have the stomach for this city. "Eat your cake. I paid a lot of money for it."

"You better hide the rest or Charlie will devour it in the night."

Worry nags at me. "He's picking up weight."

"Sorry. I'm not here much, I'm afraid, or I would've taken him out for exercise."

"I have an idea."

"Uh-uh. When you get that light bulb moment look, I get worried."

I prop my foot on the seat of my chair, hugging my knee. "He can walk the dogs."

"You mean *them*?" She throws her thumb at the door adjoining to the clinic.

"Yes! He crosses the road by himself, right? We can try with one dog first and see how it goes. I can go with him tomorrow."

"I suppose it can't do harm."

"It'll be good for him to get out more, breathe in some fresh air."

She snorts. "What fresh air? In case you haven't noticed, this is Joburg."

I'm not having my spirits dampened, not tonight. "Charlie and I'll do the first doggie walk together."

"You're a good sister, Val. Charlie's lucky to have you."

"No, I'm lucky to have him."

I'm still raw about my studies, but there's a reason I'm doing this. The reason is a beautiful, innocent boy trapped in the body of a man who sits on Kris' couch with a huge smile on his face. All it takes to make Charlie happy is a piece of cake. I should learn from him.

Gabriel

THE THERAPIST KNOCKS on my door at ten sharp, as agreed. Dorothy Botha is a short, attractive woman in her late forties.

She's wearing tight jeans and a stretch shirt, not the attire I imagined for a psychiatrist. At the rate I'm paying for the house call, I expected her to show up in Dior or Gucci.

She shakes my hand, and offers a smile. "Mr. Louw."

"Call me Gabriel. Thank you for meeting Carly at home. It's more comfortable for her in her own environment." And there's less chance for one of our enemies to discover my daughter has instability issues. They'll use anything they can against me.

I show her to the reading room where Carly sits on the couch, her legs pulled up under her. My daughter gives me a cutting look when we enter and doesn't offer Dorothy a greeting. Every part of her body languages says she's not happy about spending her Sunday morning with a shrink.

"Carly, this is Mrs. Botha. Say hi."

"Say hi," Carly parrots.

I'm about to lose my cool and give her a lecture about proper manners, but Dorothy lays her hand on my arm.

"You can call me Dorothy." She takes the chair opposite Carly and looks up at me expectantly.

I get it. She wants me to leave. "Coffee, tea?"

"No, thank you." She's pleasant, but firm.

"All right, then." I close the door, hoping to God Dorothy will accomplish what neither me nor Sylvia is able to do--get Carly to open up.

While the women are talking, or *hopefully* talking, I clear the table from our late breakfast, and feed Oscar. He's got a new brand of food, the same as Bruno. With the price on the tag, they must put gold flakes in the kibbles. The brand's worth its weight in gold, though, because Bruno's allergies have disappeared, and Oscar's coat is thick and glossy. Bruno's food is delivered to our door from our local vet. I pay the bill. No cat food is included. The specialty food isn't available at supermarkets. If Valentina doesn't order it with our daily groceries, where does it come from?

Magda walks into the kitchen, dressed up in her black and white Chanel suit. "Where's Carly? I want to invite her for lunch."

I cross my arms, and lean on the counter. "Where?"

"The McKenzies."

My back immediately turns rigid. "Not interested."

"Come on, Gabriel." She props her clutch bag on her hip. "Carly's never going to take your place. She hasn't got it in her. Our only chance is finding her the right husband."

"I said no."

She advances two steps, stopping short of me. "Do you have a cleverer idea? What if something happens to you? Or me? Who's going to take over our business? Not that gold-digging, ex-wife of yours. Word's going around she's got her sights set on Francois. If she marries him and we can't provide a successor, that slimy rat will take over as Carly's stepdad. Is that what you want?"

Acid burns my mouth. Francois is a pretty boy five years Sylvia's junior, but that's not what's bothering me. It's the idea of him playing stepdad to Carly that I can't digest.

"Answer me. Is that what you want?"

"Is that all you care about, finding a successor for the business? What about Carly's happiness?"

"Happiness?" She laughs. "Carly is my granddaughter, but by God, she's a spoiled child. You got her used to this." She waves her arms around the room. "You give her everything her heart desires. You think she's going to ever settle for less? I don't think so."

"Don't project your sentiments on Carly."

"Oh, money is as important to her as it is to me. Let's face it, even if she's not a leader, she's a Louw. She'll do her duty for our name."

"Don't you dare treat her like a pawn in your business. Carly's not going to lead the life I live."

"The life *you* live? You want to live the life of one of our debtors? Want to see what it's like on the poor side of the fence? Do you know what happens to you and your daughter at night when you don't have enough money for an alarm system that criminals can't break through?"

"I know what happens. I've seen it."

"You haven't *felt* it. Believe me, you don't want to live any other life than this life." She scrutinizes me. "You're getting soft, Gabriel. It's that girl, isn't it?"

My hackles rise. "She's got nothing to do with this. Valentina or no Valentina, I'll never marry Carly off to Benjamin McKenzie."

"I hope for your sake you're growing tired of fucking your toy."

Every muscle in my body tenses. My injured leg protests against the strain. "What's that supposed to mean?"

"A cat only plays with a mouse for so long before he goes for the kill. Why isn't she dead, yet?"

My heart drops like an ax splitting wood. "I'm not ready."

"I've been patient with you. I gave you the toy you so badly wanted. We made a deal. Now I'm giving you a direct order. Kill her, or I'll do it for you."

I almost jump on her. I'm a hairbreadth away from her face before I stop myself. "You'll do nothing for me, do you hear me?"

"You have one last chance. Make it sooner than later." She smiles sweetly. "You're not twelve any more. Don't make me shoot you in the foot."

My vision goes blurry. I'm about to strangle my own mother in our kitchen. The only thing that stops me from reaching for her scrawny, white, wrinkled neck, is Carly's figure that appears in the doorframe.

There's a chill in her voice. "We're done."

"I'm going out for lunch, Carly dear. Why don't you join me?"

"Magda is having lunch at the McKenzies," I say, knowing how much Carly hates Benjamin.

"No thanks, Gran. I've got homework." She trots down the hallway, pretending I don't exist.

When Carly is out of earshot, I narrow my eyes. "Let me handle my own affairs and leave Carly out of the business." Giving my mother my back, I walk from the room, feeling the tension in my leg.

"Softness will get you killed, Gabriel," she calls after me.

Dorothy waits in the reading room.

I close the door and take a seat. "How did it go?"

She wipes her fingers over her brow. "She's tough to talk to. Of course, I need to win her trust first." She looks at me from under her lashes. "I pick up a need for approval and acceptance. Are you spending enough time with her?"

"Not as much as I'd like."

"Busy job?"

"It's not that. Carly would rather spend time with her friends than her father."

"It's normal. Try to strengthen her self-esteem by complimenting her for homework well done or good deeds, anything positive, but be authentic. Make sure she knows you're noticing her and taking an interest in her life."

"I assure you, I am."

"I don't doubt that, or I wouldn't be here. Just make sure you show her as well as tell her. It will help, of course, if I can have a joint session with you and your ex-wife to agree on a consistent strategy that will reinforce your daughter's self-image."

"I'm afraid you won't find much cooperation from my ex-wife."

"Ah, well." She wipes her hands on her thighs and straightens. "Let's see how it goes after a couple of sessions. Try to maintain the status quo at home. Don't introduce any new or stressful situations if you can avoid it, at least not for a while."

"Such as?"

"A stepmom."

"Carly's worried about that?"

"She mentioned it. I know this is a personal question, but are you seeing anyone, maybe a lady friend your daughter doesn't get on with?"

"No." Not that Carly knows of, at least.

"Then Carly's fear is unfounded. It's not uncommon for children to feel lost after a divorce. Carly's frightened of losing you or her mother to someone else. Reassure her of your affection whenever you can."

"Of course."

"I'll see you next week, same time."

"I'll walk you to the door."

Even as I speak, my mind is drifting to a reoccurring thought. How will Carly react if she ever finds out about Valentina?

Valentina

REGRET IS NOT A CONDUCIVE SENTIMENT. Still, I can't help from feeling it when I read the letter addressed to me that Gabriel brings to the kitchen on Monday morning. Reading it with my back to him, I curl my fingers in a fist until my nails cut into my skin. I want to cry, but he's hovering at the coffee machine.

"Good news?"

I glance at him from over my shoulder. He's dressed in a dark suit with a blue shirt and yellow tie. He makes the ensemble look perfect. The tailored pants stretch over his narrow hips, which emphasizes the broadness of his chest. His unique fragrance beckons me, but I need to be alone to deal with the news.

I shrug.

"All right." He says it like a threat, making me understand he'll let me get away with my disobedience of not giving him a reply for now, but maybe not later.

I hold my breath until he has left the room. Only when I'm alone do I allow the emotions to explode inside of me. I grab the edges of the counter so hard my arms shake from the strain. The letter crumples in my fist. I scrunch it up until it's a tiny ball. Of all the sick jokes in the world, this one must have the best timing. I bang my fists on the counter, setting the bowls and knives and spoons clanging. For all of three seconds, I allow myself every single destructive emotion that lances into my heart, and then I lift the lid of the trashcan and dump the letter informing me of my all-inclusive scholarship inside. When the lid falls back with a clang, something inside of me ceases to exist. What's left is the hollow echo of a dream and nothing more than the will to survive.

Gabriel

THE LETTER that arrived from the university this morning should've made Valentina ecstatic. There's a change in her I don't understand. After doing my morning rounds at our franchises in town, I head to her friend's place where Charlie lives. The woman waiting in reception with a Miniature Doberman shrinks back when she looks up at my face. Walking past her with practiced ignorance, I venture to the food section and lift my sunglasses to read the labels. I pull a bag of the urinary diet brand Valentina bought for Oscar from the shelf and carry it to the till. A few minutes pass before a peroxide blonde in a white overcoat exits. Hard lines mar her weathered face, and her fingernails are broken. Her eyes give away nothing as she assesses me. They flitter from me to the bag of food standing on the counter.

"Can I help you?"

"Is this the best brand you've got?"

"By far."

I lean an elbow on the counter and check out the board with the rates for neutering and vaccinations. "My housekeeper buys it for my cat. I don't know the brand, but I thought I'd get the same."

Her eyes flare for the briefest of seconds before she narrows them. "Your housekeeper is a clever girl."

"She sure is, but she should've told me she's paying for the food out of her own pocket."

"Maybe she couldn't, because she knows you don't care much for your cat."

The lady with the Doberman is watching us, her head bobbing between the vet and me.

"It's true. I don't care for the hair that he sheds in my house or the fact that he tears my curtains to pieces, but my housekeeper seems to like him, so here's the deal. I'll open an account and send a driver once a month to collect the food." I point at the large breed dog food of the same brand. "You can throw in a couple of bags of that, as well."

It almost looks as if she's going to refuse me, but the state of her waiting room tells me she needs the business. After a moment of measuring me, she says, "I'll take down your details."

She writes my address and phone number down in a book. In this day and age, nobody uses a book, not even my most unsophisticated loan sharks. She has a patient waiting, and me taking a chunk of her consultation time. What she needs is a computer and an assistant. No wonder she's operating in a run-down building, charging fees lower than the going rate.

I tap my fingers on the countertop as she scribbles down my order. "You should go electronic."

She lifts her head to give me a cutting look. "I'll upgrade when I can afford it."

I don't blame her for hating me. What makes her different than the rest of the world? In any event, I'm not out to win anyone's love. I can forget about getting information on Valentina's emotional state of late from this woman. She won't give me a glass of water if I'm dying.

She slams the book closed. "Are we done?"

I let the sunglasses fall back over my eyes. "For now."

Saluting her, I take the food and walk to the door. The

Doberman whines as I pass her owner who leans as far away from me as she can without falling out of her chair.

Valentina

THIS LASAGNA CAN'T FLOP. I'm so engrossed in letting the white sauce thicken without forming lumps that I don't notice Rhett until he's right next to me. Startled, I drop the whisk. It bounces on the stovetop, rolls off the edge, and hits the ground. It's the first time he's set foot in the kitchen since I arrived. He bends down to retrieve the whisk and rinses it under the tap before handing it back to me.

"Thank you." I use my left hand to stir the sauce.

He motions at the bandage on my thumb. "How's the hand?"

"Good, thank you."

He gives a wry smile. "I didn't get a chance to apologize for driving you to the Joburg Gen. If I had any idea the place was that bad, I would've gone directly to the clinic."

"You did what I asked."

"I wasn't thinking straight. I saw the blood and kind of blanked out."

I can't help but smile. "You? Seriously?"

He lifts his palms in a gesture of surrender. "It wasn't the blood as much as it was *you*. I thought Gabriel was going to kill me."

"For what?"

"It happened on my shift."

"It wasn't your fault."

"Wouldn't have mattered. I was the messenger."

I stop stirring to look at him. "I'm sorry if I got you into trouble."

He grins. "Not as much trouble as you got yourself into. No more kitchen accidents, okay?"

"I'll do my best." I return my attention to the sauce.

He leans on the counter and crosses his ankles. "I was thinking of getting you a puppy."

"A puppy?"

"I already cleared it with Gabriel." He shifts his weight around. "I can get you one of those fluffy dogs women like. A Maltese Poodle or something."

"I don't want a dog."

He looks disappointed. "Why not?"

"I've lost enough. I don't want to care about another dog."

He uncrosses his ankles and crosses his arms, not meeting my eyes.

When he doesn't speak, but doesn't leave either, I remove the sauce from the heat, and turn to face him squarely. "Why did you shoot Puff, Rhett?"

His chest expands, as if he's taking a breath, and when he lifts his gaze again, he regards me with a level stare. "I didn't want to leave the dog to fend for himself on the streets."

"What?"

"I've seen enough of dogs to know that mongrel wasn't going to make it on his own. Leaving him would've meant a drawn-out, cruel death of starvation."

"Leaving him?"

His voice takes on a quiet tone. "When we broke into your flat that morning, it was with explicit orders."

The blood drains from my head, leaving me with a fuzzy feeling. Rhett was certain we weren't going to get out alive, neither Charlie nor me. Oh, my God. Gabriel wasn't there just for Charlie. He was going to kill us both. I put the information away in the back of my mind to deal with later. Alone.

"I don't know why Gabriel changed his mind, but I can assure you, it's never happened before."

My laugh is forced. "My mother used to say I have a guardian angel. Maybe she was right."

"If it'll make you feel better, Gabriel fucked me up good for killing your dog."

"That day you came out of the gym with a broken nose."

"Yep. Look, I'll sleep a whole lot better if you'll let me get you that dog."

The look he gives me is so remorseful that my compassion wins over my vengeance over Puff. Logically, I understand why he did it. It doesn't make it right or better, but I'm not in a position to deny anyone redemption. I'm still chasing after absolution for what happened to Charlie. Wiping my hands on my apron, I consider his proposal. Another living being will only make me more vulnerable than what I already am, because that's what caring for someone or something does.

"I don't want a dog. I want you to train me."

He looks at me like I lost my mind. "What?"

"Teach me self-defense. We can practice in the gym."

"Gabriel will kill me."

"Not if he doesn't know. We can do it when he's out."

"It's a crazy idea, Valentina."

"Is it? Have you ever stood helpless while men took the money you busted your ass for? Have you ever been held down and violated, unable to do a goddamn thing about it?"

He averts his eyes, unable to hold mine.

"Please, Rhett. I'm not going to use it against anyone in this house. I'm not stupid. I just don't want to feel helpless any longer."

He swallows. "Ask me anything else. If Gabriel finds out––"

"He won't, not unless you tell him."

He looks at me again, a war waging in his eyes. Finally, it's his guilt that wins out. "Fine, but not a word to anyone, not even Quincy."

"All right."

He straightens from the counter, but his shoulders sag. "I'll let you know when the coast is clear."

"Thank you."

"Consider us even." There's a hint of apprehension and even fear in his expression as he walks from the room.

Gabriel

THE REPORT from Anton only confirms what I already know. No one knows anything about Valentina's rape. I drop the pen on my desk and rub my tired eyes. I'm not surprised Marvin didn't go to the police. His family was shamed. The way he would've dealt with the crime was to avenge his daughter's stolen innocence by killing the man responsible. Since he died in the same year she was assaulted, I'm not sure he got around to it. Is that why Lambert abandoned his promised fiancée? Because she was spoiled goods? Find the bastard who raped her I will, but for now I have a bigger priority--Magda's threat.

Never underestimate Magda. I know what she's capable of better than anyone. If I don't kill Valentina, she *will* do it, and as punishment for my disobedience she'll do it in a way that will hurt me. I'm not shy about my habits. My mother knows I fuck like some people take up a hobby. She knows I'm territorial and the most possessive bastard on the face of the earth. She knows me well enough to understand that the thought of another man's hands on Valentina will drive me to my knees, especially after what I did to Diogo. Valentina's death is a place I can't even go. If Magda has to finish the job for me, Valentina will most likely suffer gang rape followed by a horrendous and slow death of torture. I have to find a way to keep her, but there's nowhere I can hide her where Magda's network of business associates won't find her. And then there's Charlie. What do I do with him? Where do I keep him safe? I made a deal with Valentina and, knowing how much Charlie means to her, this is one I intend to honor. Every problem has a solution. I just have to look hard enough.

Seeing that I have precious little time, I should be searching for a way to keep my beautiful toy, not slamming my study door, and stalking the hallway like a crazed man, my steps taking me where they always do, Valentina's room. It's late. Magda and Carly have long since gone to bed, but I still keep a watchful eye.

Just a few minutes. I need a break to clear my mind. Chasing improbable solutions to escape Magda's promise has sent me in circles like a dog chasing his own tail. I need to hold her, see her, taste her, breathe her, to calm the clawing fear of losing her.

When I walk into her bedroom, she steps from the bathroom, her hair wet and her body damp. She stops in the doorframe. The bandage is dry. Good. The last thing I want is more worry. I need her too much.

For a few seconds, we have a stare-down, each one of us waiting for the other to make a move. There are a million things I can do with her. I should punish her for this morning's obstinance when she gave me the cold shoulder, but I won't touch her like that when she's injured. I haven't yet made up my mind when she closes the distance between us, placing her delicate body in front of mine like a vulnerable white pawn in the path of the black stallion's hooves. The position is a physical reminder of the difference in power between us. I can throw her on the bed and eat her pussy from the inside out, I can fuck every hole in her body, or kiss her until she can't breathe. She's mine to do with as I please. I overcompensated for my looks by becoming a master of physical pleasure. I can't give her a pretty face, but I can make her scream with orgasms until there's not a breath of air left in her lungs.

Her hands reach for my shirt. I'm curious. Is she going to undress me? She grips the edges of the fabric above the first button and yanks them apart. Fuck dammit. There's a tearing sound and buttons flying everywhere. She goes up on her toes to push the shirt over my shoulders, but the sleeves get stuck on my upper arms. Abandoning her efforts with the shirt, she focuses on my belt instead, her fingers fumbling with the buckle.

My heart is beating like the hooves of that dark horse she unleashed, and I'm frightened that the beast will crush her when he lets his passion rein free, but I'm too weak to stop her. Finally managing to pull the leather from the loops of my waistband, she folds it double and pushes it into my hand. It's there in her eyes, what she wants me to do. The brown of her irises is mud-stained and murky, like a dam after a landslide.

Under normal circumstances, I'd tie her up and give her what she wants, spank her while I fuck her, but it hasn't been a normal week. When I don't move, she cups my balls and squeezes them through my pants. Her tongue is hot and wet on my stomach, licking a line of molten lava up my chest. Her small teeth latch onto my nipple. I jerk when she bites. Bloody hell. She lets go to bite into the muscle of my pec, then pulls back to study the marks she left on my skin. Her hands snake around my neck, pulling me down to her lips. The nip she gives my bottom lip draws blood. Her nails dig into my scalp. She kisses me like a mad woman, moaning and rubbing her body against mine.

As suddenly as she grabbed me, she lets go, falling back onto the bed with open thighs. Her pussy is ripe for me, wet and swollen. I follow as if she's got me on a tight leash, but before I can straddle her she rolls over and gets up on her knees, offering her ass and pussy. It is a sight so alluring I almost lose my reason. I don't move my eyes from the clean-shaved triangle between her legs as I kick off my shoes and almost tear the zipper to get out of my pants. I take no more than a second to pull off my socks. Gripping her hips hard, I drag her to the edge of the bed, placing her where I need her.

"Take me, Gabriel. Take me hard." I'm about to do exactly that when she says, "Make it hurt. Make it hurt really bad."

My lust jerks to a halt. I get off on hurting her, but her pain ultimately brings us both pleasure. I'm using pain to train to her body to need me, but I won't allow her to use physical pain to escape her feelings. That's reserved for monsters like me, and I have no intention of turning her into a monster. I need her sweet and innocent. I need her for who she is.

She looks at me from over her shoulder. "Gabriel."

Her cry is a plea while her eyes are filled with fear––fear that I won't oblige. There aren't many things I'll deny her, but this I won't give.

"Gabriel!"

Her tiny hand folds around my shaft. I'm so hard I scarcely feel the pressure of her fingers as she guides me to her asshole. I know how an ass fuck without proper preparation feels for a woman. I made my lovers describe every sensation to me in detail. The fact that she wants this shows me how badly she's hurting inside.

"Fuck me already if you're a man."

I know what she's trying to do. "Provocation isn't going to work with me, beautiful."

Grabbing her around the waist with one arm, I shift her up the mattress. When I go down on my side, I bring her body with me, pressing her back to my chest.

"Fuck you, Gabriel!"

She struggles in all earnest, trying to break free, but I trap her in the constraint of my arms.

"Let me go!"

I hold her in place and plant the gentlest of kisses in her neck.

"No! Don't you dare."

I kiss her ear, her hair, and her temple with a soft brush of my lips. "You're so beautiful, Valentina. Have I ever told you that?"

Her voice breaks. "Please, don't."

I throw my leg over hers, confining her kicking legs while I push her upper body into the mattress to kiss her spine. Sobs shake her body, but I kiss every vertebra, working my way to the curve of her ass and back up.

"Not like this," she cries. "Not gently. Not like you care."

I give her all the tenderness I'm capable of, stroking my fingers over her firm ass and between her legs, testing her folds. She's wet.

Always ready for me, just like I trained her. When I direct my cock to her entrance, she starts fighting me again, wiggling her upper body, and kicking with her legs. All I can do is hold her shoulders down with my arms and keep her legs trapped between mine while I enter her slick body, inch by slow inch until she's taken all of me. She's so hot and tight she makes me dizzy. With her thighs pressed together the friction is too much. With every stroke, I risk coming like an inexperienced adolescent.

"I hate you." Her words are muffled by the pillow, but her body is already rocking with mine. "Why can't you do it? Why don't you hurt me?"

I won't cut her air, I won't bury my cock in her ass, and I won't take my belt to her. It's my business to understand her needs, and what she needs right now is to be loved.

"Why didn't you kill me, Gabriel?"

I still. "What are you talking about?"

She turns her face to the side. "Rhett told me."

That fucker.

"That's why he shot my dog," she whispers. "We weren't supposed to make it out alive."

I start moving again, trying to still her with our pleasure, but she won't let it go.

There are tears in her voice. "Why Gabriel? Tell me, damn you."

"Because I wanted you," I grit out.

She pushes her ass up against my groin. "Is it this? You needed a fuck?"

I thrust deeper, making her moan. "You know why."

"You spared my life to make me your whore."

"Not my whore." I kiss the soft, golden skin of her shoulder. "My property."

"What's the difference?" she asks bitterly.

The difference is that property belongs. I find her lips, kissing her like she's mine, trying to show her that however much I trained her to need me, I need her in equal quantity. This time, she doesn't resist the gentleness of my touch. She kisses me back, our rhythm slow and revering. I glide my body over hers, the slickness of my sweat-damp skin making the friction smooth. The movement drives my shaft deeper. I feel her on every inch of me. A deep groan tears from my chest.

Goddammit, this is heaven. My balls pull up into my groin, and sharp needles pierce into the base of my spine. Fuck, not yet. I want to last. I still for a moment to bite back the pleasure. I drag my hands over her hair and down her shoulders, over the soft curves where her breasts are pressed flat against the mattress. She's soft and resilient and so much woman. I revel in invading her body, making her secrets and feelings mine. I push as deep as I can go, until my cock hits a barrier. A small gasp escapes her lips. I must be pushing against her cervix. Carefully, I ease back and push again. She throws her head back and whimpers, her moans changing from cries of defiance to need. Just a bit deeper and I'd touch the place in her body where miracles happen, where a child can grow from a seed in her womb. The only thing more beautiful than a woman is a pregnant woman. When your seed takes root in her womb and her breasts grow plump with the wonder of new life as her belly expands with your child, you want to love her and fuck her with your child growing between you. Valentina will scare me with the rawness of her beauty as motherhood changes her.

My body tenses with a building ejaculation so powerful it hurts. As my release explodes an idea erupts in my mind. While I empty myself in her body, I find the answer I've been looking for. I know how to irrevocably save her.

It's depraved and immoral.

It's dubious.

It's perfect.

14

Gabriel

It takes a day for my doctor to deliver the placebo birth control pills. While he's there, I make use of the opportunity to explain to him what I need for next week's house call.

From next month, Valentina won't be protected. I'm an asshole, but falling pregnant is her only hope. The one line Magda will never cross is killing the mother of her grandchild. I'm not naïve enough to believe Valentina will ever want a baby with me. She can never know I took the choice from her hands. It'll be easier to accept if she thinks it was an accident.

Being pregnant will be tough on her. I have no illusions about the psyches of 'women in waiting'. Sylvia detested every minute of being pregnant. She hated what the pregnancy did to her body. My mother never lets an opportunity go by to remind me how she suffered to give birth to me. According to Magda, the pain of bringing me into this world was worse than torture. She resented not being as agile or mobile as normal. She got varicose veins and backaches that drove her nuts. The only time that Magda sympathized with Sylvia was when she was pregnant with Carly. Yeah, it won't be an easy road, especially not for a young woman who hasn't completed her studies. I don't even want to think about our age difference. I'm heading down a hell of a bumpy road, dragging a young woman along against her knowledge and will. You don't get more depraved than that.

After my morning gym workout, I have a shower, and close myself in my study to go over the financial reports. I'm not ten minutes into my work when my phone rings. My CFO's name pops up on the screen.

"Harry, what can I do for you?"

"I just had a call from UNISA. Miss Haynes dropped out."

"What?" I heard him loud and clear, but it makes no sense. "I'm not sure I understand."

"Would you like to withdraw the scholarship, or are you willing to consider another student?"

"I'll get back to you." I end the call and get Aletta Cavendish on the line. "I just found out Valentina quit her studies."

"Oh, dear. I thought she told you."

Of course she hasn't. She doesn't know I know about her studies. "Did she say why?"

"Only that her priorities have changed."

"Is it too late to have her cancellation reversed?"

"I can hold onto it for a while, but not long. Her assignments are overdue, and the exams are coming up in less than two weeks. It doesn't help that she already failed a test."

"I know how badly she wants this degree. Give me a chance to speak to her."

"I hope you can sway her."

"I will."

"I'll be waiting for your call then."

I hang up and lean back in my chair. So, this is what's been eating Valentina. Rhett told me she even refused the puppy he offered. If she can hang in there for a few weeks longer, everything will change.

For the rest of the day, I chase leads to Valentina's rape, but doors close in my face as far as I go. It's a futile effort that leaves me agitated and exhausted. By the time I get home in the late afternoon, I'm worked up into a state that leaves Quincy with a bleeding lip after our wrestling exercise in the gym. A thunderstorm is brewing on the horizon when I have my shower, casting the sky in an ominous, purple light with a touch of gold where the sun penetrates the dark masses. Coming downstairs for dinner, Magda announces we have a surprise guest. Sylvia is seated next to Carly, her blonde hair braided in a French plait and a virginal white dress clinging to her body like a glove. She lost weight.

"Gabriel." She acknowledges me with a tight nod and a cold smile.

I kiss my ex-wife's cheek. "You look beautiful, as always."

She touches her diamond necklace, a gift from me for our first wedding anniversary. "Thank you."

I take my seat and start pouring the wine. I'm going to need a few glasses. "To what do we owe the visit?"

"Nothing. I don't need a reason to visit my daughter, do I?"

Across the table our gazes lock in a non-verbal battle. Mine is torn away from hers when Valentina enters with the starters. My maid's demeanor is one of professionalism as she serves us, but I don't miss the way Sylvia glares at her.

"I'm going over to Sebastian after dinner," Carly says, bringing my attention back to her.

I nod as Valentina hovers beside me with the asparagus. "I don't remember you asking."

"I already said yes." Sylvia drapes the napkin over her lap, challenging me to defy her.

The reason for Sylvia's visit suddenly becomes clear.

"I still don't like that boy." Magda gives Carly a hard look. "He's not our type."

"Grandma," Carly groans. "It's none of your business."

I'm too tired to deal with this tonight. "Mind your tongue, young lady. You won't speak to your grandmother like that."

"She started." Carly pouts and crosses her arms.

Magda snorts. "What can you gain from a relationship with him? Who are his parents? No-good average workers with a business in textiles."

"She's not asking to marry him," Sylvia says. "Anyway, she's my daughter. You don't have a say."

"Our daughter," I remind her.

Magda picks up her fork. "We're not going to fight over this at the dinner table."

"We're not," Sylvia says sweetly. "The decision is already made."

"It's not about the boy," I say. "It's about going behind my back without asking."

"As I said," Sylvia adds with force, "she asked me."

For once, I agree with Magda. This is not a fight that needs to play out here. I'll have a word with Sylvia after dinner about her conniving ways with Carly.

"Well," Sylvia's shoulders set in a straight line, "that's handled then." She pats Carly's hand with more affection I've ever seen her deal our daughter.

Something is up with Sylvia. She hates poverty as much as Magda, which puts Sebastian under her radar line of suitable boyfriend material.

The rest of the meal is tense. I'm relieved when the ordeal is over. Sebastian's mom comes over with her son to fetch Carly and politely declines our offer for a drink. From the porch, I watch Sylvia say goodbye to Carly.

"Be back by eleven," I call, giving Sebastian a look that tells him not to fuck with me.

When the car pulls off, Sylvia comes back up the steps and hands me her jacket to drape over her shoulders. "Good evening, Gab. I'll let you get back to fucking your maid."

I grab her wrist. "It's the last time you'll call me that, and the last time you'll make a snide comment about my maid."

Jerking her arm from my grip, she hisses, "We'll see how well your future works out for you," and then she strides to her sports car with a stiff back. She waves through the window before pulling off with screeching tires.

There was a time she called me Gab. It was a time I trusted her and believed she cared. She's a damned good actress.

"That's what you get for marrying that whore," Magda says behind me.

I look over my shoulder to see her watching from the doorstep. "You'll be wise to keep quiet now."

She only chuckles as she turns on her heel and disappears into the house.

In the lounge, I pour a stiff drink and wait an hour. There's no way I can go to bed before Carly is home. I dial the kitchen.

Valentina's voice comes over the intercom. "Yes?"

"Come to the lounge."

She steps into the room five minutes later, regarding me with mistrust where I sit in the armchair.

"Come sit with me." I hold my hand out to her.

Instead of climbing onto my lap as I would've liked, she stops at the edge of my seat, and drapes herself on the carpet by my feet. I push her head down on my thigh, stroking her silky hair. Like she accepted my pain, she's learning to accept my tenderness. I'm enjoying our tranquil moment, but there are two issues of importance I have to bring up. I don't have the luxury of waiting for her to confide in me, any longer. I've given up on hoping for her trust.

"Why did you drop out of school?"

Her body goes rigid. It takes her a moment to answer. "How did you find out?"

"Does it matter?"

"You're right," she whispers. "I don't want to know."

"You're going back."

She jerks her head up to look at me. "Don't. I've dealt with it. I don't want to go down that road again."

I fist my hand in her hair. "You'll go back."

"Gabriel." Her eyes fill with tears. "Please."

"Marie will come back. Things will go back to normal." It's a lie, but I can't tell her how I'm planning on changing her circumstances.

"Things will never be normal for me."

That's true, but she better accept it. She'll take whatever I choose to give her. My hand tightens in her hair. "You'll call tomorrow and withdraw your cancellation."

"Why?" she whispers.

Because despite everything, I still want her to be happy. "You'll obey me, like you promised."

Hurt flickers in her eyes. "Are you threatening me?"

"I'm the biggest damn threat of your life."

Her bottom lip starts to tremble. "Of course. How could I forget?"

My hand is aching to tan her ass. If it weren't for her injury, she'd be draped over my lap right now, her panties around her ankles.

"Don't push me, Valentina. You'll do as I say without question, because I know what you need, and it's my job to give it to you."

That same acceptance with which she submitted to my lashings and fucking filters into her expression. It's not so much a choice as an understanding that there's no choice.

"Good girl."

I bend down to kiss her, tasting the sweetness of her

submission as her lips quiver under mine. If I don't pull away, I'll take her right here in the lounge, and I still have plenty to say.

"There's something else you're going to do for me." I watch her face carefully as I choose my next words. "You're going to tell me about the man who raped you."

Panic flares in her eyes. Her cheeks pale, and her lips part. For a moment, she only stares at me. From her reaction, it's clear she's never spoken to anyone about it, not in the healing sense, at least.

"Who have you told?"

She swallows. "It was a long time––"

I pull gently on her hair. "That's not what I asked. Who did you tell?"

"My–my…no one."

"Let me rephrase that for you. Who knows or knew?"

"My family."

"Who in your family?"

"My mom, dad, and my brother."

"No one else?"

She shakes her head.

"They didn't make you go to a doctor, the police, a therapist?"

"My mom got me the morning-after pill."

I already know why. Her family would've tried to bury the shame. What I need are details so I can track the fucker down.

"Start by telling me where you were when it happened."

A sob escapes her throat. "I don't want to go back there."

I loosen my fingers in her hair and drag them down the long strands. "I'm here for you, baby. You're not going through this alone."

"I can't do it."

She tries to get up, but I push her down. If I could find out the truth without putting her through this, I would, but I'm at a dead end.

"You don't have to go into the details. Think of it as a movie.

Look in from the outside. Go back to the scenes and tell me where you were."

"Gabriel, no." She gets onto her knees and clutches my thighs. "Please, I beg you."

I almost falter. Valentina on her knees in front of me, begging, is more than what I can handle, but she needs to heal, or she'll never be free. The man who stole her virginity will always own a piece of her as long as she keeps it bottled inside, and the fucker doesn't deserve her peace of mind or pain. I press her face down in my lap, running my fingers through her hair.

Steeling myself, I say in a stern voice, "Start at the beginning."

She rubs her cheek on my thigh. A big tear rolls from under her long lashes, the wetness penetrating the fabric of my pants. She licks her lips and opens and closes them twice before she gets a word out.

"Mom sent me to take Dad's dinner. He was working late."

"Where?"

"At the workshop."

"Was it dark?"

She thinks for a while. "It was still light. I think it was before six, because it was right after the afternoon sitcom."

"Good. Carry on."

She swallows again. "A car pulled up."

"What kind of car?"

Her whole body goes rigid. "I don't remember."

"Don't feel, baby. Just tell me who drove the car."

"I–I don't know. I only know they were old."

They? She said only one man raped her. "How many?"

"Five. Six. I think six. I was scared. I didn't want to look at them. I kept my eyes on the ground."

"Don't feel." I brush my thumb over the tears that spill down her cheek. "What did they say?"

"I can't remember. I don't think they said much. One grabbed my arm. Daddy's lunchbox fell on the ground. His sandwiches dropped out. I remember thinking how angry he was going to be if there was sand on them."

"Go on," I say when she falls quiet, rubbing my hand up and down her back.

"They laughed. They laughed a lot."

Anger boils up in me. I feel like breaking something.

"They took me."

"Where?"

She blinks. "I don't know."

"Did they take you by car? Did they make you get inside?"

"No. They dragged me into the building. A bar."

"Can you remember the name?"

"I didn't see."

If she walked, it was not far from where she lived. "Maybe you saw when you went past there later."

"I never walked that road again."

"What did the inside look like?"

"It was dark. Smoke. It smelled of cigarette smoke. There was a counter and bar stools, and a neon sign above the mirror, I think. There was a room at the back with a pool table."

"Were there other people inside?"

"A man behind the bar. I remember him because I screamed for help, but he turned away."

"What did he look like?"

"Fat. Bald. That–that's all I remember."

"You're doing well, sweetheart. Where did they take you?"

She starts shaking, her frail body trembling between my knees. "The back."

"It's a movie. It's not happening to you. Can you see it?"

"They ripped off my clothes and held me down."

Enough. I can't stand it, but I can't let it go, either. "What did he look like?"

"I kept my eyes closed. I couldn't look."

"Only the one?"

"Yes," she says meekly.

I bite back my fury. "What happened after?"

"They left me."

"How did you get home?"

"I woke up in an alley. It was dark."

"You woke up?"

"They beat me. I must've passed out."

God help me, I will tear their limbs from their bodies and make them swallow their dicks before I skin them alive.

"I tried to walk, but I was hurting and bleeding. I didn't get far. That's where my brother found me. When I didn't get home, my mom got worried. She called my father. They started looking."

"He took you home?"

She nods, exhaling a shaky breath. "Mom treated my wounds. I stayed home until the bruises were gone. My father said he'd find the men responsible."

"Did he?"

"I don't know. I didn't want to remember. I didn't want to ask."

"Can you remember the date, Valentina?"

"Thirteenth of February."

Two months later, her father died in the car crash, and her brother suffered brain damage. The mafia who was supposed to be their family rejected them, and here she is, on her knees in front of me. I hook my hands under her arms and lift her onto my lap, cradling her head against my chest.

"They're going to pay."

The tenseness eases somewhat from her small frame as she sits in my arms, allowing me to soothe her and keep her safe.

I kiss the top of her head. "I won't let anyone ever hurt you, again."

For the first time in my life, I have no desire to take cuddling further than holding a woman in my arms. There's satisfaction greater than the high I get from sex in providing her with strength and protection. Even better is that she allows me take care of her, to be the man for her I couldn't yet be for any woman.

We sit together like this for a long time. My only desire is to carry her upstairs and lay her down on my bed, to hold her until the day breaks, but it's close to eleven, and Carly will be home soon.

My thought is scarcely cold when the front door bursts open, and Carly flies through it, sobs and tears following in her wake as she runs through the entrance and up the stairs. Valentina jerks in my arms. She scurries off my lap as fast as I'm trying to get to my feet with my useless leg. She looks at me with wide eyes, concern etched on her face.

"She hasn't seen us," I say.

I have to leave Valentina to go after my daughter. If that dickhead of a pretty college boy touched her, he'll get what he deserves. On the landing, I hear her door slam. My hip aches as I rush to her bedroom.

"Carly?" I call, knocking on the door.

"Go away."

I try the knob. It's locked. Her sobs reach me through the wood.

"Open the door, Carly."

"I said go away!"

"If you don't open this door right now I'm going to break it down."

"I don't care. I don't give a damn."

"Carly!" I'm more worried than angry, but it's the anger that sounds in my voice. "You have three seconds."

"Go to hell."

That's it. I take a few steps back and get ready to charge. I'm about to throw my weight against the door when Valentina comes running up the stairs.

"Gabriel!" She grabs my arm. "What are you doing?"

"Stay out of this."

"You'll scare her."

It's the plea in her eyes that makes me pause. I don't want to frighten Carly, but my fatherly instincts are in overdrive.

I drag my hands though my hair. "Something's wrong."

My concern is mirrored on Valentina's face. Maybe it's the subject we discussed just before Carly's turbulent entry, but we're thinking the same thing.

Valentina walks to the door and taps gently on it. "Carly? Are you all right? Your dad's really worried about you. Please come out and talk to him before he does something stupid."

A hiccup and a snort-laugh comes from inside.

Laughing is good. Whatever happened can't be that bad.

"I don't feel like cleaning up the mess he's about to make," Valentina continues, "not to mention facing your grandmother when he wakes her up with the noise."

The mention of Magda does it. Footsteps approach the door. The key turns. The door opens on a crack, and Carly's tear-streaked face appears around the frame, black mascara smeared under her eyes and her hair a mess. I have to clench teeth, hands, and muscles not to shove the door open, and march into her room.

Carly sniffs and looks between Valentina and me. "I don't want to talk about it, Dad. Go to bed."

"Not until you tell me what's wrong."

"Nothing."

I motion at her face. "This doesn't look like nothing."

"You won't understand!"

It's times like these that I hate Sylvia with an unfair fierceness for walking out on us. "I'll try my best."

"No, thanks." She adds sarcastically, "Can I go to sleep, now?"

"Fine. I'll have to drive over to Sebastian's."

"Dad!" Fresh tears build in her eyes.

I can't stand to see her tears. Moving forward, I hold my arms open for a hug, but she takes a step back into the room and starts closing the door. Only when I stop in my tracks does she let go of the door.

"Can I speak to you, Valentina?"

Valentina shoots me a look. I motion for her to go ahead. I'm desperate. I'll use any measures to get Carly to open up.

"Sure." Valentina clears her throat. "Do you want to talk in your room?"

Carly takes her by the arm and drags her inside, the door shutting behind them.

Why am I surrounded by females who are set on making my life difficult? I go to my study and activate the security system. For my family's safety, every room in the house is equipped with hidden microphones. You never know. It's less than honorable to eavesdrop on my daughter's conversation with Valentina, but only a father will understand how I feel. I pour a whiskey and take a seat behind my desk.

Carly's voice comes over the speaker. "We had a fight."

"Oh, Carly. I'm sorry, honey. Fights happen, you know."

"Not these kinds of fights."

"Was he mean to you?"

"Not exactly. Actually, he was quite polite. I just don't understand. I don't get guys."

"What did he do to upset you?"

"He broke up with me."

"Oh. I didn't know you were going steady."

"He asked me on our first date."

"Then he breaks up a few weeks later?"

"He met someone else. He cheated on me. He lied to me."

"That must hurt an awful lot."

"He says I'm too girlie for him. I'm so humiliated. I hate him."

"You shouldn't look at it like that. Someone not liking you for who you are is nothing to be humiliated about."

"He's a first-class jerk. He's dating Tammy Marais."

"I don't know Tammy, but I know you're beautiful and clever.

You're also still very young. There's lots of time for you to meet the right man."

"How do you know I'll meet someone? What if there's no one out there for me?"

"There are plenty of good men out there."

"How can I make sure they'll like me?"

"By being yourself."

"Did you have a lot of boyfriends? Do you have one, now?"

"I didn't date."

"Why not? Don't you like men?"

"I was busy. I had my studies and a job."

"Are you sorry now that you're old?"

Valentina laughs softly. "I'm not that old."

"Are you? Sorry?"

"Sometimes, but it's no use crying over things we can't change."

"I want him back, Valentina. Tell me what to do."

"You want my opinion? He doesn't deserve to have you back."

"If you don't have experience with men, how do I know I can trust your advice?"

"You don't have to trust me. Trust yourself. I'm sure you know you're worth more than lies and deceit."

"You're right. I'm worth more than Tammy Mousy Hair."

"And elegant young ladies aren't nasty."

Carly giggles. "You're no fun. I can't gossip with you."

"See? You're feeling better, already."

"I guess. Thanks for…uh…putting things in perspective."

"No worries. How about hot chocolate with marshmallows?"

"My mom won't approve."

"Hot chocolate *without* marshmallows?"

"I suppose, as long as it won't make me gain weight."

"You're a skinny thing. You don't have to worry about one hot chocolate."

"Okay. Will you bring it to my room?"

"Only if you go say goodnight to your dad. He's worried because he loves you."

"I know. It's just…I can't talk to him about boyfriends. He'll get upset."

"Tell him how you feel. If he understands, he'll be more patient."

"Will you talk to him for me, like you did for going out with Sebastian?"

"I think you can handle him all on your own."

"Thank you, Val."

"You're welcome. Go see your dad. I'll leave your chocolate on your nightstand."

I cut the security link and tip my hands together. Valentina was right all along. It wasn't necessary to make a fuss about Carly going out with Sebastian. The problem took care of itself. Valentina was good with Carly tonight. I'd trust my only daughter with her any day.

15

Valentina

After I opened up to Gabriel about my rape he became more possessive than ever, but he also lifted a weight off my shoulders. My parents' advice was to pretend that day never took place, and until Gabriel, no one knew exactly what happened. My mom didn't want to hear the details. She wanted to spare me the pain of reliving them. I would've confided in Charlie, but I didn't have a chance. After my attack, my parents did everything in their power to please me. When I said I felt like chocolate cake, my father loaded Charlie and me in the car, and then the accident that changed our lives forever happened.

Gabriel calls me to his study every night after dinner. I sit at his feet with my head on his thigh as he reads and comments on my assignments or watches the news while stroking my hair. Afterward, he takes me depending on how he interprets my needs and mood. Sometimes it's tender and sometimes hard. I revel in whatever he gives me, needing his body with an intensity that doesn't diminish, no matter how many times per night he makes me come.

Things are looking up in my life. Since Carly reached out to me about her breakup with Sebastian, our relationship is friendlier. Aletta said if I hand in my assignments, she'll hold onto my study cancellation, giving me a second chance at my dream. I can still be something other than a maid after nine years. With the bursary, I have more money to spend on Charlie and Kris. I can even afford to take them out to lunch on Sunday. I choose a restaurant in Rosebank, close to El Toro, a delicatessen shop where Marie used to buy Spanish chorizo. Magda told me to make paella on Monday, and she only eats this particular brand of sausage in the dish. Since El Toro doesn't deliver, I profit from picking up my order while spoiling Kris and Charlie.

We get a table on the terrace at Roma's and order spaghetti with scallops in basil-flavored cream. Charlie is working his way through his second Coke float. His eyes shine, and his cheeks have a healthy color. He's even lost a bit of the flabbiness around his waist.

"The change in him is remarkable, Kris."

She takes a sip of her wine. "He's a good dog walker. Plus, it saves me a pack of time."

"It makes me happy to see him like this. I wish I could do more."

"So, what's with the lunch?" she asks after we've eaten, direct as always.

"I have good news. The university granted me a full bursary."

"I thought you dropped out."

"I did, but Gabriel said Marie should be back at work soon. I'll have time to study again, and with the full bursary I won't need to worry about the shortfall."

Leaning back, she crosses her arms. "What's going on with him, Val?"

"Nothing." I pick at my napkin, tearing off small pieces. "Why?"

I can't tell anyone what happens behind the closed doors of Gabriel's house. Especially not Kris. She won't understand. Hell, sometimes *I* don't understand.

"He's been to the practice."

I still. "Why?"

"To buy cat and dog food, apparently. He's got a standing order."

"He didn't tell me."

"You're sleeping with him, aren't you?"

I jerk my head up and glance at Charlie, but he's engrossed in his drink. I can't lie to her in her face, so I say nothing.

"He's a loan shark, and you're indebted to him for nine years. You want to know what I think? I think you're his sex toy. His favorite toy. For the moment, he dresses you up––yes, I saw the parcels he carried to my house––and he covers your bills. Hey, I'm not complaining. I need the business. All I'm saying is don't fall in love with him."

I look away to where a mom and dad are having lunch with a cute little girl. "It's not like that."

"How is it? Are you parading around for him in a French maid's costume? Is that his fantasy?"

I give her a chastising look. "Stop it."

"Every boy eventually grows tired of his toys, even his favorite toy."

"I don't have a choice," I say in a lowered voice. "He's not all bad, Kris. I think he tries really hard to treat me well."

She leans forward. "He's a goddamn killer. A criminal. *The Breaker*, Val. Do you need me to remind you *how* he kills people?"

"No."

"Don't sugarcoat him because he's nice to you. Never forget who he is. More importantly, never forget who *you* are and what you are to him."

"What am I?"

"Debt repayment. You're a slave."

"Call it whatever you want, but I made a deal to save Charlie's life. I'll slave, whore, bust my ass, and work my fingers to the bone to keep him safe."

"What about *your* life?"

Kris doesn't know my history. She doesn't know how Charlie picked me up in the gutter, battered and left for dead, and carried me home for more than two miles. She doesn't know he sat next to my bed and held my hand every night after my assault when I was too afraid to close my eyes to sleep.

"I made a choice, Kris. I made a promise to Gabriel Louw. You don't break your promises to Gabriel. Give it a rest, will you? I'm doing the best I can."

"Jesus, Val. If this is your best, you're heading for a cluster fuck. You cut off your finger for Christ's sake." She wipes a hand over her brow. "How is this going to play out?"

"After nine years, I walk away, get a job, a nice house for Charlie and me, and get out of your hair."

"You're not in my hair, kiddo, but I worry about you."

"I know." I push my chair back, desperately needing air. "I'm taking Charlie for a walk."

"I'll order dessert. Tiramisu?"

"Sounds good. Come on, Charlie." I take my brother's arm and cross the Rosebank Square to stroll down the walkway past the shop fronts. Charlie stops to stare at every window. It's not as much the objects he likes as the colors.

"Charlie?"

He points at a red bicycle in the sports shop. "Loo–look."

"What?" I want him to say it. I want to know what's going on in his head.

"Pre–pretty."

"What's pretty?"

"Lo–look." He points again, getting frustrated.

"The bicycle?"

He's already moved on, stuck in front of a shelf of colorful cycling helmets.

"Li–like."

"Which one?"

He rolls his shoulders like he does when he gets annoyed and carries on down the path with a brisk pace.

I run to catch up, taking his hand. "Do you remember how you used to walk me home from school?"

He hurries on toward the street. Once Charlie is on a mission, it's difficult to distract him. He throws his whole weight into a task and won't stop until he's accomplished what he's set out to do. I'm longing for the connection we once had. I'm aching to have my brother back, to give him back to himself, but he's in his own world, and I sometimes wonder if I'm even part of it.

We stop in front of a red Ferrari parked on the curb. This is what attracted his attention. When he puts out his hand to touch the shiny bodywork, I snatch it back.

"Don't touch the car. What did I say about touching things that aren't ours?"

"That's all right," a male voice says.

I twirl around to where the voice comes from. The man facing us has blond hair and a tanned face with friendly, green eyes.

"You can touch it if you like," he says to Charlie. "It's mine."

The man is as beautiful as his car. It's the kind of sinful beauty that will make a woman forget her male companion at a party.

I tug on Charlie's hand. "We should go."

"I can take him for a spin, if you like."

"Spi–spin."

"Uh, thanks," I push my hair behind my ear, "but my friend's waiting for us."

"Pity." He holds out his hand. "I'm Michael."

I reach out tentatively, but before I can make up my mind, he folds his broad palm around mine and squeezes. When I don't say anything, he gives me an amused smile.

"Your name?"

"Valentina."

"That's pretty." He lets me go and shakes hands with Charlie. "You have good taste, eh…" He lifts a brow and waits.

"Charlie," I say.

"Pleased to meet you both. Maybe we can talk about that spin. If you give me your number, I can call when it's convenient."

"Our dessert is ready." The word 'dessert' will catch Charlie's attention. "Thank you, anyway."

Charlie lets me lead him back across the square to our table.

"Who's that?" Kris asks.

"I don't know. Charlie liked his car."

"Ditto." She waves her spoon at the plate in front of me. "Dig in. It's delicious."

It's hard to say goodbye to Charlie. At least he seems happy. I let that thought soothe me as I cross the street to where Gabriel's Jaguar waits. It's Rhett who exits.

"Hi," I say, surprised. Gabriel said he'd fetch me.

"Gabriel's busy," he says with a wink, holding the door for me.

I wait until we pull off into traffic to ask, "Where is he?"

"Business."

A shiver runs over me. Is he breaking someone's bones? Killing someone?

Rhett gives me a sidelong look. "It's better not to ask."

"I wasn't going to." I glance through the window to escape his piercing eyes.

"On the upside," he continues brightly, "we can train."

I turn back to him quickly. "Really?"

"He'll be busy until late."

My mood picks up. I have to learn how to handle myself.

Gabriel won't be there to protect me forever. Like Kris said, he may grow tired of his new toy sooner than later.

Rhett changes gears and speeds up when we hit the highway. "Why the sad face? Is your brother all right?"

"Sunday blues." I try to smile, but it's a weak effort.

We don't talk for the rest of the way. At home, I change into my shorts and T-shirt and join Rhett in the gym. It's weird to be here out of my own, free will. The gym represents a place of erotic pain and deep-seated pleasure for me. My body reacts at the thought, sending moisture to my folds. I shake my head and jiggle my fingers, physically expelling the unwelcome arousal at the memory of what Gabriel does to me here.

"Ready?" Rhett walks around me like a boxer measuring his opponent.

"Give me your worst."

He laughs. "You're a funny one."

I fling around and punch him in the stomach. "Like this funny?"

My knuckles hurt, and he doesn't even flinch. Before I know what's happening, he kicks my feet out from under me with a swift swing of his leg, making me land on my ass with a humph.

"This move is child's play, perky tits. You've got a far way to go before you can handle my worst."

"Okay, short dick." I hold out my hand for him to help me up.

He only laughs at the diminutive name. When he's halfway in the motion of pulling me up, I yank hard, using the momentum to bring him down to the floor. He does a graceful shoulder roll and flips his leg over me, pinning me face down on the mat.

He chuckles. "You've got spirit, I'll give you that, perky tits."

"Fuck you, short dick."

"Wanna see? You'll take back your words."

"No thanks. Kicking you in the balls when your pants are around your ankles won't be fair play."

He laughs again. "Yep, you're funny." He gets to his feet and pulls me up by my arm. "We'll start with some basic defense moves, and when you've gotten the hang of them, I'll teach you how to use an attacker's strength to beat him."

The minute I'm up, I kick at his feet like he did with me, but he catches my leg, holding me captive.

"You're a quick learner, and you've got more courage than brains, but let me do the teaching. I don't want to hurt you."

I hop around on one foot to keep my balance. "It'll take a bit more than that."

"As I said, more courage than brains. You're small. You've got to learn to fight clever."

"Okay."

He releases me. "Ready?"

For the next hour, he drills me. By the time he calls it a day, I'm sweating.

"You better have a shower. Gabriel will be home soon."

"I want to learn to use a gun, too."

He props his hands on his hips and regards me from under his eyebrows. "Valentina."

"It's a big, bad world out there. I won't live here forever."

After a moment, he sighs and shakes his head. "In for a penny, in for a pound."

I'm happy with my progress. Finally, I'm getting out of my vulnerable bubble. There's just enough time to shower before Gabriel enters my room.

He walks up and stops flush against my back. "How was your weekend?"

"Good."

He pushes my hair aside and kisses my neck. "We're having a dinner party at home on Tuesday. It'll be a late night."

"Okay. Do you have a menu in mind?"

"Magda will brief you. It's important to her." He doesn't need to say more. He wants me on my best behavior. "Don't forget your checkup tomorrow."

I dress the wound religiously, but it's still red and puffy.

He puts his arms around my waist and pulls my back against his chest. "Bend over and put your hands on the wall."

His tone is clipped, like when he's desperate and can't wait. My body grows deliciously warm and wet. I bend my back and brace myself on the wall. He lifts my skirt up over my waist and jerks my panties down. The metal clang of his belt sounds in the room, followed by the scratchy pull of his zipper. His cock pushes against my folds. Without warning he plunges forward, impaling me in one, hard thrust. My back arches from the friction.

"Fuck, Valentina." He holds still, either to give my body time to stretch around his too large penis or to get a hold on his control.

"Take me as you want," I pant, unable to keep still for much longer.

"Oh, I will."

Gripping my hips between his palms, he pulls out almost all the way and slams back in. Pleasure ripples through my womb. He wastes no time in working me up to a climax, fucking me hard. When I come, it's explosive, but so is his release. He grunts and keeps going until his cock is too soft to stay inside me. Only when his shaft slips out does he go on his knees and suck my clit into his mouth. It's impossible to come again so soon, but he's relentless. He has his teeth on my clit and his fingers in my pussy and ass. Our sounds mingle until there's only the unique blend of our moans in the room. He makes me come again in his mouth, driving me to the edge of pleasure. My legs can't carry my weight. When I collapse, he catches me around the waist and carries me to bed. He holds me until it's dark outside, and then he fucks me on my back and on my hands and knees until my throat is hoarse from screaming. My body is depleted. I can't give him any more, but I want more from him. I'm insatiable, and he's to blame.

My heart aches with something I can't name when he leaves me. I lie in the dark until I can't suffer it any longer. There's only one thing to do. I sneak through the dark house to his room. He's standing in the doorframe, waiting, as if he expected me. Jumping into his arms, I cling to him. I'm a stranger to myself, not understanding this woman who can't breathe without her captor. He wraps his arms around my ass to hold me up and kisses me long and sweet. Gently, he lies me down on the bed, pulling me to his chest. Only then, safe and happy, do I fall into an exhausted sleep.

THE DOCTOR'S appointment is at four the following day. As I get ready, Gabriel calls me on the internal intercom and summons me to his room. If we don't leave soon we'll be late. Why does he want to see me now? Before I can knock, he opens the door. I freeze with my hand midway in the air. A disposable sheet is laid out on the daybed, and a gurney with monitors and scanners stands next to it. The same doctor from before, Samuel Engelbrecht, waits in the room. I look at Gabriel for answers, but he says nothing. He only pulls me inside and closes the door.

"Undress and lie down," the doctor says.

I assumed I was going to see the doctor who operated on me at the clinic, and what Gabriel's doctor demands doesn't make sense. "You need me to undress to examine my finger?"

Gabriel takes my hand. "After what you told me, I want to make sure you're all right. You could've suffered internal injuries you're not aware of."

A blush works its way up my neck, warming my cheeks. "Why didn't you tell me?"

"I didn't want to stress you."

I pull my hand from his. "This isn't necessary."

His eyes turn hard. "Get your clothes off, or I'll take them off for you."

I'm so humiliated I don't know where to look. I don't doubt for a minute Gabriel will execute his threat. Angry tears burn in my eyes as I turn my back on them and pull off my trainers, uniform, and underwear. Draping my clothes over the armrest of the chair, I lie down on the daybed.

The doctor approaches with a probe. "Bend your legs."

I do so grudgingly, avoiding Gabriel's eyes. The doctor pulls a condom over the probe, lubricates it with gel, and inserts it gently in my vagina. The scanner beeps to life. He says nothing as he examines me. He only gives Gabriel a nod when he pulls the probe free. My abdomen is next. I am not sure what he's looking for, and I can't imagine why Gabriel wants to know if the rape damaged my body. After the ultrasound, the doctor takes my blood pressure and weighs me. It's when he brings a needle to my arm that I start protesting again.

"What's that?"

Gabriel takes my wrist, brushing his thumb over my pulse. "It's a vitamin boost."

"I don't need it."

"I told you already, your health is my responsibility."

There's a note of steel in his voice. He'll hold me down if he has to. I don't have a choice but to accept the injection and whatever is in it.

With the injection done, the doctor lets me get dressed and makes me sit on the bed to examine my finger. His face is blank, but he stares at the wound for a long time.

"I'm going to prescribe a stronger antibiotic. I want to see you every day."

"What's wrong?"

"A small infection," he says, as if talking to a child. "You've got to keep it still. Don't use the hand."

I bandaged it tightly when I wrestled with Rhett, and we were careful. I'm also cautious with the housework.

The doctor looks at Gabriel. "Any chance you can keep her still for a couple of weeks?"

The set of Gabriel's jaw is enough to give us the answer. Magda will never let him.

"Well, then." The doctor starts gathering his equipment. "Tomorrow same time?"

"Yes," Gabriel says.

When he's gone, I gather the courage to confront Gabriel. "Why?"

"Don't make me repeat answers I already gave you."

"Isn't he going to take his apparatus?" I motion at the gurney with the monitors.

"It'll stay here for a while."

"What are you doing, Gabriel?"

He cups my cheek. "Looking after you."

When he pulls my head to his chest, I can't resist. I can only melt against him, letting his erratic heartbeat seduce me into thinking he actually cares about more than my body.

FROM THE CAREFUL menu planning it's obvious that Tuesday night's dinner is important to Magda. She chooses a caviar mousse starter followed by salmon and spinach crumble with sweet pastries for dessert. I pay special attention to the cooking, ensuring I do nothing to jeopardize our deal. I twist my hair into a neat bun in the nape of my neck and scrub my nails, which are stained orange from the curry I often cook with. The mousse has just set when Magda rings the bell for me to serve. Balancing a tray on one hand, I push the swing door to the dining room open with my shoulder. Looking up, I freeze on the spot. The man sitting opposite Gabriel is the one from Rosebank, the one with the Ferrari. Next to him sits a pretty redhead with freckles on her nose.

"Valentina!" Michael jumps to his feet and holds the door for me to pass.

Gabriel goes rigid. Magda's mouth turns down, her Pit Bull eyes drooping in the corners.

"You know each other?" Gabriel asks, his ice blue eyes narrowed on me.

"We met on Sunday." Michael takes his seat again. "She wouldn't give me her number." He takes the redhead's hand and smiles. "Seems the fairy godmother of fate is still doing her job."

"Valentina isn't available," Gabriel replies coldly. He turns to me. "Where exactly did you meet?"

I clear my throat. "In Rosebank."

"What were you doing there?"

What I do with my free time is none of his business, and his jealous attitude is unwarranted and unreasonable, but Magda can still put a bullet in my head for back chatting or dropping a spoon, so I answer obediently. "I went to El Torro to buy the chorizo."

"I went to El Torro to pick up a bottle of Magda's favorite wine," Michael says. "You see? Divine intervention."

"She's below your class," Magda says. "We picked her up in Berea."

I walk around the table, serving the people who talk about me as if I'm not in the room. I want to dump the mousse on their laps. *Charlie. Think about Charlie.*

"I don't care where she's from," the woman says. "We're not snobbish that way."

She has a rock of a diamond on her ring finger. She must be Michael's wife. Are they into threesomes? I can't get out of the room fast enough. In the kitchen, I inhale and exhale to control my anger. I'm sick of being looked at as a piece of meat.

For the rest of the dinner, the stress mounts every time I step into the dining room. Michael gawks openly while his wife pays me compliments on my physical appearance. Magda is red in the face with annoyance. The one who scares me most is Gabriel. He's quiet. Quiet is never good.

By the time I serve the pastries in the lounge, my stomach aches with tension. My hope of escaping is squashed when Gabriel calls me back as I'm about to exit.

"Valentina." There's authority in his voice. "Come here."

Four sets of eyes are watching me. Magda sits on a single chair at the short side of the coffee table. Her stare is both scornful and hopeful. She hopes I'll disobey. The consequences should be fun to watch. Michael looks on with open curiosity while his wife has a glimmer of excitement in her eyes. My gaze locks with Gabriel's. In silent instruction, he takes a cushion from the armchair and throws it on the floor next to his feet. I don't have a choice. I walk over to him, the tightness in my stomach growing with every step. As I've done so many times before, I sit down next to him. A smile of approval warms his face. He looks at me as if he sees no one else. He cups my cheek and tilts my head to rest on his thigh. Then our brief, private moment is over. Gabriel continues his conversation in a businesslike manner while playing absently with my hair.

Magda looks like a puffed-up dragon about to spit fire. Michael and his wife are obviously used to this kind of behavior. My posture on the floor while Gabriel pets me doesn't take up more of their attention, except for the occasional envious glance Michael shoots Gabriel.

While they're discussing a lease contract for new business premises, Gabriel feeds me sips of champagne. When the tray with sweet pastries is passed around, he takes his time to study the selection and chooses a mille-feuille that he pops into my mouth. His thumb lingers on my tongue. After I've chewed and swallowed, he wipes the icing from the corner of my mouth before licking his finger clean, giving the action his full attention. There's a smile in his eyes as he looks down at me. Again, we're sharing a moment the other three people in the room aren't part of.

After the dessert, he swaps the champagne for whiskey. I'm not a big drinker. Already buzzing from the champagne, I shake my head when he presses the glass to my lips, but his fingers tighten in my hair, pulling back to arch my neck. He takes a drink from the glass and brings his mouth down to mine. I only understand his intention when he spears my lips with his tongue, forcing them open, and feeds me the whiskey straight from his mouth. I gulp and swallow in shocked surprise. He keeps my head in place to drag his tongue over my bottom lip, licking it clean. Only then does he let go of my hair. My face is ablaze with embarrassment. If Mr. and Mrs. Michael find it shocking, they don't show it. Only Magda shifts around on her seat. When Gabriel brings the glass to my lips the second time, I open without argument. Being force-fed in front of his mother and friends isn't an experience I'd like to repeat. It's as if Gabriel is making a point by demonstrating his ownership of me.

At the end of the evening, and three glasses of champagne and a whiskey later, I've gone from a buzz to feeling tipsy. I'm aware of what's happening around me, but I'm seeing double, and my nose is numb. I'm also extremely lethargic. I'm grateful when Michael gets to his feet and announces their departure.

He saunters over to us. "May I kiss the lady, Gabriel?"

Gabriel puts a broad hand on my shoulder. "You may not."

He makes a face of mock disappointment. "I understand. I would act the same if she was mine. You make me long for a sub again."

"She's not a sub," Magda bites out. "She's property."

Michael sighs, barely sparing Magda a glance. His eyes find mine. "Even better."

His wife crosses the floor to lean her head on Michael's shoulder. "If you ever grow tired of her, Gabriel, let us know. I'll be happy to offer her a position."

"That won't happen," Gabriel says through thin lips. "She's too valuable to me."

"You mean her debt is too high," Magda corrects, her glare communicating something with Gabriel I don't understand.

Michael pats Gabriel's shoulder. "Well, goodnight my good man. Next time dinner is at our place." He looks at me. "You should bring your…"

Property. Toy. Four hundred thousand rand-asset.

"Maid," Magda says.

Gabriel gets to his feet. "I'll walk you out." He addresses me with a single command. "Stay."

While Gabriel and Magda see their guests off, I remain as Gabriel ordered. My head is spinning, and I'm not in the mood for punishment tonight. When they return, Gabriel's shoulders are tense, and Magda's mouth is pulled into a hard line.

"Goodnight, Magda," he says pointedly.

Magda isn't that easily dismissed. "You embarrassed me. I won't tolerate this kind of behavior in front of our guests."

Gabriel smirks. "They didn't seem embarrassed to me."

"I'll remind you this is *my* house."

"You insisted we live here."

"For security reasons. There are a hundred or more people who'd have your head on a plate."

"Agreed. It's easier protecting us all under one roof. That doesn't mean you can tell me what to do. As you said yourself, I'm not twelve any longer."

Her nostrils flare. "Are you dealing with what we talked about?"

"I am."

"How long?"

"Soon."

She regards him for a moment in silence. I'm half relieved when she stalks from the room. The other half of me tenses now that I'm alone with Gabriel. His mood is dark. Is he going to punish me? He offers me a hand and pulls me to my feet. My legs are stiff from sitting in the same position for hours, and I stumble, crushing into his chest.

"Sorry," I mumble. Oh, God. My tongue is slurring.

He sets me on my feet with his hands on my hips, testing my balance before he lets go. When I manage to stand without falling over, he steps aside and points at the door. Interpreting it as my cue to leave, I take a few steps, but I have to hold onto the furniture to walk straight. I don't make it to the sofa before his hands stop me. With one arm around my shoulders and the other under my knees, he scoops me up and carries me to the stairs.

"The kitchen," I protest, pointing in the opposite direction.

His chest rumbles with his deep voice. "The kitchen can wait."

In front of his bedroom, he fumbles with his doorknob. When the door swings open, he carries me inside and kicks it shut. The medical equipment is still there. I vaguely wonder when the doctor is going to send for it.

Lying me down on the bed, he undresses me and then himself. His body is hard and rough, the broken lines and deep scars adding to his masculine, forbidden beauty. He climbs over me, pinning my arms above my head. The alcohol loosens my inhibitions. This is not a good idea. I may do and say things I'll regret in the morning.

"Gabriel." His name comes out as a needy gasp. "I think I'm drunk."

"Good. A drunk woman never lies."

He moves down and takes my nipple in his mouth. I arch up, crying out as pleasure ripples through my body.

He licks over the pebbled tip. "Do you find him attractive?"

His raspy tongue sends goose bumps over my skin. I strain my neck to look at him. "W–what?"

He licks the other nipple before sucking it deep into his mouth.

"Ah, God! Gabriel." I fall back, panting.

"Michael. Do you find him attractive?"

He grips my wrists in one hand and moves the other between my legs, parting my folds and stroking my clit. My hips lift to him, but he removes his touch.

"Answer me, Valentina."

I gasp as he presses the pad of his thumb on my clit. "Yes. Yes, he's very pretty."

His face contorts in a mixture of hurt and acceptance, as if he knew the answer but wanted to punish himself by hearing it. It's an unusual display of emotion. He's an open book as he stares down at me, maybe because he believes I'm incoherent, but the alcohol sharpens my awareness and senses. Strangely, my fear retreats to the far corners of my mind, leaving me perceptive to everything else, to the feelings flowing between us and especially to his fingers as he parts me and slips one digit into my wetness, taking me slowly with his finger.

"Would you like him to fuck you?"

I frown, trying to imagine Michael in Gabriel's position. The idea of any other man touching me fills me with distaste. "No."

"You can be honest. I won't punish you for the truth."

I clench my inner muscles, trying to take his finger deeper, and grind my sex against his palm. "Don't you understand what you've done to me? I want *you*, Gabriel."

The pain in his eyes doesn't ease. There's relief, but grief still sets his face into hard angles that emphasize his harsh features. The shadows of the room hide the scar tissue on his cheek, but not the somber light of his ice blue eyes as he stares at me. To me, he's perfect. I love the stark lines that define his unusual masculine beauty and even the sorrow that's permanently etched on his face. Needing to touch him, I pull on his grip, but he tightens his hold.

"Please, Gabriel." I beg him with my eyes, my voice, and my hips.

He groans as I rotate my lower body, trapping his hand between us. Slowly, the squeeze of his fingers on my wrists relaxes, allowing me to lift my hand to his face. I cup his cheek and brush my thumb over the devastating map of scars. It's frightening to look at him, but when you find the courage to look, to really look, the power of the beauty that lies underneath the physical destruction is blinding. I've seen the beauty inside of him, too. He's a good father to Carly, and he gives me much more than he takes, even if I'm nothing but property to him.

"I only want you," I whisper.

For a moment, he leans into my touch, brushing his scarred

cheek over my palm, but then he turns his head away, angling his face to the darkness.

"Gabriel." I moan in protest.

He pushes my legs open wider, positioning his cock at my entrance.

"Gabriel."

I say his name, trying to bring him back to me, to catch the moment we've lost, but he braces himself on his arms, putting more distance between us. The only connection between us is his cock that slams violently into my body. An ache spreads inside of me. He pulls back and does it again, stretching and burning me with that dull pain that tells me he's too rough. He fucks me so hard my body shifts up to the headboard. Over and over he pounds into me, and all I can do is wrap my legs and arms around him, holding on while I give him everything I've got. With every thrust he growls, keeping his face turned away from me. He's never taken me this brutally before, and even as it hurts, my soul revels in his possession. For now, I don't care that I'm property. I don't care that I'm a price tag and an empty body. I just want to be his.

"Only you," I say.

He lances into me harder, his grunts louder, punishing me for something I don't understand. The rougher he treats me, the softer I mold my body around him.

"Only yours."

He snarls, driving into me with such force I'm scared he'll break me.

"Damn you, Valentina. Don't you dare lie. Not about this."

"I want to be yours."

He grabs my face between his palms and jerks his head toward me, putting our noses inches apart without slowing the hard pace of his hips. "Look at this face. Look at me!"

"I *am* looking."

Angers pulls his features into a fearful mask. His nostrils flare, and moisture brims in his eyes. "Stop it."

"Yours."

He utters a raw cry and grinds his groin against mine. Throwing back his head, he clenches his teeth and bites off the sounds as liquid hotness fills my body. He shakes with his release, his body slick with perspiration. I need him. He made a hole in my heart, and only he can mend it. Snaking my arms around his neck, I pull him down for a kiss, but he untangles my wrists and arranges my arms next to my body. He only rests his forehead against mine for the briefest of moments before he lifts up on one elbow to look at me. Our eyes remain locked as he lets his cock slip free to fill the empty space with his fingers. Using his release, he lubricates my clit and brings me to a quick orgasm, all the while watching me.

When the aftershocks subside, he takes me to the shower and washes me. Too weak to stand on my feet, he sits on the bench with me straddling him, my head resting on his chest. The water stings my private parts, and I flinch when he soaps me down there. He towels us dry, carries me back to his bed, and then he disappears into the bathroom again. When he returns, he hands me a glass of water and a tablet.

I look at the white pill. "What's this?"

"Paracetamol. You'll need it if you don't want to wake up with a headache."

He puts the pill on my tongue and makes me drink all the water. The bed dips as he settles behind me, pulling me to his chest.

"I should leave," I say sleepily.

"I set the alarm for five." He kisses my shoulder. "Rest."

I snuggle closer, enjoying the warmth of his embrace. Even if it's only for a few hours, I'll take what I can get. I'm used to living off scraps.

I'm almost drifting off when his voice pulls me back from my sleep.

"There was this cat."

I lie still, waiting for him to continue.

"It was a kitten. Nothing special. Just an alley cat, but to me she was beautiful. She had a soft pelt, black as the night, and eyes like yellow moons. The cat showed up out of the blue at my best friend's house. He called her Blackie. From that day on, Blackie always followed my friend around. She stayed in his room and slept on his bed."

His chest expands with a breath. "I was jealous of him. I wanted the cat to come to *my* house. I wanted her to follow *me*, but she didn't, so I smuggled pieces of fish and steak to his house, luring her through his bedroom window. She ate the food, but still wouldn't follow me home. One day, when my friend was at rugby practice, I went to his house and took the cat. I locked Blackie in my room, hiding her from Magda and our maids. I made a bed for her in my closet, and I fed her treats my friend could never afford to give her. I kept her closed in for two weeks. By that time, I reckoned she would have accepted her new, more luxurious home."

"What happened?"

"The day I let her out, she ran straight back to my friend's house." He strokes my arm for a while, then says quietly, "He thought she'd run away, like strays do."

"Did she continue to live with him?"

"I don't know. I stopped being his friend after that day."

"Why?"

"I couldn't bear to look at that cat."

What is he trying to say? I turn in his arms to look at him.

He kisses my lips softly. "If you set something free, it doesn't come back to you, no matter how well you treat it."

A deep sense of uneasiness settles in my gut. Is he telling me he won't let me go?

"Sleep." He kisses me again, the gentle act conflicting with the soreness inside my body that acts as a reminder of his earlier roughness. "You'll be tired, tomorrow."

I close my eyes to hide my turbulent emotions from him. His story shocks me. It tells me three things. One, he'll take whatever he wants. Two, he believes himself undeserving of love. Three, he'll keep me for as long as my body serves him. What shocks me more is that I yearn to trust him. As long as he holds Charlie and my life in his hands, I can't. For the first time, I consider that he won't honor our deal. He's not going to set me free like the black kitten. A man like Gabriel doesn't repeat the same mistake twice. That's what he was telling me with his story. Tears build up behind my closed eyelids. I turn my back on him again so I can shed them quietly into his pillow. He leaves me with no option. If he doesn't let me go when I've settled Charlie's debt, I'm going to have to run away.

16

Gabriel

Awake long before the alarm goes off, I pull Valentina's soft, warm body closer and mull over last night. Getting Valentina drunk wasn't planned. It's too soon for her to conceive, so I wasn't risking her or a developing fetus' wellbeing. The idea popped into my head while Michael fucked her with his eyes. Sylvia was always brutally honest when she had a drink too many. That was how I found out she never loved me. It shouldn't have come as a surprise. I wouldn't have been so damn gullible if I hadn't been desperate for a woman I could call my own.

Yeah, the truth comes out when a woman is drunk, and unlike men, they don't whisper lies in their moments of passion. When a woman is a second away from coming, that's when you see her true feelings in her eyes. Valentina needs me. That's what I trained her to want. Like the kitten, I lured her with pleasure and orgasms, driving her to her limits and beyond, ensuring that no other man can ever give her what I can, because no other man will have the balls to hurt her to make her come harder. Then why am I gutted?

Women want me for my money, for sex, or for the security that comes with being connected to me. Valentina wants me because I designed it so. It's too much, hoping she'll ever want me for me. Girls like her want men like Michael and Quincy. It's nature. There's not a damn thing I can do about nature, except twist, force, and bend it my way. If I need to make her my captive forever, so be it. Soon, she'll be bound to me in blood. Our child will be a connection she can ever break.

At five, I still my bitter thoughts, switch off the alarm, and start the sad task of waking her. If I could, I would've left her sleeping in my bed. I love having her between my sheets. She groans as I wipe her hair over her shoulder to kiss the gracious curve.

"Wake up, beautiful."

"Gabriel." Her voice is sleepy.

With much regret, I throw the sheet off, letting the fresh morning air cool our bodies. Goose bumps break out over her arms. She turns on her back, rubs her eyes, and stretches.

"What time is it?"

I switch on the nightstand lamp. "Five."

She sits up and swings her legs over the bed. Her back is a perfect portrait of frail vertebrae covered with silky skin.

She gives me a shy look from over her shoulder. "May I please use your bathroom? With all I drank last night, I won't make it to mine."

"Go ahead." I want her to touch everything that's mine. The thought of her fingers trailing over the objects that belong to me makes my skin contract with pleasure, as if she touches *me*.

Her slender hand brushes over the mattress as she gets up. She takes my shirt from the chair and pulls it on. Warmth at the sight of her wearing my clothes fills my chest. When she closes the bathroom door behind her, I get up to select my clothes for the day, but stop dead. Blood spots my sheets. It's not much, only a few drops, but enough to tell me I've broken her again.

I jerk a suit from a hanger with a scowl. God knows I don't

deserve anything as beautiful and perfect as her, but I can't let her go.

The door opens, and Valentina enters. Her cheeks are pale, and there are dark circles under her eyes. She smiles at me as she crosses the floor with small steps. Before she reaches the door, I cut her off. I pull her to me with my arm around her waist, cupping her sex gently with my free hand.

"Are you all right?"

She winces at my touch. "Just tired."

Fury directed at myself combusts in my chest. "We'll go to bed early tonight."

She gives me a weak nod. "I better go before Carly or Magda wakes up."

Reluctantly, I withdraw my touch. "I hurt you."

"You wanted to."

"Not like this. You should've told me."

Her gaze holds mine. "No, Gabriel. You didn't want to hear what I was trying to tell you." Without another word, she walks gingerly from my room.

I let her go because I don't have a goddamn choice. Abandoning the suit, I pull on my exercise gear, go down to the gym, and slam my fists into the punching bag until they bleed.

IT'S GOING to snow in the middle of summer. Carly is having breakfast with us. She's unusually chatty, to the point that Magda escapes with her coffee to her study.

"Dad," she says after an exceptionally long account of her week at school, "I've got something to tell you."

My gut twists inside out. I'm not going to like what's coming. I brace myself as I wait silently with a stoic face.

"I've decided to move back in with Mom."

The blow hits me right between the eyes. I don't know what I expected, but it wasn't this. I lower my cup and take a long, deep breath to calm myself. Sylvia's unexpected visits and easy agreement to let Carly go out on dates suddenly make sense.

I'm careful to keep my voice even. "What prompted the sudden decision?"

"Mom misses me."

The guilt card is a dirty one for Sylvia to play. "You don't have to make a hasty decision. Why not think it over for a while?"

"I've been thinking about it for a long time, already. It's not like you'll only see me every second weekend. I can come visit whenever I want."

"Of course. Your room will always be here."

"Thanks, Dad."

There's no point in arguing with Carly once her mind's made up. She takes after me in that regard. I don't trust Sylvia as a mother. She's only ever proved to me she's not capable of the job, and I don't like Sylvia's new boyfriend. All I can do is be there for Carly when she needs me.

"You're not mad?" she asks.

"Of course not." Disappointed, sad, but I'm not mad at my daughter.

"I'm packing some of my things today. Mom will fetch me tonight. Will you be here to say goodbye?"

So soon? "Of course." The day, which has started out bad, goes several shades darker. "Let me know if you need a hand."

"Thanks, but I'm cool."

Unable to contain my emotions, I push back my chair. "I'll pick you up after school."

"Uh, Dad?"

I pause, waiting for her to speak.

"Me and some girls from my class are going to Mugg & Bean after school."

"Who's driving?"

"Mom."

"I'll see you before you go, then." I walk to the door before she sees the anguish I'm feeling in my eyes.

"Have a nice day," she calls after me.

Just like that, my daughter, my precious gift from Sylvia, is ripped from my house.

What I need is a fight. I take Rhett with me to drive around Valentina's old neighborhood. The chances of finding the bar she mentioned are slight. Many of the old places don't exist any longer. The neighborhood has, like so many others around, turned into a cesspool of crime. The buildings are dilapidated. Some are broken down to the ground. I requested the city plan for twelve years ago from the municipality, but like the rest of the government, they're a corrupt bunch of uneducated officials. The records have long since been displaced with the collapse of the system. It's a joke this country is still functioning. It's people like me and the rest of the thugs on the street who pull the strings. Politicians are merely the puppets. There are a million ways to go to hell, and I've earned them all.

None of the old crowd who knew the neighborhood is left. My father's cronies from way back who collected money on this beat are gone. Steven died of a heart attack with his pants around his ankles on the can. Dawie kicked the bucket when he fell down his front steps and broke his neck. Barney went out the old-fashioned way, gunned down in his front yard. Mickey passed away from cancer, and Conrad caught AIDS from the whores he pimped. My father's death, going peacefully in his sleep, is the most gentle and uneventful of them all, contrary to the violent lifestyle he led. How will my end come? Will I die for the *business*, with a bullet in my brain, or like my father in my bed?

Rhett pulls up to the curb and nods at the flaky house with the missing roof tiles. "This one?"

"Yeah." I cock my gun and slip it into my waistband. "Let's go."

Lambert has the door open before I'm strolling through the weeds in his front yard.

"Gabriel." He gives a nervous laugh. "You'll give me the wrong idea, calling on me all the time."

I motion for him to enter. Rhett and I follow. The firm click of the door when I shut it makes Lambert go tense. His yellow skin takes on a pasty color.

"What can I do you for?"

I hate his slang, but I swallow my insults. "Tell me about the bar that used to be around here."

"The bar?" His shoulders relax visibly.

"Neon sign, bald bartender, pool table at the back."

He scratches his head and thinks for a while. "Ah," he says after a moment, "that'll be Porto, but the place doesn't exist, anymore." He sneers. "Won't find much other than squatters living there."

"Who's the owner?"

"Bigfoot Jack."

The name rings a bell. My father mentioned him once or twice.

"Where can I find him?"

"Six feet under."

Shit. Another dead-end. "Who protected him?" Everyone in the hood had protection from someone. You couldn't survive otherwise.

"He was with the Jewish guys from Kensington."

"Jewish? In Portuguese territory?"

"His wife is Jewish. The big boss made a deal with the Porras to cut Bigfoot out of the loop. Why do you want to know all this stuff?"

"I'm writing a history book," I say drily.

His nose wrinkles, burying his tiny pig eyes in layers of skin. "You're shitting me."

The guy is really thick.

"Where can I find the wife?"

"Won't do you no good. Sophia's got Alzheimer's. She doesn't recognize an ant from a fly."

This doesn't help. I wipe a hand over my face.

Lambert doesn't seem to know where to put his feet. He shifts from the left to the right. "Want a beer?"

"Come on." I nod at Rhett and make my way back to the car.

Inside, my bodyguard turns to me. "Do you mind telling me what's going on?"

"I need Lambert's phone records."

"I'll call Anton."

"I already did. They've been wiped."

"From how long back?"

I give him the date on which I first visited Valentina's almost-husband.

"I know a hacker at Vodacom who's discreet. I'll call him and see what he can do."

While I'm driving, he calls his contact. Before I pull into our driveway, he has a number for me. I park and punch the numbers he reads out loud into my phone. Already by the fourth digit, I know who the number belongs to. As I type in the last digit, Magda's name pops onto the screen.

I fling the door open and make my way to the house with long strides.

"Gabriel!" Rhett jumps from the car and runs after me.

"Stay out of this," I call back.

I find Magda in her study. "Why did Lambert Roos call you?"

She leans back, regarding me from over the rim of her glasses. "He wanted to know why we're sniffing around in his territory." She folds her arms. "Why are we, Gabriel?"

"Did you know Bigfoot Jack?"

"Not personally, but everyone in the business knows who Jack was."

"What do you know about him?"

"Same as you--not much. Why this sudden interest in Bigfoot?"

"I'm trying to piece together Valentina's history, but it's all dead-end streets."

"Why?"

"I'm interested."

"Don't get attached to her, Gabriel. I've warned you, already."

"So you have."

"Are you?"

"Am I what?"

"Getting attached?"

"I don't think I'm capable of attachment."

"You've always been a soft boy, too soft for what it takes."

"What does it take, Magda?"

"Do your job."

"You mean kill her."

"As agreed."

I don't agree at all, but a text comes in from Rhett, informing me the doctor has arrived. I order him to wait upstairs and go in search of Valentina. She's walking Bruno with Quincy, and seeing them together in friendly banter only escalates my irritability.

"Hey," she says when she sees me.

Her warm smile cools at my explosive state.

"The doctor's waiting," I say.

At my tone, Quincy mumbles a greeting and takes his leave.

"I know. I suggested we get started, but he insisted on waiting for you," she tells me.

"I'm here now, so let's go."

In my room, I tell the doctor to repeat the same tests from yesterday. Yesterday, I wanted to ensure Valentina hasn't sustained internal injuries that could prevent her from having children. Today, I need to know I haven't damaged her.

"Again?" he says, his voice not giving away his thoughts.

I raise my brow in challenge. I pay him enough not to ask questions.

He turns to Valentina. "You know what to do, my dear."

"I don't understand."

"Do it, Valentina," I say more harshly than what I intended.

She flinches at my tone but obeys. Only when the doctor tells me that she's fine do I relax. I'd instructed him to inject her with a fertility treatment yesterday to increase her chances of conceiving. She'll be ovulating a week from today, and my seed will be in her morning, afternoon, and night, until it takes.

I hold out her dress for her to step into and button up the front before guiding her back to the daybed. The doctor unrolls the bandage on her thumb, exposing an angry, red wound. I don't need his confirmation to know the antibiotics aren't helping. Neither does Valentina.

She looks at me with big eyes. "I hoped it would be better today."

The doctor gives me a grim look. "She'll have to go to the clinic. Now."

My world comes to a standstill for a third time that day. I take Valentina's hand in mine. Her palm is cold and clammy. "Is there a risk of her losing her thumb?"

"I don't know. I'm not a surgeon." He pulls off the medical gloves and throws them in the trashcan. "Do you need me to call an ambulance?"

"No." I squeeze her fingers. "I'll take her."

I get Quincy to drive us so I can sit in the back with Valentina, my arm around her shoulders. Her frame is tense, but she leans into my touch when I grip her chin to kiss her lips. From spanking her, I know her pain threshold is low. That's why she was so pale this morning. I want to tell her it will be all right, but there are already enough lies between us, and I simply don't know.

On the way to the hospital, I call my personal insurance broker and get her to arrange pre-admittance at the clinic. It's peak hour traffic at five, but Quincy knows the back roads and manages to get us there in little over thirty minutes. With Valentina already admitted, we walk straight to an examination room where a young surgeon waits on us. He takes one look at her finger and orders tests to be done.

"What's the course of action?" I ask tightly.

"One thing at a time. Let's get the results, first."

"How long will it take?"

"An hour, maybe ninety minutes. We have the lab on site, and I requested the tests as a priority. I can get you a private room where you'll be comfortable, or you can wait in the cafeteria."

"Get us a room, please." I can't stand crowds, and I doubt Valentina is in the mood for hospital coffee.

A nurse shows us to a room with bright yellow walls and a single bed with a blue bedspread. Quincy takes up a position by the door while I make Valentina sit on the bed. I check the time on my phone. It's almost six. I'm about to shove it back into my pocket when it rings. Carly's name appears on the screen.

"Excuse me." I press a kiss on Valentina's temple and walk to the corner of the room. "Hello, princess. Where are you?"

"I'm home. Where are you?"

"At the hospital."

"Is something wrong?"

"I had to bring Valentina. Her wound is infected."

"Oh, no. Tell her I hope it's going to be okay. Listen, Mom's here. Rhett is loading my stuff in the car."

"Already?" I glance at Valentina. "When are you leaving?"

"We can't wait long. Mom's got something on. I can stop by next week."

I'm torn in two. I don't want to let Carly go without saying goodbye, but I don't want to leave Valentina, either.

Valentina hops from the bed and lays her hand on my shoulder. "Carly?" she whispers.

I nod.

"Go," she says. "I'll be fine."

"Give me a minute, Carly." I put the call on hold. "I'm not leaving you. Not now."

"Quincy is here. You heard what the doctor said. It may take an hour or more. Go say goodbye to your daughter. I'm a big girl. It's just an infection. I'll get a shot of potent medicine, and then I'll be back."

I stare at her face, her full lips, and her sad, murky eyes. Rationally, what she says makes sense, but I can't get myself to tell Carly I'll be home in thirty minutes.

"Go on," she urges. "Your daughter is moving out of your house. You're not going to let her go like this, without even being there."

I pinch the bridge of my nose and take a second to make my decision before taking back the call. "I'll be home in thirty minutes."

"Okay," Carly says brightly. "I'll wait for you."

I press a hard kiss to Valentina's lips. It's on the tip of my tongue to tell her I love her, but I swallow the words back just in time. A shiver of shock runs down my spine. What the fuck is wrong with me? The thought tumbled into my mind from nowhere. Habit. It must be habit. Whenever I had to leave Sylvia in a difficult situation, I always needed to reassure her of my feelings. I backtrack to the door and say, "I'll be back later."

Her smile is warm and easy. It's a smile meant to soothe. I escape the feelings crashing down on me, leaving them in the confines of the hospital room as I flee outside.

"Stay with her," I say to Quincy, "and call me when there's news. Anything she needs, anything at all, don't hesitate."

"Yes, boss."

"Give me the car keys. I'm going to the house, but I'll be back as soon as I can."

He fishes the keys from his pocket and hands them to me.

"Don't move away from this door. Keep her safe."

He flicks his jacket aside, showing me the gun that's tucked in his waistband.

I leave the hospital with mixed feelings. If Sylvia was reasonable, I would've asked her to wait, but she's not, and she'll be especially difficult where Valentina is concerned.

The traffic is a nightmare. It takes me more than forty-five minutes to get home. Sylvia and Carly are waiting outside next to Sylvia's overloaded convertible.

"Dad!" Carly runs to me when I get out of the car. "I knew you'd come. Told you, Mom."

She lets me hug her, a rare occurrence. I look at the boxes and suitcases piled up on the backseat of the Mercedes. "Wow, when did you accumulate all this stuff?"

She jabs me with an elbow in the ribs. "You should know. You paid for it."

"Can you even wear all of that?"

"It's not only clothes," she says indignantly. "There are books, too."

"What, ten?"

Sylvia walks up to us in a tight-fitting, pink pencil-skirt suit. "We have to go."

"Carly, if you need anything––"

"I'll call."

"No more than an hour on your phone per day and no dates without my permission."

"Gabriel." Sylvia gives me a hard look. "I'm her mother. I'm capable of handling these decisions."

"But we'll make them together."

She moves away, doing her best not to appear abrupt in front of Carly. "She's growing up. Accept it."

I'm not getting into a fight with Sylvia. Not today. I kiss Carly's cheek. "I love you, princess. You know that, right?"

She wipes her palm over her cheek. "Yuk, Dad! Since when are you all mushy?"

"Since my baby girl is growing up." I was going to say leaving, but I don't want her to feel guilty for spending time with her mom.

"Stop it." She swats my arm. "You'll make me cry, and I don't want my mascara to run."

"Carly." Sylvia starts tapping her foot.

The two women make their way to the car and get inside. As the vehicle clears the gates, a feeling of desolation creeps up on me. The house is empty and purposeless. Its framework stands like a big, white elephant behind me. The pool, garden, televisions, everything was for Carly. It's like a piece of me has left with my daughter.

My phone vibrates in my pocket, drawing my attention back to the present. There's a text message from Quincy.

Valentina's in surgery.

17

Valentina

I wake up in a hospital bed without a piece of me. It's not the end of the world to lose a thumb. Worse things can happen, but I'll never hold a needle and thread again. To be a veterinary surgeon, you need all your fingers. It happened too quickly for me to process. Twenty minutes after Gabriel left, the doctor returned with the news. The digit they sewed back didn't take. I had gangrene in my thumb. To stop the infection from spreading, he had to amputate above the knuckle. Fifteen minutes later, I was wheeled into the operating room.

The door opens, and a nurse enters. "You're awake." She looks at the chart by the foot of the bed and adjusts the drip in my arm. "Ready for visitors? Mr. Louw is anxious to see you."

I'm not. I want to be alone to process what happened.

"Push the button if you're in pain." She leaves a call button within reach of my good hand and calls brightly through the door, "You can see her now."

When Gabriel enters, my heart shatters. His hair is messy and his shirt creased, like he slept in it all night. The skin under his eyes is a blue-ish color. He limps to my bedside, his face an unreadable mask. Despite his tall frame and all those muscles, he looks utterly vulnerable. A deep need to soothe him makes me reach out, cupping his cheek.

"What time is it?"

"Just after six." He adds, "In the morning."

"Did you stay the whole night?"

"Of course."

"You didn't have to."

He says nothing, but turmoil suddenly twists his face.

"It's just a thumb," I say.

He grabs my fingers and squeezes so hard it hurts. When I cry out he lets go, seeming uncertain what to do with my hand. Finally, he places it on top of the bedspread.

"You're not the only one who can brag. I've got my own scar, now."

"I've already spoken to the doctor about a prosthesis."

"I don't want an artificial thumb."

"Why not? It'll look natural."

"It won't function."

"No." He avoids my eyes. "It won't."

"I don't care about how I look." When his eyes turn stormy, I try for humor. "Damn, I'll never be able to hitchhike."

A smile breaks through his dark expression. "You don't have to. You've got me."

Not forever.

He traces a finger along my jaw. "There are other things. Veterinary assistant. Nurse."

It's like telling me there are other men than him.

"Yes," I say softly, "there are other things."

TIME FLIES by during the next few weeks. Christmas comes and goes. I shared a quiet lunch with Kris and Charlie. Instead of buying each other gifts, we donated money to a charity for stray animals. Gabriel, Sylvia, Carly, and Magda had a party with their associates and friends. Magda hired caterers, so my help wasn't needed. Gabriel gave me a spa voucher for Christmas that included every imaginable pampering treatment. My gift to him was of a more depraved nature. He asked to tie me up and film spanking and fucking me. He didn't need my permission, but my free will was the gift he wanted. It was another way of twisting more submission from me, of making me fall deeper into the darkness that is us. Afterward, he made me watch it. Like the perverse being I've become, it turned me on, and the reward for my reaction was a tender marathon of slow lovemaking.

The house is quiet without Carly. She comes to visit every second weekend for a couple of hours. I can tell Gabriel misses her. After New Year, the house turns even quieter when Magda leaves for Cape Town. I don't know what kind of work she's doing there, and I don't ask. Gabriel is often out on business, leaving me alone in the mansion. Gabriel, Quincy, and Rhett treat me like an invalid, carrying the washing basket and anything else I can easily enough pick up. For some tasks, I switch to my left hand. Others, I manage with four fingers.

Marie comes back to work, her speech impaired and her disposition brusquer than before. As the traveling between home and work becomes too much for her, she moves into a bedroom in the house. I have a strong suspicion she tattles to Magda. She watches me like a hawk. For that reason, even if Magda and Carly aren't present, I still don't spend whole evenings in Gabriel's bed. Some nights he comes to me, and some nights I go to him. When we're together, I'm his sex object. His pet. When Magda enters the equation, I'm property. Gabriel is careful to tone down the affection he shows me in private when Marie or Magda is around.

Kris is supportive. She said I could still buy into the practice, even if we both know I'll never be able to afford it on a maid or veterinary nurse's salary. Aletta was sad when I told her the news. Shortly after, she informed me they awarded the bursary to another, needy student. Charlie got very involved with the dog walking. He takes the task to heart, and the responsibility seems to do him good.

It's only me who's not doing well. On a non-physical level. My checkups are good. The doctor says the infection hasn't spread. I'm stuck in Gabriel's house, submitted to his mercy, and I can't say he's mistreating me. I've come to crave the spankings and beltings. He buys my food and clothes. Anything I want, I only have to mention it, and I'll find it in my room the next day. It's as if he's trying to make up for the loss of my dreams and the dark needs he submits me to with material compensation. His gifts range from cosmetics to books and even a new iPhone.

Sex with Gabriel is always explosive, even when it's gentle. Lately, there's a lot of gentle. That's why I can't understand my growing sadness. The kinder he acts toward me, the sadder I feel. I can't bring the man in my bed together with the man who holds Charlie's future over my head. I want to hate both, but I know better. It's been a long time since I felt only desire for Gabriel. I care about him, and I hate that I do.

As always, Gabriel picks up on my mood. That night, he arranges my naked body on the mattress so he can look at me. He cups my breast gently, stroking his thumb over my nipple.

"Ouch." The sensation is almost too much to bear.

Testing the weight of my breast, he gives me a thoughtful look. "You're close to having your period."

He almost looks disappointed. It's not like he hasn't made love to me during my period. I don't understand his silent dejection.

"Yes." I turn on my side, facing the wall, relieved to understand the reason for my depressive feelings. It's just a heavy bout of PMS.

He rubs a palm over my stomach and presses his cock between

my legs. "I'll be gentle." Without waiting for my consent, he rolls me onto my stomach and settles between my thighs. "Open for me, beautiful."

I open my legs, giving him the view he wants. He strokes and teases me for a long time, until his fingers are soaked with my wetness. Only then does he push inside, slow and easy. It's then that it hits me. Since I've been back from the hospital, he's only taken me from behind. How could I have missed this before? He's fucked me against the wall, on his desk, in his armchair, in the pool, and in a variety of other, creative places, but my butt was always pressed against his groin, my face looking away from him. Is it me? Does he find me unattractive? I twist under him, starting to squirm.

"Valentina."

"Let me up."

I don't expect him to, but he obliges. He watches me warily as I switch positions, turning him on his back.

"What are you doing?"

"Looking at you."

"Why?" he says with a pained expression.

"Because I like to."

I lower myself over his cock, taking him into the depth of my body. I let the pleasure show on my face, letting him see what he does to me as I start rocking, my nerve endings coming alive for him.

"You don't have to," he says.

"Do you like to look at me?"

"You know I do."

"Then stop talking and fuck me."

It's as if a dam inside of him breaks. He growls and grips my hips, keeping me in place while he pounds into me, taking me to the edge I want to go.

As my body tightens, he cries out his climax. It's the quickest we've come together since the week he started fucking me. I drape my body over his chest, holding him inside of me. I wish I could stay like this, but I'm not naïve enough to let myself belief this will last. It matters nothing to him. He has no emotional obligation to me. He can fuck anyone he wants without explanation.

"Gabriel?"

He strokes my back. "Yes, beautiful?"

"Do you fuck other women?"

His hand stills. "Why?"

I shrug. "Don't I need tests for STD?"

The caressing resumes. "There's only you, Valentina. I told you before."

"It was a long time ago. It could've changed."

"I'll tell you if it does."

My heart feels like it has just gone through a blender. It can change. I was right. I swallow my tears, angry at my irrational feelings. I have no right to expect more from him. It's my own damn, stupid fault I fell for my tormentor.

THREE WEEKS LATER, I resume my secret training with Rhett. My amputated thumb has healed enough to undertake more strenuous exercise. I'm out of shape, even if I tried to stay fit by using the Walker in the gym. He floors me every time, throwing my ass on the mat. It's during our session on Thursday evening when Gabriel is out on business that I burst into frustrated tears.

Rhett looks at me, aghast. "Did I hurt you?"

"No." I wipe at my cheeks. "I'm just emotional."

My damn period hasn't started yet. The sooner it does, the sooner I'll get over this depressed state.

He offers a hand to pull me up. I'm scarcely on my feet when the evening's dinner pushes back up my throat. I rush to the bathroom, making it to the toilet just before I empty my stomach. Rhett runs in after me, coming to a halt next to the toilet.

Dry heaves wrack my body, making my eyes tear up.

"Jesus, Valentina." He takes a stash of paper towels and hands them to me. "Are you all right?"

"I'm fine."

Feeling slightly better, I rinse my face and wash my hands.

He touches my arm. "Are you…?"

"No." I shake my head. "I'm not sick."

"I meant are you pregnant?"

My lips part in shock. The blood drops straight from my head to my feet, leaving me feeling dizzy. "No, of course not."

I've never missed my pill. I am however a little late. Oh, God. What if? Gabriel will kill me.

Impossible.

I've been careful.

I take another towel from the dispenser and wipe my mouth, noticing how much my hands are shaking. "I think I'll call it a night."

"Can I get you anything?"

"No, thank you. I just need an early night to catch up on sleep."

He watches me leave, not saying a word.

I crawl into bed after a shower, but I don't close an eye. It's late when Gabriel returns. He strips naked and climbs into bed beside me. I'm wet for him, but he takes his time to lick and tease my folds. He doesn't stop until I've come twice, and only then does he fuck me. The way he loves my body is incredible, but my mind isn't there. My mind is searching for solutions to problems I haven't even confirmed, yet.

"Where are you?" he finally asks, kissing my breasts.

"I'm sorry. I'm just tired."

He covers my body in kisses, all the way from my stomach to my feet. He's so gentle, I want to cry.

When he's kissed his way back up to my neck, he hugs me tightly and says, "Go to sleep."

AFTER BREAKFAST, I walk to the staff unit. Rhett is sitting on the porch, sipping his coffee. He gets to his feet when he sees me.

"You look like shit."

"Thanks." I give him a wry smile. "I need a favor, please."

"Anything." He leaves the cup on the rail.

"I need you to go to the pharmacy."

His look is pitiful. "All right."

"Gabriel can't know. Do you hear me?"

"Valentina."

He walks down the steps and reaches for me, but I pull away.

"He can't know, Rhett, not until I know for sure."

He swallows and nods. "I'll be back soon."

A SHORT TIME LATER, I sit on the seat of the toilet, staring at the two blue lines on the strip.

Positive.

I'm expecting Gabriel's baby.

A mixture of feelings rushes through me. I'm faint with wonder. I'm also sick with fear. Will he blame me? He'll be furious. Worse, he'll think I did it on purpose to trap him. Gabriel will never want a baby with a woman who's property. I don't mind raising a child on my own. Gabriel doesn't have to give me a cent. I won't expect support from him, but what if he doesn't want me to have this baby? What if he forces me to have an abortion? If he drives me to a clinic, there won't be anything I can do to stop him. He still owns me, and now he owns the baby growing in me, too.

There's only one thing I can do to save the little life inside me. I quickly pack a bag, my hands trembling so much I drop my phone twice. I wrap the pregnancy kit in a plastic bag, and discard it in the trash outside where no one will look. Only Rhett will guess, but by the time Gabriel confronts him, I'll be long gone.

In Gabriel's study, I write a quick note.

I can't honor my promise. I hope you'll forgive me.

Leaving it on his desk, I pull the door close, knowing Marie won't enter his study. Then I call a private taxi. It's going to cost an arm and a leg, but I can't afford to take a minivan. I need to disappear fast. Rhett left with Gabriel a short while ago, and Quincy is walking Bruno. I walk past the guards at the gate with a wave, my bag slung over my shoulder, acting as normal as I can. They've only seen me leaving the property on foot once, but I'm leaving on a regular enough basis for them not to stop me.

A block from the house, I pause to wait. Two minutes later, the taxi pulls up to the street corner I gave the driver. Looking over my shoulder to make sure no one is following, I jump inside.

"Go, please. Quickly."

I don't glance back as the driver speeds away. I cup my hands over my stomach and stare straight ahead.

I have to.

For my baby.

CONSENT

THE LOAN SHARK DUET (BOOK 2)

1

Valentina

A baby.
I'm going to have Gabriel Louw's baby.
Gabriel Louw.
The most dangerous man in Johannesburg.
Oh, God.

I clutch a hand over my mouth to silence a sob and place the other over my stomach where our child is growing.

While the taxi takes me farther and farther away from my captor on my impulsive escape route, my mind reels with a thousand thoughts. How did this happen? Did I forget to take my pill? I'm sure I took it every day at the same time. I even have an alarm programmed on my phone. Did I slip up? How? When? I haven't taken any medicine that could've interfered with the contraceptive.

For the life of me, I can't think of an explanation. My rational mind, the part of me in denial, demands that I find proof that the pregnancy test is wrong, but my gut knows otherwise. The knowledge pounds in my ribs.

I'm pregnant.

And alone.

I have little money, no job, and I'm running from Gabriel Louw.

I'm in so much trouble. Now is not the time to figure out what went wrong. I need to think of how I'm going to stay alive.

"Where to, ma'am?" the driver asks.

When Gabriel finds out I'm missing, he'll go after my brother. I give the driver Kris' address and sink back in the seat, nauseous from fear.

He glances at me in the rearview mirror. "Everything all right?"

I lower my hand from my mouth and grip the door handle. I need to hold on to something. "I'm fine, thank you."

It feels like forever before we pull up at the clinic. I ask the driver to keep the meter running and skirt around to the back of the house where I won't be visible from any of the clinic windows. I try the kitchen door, but it's locked. I knock softly.

Please, Charlie, hurry.

For several painful heartbeats, nothing happens.

Biting my nail, I run from window to window until I spot Charlie. He's sitting on his bed, reading a comic book. I tap on the glass. The last thing I want is to scare him by pounding on the window. No reaction. I knock harder. I can't afford to attract Kris' attention. In the meantime, the taximeter is running a hole into the small amount of cash I have on me.

Tap, tap.

Finally, Charlie looks up. When he sees me, he calls out, "Va–Val."

I motion for him to be quiet with my finger on my lips and point at the window latch. Instead of opening it, Charlie hops from the bed and leaves the room.

Don't call Kris.

A moment later, the backdoor opens, and my brother steps out.

Beyond relief, I want to pull him into my arms and tell him we're going to be all right, but I have to act normal.

"Surprise, Charlie," I whisper. "I came to fetch you. We're going on a holiday, but you have to come quietly."

"Q–quiet," he whispers back, mimicking my earlier gesture with a finger on his lips.

There's no time to go through the house and gather some of his things. I lock up so Kris will be safe inside and throw the key through the bars of the open bathroom window. Hooking my arm through Charlie's, I lead him to the waiting taxi.

Inside, the driver and Charlie speak simultaneously.

"Where do you want to go?"

"Where are we go–going?"

Where are we going?

Where can I run to where Gabriel won't find me? A place like that doesn't exist. If I'm to keep my wits about me, I have to ignore that notion. I'm no longer responsible for only Charlie and myself, but also for a third life. I have no plan of action. I pinch the bridge of my nose.

Think, Valentina. Think.

"Ma'am, where to?" the driver repeats, more impatient now.

I can't afford a plane or bus ticket to anywhere for myself, let alone for two people. There's only one option left. Wherever we're going, I'll have to drive.

"Ma'am?" The man turns in his seat and gives me a piercing look. "Is everything all right back there?"

"Yes. We're going to Berea."

He regards me from under his bushy eyebrows and says with a hint of disbelief, "Berea. You sure?"

"Just drive. I'll give you directions."

He holds my eyes for another moment before turning back to the front and pulling away from the curb. I exhale in relief, and squeeze Charlie's hand to reassure him, happy that Kris hadn't seen us. Charlie has wound down his window and is staring at the buildings that whiz past, oblivious to the lump of concrete in my stomach and the maddening fear pumping through my veins.

I send a quick text message to Kris so she won't worry when she finds Charlie gone.

Charlie and I have to leave for a while. Sorry to sneak off like this, but the less you know the better. Thank you for always being a friend. Love you.

A block from my old flat, the driver stops. "This is as far as I go." He motions at the street ahead. "That's hijackers' paradise."

I pay the extortionate amount and usher Charlie out before the driver can pose the questions I see in his eyes. The minute we're on the pavement, he speeds off, happy to get out of here.

"Va–Val." Charlie kicks in his heels as I take his arm. "This is ho–home."

"Not anymore." I give him a bright smile. "This is only where our holiday starts."

I have precious little time. It's a matter of hours, minutes maybe, before Gabriel discovers me gone and puts a death warrant out for our lives. He'll track my phone and be on our tail faster than I can say disappear, but if I want Charlie to follow hassle-free, I have to make him happy.

We walk one block to a corner café where I buy Charlie a King Cone ice cream. While he sits down on the pavement to eat it, I call Jerry. The number rings and rings, and finally disconnects without going onto voicemail.

Darn it. Jerry is my only hope. I try the special number he gave me when he was still supposedly watching over Charlie. It's a number only me and some of his crime buddies have.

This time, he picks up with a hesitant, "Val?"

There's no time to beat around the bush. "I need a car."

"What?"

"A car, Jerry. Now."

"To buy?"

"Would I have called a car thief if I wanted to buy a car?"

He utters his refusal meekly. "I can't do it. What's going on? This isn't like you."

I've always condemned his shady business, but now isn't the time for my moral values to induce guilt. "After what you did to us, you owe me, damn you."

There's dejection in his voice. "Val…"

"Do you want to know what Gabriel Louw did to me because of your ignorant stupidity?"

"Oh fuck. Oh fucking fuck. You're running." His voice trembles. "You're running away from The Breaker."

"If he finds me, I'm dead. So is Charlie." And the baby I'm carrying. "Please, Jerry. You got us into this mess. Help me get out."

There's a long silence. I can almost feel the gears turn in his head. Just when I think he's going to hang up, he says, "Where are you?"

"Your place."

"Give me an hour."

"Thirty minutes."

"Goddamn, Val." He takes a breath, as if to calm himself. "Wait at the side of the building."

"Thank you. You better show up. When I hang up, we can't speak on this phone again."

He knows what I mean. I have to destroy the phone if I don't want Gabriel to track me.

"I'll be there." The line goes dead with a click.

Charlie has finished his ice cream. I make him clean his hands on a tissue and throw the wrapper in the trashcan so I can go around the corner and crush the phone under my heel. There are too many tiny parts to discern a tracker, not that I know what to look for, so I stamp on everything again, just to be sure, and dump the lot in the trashcan.

"Ready for our adventure?" I take Charlie's hand. "Let's go get our wheels."

We hide in an alcove from where I can watch the road. Thankfully, we haven't crossed any thugs, but they'll soon crawl out of their holes with the setting of the sun. I play a distracted game of noughts and crosses with Charlie, using a chalkstone I picked up in the road to draw lines on the brick wall.

Thirty-five minutes later, an orange station wagon pulls up. The bodywork is dented and the metal rusted where the paint has peeled. My jaw drops when the rickety vehicle comes to a stop next to us and Jerry exits.

"Jerry." I throw my arms in the air.

"What?" he says in an exasperated voice. "It's all I could do on short notice."

"How far will this thing get us?"

He pats the bonnet. "She's good. I checked her out. Engine is a make-over, the full Monty." He holds the key out to me. "Swapped the registration plate, too, but keep off the main roads, just in case."

"Thanks." I snatch the key from his hand. "Let's go, Charlie."

Jerry pats Charlie on the back as my brother rounds the car. "How's things, my man?"

Charlie gives him a high-five and a grin. When he's buckled up, I look at Jerry through the window one last time before pulling off, heading for the highway.

The engine makes a funny noise, and the body of the car rattles, but we make smooth progress and manage to get through Hillbrow without any hijacking attempts, courtesy of the state of the car.

Once we hit the N1, my frayed nerves finally unravel. My hands start shaking on the wheel. A hot flush travels over me, making me break out in a sweat. My stomach is so tight it aches. I fight the urge to throw up. The summer smog is brittle and dirty, but I open the window to fill my lungs with air. As always, survival mode kicks in and numbs me to the fears and dangers of our situation.

Charlie is looking through his window, humming a song. I manage to tweak the radio enough to find a Country and Western station he likes. Checking the petrol gauge, I groan inwardly. The tank is near empty. At the first petrol station after Midrand, I fill up and use my last cash to buy a few supplies from the Quick shop, which are mostly snacks for Charlie. I don't dare withdraw money at the ATM with my card. It will be too easy to track. I should have remembered to do that before I started out.

My gut twists and churns the farther we crawl away from Johannesburg, the city of gold that is ruled by a man as beautiful and ruined as the place itself, a man who'll kill us if he finds us.

When the skyline of Sandton disappears from my rearview mirror, a crippling notion of loss and loneliness hits me. The emotions throw me off kilter. Shock runs through me. I miss Gabriel. That makes me twisted and sick. It must be the hormones. Yes, I'm not myself. Uninvited tears sting my eyes. Swatting at them, I force my gaze on the road ahead.

Don't look back.

There is only Charlie, me, and my baby now.

We'll make it. We'll survive.

I have no idea where I'm heading until we hit the sign announcing the three-way split. If we carry on straight, we head north toward Polokwane. I don't know the area. The only remaining options are Bloemfontein or Durban. Durban isn't as far away as Bloemfontein, and the weather is less harsh. Without financial means, Durban is the better option. Plus, I can make it there on a tank of petrol, whereas I'll run out of fuel in the middle of nowhere, long before I hit Bloemfontein.

The sign for the N3 appears. I change lanes and enter the interchange that takes me over the highway and east. With a flick of the indicator, I decide our destiny and future.

Gabriel

THE GUY I took out this afternoon was scum, but today the violence leaves a bad taste in my mouth. All I want is to go home to Valentina, crawl into her body, and melt into her bed. Things between us have changed. No matter how much I lie to myself, she's no longer the toy I pickpocketed from her life. She's something--someone--I want enough to break every rule in the book to keep. She's no longer my captive. I'm hers.

My addiction has grown over the months to an all-consuming obsession. Despite the coldness inside of me, she awakens emotions I thought I didn't have. She makes me feel things I've never felt before--gratitude, regret, joy, and fear--and even if these feelings scare me shitless, I want more.

When I get home, I dismiss Rhett and Quincy and go upstairs for a shower. I don't want to face my girl covered in blood. Washing the stench of my sins away, I think about her and what I want to do to her body. The thoughts make me hard. If I wasn't so impatient to plant my cock in her body, I would've made myself come first so I can last longer, but my urgency is palpable. I towel myself dry quickly and dress in slacks and a shirt.

My heartbeat speeds up as I make my way to the kitchen. At this hour, Valentina will be ironing. It irks me to see her work so hard, to see her work at all, but it's not for much longer. The minute she falls pregnant, everything will change.

Silence greets me when I enter the kitchen. The counters are tidy and wiped down. Marie has already left for the day. An eerie emptiness presses down on the space. I don't like it. I quicken my step, putting my head around the scullery doorframe, but there's no one. A sickening sensation settles over my body. Every nerve ending tingles. Rushing to the maid quarters, I jerk open the door. Valentina's bed is made. Oscar is sleeping on her pillow. My leg hurts from the force I put on it as I limp to the bathroom.

Empty.

With a growing feeling of dread, I fling the cabinets open. Everything seems to be there. The cosmetics and bath salts I bought are neatly stacked. Back in her bedroom, I do the same with her closet. The clothes, shoes, jewelry, books, and other knick-knacks I got for Valentina are there. Still, something is wrong. I know it in my gut.

Standing there, absorbing the chill from the descending night, the molecules of my body go flat and cold. An overpowering sense of abandonment fills me. Then the fear hits, hot and liquid, rippling over me in a wave. If Magda did something to Valentina… If she hurt her… I swear to God I'll kill my mother.

Making my way down the hallway to my office, I dig my phone from my pocket and call Rhett.

He replies with a cheerful, "What's up, boss?"

"In my office. Now. Bring Quincy."

I hang up and rush through my office door, expecting an army or Magda, but what I see is a sheet of white paper on my desk.

All of my attention hones in on that scrap of paper. Instinct tells me everything that has just derailed in my life is summarized on there, and for three whole seconds I can't make myself move. I pinch my eyes shut, brace myself, and round my desk. It's in her handwriting. My hand shakes as I lift it to the light and read.

I can't honor my promise. I hope you'll forgive me.

Goddammit, no!

I crumple the paper in my fist and drag my hands through my hair. I feel like falling to my knees, but somehow I remain standing. Of all the things she could've done, this is the last I expected. Charlie means too much to her. My feelings are a mess of tangled, electric wires. I'm about to short-circuit, explode, and burn out. I want to find and hurt her, make her pay for her betrayal and for what she's putting me through. I'll take the skin off her backside and drag her right back. This time, I'll chain her to my bed until she understands the meaning of *property*.

Rhett and Quincy chase through the door, saving me from my dark thoughts. They both still at the state of me.

"What's up?" Quincy asks carefully.

I lower my hands to my hips. It's hard for me to speak. For a moment, I consider thrusting the paper at them, but I don't want them to witness Valentina's intimate rejection. I swallow, breathe in, and say, "Valentina's gone."

Quincy pales. "What do you mean, gone?"

It takes every ounce of strength I have to push out the words, and when I finally do, my mouth is bitter. "She ran."

Rhett's eyes go wide. "Fuck, no."

Quincy is the first to get to his senses. "Did she say something? Has someone seen her go?"

"She left a note." Since Quincy seems more in control than Rhett, I say, "Go to the guardhouse. Ask them when she left and how. With what? Did she go with a suitcase? Pull the tape. I want to know every fucking detail. Not a word to Magda or her guards." A dribble of cold sweat runs down my spine as I say it. This is the opportunity Magda has been waiting for.

Quincy is out of my office in a flash. I'm tripping over my thoughts in the orders I'm thinking up for Rhett. Track her phone. Pull her bank records for the last six hours. Put out word with our informants. Before I can voice anything, Rhett steps forward. Something in his demeanor makes me pause. His shoulders are hunched and his eyebrows drawn together.

"Gabriel…" he starts.

This is going to be bad.

He pauses and licks his lips. "There's something you should know."

Those words make me want to kill him. He knows something and withheld it from me. I stand quietly, waiting for him to continue.

"I think…" He lowers his head. "Maybe… I don't know for sure, but…"

My patience snaps. "Spit it out or I'll shoot a hole in your goddamn tongue."

He takes a deep breath and faces me. "Valentina asked me to buy her a pregnancy test this morning."

I reel in shock. "What?" I heard him fine, but I can't process what he told me. "Valentina thinks she's pregnant?" I say more to myself than him.

"If you think about it, she's been acting kind of emotional, lately."

I let the observation sink in. She's been through a lot with her accident and giving up her studies. Naturally, I attributed her sadness to those events. Now that Rhett mentions it, Valentina has been more tearful than usual. When I touched her last night, her breasts were bigger and tender, but I blamed her pending period for the changes.

Fuck me.

There are too many feelings assaulting me to make sense of anything--pride, joy, fear, hot fucking raving mad anger. If Valentina is pregnant and she ran, it can only be for one reason. I know how negative and depressed the women in my life felt about their planned pregnancies. How much worse must she feel about an unexpected one? She doesn't want the baby, and she's going to get rid of it.

Even if I expected the reaction, I'm filled with rage and heart-ripping anxiety. The rage is not for her, but for me. I could've prevented this disaster. I should've locked her up. I should've noticed when her disposition changed. I could've prevented her from killing our child, the child who is supposed to save her.

Pain rips through my insides when I think about losing an unborn baby, but I have no one but myself to blame. This is all my doing. I swapped her birth control pills for placebos. I deceived her in the most despicable way, and I'll take full responsibility for her actions. No matter if she's no longer pregnant, she's still mine, and I want her back.

"Gabriel?" Rhett has taken two steps back and is standing at a safe distance closer to the door.

"Search every trashcan on the property." There's a good chance Valentina took the pregnancy test with her, but I need to be sure. "Find that test and bring it to me."

I'm clear enough in my fucked-up state to realize I may be jumping the gun. There's a chance she's not pregnant, but I have to consider all options.

When he's gone, I call the guardhouse and bark out commands. I don't want the news to leak to Magda prematurely. Eventually, she'll find out. Until then, I need all the time I can get or Valentina is dead. I punch in the details to activate the tracker software installed on my phone. Her tracker is goddamn dead, which can only mean she destroyed the phone. To be sure, I dial her number, but it goes straight onto voicemail.

The day I kicked down Valentina's door in Berea, I gave her my phone to call her friend, the vet she's been working for. I saved the number on my phone when she was done. Scrolling to Kris' name, I dial the number with a shaking hand.

Her voice comes tired over the phone. "Kris, here. How can I help?"

"Gabriel Louw."

She goes quiet at the mention of my name.

"Is Valentina with you?"

"Why would she be?" Panic enters her tone. "What's wrong?"

I believe her. Her reaction is too genuine to be acting. "Is Charlie there?"

"You know he is."

"I think you better check."

"Even if he wasn't, I wouldn't tell you."

"Listen to me, and listen carefully. This is not the time for games. Valentina's life may be at stake."

"You useless son of a bitch. I'll bust your balls." She carries on with elaborate and colorful insults that are interrupted by a lot of barking. I assume she's walking through the clinic to the house. "I'll mince you up and eat you alive."

"Kris?" I keep my voice calm. "We both care about Valentina, each in our own way. Help me to help her."

She grows quiet at that, and for a moment, so do I. It's the first time I've admitted to anyone but myself that I care about Valentina. The words shock me, but they also free me. It's out in the open. No more hiding.

She inhales and exhales. The air that leaves her mouth is shaky. Her verdict is short and sweet. It has a sense of terrible finality. "He's gone."

Jesus.

I raise my face to the ceiling and search for calmness within myself.

"What the hell is going on?" she shouts.

"Is there a note?"

I can hear her footsteps clacking through the house. "No. Nothing." She's shuffling things around. Something hits the floor with a thud. "Fuck-all. All Charlie's stuff is here."

"Stay calm. I'll find her. Do me a favor. Call me on this number if you hear anything from her."

"Why will I give you shit?"

"Believe me, right now, I'm her only chance."

"The sad thing is I do."

I cut the call just as Rhett reenters my office, a zip lock bag in his hand. He holds it out to me. "We found it."

His solemn eyes tell me the news even before I reach for the proof. Two blue lines.

The air leaves my lungs. My weak leg twitches, and I have to grab the edge of the desk to maintain my balance.

I was right. Valentina could only have left for one reason––to get rid of a baby she doesn't want. It may just kill her if Magda has her way. It's the exact opposite of what I intended. My fucked-up, ingenious plan backfired.

Quincy comes rushing back. Words fall like verbal diarrhea from his lips. "She left on foot four hours ago. All she had with her was an overnight bag. I tried not to raise suspicion, but the guards know something's going on. I'm afraid…" He trails off as his eyes land on the bag in my hand. "Fuck. Is that what I think it is?"

"What now, Gabriel?" Rhett asks, his expression concerned. "What do we do?"

I don't hesitate in my answer. "We get her back."

"You better hurry," Quincy says. "The guards made noise. By now, Magda knows."

The stick with the evidence of Valentina's conception in hand, I march to Magda's office.

She sits behind her desk, scribbling on a notepad. "Valentina ran." Her expression is smug. "We're going after her with everything we've got. A team is already on the way to her brother."

"Stop them."

She throws down her pen. "Excuse me?"

I drop the evidence of my child in front of her. It takes her one second to connect the dots. In her eyes, I see her understanding. We both know I did it on purpose, and we both know why.

She pinches her lips together and leans back in her chair. "So, this is how you get what you want."

"Call off your men."

"You made a big mistake."

"That's your opinion, and you know I don't care about what you or anybody else thinks. Valentina is going to be the mother of my child. From now on, she's family. That wipes away her debt and keeps her and anyone remotely connected to her safe."

I don't say what I suspect, that the baby may already be gone. It doesn't matter whether I bring her back pregnant or not. Eventually, she *will* have my child, even if it takes years and thousands of rands of fertility treatments. I don't care. Somewhere in the back of my mind I know it's a lie. I do care. I do care if she wants to be a mother. More than that, I care if she wants *my* child.

Unfortunately, when it comes to life and death, we don't always have the luxury of choice or answers to our questions. Maybe it's better that I don't know the answers. I already know I'm a monster, and she hates me. What I'm doing to her is selfish, wrong, and immoral, but I've never claimed to be a good man. I wanted her from the moment I saw her. I still do. More than ever. Letting her go is the one thing I'm not capable of.

Magda is still regarding me with contempt. I'll go as far as to say with hatred. Even as she speaks, she picks up her phone and dials a number. "You foolish boy. This goes to show men can never be trusted. It's too easy to lead them around by their dicks." A ringtone sounds on her phone, followed by a curt answer. "Scott, turn back. The hit on Charles is off." She listens to a reply. "We still want the girl, but bring her in unharmed." She cuts the call and glares at me. "You do realize you've given all your power away. Now, she holds the power over *you*. I hope this makes you happy."

It's been a long time since Valentina took power over me, and a man like me can never be happy. I'll settle for being content, and I'll be that when I get my precious property back.

My mother needs to understand one thing. "If a hair on her head is harmed, I'll take it as a personal attack on me and my family. All gloves will come off."

"This can never have a happy ending."

I don't want to hear my mother's prophecy, because it hits the instinctive knowledge inside me with a bullseye. "Just make sure your men understand. She's my responsibility. Anything they find, anything they hear, sniff, guess, or divine, I want to know."

"You will. I owe you a *fuck you* for getting tangled up between that whore's legs and screwing this up for the family."

I inch closer to the desk, towering over Magda. "Careful. You're talking about the mother of my child. This is your last warning. Insult her again and you won't like the consequences."

The smile that cracks her thick layer of foundation is artificial. "I'd love to see how you explain this one to Carly."

It's a low blow. Since considering the possibility that Valentina may be pregnant, it's something I've contemplated. I'll have to lie to my daughter, telling her some rosy shade of pink bullshit story about Valentina and I falling in love, when in reality nothing can be further from the truth. There's no way to ensure Valentina will keep her mouth shut about the circumstances of how we ended up in bed. I seduced her, but I did it against her will. There's little difference between my kind of seduction and force. For all I know, she'll take revenge in telling Carly how I stole, blackmailed, and tortured her for nothing but my pleasure, only so I can feed my sick addiction to giving her pain and orgasms. Her tears and pleas make me hard, but her climaxes make me explode. The combination of the two--her pain and pleasure--is the biggest aphrodisiac. Beyond that physical part, something else has started to develop, these *things* she makes me feel, like the agony that's slicing through my gut right now.

"I'll deal with it," I say bluntly. "No one says a word to Carly but me."

"Oh," she snickers, "I wasn't going to volunteer. I'll leave the unpleasant task to you."

"Good. I'm glad we understand each other." I walk to the door and turn. My smile is as cold as her eyes. "Congratulations. You're going to be a grandmother again."

I don't wait for her reaction. I go back to my study to start my own search.

It becomes apparent I have nothing to go on. Valentina destroyed her phone in no place other than that godforsaken area where she used to live, and she hasn't touched the money in her account. Even though she couldn't afford a plane ticket, I set up a search for travelers by plane and bus. Trains going farther than Pretoria are non-existent, so that leaves me with private taxis, but none in the Johannesburg area has crossed the city borders during the last few hours. My hackers plant bugs in electronic banking and medical servers to raise a flag if her and Charlie's names pop up anywhere on the system. I inform my network of colleagues and police informants to be on the lookout and offer a huge reward for any information on her whereabouts. Then I drive to Kris' house, who's shell shocked. She shows me Valentina's text when I finally convince her I'm only trying to keep Valentina safe, and demands to know why Valentina ran. I don't tell her about the baby. For now, it's best that only Magda, my bodyguards, and I know.

I take Rhett and drive to Berea. We knock on the door of every bar and business in a five-mile radius of her old place, but no one knows anything. By the time night falls, I'm sick. My concern is so great I can't even hate her for it. I only want her back. She's got no money, and the world is a very unsafe place. Valentina may be cold, hungry, or scared. She may even be in danger. Without money, her only option is a backstreet abortion, and those don't come without health risks. Feeling defeated, I get behind the wheel and drive to an unbearably empty home.

2
———

Valentina

The drive is strenuous. Because of the state of the car, it takes longer to cross the country at a slower speed than the legal limit. My back aches, and Charlie is getting restless, but after seven hours the lights of Durban finally come into view. Just as well. We're almost out of fuel. I have no idea where I'm going. I've only been here twice on holiday with my parents as a child.

A sign indicates the beachfront. The main beach will be much too dangerous with the criminals hanging around. I opt for one in a suburb and follow the road to a dark and empty parking lot. We can't stay here in full sight. It's asking for trouble. After circling the parking once, I find a spot where I can drive off the tarmac under some overhanging trees. The hiding place isn't perfect, but it will have to do. I can't go another kilometer.

Charlie makes a lot of excited noise when he realizes we've reached our destination. I have to silence him like I did at home when we hid from the mob. Knowing he needs to stretch his legs after the long sit, I unlock the doors and help him crawl out from under the dense vegetation into the night. The tropical climate is warm and humid.

Hand in hand, we walk down the steep path to the beach. I use my penlight to illuminate our way, keeping vigilant and watching out for danger. You never know who lurks in the dark.

"Shh," I say. "We're not supposed to be on the beach at night. This is our secret, okay?"

Charlie nods enthusiastically. "Se-secret."

We stop at the bottom of the stone path to take in the scenery. The moon shines over the water, casting a light over the white foam of the waves. I take a second to register the salty air and the crush of the water as it curls and breaks.

"Do you remember the ocean, Charlie?"

"Swi-swim."

"It's night."

His tone becomes insistent. "Swi-swim."

"Tomorrow, okay? It's too risky at night."

"Swi-swim!"

I take his arm. "First you need to sleep to build up your strength."

I utter a sigh of relief when he allows me to lead him back up the path. Near the top, we climb over the sand, already wet from dew, to relieve ourselves in the dunes. Certain that the parking lot is still empty, I take him back to the car. For a second, he freezes.

"N-no."

"We're not going to drive anymore. I promise."

He shakes his curls. "No-no."

"Hey," I nudge him with an elbow, "this is our big adventure. We're camping."

"Ca-camping."

"Yes." I take his hand and guide him back to the car. "Isn't this exciting?"

I put the seats down and settle him in as best as I can, rolling my fleece into a pillow for his head and covering him with my jacket. When his soft snores fill the car, I allow my façade to drop. Pretending is exhausting. I don't know if we'll get through the night unscathed or where tomorrow's food will come from, but worrying ahead is useless, so I simply focus on getting through the night.

MORNING IS SURPRISINGLY COLD. I shiver in my T-shirt. My body aches from the uncomfortable position. Too wary of the possible dangers, I haven't slept a wink. Charlie shifts, yawns, and gives me a bleary-eyed look.

I cup his cheek. "How did you sleep?"

He doesn't answer, but he doesn't have to. The dark circles under his eyes say it all.

We crawl out from under the bushes. I bring my toilet bag from the car and find a garden tap at the top of the path to the beach where we can wash our faces and brush our teeth. I give Charlie the toothbrush I bought at Quick and help him with his grooming. Dressing behind a tree, I pull my bikini on under my dress and try not to think about the fact that Gabriel bought it for me. Charlie will have to swim in his underpants until I can make another plan.

"Hu–hungry."

"Me, too."

Not having enough money left for food, I let Charlie finish the apple from his snacks and fill up his empty soda bottle with water.

"Ready for more adventures?" I shade my face with a palm, looking up at the road that snakes past the houses to the top of the hill.

Charlie groans, but he follows as I start walking. After an hour, we hit the first small commercial area. It's a strip mall consisting of a grocery store, a Wimpy restaurant, a bank, a pharmacy, and a liquor store. I stop at every store to ask for a job, but as expected there's nothing available. With an unemployment rate of over forty percent and me not having formal qualifications or referral letters, I have zero percent chance of landing anything, not to mention that the affirmative action law isn't in my favor.

By midday, we hit another residential area and a beach. I'm famished, and Charlie is tired. We stop at a beach kiosk selling ice cream and hot dogs. I count out my last few cents on the counter, but it's not even enough to buy Charlie an ice cream.

The man waiting behind us in the queue clicks his tongue. "Eish," he says in the local dialect, "you look hungry, little miss."

I turn to look at him. He has brown, wrinkled skin, like the coloreds who are a mix between black and white.

He shuffles past us to the front, goes through his pockets, and takes out a bill, which he hands to the vendor. "Give this lady and man each a *boerewors* roll."

I gape at him, blinking back tears. From the state of his clothes and the way the soles of his shoes flap when he walks, he's worse off than us.

"No, please." I hold up a hand. "It's very kind, but I can't accept."

He makes a tsk-tsk noise and rumbles off something in Zulu to the man grilling beef sausages on the gas grill behind the counter.

Before I can protest again, the vendor places two *boerewors* rolls with all the trimmings in our hands.

I avert my eyes, ashamed that we robbed this poor man of a meal, but too starved to refuse him a second time. "Thank you."

"You're very welcome."

Charlie has already dug in. We sit down on a bench facing the sea to eat. The bread is toasted and the beef sausage thick and juicy with fat. The *chakalaka* sauce is dripping with onion, peppers, and tomato. It has just the right amount of chili to give it a bite without burning. Charlie devours his in seconds and licks every drop of sauce from his fingers. I finish half of mine and give him the rest.

The man who bought us lunch walks past, a bottle of Coca Cola under one arm and a loaf of bread under the other. A worn jacket with patches on the elbows stretches over his crooked back.

The stitches are visible where the fabric is pulling apart on the shoulders.

"Wait!" I jump up and run after him.

He turns and smiles. "Yes?"

"Do you have a number?" I wipe the windblown hair from my face. "I can call you when I get a job to repay you."

"Not necessary," he says with a shake of his salt-and-pepper head, "but you'll have a hard time finding anything here."

"You don't know of something?" I ask hopefully.

He laughs softly. "If I did, I would've told you."

"Thanks again for the food."

"Good luck." With a wave he's gone.

We're going to need more than luck.

To distract Charlie, I take him swimming. He hangs around in the shallow water until his lips are blue and his teeth are chattering before he lets me towel him dry. For a while, we lie in the sand, looking up at the clear, blue sky. It will be dark in a couple of hours. We need to head back to the car. While we walk I talk and sing to keep Charlie's mind off the effort, simultaneously watching out for unfavorable elements. At least here, in the residential area, we're safer.

At the strip mall, we sit down on the lawn of a small park facing the back of the shops to rest. This is what I tell Charlie, but I have an ulterior motive. When a waiter at the Wimpy brings out the trash bags, I tell Charlie to stay put and run across the road.

"Excuse me," I call as I near.

The man looks up. He has a skin as smooth and dark as oil and his apron is a pristine white.

"Are there any jobs here?"

He shakes his head. "*Aikona.*"

"Maybe some leftover food?"

He shakes his head again and dumps the bags in the trashcan.

"There must be *something* someone didn't finish. I'm not fussy."

"People take home what they don't eat in doggie bags." He pushes past me, heading for the door.

I grab his arm. "Please. Don't make me go through the trash."

He jerks free and slams the door in my face.

Swallowing my pride, I look around, and when I see no one, I lift the lid on the trashcan and tear open the bag on the top. The inside is a mashed-up version of breakfasts, lunches, and dinners with splatterings of coffee and milkshake. I push back my sleeve and plunge my arm in up to my elbow, but all I grab is mush. It will be easier to take out the bag, but it's heavier than I thought. I battle and grunt, and just as I'm about to free the bag from the bin, a hand closes around my throat. Uttering a shriek, I drop my loot.

"This is my beat," a voice growls.

I look up into a pair of bloodshot eyes. The man holding me stinks of brandy. His clothes are oily and his hair and beard dirty.

"Sorry," I mumble, battling to get the word out with the pressure he's putting on my windpipe.

From the corner of my eye, I watch Charlie. My heart sinks when he gets to his feet, his face scrunched up in fear.

"I didn't know." I lift my hands. "I won't come back here. Just let me go. My brother is on his way, and he's going to hurt you. I don't want trouble."

He glances over at Charlie. When he sees my brother's bulky frame moving toward us, he releases his grip on me. I scurry away as fast as I can, intercepting Charlie halfway.

"Va–Val?"

Charlie would never hurt a fly, but my threat worked.

"Let's go," I say, taking his arm and heading back to the road.

We have to wait an hour before the last visitor, a man who was jogging on the beach with his dog, leaves the parking lot where our car is hidden. Only then do we get into the car and settle for the night. Thankfully, Charlie falls asleep quickly, but I'm not so lucky. My mind works overtime. We need money. The only plausible solutions are to find a job, rob a bank, or beg. I don't want to beg or steal, but work is hard to come by.

The surprising part is I still miss Gabriel. I miss his arms around me and his mouth on my skin. My body needs him with more intensity than ever. If he was here, he would've kept me safe, like he protected me from Tiny, but what will he do to my baby? Will he blame me? Or hate me? Will he believe it was an accident, that I didn't plan this pregnancy to manipulate my way out of my debt? No. He won't believe me. A man like Gabriel never slips up, and he won't understand failure. There was a good reason why he gave me the birth control pills. He won't want this baby. He won't be forgiving or understanding. Yet, lying here, staring at the roof of our stolen car, I want to run both from and to him. He's the only man I simultaneously crave and fear.

A noise pulls me from my reverie. It sounds like an empty can being kicked on the tar. I look over to Charlie. *Please don't wake up and panic.* If he makes a sound, we'll be discovered. The metal clang becomes louder. Laughter follows. I turn on my stomach to peer through the back window. Four men are walking our way. They're kicking a beer can between them. The red end of a cigarette glows in the corner of one of the men's mouths.

I close my eyes. *Don't let them venture into the bushes.* My heart starts galloping as they come nearer and nearer, making a raucous racket. The walking and swimming must've exhausted Charlie, because he sleeps through the noise. My nails dig into my palms as I wait for them to leave, but they sit down on the side of the lot, and from the way they make themselves comfortable, they may stay for a while. They talk and talk until the conversation turns into an argument, but I don't understand what they're saying. They're speaking in Zulu. One of the men puts a six-pack of beer in the center of their circle, and they each crack open a can. Another chooses a song on his phone and plays it at top volume. Charlie stirs, but he doesn't open his eyes.

They're getting wilder, laughing and smoking pot. The smell is unmistakable. When they take out flip knives and start throwing them at stray cats, I break out into a cold sweat. On top of that, my bladder is full, and I don't know for how much longer I can hold. As long as the men are here, we're trapped. The feeling is nauseating. Right now, I'll do anything to be back in Gabriel's strong arms, except sacrifice my baby.

After a long time, one gets up and walks into the bushes, heading straight for us.

My throat closes up. I stop breathing. A short distance from our car, he stops and opens his fly. Aiming straight at us, he relieves himself in the bushes.

Don't let him see us.

A tilt of his head, one missing leaf or the shine of the moon on the body of the car, and we'll be discovered.

He shakes himself dry, zips up, and, to my utter relief, turns back to his buddies.

My body is a shaking mass of nerves. I'm shivering all over, feeling cold to my core. I stay awake, hardly breathing, watching their every move. After what feels like an eternity, they get up and walk away. The air leaves my lungs in a gush of relief. To be on the safe side, I wait ten minutes before I dare it out of the car and near the lot. There's no sign of the men. I make quick work of emptying my bladder behind a bush and flick on my penlight. On the tarmac lies a burned spoon caked with blood, an empty plastic bank bag, and several dented beer cans. We can't stay here. It's only a matter of time before we're caught, raped, and murdered.

THE NEWSPAPER HEADLINE at the stand we pass the next morning doesn't help to ease my nerves. A family was tortured to death in their home last night for their television and laptop. Charlie walks next to me, grumpy and sulky. This is no joyride for him, either. I wish I could talk to him and ask his advice. I'll give anything for a shoulder to lean on, for someone to share a small part of my burden. Determined not to sleep in the car, we walk farther today in my quest of finding a job. At the grocery store, I manage to beg a few expired loafs of bread, and this keeps us going for two days.

When Charlie swims, I rinse his clothes and let them dry in the sun. At night, we sleep hidden between the tall grass in the dunes. It's more comfortable, but colder and wet. Charlie develops a cold, but I refuse to give up hope. More than once I'm tempted to withdraw money from the bank––I still have the monthly allowance Gabriel paid me––but the minute I do, Gabriel will know where we are. I may as well sign our death warrants.

After a week, there's no more pretending that this is a holiday. Charlie doesn't believe me, any longer.

"I want to go ba–back," he begs.

I pat his leg. "Soon." What else can I say?

Another week of going hungry and washing under cold beach showers, and I finally hit the jackpot. We're outside a dry-cleaning store when a Chinese man drags a woman out by her collar, screaming in Mandarin. I don't understand a word, but from the shirt with the burned hole he holds up as he shouts, it's not difficult to gather what the rift is about. He goes back inside and returns with a handbag that he throws at the poor woman. She cries and begs in English, saying she's sorry, but the man is a statue with his finger pointing north. When she realizes her begging has no effect, the woman leaves with hunched shoulders, clutching her bag to her chest.

I jump at the opportunity. An hour later, I'm hired. The only reason the man, Ru, is taking me on is because he can pay me cash under the table. This is his way of avoiding social charges, and it suits me. There's no money trail that leads to me. The pay is low, but he lets Charlie stay with me while I work, and for half of the money he pays me per month, he gives us a room with a toilet and basin in the back. It has a door exiting onto the street so we can come and go freely when the shop is closed.

The room is dirty, but with Charlie's help we clean it with the products from the shop, scrubbing away fungus in the basin and grime in the toilet, the origins of which I don't want to consider. The mattress is stained with coffee and semen, but I cut plastic trash bags open and tape them around the bed.

The following day, we go back to get my clothes from the car, but the long walk isn't worth the effort. Someone broke into the car and stole our belongings, down to our soap and toothbrushes. When I tell Ru about our misfortune, he allows us to take clothes from the box filled with unclaimed dry-cleaning.

The money I earn is barely enough to feed two people. Our new lifestyle isn't so much different from our old one in Berea, except back then I still had my dream of making a better future for us. My dream may be dead, but my hope's still alive. We'll get through this. I work long hours, sweating over the ironing board while Charlie plays solitaire at the plastic table in the corner we use for lunch breaks. The rhythm is harsh, and my pregnancy doesn't help. I've never been more tired in my life.

I soon discover another reason why Ru's happy not to have me employed on a formal contract. He can treat me however he likes. He makes me work twelve hours per day instead of the legal eight, but I don't dare complain. It's hard to put one foot in front of the other after ironing from six in the morning to seven at night with an hour lunch break. Most evenings, I fall asleep the minute I hit the mattress next to Charlie.

After a few more weeks, three months to be exact, my jeans are stretching over my stomach, and I can't fasten the button any longer. There's nothing else in the box of unclaimed clothes to fit me, so I keep the two ends of the waistband together with an elastic band I wind through the buttonhole and around the button. Some women are lucky and don't show much for the first four or five months of their first pregnancies, but I'm not one of them. I have a definite bump. If my boss noticed, he doesn't say anything.

Nausea hits me on and off at all times of the day and night.

Sometimes I vomit, and sometimes it's only a sickening sensation in the pit of my stomach that lasts all day. I'm losing instead of gaining weight, which must be because of the vomiting. Our future may not look bright, right now, but I can work on it. We're alive. All I have to do is get through this pregnancy and have a healthy baby.

It's in April, during the first week of my second trimester, when I hand a well-groomed lady her dry-cleaning that I faint.

I come to my senses lying on my back on the floor. Someone is slapping my cheek. Shit, it stings. Ru is bent over me, speaking in loud, angry words.

"Stop shouting at her," the lady says. "She needs a doctor."

I push onto my elbows. "I'm fine."

"You're not." The woman looks down to where my sweater has moved up, exposing the pants I keep closed with an elastic band. "You're pregnant."

This evokes a new marathon of words from my boss. He spurts them at me with animated hand signs, which mostly points at my stomach.

The woman pushes him away. "Stop it right this second or I'll call social services."

This shuts him up.

"You need to see a doctor," the woman says.

"I'm fine, really." I let her help me into a sitting position.

She purses her lips while studying me. "I'm taking you."

"No, I just need a minute."

"Don't worry, I'm paying."

I want to die of shame, but concern for my baby overrides my pride. "I have to tell my brother where I'm going, or he'll worry."

"I'll wait."

I tell Charlie to stay in our room and lock the door. When I get back to the front shop, Ru starts protesting again.

"I'm reporting you," the woman says, waving a finger in his face.

Unhappy but pushed into a corner, he lets me go, leaving him in the lurch in the middle of a workday.

"I'm Cynthia," she says as we get into her luxurious car.

I don't reply, praying she won't think I'm returning her kindness with rudeness. The less anyone knows, the better.

She drives me to a fancy clinic and introduces me to a lady friend who's a gynecologist. When the receptionist asks for my identity document, I start to argue, but she tells me it's standard procedure, and I can't see a doctor if she hasn't registered my details. I don't have a choice but to hand mine over. Cynthia gives the receptionist my address, and when I say I don't have a phone, she gives her the number of Ru's shop.

As if understanding my fear, Cynthia pats my hands. "Don't worry. This clinic is very discreet. No one will know you were here."

After an ultrasound and blood tests, the doctor tells me I'm fine and my baby is healthy, but I'm undernourished. She prescribes vitamins and a protein shake, which my Samaritan pays for at the pharmacy.

"Thank you," I say when Cynthia drops me off at the shop. "I don't know how to repay you."

"You've been pressing my husband's shirts for over three months. Besides, I was going for an expensive lunch date with a friend. I'm happy to have used the money better."

Not having more words, I exit the car and make my way back inside where I'm met with a very angry Ru.

He points at my stomach. "No baby. No want no baby. Go." He waves his hands at me. "Out. Go."

My hope shatters, and my world ends. "I'm okay, I promise. It won't interfere with my work."

"Out. Tomorrow. No baby." He pushes me toward the backroom. "No baby. Tomorrow. Gone."

I unlock the door and stumble inside in tears, finding Charlie on the bed playing solitaire. I look around the shabby but clean room with the cheap sheets I bought from the flea market and the boxes covered with colorful cloth that serves as our table. I don't even know if the car is still in the bushes by the beach. Everything we had is gone, including my job.

"We'll be fine," I say, brushing my hand over Charlie's head as I walk past him to the two-plate stove. "How about scrambled eggs for dinner?"

Charlie loves scrambled eggs. I turn my back on him so he doesn't see my hopeless tears. Gripping the counter, I let them flow. It's my fault we're in this mess. If I hadn't slipped up with my birth control, Charlie would've been safe, warm, and in bed with a full belly. I have to find a new way of putting a roof over our heads and food on the table, but I'm so, so tired. I don't have the strength left to fight this never-ending battle of survival. How long before I let my brother and baby down? Tomorrow, we're back in the street. Oh, God, what am I going to do?

Silent sobs shake my shoulders as I lift my eyes to heaven and pray for a miracle.

Something.

Anything.

Gabriel

IT'S BEEN three months and a week since Valentina ran. I thought I knew agony when Sylvia left, but nothing compares to this torture. Not knowing is the worst. Is Valentina alive? Is she well? When I'm not looking for her, I get through the days by focusing on business and through the weekends by spending time with Carly.

The first breakthrough comes from Magda. I'm pouring over our financial statements when she walks into my study and throws a photo of a vehicle number plate on my desk.

"This is how she left."

I drop everything to look at the picture. For the first time in months, my frozen heart starts to thaw. My fingers tighten on the glossy paper. "How did you find this?"

"I found Jerry."

This reminds me how powerful my mother's network is. I've been trying for months to locate that orange-haired mongrel with no success.

"Where did you find him? How?"

"Does it matter?" She perches on the edge of my desk. "Connections."

Valentina hasn't touched her money, which leaves only one explanation. "He gave Valentina a stolen car. False number plate?"

"Exactly."

"And?" I hold my breath.

"Nothing so far, but I've put out word that we're looking for a car of this description. I have a few friends in the traffic department."

Since our initial argument, Magda's become a lot more cooperative. As she came to acknowledge that Valentina could potentially bear me a child, she's been putting her full weight behind the effort of tracking Valentina. For the first time ever, I have the sense that our family--at least my mother and I--are standing together. It doesn't make us like each other, but our tolerance levels are higher.

Despite my concern and anger, I admire Valentina for staying hidden for so long. The odds have never been in her favor. It was only a matter of time, and that time is now.

A DAY LATER, we have information from the Kwazulu Natal Traffic Department. The good news is they found the vehicle. The bad news is it's a burnt-out wreck. Today's flights to all airports in Natal are fully booked, and I can't wait until tomorrow.

An hour later, Rhett, Quincy, and I are on our way to Durban. I take the Jaguar while they follow with the Merc so we can split up if needed. I instruct my bodyguards to talk to the people residing in the area where the car has been found, and I visit the site. What I see raises the hair on my arms. The car has been hidden behind some bushes under trees, something clever that Valentina would do, but the state of it makes my skin crawl. There's dissolution in the vandalised carcass. The tires are missing, the seats have been ripped out, the dash torn to pieces, and the windows shattered. In the midst of the chaos, in a circle of black, burnt grass stands the broken framework of the car. There's no telling how long ago the destruction took place, but the pungent odor of soot still coats the soil. Is her body somewhere in the bushes, vandalized, too? Even if Magda's contact at the police department ensured me the area has been thoroughly searched, I can't get the ghost of that thought out of my head.

Quincy and Rhett join me an hour later. An old man living in a beachfront house saw a young woman and man matching Valentina and Charlie's descriptions hanging around the beach, but it's been days since he last saw them. I'm about to search the dunes when a text message comes in from my hacker.

Bingo.

Valentina Haynes visited a private clinic. *Today.* I stare at her address and phone number that appear on my screen, waiting for the next line to say it's a hoax, but no other information follows.

"What is it?" Quincy asks.

"Rhett, Quincy, bring the car. Follow me."

Rhett's voice is both hopeful and frightened. "You found her?"

I'm not going to jinx my luck by saying yes. I make my way with long strides to my car. Rhett catches up with me as I open the door.

He places a hand on my arm. "Gabriel?"

There are a thousand questions in the way he speaks my name, and I understand each of them. I know what he's asking. "I'm not going to hurt her. If they're both there, take Charlie for a drink until I give you further instructions."

He drops his hand, letting me get into the car.

I send the address to Anton, my PI, with instructions to get information on the dwelling. I want to know what kind of building it is, who owns it, and if tenants are registered.

The few kilometers I drive to the address on my GPS are the longest of my life. Every single traffic light is red and seems to take forever to change. It's early evening when we pull up in front of a dry-cleaning store. The store is already closed. My spirits sink. I pull up the information Anton sent to my phone. The business is owned by a Chinese immigrant. If he gave Valentina a job, she's not registered as an employee in his records. I get out and motion for Quincy and Rhett to follow, weapons pulled in case. The area isn't as bad as the city center, but you never know. If need be, I'll wait out here all night until the shop opens in the morning. It won't hurt to look around in the meantime.

We move around the building. A light shines from the single window in the backroom, but a curtain obscures the view. My pulse racing, I test the doorknob. Locked. A nod at Rhett communicates my command. He knows what to do. Stepping back, he takes aim.

3

Valentina

Wiping my eyes with the back of my hand, I take a few deep breaths and get a hold on myself. One thing at a time. Dinner first and then packing. I'm breaking the eggs in a bowl when a shadow moves across the curtained window. My heartbeat picks up and warning prickles pop over my skin. Maybe it was someone passing by in the street. Holding my breath, I prick up my ears and sharpen my gaze. No sound comes from outside. There's no further movement. Several seconds pass with nothing happening. I'm almost letting the air out of my lungs in relief when the doorknob turns.

The action is quiet and ominous. Someone is trying to break in.

I can't move. Escape. We need to escape, but the door to the shop is locked, and Ru is the only one with a key. Five more seconds and then the adrenalin takes effect. I drop the whisk, looking for a weapon. At the same time, I gauge Charlie's position. He's still on the bed, which puts him closer to the door. Grabbing the vegetable knife, I put myself with quiet steps between Charlie and the door. Thank God for Rhett's self-defense training. My experience is limited, and my physical state is weak. My only chance is to catch our attacker off-guard. As soon as the door opens, I'll stab. My hand holding the insufficient weapon shakes. Charlie looks up and notices the knife. Before I can silence him, he yells. His scream breaks my concentration. A loud thud falls on the door. The doorframe rattles. Whoever is outside now knows we know he's there. The element of surprise is lost. There's no more breaking in quietly. He's kicking down our door.

When the door flies into the room a horrible spell of déjà vu washes over me. For the second time tonight I'm frozen, but this time I'm frozen in a moment in the past. Like in my memory, Gabriel steps over the broken wood into the room. Rhett and Quincy are on his heels, but I can only focus on the man I ran from and the gun in his hand.

He found us.

He's going to kill us.

Charlie stares at the three men, confusion marring his features. Since our first violent encounter with Gabriel, after all the visits to Kris' place, Charlie considers Gabriel a friend. Quincy and Rhett block the only exit while Gabriel crosses the floor with his characteristic limp. He wears a black suit and white shirt without a tie. His body is as broad and big as I remember, and there's menace in every line of each rigid muscle. The dull light of the room isn't enough to wash out the scars on his cheek. He missed a haircut or two. Wisps of curls reach his ears.

He stops in front of me and looks down at me with the darkest expression I've ever seen. From the way his chest heaves, whatever is going on inside his head is intense. Retribution is intense. So is killing. There's only one thing I can do to try and save our lives.

I fall down on my knees and fold my arms around his legs. Looking up at him with all the begging I'm capable of, I whisper, "Please, Gabriel."

The gun in his hand shakes.

I can't control my shivering. Even my voice trembles. "It's not Charlie's fault. Please don't hurt him."

"Come on, buddy," Rhett says, taking Charlie's arm, "let's go grab a milkshake."

"Milk–milkshake." Charlie doesn't hesitate. He trusts Gabriel and therefore his friends.

They're going to shoot my brother in the back alley. I start to cry, hugging Gabriel's legs harder. "Please don't hurt him. I'll do anything, anything you want."

His stance is passive as he regards me. The only movement is a tick in his temple. "They're just taking him for a drink."

So that Gabriel can shoot me without Charlie bearing witness?

Rhett and Quincy exit the room with my brother, leaving me alone with Gabriel. My tears fall faster. My pride won't let me grovel for myself, but I'll do anything for my baby. Degrading myself like I've never done, I kneel down farther and kiss his feet, my tears spoiling his expensive shoes.

"Please, Gabriel, I beg you. Please, don't kill us. I'm sorry. I'm so, so sorry. I'm sorry for running, but I didn't have a choice."

My breath catches in fear when he grips my hair and guides my head up to meet his eyes again. Caressing my scalp with the barrel of the gun, he takes a plastic bag from his pocket and dangles it in front of my face. "Is this why you ran?"

As my eyes focus on the object, an involuntary gasp escapes my throat. He knows. I lift my gaze slowly back to his. The ice in his blue eyes pierces my heart.

I shake my head, forcing out through dry lips, "I didn't fall pregnant on purpose. I swear to God. Gabriel, you have to believe me. I don't know how it happened, but I promise you it was an accident."

He hooks his hands under my arms and pulls me to my feet. His voice is quiet. Dejected, almost. "I believe you."

I sag in his arms. How can he be so blasé? The life I carry means nothing to him. He's still going to kill me. The only question remaining is how. Gathering inhumane strength, I push away and stand up straight. "Are you going to shoot me?"

He regards me with a strange light in his eyes. "No, Valentina, I'm not going to shoot you."

I lift my chin a fraction, ignoring the warm tears that trickle down my cheeks and drip on my sweater. "How are you going to do it?"

"Do what?"

"Kill me. Strangling? A knife? Poison? Or will you break my neck?"

The ice in his eyes splinters. The fragments turn dark. "I didn't say I was going to kill you."

My thin bravery slips. "What then?" I throw the words at him. "Torture me?"

"I prefer to call it punishment." He grabs my face and digs his fingers into my cheeks. "For running. For putting your life in danger. For not talking to me before stupidly fleeing."

More tears spill from my eyes, running over his fingers. "I thought you wouldn't believe me. I knew you'd be angry about the baby."

His hold slackens. "I *am* angry about the baby." His shoulders drop as he lets me go. "You should've talked to me."

He'll force me to do what I feared all along.

"What now?" I whisper.

"Now I take you back to where you belong. We'll work through the rest when we're home."

Meaning he'll make me get an abortion. Cupping my hands over my stomach, I take two steps back.

"I beg you, Gabriel." My lips tremble violently. "Please, don't hurt my baby."

When the last word leaves my mouth, the moment freezes. Gabriel's eyes widen, and his face pales, the color making the embossed scars on his cheek stand out with an angry red. Time stretches as he stares at me in shock. The horror I never wanted to see is etched on his face, giving me insight into his soul. No, he wasn't taking me home for an abortion. He hoped I would've taken care of it, by now. He's disappointed the problem is still here, growing in my belly.

The spell keeping him immobile breaks, and he limps back to me. We're two broken people in a twisted situation with an innocent life trapped between us, a life I already love more than my own.

"Please," I beg when he towers over me, "I'll take your torture or punishment, and I promise to never run from you again, no matter what, if you let my baby live."

"*Our* baby," he says harshly.

He's right. It's his baby, too, but we aren't two people in a relationship who make consensual decisions. Gabriel decides.

"Yes, our baby," I agree. "Don't make me do something I can't live with. Please."

"You want this baby," he says with a tinge of disbelief, "knowing how it'll complicate your life?"

"It's not his fault he was conceived. It can't be undone, and I'll deal with it, whatever it takes."

His left eye jumps, and his nostrils flare. I have no idea what he's thinking, only that it's upsetting. I understand why he's unsettled. I know how this must look. Many young girls in my neighborhood got themselves knocked up to catch a man or to escape a debt. It must be hard for him to give me the benefit of the doubt and to battle the idea of becoming an unwilling father.

"I won't ask anything from you," I continue hastily, biting back my tears. "I won't make this problem yours. You have nothing to worry about. I don't expect your money or time. I will take care of everything. You won't even know the child is there."

All I see is incomprehension as he digests my words. For some reason, he seems confused––it's a lot to take in––but as he doesn't object immediately, I allow myself to feel hope.

"Please?" I ask softly.

"Why?" is all he asks in return, as if he can't get his head around my request.

"Because I already love him."

"Him?"

"I have a feeling it's a boy."

He says nothing. We stand, facing each other, while unnamable emotions play off between us. I hold my breath as I wait for his answer. My life, Charlie's life, and my baby's life are in Gabriel's hands. The next word that falls from his mouth will be the verdict that decides my child's future, the difference between life and death, and I can't do a goddamn thing about it, because I'm still Gabriel's property for the next nine years.

The sound I'm waiting for doesn't come, but he gives me better. He wraps his arms around me and pulls me to his body. The minute his strength envelops me I collapse, my knees caving in while my hands fist in the shirt under his jacket. It doesn't matter that I can't stand, because he is there to catch me. I breathe in his spicy and clean scent, enormous relief making me dizzy and, now that I'm no longer alone, also leaving me weak.

"I was so afraid," I whisper, letting out a tremulous breath and clutching his clothes as if they're my lifeline. "I was so afraid every day."

"Shh. I'm here now."

His hands are broad and strong on my back, and I sink deeper into the strength he provides. The way he holds me is hesitant. I sense he wants to say more, but after another heartbeat, he scoops me up in his arms, snatches my bag from the makeshift table, and carries me to his car.

I know men like him, and I know the gift he just offered is greater than any I could've hoped for. More than believing me when I said I didn't fall pregnant on purpose, he forgave me for running, and he's allowing me to have a baby he doesn't want. He didn't have to. He could've dropped me off at a clinic with instructions and fetched me back as his toy. Men like Gabriel don't do well with pregnant toys. A big belly won't serve his needs. Or maybe I'm done being his toy. Whatever the case, I'm filled with relief. I lean my head on his chest in gratitude.

He opens the door, lowers me in the passenger seat, and fits my seatbelt. He removes his jacket and dumps the gun in the cubbyhole. The jacket goes on the console between our seats and my bag at my feet. When he takes the wheel, I dare to ask again, "Charlie?"

He squeezes my knee. "Don't fret, beautiful. He'll be fine."

After fastening his seatbelt, he steers us into the traffic and dials Rhett on the hands-free kit with a single instruction. "Take Charlie home."

I lean my head back, for the first time in three months not worrying about dying. With the earlier adrenalin wearing off, I feel like a washed-out ragdoll. I don't care about what waits for me at home. All that matters is that we're safe.

Gabriel cups my neck and pushes my head down in his lap, my body cushioned on his jacket. I keep my eyes open and absorb his power. His thigh muscles bunch under my cheek as he steps on the clutch and changes gears. I watch his enormous hands as he grips the wheel and takes charge of my destination. The feeling I once had of placing myself in his hands, trusting him to be a good driver who'll bring me safely to my destination, is now real. I rely on him to drive us six hours straight through the night and deliver us home. There's not a doubt in my mind he'll navigate any pitfall without falling asleep or crashing the car. Gabriel is too decided, rational, and faultless for that. His chest rises and falls with steady, deep breaths, the reassurance I need that he's securely on his course and knows what he's doing. I can let my guard down. For once, I can rely on someone else to take control.

I nestle deeper into his lap, letting his warmth enfold me. Masculinity radiates from the flex of his muscles as he manipulates the powerful engine of the car. He doesn't break the speed limit, and this further reassures me. He turns up the heater and puts the radio on a classical music station that helps soothe me.

Once on the open road where he doesn't have to change gears, he brushes a palm over my head, tangling his fingers in my hair. For a while he rubs the tresses between a thumb and forefinger, and then he strokes my shoulder and arm. He runs his hand over my back and comes to a stop on my waist, his fingers playing gently over the side of the bump that used to be my flat stomach. I turn slightly to find a more comfortable position, and Gabriel doesn't change his hold on me. He keeps his fingertips on the curve of my belly, lightly, yet protectively.

The moon is visible from the passenger side window where it breaks through the clouds. It moves with us, bringing along the milky-way stars. There's something soothing about the sound of the tires rolling on the tar and the music playing softly in the warm background while I'm cocooned in a strong man's lap as the cold, dark night speeds past outside. Finally, the comfortable, luxurious safety of it all lulls me to sleep. I fall down a rabbit hole of deep, exhausted, crazy dreams where property like me is cherished.

Gabriel

ALL THE WAY from Durban to Johannesburg my insides shake. How easily I could've lost her. She's a survivor, one of the strongest I know, but even survivors eventually run out of luck. This is my fault. This is my backhanded, conniving doing. Valentina ran to protect our baby. She believed I wouldn't want it. I can't blame her. From her perspective, I'm the monster, and it's true. Only a monster would kidnap her, train her to fuck him, and then make her pregnant without her consent. Only a monster would believe the worst of her, expecting her to run to get rid of our child. A good man would've seen things for what they are. Valentina isn't capable of hurting an unborn child, even if that child is a monster's.

The guilt mauls my mind to pieces all the way home. I hate myself for who I am and for what I'm going to do, because I won't tell her. I won't tell Valentina why she fell pregnant. I'm too needy. I want a small part of her affection and approval too much. Why make her hate me more than she already does? Why make it harder on her? It'll be best for both of us to keep the untruth alive. She never needs to know. This is what I tell myself when I park the car in the driveway.

While she was sleeping, I called Magda to let her know the status of the situation. I also checked with Rhett on how Charlie was doing. They were behind me by one hour. I instructed them to let Charlie sleep at the guardhouse when they arrive. It was a long twelve-hour drive to Durban and back, but I barely feel the strain. Superhuman strength drives me where my woman and child are concerned. A glance at the dash clock tells me it's three in the morning. The house is quiet, everyone asleep. Just as well. I want time alone with Valentina before facing Magda and the rest of the staff.

My precious bundle stirs when I lift her from the car and carry her inside, but I press her face to my chest, urging her not to break her sleep. I take her upstairs and lie her down on my bed, trying not to disturb her too much when I remove her clothes. After undressing, I get under the covers beside her and pull her to my chest. My body molds around hers, every part just like I remember, except for the soft curve of her stomach that presses deeper into my groin. The rest of her has lost weight. Her bony shoulders and thin arms cut straight into my conscience, and still I'm perverse enough to grow hard. I want to both possess her and revere her by not touching her. With all the willpower I possess, I force my dick down. For now, her mind is in a subconscious world, and like the bastard I am, I hold her naked body close while she can't deny me.

Valentina

Wakefulness pulls at me, but I'm not ready to open my eyes. I'm still in my cocoon, warm and safe, only, now it's softer and more comfortable. Slowly, reality returns. I'm in a bed, in a pair of strong arms. Naked. I lift my eyelids to find Gabriel watching me. Immediately, I tense. When is he going to order me to the gym for my punishment? As stiffness invades my muscles, his eyes grow hard, and his deformed face twists into a cold mask, but he doesn't loosen his hold.

His voice is clipped. "How do you feel?"

I sweep my hair behind my ear, self-conscious about our nakedness. It's been three months and my body has changed. "Fine, thank you."

"Stay." He throws the duvet off his body, but makes sure I'm covered.

His chiseled ass bunches, and the muscles in his broad back flex as he walks to the bathroom. A second later, the water in the shower comes on.

Not sure what to do, I look around the familiar room. The same medical equipment from before is still here. I'm not going to lie in bed awaiting my punishment naked. I get up and walk to the closet to borrow one of his T-shirts so I can make it to my room with my modesty intact, but when I open the top drawer my T-shirts are neatly folded on the shelf. So are my underwear, shorts, and nightdresses. Drawer after drawer holds my clothes as well as new garments I've never seen. I lift a blouse to read the label. Everything is in my size, or at least my pre-pregnancy size.

Baffled, I go through the closet. My jeans, dresses, jackets, and pants are organized by colors.

"Those won't fit, now," his deep voice says behind me.

I jump and twirl around. Gabriel stands in the door, a towel wrapped around his waist and his chest wet with drops of water. Instinctively, I cover my breasts and below my stomach, a warm flush working its way over my body. Without looking at my naked parts, he takes a T-shirt from the top shelf and hands it to me. It's one of his.

"We'll have to do some shopping," he says.

I pull the T-shirt over my head hastily. Thankfully, the hem reaches my knees. I motion at the cupboards. "I don't understand."

"I had your things moved over."

"Why?"

He takes down a shirt and drops the towel. I have to look away as he starts to dress. "We'll rectify the clothes situation as soon as possible. I apologize about that."

More confused than ever, I say, "You couldn't know. That I'm still pregnant, I mean."

The look he gives me is a strange one. A shadow invades his eyes. He pulls on a pair of slacks, not bothering with underwear.

"How *did* you find out?" I ask carefully.

"Rhett was worried about you."

"Ah." It's a nice way of telling me Rhett ratted on me without blaming Rhett.

Feeling increasingly uncomfortable, I find a pair of panties and borrow one of Gabriel's sweatpants with an elastic waistband that accommodates my rounder waistline. I have to roll the pants up several times.

"Back to bed," he says with a dark expression.

I can't stand the tension, any longer. "Gabriel…"

He turns to me. "Valentina?"

"Just take me to the gym and get it over with."

For one second, two seconds, three seconds he stares at me,

then he crosses the floor and puts his hands on my shoulders. "I'll never hurt you while you're pregnant."

The air leaves my lungs in a gush. I'm relieved, but not reassured. "Only after?"

He doesn't answer. He only points at the bed and makes me get back in.

"Don't move."

"Charlie?"

"Later."

He kisses my forehead and leaves the room. What am I supposed to do? Sleep? Not ready to test Gabriel's patience, I stay put. The door opens not five minutes later, and Marie enters with a tray. She gives me a scowl and dumps it on the nightstand. There are eggs, bacon, toast, baked beans, and coffee. The smell of the food makes me feel sick, but I fight it down. Before I can say thank you, she's gone.

Gabriel doesn't leave me alone for long. When he returns, it's with Dr. Engelbrecht. A frown runs over his features when he looks at the untouched food, but he doesn't say anything. The doctor runs tests similar to the ones I took in Durban and notes everything on his computer.

"I know it's hard when you're feeling sick," the doctor says, "but if you don't want intravenous feeding, you'll have to eat something."

"She'll try," Gabriel says.

Once the doctor is gone, Gabriel gives me a piercing look. "Put on your coat and shoes."

"Where are we going?"

He takes his jacket off the clotheshorse, but doesn't answer.

I don't have a choice but to obey and follow him to his car. Before starting the engine, he kisses the knuckle of my amputated thumb and places my hand on his thigh. We drive in silence. It's only when we park outside a redbrick building that I dare to question him again.

"Gabriel, what's going on?"

He turns off the engine and faces me squarely, his body a block of hard muscle that takes up all the space on his side of the car. Tightening his fingers on mine, as if he's expecting me to pull away, he says in an unwavering voice, "We're getting married."

4

Valentina

"What?" I cry.

I try to pull away, but he holds fast, a silent warning creeping into his eyes.

"We're getting married," he repeats.

"Now?"

"Here, now, today."

If he punched me in the stomach, he couldn't take my wind out harder. "Why?"

He gives me an even look. "You're pregnant with my baby."

I'm feeling more hysterical by the moment. "That doesn't mean you have to marry me."

He lets go, opens his door, and comes around the car to open mine.

When I don't move, he puts his head in. "Get out of the car, Valentina. Now."

Kicking and screaming won't do me good. He'll carry me into

the building if he has to. My only chance at getting out of this is to reason with him.

I step out on shaky legs, holding onto the door for stability. "You don't have to marry me just because I'm pregnant."

He narrows his eyes. "Do you think I won't man up to my responsibility?"

"I told you, I don't expect anything from you."

He puts his nose a hairbreadth from mine. "Has the thought that I'm doing this to protect you crossed your mind?"

The sucker punch he dealt me earlier is nothing compared to this knockout.

"Do you know how many enemies I have?" he continues, grabbing my arms. "Do you know what they'll do to you to get to me? The only thing that makes anyone in the business untouchable is being family."

Everything he says is true. I know how the business works. My child hasn't been born, yet, and there's already a sword hanging over his head. The fact that he's Gabriel's child is enough to put both our lives in danger. I understand what he says, but marriage isn't what I want. It's not what Gabriel wants. Not like this. Marriage is for love.

"There must be another way."

"This is the only way. You can do it the easy way or fighting. The judge has been bought. He doesn't care if you say yes or no. We *will* be married."

His fingers dig into my arm as he pulls me up the stairs and through the door. Some of his men have followed by car and are guarding the entrance. He doesn't give me time to protest or speak until we stop in front of a door with a metal plaque that reads Judge EL Viljoen.

I hang back when he moves forward. He turns with an irritated look.

"Gabriel."

"What?"

I run my sweaty hands over the fitted trench coat that won't fasten over my bump, any longer, to dry my palms. "I think I'm going to be sick." Bile pushes up in my throat.

He cups my face. For the first time since I've met Gabriel his eyes fill with something keen to dearness. "Take a deep breath." He gives me a hard, possessive kiss and ushers me inside.

Barely five minutes later, we're married.

Husband and wife.

The nausea I've managed to hold down boils over. We're scarcely outside before I empty my stomach in a flowerbed. Gabriel is next to me, his arm around my shoulders. He holds my hair out of my face and rubs my back as dry heaves wrack my body. Tears mix with my anguish, shaking my shoulders.

"It's all right, beautiful. Breathe in and out."

I take a steadying breath and scrape some dignity from the bottom of the barrel of my control, enough to straighten my back and suppress more tears.

Gabriel takes me back to the car and fastens my seatbelt. Shell-shocked, I stare at the platinum band with the floating diamond on my ring finger that matches the one on his, except that his has a black diamond. Mine fits perfectly. There's no way he got the rings this morning. He already had them before we left the house. The hasty marriage isn't something he cooked up last night.

He gets in and traces his thumb over my jaw. "Feeling better?"

I hold up my left hand, fingers splayed. "How long have you been planning this?"

His expression becomes guarded. He starts the engine and puts the car into gear. "Since I found the pregnancy test."

"Why are you doing this? Why give up your bachelorhood to protect *me*?" Seriously, why does he care? "My debt can't be worth *that* much to you."

Instead of answering, he pulls off, his guards following. We drive in silence until we hit the road heading toward Lanseria.

"Where are we going?"

He cups my knee. "We need someplace tranquil to talk."

"Charlie--"

"Will be fine. Rhett and Quincy are taking care of him. Today is about *us*."

My worry is not completely eased, but I don't have a choice. I have to trust Gabriel. Now that we're back, I have to let Kris know. I hate that I made her worry.

"Do you mind if I call Kris?"

He takes his phone from the console holder and hands it to me.

"Thank you."

Gabriel has her number saved in his contacts. Why doesn't that surprise me? She picks up with a rushed greeting.

"Kris, it's Valentina."

"Val! Where are you?"

"Johannesburg."

"Are you all right?"

"I'm fine. We're fine."

"What happened? Did Gabriel find you?"

I glance at him, knowing he can hear her, but his face is a stoic mask.

"Yes," I say.

"Tell me what's going on. I'm going out of my mind."

"I promise to explain everything, but not on the phone."

"When can I see you?"

I look at Gabriel.

"Tomorrow," he says.

"Tomorrow," I repeat.

"Today. You owe me a fucking explanation."

"You're right." I rub my eyes. "But I can't do it now. It'll have to wait."

"Val--"

"Kris, please."

She must hear the desperation in my voice, because after a sigh, she says, "Okay. Tomorrow and not a day later. I'll be waiting."

"I'm sorry for making you worry."

"I'm just glad you're safe. We'll talk tomorrow."

I don't know how I'm going to explain. I both fear Kris' judgment and crave her support.

I hand Gabriel back his phone and look through the window. We're heading toward Magaliesburg, passing the airport.

"How do you feel?" he asks.

"Nauseous."

I swear there's a hint of a smirk on his face.

"What's so funny?" I snap.

There's a definite twitch to his lips this time. "It's cute."

"It's cute that I feel like puking?"

"It's cute that you're having pregnancy symptoms."

He places his palm on my stomach, but pulls it away immediately, as if he's worried his touch is unwelcome. The sad and sick thing is I go cold when his touch is gone. Only pride prevents me from asking him to hold me.

After thirty minutes, the road starts twisting up the mountain. I don't usually get carsick, but the winding road doesn't help. I have to focus on my breathing not to empty my stomach again.

He pats my knee. "Almost there."

I close my eyes and lean my head against the headrest. When I open them again, we pull through the gates of Mount Grace. I sit up straighter. I've always wanted to come here. I heard it's beautiful.

It's that and much more. The mountain resort is hidden in the lush hills, surrounded by a forest. The main building has stone walls and a thatch roof. Everything shouts luxury and extortionate rates. When we enter the lobby where several well-dressed guests are conversing, I feel self-conscious about my clothes, but Gabriel's arm is around my body, sheltering me against his side. A concierge rushes forward and greets Gabriel by name.

"Your room is ready, sir. Would you like me to escort you?"

"We'll have breakfast, first. My wife is pregnant, and she needs to eat."

"Of course. What may I get you?"

"Everything," Gabriel says, "and my men will order from the menu."

"Yes, sir."

Gabriel's guards follow, but they keep enough of a distance to give us privacy. We're escorted to an indoor garden where a table is set with silverware and paper-thin bone china. Evergreen creepers ornate the glass walls that give a view of the mountains and the valley.

"Not too cold?" Gabriel asks as he takes my coat.

There's a bite in the autumn air, and the day is overcast. "It's warm enough inside here, thank you."

He seats me before taking the opposite chair. A waiter arrives with coffee and an assortment of herbal teas. I opt for a mint infusion, as coffee doesn't agree with my stomach, of late. More waiters deposit silver-covered platters on the tables lining the sidewall. They lift the lids to reveal every kind of breakfast food imaginable. There are sausages, bacon, fried potatoes, eggs, porridge, pancakes, cereal, fruit, nuts, croissants, sweet pastries, cheese, and a variety of cold meat cuts. Gabriel's men are not seated with us, but there's enough food to feed ten times the small army.

"This is too much," I protest.

"I didn't know what you could stomach. Besides, I didn't want to waste time pouring over a menu. It was easier to simply order everything."

"The guards can eat with us. At least not all the food will be wasted."

"The guards are fine." He turns to the headwaiter. "Pack up whatever we don't eat and deliver it to the homeless shelter."

"Certainly, sir."

Gabriel turns to me. "There. Happy?"

"Shall we serve, sir?"

"We'll manage, thank you."

The staff exits discreetly, leaving us alone.

"We need to get some food into your body," he says. "What do you fancy?"

"Just some fruit." I look at the spread. "I'm sorry, but the smell of everything else makes me queasy."

"Don't ever apologize for how you feel." He gets up and places a selection of fruit on a plate, which he carries to the table. "Orange?" He spears a piece on a fork and brings it to my mouth. Piece by piece, he feeds me until half of the plate is gone and I assure him I can't eat another morsel.

"You didn't eat enough in Durban." His expression turns somber. "Your stomach probably shrunk. We'll have to fix that."

"It's just the pregnancy. Aren't you hungry?"

The way his gaze trails over me detonates sparks on my skin. He still wants me, and my body hasn't stopped wanting him. Not for one second. Not even after he bullied me into marriage. The conditioning of old kicks in. My panties turn damp as he takes my hand and rubs a thumb over my wrist.

As quickly as he took my hand, he lets it go. An uncomfortable silence follows as he serves himself a full English breakfast and eats while I sip my tea.

He only speaks again when he pushes his empty plate aside. "We need to talk. I know you don't want this, Valentina, but there's no turning back. You asked me why I gave up my bachelorhood to protect you. You're going to be the mother of my child. You and our child are my responsibility, and I've never been scared of my responsibilities. You're family, now. Your debt has been wiped clean. You never have to fear for your or Charlie's life again. We're going to be a family, and I know it won't be easy. All I ask is that you try. I won't deny you anything within my means to give. Ask and you'll have whatever your heart desires."

I swallow at the end of his speech. "Charlie and I, we owe you nothing?"

"You have no more debt."

What he offers is noble, but I have to understand if we're equals. "Are you saying I'm free?"

A stony expression replaces his earlier tenderness. "No."

"Then nothing has changed in terms of what I owe you."

He leans back in his chair, putting distance between us. "Oh, but it has. Everything has changed." He holds my eyes. "Before, it was nine years. Now, it's forever."

The statement startles me. I bite my lip to stop it from trembling. How clever. He changed the game, the rules, and the implications. What did I think a ring on my finger meant? I'm still a toy. The only difference is this time it's for life.

Leaning over the table, he grips my chin, but there's nothing tender in the gesture. It's dominant and brusque. "It'll be easier for both of us if you don't let your disappointment show so easily."

With a jerk of my head, I free myself. "Why must it be forever?"

"You're mine, Valentina. I'll never let you go."

"Why?" I whisper again, needing to understand so badly it eats a hole in my soul.

"I don't need a reason. When I first saw you back at Napoli's, I wanted you, so I took you. Now, I've decided to keep you."

The teacup is shaking so much in my hand I have to put it down. "What about what I want?"

"I said I'd do everything in my power to make you happy. Our time together doesn't have to be miserable. It can be good. Just accept the way it is, and things will be easier for you."

The part of me that needs to be loved rebels. "I'm still your property."

"As my wife, you'll be respected and protected."

"As long as I stay."

His expression darkens. "You ran from me once, but I won't let you run twice. The next time it happens, the person who'll suffer is

Kris. I'll ruin her, break everything she's built in her life, and kill her. Do you understand?"

The food pushes back up in my throat. It feels like a knife is twisting in my stomach.

"I asked you a question, Valentina."

Tears blur my vision. I don't want to cry in front of him. I don't want him to know he has an effect on me. Blinking away the moisture, I give him the answer he wants in a voice hoarse from suppressed tears. "Yes."

"Good." Pushing back his chair, he comes around to my side of the table and wraps his arms around me. "In time, you'll get used to it."

I don't say anything. A deep-sated knowledge presses down on me. Gabriel is a man of his word. He did what he said he would. He found a new kitten, and this time, he's not letting it go. All I can do is pull up a protective barrier around my heart. If I'm to survive this new arrangement, I need to be strong, but the first cracks are already showing. He'll break me, after all.

AFTER OUR WEDDING BREAKFAST, Gabriel takes me for a walk in the garden. True to his word, he tries to make this good for me. He has his arm around my shoulders, ensuring I don't slip on the stepping stones that are wet from dew, and points out bird species.

At the edge of a pond, we stop to admire the view.

"I was thinking," he says, "that maybe you'd like to do charity work."

I look at him quickly.

"Now that you're not studying or working," he continues, "you'll have time on your hands. I know you had your heart set on being a vet," he rubs a finger over the knuckle of my missing thumb, "but how about starting a dog rescue program? I'll sponsor all the money you need."

It's too much, too fast. I haven't made peace with my new future, yet. I need time for everything to sink in and to adjust to my new circumstances.

"Thank you. I'll think about it."

He touches my cheek. "You're pale. Still nauseous?"

"A little."

"Come on. Let's get you to the room."

I don't ask for how long we're staying or why, assuming this is our pretense of a honeymoon.

The room is spacious and comfy with decorations in neutral colors. We have no luggage, but the bathroom is stocked with everything I need, including a toothbrush, comb, fluffy robe, and slippers. The tub stands against a ceiling to floor glass window that reveals more stunning views of the valley.

"Do you mind if I have a bath?" I ask. "I've been washing in a basin for three months."

A shadow crosses over his face when I mention the basin, but he doesn't comment on it. "Sit over there." He points at the wicker chair in the corner. "I'll run you a bath."

Emotionally, I feel depleted. I flop down in the chair, watching Gabriel prepare a bath with oil that smells of lavender. My life is no longer my own, but I'm too tired to fight it. Sometimes, swimming upstream becomes too exhausting. Will it be terrible if I, just for a while, go with the flow? Maybe, when I get my strength back I'll fight again, but now isn't that moment.

"Come here," Gabriel says when the bath is filled with steaming water, holding out his hand.

Disobedience comes with a price. Pushing to my feet, I cross the floor and stop in front of him. A moment of silence follows as he looks at me, his thoughts impossible to read. When he finally acts, it's with determined, strong movements. There's nothing insecure or hesitant in the way he grips the hem of the T-shirt and drags it over my head. Burying his fingers under the elastic of my underwear, he pushes both the panties and sweatpants to the floor.

As his fingertips skim over my legs up to my hips, my body heats, coming alive under the light caress. The power of his touch is familiar. I'm both devastated and ecstatic to discover his magic still works on me. I crave his body, but feel guilty about wanting the man who tied me to him with the invisible chains of marriage, and worse, Kris' fate. As always, he leaves me no choice. I'm powerless to prevent his touch or my arousal. I'm powerless to do anything but feel.

A flutter of nervous anticipation races through my belly, burning my core as his hands fasten on my waist. Instead of lifting me into the bath, he walks me backward to the window until my back presses against the glass. The crisp chill of the autumn air penetrates my skin, but heat runs down my spine. He arranges me like a butterfly pinned for framing and takes a step back. For several seconds, he only looks at me, his gaze trailing from the top of my head to the tip of my toes. There's fire in his eyes, but it's his hands I want. I crave them on me with a desperation that makes my breath shallow and my breasts heavy. When he finally comes closer again, his clothes brush against my skin. It takes all of my self-control not to rub up against him in search of the contact I need.

Holding my eyes, he reaches between my legs. My body trembles when he lightly outlines my folds.

"I'll understand if you don't want this," he says. "I know how it is with a pregnant woman."

The fact that he's giving me a choice comes as a big surprise. It's the last thing I expected from him. But I do. I want him there and deeper. Cupping his hand, I guide his middle finger inside.

He lets out a groan and rests his forehead against mine. "You're wet. I trained your body too well."

There's no arguing that fact. Every long and frightening night of my freedom I yearned for him, for the way he now gathers my moisture and spreads it to my clit. I gasp when he presses the pad of his finger on the nub and holds the pressure without giving me the stimulation I need. Forcing my hips to be still, I wait for permission to have my release. His breath chases over my face as he keeps the stance, his hard-on a thick rod against my hip.

His jaw flexes as he grinds his teeth. I don't know why, but he fights wanting me. Me? I've given up a long time ago. I'm a realistic girl. I know I'm an object, something to satisfy his sexual cravings for dominance and manipulating my pleasure, but I've come to accept his control over my body as I'm coming to terms with my new captivity. I'll never be free or loved, and I'm not going to deny myself the only thing I have––unequalled physical passion. If this is what my life has been reduced to, I'll take what I can get. I'm not masochistic enough to refuse the breadcrumbs when I'm starving. There will be other things that can fill the hole in my heart and the hankering for love in my soul. A career, a child, finding joy and gratitude in each moment. In this moment, I can have a piece of Gabriel by giving him what he wants most. My pleasure. My submission.

Cupping his beautiful, masculine, scarred face, I guide his lips to my breast, showing him what I'm prepared to take and give.

"Valentina." My name is a broken sound on his lips. He brushes his mouth over my nipple. "Are you sure about this?"

I drag my hand through his hair, tugging on the strands. "Isn't this what husbands and wives do on honeymoon?"

He looks up at me with the kind of intention that's fierce enough to scare. "No." The word is loaded. It slips out on a huff of strained control. "This is *not* how husbands and wives behave."

I know what he means. Husbands and wives make love. They don't devour each other with a hunger that borders on obsession, on something so perversely pleasurable it feels wrong.

The air leaves his lips on a gush, a moment of sublime surrender. The fight to keep his distance melts into the kiss he plants on my breast. He groans when his tongue touches the tip. With a catch of his breath, he draws me deeper.

My knees buckle at the scorching hotness of his mouth as he

licks and bites. Gone is the cotton wool in which he wrapped me earlier, and back is the man I'm addicted to. He lets go of my sex to squeeze my other breast between his fingers. His mouth moves to that peak, sucking with a force that pulls blood to the engorged tip. When I moan, he lets go with a pop.

He rubs a palm over the curve. "Jesus, I gave you a hickey on your tit."

I don't care. My body has worn his marks before, marks harsher than the red spot on my breast. His name falls needy and breathlessly from my lips.

Contained desire replaces the predator look of a moment ago. Once again, Gabriel is in control. He kneels in front of me and hooks my leg over his shoulder. Folding his hands around my waist, he helps me keep my balance while his mouth goes to the juncture of my thighs. He watches me as he teases my folds with his tongue, running the tip over my heated flesh. When he bites lightly into my labia, I jerk and try to move away, but his big hands keep me in place. It's the grueling way in which he sucks on my clit and runs his teeth over the aching nub that has my toes curl with unbearable pleasure. He pulls back, all the while holding my eyes, and parts my pussy lips. His gaze leaves mine to study the flesh in the V of his fingers.

"You are so fucking beautiful," he whispers. "You have the prettiest cunt I've ever seen."

I flush at his vulgar compliment, but he doesn't give me time to process how I feel about the crass words, because he sinks the thumb of his free hand into my channel. My thighs tremble when he pulls out and pushes back in a few times.

"That's it, beautiful. I want to make your whole body shake with pleasure."

That's exactly what happens when he uses two fingers pressed together to spank my clit.

"Gabriel!"

My nails dig into his shoulders for support as my body prepares for release.

"I know you like this."

Yes, he does. He knows this from the first time he spanked my pussy with his belt.

"Come for me," he growls, looking up at me with dark possession.

Two more taps, and I do as he demands, coming with a violent spasm that locks my muscles and arches my back. He covers my clit with his lips and sucks me through the orgasm until I'm trembling with aftershocks. My head is tilted back, and my eyes are closed, but I feel him straighten and work open his fly.

He kisses the shell of my ear. "I'm going to fuck you right here against this window."

No one can see us––our bathroom is practically overhanging an abyss––but the thought of being seen in such a compromising position makes me tense. The slick head of his cock touches my stomach. I open my eyes to look at him. His face is close to mine, not turned away to shelter me from the scars as before.

He brushes our lips together. "What a gorgeous sight you must be with your ass cheeks pushed up against this window."

He grabs my ass and spreads the cheeks, opening me up to the view of the outside world. "What a turn-on to see those wet pussy lips." He nips at my neck, freeing his cock. "Any man on the other side of this window will come in his pants."

As he speaks, he aligns his cock with my entrance and presses an inch inside. I moan at the thick intrusion, needing him to drive deeper, but Gabriel isn't to be rushed. Male grunts and female whimpers fill the space as he enters me painstakingly slow. It takes him a while to work himself fully inside. I'd almost forgotten how big and thick he is. By the time he's buried up to his balls, he's perspiring, and his face is contorted with strain. He flattens me against the glass with his body, bends his knees, and gives a few shallow pumps.

"Mine. Mine. Mine." He accentuates each word with a shove that drags his cock over the sweet spot that makes my womb tighten with a new building need. It's too little and too much.

"Pleeaasse," I beg.

He pulls out almost completely to give me more friction, and penetrates me carefully. He cups my hips between his large palms as if I'm as fragile as our breakfast china. His heat envelopes me from the front while the cold window cools my back. At this rhythm, the contraction that announces my orgasm is a slow-detonating pool of pleasure that ripples out over my entire body.

"Ga--" I swallow the rest of his name as I come.

"Yesss," he grunts, "come on my cock."

My inner muscles clench around him as he speaks the wicked words. My skin is still tingling from the orgasm when he pulls free, turns me toward the bath, and places my hands on the edge of the tub.

"Hold on for me."

With much gentleness he enters me from behind. His thumb presses on the pucker of my ass, adding extra sensations as he pumps in and out of my body, swaying us both with an easy rhythm.

"Look at that," he says, grabbing my hair and turning my head toward the mirror on the wall.

The muscles of his legs and ass bunch as he pulls out, drives in, and grinds our groins together, over and over. The motion makes my breasts sway. Holding onto one hip, he palms a breast and rolls my nipple, making me contract around him.

He groans and pinches. "Yes, squeeze my cock just like that. Make me come."

When I clench my inner muscles, he falls forward with a curse, catching his weight with his palms on the edge of the tub. His chest is pressed against my back. Even if I can't take him any deeper he thrusts his hips up, claiming every piece of me he can.

I feel the exact moment he snaps, the moment every part of his body goes rigid and his cock grows thicker inside me. When he reaches for the bath oil, I'm reminded that Gabriel is still the hard lover from before. I squirm when the cap lifts with a click, but he holds me down with a hand between my shoulder blades and squirts the liquid down the crack of my ass.

I know what this means even before he penetrates my dark entrance with a finger. For a while he takes me with shallow pumps, and then his finger slips in all the way. When I'm used to the sensation, a second finger joins the first, and then a third.

"Will you be a good girl if I let up, Valentina?"

No matter how well he prepares me, anal will never be my favorite, but Gabriel loves it. I want to give him this. I look back at him from over my shoulder and give a small nod.

"Good kitten."

He lifts his palm from my back and grabs the root of his cock, positioning it at my tight entrance. His free hand moves between my legs. It burns when he opens me with the broad head of his cock, but his deft fingers are manipulating my clit in just the right way, rolling the over-stimulated nub with the perfect amount of pressure. The way into my backside is a slow process that takes a long time during which he stops frequently to let me adjust. When the burn gets too much, he pinches my clit, setting my nerve endings off with a good kind of pain. By the time his whole length is buried inside, I'm shaking, but the pleasure is always bigger than the pain.

"I want to make this good for you," he says in a strained voice.

I cry out when he starts moving, feeling a dark and demented pleasure work its way through the pain up my spine. I gnash my teeth together as he increases his pace, trying to accommodate the carnal feelings so different from my usual orgasms. I crave with ferocity, but I don't know what. It's only when he plunges two fingers into my pussy and scissors them that I understand what my body wants. I need to come so badly it feels like torture. I'm on the edge, but the anal penetration isn't enough.

"Touch yourself," he commands, understanding my body better than I do.

I find my clit and rub while he fucks me with his fingers and cock. I'm not cognizant of time or place, only of him and our bodies as he pushes me to the darkest of pleasures, to a point where no person should go. He fucks me into floating bliss, always pushing the boundaries to physical highs I'm frightened I won't survive but somehow always do, and he's right there with me as he curses and cries out his climax. Coming inside me while driving me past my limits and beyond, he makes me lose myself in the best and worst way possible.

Before I can guard my tongue, the words tumble from my mouth, drowning out even the powerful orgasm burning through me.

"I love you, Gabriel."

5

Gabriel

A man like me can only hope for the words she utters, but they catch me off-balance. I stumble back, ripping my cock too quickly from her ass and making her whimper. She freezes. Her back is no longer rising and falling with the heavy breaths of earlier. She's as shocked as I am. The statement tumbled from her mouth without premeditation. Unlike my usual type of woman, she didn't express the ultimate sentiment of affection to manipulate me, because there's nothing to manipulate. Her fate is sealed. The ring on her finger is the proof. She's mine—forever—but the spontaneity of the words doesn't make them truer than when Sylvia or Helga spoke them. This is what I trained her to think. To believe. Sex and emotions go hand in hand for women. My weapon with Valentina has always been sex, and her words confirmed I won the war. Yet, instead of feeling victorious, I feel like a jerk. Bleak, cold self-loath fills my gut.

Covering her body with mine, I fold my arms around her and give her the only thing that can make me feel better––the truth.

"You only think you love me because I trained you so." I kiss her neck to soften the ugly deliverance.

Finally, her chest expands as she inhales. When she pushes up, I don't prevent her.

She turns in my arms to face me. Pride clashes with embarrassment in her pretty, big eyes. "You're right," she lifts her chin, "because I hate you more."

There it is, the naked truth, stripped from pretenses and a dollied-up version of our unconventional relationship when sex is taken out of the equation.

I cup her face. "I know, beautiful."

The sad part is, I do. I always did. The minute I saw her and decided what I was going to do with her body, I knew she would hate me. I just wasn't prepared for how much it would hurt, and that comes as a surprise. Sure, I care about her like I've never cared about another woman, not even my ex-wife, but the plan was always to maintain my superior position of power over her. Feelings were not supposed to weaken me. How could I foresee this petite woman would make me feel so many different things in the short span of half a year?

I'm crowding her space, not backing away so she can move, but she's not trying to escape. She faces me bravely with her pale cheeks and blurry eyes. I recognize the emotion in that expression. Defeat. It's the point at which she realizes how utterly I've ruined her. She needs me, and she hates it, but she doesn't shy away from the reality. She embraces the pain and makes it her own with that same sense of survival that allowed her to accept my ownership, give up on her dream, and carry my unwanted baby.

In return for her life and body, her dreams, and one-sided, warped love, I wrap my arms around her and give her comfort. She doesn't deny herself the little I offer. She buries her face in my chest and leans against me, allowing me to support her weight. I scoop her up in my arms and lower her into the water before getting undressed and into the tub myself. I pull her back to my chest so that her head rests on my shoulder. The water covers everything except the contracted tips of her breasts that float like enticing cherries on the milky water. I lather soap into the sponge and drag it over her smooth shoulders and the crests of her breasts. I wash gently between her legs where it will be tender and rub my palms over the toned muscles of her thighs. It's on her stomach where I linger the longest, folding my hands around the miracle unfolding in her womb.

I'm amazed that she allows me to touch her at all and pathetically grateful. I couldn't come near Sylvia from the minute she fell pregnant to the day Carly was born. Reluctant to break the moment, I don't have a choice when the water starts to cool. I pull the plug, help her from the tub, and hand her a towel. We dress silently, both lost in our thoughts. When I look back at her, my heart fills with an overwhelming, intense fucking sadness. Against the expanse of the window, she looks lost and unbelievingly neglected, a bride in my oversized clothes. Fragile, damaged, and irreparably broken.

"Come to bed." It's midday, but I want to hold her.

She blinks as if returning from someplace far. I don't like it. Even the moments she retracts within her head are too far away for my liking. With the backdrop of the mountains and wild nature, she's terrifyingly destructible. Small and vulnerable. The swell of her waist reminds me that her delicate condition makes her ten-fold more frail. An overpowering sense of protectiveness consumes me. The fear that something should happen to her or that I could lose her pushes a burning sensation up in my throat. The thought of anyone's hands on her other than mine will drive me to my knees.

Suddenly, I need to know. I told myself if I could have her back it would be enough, that I wouldn't ask questions, but I'm not strong enough to stand by my intention.

"In Durban, did you touch another man?"

She gives me a startled look. "No."

"Nobody?"

"The only man who's ever touched me is you." She looks uncomfortable. "Except for that one time."

I cross the floor and kiss her lips to shut her up. I don't want her to think about the rape. Due to all of my energy having been focused on finding my runaway girl, I haven't made progress with tracking her assailants. Enough of those thoughts. I took her body hard, and she needs to rest. Maybe I need to hold her more than she needs to be held, but it doesn't matter. I take her hand and pull her down next to me on the bed. Fully clothed, I put my arms around her and cradle her against my body. She relaxes, her limbs molding around mine like puzzle pieces that fit just right.

"What would you like to do later?" I ask, stroking her hair.

"This is enough, Gabriel."

I kiss the top of her head. It can never be enough. I can never get my fill of her, and that scares the fuck out of me.

We nap for a couple of hours, have a late lunch, and take one of the short hikes to the waterfall after I checked with the hotel guide that the walk isn't too strenuous for my pregnant bride. The air and exercise do us both good. I needed to clear my head from Valentina's gut-eating revelation of love and hate, and she has a glow on her too-pale cheeks when we get back at sunset. Not willing to share her with others, I selfishly order dinner to be served in front of the fireplace in our room. When the staff have cleared the dishes and stoked the fire, we play a game of Scrabble. Our behavior strikes me as odd. This isn't something I'd ever have done with Sylvia, and certainly not on a honeymoon, but we aren't a normal couple celebrating our newly taken vows.

Even if my need for Valentina is already fierce again, I take her to bed without fucking her. In her fragile state, I'm worried of wearing her out, and after this morning's marathon tonight seems too soon. Despite not satisfying my sexual urge, I'm wholly and strangely content to simply sleep next to her, a definite first for me.

When the sun wakes me with a pale glow that sifts through the large windows of our room, I can't pretend that our mountaintop castle of glass is forever, any longer. The fairy tale of last night is over. It's time to go back to reality and all the problems our new situation will bring, including breaking the news to Magda and Carly. I start with Magda, sending her a text message to inform her we're married. Let her make of it what she will.

Valentina is quiet on the way home. The first thing she does upon our arrival is to check on Charlie. Her worry was for nothing. He's in his element, playing a game of cards with the off-duty guards in the staff quarters. The walk to the house seems like a good time to bring up our living arrangements.

"Charlie will live with us from now on."

She stops dead and gapes at me.

"Aren't you happy?"

"Of course, I am. I just assumed he'd go back to Kris."

"You're my wife. That makes him family. He can take one of the rooms upstairs. I'll send someone for his things, today. You can take charge of redecorating or whatever it is you women do."

"Thank you." She squeezes my fingers.

I bring her hand to my mouth and kiss her knuckles. "I don't want you to do anything strenuous while you're pregnant. No physical labor."

"I'm pregnant, not sick."

"I won't take risks with your health."

At my stern tone, she remains quiet.

The clothing consultant is waiting for us at the house with a selection of pregnancy outfits for Valentina to choose from. I thought it easier for her to shop at home than do the tiring clothes hunting. It wasn't my intention to stay while she tries on some of the dresses, but I find tremendous joy in sitting on the couch while she parades for me. Being conservative in her spending, I have to talk her into taking more than a couple of pants with adjustable waistbands and A-line dresses. My favorites are the fitted ones. It'll show off her belly beautifully. Sitting there and watching her, my chest expands with pride. She's going to make me a father, a precious gift I thought I'd never have again.

With the consultant gone, I hand Valentina the ideas I jotted down for her to start an animal rescue program, as well as a new phone. She's a bright and ambitious woman. The last thing I want is for her to be bored. We rehired our old cleaning company plus a server for our evening meals, and Marie is back in the kitchen. My wife will not dirty her hands like she was forced to when my mother made her our maid.

Think of the devil, Magda walks into the lounge as Valentina tells me she's going upstairs to change out of my clothes.

"Val." Magda approaches stiffly. She doesn't hug Valentina or kiss her cheek like she did with Sylvia when I brought her home after our wedding, but she makes an effort to be polite. "Welcome back." She motions at Valentina's stomach. "How are you?"

My petite wife's hands fold over her belly in a protective manner. "I'm fine, thank you, Mrs. Louw."

"Call me Magda. We're family now."

"All right, Magda."

Magda brushes her hands over her dress. "I'm going to be brutally honest, because there's no other way of saying this. I'm not happy with the turn of events, but whatever our past, whatever your debt, that's behind us. You're a Louw, now, and family comes first. You'll have all the benefits that come with our name, and in return I expect you to be loyal. Understood?"

"Yes."

Magda is worried that Valentina will rat to the wrong people in government, people who abide by the law, or worse, our enemies.

I put an arm around Valentina's waist. "She understands."

"Good." Magda looks between us. "I'm also not happy about the way you snuck off to tie the knot. And like this." She motions at

Valentina's attire and pulls up her nose. "Really, Gabriel, shame on you to make a lady marry you in such a state. It should've been done properly, in a church, with guests, and with the public exposure my son deserves. The best we can do now is a newspaper announcement."

I don't argue, because she's right. Shame on me. Like every other woman, Valentina deserved a pretty white dress, flowers, a three-layered cake, and the whole nine yards, but I was too frantic to secure her safety. Plus, I wanted those invisible handcuffs on her the second she was back in my bed, where she belongs.

"Well, then," Magda gives a tight nod, "shout if you need anything."

When my mother's stifling presence is gone, I put my hands on Valentina's shoulders and turn her to me. Her muscles slacken as the tension leaves her body. Magda makes her nervous.

I brush a thumb over the smooth skin of her cheek. "I have business to take care of this afternoon, and I won't be home for dinner. I'm going over to Sylvia's to break the news to Carly."

Apprehension fills her eyes. "How will she take it?"

"She'll be fine." I give her a reassuring squeeze, even if I have my doubts. "If you're going over to Kris', or anywhere for that matter, the guards will go with you."

She doesn't contest the new invasion of her privacy. Valentina already knows when a battle is not worth fighting.

I kiss her lightly. "Call me if you need me or if you're not feeling well."

"I'll be fine," she says in a chastising tone.

I chuckle and kiss her again. She will be. She's too strong to be anything else.

Valentina

THE AIR in the house is suffocating. No matter where I turn, Magda is there.

"What on earth are you wearing?" she exclaims when I come downstairs in a calf-length wool dress with boots. "This shows every roll and bulge on your body. You want to hide your stomach, not draw attention to it. Try a short dress that you can wear like a blouse over a pair of slacks, and go for flats. These heels," she waves at my boots, "look like a prostitute costume for Halloween. A scarf is always good to round off your appearance. I'll take you to Hermes in Sandton tomorrow. They have a new range in neutral colors for winter."

In short, she wants me to dress like her. Ignoring her comments, I escape to the kitchen for a cup of tea. Marie enters with a bunch of coriander as I switch on the kettle.

"How are you doing, Marie?"

Her mouth droops on one side. "Shlut."

It takes me a while to figure out what she said. Suddenly, my thirst for a warm drink is gone.

"Where's Oscar?"

She doesn't answer.

I find him sleeping on the dryer. "Hey, baby. I missed you." I scratch behind his ear and am rewarded with a purr.

Curiosity drives me to my old quarters. The room is bare. The bed has been stripped, and the curtains are gone. It feels unreal to see the space so empty. A part of me belongs here. Strangely, I'm sentimental about my first intimate moments with Gabriel that took place in this room. I recall with uncanny clarity the first night he came to me. If he were a less skilled lover, would my reaction to him have been different? Somehow, I doubt it. The truth is I'm as attracted to Gabriel as I'm frightened of him. His darkness has long since invaded my heart, making me a soul mate to the unspeakable needs that drive him.

From far-off, Magda calls for me. I escape outside to see Bruno. At least he's happy to have me back. After playing with him for a while, I follow the path to the staff quarters. Quincy is with Charlie.

He gets to his feet when I enter. "Mrs. Louw."

"Please, I'm still Valentina."

He gives a small nod. "How are you?"

"I'm good."

"Are you?"

"Yes, of course." My smile is forced as I move to Charlie. "Still playing cards?"

"He plays a mean game of poker." Quincy laughs. "He cleaned out the coin jar."

"Thank you," I say gratefully. "I'll take him off your hands as soon as I get back from Kris'."

"No sweat. We're having fun. Gabriel mentioned that you'd go. The guards are ready when you are. Shall I call Kris and let her know you're on your way?"

"That will be kind, thank you."

It took time getting used to Rhett or Quincy driving me around when Gabriel wasn't available, but now I have an entourage of two cars and seven men.

"Isn't this over the top?" I ask my driver.

He doesn't answer, and for the rest of the way we're silent.

Kris comes outside the minute we park. The men take up positions around the property.

"Val!" Kris takes me into a hug and holds me at arm's length. "Are you all right?"

"Perfect."

She glances at the men. "Are they really necessary?"

"Gabriel seems to think so. Let's go inside."

She takes my arm and leads me to the practice. "I cleared my schedule when Quincy called. I just have to finish the midday medications."

"Oh, Kris, you shouldn't have." She needs the consultation money.

"I want to talk to you without interruptions."

"I could've come tonight."

"I couldn't wait. Come on, take the tray."

I take the tray with the pills, syrups, and syringes, and follow Kris to the hospital kennel. Boxes are stacked in the corner and on every free surface. Reading the labels, I shoot her a questioning look. "A computer? And printer?"

She administers an injection to a Pug. "More like computers and printers, as in plural."

"Did your ship come in?" Nobody deserves it more than Kris. "Did you inherit money from a long-lost uncle?" I tease. "What happened?"

She finishes with the injection and closes the cage before turning to me. "Gabriel, that's what happened."

"What?"

She waves her arm at the boxes. "All of this is from him. It came last week. There are also an ECG and X-ray machine in the backroom."

"Where are you going to put all this stuff?" The practice is bursting out of its seams as it is.

"An architect came to see me about plans for extending. The plans include a reeducation pool, Val."

I gape at her. "Gabriel?"

"Yes."

"Did you accept?"

"No."

"What did he say?"

"He told me to drive everything to the garbage dump if I don't want it." She carries on with her administrations.

"That sounds just like him."

"Why did he do it?" she asks, wiping her hands on her overcoat and giving me a piercing look.

"He didn't say?"

"Nothing."

"Shall we have some tea?"

"All righty."

We finish the round of medicine and go to the house. In the kitchen, she takes two beers from the fridge.

"No thanks. I'll stick with tea."

I switch on the kettle while she cracks open the can and watches me from under her lashes.

"What the fuck, Val?"

I sigh and lean against the counter. "I'm really, really sorry about running off with Charlie like that. I couldn't tell you. I didn't want to put your life in danger."

"Gabriel stormed in here looking like a madman. The guy is normally a freaky, frightening shit, but the way he looked that day scared the bejesus out of me. Why did you run?"

"I thought… I was worried he'd make me do something I didn't want to."

"Like what?"

I grapple for words, trying to find the most tactful ones.

"Like what, Val?"

"I'm pregnant."

"Jesus." She turns her head to the ceiling and drags a hand over her face. When she locks eyes with me again, there's sympathy in hers. Her gaze slips to my stomach. "How many months?"

"Four."

"Too late for an abortion."

"I didn't want one."

"Why not? Did you fucking plan it?"

I give her an incredulous look. "Of course not. I took my pill every day." I fiddle with the teabag. "I don't get where I went wrong."

Her sigh is labored. "It happens. The pill isn't one hundred percent effective. There's always the one percent exception, but why did you let the pregnancy come this far? No one would've blamed you if you'd ended it. Your circumstances aren't exactly normal."

"It's not the child's fault."

"Neither is it yours." Her voice turns bitter. "It's Gabriel Louw's fault."

"It takes two to tango."

"I'm not naïve, Val."

"He didn't rape me."

"No?"

"No!"

"Can you honestly tell me you gave him your consent?"

"Yes. Actually, I begged him." I take down the tin with sugar so Kris won't see the shame in my eyes.

"I told you he was fucking with your mind. Please don't tell me you love him."

I can't face her. "I told him those exact words yesterday."

"You did not."

"I also said I hated him more."

"What is this? A love-hate thing?" She walks to my side and lowers her head, searching for my eyes. "What do you think you have with him, Val? You still owe him money, and nine years of slave labor."

I pour the water over the teabag. "He wrote all of that off."

"Because of the baby?"

Cupping the mug, I turn to her. "We got married yesterday."

Her jaw drops. Her gaze goes to the ring on my left hand. For several seconds, she only stares at it, as if she can't make sense of what it is. Finally, she clasps a hand over her forehead and starts pacing the room. Neither of us speaks while she processes the news.

When she finally stops, it's to stare at me with incomprehension. "Explain it to me, because I don't get it."

I shrug. "I'm going to have his baby. Making me family was the only way he could protect me."

"Are you listening to yourself? You're a member of the Louw family. You're mafia, Val."

"They're not mafia. They're loan sharks."

"What the hell ever. Same difference. You married into the mob."

"Well, it's done. I can't take it back."

"Damn right, you can't." Her gaze shifts back to my stomach. "How does he feel about the baby?"

I swallow. "I'm sure he's not ecstatic, but he was man enough to face his responsibility." I don't say marriage had a lot to do with Gabriel's obsessive possessiveness of me.

She holds up a finger. "Let me get this straight. You found out you're pregnant, but couldn't get it over your heart to terminate it, and frightened that Gabriel would make you have an abortion, you ran, taking Charlie with you, because you knew Gabriel would come after him when he found you gone. And then?"

"Then I got Jerry––You remember my old neighbor?––to give me a car, and we drove to Durban. That's where Gabriel eventually caught up with me."

"And instead of killing you for running, he married you."

"Yes."

"Do you know how fucked-up this sounds?"

"I know the situation isn't ideal, but Charlie is safe, and so am I."

"My God, Val, you're going to be a mother. Is this what you want?"

"Maybe it's not what I would've chosen, at least not for another few years, but it happened, and I'm dealing with it as best as I can."

"What about your life?"

"What about it?"

"Is it going to be centered around the mistake you and Gabriel made?"

"My child is not a mistake."

"That's not what I meant. A life without love can get terribly lonely."

"I'll have my baby, won't I?"

"I'm not sure you will."

A feeling of dread creeps over me. "What do you mean?"

"You grew up with the business. You're not stupid. This child will be Gabriel's first and yours second. If his family is against you, they may not give you much of a say in how you raise him. In fact, if they want to, they can take him away from you."

"He's mine." I put a hand on my stomach. "Nobody takes him away from me."

"That's not how the family works," she says gently.

She's right. Gabriel holds all the power, but I can't face it. Not now.

"Listen, Val, just do me a favor. Get a job. Find something to occupy your mind, something that'll make you happy."

I sound immaturely bitter. "For in case I end up not having a child to take care of, you mean?"

"I care about you, kiddo. That's all."

"I know." I look away. "Gabriel wants me to run a charity project for strays."

"Do you?"

"I don't know. I've kind of lost my passion."

"Maybe it'll come back."

"Maybe."

"I'll always be here for you, no matter what. You know that, right? I just don't want you to look at the situation with blinkers and get a shock when reality hits."

"I know."

"Hey," she nudges me, "have you had lunch?"

"No."

"How about I cook us something and we talk about disposable versus echo-friendly diapers?"

"I have a better idea. I'll take you out to lunch and baby shopping."

"Don't grab the arm when I offer the little finger. There's a big difference between talking and actually walking through aisles filled with bottles and pacifiers."

"We'll also talk about your new practice. Are you going to keep the equipment Gabriel sent?"

"I haven't decided, yet."

I leave the tepid tea on the counter and take her hand. "You'll have to hire more people if you do."

"And set up a baby playpen for when his mom comes to visit."

I swipe at the tears building in my eyes. "Damn hormones."

"Here." She fishes a tissue from her pocket. "The best remedy to get over pregnancy hormones is tiramisu at Roma's."

"Yuk." I make a face. "The thought alone of coffee liquor and cream makes me sick."

"It's for me, not you. Looks like I'll need a double portion, today."

A laugh bubbles from my throat. "You're horrible."

"Love you too, kiddo."

Gabriel

On the way to Berea, I call Dorothy Botha. The psychiatrist greets me by name when she answers.

I dive straight in. "I need advice. When's a good time to call?"

"You can speak. I'm not with a patient."

"I need to break important news to Carly, and I was wondering how to go about it."

"What kind of news?"

"I got married, and my wife is pregnant."

A silence follows. "Does Carly know about your relationship?"

"We kept it secret. She was our maid."

"I see." The silence stretches even longer. "Does Carly like her?"

"Let's just say she doesn't hate her. After what you said about Carly's insecurity of losing me or her mother to a new spouse, I want to make sure I handle this correctly."

"I'm afraid it's too late. You handled it wrong the minute you decided to get married in secret. Carly hasn't been a part of the unfolding relationship or the events that led to your decision."

"Things were complicated. What do you suggest?"

"In a situation like this, I'd say go for honesty."

"Impossible. This is not a rose-colored fairy tale, Ms. Botha."

"If you can't tell all the facts, be as honest as you can. Tell Carly why you excluded her and be frank about your feelings. It may help her to express how she feels about your rash decision. Expect a negative reaction, and whatever you do, don't get upset. What she'll need is love and understanding. Give her time to deal with the news and to adjust, but make it clear that your decision won't change, if that's the case. It's important to show her stability and to reassure her that your love for her is unaffected."

"So, I just blurt it out?"

"No, you use tact. Give her a prompt to prepare her, something like, 'Carly, you remember Ms. So-And-So?'"

"Got it."

"Good luck. I'll chat to Carly about it during our next session."

"Thank you."

"My pleasure. Oh and congratulations."

I rub my aching neck muscles when she hangs up. As I've said to myself so many times during the last few days, I only have myself to blame.

The first thing on my agenda is to have a word with Jerry. I've been looking for him ever since the burglary at Valentina's old flat, the scruffy bachelor apartment I now own. The cockroach has been hiding from the day I took Valentina, but now that Magda has found him, he crawled out of the drainpipes, thinking he's safe from me. There are things that don't add up, and I want answers.

As per my instruction, Rhett and Quincy follow in the Merc. I needed privacy for the call I made to Ms. Botha. They park behind me in front of Jerry's building. The beggars on the sidewalk recognize my face. They scatter when I exit. From windows higher up, mothers shout in Xhosa and Sotho for their children to run inside.

Scott, my mother's bodyguard, gets out of the Merc with my two guys. This wasn't the plan.

He greets me with a curt nod. "Mr. Louw."

"Scott," I say, acknowledging him, and turn to Rhett. "What's the meaning of this?"

"Mrs. Louw sent him with us."

My mother has never sent a babysitter before, and she didn't send Scott out of motherly concern for my wellbeing. I've been in situations a lot more dangerous than this one. In any event, we're here, and I don't want to waste time.

"Quincy, stay with the cars," I instruct. We may be feared, but some dumb idiot or teenager on a drug high may get it into his head to steal the vehicles or the tires.

"Yes, boss." He takes out his gun, making sure it's visible.

"You guys come with me."

We climb the rusted steps to Jerry's floor. I pull my gun while Rhett bangs on the door.

"Who is it?" a voice calls from inside.

I don't feel like breaking down a door, today, so I cock my head at Scott who replies.

"It's Mrs. Louw's guy, Scott."

The key turns in the lock, and the door swings open. The minute the cockroach sees me, he reverses the action, trying to shut the door, but my foot is already wedged between the wall and the wood.

Knowing he's trapped, he swallows and backs up into the room. "What do you want?"

We enter the interior that looks and smells surprisingly clean.

"I'd like to ask you a few questions." I close the door and lock it.

His eyes follow the action. "About what?"

"Where were you hiding these last few months?"

"I wasn't hiding."

"No?" I move around the room, taking in the shelf above the television stacked with decks of cards and an early edition of Monopoly. I love this edition. Eloff Street, one of the main arteries of Hillbrow, is still a prized property in this board game.

"I was visiting family," he says, his eyes darting between Rhett, Scott, and me.

"Right." I lift the Monopoly lid. All the pieces, including the car, hat, shoe, iron, and cat, are there. "Or maybe you ran because you thought after taking Valentina I'd come for you."

He utters a nervous laugh. "Hey, I didn't do anything wrong."

"You took Charlie gambling, didn't you?"

His face pales a shade, but he keeps up the bravado. "Where's the sin in that?"

"Let's see." I take out the silver cat and study it in the light. "Maybe the fact that he's got brain damage and doesn't know the meaning of debt?"

The way he licks his lips reminds me of a lizard catching flies. "I don't understand."

"What don't you get?"

"Why are you here, asking about this?"

"Who broke into Valentina's flat?"

"I only heard about it from the neighbors. I told you, I wasn't here."

I advance on him, swinging the gun by the trigger guard. "Why did you give Valentina a stolen car?"

"Because I felt bad, okay?"

"Bad about getting her and her brother killed?"

He backtracks until his legs hit the couch. "You killed them?"

"I was going to, but you knew that."

"I didn't know for sure." He lifts his palms. They're sweaty and shaking. "Look, I didn't know a goddamn thing. I only did what your mother told me to do."

I freeze. I heard him perfectly well, but reflex makes me ask, "What?"

At the same time the word leaves my mouth, a shot rings out.

6

Gabriel

The body remains standing for two beats before it falls backward onto the couch. Jerry's corpse is staring wide-eyed at the ceiling, his mouth forever shut.

Slowly, I turn. Scott has his gun raised. The barrel is still smoking.

Anger makes my jaw lock tight. It takes three calming breaths before I can speak. "What the hell just happened?"

Scott lowers his weapon. "He was disrespectful."

If Scott was my man, I'd put a bullet in *his* brain, but he answers to Magda. In two strides I'm in front of him. I can't shoot him, but it doesn't mean I can't do *this*. I pull back and plant a fist under his jaw, sending him crashing into the coffee table.

Rhett aims his gun at Scott. His first priority is protecting me. Scott may be working for my mother, but, right now, in Rhett's eyes, he's an enemy. One wrong move and the curly head is dead. Scott knows it. From where he lies on the floor, he drops his weapon and raises his hands.

"No hard feelings," he mumbles, moving his jaw from side to side.

I walk closer and stop over him, gritting out my words. "I wasn't done."

"He wasn't going to tell you anything," Scott says.

Bullshit. He was going to tell me a whole lot more, and I want my answers. Going down on my haunches, I grab Scott's right hand and push back his middle finger. "Guess what, Goldie Locks? You're going to stand in for the man you killed."

He grunts when I apply pressure. "You can't touch me. I'm on Magda's payroll."

This does it. Black dots pop in my vision. "The thing, you see, is I don't give a fuck."

Uncertainty creeps into his eyes. The way his pupils are bouncing around as he takes stock of the room tells me he's considering his options. Fight or flight. He tries to pry his finger free, but I push back more. Before he snatches the gun on the floor, I use my free hand to slide it in Rhett's direction. When his fist comes up, I grab and squeeze until he gnashes his teeth.

"Why did you shoot him, Scott?"

He spits next to my feet. "Fuck you."

"If that's how we're playing, very well." A bit more pressure and his finger snaps above the knuckle.

A chilling cry fills the room. For such a big man he has a high-pitched voice. He'll make a good soprano.

I let go of his fist and move to his thumb. "You have nine fingers and ten toes left. This can take a while."

He grunts and wheezes as I bend the digit back. His muscles tighten. He thinks I won't see the blow coming, but I've been on the block far longer than him. I duck when his fist whizzes past my face and retaliate with a few punches in his ribs. Another one in his stomach takes out his wind.

"Fuck. Ouch." He coughs and gurgles. "Fucking shit."

Snap. That was his thumb.

His cry is ugly this time. From the doors slamming and the feet running on the landing, I gather people are fleeing the building. A gunshot is nothing new. Most people wait it out, hiding behind locked doors. Screams, they're a totally different ballgame. Nobody wants to be tortured, and if the neighbor isn't talking, chances are whoever is making him scream will come for you.

Scott is rolling around on the floor, curling into a fetal position. "You shit. You broke my thumb."

"If I do both trigger fingers you're out of business. Won't be much of a guard without a trigger finger, will you?"

"I know fuck-all." He grunts through his pain.

"I'll ask you one last time. Why did you shoot Jerry?"

"I was following orders."

I jerk him into a sitting position. "Whose orders?"

"Mrs. Louw's. All I know, is she told me to take care of him." His look is cutting. "It's not my job to ask questions."

I believe him. Rhett gives a small nod. He agrees.

"Take him back to the car," I say.

As Rhett is helping a bent-over Scott downstairs, I go through the flat, but find nothing of interest. Popping the Monopoly cat in my pocket, I close the door and join the men.

"Drive Scott home," I tell Quincy. "Rhett, keep a gun on him, just in case."

Scott is fuming when they bundle him into the back, but he's quiet. He's too clever to insult me again.

Pulling off ahead of them, I race north on Jan Smuts Avenue with the speed of the devil. I need more answers, and Magda will give them. She's working at the loan office in Yeoville today.

I barge straight into her office without knocking. "Why did you order Scott to shoot Jerry?"

"Gabriel." Her manner is non-startled as she gets up and rounds her desk. "He was a nuisance."

Mad anger coils through my insides, pulling my gut tight. "A nuisance? That's enough reason for a killing?"

"That's not it, and you know it. He was starting to cause problems."

"You know what I think?" I close the distance. "I think you wanted to shut him up."

A laugh bubbles from her throat. "Shut him up?"

"He was about to tell me what you ordered him to do."

"Me? Give him an order? Are you out of your mind? The only contact I had with Jerry was to get more information on Charlie Haynes' whereabouts."

"I find that hard to believe."

"You'd believe that low-life car thief over me? Jerry was scared. Of course he'd spew all kinds of bullshit." She crosses her arms. "Believe what you will, I did your job for you. Jerry gave your wife a car––a stolen car, may I add––to run away from you. If you were man enough he would've been dead the minute I gave you the information."

"My first priority was finding Valentina. After that I had other priorities."

"Like fucking her?"

To prevent myself from strangling Magda, I plaster my fists at my sides. "You won't speak about my wife like that."

"Calm down." She drops her arms. "Since when can't I call a spade a spade?"

"You're vulgar."

"I'm honest."

"Are you?"

"I don't have time for your games. Scott killed Jerry because we had to show the world no one messes with one of us, and Valentina is one of us. Giving her a car was as good as messing with you or me. The next time she runs, her friends will think twice about aiding her in her silly quests."

"It won't happen again."

"It better not. It won't look good for you if your own wife runs away." She walks back to her chair and sits down. "Anything else?"

My words are measured. "Not today."

"Good. Now get out of my hair. I have work to do."

At the door, I say over my shoulder, "Oh, by the way, Scott has a couple of broken fingers."

The charcoal lines around her eyes crinkle. "That was a childish thing to do."

"He may also have a few broken ribs." The words give me enormous satisfaction. "If he ever gatecrashes one of my parties again, on your invitation or not, he won't leave alive." I wink. "Keep that in mind if you value him as a member of your staff."

Her eyes are spitting venom as I shut the door.

In my study at home, I add Jerry's Monopoly cat to my jar of charms. One for each life I've taken. I may not have pulled the trigger, today, but the intention was there. In my book, intention is as good as action.

The jar is disturbingly full. It sits on the corner of my desk to remind me of who I am. I can put a face to every memento in that jar. I tell myself every one of them was justified, a necessary kill in this constant war of survival, but I'm losing my appetite for the killing. My path has been set, and I've been following it as my heritage demands. With this new path I'm walking with Valentina, it feels as if I'm veering farther and farther away from where I came. I don't know where the hell I'm going, but I know I can't go back. I want to walk this road with her too much, her and my baby.

The afternoon drags on with affairs that keep me occupied until late, and when I finally pull into Sylvia's driveway it's close to seven. Dinner is served at eight. I'm hoping to get the big talk with Carly out of the way before we sit down for the meal.

Sylvia waits at the door, a hand on her hip. "Hey, Gab. Gabriel," she corrects, catching herself. Her smile is sweet and filled with the womanly self-assurance of someone who knows she's physically desirable. "You had me wondering about this hasty dinner all day."

"I didn't mean to give you extra work."

She laughs softly and holds out a hand for my jacket. "Don't fret. My cook did all the work." She deposits the jacket on the coat stand. "Are you going to tell me the reason we're having dinner with Carly, or are you going to make me sweat it out another hour?"

"Where's Carly?" I look around the foyer and up the staircase. I don't want my daughter to overhear anything prematurely.

"In her room. I'll call her down in a second. Shall we have a drink?"

She's already on her way to the lounge. I follow, looking around the foreign space. I've been in Sylvia's house a few times, but it still feels unfamiliar. Overly stuffy. Too perfectly decorated. No pets, books, or shoes lying around. Nothing to hint at life. Carly's toys were never splayed on our stairs or even the playroom carpet. Will Valentina allow life into our home? My chest fills with something warm and light as I picture trains, fire engines, and stuffed toys littering our floors.

"Here you go." She hands me a glass of Scotch on the rocks and takes one for herself, which she clinks to mine. "Now, tell me the purpose of this secretive family meeting."

It's probably better that I prepare her before I speak to Carly. I mull over the words, but there's no easy way of saying it. Finally, I settle for short and sweet. "Valentina and I got married yesterday."

Her hand stills with the glass halfway to her mouth, her red nail varnish standing out against the white of her skin where she grips the tumbler. Her eyes grow large, and her lips thin.

"She's going to have my baby."

Pulling back her arm, she slaps me across the cheek. I saw the blow coming. I could've stopped it, but I allowed her the violence as an outlet for her shock.

"You son of a bitch. How dare you humiliate our family like this?" Her voice rises. "You married the *maid*?"

"You know making her our maid was Magda's idea of getting the payback she believed we deserved."

"She caught you, didn't she?"

"Actually," I give her a cold smile, "I caught *her*."

"Why?" She bangs the glass down on the mantelpiece, drops of alcohol sloshing over the sides. "You could've had Helga or any other woman of your social standing."

"I don't want any other woman." My words are measured. "I want *her*."

"How old is she?"

"Twenty-three."

"Is this some kind of midlife crisis? Is this why you have to go for a girl fifteen years younger than you? You have to prove to yourself you still have it?"

"Is that why you're getting engaged to a younger man?"

"Fuck you, Gabriel. It's not the same."

"No, it's not, because your decisions when it comes to relationships and marriage are not based on love or affection, but on which move will serve your financial and political position best."

"Love and affection?" She utters a laugh. "Are you telling me you *love* her?"

"I don't know about love, not anymore, but whatever I feel is the closest thing I've ever felt to being happy."

"You're a fool."

"I was a fool for loving you once."

"You still do."

"Maybe––you'll always be the mother of my child––but I want her more than any woman I've ever wanted."

The color drains from her cheeks. Rage fills her violet-blue eyes, but she maintains a calm voice. "I will *not* acknowledge that woman or her child."

"It's my child. Your disagreeable nature will make things more difficult for all of us, but that's your choice."

She pushes out her chin. "I'll call Carly and give the two of you a moment. Come through to the dining room when you're ready."

As her heels click over the marble, I take a long sip from my drink. A moment later, my daughter comes bouncing down the stairs.

"Dad!" She gives me one of those rare hugs. "Dinner in the week? At mom's house? What's going on?"

I leave my drink on the table and pull her down next to me on the couch. Through the open door, I spot Sylvia making her way to the kitchen. When our eyes meet, she gives me an accusing look.

I pull my attention back to Carly. "How's school, princess?"

"Good. You've seen my grades."

"How about living with your mom? Is it working out well?"

"Yes. Is this about asking me to move back to your place?"

"Of course not." I'm stalling for time, but by God it's difficult to broach the subject. "I have news." I put a bright smile on my face. "Very exciting news."

"Dad," she sweeps her hair behind her ear, "what is it?"

"I got together with someone."

"As in dating? That's great!"

"Actually, it's a lot more serious than dating. We already took it to the next level."

"You're engaged?" She shrieks. "Oh, my God! Who is she?"

"Not engaged, Carly," I say gently. "I jumped the gun and married her."

Her smile drops. She stares at me with the disappointment I expected but hoped not to see. "You're married?"

"Yes."

"W–when?"

"Yesterday."

"I–I don't understand. Why didn't you say something? Why do it in secret?"

"It was an impulsive decision. It's not that I didn't want you there for an important event. It just happened on the spur of the moment." This is the closest to honesty I can get.

Her mouth pulls down. "Oh, my God, I have a stepmother."

"I don't want you to think of her as a stepmom. Sylvia is your mother. She's my wife, and it'll mean a lot to me if you can be kind to her."

Her bottom lip starts to tremble. "Who is she? I mean, do I even know her?"

"Yes, you do."

A frown pulls her eyebrows together. "Who?"

"It's Valentina."

Before the name is out she's on her feet. "Dad, no! How could you? She's our maid!"

I get up and place my hands on her shoulders. "Carly, calm down, please, and listen to me. There's nothing wrong with being a maid."

"She irons my clothes and cleans my room, for God's sake!"

"She *was* our maid. Not any longer. We have a cleaning service for that, now."

"A maid! Could you not have made a less humiliating choice?"

"There's nothing humiliating about being a maid. Valentina was studying to become a vet before she started working for us, and she only came to work for us because she owed a lot of money and didn't have a choice."

She jerks free from my hold and turns her back on me.

I groan inwardly. "I thought you liked her."

"Is it the money? Did she marry you for your money?"

"No."

She twirls to face me again. "What then?" Her laugh is wry. In this moment, she looks so much like her mother. "Don't tell me you're in love."

"She's going to have a baby," I say softly.

Like Sylvia, her eyes grow big. Shock washes over her features, leaving her pale and silent.

I take her hand. "This doesn't change how I feel about you. I'll always love you. I'm sorry you had to find out like this, but I hope you'll accept Valentina as a part of this family."

She pulls away, clasping her hands behind her back. "I'll be seventeen in a month. You don't think it's a bit late to start a new family?"

"It's not a new family, princess. We're all family."

"She's *not* my family, and she'll never be!"

With a sob, she runs from the room. I'm torn between going after her and giving her space. I decide on the latter. I guess that went as well as it could. In time, she'll come around.

Sylvia leans her hip against the doorframe and swirls the liquor in her glass. "Congratulations, Gabriel. I hope you're happy."

She watches me with contempt as I cross the floor, a look not unfamiliar to me. It's the same one she gave me in bed, right before I touched her.

Craning her neck up at me, she continues, "I suppose dinner is off. I don't know about Carly, but if she feels like I do, she's lost her appetite."

"I understand."

She flattens her body in the frame for me to pass. As I go for my jacket, I'm acutely aware of my limp and the way her eyes burn on my back.

"Goodnight, Sylvia. I'll call Carly tomorrow."

The ice clinks in her glass. "You do that."

I see myself out and drive the short distance home. I like to tell myself Sylvia bought a house close to ours for Carly's sake, but it's always been the prestige of the neighborhood. Like Magda, Sylvia comes from a long line of descendants where money is everything and cast is determined by birth. The house staff doesn't mix with the proprietors. In her eyes Valentina will always be the servant.

Up until today, I never realized how many of Sylvia's values are embedded in Carly.

When I get home, I find Valentina on her knees in our bathroom with her head over the toilet.

Rushing to her side, I wipe the hair from her face. "Damn, Valentina. Are you all right?"

A feeble wave of her hand is supposed to send me away. "Just morning sickness." Her body convulses, but her stomach must be empty, because nothing comes out.

Concern burns in my gut. "I thought this was only supposed to happen in the morning."

She takes two steadying breaths. "All times of the day." Her laugh is weak, but not without humor. "This baby doesn't like pasta."

I wipe my hand over her clammy forehead. "What did you eat?"

"Fettuccini with cèpe mushrooms. I had lunch with Kris at Roma's." She turns around and slumps against the toilet. Her face is pasty white and dark rings mar her perfect eyes. "About that…" A stern look invades those bleary eyes. "What are you doing sending Kris all that stuff?"

I bent down and lift her into my arms. Even at four months pregnant she weighs nothing. The worry weighs heavier on my shoulders. She looks exhausted. From the way her body is reacting, I poisoned her with my seed. I let her down on the rug and start to pull the dress over her head. Obediently, she lifts her arms.

"I asked you a question, Gabriel."

I unhook the clasp of her bra and push the straps down her arms. "She's your friend."

"Is that your motivation for spending a fortune on her practice?"

The panties follow next, but her boots prevent me from removing the stockings. "The way things were going, her practice wasn't going to survive much longer."

"If I stay, Kris gets a revamped practice, and if I leave, she's dead."

"Yes."

My answer is harsh, but she needs to understand the lengths I will go to. The knowledge that she's here against her will is a bitter pill to swallow, but I will gobble down flames, fire, and toxic waste if that's what I have to do.

I crouch down to unzip her boots. "Why bring it up? Are you planning on leaving?"

"No."

Right answer. "Then let Kris enjoy the gift and stop worrying about it. Except for the nauseating pasta, how was your lunch date?"

Her expression brightens. "Good. I missed Kris. She's a good person, you know."

"I don't doubt it."

I remove her boots and then the stockings, allowing my fingers to linger longer than necessary.

"You're back early." Her look is thoughtful. "How did Carly take the news?"

"Not well, but she'll come round."

"Oh, no, Gabriel. I'm so sorry."

"It's not your fault."

"It is. If I hadn't gotten pregnant––"

My gut twists with guilt. "I don't want to hear you talk like this."

If I were going to come clean, now would be the time, but my decision is made. She opens her mouth, but I still her with a finger on her lips. No more talk of our inside-out, right-in-every-wrong-kind-of-way relationship. No more talk, at least not for the rest of tonight, not while her naked body is right in front of me. Going down on my knees, I cup her hips and pull her toward me. She gives two tiny steps, but the momentum makes her stumble into me. I press my lips against her abdomen and hold them there until her gasp startles me.

"Oh, wow." She utters a delighted giggle. "I felt him."

My throat tightens with an unknown emotion. "The baby?"

"He moved." She stares at her stomach in wonder. "It felt like butterfly wings."

We laugh together as I splay my hands over the tight skin of her belly while she cups her hands over mine. I'm unable to process the wonder unfolding beneath my palms. She's a miracle, and she makes my life happier for this incredible gift.

"Do it again," she says, lifting her hands to give me access.

I plant kisses all over her belly, starting with her navel and ending on her pubic bone.

She says my name like it's a happy word. A ten-megawatt smile burns on my face.

"Did it work?"

"Yes." She laughs again, her eyes filling with reverence. "Oh, my God, Gabriel." She takes my hand and moves it back over her stomach. "Can you feel it?"

"It's too early, beautiful. Tell me what it's like."

"It tickles inside."

A happy glow transforms the pale face with the dark rings. It's a beautiful moment I don't deserve, but I take it greedily. I'd stay on my knees forever to be part of these magical milestones Sylvia wouldn't share with me. For another moment longer, I hold her to me, pressing my face against her warm skin, inhaling the raspberry fragrance I associate with her. I'm reluctant to let go, but she's probably tired and weak from the bout of sickness. Tearing myself away, I run a shower. There's enough space for us both to stand comfortably, but I sit on the bench and drape her over my body, unwilling to break our contact. She lets me take care of her, washing her body and hair.

When we're both dry, I carry her to our bed. My only intention is to hold her while she rests, but when her hand wraps around my shaft, my willpower dissolves. I roll over her, keeping my weight on my arms, and kiss her lips. She gasps as my cock sinks into the heat of her pussy, and then there are only moans as I make love to her, slowly and reverently.

COME MORNING, I force myself to leave our bed. Valentina is sleeping, and if I stay another second, I'm going to wake her with my cock in her pussy. Again. We made love until late, and she needs her sleep. I can't act like a goddamn horny teenager around her all of the time. The problem is I want her more than ever. With enticing curves and pretty features, she's always been my perfect little toy, my pet, but now she's a goddess. When I fell for her, it was for her strength and loyalty. This time round, I'm smitten by her unconditional love for the life she carries and her uncomplaining nature in dealing with the pregnancy curveballs.

Some women get sick, some feel tired, some have backache, and some develop cravings, but Valentina has everything. This pregnancy came at her with the full-blown force of a hurricane. I'm in the shower when she storms into the bathroom and vomits her guts out.

I'm out in a flash, wrapping a towel around my waist. I let her finish before helping her up.

She wipes the back of her hand over her mouth. "I'm sorry you had to see that."

Tangling my fingers in her hair, I push her cheek against my chest. "You've got nothing to be sorry about. We're in this together, baby."

She puts an inch of distance between us and gives me a grateful, guilty kind of smile that shatters my heart, because I don't deserve one drop of her thankfulness and especially not her guilt.

She touches her wild morning hair. "I must look a mess."

"You've never looked more beautiful."

This time her smile blinds me with its radiance. She cups my cheek on the scarred side of my face. "You're sweet."

"Sweet?" I advance on her, trapping her against the vanity. "Is that how you'd describe me?"

"Like sugar."

"Sugar, eh?" She shrieks when I catch her around the waist and lift her onto the counter. "You're doing serious damage to my reputation."

"Just a big, old, fluffy, sweet bear," she taunts.

"Old? Fluffy? Now you're asking for it." I tickle her sides, inviting more shrieks and a wild bout of screaming.

"Stop," she says through tears of laughter, trying to catch my wrists.

I catch hers instead and pin them to the mirror above her head. I want to look at her. She's insanely gorgeous when she wakes up and even more so when she's happy. Laughing tears cling to her eyelashes, making them appear darker. Traces of the same wetness run over her flushed cheeks. Silky hair tumbles in curls over her shoulders. Her breasts are firm, their new weight pulling them slightly down. Under my unabashed scrutiny, her nipples harden, pulling her areolas tight. I'm standing between her legs, her knees brushing up against my hips. My cock stirs. My breathing quickens. The mound of her shaved pussy presses against my dick where it rises under the towel. I rip the towel from my body and cover the taps to protect her back before bending her knees and placing her heels on the edge of the countertop. She's spread wide, and it's all for me.

I place the pad of a finger on her clit. "Mine."

"Yours," she echoes, her breathing shallow.

"I want to make you burn."

"Then touch me."

The laughter and playfulness are gone. That's exactly what I'm going to do. Touch her. I shouldn't, but I'm not strong enough to resist. My conscience says she needs to rest, but my lust says she's awake, anyway. Fuck my good intentions. I need her. I need her pleasure. I need her *intense* pleasure. It's too soon to take her like at Mount Grace. Fucking her ass like that, I kind of lost it after not having had her for so long, and I don't want to lose it again. I don't want to hurt her, at least not in a non-erotic way.

I squeeze her wrists. "Keep your hands up."

Fear mixes with excitement in her eyes. She wants this, because this is what I taught her. This is how I made her. It's all she knows.

Reaching over her for the wall cabinet, I take out the orgasm oil I saved for an occasion like this. I unscrew the cap and deposit the bottle on the counter. She watches me with wide eyes, licking her lips nervously.

All of my attention hones in on her pussy. Carefully, using the fore and middle finger of one hand, I part her lips, exposing the treasure buried between them. Her clit is engorged. Wetness glistens around her slit. She's turned on. Hell, so am I. My cock is about to combust, and I'm only looking at her. Holding her open, I turn the bottle upside-down and wait for a drop to form at the dripper nozzle.

I catch her gaze, silently commanding her eyes to hold mine. "This is going to feel warm, but it's perfectly safe."

She communicates her trust with a small nod.

"Good girl."

I drip the stimulant oil on her clit and massage it into the nub. Her flesh swells and turns a shade darker. Heat penetrates the calloused skin of my fingertip. I can only imagine how hot her delicate clit must be burning. The sight of that delectable flesh turning to a torturous blaze under my ministrations is enough to make me ejaculate without touching my dick, but I tear my gaze away to read the expression in her eyes. Her head is resting against the mirror, her face turned to the side. Two more seconds, and the hotness will turn into a quick-lasting, intense inferno. Right on cue, her eyes fly open. Red blotches color her cheeks.

She utters a low moan. "It burns."

"I know, baby."

I stop the massaging, giving her time to absorb the sensation. As the intensity climbs, her clit swells. Her feet slip from the counter. She tries to relieve the sensation by closing her legs, but I need to watch. Pushing open her thighs, I trap her body with the weight of mine and press my oil-coated finger on her asshole.

"Want to burn here, too?" I ask, kissing her shoulder.

"No." She squirms under me. "Please."

"Then keep your legs open."

She rotates her hips, trying to press her burning parts on the cold marble, but I catch her legs to keep her still. She gnaws on her bottom lip and tries to be quiet as she rides the wave that burns through her genitals, but her whimpers are becoming louder.

"Please, Gabriel. I need to come."

The stimulant makes her clit pulse with need, and the bite of heat will only make it hotter when she comes. Her pussy is wet with her arousal, the lips dark pink and swollen, inviting me to sink my cock into the soft, warm depth beyond. On the brink of exploding, my cock spills pre-cum. I part her folds with one hand and flick her over-stimulated clit with my nail. Every time my nail connects with her skin she dilates a little more and screams a little louder. I count every flick, measuring the pressure carefully. Too hard or soft and she won't find release like this. She comes on the eleventh count with a wail that lifts the roof. Her pussy contracts around nothing but air, but it won't be empty for long. I press the head of my cock on her clit, rubbing in circles to prolong the orgasm. She clamps her legs around my hips. The heat that drove her to this high penetrates the tip of my penis and burns down my shaft in a slow, agonizing mixture of painful pleasure. The urge to spear into her is fierce, but I count to five, take a few deep breaths, and enter her carefully.

Her pussy is tight, hot, and wet with a distant echo of a burn. I stop when I'm buried to the hilt. This is what I always want, to take her so deep she doesn't know where she begins and I end.

There's an endless need to my rhythm as I start pumping. She drops her arms to grip the basin for support as I shove into her, making her back collide with the mirror. I need her to come again, with me this time. Having made it my business to understand her body, I know how to make that happen. Gripping both nipples between my fingers, I use the hard tips as leverage to bounce her curves. The clench of her pussy on my cock is the reaction I'm after. I thrust harder and pick up my pace. Her body tenses, and her legs hug me tighter.

"Come, beautiful." I release her nipples and grab her breasts in my palms, kneading the flesh as my own climax starts to build at the base of my spine. "Goddamn. Fuck."

My load explodes like hot jets of lava. I bite back another curse and fall over her, trapping her body between my arms.

"Goddammit, Valentina." I rest our foreheads together while I catch my breath.

By the time I feel more or less steady, she's still lying back against the mirror, her muscles like mush.

"Don't move."

I turn on the shower and rinse us both, taking care to wash her gently. When she's dry, I coat her genitals with a vaginal balm to alleviate any lingering burn and just to be sure her asshole, too.

Wiping my fingers on her inner thigh, I search her eyes. "How are you doing?"

Her smile is soft and sleepy. "Mm."

I wish I could take her back to bed, but our first appointment will be here in thirty minutes. We don't have time for more than a chaste kiss. "Get dressed and come down for breakfast. You need to eat. After breakfast, there's someone I'd like you to meet."

"Who?"

"Just do as I say."

"I'll go check on Charlie, first. It was his first night in his new room."

"Let him sleep. He was up late with Rhett, watching movies."

"This is new to him."

"He'll be fine."

"I just--"

My palm lands on her naked backside. *Smack.* "Are you deliberately provoking me to spank your ass?"

For a crazy moment a new bout of lust flares in her eyes. It looks as if she may consider that forbidden spanking, but then she turns to brush her hair.

My phone buzzes on the nightstand with a message from Magda. Our appointment arrived early. Thank God Valentina doesn't ask more questions. I have no idea how she'll react to the man waiting for us downstairs.

7

Gabriel

By the time I get downstairs, Christopher van Wyk and Magda are conversing in the lounge. Magda introduces us. He's a close friend, and this was her idea.

"I'm early," he says, shaking my hand, "but I didn't know how traffic would be from Pretoria."

"Why don't you join us in the dining room?" I offer. "We can talk over breakfast."

Magda is in the middle of pouring coffee when Valentina comes down the stairs. Like a fool, I stop what I'm saying to stare at her through the open door. She's crazily, inhumanely, angelically beautiful. Her hair has more volume, and her face has a pregnancy glow. Maybe some of it is the post-orgasm endorphins coursing through her blood, but the pearly quality of her smooth skin is something I've only seen with expecting mothers. The blue dress is fitted, showing off the roundness of her full breasts and stomach. There's a spark in her eyes as she looks straight at me, a telltale sign of secrets, of moments in bathrooms only we share.

"You were saying?" Christopher urges.

"I–uh…"

Valentina saves me by stopping in the door.

I get to my feet. "Let me introduce you to my wife. This is Valentina. Valentina, meet Christopher van Wyk. He's a hypnosis psychologist."

Christopher comes around the table to shake her hand. "Pleased to meet you, Mrs. Louw."

Magda tenses when Christopher attributes Valentina with our surname, but she plasters a smile on her face. "Christopher is a friend. I wanted you to meet him, Valentina."

"Me?" Valentina takes the chair I hold for her.

"Since Charlie is now part of the family," Magda says, "I want to look into all possible treatments."

Valentina looks at me quickly, a question in her eyes.

"I didn't have time to tell you." The truth is I didn't want to give her the opportunity to refuse.

"We've already tried everything," she says politely.

"Not hypnoses, I'm sure," Magda says.

"No, not hypnoses, but I've met with all the specialists in Johannesburg. Nothing can reverse the brain damage."

"We're not talking about repairing damage," Christopher says, taking his seat again. "We're talking about making sure he's comfortable and happy."

"I assure you, Charlie is as balanced and happy as he can be."

"Hypnoses can help him be more autonomous." Magda brings her cup to her lips. "He needs more stimulation and friends. There are wonderful institutions in Johannesburg that can provide that."

Alarm flashes across her pretty features. "Gabriel, you said he could live here."

"He can." I cup her hand. "I only want you to consider all possibilities now that money is not an issue."

"He needs me." She glances at the people around the table like a trapped rabbit. "I'm his only family."

"Shh." I pull her chair closer to mine and put an arm around her shoulders. "I don't want you to get upset. The decision remains in your hands."

"You'll let me decide?"

"Of course."

Her tense shoulders relax a fraction. "What does the treatment entail?"

"A few sessions of hypnoses," Christopher says, "during which Charlie will go into a state of deep relaxation. He'll come out of the sessions feeling centered and at peace. I've used my technique in similar cases to help with insomnia, loss of appetite, speech problems, ticks, repetitive actions, involuntary cussing, anti-social behavior, and incoherent thoughts."

"Charlie has a short attention span, and he repeats syllables, but he eats and sleeps well."

"We'll do an extensive evaluation beforehand," the doctor says.

"If it's in Charlie's best interest…" She looks at me.

"It is," I say. "There are also legal issues you neglected, such as declaring Charlie financially incompetent and formalizing your guardianship. We'll look at that after breakfast."

Her gaze flickers between Magda and me. She doesn't trust us, and I don't blame her. She always took care of her brother without help, and we were going to kill him, after all.

"You're not alone any longer," I whisper in her ear. "I'll take care of everything."

Valentina

AFTER BREAKFAST, Gabriel gives me documents to sign to declare Charlie financially incompetent and to secure my guardianship. I'm eager to see how my brother is doing this morning, but Charlie wakes late. I'll have to have a word with Rhett about the movie nights. Charlie is happy with his new bedroom, especially the flat screen television mounted on the wall.

I make Charlie a breakfast of tea and toast, and introduce him to Bruno, but the two don't hit it off. Bruno must sense Charlie's apprehension. Usually, Charlie doesn't venture outside unless lured by someone dangling a reward in front of his nose, but I give him strict instructions about asking before going to the garden. I don't think Bruno will attack him, but I prefer to be over-cautious. To get Charlie out of the house, I decide to take him shopping with me after lunch.

When I tell Gabriel about my plan, he's pleased that I'm getting out and spending money. He walks us out and hands me a set of keys.

My fingers fold around the key ring. "Keys to the house?"

"Yes." He chuckles. "And your wheels. Sorry it wasn't ready when you arrived, but there was no stock on the floor. I had to order it."

There are five cars parked on the curb of the circular driveway. To who do they all belong? Maybe the guards or Magda and the cleaning service staff.

"Go on," he says, indicating the remote in my hand.

When I press the button, the indicator lights of a Porsche Cayenne Turbo lights up.

"That's very kind, but--"

"Don't say you won't take it," Gabriel says darkly, "because it's my job to provide for you."

"All right, I won't say I won't take it, but it's a big car. I just need something small."

"It's a safe car with enough space for a pushchair, carrycot, feeding chair, nanny, and whatever else women need when they go out with a baby."

The wayward look of panic in his eyes as he rumbles off the items makes me laugh. I punch him playfully on the arm. "I won't need more than a pushchair and definitely not a nanny."

"No?" He seems surprised.

"My mom and I were close."

He still looks at me with his brow raised in question.

"I want to raise my child myself. I want to experience everything, both the hard and joyful parts." Kris' words suddenly haunt me. I wrap my arms around his waist and look into his eyes. "You'll let me take care of our baby, won't you?"

The tenderness in his touch as he brushes the hair from my face reassures me. "Anything you want. As long as it doesn't tire you too much."

Going on tiptoes, I kiss him. "Thank you for the car." I learned my lesson. There's no point in arguing.

"My pleasure. Drive safely."

He nods at the guards standing next to a black Mercedes as Charlie and I get into my new car. I know they'll follow, but I also know it's for our safety.

"Mi–milkshake. Can we have mi–milkshake?"

"We're going to buy Gabriel a gift, but we can stop for dessert. In fact, we can do better than milkshake. How about a banana split?"

Charlie's mouth drops open. I swear there's a drop of drool on the side. I pat his leg. "I know. You haven't had many of those. Not nearly enough."

We drive to a nearby mall in Rosebank. After Orange Grove, Rosebank is the suburb with the largest Jewish settlement. It thus comes as no surprise that I run into someone from the Jewish business from way back.

"My goodness," Agatha Murray cries, "aren't you the Haynes girl?" She looks Charlie up and down. "You must be Charles."

"That's right. How are you?"

"You probably don't remember me."

It's hard not to remember her. Agatha has the same look from when she removed her false teeth and slurped her tea from the saucer in our kitchen. From head to toe, she's dressed in black, always a lacy dress with a cloak and hat. She's been dressed that way since her husband died, a long time before Dad passed away. She must own a thousand hats. I've never seen her with the same one. Today, she wears a box style creation with a crow feather bouquet and a big, faux diamond that keeps the lot together.

"Oh, no, I do remember," I say.

"Sad about your parents. So wrong."

Charlie starts to shuffle his feet. He's getting impatient.

"And Charles," she says when her eyes are drawn by his movements. "What a tragedy."

Tragedies are not on my topic list for the day. This morning's meeting with Christopher already made me feel guilty enough. "Nice running into you."

"I suppose Charles would've taken over the business if not for the accident. He was always a big chunk of a boy, all muscles and the tallest of his class. Do you think he would've become the big boss, maybe run the mafia?"

I glance around to see if we're being overheard and keep my voice low. "I'm glad he's not part of that criminal lifestyle."

"Criminal or not, at least you wouldn't have ended up as poor as church mice. Are you still in Berea?"

"We moved."

"Where to?"

"I really have to go."

Bony fingers close around my left hand. Before I can pull back, she lifts my ring finger to the light.

"Will you look at that?" She gives a hen-like cackle. "From the size of this rock it's not Lambert Roos' ring." She studies the ring, turning my hand left and right.

Self-consciously, I pull away.

"Lambert didn't have a choice, you know. He wanted to marry you. He wasn't all bad, back then." She sniffs. "A bit lazy, but not all bad. Everything was set up for your engagement the day you'd turn eighteen, and the next thing you know, the Portuguese break down their door and threaten to kill everyone if they take you in. Said it would be a war between the Jewish and Portuguese. Just like that, they cut you loose. I think the payoff also had a lot to do with it."

"What?" I forget about Charlie's fretting and my irritation. "Why?"

"Don't know. Probably money. Money's always the motivation in the business, isn't it?"

I stare at her open-mouthed. My father was part of the Jewish mob, but they had an agreement with the Portuguese in the south.

"Anyways," she waves a hand, "all water under the bridge. That life is gone. Not many of the old gang is left." Her eyes take on a far-off look.

"I–I'm sorry. I have to go." Grabbing Charlie's arm, I drag him along the walkway.

"Wait! You haven't told me who you married."

Not wanting to listen to more, I rush head-on into a flow of pedestrians. Scratching open the old wounds of how my father died was too painful. I do my best to shake her words as I sip a fruit juice while Charlie gobbles down a banana split with all the trimmings. While we are in the café, Kris calls, asking how I am, and somewhat manages to distract me from my guilt trip.

"I need help at the practice," she says. "Can you come back?"

I owe her. "I'll be happy to. Can I bring Charlie?"

"I was hoping you'd offer. He did a great job walking the dogs."

We agree that I'd start next week on my old salary. I don't need the money––Gabriel transferred a ridiculously big amount to my account––but spending his money doesn't feel right. I should earn my own.

"Come over for lunch tomorrow," she says. "We'll talk about the logistics."

After our dessert, we hit the shops. I want to get Gabriel something for his birthday. We haven't spoken about it, but the big party, the one where I was supposed to work, took place while I was in Durban. It's pathetic, but I care. I can help it as little as I can help how he makes me feel with his touch. Even as I crave my freedom, to be allowed to make choices like any other human being, I meant it when I said I love him. I lied when I said I hate him more. My love for him has quietly blossomed inside of me, growing from the tiny kernel he planted. By the time I noticed the tree it was too late. It hurt when he told me I didn't mean it. Maybe that was why I retaliated by saying I hate him, and the fact that those hurtful words didn't have any effect on him wounded me even worse. Yet, always true to his word, he's making this good for me, and this is the happiest I've been in a very long time, since that tragic day on the thirteenth of February. Giving him something for his birthday is my way of showing appreciation. The only problem is that I have no idea what to get him. Gabriel has everything.

We walk around the mall until Charlie gets tired, and I have to make a decision. Coming to a stop in front of a bookstore, an idea hits me. It doesn't take long to find the book I'm looking for. I pay and have it wrapped. Forty minutes later, we're home.

With Carly living at her mom's, Magda has dinner served later. It allows her and Gabriel to work late. Charlie won't last that long, so I cook him spaghetti bolognaise and serve it with a salad in the kitchen. We unpack his clothes Gabriel's men brought over from Kris' and explore his new gadgets, which include a PlayStation and a stack of games, courtesy of Gabriel. He's settled for the night when Gabriel comes home after nine. Dinner is not until ten. He'll work another hour in his office. The gift clutched behind my back, I knock on his door.

His deep voice is laced with impatience. "Come in."

Uncertainly, I pause in the doorframe. He looks stressed and busy. I'm disturbing him.

Leaning back in his chair, he works his tie loose with one hand and holds the other out to me. "Come here."

I walk around his desk and stop next to him.

He stretches his neck to look around me. "What do you have behind your back?"

"A gift."

"A gift?"

"For you," I say shyly. He's going to think it's a silly idea.

"For me," he parrots. Warmth fills his eyes and then appreciation as he trails his gaze slowly over me. He pats his knee. "Then you better come over here and give it to me."

One more step puts me between his legs as he opens them to accommodate me. With his hands on my hips, he lifts me onto his lap, making me straddle him. The dress rides up over my thighs, exposing my underwear. I still have my hands clutched behind my back, so he can't let go of my waist without risking my balance, but he stares at the triangle between my legs as if he wishes to touch it with every fiber of his being.

"That's a real pretty gift," he muses. "I can't wait to open it."

The knowledge of how much he wants me fills my core with heat and my heart with a deeper kind of warmth. I bring the present from behind my back. "This is what you need to open."

A smile tugs at his lips as he lets go of me with one hand to take the gift. "What's the occasion?"

I cup his face, feeling the roughness of his beard between my palms, and kiss his lips. "Happy birthday. I'm…" It's hard for me to say this, but I have to get it off my chest. "I'm sorry I wasn't here. I'm sorry I ran. I'm sorry I put our lives in danger. I should've spoken to you, trusted you, but--"

"Shh." He stills me with a kiss. "There's nothing to forgive." His expression becomes pained. "No more of this talk, understand?"

I nod.

He holds up the gift. "You want me to open this now?"

"Whenever you like."

"Grab the armrest. I don't want you to fall."

When I do as he's instructed, he tears the paper away and holds the book up to read the title. "Baby names."

"I didn't know what to get you. You have pretty much everything, so I thought you could choose his name."

In our kind of families mothers name their babies. It's an unwritten and unbreakable rule. Their reasoning is that as long as they suffer the pain of childbirth, the choice is their privilege and right. The pain of childbirth has always been a foolproof bargaining chip, and the details thereof is an argument men aren't prepared to take on.

Gabriel swallows hard. He stares at me with a piercing gaze. "You'll let me?"

"It's not a real gift, but--"

The book falls onto his desk, and his arms come around me. "You'll really let me?"

"If you're fine with it."

"Valentina..." He presses our foreheads together. "You have no idea how much this means to me."

"I was hoping."

"Thank you." He gives me the gentlest of kisses, his trimmed beard scraping my skin. "It's a beautiful and unselfish gift."

"Do you have any ideas, yet?"

His lips tilt in one corner. "You're not supposed to say until the baby is born."

"I'll never be able to wait that long!"

He nips my bottom lip. "Looks like you dug yourself a very deep hole, but don't worry, you have five months to conquer your curiosity."

"You're evil."

The smile vanishes, and his expression turns serious. "Yes, I am, but no matter what I am, you're mine."

Before he can say more gloomy things, I kiss him again, running my fingertips over the rough ridges of his scars. He's my darkness and my love, and he has no idea how truly I am his.

Gabriel

My men inform me of my wife's run-in with Agatha Murray. It's accidental, or I would've picked up a call to or from Agatha's number on Valentina's phone. Yes, I'm a creep. I check my wife's calls, but it's as much for her protection as my peace of mind. Our business is dangerous. Even if most men play by the rules and only a crazy idiot will lay a finger on my wife, there are always the nutcases who would cross the line. Besides, she's still a forced wife, one I keep on a tight leash of pleasure and threats, and I prefer to be prudent when a mob family member like Agatha suddenly walks onto the stage.

Not wanting to raise the issue in front of Magda, I search out Valentina after breakfast. She exits Charlie's room with a laundry basket. What the hell? The thing is so big it blocks her view. She almost bumps into me. The collision is only prevented because I catch her waist.

Worry makes my voice sound angry. "What are you doing?"

She blinks. Her big, innocent eyes are wide. " Laundry."

I take the basket from her hands. "You're not supposed to carry heavy things." Scrap that. "You're not supposed to do the laundry."

A sweet smile flirts with her lips. They're full and pink, and so fucking kissable. "There's nothing wrong with my hands."

"I don't care. We have a service for this."

"Don't be difficult."

"You haven't seen difficult, yet." I put the basket aside, tangle my hand in her hair, and drag her to me. "I can show you, but it'll cost your tears and pleasure."

Those soft lips part. She moans. A soft ripple runs over the delicate skin of her throat as she swallows. When I pull her head back farther to look into the dark pools of her eyes, she sags against me, her body warm and supple. Her pupils dilate a fraction, and her gaze becomes lustful.

My words turned her on. Me, there's no word for what I am.

Combusting, maybe. Exploding. Trapped between our bodies, my dick pulses against her stomach, showing her how she affects me. What I want is to rip off her clothes and fuck her right here against the wall. I may go crazy if I don't.

Dragging my lips over her throat, I kiss a path up to her jaw. "Would you like that, beautiful? Do you want a bite of pain with your pleasure?"

Her breath catches. "Yes."

I graze her earlobe with my teeth. "Why?"

"It feels good."

The sadist in me roars. I want to spank her, whip her, belt her, but not while she's pregnant. The confirmation that she wants this is enough. Letting go of her hair, I catch her face between my palms and crush our mouths together. My tongue spears through her lips without waiting for her to open. She whimpers, and I swallow every sound. My hand moves up under her dress, finding the elastic of her underwear. My fingers are a hairbreadth away from penetrating her pussy when someone clears a throat behind me.

Fuck. Not now. I let Valentina's lips go with a sound close to a growl, blocking her body with mine until I've lowered her dress to protect her modesty.

Magda walks past us with a scowl. "You have a room, for God's sake."

That was a bucket of cold water on our moment. Valentina's cheeks burn like light bulbs. She averts her eyes and tugs a strand of hair behind her ear.

"We have a meeting in ten," Magda calls from the end of the hall.

Taking my wife's hand, I intertwine our fingers. "No more laundry or any housework for that matter."

"Laundry isn't hard work."

My tone doesn't leave room for arguing. "No laundry."

She consents with a huff.

"My men told me you ran into Agatha Murray, yesterday."

"Oh." Her brow furrows, as if the memory is unpleasant. "Yes."

"You look upset. What did she say to you?"

"It was nothing."

"Valentina, don't lie to me."

"Nothing important, anyway."

"It is to me."

Her shoulders sag. "You're impossible."

I take her other hand and pull her body against mine. "I have a video conference in five minutes. Start talking."

A sigh moves her breasts against my chest. "She said the Portuguese threatened Lambert's family with a war if they took me in. Apparently, he was bribed not to marry me."

Every muscle in my body tenses. What the hell do I make of the information? It's as I suspected. Lambert didn't turn his back on his promised bride because he didn't want her. He was fored to. The question is why.

The kiss I place on her lips is gentle. It's my way of rewarding her honesty. "Be a good girl today. I'll see you for lunch." I squeeze her hands and set her free.

"Gabriel?"

I grin like a teenager. God, I love it when she says my name, especially with that sliver of shyness, as if she's about to ask me for something and she thinks I'll refuse her. If she only knows, I'll bust my balls for her.

"Valentina?" I let her name roll over my tongue.

"I won't be here for lunch today."

"Where are you going?"

"To see Kris. With all the extensions in the practice…" She wrings her hands together.

"What is it?"

"She wants me to work with her again."

Kris did what I'd ask of her. This will be good for my girl. She's not the stay-at-home type. "Do you want to?"

"I'd like that."

"Good."

Her face lights up. Everything sparkles from her eyes to the happy blush on her cheeks. "Really?"

"Really. Be safe."

Her look turns serious. "You, too."

My cock rages in protest as I walk away from her. I'm done. Finished. Beaten. There's no more walking away from her. Ever. I can't exist without this scrap of a woman.

Valentina

I MORE OR less abate my nausea with two crackers and ginger ale before getting ready to meet Kris. Charlie and I are halfway to my car when Rhett comes jogging up the driveway. From the way sweat drips from his body, he's been out for a long run. Things between us have been awkward since Gabriel brought me back, mainly because I've been avoiding him. It's not his fault, but I'm still upset that he betrayed me. In the end, before I ran, I felt like we were becoming friends.

"Hi," I say to be polite without breaking my stride.

He grabs my wrist as I pass. "Valentina."

I look back over my shoulder. "Yes?"

"Can I talk to you?"

"I have a lunch appointment."

"It'll only take five minutes."

From the steel in his gaze, it's clear he's not going to budge.

"All right."

He relaxes marginally and releases my grip. "I had to tell Gabriel."

"I understand."

"You don't. Magda's men were going to kill you. The only way to keep you safe was to play that pregnancy card. Magda will never hurt the mother of her grandchild."

"Oh." Understanding blooms in my senses. "I thought Gabriel… I thought he…"

"Was going to force you to get rid of the baby?"

"Yes."

"Well, now you know."

"I owe you a thank you, then."

"I'll settle for you not being angry with me."

"I wasn't angry. You work for Gabriel, and your loyalty lies with him. I just felt betrayed."

A look of hurt washes over his face. "I didn't want to compromise your trust, but as I said, if I'd kept my mouth shut you would've been dead."

I look at Charlie quickly, but he doesn't react to the statement.

Rhett holds out his hand. "Friends?"

"Friends."

We shake on it.

"How are you doing?" His gaze trails to my rounder belly.

"I'm good when I'm not nauseous, vomiting, or crying for nothing."

He grins. "I hope you're giving Gabriel a go for his money." His face sobers. "Is he treating you all right?"

"Yes." I don't want to discuss my relationship with Gabriel. "Very well."

"Good." He pats Charlie on the back. "I have to get ready for door duty. See you around."

The atmosphere between us is lighter. There's some of the old banter in his manner as he calls back, "At least the baby saved me from training you."

"Not by a long shot."

He turns and skips backward. "How come?"

"The minute he's born we're back to basics."

He groans, but there's a grin on his face as he jogs away.

WE FIND Kris in the kitchen, frying veal schnitzels. The smell puts me off, but I swallow down my nausea.

"Sit down," she says. "Food's almost ready."

"Yum–yum." Charlie takes his usual seat at the table and sticks a napkin into his collar.

I pour the water while Kris dishes up rice, schnitzels, creamed spinach, and cinnamon pumpkin mash.

"So," she says between two forkfuls of food, "I've decided to go for it."

"The plans for extending?"

"The pool, the new operating room, the bigger kennel, everything."

"Good for you."

"I reckoned it's rude to stare a gift horse in the mouth."

My suspicion grows. Kris is too much of a principled person to change her mind overnight. "Is Gabriel behind this?"

She makes big eyes. "You know he's paying."

"I mean, did he tell you to do this for me?"

Caught out. Her cheeks flame. "He might've mentioned it'll be good for you to get back into a business you enjoy."

"You'll shove your pride and do it for me?"

She reaches over the table and cups my hand. "He's right, you know. Giving up your studies was damn hard. Nobody knows how much that meant to you better than me. You lost a thumb, and you can never be a veterinary surgeon, but so what? What's wrong with being a clinical vet?"

"That's not what I had my heart set on."

"Then get your heart set on something else." She points her finger at me. "You still have the passion. I can see it in your eyes."

"I'm not going back to uni."

"Are you sure?"

"I don't have the heart for it any longer."

"What about something different in the field?"

I stab at a piece of meat. "What's your idea?"

"Practice management."

"You want me to run your practice?"

"If you're not going to be a vet, so be it. I can do with another vet on the staff, but I need someone to run the business more. It will free up my time to be a vet and not a manager."

My interest is piqued. It sounds challenging and exciting.

She scoops up the rice with a piece of bread and pops it in her mouth. "More, Charlie?"

"Mo–more. It's goo–good."

She places another helping on his plate and holds the spoon to me, but I shake my head.

"We'll need a receptionist," she says, "and a vet nurse, maybe even a bookkeeper, and a makeover. A nicer reception area. I'd like to run a rescue center in conjunction with the practice. We have enough space in the back where the vegetable garden used to be. God knows, I don't have time to plant a blade of grass, anyway."

I can't help but laugh at her contagious enthusiasm. "Slow down. We'll first need a financial plan."

"We?" She puts down her knife and fork. "Does that mean you're in?"

"All right, I'm in."

She grabs my hand on the one side and Charlie's on the other. "The three musketeers."

"The three of us," I echo.

"Way to go, kiddo."

Charlie, who picks up on the vibe, chants with Kris. "Way to go–go." Laughter transforms his face. For a moment, he looks exactly like he did at the age of fifteen, before the accident.

I cup his cheek. "You like being a dog walker, don't you?"

He agrees by banging the end of his knife on the table until I have to put my hand on his arm to still him.

"Finish up," I tell him. "Kris has to go back to work."

She looks at my untouched food. "Still feeling queasy?"

"Yep. There's no telling when it will pass. I wish I was one of those lucky women who only felt sick during the first trimester or not at all." A thought strikes me. "I hope I won't let you down when it gets time to deliver this baby. Nobody in their right mind will employ a pregnant woman, let alone for such an important job."

"We'll work around it. Don't worry."

"Thank you." I mean it. Kris has always been my lifebuoy, and she's just thrown me a big one, thanks to Gabriel.

She pushes her plate aside. "How are things going at home?"

"Good." I can't help the smile or heat that creeps onto my face when I think about Gabriel's reaction this morning. "Wonderful, actually."

Her brow lifts. "Really?"

"Why do you ask as if it's impossible?"

"Wonderful in what sense?"

"Gabriel is good to me. He's kind, attentive, generous, loving…"

"Loving?"

"Yes."

"You forgot to mention controlling, possessive, and jealous."

"Yes, he's controlling, but in a protective way." He'd also threatened my best friend's life, but she doesn't need to know. As long as I stick to my end of the bargain, Gabriel will keep his word. "Let's not forget this new practice management wouldn't be possible without his generosity."

"True, he does a hell of a good job of taking care of you, but that's material."

"As I said, there's more to him than his money."

"You fell for him."

There's no more denying it. "You know I have."

"De-dessert," Charlie says, licking his plate clean.

"Don't do that," I chastise. "It's not polite."

"There's flan in the fridge," Kris says without turning her

attention away from me. "Help yourself, Charlie." She takes my hand again. "Val, what are you doing? Playing house?"

"What's wrong with that?"

"It's nothing but role play if he doesn't love you. Does he?"

I avert my eyes. "Probably not."

There's understanding and sympathy in her tone. "There's your answer."

"The thing is we're living together, we're legally married, and we're going to have a baby. Most of the time, we're happy. I'm not going to fight it any longer." Anyway, I don't have a choice. "We can't always have everything we want, but we can be happy with what we have."

"Okay." She squeezes my fingers and lets go of my hand. "I'm behind you. One hundred percent. No more questions asked."

"Thank you," I whisper.

"I may not agree with what Gabriel does for a living, but I'm grateful to him for pulling you out of Berea. That area is only getting worse. With Jerry being murdered and everything that--"

"What?" I grab her arm, my fingers digging into her flesh. "What did you say?"

"Shit. You didn't know."

"Jerry?"

"Yes."

"When?"

"Yesterday. I'm sorry, Val. I thought Gabriel told you." She adds apologetically, "Maybe he doesn't know."

Gabriel must know. Berea is his territory. He knows about everything that happens there. A sickening knowledge grows in my gut.

"How?" I ask.

"Shot between the eyes. A neighbor found him in his flat."

"Do they have a suspect?"

"The newspaper article didn't say. I don't think the police are going to make a big effort for a car thief murdered in Berea."

They won't. A killing happens every twenty-five minutes. Jerry is one thief less to deal with, and nobody cares if his killer is caught.

Suffocation hangs like a cloak over me. The air in Kris' kitchen is suddenly too thick to breathe.

Checking my watch, I keep my face even. "We'll let you get back to work. Thanks for lunch." I'm already on my feet, clearing the table.

"Leave that for me," Kris says. "I'll do it tonight."

"I'm not letting you come home to a dirty kitchen."

With Charlie's help the dishes are done and dried by the time Kris is ready to reopen the practice. I walk to the car on shaky legs, barely conscious of what's happening around me. Gabriel's guards parked across the road acknowledge me and get into their cars when we do. I make sure Charlie is buckled up and drag a few deep breaths into my lungs. Alone with Charlie who won't notice, I let the truth crash over me. My hands shake on the wheel as what Kris keeps on reminding me––the same thing I ignored and tried to forget––hits me hard.

My husband is a murderer, and he killed the man who helped me escape.

8

Valentina

The drive home passes in a haze. I can't remember if I stopped at any traffic lights. All I can think about is that Jerry is dead because of me, and my husband killed him. Yes, Jerry was a scumbag who got me into this dire situation, but it doesn't mean he deserved to die.

I put Charlie's favorite cartoon on in his bedroom and storm to Gabriel's office, not caring that my face is streaked with tears or that my mascara is running. Gabriel looks up when I open his door. The smile freezes on his face as he takes me in. He pushes to his feet, the ever-present flinch giving away the strain the action puts on his leg.

"How could you?" I cry.

"Valentina." His voice is harsh, authoritative. "Calm down."

"Don't tell me to calm down. You killed Jerry!"

A mixture of sympathy and regret soften his features. "Who told you?"

"It's in the news." The last thing I want is to implicate Kris.

Rounding his desk, he takes my shoulders. "I should've told you, but I didn't want to upset you."

"Why? Was it because he gave me a car?"

"It's not what you think."

I slam my palms on his chest. "You son of a bitch."

He catches my wrists. "Calm down, please, or I'll be forced to tie you up."

At that, I still. Gabriel never makes idle threats.

"Will you be quiet if I let go?" He sounds genuinely concerned. "All this screaming and crying can't be good for the baby."

I want to hate him, but I can't. Not even when I think he shot Jerry. My shoulders slump.

"Will you listen?" he asks.

"Yes."

"Calmly," he insists.

I don't have a choice but to agree. "Calmly."

He lets go of me slowly, testing me. When I don't move, he brushes his thumbs over my cheeks, wiping away the tears. "It was Scott who shot Jerry."

"Magda's bodyguard?"

"Yes."

"Why?"

He takes a deep breath and holds it for a moment.

"Tell me," I urge. "The truth."

"He helped you run, and he shouldn't have. She had to make an example of him."

There is doubt in the way he speaks the words. I get the feeling he doesn't believe himself. "You were there?"

"Yes," he says gravely.

Pushing his hands away, I cover my face. "Oh, my God, Gabriel. It's my fault. He died because of me. Why didn't you stop Scott?"

"He didn't give me a chance. Valentina, look at me." He grabs my arms and pulls my hands away from my face. "Jerry was no saint. He got Charlie into this mess."

My look is cutting. "You mean he got me enslaved to you."

His glacier eyes turn hard, and his hold tightens to the point of pain. "You don't understand the meaning of the word slave. I made you a princess, but if you want to be treated like a slave, that can be arranged."

Of all the cold, hard truths, this one cuts the deepest, because it's another affirmation of what Kris keeps on telling me. Gabriel doesn't love me. I'm an object. He can turn me from princess to slave as his mood changes.

The pain in my heart makes me lash out at him in anger. "What I want doesn't matter, anyway. You'll do with me as you please."

"What you are to me is entirely in your hands. You can live in comfort and be cherished or be chained in my basement and sleep in a cage."

"But I can never leave."

"No, you can never leave."

"Then I'm nothing but your prisoner."

"That's one way to see it. The other way of looking at it is that you're my wife."

Sobs push up from my chest and find their way to my lips. I was doing so well on make-believe until a couple of hours ago. How can it hurt so much? Why didn't I listen to Kris? Why did I make myself vulnerable? Now it's too late. I fell for him, and it fucking hurts that he's not falling right back for me.

"I don't understand." I wrap my arms around myself and take a step back. "Why me? Why are you doing this to *me*?"

He eliminates the space between us with one, easy step. "I already told you, I don't need a reason."

"I hate you!" I accentuate the statement with a fist on his chest.

His words are tender, compassionate. "We've already established that."

I don't have the strength to fight alone any longer. I can't fight him and myself. He made me fall in love with him knowing he'll never love me back. How can any man be so cruel?

"Please, Gabriel, if you feel anything for me, anything at all, set me free." It's my only hope at salvaging what's left of my heart.

His wraps his arms around me and pulls me close, carefully, as if I have wings of rice paper. The embrace is what he offers. This is his answer. He won't set me free. What I get in return for love is a consolation hug.

"I hate you," I say, sobbing in his arms, hating myself more because I can't even mean the damned words.

He kisses the top of my head. "I've got you, baby."

The man who inflicts the pain is the man who offers the balm, holding me against the warmth of his body and whispering soothing words in my ear. Gabriel is a constant that never changes. He takes care of me now like he does after lashing me with his belt or palm. His behavior when he emotionally hurts me is the same as when he physically tortures me. I don't have the strength not to take this olive branch he offers. I don't have the strength not to fall into him. As always, he's there to catch and carry me through his cruelty. As he lifts me into his arms and moves toward the stairs, I already mourn my surrender.

Gabriel

EVERY LIVING BEING fights for one thing. Freedom. I claimed a woman and took that away from her. Instead of putting her in a cage, I clipped her wings to prevent her from flying away. In time, some caged creatures are tamed. Some remain wild forever. Valentina falls in the latter category. Her spirit is too strong, but my will is stronger. My need is fiercer. I'll break her, over and over, make her submit to me time and time again, until we both blow out our last breaths.

She's my black kitten.

She's my forever.

Her tears move me, but not with the perverse lust I feel at her erotic pain. This pain cuts me. I carry her to our bedroom and nudge the door open. This is one of those occasions I want to love her gently, giving her comfort to make up for what I won't give-- the freedom she is fighting for. The love she deserves.

Making quick work of undressing us both, I lower her to the bed and cover her body with mine. I feel between her thighs to test if she's ready and find her slick. Always wet for me. I don't wait. I put my cock at her entrance, part her folds, and pierce her pussy.

When she moans and writhes I give her more, and when she starts panting I give everything, taking her body to a place where pleasure is freedom. She clings to me with her arms and legs while her orgasm crushes through her. Our coupling is uncomplex, pure, and complete. Trapped in each other, our bodies connected, for a few blissful moments we both forget.

Valentina

COME MORNING, I go back to pretending. It's the only way to survive. It's not like anything other than my heart is suffering. Lots of people are worse off. Look at poor Jerry. I have it good. I'm lucky. It could've been me with a bullet in my brain. Who needs freedom and love? I'm done wallowing in self-centered pity. There are other people to consider.

Today is the first day of Charlie's new treatment. I gave my consent, because I couldn't come up with any arguments why we shouldn't try. We have nothing to lose. I wait anxiously outside the television room where Christopher is working with Charlie. I asked to stay with my brother, but Christopher said it would hamper his efforts and inhibit Charlie. Gabriel sits next to me in the hallway on Magda's infamous Louis Vuitton love seat, the one

Oscar almost ruined, holding my hand. He acts like a good husband, and we don't speak about yesterday.

I jerk from my thoughts when the door opens. Christopher exists first.

"How did it go?" I ask, jumping to my feet.

"Very good. We made progress."

"Really?"

Charlie follows. He looks happy, calm, and very awake, awake as in present in the moment.

"Hey." I touch his arm. "How do you feel?"

"Gre–great."

"Are you hungry?"

"Sta–starving."

"How about a burger?" Gabriel asks. "I can start the barbeque."

"Bu–burger."

"Wood or gas?" he asks.

"Woo–wood."

Charlie loves a wood fire. He can stare at the flames for hours.

"Let's go take care of lunch, then. Afterward, we're up for a game of football with the guards."

Gabriel takes Charlie and leaves me alone with Christopher. As much as I resent my husband, I love him for this.

"Do you think the sessions will make a difference?" I ask.

"I do." The doctor shifts a briefcase from one hand to the other. "We'll start with general relaxation exercises and then work on speech."

"How much of his old memories does he have left?"

"It's hard to say. I can only know if I take him back into the past. Why do you ask?"

"I just wanted to know if he remembers us the way we were before the accident."

"Ah." He puts down the briefcase and removes his glasses. "Mrs. Louw––"

"Valentina, please."

"Valentina," a note of caution slips into his voice, "it'll never be like before."

"I know. I was just hoping…"

"It's normal to miss the old personality, the person before the brain damage, but it's not conducive to dwell in the past. It's better to accept the present and to optimize on what we've got."

"I understand." I miss my brother so much. I long for the Charlie I destroyed.

He looks at me with scrunched-up eyes. "Maybe you could use some hypnotherapy yourself. You lived through a traumatic experience with the accident, and the trauma is often ongoing for the ones left to take care of the injured."

"Oh, I'm fine."

"It won't do harm trying. Isn't that what we said for Charlie?"

"Really, I'm all right."

"Let me know if you change your mind."

I hold out my hand. "Thank you. May I walk you out?"

His handshake is firm. "I want to say goodbye to Magda before I go, but don't worry, I know my way."

Gabriel

WE'RE at the dinner table. Magda is at the head and Valentina opposite me next to Charlie. Our server enters with the wine.

"No wine for Charlie or me, thank you," Valentina says, as every night.

"Water, ma'am?"

"Sparkling, please."

Magda raises a finger. "Still. Sparkling will give you indigestion."

Valentina doesn't argue, but I pour my wife a glass of sparkling water. Magda's look is condescending, as if I'm a child who obstinately defies her for the sole purpose of creating conflict.

When the roast is served and Valentina adds salt, Magda says, "Not so much salt. It's not good for the baby."

I pin Magda with a look. "Her blood pressure is fine."

Magda takes a sip of wine. Her gaze moves over Valentina. "You couldn't fit a tighter dress?"

The black dress was my choice, and Valentina looks stunning in it. It shows off her growing belly just the way I like. I want the world to see she's carrying my seed in her womb.

Valentina shifts on her chair, but I wink at her. "I like it."

Magda makes a sarcastic sound. "You would."

"May we please eat in peace, now?" I ask pointedly.

Pinching her lips together, Magda gives me the stink eye.

For a while we eat in silence, except for the noise of Charlie's cutlery. He has a habit of hacking everything on his plate to tiny pieces.

Halfway through the meal, Magda is on her third glass of wine. From time to time she shoots an irritated glance in Charlie's direction, her eyes focused on the knife he drags through the meat.

As if she can't stand looking at him butchering his meat any longer Magda turns sideways in her chair, cutting Charlie from her peripheral view. "Any news from Carly?"

The food goes stale in my mouth. Magda knows it's a sensitive subject and one I don't care to discuss at the dinner table. I swallow and take a drink. "Nothing new."

"I miss her." Magda sighs. "When is she coming home? Isn't her weekend visit long overdue?"

Charlie drops his knife. It makes a loud clang as it hits the plate. Magda jerks. She pinches her eyes shut for five seconds, probably counting to get control over her patience.

"I said--" she starts.

"I heard what you said. Sylvia and I don't work like that, and you know it. Carly is old enough to decide when she wants to visit. She knows her room is always ready."

"Maybe you should force it, Gabriel." Her gaze keeps on flittering to Charlie who's pinching each miniscule piece of food on his plate with a loud clank of his fork. "You're too easy on her."

Charlie takes a bite and chews exactly ten times before he swallows. He repeats this with every morsel.

Magda turns to Valentina. "You should take the room on the left of yours for the baby. Have you thought about decorating?"

Valentina glances at me. "Gabriel and I haven't discussed it, yet."

The sweet, incredible woman she is, she'll allow me to be a part of creating a room for Connor. That's what I decided to call him, after my great-grandfather whom I greatly admired.

I give her a smile, telling her how much she pleased me. "What would *you* like?"

"I was thinking bright colors like green and blue with a jungle theme. Something happy."

If she wants monkeys and elephant tusks on the walls she can have that. She can have anything she wants.

As usual, Magda has to throw a spike in the wheel. "Green and blue?" She chortles. "It won't fit with the rest of the house decor. I saw a beautiful crib in whitewashed wood with a beige, hand-embroidered duvet. It will look perfect with off-white walls and sand-colored curtains. We should replace the carpet with tiles. A carpet will get too dirty with a baby."

Valentina sits up straighter. "Thank you for your input, but it's not my style."

It's the first time Valentina defies Magda so openly, and Magda doesn't like it. I, on the other hand, am ecstatic that my tiny wife has enough backbone to stand up for what she wants.

"Well," Magda looks between us, "this is still *my* house."

It's a winning statement to an argument. There's not much

Valentina can say to that, and the smug look on Magda's face says she knows it.

I've been toying with the idea of getting our own place, and now my decision is made. The atmosphere in this house is way too tense.

Gabriel

It takes another three weeks of cajoling before Carly agrees to come over. She doesn't agree to a weekend visit, but I settle for the Saturday lunch she proposes. To make it as relaxed as possible, I plan a barbeque by the pool. It's late autumn, and the water is too cold to swim, but the day is sunny and pleasantly warm. An outdoor lunch will do us all good.

Carly doesn't say a word in the car on the drive to our house.

In the driveway, I switch off the engine and turn to her. "Is there anything you'd like to talk about before we go inside?"

She stares straight ahead with her arms crossed over her chest. "Like what?"

"Like the fact that Valentina and I are married and we're going to have a baby."

"You said it all, didn't you?"

"Don't be a wisecrack. Do you want to talk about how it makes you feel?"

She shoots me a dirty look. "Embarrassed?"

"I'm sorry if my choice embarrasses you, but she's a good, strong woman, and I'm proud of her."

"Like you're proud of Mom?"

"This has nothing to do with me and your mother. Your mother chose a different path, and I accepted it. So should you."

Turning her face away from me, she picks at the hem of her blouse. "You treat her differently."

"How?"

"You love her more."

"Please don't compare her and your mother. It's not fair to either."

"Did you love Mom?"

"Very much."

"Why did it change?"

"People change. Sometimes, we grow apart or want different things."

"Did Mom want different things, or was it you?"

"Pointing fingers and laying blame won't help. It is what it is. We need to accept it and move on."

She snorts. "You certainly have."

"Would you rather see me alone for the rest of my life?"

"Not alone. Just with someone different. She's a gold-digger."

"Listen to me, Carly. Valentina didn't ask to be put in this situation. If it's anyone's fault, it's mine. This is hard for her, too. Will you at least try to make an effort?"

"That's why I'm here, isn't it?"

"Good. I appreciate that. Before we go inside, there's more you should know."

She turns her head to me quickly. "More? How much worse can this get?"

"Carly," I say sternly. I'm trying to be patient, but her attitude doesn't help.

"Okay, okay." She rolls her eyes. "I'm listening."

"Valentina's brother is staying with us."

She gasps. "Are you moving her whole family in?"

"Just her brother."

"Why must he live here?"

"He has brain damage and needs a lot of care."

"Oh, dear God." She makes a face. "A disabled person in our house?"

"I'm proud of the way Valentina takes care of him."

"Give her a gold star on her forehead or something. Doesn't she have other family who can take him in?"

"No and that's not the point. I offered."

"How crazy is he?"

"He's not crazy. He lost some of his cognitive functions. Mostly, he repeats parts of words."

"This is going to be the Mad Hatter's crazy tea party."

"I won't tolerate this kind of talk, understood?"

She blows out a puff of air. "Can we go inside, now? It's hot in the car."

"Remember what I said. This is not Valentina's fault."

She gets out and slams the door. I take a few deep breaths. Admittedly, I haven't expected her to be ecstatic. I don't blame for her being upset, but I can't stand by and let her be mean to Valentina for something that's my fault.

I grab Carly's bag from the back and follow her inside.

"We're outside," Magda calls when the slamming of the door announces our arrival.

Instead of heading to the deck, Carly snatches her bag from me and veers toward the stairs. "I'll meet you at the pool. I'm going to change."

Some of the tenseness leaves my body when I step outside and see Valentina. She's dressed in a tight dress with her hair pulled back. God, she's beautiful. The size of her belly doesn't faze her, but Valentina has never been conscious of her physical beauty. The fact that she doesn't know how desirable she is only makes her more desirable to me. A tendril that escaped the elastic feathers over her temple and a flush marks her cheeks--telltale signs that she's been busy. She's bustling around the veranda table, which is laid with green crockery and bright yellow napkins. A bunch of sunflowers is the center decoration. Magda is lying on a deckchair, reading a book, and it looks like Charlie is doing origami the way he meticulously folds the paper napkins.

I cross the deck and pull Valentina to me with a hand on her hip. "Hey, beautiful."

She smiles at me. "I made potato and beetroot salad with garlic bread. There's mud pie for dessert. Do you think it'll do?"

"Perfect."

I make sure she gets how much I appreciate her efforts with a soft kiss. The red of her cheeks darkens.

She first glances at Magda and then at the sliding doors. "Where is she?"

"Changing. She'll be down in a minute."

Carly takes her time to join us. By the time she walks through the door wearing a swimsuit and sunglasses pushed back on her hair, I'm on my second iced tea.

She kisses Magda's cheek, but ignores Valentina and Charlie.

My blood starts to simmer, but I remind myself I'm solely to blame. Forcing patience, I count to ten and say, "Carly, don't you have something to say to Valentina?"

She turns to Valentina as if she only notices her now. "Oh, yes." She flops down in a chair and flips her sunglasses over her eyes. "Get me a lemonade. Plenty of ice. While you're at it, bring me a towel."

9

Gabriel

My vision unravels at the edges. Who is this mean girl? Carly has always been difficult, but this disrespect crosses a new line. The tea sloshes over the edges as I slam the glass down on the table. In two strides I'm next to Carly, pulling her up by her arm. She looks at me with a start, her cocky attitude slipping. Magda drops her book and jackknifes into a sitting position.

"Dad!"

Carly protests as I drag her through the sliding doors back into the house. It's time the two of us had a talk. Not like the talk we had in the car. A serious talk.

The first available room is the reading room. I push her inside and am about to slam the door when Valentina rushes up.

"Not now," I growl. This is between Carly and I.

Her soft hand on my arm pauses me, and it's the look in her eyes that makes me falter. I can't resist this begging, wide-eyed appeal.

"Just five minutes," she says.

Educating Carly in manners is my responsibility, but it's also Valentina's right to stand up for herself. With much difficulty, I remove myself from the room, but I can't move farther than around the door where I stop to eavesdrop shamelessly.

"You're upset," Valentina says.

"Damn right, I am."

"I understand. The news about the baby must be hard to deal with. It came as a shock to me, too."

"You only got pregnant to trap my dad."

"It was an accident neither of us planned."

There are tears in Carly's voice. "How long have you been sleeping with him?"

"That's private," Valentina replies gently, "and not your business."

"Did you seduce him?"

"No."

"Then what?"

"I don't understand your question."

"He said you didn't ask for this." There's a long silence before Carly speaks again. "Did he … force you?"

My heart stops beating. Valentina hates me. She has no reason to protect my daughter from the ugly, raw truth. Yes, I forced her. I made her beg first, but I gave her no choice. Not really.

The tremble in Valentina's voice is so minute, if I didn't know her as well as I did, I would've missed it. "Why would you ask that?"

"It happened to friends of my mom. The maid is pregnant with the husband's baby, and she said she didn't have a choice because he forced her."

Valentina's voice is firm and reassuring. "It didn't happen to us."

"He didn't … rape you?"

"Absolutely not. Please don't think about your father that way."

"So, you're not a victim."

"No, I'm not."

"If you're not a victim, I can't feel sorry for you."

"I'm not asking you to feel sorry for me. I'm asking you to try for us to get on."

"Why? Why should I? I don't even like you. You're lower class and poor."

"Fair enough. Then try for your dad's sake."

"I'm not doing anything for his sake. He didn't talk to me before marrying you to see how I would feel, so why should I consider his feelings?"

"He loves you, Carly. Don't push him away. If we put a bit of effort into it, we can all get along."

"Give me one, good reason why I should get along with *you*?"

"You're going to have a baby brother or sister. Doesn't that count for anything?"

Carly goes quiet. For several seconds, neither of them speaks. Finally, Carly says in a broken voice, "I've always wanted a brother or sister, just not from you."

"We can't change that it's me, but I'm sure this baby is going to love having a big sister."

Carly sniffs. "You think?"

"I do. I was hoping you'd help me with some baby shopping."

"Those tiny shoes and cute bunny-ear pajamas?"

Valentina laughs. "And a teddy bear. Every baby needs a teddy."

"Oh, my God, I know exactly where to go. Tammy's big sister had a baby last month. You should see the cute baby dresses and matching headbands we got for her. Can I help with the room?"

"Yes, you may."

"Not the painting, though. Oh, and I'm not changing diapers."

"No paint. No diapers. Got it."

Carly excitedly babbles on about baby powder, mobiles, and blankets.

For the first time in months, I hear Carly laugh. I lean my head back against the wall and swallow hard. I don't deserve Valentina's cover-up, but I take it anyway.

Valentina

WE PARK in front of a two-story house with a circular entrance hall like an abstract castle tower. The pillars framing the entrance are a modern, off-kilter version of the Arc de Triomphe. The house is painted gray, black, and burgundy. I've never seen anything like it.

"Where are we?"

Gabriel turns off the engine, but doesn't answer. He exits and comes around to help me from the car. It was a long drive to the northern suburb of Broadacres, and we got stuck in traffic. I stretch to relieve the ache in my back. His hand moves to my lower back, his fingers gently massaging the sore muscles.

At the glass doors, he hands me a key with a red ribbon looped through the hole.

"Gabriel, what is this?"

"Our new house."

Incapable of forming words, my gaze shifts from the keys to the doors. Behind the glass, there is a large, open-plan, furnished space.

"Aren't you going to open it?" he asks with a quirk of his lips.

I fumble to fit the key in the keyhole and eventually manage to let us inside.

Our footsteps echo on the slate tiles. A spiral staircase leads from the tower to the first level. To the left is a lounge and at the back a kitchen. The finishes are in industrial steel.

"Come." He takes my hand and walks me through the house.

The ground floor includes a wine room with walk-in fridge, an office for Gabriel, a soundproof cinema, an indoor barbeque facing a heated pool, a Jacuzzi, bar, bathroom, sauna room, and gym. The kitchen leads to a pantry and scullery, and the scullery to maid quarters and a double garage.

He gauges my reaction as he leads me upstairs. "Do you like it?"

The decoration is minimalistic and modern. I can see why Gabriel would like it. "It's very impressive."

Satisfied with my answer, he shows me four spacious bedrooms, each with an en-suite bathroom.

From the main bedroom, we step onto the balcony that has a view on the pool.

"Charlie can have the bigger bedroom on the right, and we can break a door from ours to the one on the left for the baby."

I lean on the balustrade and look up at him. "Why?" Magda has a big house, and up to now Gabriel has been content to live there.

"I want you to be happy. I want you to buy what you please, decorate as you like, and paint the walls green if that's your thing."

I have to laugh. I can't imagine the gray walls of this house being a crazy green.

He cups my hips and presses our lower bodies together. "Just promise me the nursery will have a jungle theme. I kind of have my heart set on it."

More laughter bubbles over my lips. Baby and decoration talk is so unlike Gabriel.

"I want this to be good for you, Valentina." He brushes the hair from my face. "Having a baby won't be easy. I want you to be as comfortable as you can be."

"Thank you," I whisper, not for the house, but for his efforts.

He kisses me and smiles against my lips. "Does that mean you like the house?"

"I do."

"Then we move next week."

I weave my fingers through his thick hair, keeping him in place. "I don't care where we live, as long as you never stop touching me."

The smile is gone. His expression sobers. "I trained you so damn well."

"Does that mean you like it?" I ask, throwing his words back at him.

"Like it?" Heat invades the icy blue of his eyes. "I love it. I fucking live for it."

As his fingers go to the zipper of my dress, I melt for him, wanting what he can give me long before he offers. Whether he drags me to Berea, Broadacres, or hell, it doesn't make a difference. As long as he feeds on my pleasure, his arms will keep me warm, and I can go on pretending he gives a damn about more than my body.

THE MOVE TAKES place the following Monday. By Tuesday, we're settled. Since the house came fully furnished, all we had to transport were our clothes and Gabriel's office equipment. On one of the nights Gabriel works late, I invite Kris over for dinner to show her our new home. I would not have felt comfortable inviting her to Magda's house. At least here, I can do as I please. The freedom feels amazing. The irony of that sentiment doesn't escape me. I'm anything but free, but as the days go by and my stomach grows bigger, a new numbness dulls my senses until I don't think about my captivity, any longer.

The intercom buzzes as I'm caramelizing the sugar with a kitchen blowtorch over the crème brûlée. Oscar, who now lives with us—as does Bruno—jumps from the priceless silver bowl on the coffee table.

"I'll get it," Rhett calls from the gym.

Rhett and Quincy reside with us in the staff quarters meant for the maids. Each has an independent studio with a kitchenette and bathroom. Gabriel insists that one of them stays with me when he isn't home. The guards stationed at our gate aren't live-in. They work on a shift basis. The living arrangements with Quincy and Rhett worked out well, since I don't want a live-in maid and prefer to take care of the cooking myself, maybe because of the memories that role evokes. Due to the size of the house, we were forced to hire a cleaning service that comes in twice a week. The rest I can handle between working at Kris' clinic and completing a mini MBA to help me master business management. The household, work, Charlie, and studies keep me busy, but I've never been an idle person, and I like to feel useful.

"Here's your guest," Rhett says, holding the door for Kris.

"Thanks, Rhett. Dinner is almost ready. Would you like to join us?"

"Yeah." His smile is enthusiastic. Rhett loves home cooking. "Let me grab a quick shower."

Going over to Kris, I give her a hug. "How was the traffic?"

"Not too bad." She looks up at the double volume entrance, turns in a circle, and whistles through her teeth. "Wow."

"Do you like it?"

"Too modern for my taste, but it's ... wow."

"Charlie, come say hi," I call into the cinema room. "Kris is here."

Charlie bounces through the door and takes her in a bear hug as if he hasn't said goodbye to her at the practice only three hours ago.

Kris sniffs the air. "Smells like Beef Stroganoff."

"Good olfactory skills. Wine or beer?"

"Beer."

"In the fridge. Help yourself."

Kris grabs a can and looks around while I set the food on the table.

"There are an awful lot of glass doors and windows."

"I love the light."

"What about security? I don't see burglar bars."

"Each door and window is fitted with a bulletproof metal shutter. No metal cutter can get through the steel. In case of an emergency, we can bring them down in seconds with the push of a button. We have a control panel in the kitchen and upstairs in our room."

"You don't fool around."

"You know Gabriel."

"Yeah, this sounds like him. That man is crazily protective over you. I don't want to see how he's going to be when the baby is born."

Rhett enters the kitchen, his hair wet. "Is that Stroganoff I'm smelling?"

"Spot on," Kris says.

He rubs his hands together. "Shall we eat before it gets cold?"

Kris chuckles. "Hungry?"

I dish up, and Charlie serves the water. Rhett doesn't drink when he's on duty.

"Val tells me she can shoot a bullseye. Is it true?" Kris asks Rhett.

He gives me a chastising look. "You're not supposed to advertise it."

"I only told my best friend." I grin. "I was proud."

I'll have to pick up the self-defense training after the birth, but I convinced Rhett to take me to the shooting range when Gabriel stays out late for business.

"My lips are sealed," Kris says, "and I think it's a good thing that Val knows how to defend herself."

Rhett gives Kris a half-smile. His ass will be on the line if Gabriel finds out.

"How's Charlie's sessions going?" Kris asks, thankfully changing the subject.

"Good." I pat Charlie's hand. "Christopher says he's making progress. Aren't you?"

"Pro–progress."

Kris raises her beer. "To Charlie's progress and the best practice manager in the world, who can now also shoot like a pro."

Our laughter is interrupted by Rhett's phone.

"Excuse me." He looks at the screen. "It's Quincy. I have to take the call."

He leaves the table and walks to the far corner of the lounge, but the acoustics of the open space carry his words to us.

"What?" He pauses to listen. "Okay. Sure. No worries. I'll tell her."

My armpits zing with pinpricks of foreboding. "Is Gabriel all right?"

He walks back to the table, his expression troubled. "It's Carly. She's been arrested for possession of drugs. Gabriel is at the police station. He'll be home later than planned."

Kris covers her mouth with a hand. Only Charlie eats without a care in the world. My appetite for food is gone. All I want is to be with Gabriel.

"There's nothing we can do," Rhett says. "We may as well enjoy our meal."

By the time Kris leaves, there's still no new news from Quincy or Gabriel. Rhett goes to bed, and I watch a movie with Charlie to distract myself, but I can't concentrate on anything. Finally, there's nothing left to do but ship Charlie off to bed and wait. I shower and change into a nightdress before making myself comfortable on the sofa in the lounge with a book. My gaze keeps on flickering to the door, watching for Gabriel's headlights at the gate.

It's well after three in the morning when he returns.

When I open the door, he grabs me to him and buries his head in my neck. "What are you doing up?" He kisses the soft spot on the curve of my shoulder. "It's late."

"Is she all right?" I pull away to look at him. "Did the police lay charges?"

He closes the door and turns all three deadbolts before taking my hand and pulling me to the bar. He pours me a tomato juice, for which I developed a sudden craving, and a Scotch for himself.

"No charges."

"Did your lawyer get her off?"

"Not my lawyer. Magda."

He doesn't have to say more. Magda has questionable connections with the police.

He sits down on one of the barstools and pulls me onto his lap. "The police raided a nightclub." His icy eyes turn stormy. "They found a gram of coke on her."

"Oh, Gabriel." I place a hand on his cheek.

"She's sixteen, for God's sake." He cups my hand and rubs his jaw over my palm. "Sylvia said she didn't know. She said Carly sneaked out."

"The drugs?"

"Carly said a friend gave it to her. She swore she tried it only once. Tonight was supposed to be her second time. I think the arrest was a good lesson. It scared the hell out of her, especially since she's under the legal age for access to that club." He absentmindedly strokes my hair. "She promised me she'd never do it again, but how can I trust her, now?"

Wrapping my arms around him, I lean my head on his chest, offering him the little comfort I can.

"Valentina." He grips my chin and tilts my face up to him. "I don't know what I'd do without you."

Like he's always there for me, I'm there for him. He knows he can count on me, no matter what. It's an invisible bond that becomes stronger with each passing day. I don't know if it's the baby or the time we spend together that brings us closer, but it doesn't matter. I've never felt more connected to anyone than I feel to Gabriel, and that scares me.

"Don't leave me," I plead.

It's an irrational fear I contribute to my pregnancy hormones and a strange request coming from someone who begged to be set free less than a month ago. I want to stay, but out of my own free will, and until Gabriel lets me go, he'll never trust or believe me when I say I love him and I won't run.

Instead of pointing out the shift in my demands, Gabriel brings our lips together and kisses me tenderly. "Never. I can never let you go."

Embracing that knowledge, I lean into him, immensely grateful for my imperfect world.

Gabriel

THE MONTH that follows is the happiest of my life. I have setbacks with Carly, but our relationship has never been better. She visits every weekend. Valentina suggested she chooses a room and decorates it herself, which Carly appreciated. We celebrated her seventeenth birthday with a quiet lunch at home, and afterward she did baby shopping with Valentina. Although she'll never see Valentina through my eyes, they're getting along, mostly due to Valentina's efforts, for which I'm forever indebted.

Business is calm for a change. Magda has finally accepted my decision to move and for once we're not knocking heads. The distance is what we needed. We get on better not living under the same roof. Quincy and Rhett dote on my wife, and only her devoted attention to me and me alone makes me swallow my jealousy. We had a door fitted between our room and the nursery, and Valentina bought the paint. Bright green. I'm sure it's just to piss Magda off, but I'm game.

As far as the world's concerned, we're newlyweds. Hell, as far as I'm concerned, this is as normal as it gets. I can't keep my hands off her, and she needs my invasive advances. I can love her hard or hold her in my arms watching a movie. It doesn't matter whether we're swimming with Charlie or clearing the table after our meals, I love every minute with her. I love the way her belly swells with the life we created. Every time I look at her, I have this godawful fear that it's not real, that it's too good to last. Like an infatuated person I drift on the cloud I fabricated, blind to anything but my wife's pleasure and my own euphoria.

On one of those warm and sunny winter mornings the Highveld is famous for, we're lounging by the indoor pool. I have Valentina's legs in my lap, massaging her feet. She moans as I work on her pressure points. I steal glances at her bikini-clad body. With her six-month belly she looks both like a pinnacle of strength and vulnerability. Charlie discovered a love for water. He's a strong swimmer. Nevertheless, I keep an eye on him as he's doing laps from the shallow to the deep end. Later, I'll fetch Carly for the weekend. We have a barbeque planned. There are only us, Rhett and Quincy, and a couple of Carly's girlfriends. Afterward, the plan is to relax with a couple of movies. I'm looking forward to the afternoon. The low-key, family time is exactly what I need. Oscar jumps from my towel as my phone vibrates.

I check the screen. Sylvia. Carly must be running late, as usual. I flip the button to answer and am met by a noise so foreign and bizarre that my mind refuses to place it. I sit up, every muscle going tense.

"Sylvia?"

A series of incoherent words mixed with hysterical sobs follow. I move Valentina's feet aside and stand, my only awareness the acute pain that shoots into my hip and the numbness that settles over my heart.

"Sylvia, take a deep breath and tell me what's wrong."

Her sobs become more distant. There's a scratching noise before another voice comes on the line.

"Mr. Louw?"

"Who are you? What's going on?"

"I'm a paramedic, sir. Mrs. Louw is not in a state to speak, right now. We have to ask you to come to the Garden Clinic."

"What happened? Who's hurt?"

"It's your daughter, sir." There's a short, horrifying pause, and then the words I can't face. "I'm terribly sorry."

10

Gabriel

My chest shrinks. My ribs constrict my heart. Static noise buzzes in my head.

My little girl. *My little girl.*

"Gabriel?"

Valentina's voice reaches me through the ringing in my ears. The sound is far-off and distorted.

Only thirty-seven years of experience allows me to put one cognitive thought in front of another. Tell Quincy to stay with Valentina. Get the car. Drive to the clinic. Call Magda on the way.

"Gabriel?"

I turn to my pregnant wife, seeing nothing but her belly and our unborn baby. "It's Carly," I say on autopilot. "She's in hospital."

"What happened?" she asks in a small voice.

"I don't know." But I do. Please, no. No. Dear God. I can't survive it. There's still hope.

She pulls a wrap around her body. "I'll come with you."

"No."

The word is harsh and angry. It wasn't my intention, but I can't control my intonation. I need space. I need to break down in the car so I can be strong before I get to the clinic. Sylvia won't want Valentina there, and I don't have enough presence of mind to deal with what awaits *and* protect Valentina. Most of all, I don't want to expose Valentina to a hospital with germs and a stressful situation in her fragile state.

Hurt invades her eyes, but she quickly clears it. "All right. Let me know, please. Let me know if you need me. Anything."

Drops of water splash over the side of the pool where Charlie is swimming. The white smell of chlorine fills my nostrils. The lazy buzz of a bee turns at my ear. Oscar licks his paw and washes his face. A breeze stirs the lavender in the hothouse at the edge of the pool and carries the scent through to the deck. The clean flower fragrance is infused with the fresh odor of a mowed lawn. The smells mix with the chlorine from the water to create a summer perfume right in the middle of winter. Our little artificial paradise. Every detail is magnified. Every impression is clear and clutter-free. It's the adrenalin from the shock. I take everything in and imprint it in my mind, instinctively knowing things will never be the same. Life will never be as carefree and happy as it was this morning.

I give Valentina a peck on the lips. "Lock the door behind me."

In the lounge, I grab my shirt and pants from the back of the sofa. Stripping from the wet swimming trunks, I leave them in a mangled puddle on the floor and pull the pants on without jocks. While I button up my shirt, I call Quincy on the phone. I'm not wasting time walking to his room.

"I'm going out." I grab my wallet and jacket from the kitchen. "Keep an eye on Valentina and Charlie. They're by the pool."

Once I clear the gates, I floor the gas, breaking every speed limit and pissing off more than one minivan taxi. It's only a matter of minutes before I turn myself into a road rage victim.

I use the voice control to call Magda.

"I'm on my way," she says. "Sylvia's boyfriend called me."

The parking lot at the clinic is thankfully empty. I curse my leg as I run too slowly to the entrance and barge through the doors.

"Carly Louw," I announce at the front desk.

The receptionist avoids my eyes. "Lounge number six, sir."

"It's Louw," I repeat. "My daughter has been admitted." She'll be in the emergency wing, in an operating room, or in intensive care. Not the lounge. Please God. Not the lounge.

"The others are waiting for you, sir. Lounge six."

Not the lounge. Not the lounge.

"Sir?"

"Yes." I turn toward the private rooms, every step slower than the last.

Not the lounge.

My palm flattens on the door, right under the six. Once I push the door open, I can never go back. Once I cross the threshold, my life will never be the same. But the world turns under my feet and around me, and there's no choice but to move forward with time. I apply the necessary pressure, propelling myself into the room.

The door clicks softly behind me with a bizarre finality, enclosing me into the reality sealed in the lounge. My gaze goes around the space, my eyes connecting with each person who shares my fate. Sylvia is hunched over. Francois, her boyfriend, strains under the effort of holding her up. Magda stands next to them, her Gucci handbag swinging uselessly back and forth in her hand. Facing them is a chaplain. He stops talking at my entrance. Magda's eyes find mine. This is what my eyes must look like—barren and empty. She gives me a small shake of her head, preparing me.

"Mr. Louw." The chaplain bows his head and grasps my shoulder. "I'm sorry."

They still have to say it. Someone has to tell me.

Sylvia lifts her head. Anger and blame twist her features, but not acceptance. I feel so much sympathy for her, right now. That's the worst suffering––the road to acceptance.

"Tell me." Don't tell me. Until it's spoken, it isn't real.

The chaplain squeezes my shoulder. "Your daughter ... eh..." he glances at a piece of paper on top of the Bible he clutches in his hand, "...Carly, is gone."

"Gone?" I say.

The clergyman falters under my hard look.

"Gone where?"

"Mr. Louw."

He says my name like it's an appeal. An appeal for what? An appeal not to make him say it?

"What?" I challenge.

It's Sylvia who steps forward. "She's dead. She's dead, Gabriel. She's dead!" Flinging herself at me, she hits my arms and slaps my face. "It's you! It's you! It's all your fault!"

I take her blame and punches, wishing to God she'd hit me harder so I won't feel the torch burning a hole through my heart.

The chaplain and Francois reach for her simultaneously, trying to pull her off, but she renews her attack, shouting and sobbing with snot flying from her nose. I hold out an arm, holding both men off.

"Why?" she cries, looking at me for an answer. "Why, Gabriel? Why?"

Why? Yes, please, someone, tell me why. I don't know. I can only look at her.

At my silence, she collapses against my chest, grabbing fistfuls of my jacket. "I'll never forgive you. It's you. It's you and your games. You and your wife and new baby."

At the mention of my wife and child, I loosen myself from her grip, holding onto her elbows to keep her stable.

Francois takes her shoulders, and Sylvia allows herself to be led to the corner where he rocks her in his arms.

Magda regards me with a stoic, pale face. "She overdosed on sleeping pills."

I can only manage a nod in both acknowledgment and thanks. I needed to know.

"They pumped her stomach," she continues, but doesn't say more. She doesn't have to.

"Would you like me to pray for her?" the chaplain asks.

Praying won't change that she's *gone*. Dead. Praying won't bring her back.

"We should discuss the funeral arrangements." I need to do this. I need to keep busy.

Francois shoots me a 'you can't be serious' look.

"About counseling––" the chaplain starts.

I don't hear more. I'm already out of the door. Counseling will help as little as praying. No one in that room can console me. I can't console them. I just want out.

SO YOUNG.

Her face looks angelic. Peaceful.

The doctor draws back the sheet to cover her. "We made arrangements for her to be transported to the morgue." He hands me a hospital bag with her belongings. "I'm sorry for your loss."

I nod without cutting my eyes away from the shape under the sheet.

"Whenever you're ready," he says.

The door shuts with an agreeable click. At last, I'm alone with my girl. I move the sheet aside to take her hand. Her skin is cold when I press my lips to it.

"I'm sorry I failed you, Carly."

My voice breaks. Scorching tears burn my face and trickle down my neck into the collar of my shirt. Inside, I'm pulp. A mushed bruise. It's only my conditioning that allows me to construct a stoic wall on the outside. I've taken plenty of lives, but I've never lost one. My dad, yes, but that was different. We weren't close. I've never been cut open, exposed, and left vulnerable. I'm a hollow shell of weakness, easy prey for any enemy, and I dare them all to take me on, take me out, and end this misery for which I'm solely to blame.

I failed.

Where did I go wrong? Was I too hard on her? Too soft? Why did I not see it coming? Did I spend too little time with her? Was I too self-absorbed? Was it my lifestyle? Did she find out what I do for a living? I should've refused when she said she was moving back to her mom. I should never have driven her home the day she confronted Valentina before we even started the barbecue. I should've insisted she stay. I should've forced her to talk. I should've been more patient. I should've taken her home with me after the drug scare. I shouldn't have ignored my gut. I shouldn't have lived in my ignorant bubble of selfish happiness.

Regrets, regrets.

Someone, God, anyone, please fucking tell me where I went wrong. I want to tear the sky in two and scream at life for explanations, but all I do is go down on my knees and press my forehead to my daughter's dead hand. I pray to know. I *need* to know, but there will be never be an answer. No understanding. No absolution. No forgiveness. Only guesses and guilt. Only should haves and what ifs.

When they come to take her, I find Magda waiting in the hallway. The exterior she works so hard on maintaining breaks, and her unspoken accusations show through the cracks.

"Francois took Sylvia home," she says. "The doctor gave her a tranquilizer."

"I'll take care of the funeral arrangements."

"You better. I doubt Sylvia will manage."

"Can I give you a lift?"

"Scott will drive me." She hesitates. "Will you be all right?" Her voice breaks on the last word.

For a brief moment, she pulls me to her, enveloping me in her embrace. It's the first time my mother put her arms around me. It feels foreign, and after a heartbeat she pulls away. The cracks in her veneer break all the way open. Tears stream down her cheeks, running black mascara rivulets through her foundation.

"I'll never forgive her for what she did to this family."

It takes me a second to understand who she's talking about. It's easier to shift the blame, but not even Magda can be so blind.

"It's not Valentina's doing."

"It's the baby," she whispers, "and everything else."

Dumping *everything else* in my lap, she leaves me with that heavy burden and walks away. She's right, of course. I've always fucked up everything in my life. My relationships. My daughter. Valentina. *I* should be under that white sheet. It's me who doesn't deserve to live. Albeit, ironically, here I am.

Parking in the garage at home, I sit quietly for a long while. The life has been sucked out of me. I'm numb. I can't cry, rant, or rave. I can't sleep or eat. I can't work or think. Most of all, I can't face myself. I sit in my car, because I simply don't have the willpower to do anything else.

The door connecting to the house opens and the light comes on. Valentina stands in a pool of tungsten brightness that shines through the thin fabric of her nightdress. It throws a spotlight on the roundness of her body, the lies and mistakes I planted in her belly.

"Gabriel."

My name is a sob. She must've heard. Scott or someone from Magda's staff would've called Quincy. She doesn't come closer or speak. She waits for me to make the first move, to see what I need.

Steeling myself, I force my body to comply and exit my car. Her arms reaching for me are too much. I don't deserve her sympathy or soothing. I did this to her. I did this to Carly. I'm destruction.

I'm a monster. A look of pain filters into her eyes when I sidestep her embrace.

"It's late," I say, facing away from her. "Get some sleep."

As I stalk away, her soft whisper reaches my back.

"I'm sorry, Gabriel."

I keep on walking. It's what she wants. It's best for her.

I take a blanket and pillow to my study. There's not a chance I'll sleep, but I need the pretense of routine like I need the Scotch I pour. I down the hard liquor and pour another, then another. Alone, I fall on my knees and wail into the pillow, grieving for the life I created and destroyed.

At some stage, I must've passed out, because I wake with a headache from hell and my throat on fire. It's five in the morning. Quietly, I walk through the big house, going from room to room of nothingness and empty meaning until I've done the full round and am back in my study. The bag from the hospital sits on my desk like a shrine, a reminder that will never let me go.

My hands shake as I reach inside. It's like plunging your arm into a box full of snakes. I don't know what I'll pull out or how it will poison me with further self-blame and sorrow, but I can't stop myself. I remove a white tank top and blue shorts. Underwear sealed in a plastic bag. Her favorite pair of sandals. A raw sound leaves my throat. The clothes are familiar, yet strange. Not on her body, they look like someone else's, and the estranged sentiment scares me. I want to hold onto every memory, not lose a single fiber of intangible emotion or the lifetime of movie reels imprinted in my head. Her first tooth, her first smile, her first step. God, it hurts. It cuts and cuts until I'm nothing but meat shredded to the bone.

I fall into my chair, fighting my shirt collar and tearing at the button strangling me. I'm sorry. I'm so fucking sorry. Forgive me, Carly. I'll never forgive myself. My hands curl into fists. I bang them on the desk so hard my knuckles bleed. I want her back. I want to turn back time. Smoldering anger burns through my body, shaking my muscles. Every ounce of that thick, black fury is directed at myself. How could I not know? How did I not see?

It takes several deep breaths before I somewhat calm myself. I have to behave rationally. For everyone else's but my own sake. I have to wear the mask and carry on.

My attention goes back to the paper bag. Turning it upside down, I give a shake, longing for more. Something. Anything. A sealed envelope drops out with a clank. Inside is something bulky. I run my fingers over the paper ridges. It feels like a chain. I break the seal and let the object slide out. It's Carly's platinum butterfly pendant, the one I gave her for her seventeenth birthday. Picking up the chain, I hold it up to the light. It dangles from my fingers, the butterfly soaring like a pendulum from left to right, right to left.

"Fly free, princess." I press the silver wings to my lips. "Goodbye."

Goodbye. This is where I make my peace, find my acceptance. It'll be a long road to healing, and I honestly don't know if I can do it. Holding the pendant over the jar of keepsakes, I let the chain run through my fingers, allowing it to slip from my grasp, link by link. It drops with a clink on top of the mementos. This is where it belongs, with all the other lives I took. I wring my hands together, intertwining my fingers until it hurts.

This was the last time.

The last one.

I'm done killing.

Valentina

THE NIGHT IS one of the longest of my life. I toss and turn and tiptoe downstairs several times to check on Gabriel. The door of his study remains closed. Not a sound comes from inside. Only a shard of light seeping from under the door confirms his presence. What do I do? How do you make something like this better? Sick with helpless grief and self-blaming worry, I pace between the kitchen and lounge until the first light pierces the awful night.

The sun is weak today with mist clouds gathering in the sky. The day feels broken. Everything feels broken. My heart shatters for Gabriel. I burst into tears every time I recall Quincy's horrible words, the way he looked at me with concern and pity as he stuttered the news, because I play a guilty part in this tragedy. The pregnancy was hard for Carly to take. Even harder was the implied meaning that her father and I were intimate in secret, right under her nose. If I hadn't fallen pregnant, none of this would've happened. Carly would've been blissfully unaware and maybe still alive. Yes, definitely alive. The more I think about it, the more I cringe in shame and burning sin. This is my fault. If I didn't beg Gabriel to selfishly let me keep the baby he never wanted, this wouldn't have happened. Will Gabriel ever forgive me? Can I forgive myself? I can't deal with the answers, so I focus on the most pressing matter––taking care of Gabriel.

My gaze alternates between the rising sun obscured behind the clouds and the study door. When the door is still closed by eight, I take a hasty shower and check on Charlie before starting the tasks of the day on autopilot. I feed Oscar and Bruno and cook breakfast for Quincy, Rhett, and Charlie.

Quincy watches me from under his lashes as I prepare a tray for Gabriel. "How is he?"

I avert my eyes. "I don't know."

"He hasn't come out of his study," Rhett says in understanding.

I add sugar to the tray. "He needs time."

"Of course." Rhett gets to his feet and reaches for the tray. "Let me take that for you."

"I've got it," I say hastily. "Finish your breakfast."

What I mean to say is that I need to see Gabriel. I ache to see him, to soothe him, to tell him how sorry I am, if he'll even listen to me.

At the door, I balance the tray on the table in the hallway and knock.

His voice sounds simultaneously strong and tired. "Who is it?"

"Valentina." I clear my throat. "I brought you breakfast."

The sound of his chair scraping over the floor reaches me through the door, followed by his uneven footsteps. The door opens on a crack.

"Gabriel--"

"I'll take it."

Picking up the tray, I hand it over and lick my dry lips in preparation for what I want to say, but the shadow of the door falls over me as he shuts it in my face with a curt, "Thank you."

"You were right," Rhett says behind me, making me jump. "He needs time."

I flush with shame that Rhett witnessed the rejection of my condolences. It's a clear reflection of Gabriel's judgment. I feel like guilt is carved on my chest. First my father and Charlie, then Tiny and Jerry, and now Carly.

"Yes." I take several steps away from the door. "He needs space."

"Val." Rhett reaches for me. "Are you all right?"

"It's not me who's suffering." Tears burn in my eyes. "I wish I could take it away for him."

"I know." He gives my shoulders a reassuring squeeze. "I know how you think, Val. It's not your fault."

Unable to look him in the eyes, I turn my face to the side.

"It's not your fault." He accentuates his words with a gentle shake.

"Sure. Yes." I twist free. "I'm going to start lunch. We'll probably have visitors popping in throughout the day."

So many people stop by to pay their condolences I lose count. Business associates, mafia, government officials, employees. They all arrive in dark suits with respectful faces and expensive flowers, muttering words of sympathy and solace. Gabriel sits in the lounge, receiving the drips and drabs of guests who never dwindle enough to grant him a moment of solitude. The only way I can make myself useful is to bake savory and sweet pastries and prepare salads and casseroles, which I serve as the hour of the day demands. Savory snacks in the morning, lunch from twelve to two, and sweets in the afternoon with tea. Quincy and Rhett help to load the dishwasher and unpack the crockery in a continuous cycle. Charlie is happy to take charge of brewing fresh tea and coffee.

Magda arrives shortly before teatime. Despite her brave composure her face is ashen. We face each other in a strained atmosphere by the door. Since our move, she hasn't been over to visit, not even to see the house. No matter our history, my heart aches for her loss.

I place a hand on her arm. "Magda, I'm sorry."

She shakes off the touch. "If it wasn't for you…"

My stomach dips, and my insides twist, guilt eating at my gut. I step aside to let her in. "He's in the lounge." I motion at the group crowding the sofas.

Sylvia arrives a few minutes later on the arm of her boyfriend. Her hair is neatly plaited in a French braid, and she's wearing makeup, but she looks haggard. Her eyes slice through me, and then her gaze drops to my big stomach. The way she looks at me makes me feel dirty, like I cheated or did something wrong. Was I wrong in surrendering to Gabriel's advances? Shouldn't I have been stronger? A better person would have resisted. Indefinitely. I feel like I'm standing in a spotlight about to receive judgment.

"This is her," she says to Francois. "This is the reason my Carly committed suicide."

11

Valentina

The subdued conversations around us drone out Sylvia's words. Nobody but her friend and I heard. For that, I'm profoundly grateful. I'm not sure I can handle the whole room's eyes on me in the midst of Gabriel's grief.

A switch in her flips, and I no longer exist. She looks right through me. Like Magda, she walks to Gabriel's side to receive the sympathy and support she deserves. I didn't expect anything different, but it makes my standing clear. Gabriel and I may be married, but only in name. To everyone else I'm still the maid, the slave, the toy, the imposter. I can't even deny it. All of those things, I am. The only people who pay me kind attention are Michael and Elizabeth Roux.

Elizabeth hugs me by the door. "How is he doing?"

I can only shake my head.

"Come here." Michael takes me in bear hug, holding me for two seconds to his big body.

Up to now, I haven't realized how much I needed a hug. There's nothing sinister in the gesture. The only vibe he gives off is of platonic affection. I immediately like him more.

Elizabeth hovers a palm above my stomach. "May I?"

I try to give her the bright smile of an expecting mother, but my effort flies half-mast. "Sure."

She places her hand on my belly and looks at Michael with sparkling eyes. "Oh, my God. I swear I feel the baby kick."

"He's been kicking up a storm since this morning."

"You're beautiful, Valentina. Truly stunning. Isn't she, Michael?"

"Breathtaking," he says with a kind light in his eyes.

"I think I'm making the baby active." Elizabeth removes her hand. "He obviously likes me." She looks toward the lounge, taking in the guests. "Poor Sylvia." Her attention returns to me. "Poor Valentina. She hates you, doesn't she?"

"Is it that obvious?"

Elizabeth makes a sad face. "The way she looks at you…"

"I deserve it."

Michael grabs my hand. "No, you don't, and if you ever say something so self-degrading again, I'll get Gabriel's permission to spank you myself."

A baritone voice resonating from behind us makes me jump.

"What was that, Michael?"

The three of us turn in unison. Gabriel is standing two steps away, his white shirt and black tie pristine, as if he hasn't been wearing it since early this morning. He appears together, like he has a handle on everything. Only the haunted look in his frozen-over eyes gives him away.

"I was just telling Valentina not to put herself down," Michael says.

Gabriel's eyes find mine. They penetrate my soul, making me cold inside. "Is that so?"

"Our deepest condolences, my man." Michael places a hand on Gabriel's shoulder. "There are no words."

"No, there aren't," Gabriel says.

"Gabriel." Elizabeth embraces him. "If there is anything, anything at all..."

"Thank you."

"Congratulations on the wedding," Michael continues. "We're happy for you."

"Yes," Gabriel says without looking at me.

Inwardly, I cringe. If I had any doubts about Gabriel's feelings toward me, I don't any longer. He thinks like Magda and Sylvia. It's only his sense of responsibility and honor that prevents him from tossing his true thoughts in my face.

Elizabeth saves the moment by asking Gabriel questions about the funeral planning. All the while, he ignores me without ignoring me. He pretends I'm not standing next to him, but we're so aware of each other our bodies hum.

The atmosphere is uncomfortable. The stress is too much. Every muscle in my body is clenched. A band tightens around my abdomen, squeezing and holding for three seconds before releasing. After two beats the pattern repeats, but it doesn't hurt. My first Braxton Hicks contractions.

Needing to escape the tense situation, I offer to get Elizabeth and Michael a drink, but Gabriel stops me before I can walk away.

His fingers curl around my upper arm. "No."

I stare at him in surprise. "Excuse me?"

"Go upstairs and rest."

Is he trying to ship me off? Is he ashamed of me? Of everyone seeing the evidence of what happens between us in the size of my belly? Hurtful feelings scorch through me, but this isn't the time or place. This isn't about me. Or us. This is about him and Sylvia. This is about Carly.

"All right." I smile brightly for his guests. "Let me know if you need me."

I purse my lips as another contraction hits. Gabriel holds my gaze for two more seconds, his eyes too knowing, too piercing. When the invisible vice on my belly snaps, I offer Elizabeth and

Michael a polite greeting and free my arm from Gabriel's hold, turning for the stairs, but he doesn't let me go. His palm presses on the small of my back.

"I'll walk you."

I can't be alone with him, right now. I'm afraid of the intensity of what I felt a moment ago, and most of all of his honesty. "I'll be fine. Stay with your guests."

And he does. He turns around and walks away.

In our room, I sit down on the bed. My hands smooth out the comforter that knows our secrets, our shame. Grief and blame tear me apart. My heart breaks a thousand times over for the man downstairs. I'm powerless to console him. How can I? I'm an ugly, dirty link in a chain of events that led to Gabriel's daughter's death.

Gabriel

MAGDA IS GETTING impatient with me. She taps her nails on the desk upstairs in Napoli's. "It's been a month. You have to move on."

A month since Carly is *gone*, and I can't get my shit together. With moving on, Magda means killing, of course. Some jackass in Braamfontein crossed the line when he burgled our office. A month ago, I wouldn't have hesitated. I would've taken the idiot out without blinking an eye, but I made a promise to myself, for Carly, and I won't betray my daughter's memory.

I turn my back to her, facing the window that overlooks the gambling floor below. "Told you, I'm done. I'm out."

There's anger in her voice. "Without you, we'll go under."

"You have Scott and a thousand others you can recruit."

"*You* are my son. Albeit a useless one, and thanks to--" She cuts herself short, gulps in some air. A shaky breath slips into the silence. "Now we don't have an heir."

Damn right, we don't. My son won't end up like me, just like it was never my intention to marry Carly off to a criminal worthy of running our shady business. What Magda won't see is that we never had an heir, and we never will.

"It's your business." I turn back to face her. "Do with it what you will, but I'm leaving."

Scorn deforms her mouth. "What will you do? How will you live?"

She's got me by the balls and from the way that scornful smile grows into a spiteful grin she knows it. I have no idea. I have a wife and soon I'll have a child to take care of. People hate me. Enemies have grudges. I need to keep my family safe, and the only way to do it is to have money. State of the art alarm systems, ammunition, and guards cost bucks. Big bucks.

I cast out my feelers carefully. "I could still run the office, take charge of our business affairs."

She throws me a snide look. "In our business the only bosses respected are the ones who get their hands dirty."

"We could clean up the business."

She slams her fist on the desk. "This isn't how this city works, and you know it." She points a finger at me. "Try and run a clean loan shark business and see how far you get. The competition will ruin you in a day, and if they don't, the police and government will. They'll take kickbacks from someone willing to pay it, and we'll be finished. Over."

The sad part is she's right. If you can't do bribes and play dirty, you're going down.

"I will not see my hard work to build this company up to where it is go down the drain." She accentuates her statement with a nail she pushes on the polished wood of the desk.

I won't break my vow. That leaves only one option. "I'm sorry, Magda. I guess that means you're on your own."

Her body goes rigid. Pushing back her chair, she rises stately. It looks as if her back is about to snap. The fine hair on her upper lip and chin trembles. Her nostrils expand and shiver like a buck smelling lion.

She presses her palms flat on the desk, regarding me from over the rim of her glasses. "You're making a mistake."

"This is the only right thing I've done in my life."

Her arms are shaking so badly she has to lock her elbows. I've never seen her this mad.

"It's *her*, isn't it?" she hisses. "It's *her* idea. *Her* doing. *She* planted this in your dim-minded head."

My defenses rise. "Leave Valentina out of this."

Her eyes narrow to slits. "I should've known. Should've guessed this is her game. She's always been too holy for us."

I take a step toward the desk. *"Leave her alone."*

"This is what it's come to, then?" She straightens, balling her fists at her sides. "You'll choose her over your family, over your own mother?"

"She *is* my family, and yes, she comes first."

Magda reels at my words. I may as well have slapped her. The color of her skin takes on an ashen tone. For a few seconds, emotions suspend between us—shock, betrayal, disappointment, anger. They pollute the air and poison the blood that's supposed to be thicker than water.

When there's no other expression but disillusionment left on her face, she says flatly, "Get out."

I throw her words around in my mind. *This is what it's come to.* To be honest, we've always been heading this way. I was always the son who disappointed. She took my choice and gave me a gun, but I'm not that boy any longer. I'm the man Magda bitterly hoped I would never be.

Rapping my knuckles on the desktop, I give her my resignation with a tight nod and turn my back on her and the future I've been building all my life. A part of me feels sorry for her. Not only did she lose her only granddaughter, but also the ambitions she had for her son. I won't be her successor. I won't salvage and nurture the business she busted her balls for. It will go with her to her grave, and what I've done for this business will take me to hell.

Outside, I stop on the landing for a breath. I lean my palms on the balustrade and inhale deeply. This is where it all started. This is where I laid eyes on Valentina for the first time. She looked so young and damn innocent in her white uniform and so strong. She was standing right there, at that table, and when the croupier grabbed her arm, I wanted to chop off his hand for laying a finger on her. The minute I looked into her scared but defiant eyes, I wanted her. She was a challenge and a mystery. She was brave and naïve. So damn hot and so damn untouchable. Unobtainable, and yet, just there, within my reach. Every contradiction in the book. The woman I wanted, and the woman I had to kill.

It seems like three lifetimes ago, but it's only been a year. If I were a better man, I'd right the decision I took here that night by setting her free. I'd cut her lose like I cut the cords with The Breaker, but I'm not a good man. I can never let her go. This is my unrepented evil. She's my biggest sin.

Looks like we came full circle. It ends where it began. With her. Somewhere in between, I lost Carly. My marriage, the baby, the changes in our living arrangements, it was too much. My ruthless lust for a woman I stole drove my daughter away from me, pushed her right over the edge. My burden doesn't feel lighter when I descend the stairs and walk the hell away from who I used to be. It only grows heavier the nearer I come to the house. I can't lay that godforsaken burden down, because it will mean I have to set Valentina free, but I can't look at her, either, because it means I'll have to face my guilt.

Valentina

As the days move on, Gabriel grows further and further away from me. He's closed up in himself, and no amount of probing or baiting can lure him out. To suffer the loss he did is shattering, and the grief is devastating. He eats well and exercises every day. His body is the same rock-hard, strong one I remember, but the man inside has changed. Is he even in there, in the darkness that's become his mind? No matter how much I talk or touch, I can't get through to him.

From the dark circles marring his eyes, I know he's not sleeping, even if he no longer sleeps next to me. After the funeral, he moved into the spare bedroom. He doesn't go to work or see friends. He stays at home all day, but well away from me. When he's not closed in his study or working out in the gym, he's doing DIY work around the house. I watch him with his shirtless body up on the ladder, and my body doesn't care that he's still in grief or that he blames me. It only wants what it's being denied––my husband's touch.

Abstractly, he's never been my husband, of course. Our house of cards, my make-belief reality, has come crushing down, and the man who taught me to be hungry for his caresses is now withholding them from me. This makes me sad. Since he hasn't been inside me for weeks, I feel obsolete, like a purposeless burden. When he didn't give me a choice, I didn't want to be his toy or his wife, and now that I'm neither, I desperately want to be one or the other, preferably both. I'll settle for anything he gives. There has to be hope, because he still gets hard for me. It's difficult to hide when he's working out in his sweatpants or swimming in his trunks.

Tonight, I cook his favorite dishes––lamb roast, green beans with bacon, and fried potatoes––and set a table with candles outside. Rhett, Quincy, and Charlie are dining inside, as usual. The falter in Gabriel's step when he comes downstairs and sees the romantic setting in the garden almost has my courage failing.

Meeting him at the bottom of the staircase, I take his arm and lead him outside, not giving him the choice of heading for the dining room.

Without a word, he seats me and takes the opposite chair.

His gaze moves over the meal. "What's the occasion?"

"Just dinner."

For the first time in a month he meets my eyes directly. "Just dinner?"

"And spending time alone. We're always with the others, not that I'm complaining. I like them, but..." Damn. My courage fails me.

The look on his face stops me before I can work up the nerve to finish my sentence. A veil falls over his eyes, and a shutter clicks in place. The silence stretches as he regards me with an emotion that slowly breaks through his unreadable expression. Under the thick surface of his mask, I recognize pity.

He pities me. He must think I'm pathetic. Irrational anger spreads through my veins. This is his doing, what he made me. If I'm needy, it's his fault. If I want him, he's to blame. How dare he sit there and judge me, feel sorry for me for wanting him? Tears prick at the back of my eyes. No matter how fast I bat my eyelashes, I can't blink them away. One slips free, two... Goddamn. Do I have to show weakness after weakness?

The mask slips another fraction as he reaches across the table and takes my hand. "Don't."

Don't cry? Don't want? Don't feel? I want to shout and hurt him like I'm hurting, but I sniff my tears away and force my irrational hormones down.

"I'm trying so hard..." My voice cracks on the last word. I can't carry on speaking for the fear of sobbing all over the roast.

He rubs a thumb over my knuckles. "You don't have to try, beautiful."

I don't have to try what? Staring at him through my tears, I will him to explain, but he doesn't.

He brings my hand to his mouth and kisses the back. "You need your strength. Shall I dish up for you?"

My heart shatters into tiny shards. It takes everything I have to take my rejection gracefully and not jump and fight him like a bitch in heat. I nod. When he's busy dishing food onto my plate I quickly wipe my eyes with the back of my hand. It'll be easier for him to just let me go.

"Gabriel?" I wait until he faces me. "Set me free."

His eye turn hard. "I already told you it's not going to happen." He puts down the spoon. "Eat. Your food's getting cold."

I vowed to take whatever I could get. Looks like I'm settling for being an unwanted responsibility.

KRIS PICKS up on my change at work. She drags me outside to the garden table for lunch and sets down a box of chow mein takeout in front of me. I feel bad that Charlie is eating alone inside, but when I mention it, she shakes her head and points a chopstick at me.

"Stay put. We're going to talk."

I groan.

"You can give me that look all you like," she shakes out a napkin in her lap, "but you're going to spill the beans. What's eating you?"

"Hormones." Lately, I've been using that a lot as an excuse.

Her chin sets in the way that says she won't give up. "How are things at home, with Gabriel, I mean?"

I don't want to saddle Kris with my problems, but I do need a friend to confide in. "Not well. He's a walking corpse."

She stuffs her mouth with noodles and mumbles, "Sounds kind of normal with what he's going through."

Immediately, I feel selfish and bad for thinking of my needs when I should be placing his first.

"Mourning takes time," she says.

"He hasn't been back to work, and he hardly leaves the house."

"He doesn't need to work if he doesn't want to. He's got enough money."

"I'm worried about him sitting in his study all day."

"I'm sure he's doing stuff."

"I wish I knew what to do to help."

"Give him space." She takes another big bite. "And be patient."

When I don't say anything for several seconds, she stops eating and looks at me again. "You want things to work out with him, don't you?"

This is the crux of the problem. "Yes," I whisper.

"You feel you shouldn't because of how the two of you started."

"I don't know what I feel. I only know I want this to be real. I don't want to pretend, anymore. I want a real husband who loves me for me, not an owner who married me so his enemies won't decapitate me."

"Whoa." She laughs. "It sounds harsh when you put it like that."

"But true."

"Yeah. Harsh, but true. What are you going to do?"

"I was hoping you'd tell me. What should I do, Kris?"

"I guess it depends on what you want."

"I want him."

"Then fight."

"Fight?"

"Yes. Give him another few months to mourn and then start walking around naked. That should catch his attention."

I swat at her with my napkin. "We have other people living in the house."

"I know. Maybe that's part of the problem. You need time alone. Send the guys away and bring Charlie over to me."

"You're a good friend."

"I'm practical."

"You're still a good friend."

She checks her watch. "Eat your food. We're back on in five. See? I'm practical."

That gets a laugh out of me.

Pulling weeds from the vegetable garden, I sit flat on my ass on the ground as I can't bend down anymore. Dr. Engelbrecht, who does a house call every second week, tells me I'm gaining too much weight. Some of it is water retention, but for the most part it's unhappiness. I gobble down ice cream with peanut butter sauce when I'm sad, at least since I'm pregnant. The extra weight restrains my movements, and I still have two months to go.

The July midday sun beats down on my head. Even in winter, it's hot. I seem to have an internal heater inside, making things worse. Unless I want to faint from overheating, I better seek out the cool interior of the house. As I'm battling to lift my heavy body, a pair of hands clasps my elbows and helps me to my feet.

I look up into Quincy's face. "My knight in shining armor. Thank you."

"Where's Gabriel?" He looks pissed off. "Wait, don't tell me. In his study."

"This is hard on him, Quincy." I don't know if I mean me, the baby, or Carly's passing. Probably all three.

"Yeah." He motions at my stomach. "This is not hard for you."

"It's not the same."

He looks like he wants to argue, so I say quickly, "Charlie has a session with Christopher. I'm going to make a fresh pitcher of iced tea."

"Need help?"

"I'm good, thanks."

He watches me broodily as I make my way back to the house. Christopher is already there, chatting to Rhett. I show the doctor and Charlie into the cinema room with an uneasy feeling. The last few sessions left a mark on Charlie. He was agitated afterward, but Christopher wrote the mood swings off to a normal mid-phase of the therapy. Today, I wait by the door, immediately noticing the tense set of Charlie's shoulders as he exits.

I grab his arm before he can escape. "How did it go?"

"Po-pool." He jerks free and skirts around me, heading for the sliding doors.

"I made iced tea," I call after him. "It's apple and cinnamon." Charlie's favorite.

He gives me a backward glance, but walks away with quick steps. He's irritated and won't be swayed.

Christopher follows next. "Well, I'll be on my way, then."

"Can we please talk for a moment?"

He glances at his wristwatch. "I have another appointment."

"Five minutes?"

He can't refuse me without being rude, but the corners of his mouth turn down. "All right." He puts his briefcase down and takes the tea I offer.

"Charlie's been irritable of late. To be exact, since your last four sessions."

"I told you it's normal. We hit a barrier in his development, and breaking through it is hard work, but once we're through he'll be fine. Better than fine."

"What are you working on?"

"I'm not at liberty to discuss that. It may compromise our goal if you interfere." I open my mouth to object, but he stills me with a hand in the air. "Trust me, all caring relatives interfere. It's human nature. We can't stand seeing our loved ones suffer. Just remember that all great results come with hard work."

I'm not reassured, but he downs his drink and leaves the glass on the table. "Great iced tea. It reminds me of my grandmother."

"Thank you," I mumble as he sees himself out.

I'll give it two more sessions, and if Charlie is still worked up, I'll stop the treatment. Sometimes Charlie gets impatient, especially when he can't express his feelings, but mostly, he's just a big, huggable bear. I don't want him to be unhappy, ever.

Gabriel

DAYS WEAVE into nights and nights into days. Time is one, slow, never-ending, torturous cycle. Most days, I pour over photo albums with pictures of Carly from when she was born up to her death. I study each picture, hunting for details and information I may have missed before, like on how many photos she wore her blue T-shirt with the red heart. I never realized how much she liked it. Had I known, I would've packed it in a box and kept it with her first baby shoes, her favorite rattle, and the doll she slept with until she was five, the one whose hair she cut off, believing it would grow back. My life is a box of memories. Full, yet empty.

I'm making an effort to carry on with my life. The money in my bank account won't last forever. I accepted a management job at one of Michael's firms, which is nothing but charity from his side. He's turned out to be a good friend, and no matter how hard it is to pull my head out of the sand, I refuse to disappoint him.

Magda and I are still not on speaking terms. She sent me an email stating whatever happened between us, her grandchild will always be welcome in her house, and she hopes I'll change my mind.

Tough luck. I'm on my way to a new future that doesn't involve loan sharks or breaking bones. I need to do this for me, but also for the people who depend on me to take care of them.

I'm about to leave for my first day on the new job when Quincy steps into my study.

Adjusting my tie, I say, "I'm running late."

The wide stance he takes makes me look, really look, at him. His fists are balled at his sides and his jaw is flexed. He is mad. Furious.

"We're going to talk, Gabriel. Now. This has gone on for long enough."

"Talk about what?"

"You want me to spell it out for you?"

What the fuck is eating him? "Why don't you?"

"Your neglect of Valentina."

It takes a moment for his words to register. "My neglect of––" And then they sink in. "What?" I glare at him. "It's none of your business."

His stance becomes wider. "Is she your wife or isn't she?"

My temper starts to slip. "Of course she's my wife."

"Then act like a husband, and if you can't, let someone else."

I see fucking red. Burnt black with orange, melted edges. "Keep out of my business," I growl, "and out of my wife."

"She deserves better. You got her pregnant. Now treat her right."

Grabbing his lapels, I lift him off his feet. "If you're wise, you'll shut your mouth."

He doesn't look scared in the slightest. "Can't face the truth? Not man enough to hear it?"

Before I can stop myself, I slam my fist into his jaw. He goes flying, hitting the floor with a thump. At that very moment, the object of our discussion walks through the door. Valentina freezes, looking from me to Quincy who is sprawled out on the tiles. It's him she rushes to.

"Quincy! Are you all right?" She gives me a startled look. "Gabriel, what's wrong with you?"

The jealousy I had tapered down to an art during the last few months bubbles back to the surface, ugly and acidic in my throat. She's *mine*, and she's carrying *my* child. Nobody gets her, no matter how much better a man he is.

Before I say or do something I'll regret, I leave Quincy in her concerned hands and set off for work. I'm not going to tell her about it until the time is right, until I know it's working out. She doesn't need to worry about where the money is going to come from.

THROWING my full weight behind my resolution, all I eat, drink, and live for is work. I'm adjusting well in the company and get on with Michael. I respect him as a friend and boss. Elizabeth is his second-in-command. She often asks about Valentina, but gives up when she gets nothing out of me. It feels strange to work my way up in someone else's business, but I'm grateful for the challenge. It keeps my mind off darker thoughts. The kinder they are to me, the harder I work to earn it. I want to prove my worth to them, but mostly to myself. This isn't my father's business or my mother's money. I'm earning my own way, and it's harder than I thought. I spend long hours at the office, coming home after eleven when the rest of the house is asleep, and leaving before they wake. Little by little, day after day, I stitch back a resemblance of a life.

Valentina

IT'S seven in the evening when Magda's car pulls up to our gates, and Scotts announces her through the gate intercom. What is she doing here? Did Gabriel invite her for dinner? Since the funeral, she hasn't been back to the house. Even if Gabriel doesn't say as much, they must have had some kind of fallout.

I brush down my dress, a nervous habit that stuck with knowing how much she disapproves of my choice of clothes, and meet her at the door.

Her manner is urgent. "Is Gabriel still at work?"

"You'll know better than me."

"Me?"

"He works with you, doesn't he?"

"He hasn't told you?" She makes big eyes. Behind her faked

expression, she seems pleased. "He works for Michael and Elizabeth Roux, now."

Wow. That's like pushing a needle under my nail and twisting it. The fact that he didn't tell me something this important hurts in ways I don't care to examine.

"Come in." I step aside, wondering how much I should ask. I don't want to give her ammunition to shoot down the already crumbling walls of whatever warped relationship Gabriel and I have left. I'm holding onto the ruins with both my hands, digging my nails into the broken bricks as I dangle over the wall, but I'm not sure cracks of that size can ever be filled.

She looks around the space. "Where's everyone?"

"Charlie is upstairs, and Rhett is in his room."

"Quincy?"

"With Gabriel."

"Ah. Good. I was hoping we could talk alone. Can we go somewhere private? I don't want to be interrupted."

An itch crawls down my spine. I should say no, but my gut is stirring, and red flags are waving in my mind.

"In here." I lead her to Gabriel's study, the nearest room with a door.

"I'm surprised he didn't tell you he left our company," she says once we're inside. "Then again, he doesn't tell you much, does he?"

Why did he hide it from me? And Rhett and Quincy? Are they in on this, too? I can't help how defensive I sound. "What's that supposed to mean?"

"I bet he never told you why you fell pregnant."

That itch from earlier spreads over my skin, making every nerve-ending tingle in alarm. "What?"

"He replaced your birth control with placebo pills." She pushes a USB key into my hand. "Here's the proof, and the reason why he chose *you*."

12

Valentina

Gabriel did what? I don't believe it. He wouldn't. Never. Why is Magda doing this? My gut warns me this is only the beginning. Magda planted a path of destruction in my palm, and my feet are firmly on it. My fingers clamp around the key in my hand that will, if true, destroy me. The heartache I felt at Gabriel's rejection is nothing compared to the pain slashing through my insides. I prefer a hundred lashes of his belt to this. Anything, but not this. If Magda is right, he purposefully deceived me. He lied to me. Worse, he let me believe it was my fault. My nails cut into the skin of my palm around the piece of plastic. I ache in every corner of my soul.

"I'll leave you to it." Magda walks to the door. "I assume you prefer to watch this in private. If I were you, I wouldn't waste time in packing my bags." A victorious smile marks her grand exit.

For some time, I stand rooted to the spot. My body trembles, and chills run over my skin. This is game over. It hurts, really hurts. Why me? The answer I want is in the palm of my hand. Releasing my fingers one by one, I stare at the black object with Magda's company logo. My hand shakes as I carry it to Gabriel's desk and open his laptop. When the screen comes to life, I hesitate. Once the key hits the slot, there's no turning back. I won't have a choice but to face the facts. My hand hovers next to the slot.

How could you Gabriel?

I insert the key and bite my nail.

As the file is loading, Charlie appears in the open door.

"I'm hu–hungry."

"I'll be right there. How about folding the laundry while you wait?" Charlie loves pairing socks.

"Lau–laundry." He disappears in the direction of the scullery.

I turn my focus back to the computer. A folder named *Valentina* sits menacingly on the screen. Shiver after shiver creeps over my arms. It's eerie to see my own name and wrong to open something that doesn't belong to me, something that Gabriel is clearly hiding. I make a last brave effort to abort my mission, which is driven on the ugly fuel of curiosity, pain, and humiliation, but my finger is already hovering over the mouse. Will Gabriel give me honest answers if I question him? Probably not. The final thought that sways the balance and brings my finger down is the knowledge that Magda knows more than me.

Click-click.

The folder opens. My heart stops pumping for a beat. I hold my breath and bite my lip. The folder contains two files. The one is titled *Birth Control* and the other *Evidence*. I open *Birth Control* first. It contains a sound file. Confused, I click on it. It's a recording of a telephone conversation. The voices belong to Gabriel and Dr. Engelbrecht. They're discussing my health. Guilt and fearful anticipation heat my cheeks as I listen in on a conversation not meant for my ears.

"I want a placebo birth control pill," Gabriel says.

"You want her to fall pregnant?" Dr. Engelbrecht asks.

Gabriel doesn't hesitate. "Exactly." He doesn't even sound ashamed. No remorse, no explanations.

"Tomorrow?" the doctor says.

There is a smile in his voice. "Perfect. We need to repeat the examination to make sure she's healthy and susceptible. I want her to have a fertility shot to help things along."

It takes a full minute to register the words. I rewind and play the conversation over. Over and over. With each repetition more anger boils through my veins until my body feels like a coal stove ablaze with a fire. Shaking uncontrollably, I go back to the beginning and listen to the conversation again. I can't help myself. I keep on lashing my soul with the hurtful truth, punishing myself for my naïve ignorance. My heart doesn't want to accept what I've heard, even if my mind already believes it. I cover my mouth with a hand and place the other on my stomach, over Gabriel's planned intention, the baby I love more than myself. I feel sick. When I've played the conversation back at least ten times, I stop. I've listened to every nuance and intonation of Gabriel's voice, searching for feelings and motivations that aren't there. Why did he do it? Why did he lie to me? Why me? Magda's words spin in my head. *And the reason why he chose you.*

It takes every ounce of courage I have left to open the second file. This one is a video clip. Fear snakes down my arm, making it feel heavy as my finger pauses above the keyboard, but my hand has a life of its own as it moves down and hits enter.

The image is grainy and blurry, but slowly comes into focus. It's not a feed from a security camera as I expected, but a home movie. The lens is pointing at the floor. Whoever is carrying the camera is walking. A pair of polished, black shoes fall on the wood. There are voices in the background. They are excited, loud. There is something else, another voice my mind refuses to decipher. A feeling of foreboding heats my body, making my palms clammy. I want to turn the recording off, but I can't. The unfolding pictures hold my eyes as if they're glued to the screen. The shouting becomes louder, clearer. There's cheering. The camera lifts, and the room comes into focus.

"You got that, Barney?" a voice says.

"Yeah, hurry up. I'm rolling."

The walls are covered in wood paneling with framed pictures of dressed-up dogs playing cards. In the center is a big table covered with green felt. A pool table. My mouth goes dry. My body temperature drops ten degrees, and ice lodges in every pore of my skin. Frozen in horror, I watch as four men drag a struggling girl onto the table. Two of them grab her arms, and two her legs, while a fifth starts tearing her clothes. Her screams are futile. The more she pleads, the harder they laugh. Sobs wrack her thin body. She tries to kick and gets a fist in the stomach. Her eyes are pinched shut as the man who destroyed her clothes works his pants over his hips. He's fat and gray. She keeps her eyes closed as he does the unthinkable, but I don't. I watch every violating move of his body, every painful slap of his palm as it falls on her cheeks. Through the lens, I watch each face that looks on, that laughs as it's his turn to smile for the camera. The coldness spreads through my limbs when the man in the center, the one with his pants around his ankles, falls over the girl's body. Something hot and wet runs over my face and explodes in drops on the keyboard. The camera moves around the table, capturing every angle of the unmoving body that lies on top. When it comes to the side where her dark hair trails over the edge, the rapist stands up right in front of me. His head is bent, obscuring his features as he pulls up his pants and fastens his belt. Then he lifts his face and looks straight at me. My throat constricts. I try to swallow, but I can't. I can't breathe. The cold spell of my body ripples over my skin, freezing me inch by inch, until I can't move a finger or toe. When the extreme coldness reaches my scalp, it's replaced with scorching heat. I've seen the face of my rapist many times before. Right here, in my husband's study. It's standing on his desk, looking back at me now. Paying witness to my shock, he regards me with a mocking smile.

Owen Louw.

Gabriel's father.

13

Valentina

Everything happens at once. A painful contraction folds me double. A dull ache drives into my brain until my vision turns blotchy with spots. And my water breaks.

It's too early.

These are nothing like the Braxton Hicks contractions I got used to. The pain drives me to my knees. Gnashing my teeth together, I wait it out, and when the band of agony lets go, I grab the desk and pull myself up. I use the desk phone to dial the emergency number, inhaling and exhaling while I wait. Just as someone takes the call, the second series of contractions hits.

I clench my teeth and groan.

"Hello?" the operator says. "Can you hear me?"

Please don't hang up.

Click.

Damn. No! Putting one hand on the furniture, I use the desk, chair, and wall for support to make my way to the lounge. Dizziness slows my progress. My head hurts as much as my abdomen. Just then, Charlie exits the scullery with a basket full of socks.

"Go get Rhett," I say as calmly as possible, even as every bone in my body is shaking. There's a good chance I'm going to lose the baby.

Charlie takes one look at me and drops the basket. "Va–Val!"

"It's okay. Where's Rhett?" I continue to the kitchen, but another contraction stills me before I can get to my phone that's lying on the counter.

It hurts like nothing I've felt. My head is going to explode. I count through it. One, two, three, four, five. Another few steps. My cry isn't loud, but it's a wretched sound. "Rhett?"

He flies from his room, his hair wet and a towel wrapped around his waist. "Val, did you call me?" His eyes fall on the wetness on my legs and feet, and then they grow large.

"The baby," I whisper, tears dripping from my eyes. "Call an ambulance."

The thought that runs on repeat through my mind shows in the way he shakes his head in silent denial.

Too early.

We don't stand a chance with a premature home delivery. If I don't make it to a hospital on time, my baby is dead. I cry harder as Rhett gets our private ambulance service on the line and gives them our address, but the crying only makes the pain in my head worse. All the while he rubs my shoulder. I'm grateful for that point of human contact. I'm scared to go through this alone.

"They're on their way," he says in a clipped voice when he hangs up.

"Call Kris. She needs to stay with Charlie." I grunt as another contraction pulls my abdomen into a sharp point of pain.

Breathe. In, out. In, out.

While Rhett makes the call to Kris, I speak to Charlie. "I'm going to hospital, like we talked about. You're going to be all right.

Kris is coming to see you. Ask her to cook whatever you like. There's lots of food in the fridge."

"She'll be here as soon as she can," Rhett says on a huff.

"Can you be brave for me?" I ask Charlie.

"Bra–brave."

"Good. I love you so, so much." I want to say more, but I can't speak through the next contraction. I have to lean on Rhett for support. Impatient for it to lift, I blow out a breath and drag in air. I have little time before the next one comes. "You've always been a good, big brother to me, Charlie. Never forget how much I love you."

"God, Val." Rhett's voice is choked. "Don't talk like that."

"I'm good." I give him a reassuring pat on the arm. "I just want him to know."

"He knows." Rhett shoots a worried look at Charlie. "How about watching a movie until Kris comes?"

"O–okay."

As Charlie heads for the cinema room, Rhett carries me to the sofa. He pushes a pillow under my head and strokes my hair. "You're strong. You're going to be fine."

My smile is weak, because my heart is not in it.

Please don't let my baby die. Please don't let him pay the price.

Rhett has his phone pressed to his ear when sirens sound in the distance. "Damn you, Gabriel, pick up," he mutters under his breath.

I don't know how I feel about Gabriel being here, right now, but this is still his baby, too.

"Quincy?" I offer, grinding my teeth through the pain.

He's already scrolling through his contact list when the intercom buzzes, but gives up on the call to open the gate from the control panel in the kitchen. Rhett rushes for the door and lets the paramedics in. Despite the fact that he's still only wearing a towel, he runs next to the stretcher as they wheel me to the ambulance.

He grips my hand. "I'm not leaving your side."

"No. Stay with Charlie." He could drown in the pool or explode the gas in the kitchen. There are too many potential accidents waiting to happen in this house. When it looks as if he's going to argue, I beg. "Please, Rhett."

Reluctantly, he gives in, but his expression lets me know he's not pleased.

"I'll call Quincy," he calls as the paramedics load me into the back of the ambulance and one of them takes up a position next to me.

We're speeding off when the medic starts bombarding me with medical questions about my health history and the pregnancy while he listens to my heartbeat and takes my blood pressure. His eyes flare when he reads the gauge.

"Except for the contractions, do you have any other pain?"

"My head hurts."

"Blurred vision, seeing spots, or sensitivity to light?"

"Spots."

His frown deepens. "Nausea or vomiting?"

"Nausea, but I've been nauseous since the beginning of the pregnancy."

"Dizziness?"

"Yes."

He connects me to a tocometer to measure my contractions and tells me he's sending the information to the hospital ahead of my arrival. He doesn't say there's nothing to worry about, and I'm glad he doesn't give me meaningless reassurance.

Thanks to Gabriel's private medical insurance, I've been pre-admitted for the delivery at the brand-new Broadacres Clinic a short distance away from home. We clear the gates less than twenty minutes later. A male nurse is waiting at the emergency entrance to escort me to an examination room in the delivery wing where an obstetrician takes immediate charge. With him are two nurses. He's studying a tablet as one nurse helps me undress and pull on the hospital robe while the other prepares a drip. The nurse helps me into a bathroom for a urine sample before leading me to a gynecology chair where the doctor takes a blood sample and does a physical examination. The look in his eyes when he finally lifts his head reflects my fears.

"Mrs. Louw," he says in a soothing voice, "you're nine centimeters dilated, and your contractions are two minutes apart. You're in the active phase of labor. It's too late for an epidural. We're going for natural unless there are complications, all right?"

"Can't you stop the contractions? It's too early for the baby."

The way he looks at me is so calm that his next words floor me completely. "You have severe preeclampsia. Are you familiar with the term?"

I frown at him. "Vaguely."

"Your blood pressure is too high. If you don't deliver the baby now, you risk developing eclampsia or seizures, which can be life threatening." He softens the blow with a pat on my leg.

"What?" Shock resonates through me. "My baby! What about my baby?" I bite my lip as pain sharper than before contracts my body.

"We're going to do our best. The rest is in God's hands." There's a sense of urgency but also confidence in his movements as he starts to prepare, pulling on scrubs and a hair cap. "Can we call someone to be with you?" He glances at the screen of the tablet. "You have only your husband listed."

The only people I want are Kris and Charlie. They're the ones who stood by me regardless, who never lied to or deceived me, but this isn't a situation I can expose Charlie to, and it's better that Kris takes care of him.

"No," I say, "there's no one else."

"Get the anesthesiologist on standby," the doctor says to one of the nurses.

The nurse pushes a needle into my arm and connects it to a drip while the doctor takes a seat in front of my bent legs.

"Push when I tell you," he says. "On the count of three. One. Two. Three!"

The contractions are coming faster and harder. I need all my energy to breathe through them. I don't have enough strength left to think, let alone to talk, so I put everything out of my mind except the one task required of me--delivering this baby.

14

Gabriel

The meeting runs overtime. While our investor drones on about the real estate market, I check my watch. It's almost eight. My phone vibrates on the tabletop. I glance at the screen. It's a message from Quincy.

Call Rhett.

Something's up. Being in a meeting, I'd ignored Rhett's earlier call, but both my bodyguards won't be trying to reach me if it's not important. Excusing myself, I leave Michael to chair the meeting and make the call in the hallway.

Rhett's voice is strained. "Valentina's on her way to the Broadacres Clinic."

Every sinew in my body is a string about to snap. "What happened?"

"Her water broke."

I go cold. I clench the phone so hard my fingers hurt. "Hold on." I shake like a puppy in a storm. My leg is dead weight dragging behind my body as I hurry back into the meeting room and whisper my emergency in Michael's ear.

"Go," he says, grabbing my shoulder, "and let us know." His eyes are laced with concern as they follow me out of the room.

In the hallway, I text Quincy, telling him to bring the car around, and revert back to Rhett's call.

Speaking as I walk, I ask, "Where are you?"

"At the house. I'm waiting for Kris to arrive to stay with Charlie. As soon as she gets here, I'll go to the hospital."

"How did this happen? Did she lift something heavy?" Dear God, did she…? "Did she fall?" I should've been there, dammit. Maybe she tried to clean under the bed again or carry the laundry basket downstairs.

"I don't know." Rhett sounds lost. Frightened. "Magda arrived, I went for a shower, and the next thing I knew, Valentina's in labor."

"Wait." Magda arrived? My hackles grow ten inches long. "What did Magda want?"

"I don't know. I assumed it was a social visit."

It doesn't add up. I'm in the lobby, scanning the street for Quincy. "Did you see her?"

"No. I only opened the gate. Valentina met her at the door. I went for a shower to give them privacy."

"Is she still there?"

"She left before Valentina's water broke."

Spotting the Jaguar pulling up to the curb, I race for the passenger side. "Good." I don't want Magda there when I'm not home. I get inside and cover the phone with a hand. "Broadacres Clinic," I say to Quincy. "Hurry. Valentina's having the baby."

Quincy pales. He puts the car in gear and takes off with screeching tires.

"I'm on my way," I say. "We'll be there in twenty."

Luckily, at this hour, there's little traffic. We take the quieter roads and make it to the clinic in just under my predicted time.

Quincy drops me off at the front entrance. "Go. I'll park the car."

As a short month ago, I rushed to the reception desk, but this time I ask for my wife. As a month ago, the receptionist tells me to stay put. A doctor is on his way to meet me. I turn to stone. My organs transform into lead. I haven't been directed to a lounge, but it's the same.

A young man in a white coat approaches me. He doesn't waste time with a greeting.

"Mr. Louw, your wife is in labor."

I'm like a lion ready to pounce. I want to be with my woman. "I know. Take me to her."

"Shortly." His tone is assertive. "First, I need to bring you up to speed." He turns and starts walking, not looking to see if I'm following.

When we enter a small visitor's room, everything inside of me turns heavy. My stomach is a ball of granite. My chest cavity is filled with rocks.

He closes the door and turns to me. "Your wife has severe preeclampsia as a result of hypertension. The only way to prevent further risks is for the baby to be delivered immediately, but we're battling to stabilize her blood pressure. We're administering magnesium sulfate intravenously. If her body doesn't react to the magnesium, she may develop eclampsia. In other words, she may have seizures. We've already explained the condition and possible consequences to her. Before you go into the delivery room, we need to do the same." He takes a breath and plows forward. "There's a chance she may not survive the birth."

My legs turn to stone pillars. My fault. My doing. "How big a chance?"

"Right now, I'd say fifty-fifty, but it depends on how she reacts to the medication."

My first irrational reaction is anger. "Our private doctor examined her every two weeks. Why didn't he pick this up?"

"Preeclampsia often only starts at the onset of labor."

"She wasn't due for another two months. What went wrong?"

I'm screaming at nature, at God, and at the day I replaced her birth control pills with placebo ones. If I can find what triggered the untimely contractions, maybe I can go back in time and change it. Maybe I can find the mistake and flog myself to reverse this process, to take her back to before her water broke. Or maybe I simply need to punish myself for not carrying that laundry basket for her. If I flog my back to bloody strips for letting her bend down and clean under the bed, maybe God will forgive me and spare her life.

"It's hard to say," the doctor says. "A physical shock could've triggered the birth, emotional trauma, illness… there are many factors. What matters now is that you support her." He grabs my shoulder. "You have to be strong for her, Mr. Louw. It's what she needs most."

I haven't realized that big, fat, slobbering tears are streaming over my face until he hands me a tissue from a box strategically placed on the table. If she dies… No, no, no. I can't face it.

"Ready?" The doctor gives my shoulder a squeeze. "We should go."

Another minute later, I'm showering and scrubbing in a change room, donning the scrubs a nurse put out for me. My chest is so tight it's difficult to breathe. The beat of my heart is like the slap of a hammer on a block of marble, chipping away at the corners and edges, carving deep grooves into the memories of my moments with Valentina.

Please, God, save her.

I'll give my life, instead. Don't make her pay for my mistakes. Don't let her pay the ultimate price for my selfish lust and hardheaded will to keep her. Save her and I swear I'll make this right. I'll take a vow on my knees to undo every wrongdoing, every self-serving sin I committed against her. Even if it kills me, I'll set her free.

I'll let her go.

Fuck, that thought cuts crisscrossed lashes into my heart. Retribution is a bitch, and I deserve every bit of it.

"Let's go, Mr. Louw."

The nurse leads me down a long hallway with too bright lights. It's like walking down a tunnel toward the end. There's mercy in life and peace in death. I don't want her to have peace yet, not before she's lived the full and happy life she deserves. I want her to grow old and see her grandchildren married. I want her to have whatever she wants. I want her to have the mercy.

The woman in the white uniform holds a door and motions for me to enter. My world crashes to pieces before those pieces are reconstructed to form the picture facing me. My wife lies on a bed, straining with all her might. Her face is as white as pottery clay, and her slender legs are shaking in an unnatural way, as if she's having a fit. She's trying to give life to the baby I put in her womb, and suddenly her frail limbs look too vulnerable for the task. Her hair is plastered to her brow, and her skin shiny with perspiration, but the set of her mouth is determined. Strong.

Jerking from my immobile state of shock, I rush to her side and take her hand. The stump that used to be her thumb is another reminder of who I am, one more piece I took away from her.

"You can do it, beautiful."

What lies in front of me is a broken creature, an angel with torn wings and pieces of her soul and body missing. Despite the injuries, she still fights to fly. I lift her hand to my mouth and kiss her fingers. Her skin is cold.

"Please, Valentina." I beg for forgiveness. I beg for her to fight harder and not to leave me. "Fight," I whisper.

For all her brave efforts, things are going wrong. The nurses are tense, and the doctor's instructions are strained.

"The baby's not descending," the obstetrician says.

Valentina wails when he pushes a forearm on top of her abdomen and works it down. I want to tear the motherfucker's limbs apart. I want to rip the cause of her pain away and crush his skull against the wall. It's only sheer willpower that prevents me from stabbing him with the scalpel. My anger is directed at the wrong person. The root of all this agony is standing next to the bed, clutching her hand.

"Emergency caesarean," the doctor declares with a new note of urgency.

One of the nurses lays a hand on my arm. "Please move aside, sir."

I jerk free. "I'm not leaving her."

"Mr. Louw," the doctor's voice is stern, "for the sake of your wife and child's lives, leave. We don't have time."

Grabbing her face, I kiss her like I may never kiss her again. There's too much to say, but no time, because orders are being called, and Valentina is pulled from my arms onto a gurney. I strain to hold back when they take her. Walking next to her, I keep one hand on her stomach and grip her fingers in the other.

I press her palm against my mouth, stifling the emotions that won't let me speak, because I have to say this.

"I love you." Each word is broken. Each word is meant. Each word is beautiful in its own, ugly, wrong way.

We approach the operating wing doors.

"You can wait in the visitor's area, Mr. Louw."

"Wait." Valentina grips my wrist. "What's his name?"

"Connor," I say, fighting to keep my voice from breaking. "His name is Connor."

And then she's gone.

The doors to the operating wing swing shut, and I stand alone in the long hallway with the bright lights.

TEARING out of the hospital clothes, I pace and pray, repeating my vow. I feel like dying. Is this punishment for my sins?

Rhett and Quincy arrive. They're here more for Valentina than me, and I can't blame them. She has that effect on people.

"How's Charlie holding up?" I ask Rhett.

"He's fine. Kris is cooking dinner. You don't have to worry about him."

"Val?" Quincy looks as if he fears my answer, but couldn't stop himself from asking.

"I don't know," I say honestly. I give them a brief explanation of the situation.

"Fuck." Quincy clenches his hands together and flops down in the nearest chair.

"Coffee?" Rhett asks.

Sensing he needs to keep busy, I agree.

Armed with dark, bitter coffee, we nurture our fears, thoughts, and blame as we wait. When I can't stand it, any longer, I limp up and down the hallway. It's taking too long.

I've lost count of time when the door at the end of the hall opens and a doctor exits. Quincy and Rhett get to their feet. They stare at the doctor as if he's grown horns. With sure steps, he walks over, stopping short of me. His look is direct and factual, void of emotion. Standing--praying, hoping, despairing--I await the news. The stones are grinding on each other in my chest. Every breath I take hurts.

He looks at the three of us. "Mr. Louw?"

"That's me."

"It's a boy."

15

Gabriel

"It's a boy," I murmur.

I'm a dad.

Rhett, Quincy, and I stare at the doctor. None of us speak. We wait in the worst silence of my life.

The obstetrician gives me a tired smile. "Your wife pulled through."

The earth tips under my feet. I have to grab the chair back to stay upright.

She lives.

A boy.

Thank you, thank you.

I'm conflicted and raw, knowing the sacrifice I'll pay for her life, but my joy far outweighs the torment of giving up my child and the woman I love.

"He was born at thirty-six past three," the doctor continues. "One point one kilo. Thirty-nine centimeters."

My voice is gravelly. "How are they?"

"They're both doing well. You can see your wife in an hour, when she comes to. Your baby has been placed in an incubator. A nurse will take you to see him."

"He's only twenty-nine weeks. What complications can be expected?"

"Anything, but, statistically, survival rates for his age are above ninety percent and disability less than ten."

I swallow past the lump in my throat. "Thank you."

He pats my back. "Wait here. And congratulations."

Rhett is at my side the minute the doctor is gone, grabbing my arms as if he senses my physical weakness. "Congratulations, Gabriel."

A smile transforms Quincy's face into a goofy mask. "You have a son." He pulls me into a hug and slaps my back. "Well done."

"She's alive," I say, still needing to convince myself. "She's going to be all right."

There's a note of pride in Rhett's voice. "She gave it a good fight."

"She's a strong one," Quincy agrees.

They wait with me until the nurse returns to take me to my son. I stop in front of the incubator that separates us. For now, this is as close as I can get to him. He has patches on his tiny chest, a pipe in his nose, and an IV in his leg. Damn, he's small, drowning in the white diaper. So fragile. So perfect.

I place my palm on the glass. "Connor." I ache to touch him, to hold him against my chest and feel his heart beat in his brave little chest. "You made it. You're going to grow up big and strong. A good man." With a mother like his, he won't have a choice.

Big, shameless tears run through my beard into my smile. They're happy tears. Tormented tears, tears to welcome, and tears to say goodbye.

He looks just like me, at least the me before my scars, but he has Valentina's full lips. I don't know for how long I stay like that, drinking in his features while he sleeps like only the innocent can, but my hip is aching from the long stand when a nurse touches my arm.

"Would you like to see your wife?" she asks in a bright voice. "She's awake."

Would I like to see my wife? What kind of question is that? I don't bother to reply. I don't even have flowers or a stuffed toy. No balloons or diamonds. Only lies, deceit, and freedom.

The nurse stops in front of a door in the maternity wing. "Here you go. She suffered blood loss and is still weak, but you can stay as long as you want. No visiting hours apply. Don't tire her, though."

That's part of the advantage of a private clinic and room. I brace myself and push the door open. Valentina is surrounded by white sheets. Her eyes are closed, and her lips slightly parted. Her breathing is even, but her skin reflects the color of the sheets. My gut turns inside out. It's hard to see her like this.

I make my way over quietly, trying not to disturb her, but her eyelashes lift when I reach the edge of the bed. For three hammering heartbeats, she stares at me, her soft eyes awash with emotions. Fuck, that look unsettles me. The twisted, tormented expression coils around my chest and squeezes the air out of my lungs. The single tear that slips from her eye and spills down her cheek is a stake in my heart that leaves a hole that can never heal.

I grab her fingers and squeeze. I want to climb on top of the bed and hug her to me, but I don't want to disturb her wound and hurt her. Instead, I will myself to be content with perching on the edge.

I stroke the hair from her brow and trace my thumbs over the fragile skin under her eyes. "How do you feel?"

"Did you see him?" she croaks.

"He's perfect, Valentina. So perfect."

She lets out a gush of air that makes her shoulders sink back into the mattress.

"Rest." I kiss her cracked lips. "I'll be right here."

Her eyelids flutter close, and her breathing changes. In a second, I lose her to sleep. It's the anesthetic still in her system. Unable to tear away, I lie down next to her body and carefully pull her to me. I watch her until a new shift of staff comes on duty and a nurse pops her head around the door.

"The doctor is going to examine her, now, if you'd like to go home and have a shower," she offers in a curt manner. "Maybe you'd like to eat something, too. You'll need your strength to support your pretty young wife and that handsome son of yours."

Dragging a hand over my beard, I look down at my crumpled shirt and suit. I must look a mess. My mouth tastes foul, and my throat hurts. Hunger hasn't crossed my mind, but I feel unstable as I get to my feet. I'm reluctant to leave her, but get out of the staff's hair so they can care for the precious creature on the white bed.

On my way out, I check on Connor. After washing and warming my hands, I lay them on his back. He's so small my palm envelops his whole upper body. Dearness, pride, protective instinct, and love hurt my chest.

I pass my first diaper changing test, and when I place Connor like the nurse shows me, he holds onto my thumb with his fist, his grip surprisingly strong. It physically aches when I have to pry his miniscule fingers loose.

I put my fingertip on his heart. "I love you, son."

No cell phones are allowed in the maternity wing. Outside, when I switch my phone on for the first time again, there are ten missed calls from Kris. Damn. In my panic, I completely forgot to let her know the status of events.

Quincy sits in a chair against the wall when I enter the reception area. He jumps to his feet when he sees me. "How are they doing?"

The smile that cracks my face is a string tied to a helium balloon. I'm going to float right up to the clouds. "Good. She's tired. He's perfect." I take in his disheveled hair and five o'clock shadow. "What are you still doing here?"

"Wasn't going to leave without you. Rhett went home to check on Charlie. Kris was going ape shit. She freaked out when she couldn't get hold of you, so Rhett told her the news. I hope you don't mind."

"Thank you." I mean it like never before. I don't know what I would've done without these two men. And Kris.

"You're welcome. You look like shit. I'll drive you home."

It's nearly six in the morning. A new day has dawned. The rays of the sun wash over the windowsills like the hands of a clock, marking my time that's running out. It feels as if I spent ten thousand nights in here, and every step I take toward the sunlight is heavier than the one before. Each mile I put between us is a mile closer to never. I swallow the knowledge of what I have to do, putting it away to deal with later, alone. For now, we need to celebrate life.

At home, an excited Charlie and Kris meet me at the door.

Kris embraces me, tears spilling down her cheeks. "Congratulations. I was going out of my mind. Tell me everything. I made breakfast."

She leads us to the table by the kitchen and makes me relay everything that happened over eggs, bacon, and toast. I only focus on the medical aspects and go into a long and detailed description of Connor, leaving out the part of how this is going to play out. When they've oohed and aahed, I kick-start myself into action. Kris can't afford to close the practice for the day and knowing how little sleep she got last night, I offer to organize a temp through Dial-a-Temp for the day, but she stubbornly refuses. We still have to talk about Valentina's maternity leave and how it will impact Kris' practice, but I put it on the backburner for now. The priority is for Valentina and Connor to rest and grow strong.

Feeling better after a shower and changing into a clean suit, I dial Michael and inform him of the news. I have five days of paternity leave, but will swing past the office later this afternoon to tie up a few loose ends.

Five days to say goodbye. That's what I give myself. I'm not going to brood over it. Not yet. There are shitloads of things to do in five days. The nursery isn't ready. Except for a few outfits and a box of diapers, we haven't gotten around to the baby shopping. Valentina needs a crib, pushchair, carrycot, car seat, breast pump, and various other devices that babies require. After doing some shopping, I want to go past the clinic again. Eager to get on with the chores so I can get back to the two people I care most about in the world, I get some of the cash I stashed for the baby shopping in the safe from my study. I'm about to walk out of the room when my open laptop catches my attention. I always keep it closed when I'm not using it. It's a security thing, knowing how easy a hacker can access the webcam and study what's going on in our house. Every hair on my body bristles. Someone snooped around. There's information on that computer that can implicate me in crimes and murders. Deliberately, I haven't erased the evidence of financial embezzlement and bribes we made for Magda's business. You never know when you may need it, like to blackmail yourself out of a dire situation when your life is threatened.

Treading carefully around the desk, I study the top for signs of disturbances, but all the papers and files are in place, painstakingly neat and square, just as I left them. I hit a random button to repower the screen. A folder I don't know appears. The name sets my heart racing. I nearly go into cardiac arrest when I open it and read the file names.

Fuck. Shit. No.

My eyes fall on the black stick with the Louw Unlimited logo inserted in the USB flash drive.

Magda.

Magda told Valentina. She told her what I did. According to the files staring back at me, she did more than that. She gave Valentina the fucking evidence. Throwing the pile of bills on the desk, I clench and unclench my hands. I do this several times to prevent myself from hitting something. Valentina knew. She had our baby knowing what I did to her. Magda had no right. Why? I never meant for Valentina to suffer the awful truth. Goddammit! I take my anger out on the chair, kicking it until a sharp pain rides up my leg and lances into my hip.

What did Magda show Valentina? A recording of my conversation with the doctor? I open the file with a shaking hand. Just as I thought, an audio file of my call to Engelbrecht opens. I listen to the whole, dire speech, hearing what Valentina heard, trying to imagine what she felt, what she thought. I kind of guessed what the content of that file was even before I clicked on it, but I have no clue what the so-called *Evidence* folder contains. What other proof is there of my deceit?

A nasty foreboding sits in the pit of my stomach. This feels heavy. Dirty. Suddenly, I'm impatient. In my haste to open the file, I miss-click and have to do it again. What opens is a video clip. A blurry picture fills the screen. It looks like a low-quality home movie. As the images unfold, ice-cold dread fills my veins. The dread turns to boiling hot, melting fucking lava. Anger explodes in every blood vessel of my body. Rage makes me shake. My organs tremble as I witness a younger version of Valentina in her worst nightmare. I recall the uncontrollable shiver of her body as she knelt before me and told me her secret. I feel her pain and see her humiliation as six grown men caused those feelings for their pleasure. I want to kill them like I never wanted to kill. I want to make them suffer a thousand times more. I want to chop off their limbs and throw them at Valentina's feet. I will drag them through stones and thorns until they don't have an inch of skin left on their bodies. I simmer in my fury, forcing myself to watch every cruel second, wishing that every second is the last of her torture. It's gruesome to behold and sheer agony to witness, but I push on, because the video contains something I've been after for the better part of a year––the identities of Valentina's assailants.

Somewhere in the back of my mind a warning pops up. Something is familiar, but I can't place it. When one of the fuckers speaks again, the fog lifts from my mind. I know that voice. Barney. He was—oh fuck. No. One of my father's cronies. One by one, their ugly faces drift onto the screen. The whole damn team. If my father covered up their crime, if he shoveled dirt over the despicable act he's no better than them. Then the camera turns, and I look into the eyes of the man who raped Valentina—the man who gave me life.

Sweet mother of Jesus. Shocked and sick, I fall into the chair, staring at the black screen. Several facts pierce my mind like burning arrows. One, my father raped Valentina while his friends held her down. My own fucking father. Two, Magda knew. She knew about the rape, and she never told me. Three, this has something to do with why Magda wanted Valentina dead. The debt was only a smokescreen. And four, what Valentina saw in this folder triggered a shock big enough to set her into labor and risk both her and my baby's life.

Charcoal flecks of burnt-out ashes drift in front of my vision. Slowly, determinedly, I rise to my feet. I lock the USB stick in the safe and take my keys. Magda works in Brixton today. The drive there takes too long. It's mid-morning when I park in front of the loan office. Only the Merc is outside, meaning Scott is my only obstacle before I get to Magda.

I slam my hands on the glass doors and push them open. Scott, who sits behind the front desk, jumps to his feet, reaching for his gun. Before he can grip the shaft sticking from the hip holster, I plant a kick in his stomach and a fist on his jaw. He falls backward, his body connecting with the wall. I use the momentum to grip his hair and throw him face-down on the floor. With a knee in his back, I restrain his wrists and wrestle the pistol from his holster. I flick off the safety, cock the gun, and push it against his temple.

He stops struggling, knowing he's as good as dead. "What the fuck, man?"

"Where's Magda?"

He grunts as I push up his arm. "Back office."

"Who's with her?"

"She's alone."

She usually is. The office is soundproof. She won't hear me rough up Scott unless she walks through the door.

"Why did she go to my house, yesterday?"

"I don't know." He curses and whimpers in pain. "You're breaking my arm."

"That's the idea," I snarl. "Where did Magda get the tape?"

"What tape?" He turns his head to the side and gulps air through his mouth. "Ah, fuck, that hurts."

"The one she left at my place. Yesterday."

"I don't know what you're talking about."

I push harder, inviting more swearing, this time mixed with snot and tears.

"An old tape. Home movie."

"Fuuuuck. Stop."

He squirms like a worm. I let go an inch, giving him room to breathe and speak.

He pants and hisses. "I dug up a video tape in the graveyard."

"Which one?"

"Rosettenville."

"Which grave?"

"Haynes, Charles."

I shove again, inviting a howl. "He's not dead. If you lie to me, you son of a bitch––"

"It's his plot," he screams, "for when he dies."

"When?" I accentuate my urgency with putting strain on his elbow. "When did you dig it up?"

"Ah, fuck! For the love of God." Air wheezes through his teeth when I let go. "Yesterday."

"How did you know it was there?"

"Charlie."

"He told you?"

"He told the shrink."

"Who, Christopher?"

"Yessss."

That bastard. That's why Magda insisted on the hypnotherapy. She needed to find a tape she was looking for. Some pieces fall into place, but there's still a big, dark hole in the middle of the picture.

"Why did she give the tape to my wife?"

"I don't know! I don't even know what's on the tape."

I reached my limit with Scott. He doesn't know more. Gripping the gun by the barrel, I bring the shaft down hard on his head, knocking him out cold. Just in case, I retrieve the cable ties Magda keeps with various other torturing tools in the bottom drawer and tie his hands and feet. I put out a closed sign and lock the front door before heading to the back office to get my answers.

Magda hops from her chair and rounds her desk, calling for Scott before the door shuts behind me.

I advance on her. "He can't help you."

Her eyes slip to the gun in my hand. "Be reasonable, Gabriel."

"Like you were when you gave Valentina the tape?"

She pales to the color of whitewashed wood, the surface of her skin uneven and rough. "She showed it to you?"

The diabolic side of me wants to play with her. A rabbit and a fox. "Were you hoping she wouldn't?"

She holds up her palms. "All I wanted was for her to leave. I only wanted my son back."

My voice grows louder with each syllable. "You thought she'd run knowing my goddamn father raped her."

"Yes, I thought it would drive her away. You haven't been yourself since she came into your life. She's destroying you, just like she destroyed your father."

"*She* destroyed *him*?" Every one of my limbs is shaking. "He's the one who took her innocence, her youth--God, Magda, they beat her to an inch of her life--and *she* destroyed *him*?"

Her eyes are magnified behind her glasses. "She seduced him!"

"She was thirteen fucking years old," I grit out.

"I saw the way he looked at her, even when she was that young. Do you know how that feels? It's the way she walks, with her ass swaying and her tits pushed out. It's what she wears, those short skirts and tight tops." She points a finger at my chest. "She did it to him, and she's doing it to you."

I can't believe what I'm hearing. "How long have you known?"

She looks away.

"You will tell me," I say. "Today's the day we come clean."

"You weren't supposed to find out, not like this."

No. Neither was Valentina. God, not like this. "I did, so start talking."

She faces me slowly. "What are you going to do with the tape?"

She needs to understand how serious I am. I'll frighten her into talking, and if that doesn't work, I swear to God I'll torture my own mother. "It will go to the authorities, the ones you don't own."

She trembles from the hem of her dress to her neatly trimmed hairline. "It'll destroy us."

"We're already destroyed. It's over, Magda. We're over. The business is over."

Her Adam's apple bobs as she swallows. "Don't do this, Gabriel."

"Why not? My father is a rapist. My mother is a criminal, and I'm a killer."

"We do what we must to survive."

"Don't fucking justify our sins."

"You say that because you're under her spell, just like your father."

"No, Magda. I'm in love with her. I love her like I've never loved a woman. I'll go to hell for her, and I won't blink an eye to send you to jail for what you knew and covered up, so start talking."

For five full seconds she stares at me. Just when I think she's not going to answer, she says, "Your father thought he killed her. He said no one needed to know, so he told Barney to destroy the tape. Only, Barney never did. He held onto it, as a bargaining chip, maybe to blackmail your father with later, who knows? Valentina survived. We learned about it when she was already well on her way to recovery, because Marvin and Julietta kept it quiet. Your father--"

"Stop calling him my father." I can't stand to be related to him.

"Owen was sure Val knew their names. He arranged a hit to take out the whole family."

Ugly words sit on the tip of my tongue, but I will them away so she can finish this nightmare of a story.

"Before the hit could take place," she continues, "Barney ended up dead. Shot down in his own front yard. Then Marvin paid Owen a visit and said he had the tape. Got it from Barney. He gave us a printout that clearly showed your--" She catches herself. "That showed Owen's face as proof. He said the tape was hidden, and if we touched his family, it would go to the police. At the time, when Owen was running the company, we didn't have many connections in the force. The police were waiting for a reason to arrest Owen. Even a speeding fine would've done. We didn't have a choice but to call off the hit."

Now I understand why Magda worked so diligently to buy her way through the police force. There was method in her madness of having as many of them in her pocket.

"What was the payback?" Marvin would've wanted revenge and compensation for what had been done to his daughter.

She gives me a long, sad look. "You."

I stumble a step, the full weight of my body pressing on my half-lame leg. "What?"

"The deal was that you'd marry the ruined Valentina, and Owen would give half of the business to Marvin."

I battle to take in the information, but it makes sense. Marvin would not only get an upgrade in terms of a suitor for his daughter, but also a hell of a payback, not that any money could make up for what they did.

I force the question from my dry lips. "What happened?"

"Owen wasn't going to let himself be blackmailed. Charles was fifteen and a dangerous factor to be reckoned with. He was protective of his sister. I told Owen Charles would never let this go. He would bide his time and take revenge. Not having a choice, Owen agreed to Marvin's demands, but the minute Marvin was gone, Owen called in his guys and told them to find the tape and kill the Haynes'. Instead of a hit, it was supposed to look like an accident."

"The car that went off the bridge…"

"Our men cut the brake cables."

"Julietta?"

"The bank robbery was staged. She was the real target."

"Why did Owen let the children live?"

"Owen spoke to Val at Marvin's funeral. It was clear she didn't recognize him. She didn't put two and two together. You've seen from the tape…" She looks away again, unable to meet my eyes. "You've seen from the tape she never opened her eyes, and Charles wasn't himself any longer."

"Why take the risk?"

"Owen wanted that tape, and Lambert Roos told us Marvin had given it to Charlie to hide. Charlie was the only one who knew where it was. We tried talking to him after the accident, but Charlie couldn't remember. He didn't know what we were talking about. He was totally incoherent. A complete vegetable."

"The mafia cast the Haynes kids out, and Lambert rejected Valentina. Owen ordered them to do it, didn't he? Was it because Valentina was betrothed to me?"

"I had no intention of ever bringing that woman under our roof. Do you think I wanted a constant reminder by looking into her face, every day?"

"Then why tell Lambert to break off the engagement?"

"Owen didn't want them to have the Portuguese mafia's protection. If the truth came out, it would be a war between us and them." Her eyes turn flat and shiny like silver coins. "No one was allowed to take her in, but no one was allowed to touch her or her brother, either. He said it was just until he'd found the tape, but I knew it was for a different reason."

"What reason?"

"He became obsessed with her."

"Why would you say that?"

She opens the top drawer of her desk. Taking out a scrapbook, she throws it in my direction. I stride to the edge with more doom than curiosity in my heart, but we've come too far not to break the lid wide open and let all the maggots out. Flipping open the pages, I reel in shock as I stare at photo after photo of Valentina, all taken from afar. I only get to the third page before my gut turns on itself and bile pushes up in my throat. That explains how Valentina survived—relatively--unharmed in Berea.

Magda splays her fingers and rests her fingertips on the desktop. "We kept on looking, searching everywhere. We turned their house upside down and swept every nook and cranny of Marvin's workshop, but the tape never turned up. Yet, Owen kept on delaying their killing, using that damn tape as an excuse."

"When Owen died you ordered Charlie and Valentina dead to prevent them from ever talking and to take revenge on Valentina for your unjustified jealousy. The debt was just an excuse so no fingers from the mob family could be pointed at you."

"Yes. I paid Jerry to take Charlie to Napoli's."

"That's why you had Scott shoot Jerry. No witnesses."

"Yes."

"The break-in in Valentina's flat?"

"We'd searched the flat before, but when I heard she was selling it, I had to be absolutely sure the tape wasn't there."

Then I fell for Valentina, not only unknowingly honoring Owen's promise to marry his only son off to the girl he raped, but also making Magda's biggest nightmare come true, dragging the memories of my father's hideous crime over her doorstep. What a big fucking ironic turn of events.

Her voice shakes. "I told you not to fall in love with her. I begged you."

I'm dead inside for the people who conceived and raised me. My family no longer exists.

"Your brilliant plan to have Charlie hypnotized worked."

"It did. He told Christopher where the tape was hidden."

"And then you thought you could kill Valentina by showing her in brutal detail what the father of her husband did to her?"

"I'd never kill the mother of my grandchild. I only hoped she'd leave you."

"Well, you almost killed her."

"Almost?" she asks in a small voice, very unfitting for Magda.

"Valentina went into labor yesterday from shock. Not only did she almost lose my baby, she also almost died."

Joy flares in her eyes. It's brief, lasting only a split-second, but I don't miss it. She would've been glad if Valentina was dead, maybe even relieved if my child was dead, too. This, I can't forgive. I don't care that she shot me and turned me into a killer. I enjoyed being feared. I won't lie. What I won't accept is a threat to my child and the woman I love, the woman this family has wronged in every way. We took her virginity, her parents, her brother, her home, her money, her fiancé, and her protection. We brutalized her, disfigured her body, destroyed her studies, her dreams, and her life. I forced my child into her body, and now she knows. She knows the ugly truth.

Magda breaks my train of thought. "What are you going to do, Gabriel?"

"Make this right."

"I see." Her tall, straight body hunches. She looks fifty years older. "This is what it comes to, then."

"It should never have started." Owen should never have laid a finger on Valentina.

Her gaze is desolate as it searches mine. "What now?"

"It's in Valentina's hands. It's her call if she wants to lay charges or send the tape to the Jews."

She purses her lips, as if in deep thought. After a while, she asks quietly, "Boy or girl?"

"It's a boy. His name is Connor."

"Connor. You kept it in the family. That's nice. Gabriel..." She hesitates. "There is something you need to know about Carly's death. I don't think the baby was the reason for her suicide."

"What are you talking about?"

"Sylvia and Carly came over for lunch the day before she passed away. They had an argument about Carly going out to a party with her friends. Sylvia wouldn't let her go. She said after what happened with the drugs she couldn't trust Carly. Carly was being dramatic, accusing Sylvia of ruining her life. She said she'd rather be dead, and if she were, Sylvia would be sorry. I don't think she meant to overdose on Sylvia's sleeping pills. I believe it was another one of her attention seeking stunts that had gone terribly wrong."

I don't have to ask why she didn't tell me before. She wanted me to feel guilty about keeping Valentina. It was a matter of, 'See, I told you so.' Nevertheless, some of the weight lifts off my shoulders.

"Thank you for telling me."

She nods.

I look at her one last time, because when I walk out of here, I never want to lay eyes on her again.

"Goodbye, Magda."

She doesn't answer. She's still nodding, her head bobbing up and down, when I leave her office without bothering to close the door. I don't get as far as the front desk when the shot goes off.

16

Gabriel

The all too familiar sound of a bullet leaving the barrel of a gun tears through me. I stop dead. The metal explosion vibrates in my skull before the walls absorb the last echoes. My first reaction is to listen. For sounds of life? That she missed? I don't know.

Silence.

My body is heavy. I'm slow in turning and heading back to the office. My fingers hesitate on the knob of the open door. I can't breathe. It feels like I'm ten years old, under water in the swimming hole, counting to sixty. The weight of the door moves in my hand. I don't want to push it open wider, but I don't have a choice. Just like when I was twelve, Magda took my choice away when she pulled that trigger. The door swings open all the way, a crack of light falling over my shoes. I know what awaits, but the sight shakes me. Magda is slumped face-down on her desk, blood everywhere. In her hand, she clutches the gun with the ivory shaft, the same gun she used to shoot motivation into me.

Her unmoving body looks unreal. She's too strong to be splayed out like this. Too proud. Too much of a fighter. This must've been the end of the fight for her. It sure as hell is for me. My chest deflates and rises. Air fills my lungs, one painful drag after another, while her words tumble around in my skull.

This is what it comes to.

Pulling my phone from my pocket, I dial a friend, Captain Barnard at the Brixton police station, and explain what happened, minus the back history surrounding my father. Minutes later, detectives swamp the office.

Barnard gives Scott, who is coming to, a sidelong glance. "What happened to him?"

"I restrained him for questioning."

He writes something on a notepad and regards me from under his brows. "You and Magda had a fight?"

"A disagreement."

"What about, if I may ask?"

"A family matter that concerns my wife."

"I see." He continues to scribble. "Did you kill her?"

"No."

"It's suicide then?"

"Yes."

"Ah ha."

"May I go? My wife just had a baby."

"I'll let you know if you need to come in for further questioning."

Barnard's tone borders on boredom. He wasn't a friend of Magda, which is why I called him. He resented the criminality her loan shark business brought to an already crime-ridden Brixton.

Fighting claustrophobia, I rush outside and stop in the sunlight. What do I feel? Guilt? Relief? Sorrow? Pity? Magda and I were never close, but she was my mother. Good or bad, family is family, and I alone am left to carry the sins of ours. My life is falling apart, so I do what I've always done. I carry on.

The world weighs on my shoulders when I call Rhett to give him and Quincy the news before they see it in the media. Rhett offers to fetch me, but I decline.

"I do have another favor to ask," I say.

Rhett is a reliable rock, as always. "Shoot."

With the funeral to take care of, I won't get around to everything. "Can you and Quincy help with some baby shopping?"

He hesitates for a heartbeat. If it weren't for the circumstances, the fear in his voice would've made me smile. "What kind of shopping?"

"The stuff babies need. You know, a pushchair, car seat, crib, those kinds of things."

He swallows with an audible gulp. "Uh … I guess."

"Good man. Take my cheque book." Rhett has signing power. "It's in my office."

"Wait," he says when I'm about to hang up. "What colors? What models?" His tone rises with a hint of panic. "Where do you buy stuff like that?"

"You'll figure it out. It'll make Valentina's life easier when she comes home."

Mentioning Valentina seals the deal. There's no lengths my guards won't go to for my woman.

With my bodyguards taking care of the shopping, I have time to go home and pack clothes for Valentina and Connor before stopping at a florist and jewelry store. Armed with a pair of diamond earrings, a chocolate bouquet, a humongous flower arrangement, and a giant stuffed crocodile, I drive to the clinic. Diamonds in my pocket, flowers under one arm, crocodile under the other, chocolates gripped in my hand, and an overnight bag swinging from the other, I walk through Valentina's door.

She's propped up on the pillows in bed. I stop to take her in. Her long lashes fall over her cheek as she stares at her hands. Chocolate-and-wine-colored curls tumble over her shoulders, partially obscuring the soft curve of her breast under the hospital robe. The bronze glow is back on her cheeks, this morning's paleness gone. The sight of her makes me weak. I must be turning into a big fucking crybaby, because I'm fighting back tears for the third time since yesterday. Just as I think she's not going to look at me, her lashes lift, and her brown eyes meet mine. Rivers of sadness flow through their depths, leaving muddy traces I swear I can see all the way to her soul. Reluctant to start the unavoidable subject we need to discuss, I stall for time by placing the crocodile at the foot end of the bed. "For Connor."

A smile plucks at the corner of her lips. "You don't think it's too small?"

I shrug, shifting the weight of the flowers. "I thought it would go with the jungle theme."

Her gaze moves to the white and blue lilies.

"For you." I put the flowers on the bureau against the wall. "They smell good."

"Thank you."

I leave the chocolates next to the flowers and unzip the bag. "I packed you and Connor some clothes." I transfer the items to the closet. "If I forgot anything, just say, and I'll bring whatever you need." I finish by unpacking her toilet bag in the en-suite bathroom.

When I return, I catch her big, questioning eyes on me. Unarmed, with nothing weighing down my arms, I'm exposed and vulnerable. I have no choice but to give her what she really deserves––the truth.

My bad leg aches when I cross the floor and stop next to the bed. I can't help myself from reaching out and cupping my woman's cheek. For a heart-stopping moment, she presses into my palm, and then the heat of her skin is gone.

I let go, my fingers trailing over her jawline and down her neck. "How do you feel?"

Her lashes lower, half-moons obscuring her expression. "I'm good."

A wall breaks within me and emotions flood my composure. My voice trembles. "I'm sorry." Flopping down on the chair next to the bed, I grab her hand and press her fingers to my lips. "I'm so fucking sorry." For deceiving her, for the pain she suffered, for almost losing her to death. After Carly, I wouldn't be able to cope with losing her or Connor, too.

"Why?" Her breath catches on a sob. "Why did you do it?"

The question is loaded. There are so many answers to that one, single question I don't know where to start.

"I know everything, Gabriel."

Not everything. And it will kill me to tell her. I nod and swallow, trying to find my voice. "I know you know, beautiful."

Tears make her eyes shine like gold nuggets in the clear water of a river. "Why didn't you tell me?" Her hand trembles in my hold. "Did you get a kick out of making me relay the whole, ugly affair? Why me, Gabriel? Did you need to finish what your father had started?"

A wave of sickness rolls over me. "God, no. No, Valentina. I didn't know it was him until I found the USB in my computer this morning. I've been chasing the men who did this to you since the moment you told me. You have to believe me. I swear to God, if they weren't already dead, I would've killed them with my bare hands for what they did to you." My tone drops to a whisper. "If I could, I would've made my father pay."

"How...?" Her voice breaks. It takes a moment before she can speak again. "How did Magda find the tape?"

I stare at her for three full seconds. Longer. This is the part where she'll hate me even more, if that's possible. "Charlie."

"Charlie?"

"Your father killed Barney for the tape. He gave it to Charlie to hide."

"Barney. He was with your father." The color leaves her cheeks. "My father killed Barney? And Charlie remembered?" Her eyes grow large as understanding bleeds into them. "The hypnoses?"

"Yes," I say somberly. "That's how Magda found out Charlie buried the tape in the graveyard, in the plot your father had bought for him."

Resolution marks the square set of her shoulders as she steels herself for what's to come. "You better start from the beginning."

I tell her everything Magda said, leaving nothing out. I tell her my father was a sick bastard obsessed with an under-aged girl, and his obsession led to the destruction of not only her, but also my family. I tell her how the mafia paid and threatened Lambert Roos to call off the betrothal, and that I was supposed to take his place, ironically *have* taken his place. I tell her about Jerry, the trap Magda set for Charlie, and maybe the hardest part, that I was supposed to kill her, but that she already knew. She knew the nasty fact and still tried to build something with me. This is how big her heart is, but no heart can be big enough to process and forgive the depth of what I'm laying at her feet now.

She hears me out to the very end, and when my words dry up, she asks, "Why did you trick me?"

I rub her fingertips over my lips, back and forth, back and forth, pleading with my eyes for understanding as I gather my words.

"It was the only way to save you."

"From Magda."

"Yes."

"Why did she do it? Why show me the tape?"

"Giving you the tape was her way of trying to drive you away. I don't believe it was her intention to force you into early labor."

She stares at me for the longest time while silent tears streak her cheeks. Finally, she whispers, "What now, Gabriel?"

There's so much loss in her tone. The words sound broken coming from her lips. What now? How does one move on after something like this? How does she pick up the pieces of her life and build a new one? My heart aches for her, but my girl is strong. She's loyal, determined, loving, and brave. She'll make it.

"Magda is dead. She put a gun to her head when I confronted her this morning."

Her complexion pales further. "No."

No longer able to keep my distance, I climb next to her onto the bed and pull her into my arms. The minute my body molds around hers, she snaps. Big, insufferable sobs shake her shoulders. I soothe her the only way I know, holding her close. I push Valentina's head against my chest, willing her to purge her soul with bitter tears.

Valentina's cries must've alarmed a nurse who comes into the room and asks if we're all right. Taking in Valentina's state, she addresses me. "Post-natal blues. If it doesn't go away within a couple of days, call her doctor." She straightens the bed sheets and leaves without posing further questions.

I take the box from my pocket and place it on Valentina's lap. "I wanted to get you something memorable so you never forget how brave you were." I kiss her lips. "Always remember that you fought and survived."

The words are charged. We both know what I really mean. She survived my family. If she can survive Gabriel Louw, she can survive anything.

"Open it, please," I say when she doesn't reach for the box.

After a second, she pulls the ribbon free. Painstakingly slow, she removes the wrapping paper and regards the golden logo on the velvet for what seems like ages before she lifts the lid.

She bites her lip. "I can't."

"Don't say no. This is for me, not you."

"Will it make you feel better?"

Nothing can make me feel better. "Yes."

She lifts the diamonds from the box and fixes them in her ears. They suit her perfectly. She looks like she was made for flawless, brilliant stones. I take my time eternalizing the picture in my mind.

"Thank you," I say, feeling those two words to the bottom of my soul.

I'm not ready to go, but there's much to take care of. A lifetime's planning needs to happen in five days. I take her telephone from my pocket and leave it on the nightstand. Cupping her face, I kiss her forehead. The past is a thick, dark cloud stifling the air between us. Nothing can be said or done to take it away. All I can hope is that my decision will make it better.

Valentina

INSIDE, I'm hacked to pieces. My soul is broken. There's nothing left of the woman I once was or the one I could've been. I'm still a burnt-out volcano—ashes and black—but where that burn was fueled by fear and anger when Gabriel first broke down my door, now it's the result of inconsolable sadness. The crater that used to be my heart is bubbling with emotions of loss, shame, deceit, and worthlessness. I've lost so much of myself I don't know if there's enough left to build myself up from the cold embers of destruction. Gabriel's father took something from me I was supposed to save for the man I'd one day love. He took more than my innocence. He took my ability to have a normal relationship with a normal young man. Maybe that's why I fell for Gabriel. Maybe I can only have unhealthy, unequal, anything-but-normal relationships with older, twisted men. Owen Louw took my joy for life and gave me nightmares and shame instead. Because of a moment in time when he took something he shouldn't have wanted, I lost my parents and my future. I lost my beautiful Charles to a boy in the shell of a man. Because of Owen's crime, we became outcasts who lived in poverty with the cruelty of people like Tiny. When the time came, we would've paid the ultimate price––our lives.

Then there was Gabriel. Because of him, Charlie and I didn't die the day he came for us. I'd like to believe there was more than lust. A small part of me likes to think it was the kernel of something greater, something deeper. I have to believe he feels more than a physical attraction or even a sick obsession, because the seed of pleasure and pain he planted in me germinated to undeniable attachment and care. The fragile stalk of affection that shot up in my heart from the rotten secrets of our past grew as thick and sturdy as a tree. That tree may have sprouted in the fermenting layers of deceit, but that very compost made the branches rise high and strong. The addictions Gabriel gave me are woven like ivy around that trunk. They are grafted with the plant and the roots. They are part of who I am. In the center of it all is one, encompassing emotion. Love.

Despite everything, I love Gabriel. It'll take time to forgive and deal with my past, and great effort to work toward trusting Gabriel again, but there's positive in the negative. If not for that fatal day of thirteen February, I'd be married to Lambert Roos, living a loveless life in a run-down house in the south of Johannesburg with five or six kids, putting red lipstick on just to get through the day. If Magda hadn't orchestrated Charlie's debt at Napoli's, I wouldn't have walked in the night I laid eyes on Gabriel. If Gabriel weren't supposed to have killed me, he wouldn't have saved me. I'll always mourn my parents and what happened to Charlie. My scars will never fade completely, but my past doesn't have to dictate who I become. I choose not to be a victim. Owen may have broken my body and ruined my youth, but I won't give him my spirit.

Gabriel broke me, and he made me whole again. He taught me the meaning of love and gave me a beautiful baby who takes that love to a whole different level. When he took me from Berea, he didn't give me a choice, and I've floated in the blameless absolution he offered for far too long. Gabriel's prisoner or not, it's time to take a stand. Back then, I took an unwilling vow to pay off the debt for nine years. Now I'll make my promises willingly. I'd never want a killer as a father for Connor, but Gabriel works for Michael, now. There's nothing left standing between us. I *choose* this love. It's mine to have and to hold, and I'll give it my damnedest best shot until death do us part.

Gabriel

THE NEXT FEW days pass in a blur. Between painting the nursery and arranging Magda's funeral, I stay with Valentina and Connor as often and long as possible. Quincy, Rhett, and I have the baby equipment covered, or at least I think so. I have no clue if the milliard things we bought remotely covers everything, because I hadn't been involved in preparations for Carly. That was taken care of by a nurse and interior decorator. Readying a room for Connor gives me immense pleasure. I install a baby monitor with webcam so Valentina can watch him from anywhere in the house. I put up barriers at the top and bottom of the stairs, protective covers on all the corners of the tables and counters, and baby locks on the cupboards with cleaning and hazardous products. I fix a lockable cover on the Jacuzzi, put bars in front of all the upstairs windows, and install an alarm and fence around the swimming pool. Certain that the house is baby safe, I pull out all the poisonous plants in the garden, as well as cover up the fishpond. I read on the internet a toddler can drown in as little as two centimeters of water. I take Charlie to visit Valentina and Connor and prep him on being a good uncle. Rhett and Quincy are at the hospital more than home, eager to try out all the contraptions they bought and disappointed when they're told they'd have to wait until Connor can maintain his body temperature and has gained sufficient weight.

Magda's funeral is the day before Valentina comes home. I

arranged it like this on purpose, not wanting her to be a part of the event. Magda doesn't deserve her parting wishes, and I doubt Valentina would want to pay her any. The service is private, for family only, which means just me. It's not that I don't want her friends and business associates to pay their respects. I just can't face the sharks who'll circle the waters, waiting eagerly for bits of bait as to how I'm going to handle the business promotions, new appointments, pay-offs, and bribes. It seems fitting that it's me alone to witness Magda's weakest moment, when her coffin is lowered into the earth. Even in death, she takes her rightful place next to my father, the way she'd bought the plots years ago. The old graveyard in Emmarentia is full now with no more space for a soul. My body won't rest here, and that, too, seems fitting. I said my goodbyes before she died. I cut my ties the day in Napoli's.

In the late afternoon, Magda's attorney reads her will. It doesn't come as a surprise that she'd added a clause. I'm still her sole heir, but the wealth can only be bequeathed or redistributed in the event of my death. Always thorough, Magda made sure I can't give Valentina or my only surviving child a cent. Magda's hate for the girl we ruined stretches beyond life, all the way to her grave. Valentina can't lay a finger on the Louw family fortune, not even as my lawfully, wedded wife, since we got married outside of community of property. Not until I'm dead. Which poses a problem if I'm to give her the freedom I pledged on her life. There's no way I'm sending her and my child penniless into the world.

I guess I'll just have to die.

17

Valentina

Every day Gabriel visits us at the hospital. Kris, Charlie, Rhett, and Quincy are frequent visitors, too, but no one is as caring and considerate as Gabriel. I only have to mention thirsty, and I have a bar fridge in my room stocked with every imaginable brand of mineral water and fruit juice. Even when I don't say anything, he spoils me with gourmet meals from my favorite Italian delicatessen and raspberry scented bath products. He massages my back and rubs my feet. When he's not with me, he's kangarooing Connor and changing his diaper. I see the good father who loved––still loves––Carly, and get a glimpse of how life can be.

On the day of my discharge, Gabriel waits for me with a bunch of blue and white balloons. Such thoughtful and kind actions, but I want him to stop these exaggerated efforts to make up for the past and simply be himself. I just want us to be. In time, things will fall into place, and we'll find our measure of normality. I have to hold onto this belief.

To Gabriel's protest, I decline the wheelchair. I started walking a bit every day, eager to gain back my strength. Rhett and Quincy help cart everything from the room to a pickup Rhett organized for this purpose. With the gifts I accumulated, it's not a light task. Even if I'm happy to go home, it's hard for me to leave without my baby. Clutching Gabriel's hand, I pull back when we reach the main doors of the clinic. Being as in tune with my emotions as he is, he understands the reason for my panic.

Strong arms fold me into a safe and warm cocoon. "He'll be fine." He kisses my lips. "He's a fighter, like his mother."

That evokes a smile, which seems to please Gabriel, but his own is weak in return. I wish I knew what's going through his head. Magda's suicide and the knowledge of what his father did must be excruciatingly tough on him. It's going to be hard to work our way to happiness, but I have a truckload full of determination and endless love in my heart.

I intertwine our fingers. "Shall we go home?" I want him to know I'm ready, that I'm taking this next step willingly.

He swallows and nods, but doesn't move toward the door.

"Gabriel?" I loosen his arms so I can step back and look up at him.

His expression shifts. His scars scrunch up with the narrowing of his eyes, as if he's studying a portrait to commit it to memory. His beautiful, disfigured face softens, and the set of his jaw slackens as his translucent blue gaze drifts over me. This is huge. I don't know what this sudden look of sad affection means, but I know it's the kind that can rip your feet from under you. Just as I'm about to speak, a smile wipes the dooming sorrow from his face.

His voice is unfaltering and strong, washing away my fear. "After you, beautiful."

During the drive he tells me about the changes he made at home.

"I know you want to breastfeed, but I got an electric steam sterilizer, just in case Connor has to drink from a bottle for a while longer." He glances at me. "And a food processor for later when you want to make puree. If you want to, of course. There's nothing wrong with buying ready-made baby food. I just thought––"

I cup his knee. "Thank you, Gabriel. Everything will be perfect."

At home, he takes me on a tour to show me what he mentioned in the car, insisting on carrying me up and down the stairs. It's as if he's lecturing me before going on a long trip. Despite my earlier burst of energy, I'm tired by the time we finish and happy to take a short nap.

The men prepare a welcoming dinner of burnt lamb chops and lumpy mashed potatoes. I feel cherished and something I haven't felt in a long time––welcome. This is home. This is *our* home.

After dinner, Gabriel carries me to the shower and washes my hair and body. He takes extra care with drying me, careful not to press on my stitches. Kneeling at my feet, he stares at me with a molten look in his eyes.

He plants a trail of kisses up my legs to my thighs, his palms following the path. "God, you're beautiful."

"I have a lot of flab to get rid of."

"There's nothing to get rid of." His hands glide over my hips. "You're perfect."

I brush my fingers through his thick hair. "You're a liar."

"Not about this. Not about you." He places a gentle kiss under my incision. "This amazing body gave me a beautiful son." His eyes fill with regret. "I'm sorry, Valentina, but I'd do it all over again to keep you safe."

"It's okay." I cup his cheek when he presses his face to my stomach. "What you did was wrong, but I don't resent having Connor."

There's more to discuss, but we have time, and for now I forget everything as his fingers move to my center.

"We're not supposed to…" I moan when he parts me gently.

"I won't penetrate you. Just a taste."

His tongue licks over my folds, finding my aching clit. The hot wetness of his mouth feels amazing, but the pleasure makes my womb contract, and that hurts. I groan in frustrated disappointment when he stops.

"Sorry." He gives me a sheepish look. "I couldn't resist."

He picks me up and carries me to the bed as if I'm made of paper-thin glass. Shifting in behind me, he holds me to his body, skin against skin, until I drift off to the promise he made in the clinic when he whispered he loved me. When I said those same words to him, he didn't believe me, but it doesn't matter. I have all the time in the world to convince him. One day, if I'm lucky, I may hear those precious words coming from his lips again.

I WAKE UP ALONE. The sheets on Gabriel's side of the bed are cold. He can be in the shower or working out in the gym. Only, I know he isn't. There's an instinctive knowledge in my soul. A dark feeling folds foreboding wings around me. My heart flaps in the cage of my ribs.

"Gabriel?"

I get out of bed and pull on a robe. Making my way downstairs as fast as my stitches allow, I call his name again, but all I get is my echo in the empty space.

"Valentina?" Quincy steps into the kitchen, concern etched on his face. "Is everything all right?"

"Gabriel." I walk to the kitchen as if I'm walking on pins. "Gabriel's gone."

"Hey." He rushes to meet me and takes my arm. "He left early to take care of business. He'll be back after breakfast."

I sit down in the chair he pulls out for me. "Where did he go?"

"The Brixton office."

"With Rhett?"

"Yes."

Even knowing Rhett is with him doesn't make me breathe easier. "Why?"

"With Magda gone, there's a lot to iron out."

We haven't talked about the business or what his plans are, yet. Maybe he feels it doesn't concern me. "He works for Michael. Does that mean he's going back to the loan business?"

Quincy looks uncomfortable. "I don't know about that. You'll have to ask him."

There's still such a huge gap between Gabriel and I and where I stand in our relationship.

"Can I make you a cup of coffee?" Quincy asks with a scrunched-up brow. "Maybe tea?"

I clutch my stomach and push to my feet. "I need to speak to him. Now." I can't shake this horrible feeling crawling over my skin.

"Whoa." He pushes me back into the chair. "Stay put. Gabriel will skin me alive if you tear your stitches. I'll get your phone. Where is it?"

"Thank you," I whisper. "On the night stand in the bedroom."

"I'll be right back." He bolts up the stairs, taking them two by two.

I don't care that the bed is unmade or that my clothes are scattered over the floor where Gabriel dropped each item last night after meticulously studying every inch of my body, not as if he was saying goodbye. Worse. As if he'd never set eyes on me again. My throat tightens. I grip the chair, battling to breathe.

Quincy comes bouncing down the stairs with my phone and holds it out to me. "Here you go." He does a double take. "Jesus, Val. You're as white as a sheet. Are you okay? Shall I call a doctor? Gabriel said I must call Dr. Engelbrecht if you don't feel well."

I take the phone with a shaking hand. "I just need to hear his voice."

I scroll through my call list and push the dial. Pressing the phone to my ear, I wait impatiently for the call to connect. If only I can speak to him, this irrational fear will let me go. My world will be all right, my life aligned.

Hope plummets with an uneasy turn of my stomach when his phone goes straight onto voicemail.

"Gabriel," I wet my dry lips, "please call me. I need to hear your voice. I need to tell you things, too many things I can't say over the phone." I start to cry. "I want to tell you how much I love you, and that I'm staying because I want to. I want to give this relationship my best shot. I want to make the vows I took real. Please, please, Gabriel, don't take this chance away from me. Don't leave without giving me a chance to say this. You owe me, do you hear me? You owe me this chance." My tears run in rivulets down my face. "Please, call me back." I hang up, utterly devastated. Lowering my head to my hands, I weep like never before.

"Val." Quincy's breathless voice reaches me through my sobs. "Good God. What's happening? What can I do?"

Through my tears I see him crouch down in front of me.

"He's at work, sweetheart. He'll get your message and call you back when--"

The ringtone of his phone cuts him short. The sound is loud and obtrusive, like bad news.

His face freezes when he glances at the screen. His voice is ominous. "It's Rhett." He forces a smile on his face, but his heart isn't in his words. "See? He'll tell you everything's fine." He straightens and walks to the corner, keeping his back turned to me. "What's up, Rhett?"

For a while he doesn't speak. He only listens. The set of his shoulders grows tighter and tighter. They pull inward, and his head lowers between them until it hangs from his neck like a wilted leaf. He turns an inch, as if he wants to look at me, but he doesn't. He cuts the call and drops his hand without saying a word. He doesn't have to. It's written in his body language. When he finally faces me, the sorrow I see on his face weakens my knees.

"Val." He swallows and looks away, then returns his eyes to mine. "You have to be strong."

18

Valentina

My head moves from side to side automatically, already denying the words Quincy hasn't spoken yet. "No."

He walks back to me, drops the phone on the table, and takes my hands. "There was an explosion."

Heat boils through my veins and freezes over. I stare at Quincy in a silent stupor.

"I…" His Adam's apple bobs, and his eyes blur behind a veil of moisture. "I'm sorry." His voice lowers to a whisper. "Gabriel was in the building."

I can't think. I can't process what he said. Only my body is reacting to the vicious words, starting to shake uncontrollably.

"Rhett is on his way with a police officer." He blinks several times, but his tears overflow. "You've got to be strong, now, stronger than you've ever been."

I don't feel strong. I'm not strong enough for this. This can't be happening. From afar, someone calls my name.

"Val." Quincy gives my shoulders a gentle shake. "I'm going to help you upstairs. You're going to get dressed."

I move on autopilot. It's all I can do to keep myself together, but like a mended vase full of glued cracks, my foundation is already weak. Nothing is coherent, and nothing is powerful enough to protect me from this onslaught. It's Quincy's steady hand that gives me guidance, leaving me in the dressing room to finish a mundane routine so I can face the world.

Randomly, I take clothes from hangers, not giving thought to color or style. I don't remember dressing or brushing my teeth, but my breath tastes like mint, and my hair is untangled when there's a soft knock on the bedroom door. I open it to find Rhett standing on the doorstep, looking forlorn and haggard. His shoulders shake as he takes me into a brief hug, taking care not to press on my wound.

"There's a sergeant downstairs," he says when he manages to regain his composure.

"I know."

Taking my arm, he helps me to the lounge where a woman in a blue uniform waits. Looking at her young face, I feel sorry for her. What a terrible task.

"Mrs. Louw," her voice is steady, respectful, and filled with sympathy, "I'm terribly sorry to inform you that your husband perished in an explosion this morning."

Perished. What a strange choice of words. Like food or a lifeless commodity. "Won't you please sit?" I take a chair because my legs won't carry me.

She perches on the edge of the sofa and glances at Quincy and Rhett who hover at my side. "Do you prefer we speak in private?"

I follow her gaze. Like a watch losing time, I'm a second late in making intellectual connections. "Oh," I say as I catch her drift. "They're employees and friends. You can speak in front of them."

"Very well." She shifts her attention back to me. "An investigation will have to be conducted, but we suspect foul play."

Something inside my chest pinches. "You mean it wasn't an

accident?"

"We found evidence that says otherwise."

"What kind of evidence?"

"Plastic explosives."

I clamp a hand over my mouth. "Oh, my God."

"Your husband had many enemies." She says it like a statement. "Did he have any threats, of late?"

I can think of a hundred people off the top of my head who would've threatened Gabriel, especially with Magda gone, but that's not where my thoughts are dwelling. "The body." I sink my nails into the fabric of the seat when I think of him blown to pieces. "Did you find a body?"

"Not yet, but the debris hasn't been combed through."

I look at Rhett. "He could've gotten out."

Rhett's look is haunted. "I saw him go inside, Val. There's no other way out. No backdoor or windows."

Anger surges in me. "What the hell was he doing there? Why did he go back?"

Rhett places a hand on my shoulder and says gently, "He had to deal with the business after Magda's death."

The sergeant clears her throat. "What time did your husband leave the house this morning?"

I turn back to her. "I don't know. When I woke up he was gone."

"We left at six," Rhett said, "as I already told you."

She ignores him, keeping her attention fixed on me. "I'll let you know what we find." She reaches inside her pocket and pulls out a business card. "In the meantime, if you have any questions or information you think may be helpful, don't hesitate to call."

I take the card with numb fingers, staring at the name without seeing it.

"Good day, Mrs. Louw." She gets to her feet. "Again, I'm truly sorry for your loss."

Rhett sees her to the door while Quincy stays at my side.

"Who did it?" I ask Rhett when he returns.

"If I knew, Val, he'd already be dead."

I hug myself to contain my shaking. "Someone knew he'd be going there."

"Everyone knew," Quincy said with a note of despair, "and the sergeant is right. He had many enemies." His tone darkens. "As do you."

"He's not dead. I don't believe it."

"Val." Rhett goes down on one knee, putting us on eye level. "He's gone. He walked in there, and two minutes later an explosion rocked the place." He shakes his head. "I'm so fucking sorry. No one and nothing could've survived the blast."

The connection between us is still there. Could it be like a ghost limb? Would I feel the itch long after my soul mate has been amputated, like with my thumb?

Before I can analyze my thoughts, Charlie comes downstairs wearing his batman T-shirt and pajama bottoms. I go to him with outstretched arms, needing his comfort even if he doesn't understand. I lean my head against his chest and whisper, "Gabriel's gone."

"Gabriel's go–gone."

At the affirmation, my whole being shatters. My legs cave in. Like a lump of dead weight, I plummet to the floor. All I want is to curl up and stay there, but at witnessing my distress, Charlie starts pulling at his hair. He needs me. Connor needs me. In a flash, Quincy and Rhett are there, helping me to my feet.

"We've got you," Quincy says. "You're going to be all right, do you hear me? It'll take time, but eventually you'll be all right."

The words don't soothe me, because I don't believe them. Without Gabriel, nothing will be all right, so I put my strength in hope, in this strange connection that still seems to simmer between us.

"We'll find him," I say to Quincy, "and *then* I'll be fine."

A look passes between him and Rhett.

"There's been too many damn funerals in this family," Rhett grits out, "and I'll be damned if we add another one to it." He marches me over to the kitchen and calls for Charlie to follow. "First things first. You have to eat. I'm cooking."

THE POLICE GIVE clearance for the Brixton office two months after the explosion. It didn't take two months to sift through the debris for evidence. They just didn't have the staff to attend to it before. What they give me is a report and a plastic bag with Gabriel's distorted wedding band, the only item they salvaged. This token–– his ring––announces that he's gone for real. Had I not believed so strongly he's alive, I would've collapsed on the spot. The police report states human remains were recovered, but are unidentifiable. The only link to the body destroyed in the blast, confirming the deceased's identity, is the platinum ring. Officially, Gabriel has been declared dead. Officially, I'm a widow.

Gabriel has always been a meticulous planner. It doesn't come as a surprise that he has his funeral organized to the last detail, leaving nothing for me to do but mourn. Dressed in black, with Kris by my side, I stand at the edge of a grave as an empty coffin is lowered into the ground. As long as Gabriel is not inside that coffin there's a chance he's alive. Until I see his body with my own eyes, I refuse to believe it. Dr. Engelbrecht says I'm in denial, but he doesn't feel the bond I feel with Gabriel. He says denial is the first step in the grieving process, and it's perfectly normal, but he doesn't know I've been grieving since I turned thirteen. If he knew my intentions, he'd say nothing about what I feel is normal and I should be locked up in an asylum. I intend to spend every cent at my disposal to find the man who stole me. In my heart, I'm certain he's alive, even as Rhett assures me every day that Gabriel entered that building. Rhett went as far as to get the tapes from the street security cameras that monitor the building, showing Gabriel's broad shoulders disappear through the door. My husband must be Houdini, then.

A touch on my arm pulls me back to the present. Diogo's face hovers over mine.

"I'm sorry for your loss, my dear. Now that you're alone, let me know if you need a shoulder to cry on."

Rhett, who's never far, steps forward, but I hold up a hand. "No, thanks. I tend to avoid rapists."

Kris jerks with a start. She looks like she wants to say something, but Diogo places his body between us, blocking her from my view.

He laughs, the sound soft and hollow. "Careful with the accusations. I may decide to sue you for name slandering."

"I'd never make an accusation without the evidence to prove it. As it happens, I have the footage from the security cameras showing you with your dick hanging out trying to *jump* me against the wall. Isn't that how you put it?"

He glances around and lowers his voice. "No need to get your claws out. I'm only offering my support."

"Your support is unwanted. If I find you and your support anywhere near me again, I'll splash that tape in all the places that matter and turn you into an overnight news celebrity. I'm sure one of the boys will enjoy *jumping* your ass against a prison wall."

He points a finger at me. "Watch it, little girl. I don't take to threats kindly."

"Oh, it's not a threat. It's your new reality. If anything happens to me or anyone related to me, those files go footloose. Call it my personal insurance against *jumpers* like you."

Rhett and Quincy are enjoying the show, but their smiles don't diminish the ferocity of the warning looks they fix on Diogo.

Fire shoots from his eyes. All that's missing is smoke billowing from his nostrils as he twirls around and stalks away.

Inside, I'm shaking. Of course, it's all bluff. I don't have the tape. I don't enjoy playing this game, but I expected it. When someone as powerful and wealthy as Gabriel goes down, the vultures move in.

Captain Barnard, who's standing nearby, walks up. "I'm sorry about your husband."

"Thank you."

"This isn't the time or place, but call me in a couple of weeks if you'd like to clean up the loan shark business. We'll strike a deal. I'll offer you immunity in exchange for information."

"I don't need immunity. I'm not guilty of anything."

"Of course not. I sense an honest, good woman in you, Mrs. Louw. I hope you'll do the right thing."

"So do I."

When he tips his hat and walks off, Michael and Elizabeth Roux step up to offer their condolences.

Elizabeth stares after Barnard. When he's out of earshot, she says, "What did Diogo want? I bet it wasn't to offer sympathy."

"Nothing," I say.

"If he as much as looks at you again…" Michael leaves the threat hanging.

"Don't worry." Quincy takes my arm and pulls me away from Michael. "We've got her back."

"Anything you need," Michael continues with an unfazed air, "you just have to say. Elizabeth and I are here for you."

"You're coming to our place for dinner on Friday night," Elizabeth says.

"That's very kind, but--"

"No buts. I'm cooking, so it won't be anything fancy. Just a dinner between friends where you can be yourself and let your guard down." She glances at Rhett and Quincy. "Since they don't seem to let you pee alone, bring your bodyguards, too."

"They're not bodyguards, not any longer."

"Whatever." She turns to the men. "You're more than welcome, guys. Take care of her." She kisses my cheek. "Call me anytime you need a friend."

"Any last words?" the minister asks as the crowd starts to thin around the grave.

I stare at the heap of freshly turned earth. "This isn't over, Gabriel Louw."

The minister gives me a piercing look, but he doesn't say anything. He's probably happy this is over so he can go home to his comfortable slippers and newspaper.

"Ready?" Rhett asks.

"Yes." I turn away from the open hole in the ground.

"Where to? Home?"

Gabriel stipulated in his funeral plan there was to be no reception after the ceremony. I'm thankful I don't have to put on a show for the vultures.

"I'm going past the clinic to see Connor."

"I'll drive."

"I have a car."

"I'm not letting you go alone." He says it like he means business.

Kris comes around and takes my hand. "He's right. We'll both come with you, and then I'm cooking you dinner at home."

I only nod gratefully. I can do with her support, even if she's already given me so much.

As we make our way to the cars, there's a part of me that stays behind in that graveyard. It hurts, but not the kind of hurt when you lose the love of your life. It hurts with loneliness, and at the same time it burns with hope. Tomorrow morning I'll take Gabriel's ring to a jeweler to have it fixed and polished.

THROWING my full weight into dealing with the aftermath of Gabriel's *disappearance* as I came to call it helps me cope. There's enough to keep me busy so my mind doesn't dwell on his absence. For starters, there's Connor. There's always Charlie. There's my work at Kris' practice, which I put on hold. We agreed to employ an assistant, and now that Kris is earning more she can afford to employ another vet. The most challenging tasks are taking care of Gabriel's estate and the business.

As it turns out, I inherited everything––the houses, the cars, the business, the assets … and the debt. I don't think Gabriel realized the dire situation the business was in. The Louws lived well above their means, and bribe money made a big dent in their coffers. Magda did a good job of hiding it. Because of the ongoing investigation into the sabotage, Gabriel's assets and estate are frozen. My only income is the salary Kris pays me. Thank God for paid maternity leave.

The house will have to go. There's no way I can sustain it on my salary. The mortgage Magda took out on her house in Parktown to keep a drowning business afloat requires that the house be sold. One week later, both houses go on the market. I call Sylvia to ask if she wants anything––maybe there's something of sentimental value to her––but she slams the phone down in my ear.

The big, old place in Parktown has to be packed up. It takes Kris, Charlie, Quincy, Rhett, and me a full week of strenuous labor to wrap precious crockery and glassware in paper and ship sealed boxes to antique stores. I use the money I get for the furniture and houseware to pay off the most pressing debts. That same week, to my great joy, Connor comes home.

Our house is next. As soon as I secure a buyer, I rent a modest house in Northriding, a cheaper area, but still in the safer, northern suburbs. Then comes the hard part of paying off the staff. Marie left when Magda passed away, and Gabriel got rid of the guards who remained on Magda's property. I terminate the contracts with ours and pay them a bonus to soften the blow. When I propose the settlement to Rhett and Quincy, they stubbornly refuse.

"I can't pay you what Gabriel paid you," I say. "In fact, I can't pay you at all."

Quincy crosses his arms. "I'll settle for profit share."

"In what? The loan shark business is in so much trouble it'll take years to recover."

"Then I'll settle for years." He winks. "What can I say? I have faith in your business ability."

"I'm with him," Rhett says.

"It's a foolish decision, guys."

Rhett raises a brow. "This is what Gabriel would've wanted."

"What about what you want?"

"Profit sharing sounds good to me."

With that, our discussion is settled. Rhett and Quincy stay on to protect me and Connor, sharing one of the two bedrooms in my tiny, rented house, while Charlie, Connor, and I share the other. It isn't right, but no matter how much I argue and bargain, they won't change their minds.

With the move behind us, I dive headfirst into the business. Not knowing enough about finance, it soon becomes clear that I'm going to need a financial adviser to help me navigate through the minefield of contracts and debts. Michael and Elizabeth are a great help, going through the legal jargon and explaining things to me in simple terms. Gabriel was busy after Magda's death. He cleared the illegal portion of the business, cutting loose the government and police officials who received regular kickbacks from Magda. He settled territorial squabbles by putting contracts in place that operate on a commission basis. Conveniently, all evidence of corruption and crime was destroyed in the explosion that leveled the Brixton office, leaving me as safe as I can be in this city and business. If I had dirt on the big shot politicians and judges, I wouldn't have lived long. Disturbingly, Christopher, the hypnosis psychologist, disappeared after Magda's death. I can only hope he fled for his life and not that Gabriel revenged his underhanded dealings. In any event, all traces of Magda and her cronies are wiped out. What is left is the legal side, albeit a business I don't care to exploit. It still involves using crippling interest rates to rob already poor people.

Acting against Michael's advice, I lower the interest rates across the board and write off the debt of those debtors who already paid interest equal to their capital loans. There will be no more bone breaking and violence. I close all the offices except for the one in Auckland Park to save expenses and retrench the staff. Magda hired them, and I don't trust them. Rhett and Quincy help out with the bookkeeping, even if it isn't their forte. We can't carry on like this indefinitely, and I can't afford to simply shut everything down. I need money to pay Rhett and Quincy, and I need to survive. I need a future for my child and brother. I need *lots* of money if I'm to find Gabriel. What I need is a change of direction and a CFO. The problem is that I can't afford to employ a decent CFO. I need a different strategy. I run my idea past Michael when he pops in to see how I'm coping, which has more or less become his Monday ritual.

"I need a bright, young university graduate with ambition and nothing to lose."

Michael regards me from across the desk in my office with a doubtful gaze. "On a minimal wage?"

"Don't forget the profit sharing."

"Your business is unstable, and you're an unknown player with no connections. The country's economy and politics are in shambles. No local or foreign investor will give you the time of day. What you should do is collect the interest from your active lendings."

I glance at Charlie who's playing cards at a table in the corner and lower my voice. "I'm not going to put people out of their houses or slit their throats if they can't pay."

"What *are* you going to do? I assure you, the majority won't pay unless you put the fear of the devil in them."

"Write it off as bad debt."

He taps his fingers on the desk. "You're not running a charity,

Val."

"I won't do to others what happened to me."

He sighs heavily, leans back, and straightens his tie. "Your intentions are noble, but you're heading for bankruptcy."

I rub my forehead, feeling a headache coming on. "I know." This is more frightening than I thought, but I won't sink to the level of crime or violence. Never.

"Why don't you just accept my offer?"

Connor starts fussing in his carrycot on the carpet next to me. I pick him up and throw a cotton blanket over my shoulder so I can feed him discreetly. I don't have an issue with public feeding, but if Gabriel didn't want Michael to kiss my hand, I think he would've been jealous of sharing the intimate image of Connor on my breast, and it's extremely important to me to protect Gabriel's feelings, even in his absence. Especially in his absence.

"Val?" Michael raises a brow, reminding me he's still expecting an answer.

"I can't take your money." Michael kindly offered to take care of me and Connor as a way of paying his last respects to Gabriel, but my pride will never allow me. I have to make it on my own. This is my mess to sort out.

He sighs again. "You're adamant about this, aren't you?"

"Absolutely."

He pinches the bridge of his nose. "I have a contact at the business school. I'll speak to him and see if he knows any suitable candidates."

My smile is all teeth. "Thank you."

"Don't get your hopes up." He gets to his feet. "If you pay peanuts…"

"Yes, yes, I know." I roll my eyes. "I don't want a monkey. I want a clever worker who'll help me grow the tree to harvest the bananas in good time."

He makes a face. "That's the worst analogy I've ever heard. Please don't mention that in your interview."

"You brought up the peanuts."

He laughs and shakes his head. "I have to go. Dinner, our place, Friday night?"

Like every other Friday night, I accept. Our dinner dates became a standing arrangement, just as Saturday nights at Kris' place turned into a weekly institution. Charlie, Rhett, and Quincy are always included. I can't go anywhere without them, anyway. It's my friends' way of taking care of me, and sometimes those nights are all that keep me sane. I miss Gabriel with brutal intensity. Every day without him is torture. Work keeps my mind off him during the day, but it's at night, alone in bed, that I break a little more with each passing hour.

Michael kisses me on the forehead. "Hang in there. It gets better."

I can only nod. If I speak, my voice may break. I wave goodbye as he blows me a kiss from the door and calls out a greeting to Charlie.

Quincy walks in as he leaves. "I brought lunch." He places a plastic container with a fork on my desk and another one on Charlie's. "Pasta and cheese salad."

The salads are his and Rhett's humble effort at cutting costs. I know they miss their double burger take-outs.

Blinking away the tears that always come when I think of Gabriel, I give him a grateful smile. "Whatever would I do without you?"

He winks. "You're welcome. When that little man has done eating I'll take him for a stroll so Rhett can do the vacuuming."

"I can do the vacuuming."

"No sweat. You're busy."

Connor has stopped suckling. He's about to fall asleep on my breast, so I remove him gently and adjust my clothes. "You don't need to coddle Connor. He'll probably sleep right through the vacuuming."

Quincy looks at me as if I'm mad. "With that noise? You can't expose his ears to that. Nah, give him here." He takes my little bundle, sniffs his butt, and declares solemnly, "He's clean," before buckling him into his stroller and tucking a blanket around his body. He adjusts the umbrella that attaches to the side of the stroller and pulls the protective plastic cover over the hood.

"For the pollution," he says, taping a disposable hospital mask over the holes of the breathing gap.

While I dig into my salad, he loads a baby bag with diapers, wet wipes, a bottle of expressed milk in an insulation tube, a rattle, and a burp cloth. Lastly, he adds a variety of pacifiers, probably all the models on the market. I don't know why he still bothers, because Connor always refuses them. By the time he's ready, Rhett walks in with the vacuum cleaner.

Rhett drops the vacuum and stalks to the stroller. "He's not covered enough." He takes his mobile phone from his pocket and checks the weather. "It's only twenty degrees with fifteen kilometers of wind." He starts unfastening the plastic cover. "Put another blanket and a beanie."

"He'll be too hot under the plastic," Quincy protests.

"Ho–hot," Charlie says.

"He'll get sick with the wind coming through the gaps. I told you we should've taken the Chicco model. The plastic fitted all the way to the footrest."

"But that one had four wheels, and my research stated clearly that three wheels are easier to manipulate. Don't forget that Maclaren is better on the baby's back."

"The frame can't fit a carrycot or car seat like the Chicco."

"Guys," I get up and round my desk, "Connor is happy. Look at him."

They both look down into the face of innocence. Connor is sleeping, his little chest moving with strong, steady breaths. With that angelic face you'd never think he could lift the roof with clenched fists and angry bawling when his food doesn't come fast enough.

You're so much like your daddy.

Rhett slams a hand on his forehead. "Dickhead, Quincy. You haven't changed him before he fell asleep, and now he'll get diaper rash."

"You think?" Quincy shoots me a worried look.

"He'll be fine." I push Quincy toward the door. "Bring him back if he starts crying, and be safe."

If it weren't Quincy, I would've objected to taking my baby for a walk to the park opposite the street. It's much too dangerous to walk outside, even in broad daylight, but Quincy is not the average man, plus he's armed with three guns, a couple of knives, and Bruno.

The minute they're gone, Rhett starts vacuuming with the speed of superman while I go back to the books, pouring over balance statements.

He nudges my feet with the vacuum pipe. "Lift."

I cross my ankles on the desk, waiting for him to finish. The gun he always carries in the back of his waistband shows as the hem of his sweater shifts up with his movements.

When he switches off the machine, I say, "I'd like to start training again." Even if Gabriel cleaned up the business, it still remains risky because of the old stigma. People may hold vendettas. Besides, the city will always be dangerous.

He props his hands on his hips. "I agree."

His easy agreement surprises me. I expected him to argue, but the fact that he doesn't, tells me how volatile and vulnerable my situation is.

"What does Dr. Engelbrecht say?" he asks. "Are you ready?"

"I'm ready."

"Tonight." He seals the deal with a nod. "I'm going to check on Quincy." He pulls the gun from his waistband and leaves it on my desk. "Lock the door behind me."

I haven't been to Berea since the day Jerry gave me a stolen car, but it doesn't mean Berea won't come to me.

I HAVE an hourly interview with the five candidates for the CFO position I got from Michael's contact at the business school. Rhett is rocking Connor, and Quincy is playing darts with Charlie in my office. Not the most professional image, but both men refused to budge for the interviews.

The first man is in his fifties. He lost his job when the company he worked for folded, and at his age, especially with the high unemployment rate and affirmative action law, it will be tough for him to find another job. As he has a family to feed, my terms don't work for him, so we move on to number two.

A young graduate, I take an immediate like to his enthusiasm. He's not overly keen on working for a minimal wage with the long-term, uncertain promise of risky profit shares, but before he can make up his mind, Rhett shakes his head.

"Uh-uh. He won't do."

I turn in my chair. "Excuse me?"

"He's a no go." Rhett takes a threatening stance, which has the guy opposite me cower.

"Can you please give us a second?" I direct the young man to the entrance and close the door. "What are you doing, Rhett?"

"He was checking out your boobs."

"What?"

"He looked at you in *that* way."

"I agree," Quincy chirps in. "He won't do."

"Jeez, guys, give me a break. I'm trying to employ someone for the lowest of salaries to help us make big money."

They both give me their obstinate stares.

"Can we just get through the interviews without any comments from you?"

Neither answers.

I sigh and stick my head around the doorframe. "You can come back in."

The young man gives me an apologetic smile. "I thought about it while I waited, and I'm sorry, but it's not for me."

He leaves without saying goodbye.

"Now look what you've done," I exclaim on a huff.

They look too damn pleased with themselves, as if they fought a wolf off a lamb.

For far too long, I avoided the Brixton site. I choose a Saturday when I can leave Charlie and Connor with Kris. I don't want either of them to witness this.

Quincy and Rhett flank me next to the second-hand Honda I took possession of this morning. I sold the Porsche to minimize expenses. The three of us stare at the destroyed building. Emotions float between us. Of all the people in the world, they're the only two who understand what I feel, because they must be feeling a part of it. Rhett takes a shaky breath. He was guarding the street when the blast hit. The roof and parts of the walls are missing. What used to be the windows and door are gaping holes, revealing an expanse of blackness inside.

When I take the first step, the guys follow. They let me go at my own tempo, staying a step behind. The power of the destruction is devastating. Going through the doorframe is like walking into a vortex of death. Everything is a shade of black––shiny onyx and matt charcoal with smears of greasy oil. Guilt suffocates me. I wanted a way out. At some point, especially during the early days, I would've wished for this. Not so, now. I only want Gabriel back. Broken filing cabinets lay on their sides, their drawers flung out. The cushionless frameworks of upside-down chairs surround us. It's like standing in the eye of a twister of pain. My heart rate spikes, and my breathing quickens.

"There's nothing for us here," I whisper.

"Let's get her the fuck out." Rhett turns me in the opposite direction and propels me through what used to be the door.

In the street, I gulp in air, fighting to contain the panic attack. Feeling sick, I rest my hands on my knees.

"It was a bad idea to come," Rhett says.

Quincy hands me a tissue. "She needed the closure."

This isn't my closure. This is only the beginning. If it's the last thing I do, I will find Gabriel. I just need to make some damn money.

A scruffy pair of heavy-duty, construction boots fall in my line of vision.

"Hey," Quincy draws his gun, "stop right there."

My gaze trails up over mustard-colored pants and a white shirt with oil stains to a round face supported on a double chin.

"Howzit, Val?"

I wipe my mouth and straighten. "Hello, Lambert."

"You know Roos?" Rhett asks with a hint of surprise.

It's Lambert who answers. "We're childhood friends. Grew up together in the hood."

I never expected to see him again. "What are you doing here?"

"Just wanted to say I'm sorry." He looks at his feet. "I heard you married big."

"Sorry for what?"

"For never saying something."

"Who told you?"

"Marvin. Said he'd kill me if I open my flytrap, and if he couldn't get to me, Mr. Louw's people would."

"It's history, now."

Quincy and Rhett's heads turn between us. I want to leave the past in the past, not flaunt it at their feet.

"Does that mean you forgive me?"

"You didn't have a choice, Lambert. There's nothing to forgive."

"You're not going to come with your goons," he looks at Rhett and Quincy, "and shoot me in the back while I'm sleeping?"

"No."

"Okay." He shoves his hands in his pockets and rolls on the balls of his feet, still not meeting my eyes.

"Goodbye, Lambert."

"Yeah. Cheers, I guess."

Rhett gives him a look that says, 'Don't fuck with me,' as we walk back to the car.

"Who's he?" Quincy asks.

"My almost-fiancé."

"Jesus. Good riddance," Rhett mumbles. "If he looks in your direction again, I'll put a bullet in his––"

"No more violence," I say.

"I was going to say a bullet in his big toe, out of self-defense, of course, if he attacks."

I can only smile as Rhett holds the door for me.

"I wonder where he could hide?" I muse to myself as I start the engine.

"Your almost-fiancé?" Quincy asks.

"Gabriel."

A thick silence descends on the vehicle. Neither of my companions says a word.

At home, I work out in the gym, building my strength and endurance as I do every day now, and enjoy the luxury of a long, uninterrupted shower with no baby fussing or hungry hurls before we head out to Kris' place for dinner and to pick up Charlie and Connor. When I step into the kitchen, Quincy and Rhett are leaning on the counter, their arms crossed.

"I know this look." I prop my hands on my hips. "What have I done?"

"We think it's time you go on a date," Quincy says.

"Whoa. I thought men were strictly forbidden."

"Assholes are. The others who aren't assholes have to pass a test."

I huff. "Thanks for offering your assistance, but I don't need a date."

"We know a guy––" Rhett begins.

"What are you?" I tap my foot in annoyance. "A dating service?"

"It'll do you good," Quincy says.

"No, thanks. Can we go? Kris made chicken a la king, and I'm starving."

Rhett is nothing if not insistent when he wants to be. "Why not?"

I lift my left hand and splay my fingers to show my wedding ring. "Because I'm married."

"Val," there's a plea in Quincy's voice, "you're widowed."

"One date," Rhett says. "If you don't like the guy, we'll find someone else."

"Thanks for your concern, but if I need an escort service, I'll let you know."

I don't give them time to answer. I stride to the garage as if I don't have a care in the world when I'm tearing up inside. I can't stop hurting. I can't stop wanting Gabriel back. Three months have passed, and I haven't made any headway in tracing him. I did my own internet searches and asked around, but nobody has seen Gabriel since the morning of the explosion. I need a PI. For that, I need money, and for money I need the business to work. I refuse to give up on Gabriel.

"All in good time," I say to myself.

"Yes," Quincy agrees eagerly. "In good time."

He has no idea.

ANOTHER CHRISTMAS COMES AND GOES. Kris employs a new practice manager. We agreed it's better that I resign to focus on my inherited business. It takes me four months to understand the funds in which Gabriel invested the capital and return on investments, and another month to analyze them. A small, maverick type stockbroker company, McGregor and Harris, made the best return at a growth of twenty-five percent. The bank is paying a measly one percent on our tied capital, and our long-term investment policies are losing money at minus eight percent.

I call McGregor and Harris and set up a meeting with one of the two shareholders, Herman Harris. Their office is a humble room in a brand-new office block in Midrand. Harris gives my guys, as I came to call Quincy, Rhett, Charlie, and Connor, a curious look when we pile up in the narrow hallway in front of his door.

"Charlie and I'll take Bruno for a walk," Rhett offers, taking Connor from Quincy's arms.

Harris stares at my baby. "You call him Bruno?"

"That's the dog," I explain.

"Wow." He scratches his head. "You brought a dog, too?"

I shrug. "My entourage."

"Come in." He steps aside. "We only have two visitor's chairs."

"That'll be enough."

I study Harris as he directs us to two office chairs. He's a lot younger than I expected. Definitely still in his twenties.

When Quincy and I have taken our seats, I dive straight into business. "Mr. Harris, you've--"

"Herman, please." He runs a hand over his suit. "I'm a casual guy. I only dressed up for this meeting. Usually I'm in a T-shirt and jeans."

"Thank you, although, it wasn't necessary. I don't mind casual. As I was saying, you've been running one of my husband's investment funds for the past five years."

"My condolences. My partner and I were shocked when we heard the news."

"Yes. How do you make twenty-five percent when other companies make five?"

"Your late husband gave us a small amount of money to invest at high risk. The high risk paid off."

"You play the stock market exceptionally well."

"We study the trends and know how to predict them." His eyes sparkle. This is clearly his passion. "All our clients are low capital, high risk investors, which allows us to play around quite a bit. We invest the combined capital of our clients by buying up low-cost shares that show potential for big growth."

"How does your process work?"

"If I tell you, I have to kill you." He laughs at his own joke.

"What I mean to ask is how can you be sure of your predictions?"

He swivels a big computer flat screen toward me. "We wrote a software program that takes various internal and external socio-economic and political factors into consideration. It's better than any other software program out there. It maps trends we can analyze and feed back into the program, always bettering itself. Then there's this." He wiggles his fingers. "The magic touch. Intuition. I have a nose for these things."

"I have a proposition for you. I want you to scrap the trust fund management fee you charge us."

He scrunches up his nose. "You want us to manage your investment for free?"

"Not for free. I'm prepared to pay you ten percent of the profit you make on our invested capital."

He laughs and scratches his head. "That's a clever business proposition, but ten percent of what you earn in profit won't cover our fee."

"What would you say if I told you I want to move all of our investments to your company?" By law, I can't cash out the money before the investment term is up, but I can transfer it to a different investment fund.

He sits up straighter. "All of it?"

"Everything."

"How much are we talking about, exactly?"

I take out my phone and email him the document with our investment summary I prepared before the meeting. He opens the message when it pings on his computer screen, his eyes moving from left to right as he reads. When he gets to the bottom, his mouth hangs open.

He looks back at me. "All of this?"

"Herman, I'm going to be honest with you. I don't have the cash flow to pay your fee. In fact, I don't even have the money for the monthly investment debit order. If I don't take a risk, and I mean a huge risk, I'll lose everything. You may not lose much when one of your small investors goes under, but you can win so much more if you get this right. The way I look at it, it's a win-win for us both. Besides, I believe good, hard work should be rewarded, and I like what I've seen of your work so far."

Quincy speaks for the first time. "It's a young company, Val. You don't know if they're going to make it."

"I don't know if we're going to make it, either. Magda's company came from Gabriel's father's father, but it's not the same company, any longer. With all the changes I implemented, it's as rookie as it gets. At least this way Herman and I are both personally invested."

"I love your balls." Herman gives me a look of approval.

This could be the biggest business mistake of my life, but since we stopped killing and threatening, our debtors aren't paying, just like Michael predicted. It's either this risk or closing our doors.

"Is that a yes?" I ask.

"Deal."

He extends a hand, and we shake on it.

"I'll have the paperwork drawn up," he says.

Less than fifteen minutes after entering the office, we leave, adrenalin pumping through my veins.

"Damn, Val." Quincy shakes his head. "I hope you know what you're doing."

"So do I." Quincy's profit is on the line too. "By the way, I have something for you and Rhett." I take the contract from my laptop bag and hand it to him.

After reading, he looks at me much like Herman did, his mouth agape. "Twenty-five percent?"

"Yep. We're splitting it four ways––me, you, Rhett, and our future CFO, if we ever find someone willing to work for dubious profit shares."

He lowers the paper. "It's too much. The company is yours."

"We're equal partners, all of us."

"But you have Charlie and Connor to take care of."

"One day you'll have your own family to care for. Let's just hope the gamble works."

Rhett and Charlie, who spotted us waiting by the car, return with Connor and Bruno.

"Come on," I say. "We're going out."

"Out?" Rhett bends his knees to put us on eye level. "Out where?"

"Wherever you want to go. We have shit to celebrate."

"Val!" Rhett frowns at me. "Don't cuss in front of Connor. What celebration?"

"Your contract." I give him the piece of paper. "Sign on the dotted line so we can go."

He gapes at me as if I have alien antennas on my head.

I strap Connor into his car seat while Rhett and Quincy seem to search for words. When I'm done, I straighten, stretching my back. The week has been rough. I can do with downtime and greasy comfort food. "Whereto, guys? It's your call."

"Spur," they say in unison.

"The Spur?"

"Spu–Spur." Charlie bounces up and down. He loves the Spur.

"You want to go to the Spur?" I repeat.

"There's a baby playground," Quincy says, "with face painting and everything."

"Connor's too young for face painting," Rhett says, "and you don't know what toxins are in that paint."

"I bet he'll love the slide."

"He's not going on that microbe infested super tube."

I bundle them in the car while the arguing continues.

"Mil-milkshake."

"Fine. Forget about the damn slide. There are games."

"Dude, he's not playing computer games until he turns eighteen. It's bad for the brain."

"He can't be a social outcast. Guys play games. It's what *we* do."

Connor cooes as if he knows he's the center of the heated discussion.

I text Kris and invite her to join us. Then I put the car into gear and lose myself in the safe bubble of squabbling voices. My body warms with a pleasant feeling of friendship and acceptance. If Gabriel weren't gone, my happiness would've been complete.

THE MONEY from Gabriel's estate eventually comes through when the unresolved police investigation is closed and his assets are no longer frozen. It's barely enough to pay off the last of our debts, but it prevents me from having to declare the company bankrupt, which will leave me financially crippled for the next decade, as I wouldn't be able to get a loan or buy anything on credit.

Michael questions the wisdom of my moves, but he does send more candidates for the CFO position my way. After the twentieth interview, I finally meet an MBA graduate who's willing to take the plunge. Simon Villiers is clever, optimistic, and energetic--all the qualities I want in a man who is about to start his first job with barely enough money to make ends meet and twenty-five percent of--for the moment--worthless shares.

The spikes in the wheel are Rhett and Quincy, as usual. As shareholders, I need their agreement to employ Simon. I can almost see how Rhett's head is working as he studies the attractive blond man sitting at the opposite side of my desk.

Rhett gives Quincy a small shake of his head. "Too attractive. Did he look at her in *that* way?"

"I think he did," Quincy says.

Simon shoots them a puzzled look.

"You're in?" I ask Simon, eager to draw his attention away from the sideline comments.

"I'm in."

Rhett hooks his thumbs in his belt and takes a step forward. "Hold on a second. This interview isn't over. My turn."

I sigh inwardly.

"Do you have a girlfriend?" Rhett asks.

"What?" Simon's face scrunches up. "What does that have to do with my competency?"

"Just answer the question," Quincy says.

"It's discriminative," Simon retorts. "You're not allowed to ask me that."

"Well, guess what, cupcake?" Rhett advances more. "Whoever is going to fill that chair," he points at the desk next to mine, "is going to become part of the family, so excuse me for wanting to understand how *your* family is mapped out."

"All right." Simon gives Rhett a dashing smile. "Actually, I'm gay."

The looks on Rhett and Quincy's faces are priceless. All I can do is sit back and enjoy their reaction.

"Oh." Rhett glances at Quincy. "In that case, he'll do."

Quincy, who sits on the sofa in what we call our relaxing corner, pushes the stroller over the carpet with a gentle kick and reels it back in with a rope he tied to the handlebar, his invention of putting Connor to sleep. "Yeah, definitely."

"How about you, Rhett?" Simon asks in a seductive voice, getting his own back. "Are you single?"

"I'm … uh … yeah. I'm straight."

"Okay." Simon turns his attention back to me. "Where do I sign?"

I would've hired him from the way he handled Rhett alone. "Here." I push the paper over the desk to him. "Welcome to the company."

SLOWLY BUT SURELY, with Simon's help and the Harris investments, the money starts coming in. We're relying on legal loans with reasonable interest rates and make our profit through clever investments. It's exactly like running a bank. The business is not my passion, but it pays for what becomes my passion--finding Gabriel.

I don't tell my business partners or friends about my search. They don't believe Gabriel is alive, and I'd risk getting locked up in an asylum for insisting he is, so I keep my mouth shut. When there's enough money in the bank to pay for the roof over our heads and the food on our table without going into overdraft, I use what I can from my income to hire a private investigator. We start with checking passenger lists at the airports and finding a match for Gabriel's description. With his physique, it would be hard to go unnoticed. For months, nothing turns up. I go as far as endorsing Captain Barnard's efforts to clean up the areas of the city where we have branches so that he pulls all the street surveillance tapes of the day on which the explosion took place. I want to be sure I missed nothing. The tapes show Gabriel entering the building, the blast, and nothing else, but there's a blind spot at the back of the building where the cameras don't reach. With no exit at the back, he would have had to either go over the roof or underground. Barnard gets me the blueprints of the building from the municipality, but that only shows the structure. No secret passages. No sewerage or drain systems. No fire escapes from the roof.

I'm starting to lose the last thing I have left. My hope.

19

Gabriel

Staging my death was easy. After climbing through the trapdoor in the ceiling, all I had to do was move the roof tile above the hole I made beforehand and scurry over the roof and down the back of the building where the street cameras aren't angled before setting off the explosives via remote. The blast wiped away my tracks as well as all evidence that could have incriminated me or endangered Valentina's life. Rhett, who was keeping watch in the street, didn't know about the body I recovered in Hillbrow the previous night and stored in the bathroom at the back. I placed the corpse close to the explosives, knowing the explosion wouldn't leave fingerprints or dental records, and fit my wedding ring on the dead man's finger. The fire would wipe out any identifiable traces, but not the platinum band that betrothed me to Valentina for life.

For life.

Leaving Valentina and Connor is the hardest thing I've done after saying goodbye to Carly. It chops away at my insides, leaving me as broken as the people I'd tortured. Keeping Valentina forever was a dark, dubious, and beautiful dream, but that life is over. With the money from my will and the inherited business, she and Connor can live comfortably. I'm one hundred percent sure Rhett and Quincy will stay on in her employ. They love her enough to follow her to the end of the rainbow and beyond. The business is clean. I got rid of the bad elements, cut the ties, and blew the evidence to pieces. Valentina can run the loan office without being arrested or murdered by the Portuguese or Jewish mafias.

I wanted to confide in Michael, but it would've been too risky. No one can ever know. To the world, I'm dead. Valentina needs the money and a fresh start—without me.

Damn, the thought hurts. I press a hand on my chest, rubbing away the physical ache where I lie in a hospital bed in Switzerland with my body and face in bandages. New technology allowed for extensive corrective surgery to my face and hip. When I recover, I'll have new features and an almost-good body.

The self-sustained *injuries* are not as much a gift to myself as a way of bringing me back to life. I've already taken on a new identity. I'll go back to South Africa to keep an eye on Valentina and my child. This is my new life purpose, and the only motivation that keeps me going. There are too many dangers out there for a woman alone. Not that she'll be alone forever. Not a woman like her. She's much too appealing. Too beautiful. Too strong. Too loving. It will be tougher than burning in the flames of hell, but I'll endure seeing her in the arms of another man as long as she's happy. For the rest of my miserable life, I'll hide in corners and shadows, following the woman I love, ensuring she's safe on street and in her bed at night. I'll watch over her and Connor like a guard dog. I'll always love her, but this time only from afar.

Weekly updates about her welfare reach me via email. My informant is an ex-Recce. The guy is a nutcase, but he's one hundred percent reliable. Reading the latest report, I utter a loud curse. The nurse, who is changing my sheets, gives me a reprimanding look, but I don't give a fuck. I pay enough for the private room to swear as loudly and as much as I like. The pain from my surgery that's usually acute turns unbearable. It happens whenever I clench every muscle in my body.

The reason for my self-directed anger blurs on the screen in front of me. I blink and reread the last paragraph. My assets are frozen, an unfortunate result of the forensic investigation, which I didn't have the damn foresight to predict. Until the case is closed, Valentina is penniless.

I ache to be there. The need to take care of her is overwhelming, but I'm unable to come near her. All I can do is watch her struggle from a computer screen on a different continent, and it fucking destroys me.

IT TAKES another nine months of excruciating waiting, physiotherapy, and healing before I can close the distance between Valentina and I. Needing a new source of income, I launched an investment company while I waited to heal. It's awkward not to be able to buy what I want without reflecting on my balance statement, such as airfare to South Africa. By the time I leave the clinic, the small company I manage online starts showing a profit. Before my *death* I researched various offshore companies and came up with a list of promising startups. I anonymously invested money in a company manufacturing a relaxation drink, more or less the opposite of Red Bull, which proved to be an instant success. A little bird in Johannesburg told me that the gold resources are almost depleted, hence I bought up shares before the crisis hit, and the gold price skyrocketed. By fluke, I stumbled upon and acquired a small insurance firm on the brink of bankruptcy that specializes in diamonds and gemstones. I also went to considerable lengths to create a cyber history for my new identity.

When the bruises on my face are healed, I have enough money to buy a ticket to South Africa and lead a modest life. Standing in front of the mirror of my one-bedroom, rented apartment in Zurich, I study the man staring back at me. Instead of a full beard and moustache, he has a goatee. The skin on his cheeks is smooth. The scar that used to cut from his eyebrow to his jaw is gone, and the gap in the eyebrow once more covered with the same dark brown color as the hair on his head. His cheekbones are higher and his nose straighter. His eyes are green, thanks to contact lenses, and his features are set in symmetrical order. Where his left eye used to sag a fraction, both eyes are now aligned. The man is attractive, handsome even, and a complete stranger.

Perfect.

If I don't recognize myself, no one will.

The new suit is cheap, but it fits. Even in the clinic, I stayed in shape, working out every day as much as my wounds allowed. The strict exercise regime has nothing to do with vanity and everything with being able to protect my family. With a last look to ensure my tie is straight, I grab my fake South African passport and a single suitcase before closing the door on the Zurich flat forever.

MY FIRST PRIORITY when I arrive on South African soil is to secure a place to live. I rent a small house in a security complex in Midrand and buy a secondhand car with cash. Furnishing the two-bedroom house takes no more than a couple of hours at a big chain store. The next day, a fridge, recliner, and bed are delivered. Getting my hands on a firearm is a lot less complicated than what it should be. I know where to go, where no questions are asked. I don't care that the weapon isn't licensed or probably stolen. I only need it for extreme measures, in case Valentina or Connor's life is in danger, and I don't plan on getting caught. At least not alive.

On day two I'm like an animal in a cage, pacing from the kitchen to the bedroom and back long before the sun rises. I shouldn't go near her, not until I have my shit together, but I can't wait a second longer. Fuck that. I won't get too close. I'll only watch her from a distance, make sure she's all right. I shower and change into my only suit, brush my hair to perfection, and then mess it up again. I'm as nervous as a teenager going on his first date, and I'm not even going to speak to her.

My hands shake as I pull the car out of the garage and take off in the direction of Northriding. I park three houses from hers and wait. It's Saturday. There's no telling at what time she'll leave the house, if at all.

At seven-thirty, the front door opens. I move to the edge of the seat, clutching the steering wheel so hard my hands hurt. I hold my breath, counting in my head. Counting calms and helps me focus. It's a habit I perfected in the Zurich clinic.

One, two, three, four--

A man steps out.

My vision explodes in shards of black fury. I knew it was a probability. Every man will be on her like a bee on honey. I told myself I'd deal with it, but I didn't take into consideration how the reality of actually witnessing a man in her house will play havoc with my emotions. I battle to hold it in. I count to ten and back to one. I want to tell him to stay the fuck away from my wife. Only, she isn't my wife.

She's your widow. Get a grip, Gabriel.

She has every right to date, but fuck it. I can't face it. I'm about to put the car into gear and drive away when the man turns. Rhett. Relief bursts like a tide in me. A second later, Quincy exits, carrying a car seat with a baby strapped inside.

My heart stops beating. I strain forward for a better look. Connor. He looks just like the old me. He is so damn perfect, not because he resembles the face I was born with, but because he is part of me and *her*.

A dainty foot clad in a black boot steps over the threshold. A long, slim leg follows, and then a woman walks onto the porch. The pieces of my fallen-apart world snap back together. Nothing matters, not the old life I worked so hard to delete or the redefined one I so carefully constructed. As before, as every moment in her arms, there's only her. She's wearing a pair of tight jeans with a fitted red polo neck jersey and a black coat. Her body is toned, slimmer than I remember. Curls the color of ruby wine and dark chocolate tumble over her shoulders and frame her delicate face. I pivot to her like a planet in orbit. I want to jump out of the car and rush over the lawn, take her in my arms and kiss her dizzy, but the husband she had is nothing more than a bad memory. I slam my palm on the steering wheel, feeling the pain in my soul. This is the price I bargained for her life, and I'll be damned if I don't honor my vow.

The trio loads Connor and shitloads of baby stuff into a Honda. I don't know how they fit everything, but eventually they're all in. Valentina drives. Keeping a safe distance, I follow them south. It's when we near Bryanston that I understand their destination. Parking in the lot of a weekend bio market, they take their load from the car. I stop two rows away where I have a good view and roll down the window. First Rhett assembles the stroller and lifts my son inside. There's a great deal of bickering between him and Quincy about whether the cover should be up or down. Eventually, Valentina puts a diaper bag in Quincy's hands and a basket in Rhett's before taking the stroller from the disgruntled men and pushing it over the grass toward the stalls.

"He needs another blanket," Rhett calls after her. "It's only sixteen point seven degrees with a wind at five kilometers per hour."

She ignores him, swaying her hips as she maneuvers the off-road stroller over the polls of wild grass and dry heaps of upturned earth as if it's a breeze.

"Val!" Quincy runs to catch up. "Put up the umbrella. He'll burn."

I can't help the smile that creeps onto my face. It's the first time since *dying* that my mouth curves into anything that remotely resembles warmth or friendliness. The pussies. I never imagined they'd turn into two such fuss balls, but I'm right there with them, suddenly worried that Connor will burn in the autumn sun. This is South Africa, after all. There's a big hole in the ozone layer right above our heads.

A young guy in a beige trench coat stares at my woman as she strolls past.

That's my wife, you dickhead.

The vulgar ogre turns his head to look at her ass. I'm about to jump from the car and rub his face in the dirt when Rhett and Quincy give him a glare that makes him look away.

Good.

I breathe easier. I should stay in the car, but my desire to get a closer glimpse is too big. Connor is bundled up in blankets, so I couldn't get a good look to see if he's grown taller. And Valentina... She's changed. There's a new kind of self-assurance about her. If I didn't know her so well, I'd have missed the tight set of her shoulders, indicating that her life is far from easy or stress-free. She's a token of strength and resilience, of the love and loyalty that drew me to her in the first place.

I get out of the car, lock up, and trot toward the rows of stalls. Snaking my way through organic pumpkins, jams, honey, and home-baked breads, I follow the small group. They stop at a coffee corner to greet a couple who are having scones and what looks like Rooibos cappuccino. The woman has bleached blonde hair and the hulky man wears a washed-out Spiderman T-shirt over a sweater. Kris and Charlie. After exchanging a few words, Valentina and her entourage leave Kris and Charlie. Valentina stops at various stalls, conversing with the vendors while Rhett and Quincy keep an eye out and carry the produce. I'm relieved that my men are protecting her like bloodhounds. To the unknowing eye, they're just two guys trailing after a woman, but I know they're scouring the area and sniffing the air for danger. From the reports I received in Switzerland, I know Valentina can't afford to pay them, which means they must stay out of loyalty and love, the very characteristics I admire in my wife. It looks like she cultivates them in everyone who crosses her path. Look at me. Here I am, tailing her like a hungry wolf, desperate to protect and care for her.

Circling around the farm produce, I move one row up and walk down the other side so I can cross the object of my obsession for a closer look, but when I reach the spot where they were seconds ago, they're gone. Shit, where are they? I turn in a quick, frantic circle, and smack into someone with my back.

Twirling, I catch the woman I bumped into before she stumbles. The apology dries on my lips. Valentina stares up at my face. For a defining moment, the world falls away as we look at each other. My body goes as stiff as a stick. Will she recognize me? Her eyes search mine as if she's trying to make a connection, but then they go blank. My disguise works. She doesn't have a clue. Holding her so close, literally in my arms, makes me heady and drunk. Every follicle on my body pricks, coming alive with static electricity that crackles over my skin. A whiff of delicious raspberry reaches my nostrils. The silkiness of her hair brushes over my fingers where I still clutch her arms. Her lips part slightly, dragging my attention there. It takes every fiber of my being not to bend down and suck those lips into my mouth.

Valentina finds her tongue first. "I'm sorry." She steps back, breaking our awkward stance. Her eyes remain friendly, but caution slips into her expression.

Good girl. She's right to be wary of strangers, especially strangers who touch her and stare at her for a few seconds too long.

I drop my arms and force a smile onto my face. "The apology is mine. I didn't see you." God, I can't get enough of her. I don't want her to go yet. Just a bit longer to drink in her face and the warmth of her presence. Before she can turn away, I say, "I hope I didn't hurt you."

Her laugh is soft. Husky. "It'll take more than that."

Rhett and Quincy step up from behind, giving me the evil eye, but I ignore their thunderous faces, plunging on before she gets away.

"Is this your baby?"

Warmth floods her voice. "Yes. This is Connor."

I peer inside the stroller and almost choke on my emotion. My son gives me a full-blown smile. A smile. He smiled at me. I swallow down my pansy tears and jubilant laughter, keeping my voice even. "How old is he?"

"Ten months."

Connor grabs the finger I hold out greedily. I chuckle. "He's handsome."

"He is," she says with pride. "Looks just like his daddy."

Something pierces my heart. I straighten and look at her left hand. She's still wearing her wedding ring. I grow warm and fuzzy inside like I have no right to. I have no right to be happy for her grief or loyalty, not that she'd give me either.

Not ready to let her go, I grope around for a subject in my head when my gaze falls on the overflowing basket in Rhett's hands.

"You don't joke around with the shopping."

She wipes a stray curl behind her ear. "It seems like a lot, doesn't it? But my guys," she winks in Quincy and Rhett's direction, "eat like horses. I prefer to support the local farmers, plus it's organic."

That sounds just like her.

"What about you?" She eyes my suit. "You're not dressed for market shopping."

"I'm meeting someone."

"Oh, I better let you go, then."

Don't.

Tilting her head, she regards me with a quizzical expression. "Have we met?"

The mask on my face stays in place as I hold out a hand. "Gregor Malan."

She accepts my proffered hand and gives a firm shake. "Valentina Louw."

More warmth spreads over me as she uses the surname that stamped my possession on her, like my lips, my cock, my belt, and my seed. Fuck, I need to get a grip.

"It was a pleasure bumping into you, Gregor Malan."

Her smile is so fucking sweet I want to lick it from her lips. "Like the apology, the pleasure is all mine."

Only pure willpower enables me to take the first step, and the second, and the third, each farther away. I shouldn't look back, but I'm only human and a lustful man at that. When I glance over my shoulder, Rhett and Quincy are on my ass. Good boys. They'll come second if they're stupid enough to take me on, but I sure as hell appreciate that they keep the wolves at bay.

Rhett blocks my way. "We'd like a word with you."

I glance at Valentina. She stopped at a fruit stall with her back turned to us. "You left your friend unprotected."

Quincy widens his stance. "It'll only take a minute."

"Are you interested in her?" Rhett cocks his head in Valentina's direction.

This is the part where he plants a fist on my jaw for saying yes. I look him straight in the eyes. "Yes."

"Why?" Quincy asks.

What the fuck is this? "What do you mean, *why?*"

"As in a nice piece of ass for tonight or as in an amazing woman for life?"

My anger surges at the mention of her ass. "If you ever speak about her like that again I'll break your arms and legs."

Rhett and Quincy look at each other with big grins.

"I think he'll do," Quincy says.

Rhett looks me up and down. "Worth the shot, maybe."

"What's your fucking problem?"

"Here's the deal." Rhett comes closer and lowers his voice. "Valentina's had a real tough time, lately. Her life's been pretty much shit. If you checked her out because you think she'll be a nice diversion, we're going to bust your balls and break your dick. If you're good husband material, we're prepared to set you up on a date."

I can't believe my ears. "Set me up on a date?"

"Consider it a preliminary testing," Quincy says. "We'll hang out with you, you know, check you out. If you meet our criteria, we'll let you see her."

Rhett pushes a finger in my face. "Only if your intentions are serious. You play with her, you play with me."

"She's a young mom, recently widowed," Quincy continues, "so show some respect."

"What are you guys? Her dating agency?"

"Friends," they say in unison.

"I see." I don't. I want to bash their heads in for setting Valentina up on a date with a man she doesn't know, even if that man is me.

"Aren't you supposed to keep men like me away?"

"She's a good woman," Rhett says. "She deserves to have someone."

As much as I'd like to jump at the opportunity, it will make me the man I used to be, the man who manipulated her into wanting and loving him. The whole idea of dying was to set her free.

"Some friends you are," I bit out. "Keep men like me the fuck away from her, do you understand?"

"You're not interested?" Rhett asks.

"Damn." Quincy wipes his brow. "That's a damn shame. I like him."

"Guys?" Valentina walks up to us. "What's going on?"

"Nothing," Rhett says. "We just talked men stuff."

"Shall we go find Kris and Charlie? Connor is hungry."

"Yeah." Quincy takes the bag of fruit from her. "Let's go."

As nonchalantly as I can, I walk away, focusing hard on not showing the slight limp that remained.

Don't look back. Keep going.

Shit, I can't do it. When I turn, Valentina stands quietly between the hand-dyed tablecloths, watching me.

20

Valentina

The breath is trapped between my ribs. I can't draw in enough air to make my lungs work. There's something about Gregor Malan. His face is not Gabriel's and his walk is different, but he has a limp, albeit slight, and his build is the same. Everything about him screams Gabriel. If Gabriel himself didn't tell me he couldn't risk more plastic surgery, I would've bet my life the man who bumped into me is my husband. Either that or the angels had pity on me and sent me a lookalike to relieve the burning pain always present in my chest. Only, no substitute will ever do. If I can't have Gabriel, I don't want anyone. My love for him is too complete. Too perfect. I guess he finally broke me. Ruined me. For everyone but him. Yes, I'm damaged beyond repair, the broken toy destined for the garbage dump, but I'm *his* toy, and broken or not, he *will* take me back. As soon as I can find him.

"Everything all right?" Kris asks when we get back to her and Charlie.

My smile is automatic. "Fine."

"We'll put the stuff in the car," Rhett says. "Come on, Charlie, give us a hand."

The men walk off with our shopping and Connor, considerately leaving Kris and I alone.

"Out with it," she says, pulling me down in the chair next to her. "I know that look."

"What look?"

"You're brooding."

I clutch my hands together. "I just saw someone who reminded me a lot of Gabriel."

Caution flickers in her gaze. "Val, don't go looking for him in another man, because you'll only end up disappointed. No two people are the same."

"Exactly. I can't be with anyone but him."

She cups my hand. "It's only been ten months. Give it time. Someone else will come along."

"My mind feels screwed up. The things Gabriel did to me, I hated him for them, and now I crave the pain that brought me pleasure. What other man in his right mind will understand what I need?" I rub a finger over my amputated thumb. "My body is mutilated and my stomach scarred with the stretch marks of his baby. Don't you see, Kris? I'm damaged in every possible way. No one else can ever want me. Gabriel was my monster, and he made me imperfect and broken in his image. We're perfect for each other."

"Don't talk like this." She pats my hand. "You fell in love with him. It's natural for you to feel this strongly about him, even if what he did was wrong."

"I didn't fall in love with him. I'm addicted to him, but if--*when*--I find him, I'm planning on falling head over heels for him like I couldn't the first time. This time, there'll be no holding back."

"Oh, Val." Her look is concerned. "You need to see a

psychologist who can prescribe antidepressants to help you cope. There's no shame in relying on medication. You don't have to get through this on strength and willpower alone."

"I don't need a doctor." I push out my chin. "What I need is a date."

"I thought you said you didn't want anyone else."

"I don't."

Her eyebrows pinch together. "I don't understand."

"I need a date with the man I met here."

"No, no, no. You're not going on a witch-hunt for a Gabriel incarnation. That's just plain unhealthy."

"Told you I'm damaged. There's not a healthy thought left in my head."

"I don't know what you see when you look at yourself, but I see a beautiful, strong, generous, and loving woman, a woman who'll unselfishly do anything for her brother and child."

Quincy calls from across the field. "Val, let's go."

I give Kris a quick hug. "You're a good friend. Have I told you how much I appreciate you?"

"All the time."

Quincy comes jogging toward us. "I changed Connor's diaper and gave him his bottle, but he's starting to complain."

"It's his nap time. He must be tired." I get to my feet. "Thanks for meeting us, Kris."

"See you Saturday?"

"Sure. Come over for dinner and a board game in the week."

Walking back to the car, my step is lighter than what it has been in ten months as a plan takes shape in my head.

TRACKING MR. MALAN IS EASY. From what I can find on the internet, he runs a one-man, obscure insurance company specializing in high-valued gemstones. It's a risky business, but with only a handful of topnotch clients such as De Beers and Anglo American he must be making a good living. According to his social media profile, he grew up in central South Africa, near Kimberley, which, on paper, explains his connection to the diamond industry. I have my doubts about the bland and straight-lined history mapped out on my computer screen. Mr. Malan obtained a business degree from the University of Bloemfontein, after which he ran a small jewelry manufacturing business that dissolved with the owner's death, hence his new project. There's only one way to find out if my suspicion is founded.

Closing the office door for privacy, I balance Connor on my lap and dial the number listed for Dimension Insurance.

He answers with a short-breathed, "Yes?"

Everything about that voice makes me go still inside. The way the deep baritone vibrates through my body sends sparks to my nerve endings. Every follicle contracts. Every hair stands erect.

"Hello?"

I jerk back to life. "It's Valentina Louw. Did I catch you at a bad time?"

The pause on the other end of the line lasts only a millisecond, but it's enough to notice. "No. I was just working out."

I can hear the uncertainty, the questions, and the hunger in his voice. We're too much in tune, the nuances too clear for me to imagine them all. "I can call back later."

"That won't be necessary. What can I do for you?"

"I looked you up on the internet."

He utters a dry chuckle. "I gathered." More caution. "Why?"

"You run an insurance company."

"That's right."

It sounds as if he's opening the fridge. A can pops. The sound is followed by soft swallowing. My imagination does wicked things to me, putting images in my mind of Gabriel leaning against the counter, drinking beer. His Adam's apple moves as he swallows. All the while he watches me with the sexual intent that tells me he's going to bend me over the counter and take what he wants, but not without giving me what I crave, first.

"Mrs. Louw?" I swear there's a cocky grin behind the carefulness in his tone.

I fan myself with a piece of paper from my desk. "I have business for you."

"What kind of business?"

"Diamonds. I prefer we meet to discuss this in person rather than over the phone."

"I..." His sigh is filled with regret. "I'm not the right man for the job."

His words can't be further from the truth. "I'll be the judge of that. Tomorrow, four o'clock?" I close my eyes and hold my breath.

"I work from home." He makes it sound like a protest.

"Not a problem. I have your address."

"Of course you do." This time, he sounds downright amused, but then his tone changes, again. "Mrs. Louw, I--"

"See you at four tomorrow, then."

I hang up before he has time to conjure a reason why I shouldn't knock on his door. If Gregor is Gabriel, I plan to expose him. He better be ready. I'll barge through his door like he once did through mine, swinging a weapon much more powerful than a gun.

ALL THROUGH THE NEXT DAY, I have a lump of concrete in my stomach. Since we're fumigating the office, we have to close early--the perfect excuse to go home and get ready. While Connor naps, I shower and change. My hands shake when I apply make-up and dry my hair. Even the weather plays along for ambience with a powerful thunderstorm, probably one of the last before the dry winter spell. The thunder wakes Connor. I feed and change him, and get in some quality cuddle time. At three-thirty, I button up my trench coat and grab an umbrella. Connor should be good for a couple of hours. Carrying him downstairs, I go in search of the guys and find them playing poker in the kitchen.

Rhett gives a wolf whistle when he sees me. "Wow. You cleaned up nicely."

"It's only make-up." I shift Connor to the other hip, suddenly feeling self-conscious. Have I gone overboard?

"Pre–pretty."

"Thanks, Charlie."

Quincy's gaze runs over me. "Stockings and heels? I didn't know we're going out."

"Ou–out." Charlie looks at the window where thunder lights up the sky. "It's rai–raining."

"We're not going out. I am."

"Uh-uh." Quincy pulls his mouth in an obstinate line. "You're not going anywhere without one of us." He pushes back his chair. "I'll come."

"You can't come."

He gives me a baffled look. "Why not?"

"I'm going *out*."

Rhett stops stuffing his mouth with potato chips to look at me. "Out as in on a date?"

"I guess you could call it that."

"Oh. Wow. Yes. Okay." Quincy and Rhett exchange a look. "Great."

"That's cool." Rhett says. "I'll drive you."

"Rhett." I lift my brow.

"What?"

"I'm not going to relax knowing you're sitting outside in the car."

He scrunches his forehead and rubs his lips together, as if he's thinking. "It's dangerous, out there."

"You taught me how to handle myself, didn't you?"

"Yes, but––"

"Don't you have confidence in my ability to defend myself?"

"You're mean with those tiny fists and a gun, but…" He rubs the back of his head. "I don't know."

"I appreciate how well you're looking after me, guys, really I do, but if you want me to go out and meet people, you've got to give me a bit of freedom."

"She's right," Quincy says on a sigh. "We can't chaperone her on a date."

"I'll be out a couple of hours, max."

"All right." Rhett seems simultaneously happy and uncomfortable with the words. "Call us if you're running late."

"Do you mind watching Connor? I would've asked Kris, but she's working."

"Of course not." Quincy holds out his hands. "Come here, big guy. Uncle Charlie is going to teach you how to play poker, and Uncle Quincy is going to teach you how to win."

"Be careful on the road with the rain," Rhett says, his expression worried.

"I'll be fine. Thanks for Connor."

"Don't mention it." Quincy winks. "Go on. Have fun."

"There's a bottle in the fridge if Connor gets hungry before I'm back. If he gets difficult, call me."

"We know how to handle a baby." Quincy balances Connor on his knee and shoos me away with one hand. "Off you go."

"You guys are the best. I don't know what I would've done without you."

"You're making me all emotional now," Rhett complains.

"Later, Charlie." I blow him a kiss and leave before my nerves fail me.

On the drive to Gregor's place, I contemplate the outcome. If he's not Gabriel, he may not appreciate my approach, but I'm certain it's him. I can't help but feel sure of myself.

Gregor's house is in a neat, raw-brick security complex. I have to sign in at the gate, and the guard has to call his unit for permission to let me through, which warns him of my arrival. Gregor may still refuse me, but after talking on the intercom system, the guard pushes a button that lifts the boom.

As I take the long driveway up to his house, the electronic gates open. I drive in and park in front of the garage. The front door opens before I'm out of the car. Gabriel--Gregor--stands in the frame, dressed in dark slacks and a fitted shirt. The sight of him takes my breath away. This new model of Gabriel has a shorter beard and hair, but the color is the same. His face is strikingly handsome, throwing me somewhat off kilter and adding the spark that fuels my doubt. Beneath the clothes, I can guess the lines that define his muscles.

His stance is casual, but his shoulders are tense. He watches my approach with a boredom that's feigned, because his eyes miss nothing. They look at me in the way Gabriel first looked at me in Napoli's and the way he did when he broke into my flat. Like that first time, he tears open my soul and looks right through me, but there is one difference. The roles are reversed. This time, I'm coming to him as the hunter, and he's the vulnerable prey.

He doesn't speak until I'm right in front of him. "Mrs. Louw."

"Mr. Malan."

His green eyes scrutinize me. The color is disconcerting, not the iced blue I'm looking for, but he's wearing contact lenses.

"I think this is a mistake. Whatever you think my company--"

I climb onto the step, putting my body flush against his. "I'll have a glass of water, please."

The sharp intake of his breath is all I get before he backs away, giving me clear entry into his house. Prowling around, I take in his domain. The lounge, dining room, and kitchen are open-plan. The space is furnished with nothing but a reclining leather chair and a fridge.

He regards me from hooded eyes as he walks to the fridge and retrieves a bottle of mineral water. Taking a glass from the cupboard, he pours the water and hands it to me.

"Thank you." I make sure our fingers brush when I take the glass.

His eyelashes flutter. "About your business––"

"So, you're from Bloemfontein."

His eyes narrow, and his lips twitch. He doesn't like it when I defy him by interrupting and controlling the conversation, but he lets it slide.

"What else did you read about me?"

I take a sip of the water. "Everything I could find."

For a second his gaze fixes on my lips as I drink, but then he drags it away.

"How about you, Mr. Malan? Did you read everything about me?"

"I didn't have to."

I take another sip. "How so?"

"You're a known figure in this town."

"I am?"

He walks around the island counter, stopping short of me. "You said you had business. I did my homework, too. Your specialty is high-risk investments. I didn't see diamonds in your portfolio."

I lift my left hand and show him my wedding ring. "I'd like to insure this. It's very valuable to me."

He stares at it. "I don't deal in personal insurance. For that, you'll have to call Auto and General."

Leaving the glass on the counter, I place my palm on his chest and slide it down his rock-hard stomach to his even harder erection. When I cup his length, he remains motionless, regarding me with expressionless eyes, but his cock twitches in my hand.

"And for this?" I whisper. "Do I have to call someone else for this, too?"

His green eyes darken at my words, but he doesn't take the bait.

Gently, he removes my hand and puts a step between us. "As there seems to be nothing I can help you with, I think it's better that you leave."

"Nothing?" I start to unbutton my coat. "It's been a long time. Ten months, to be exact."

A vein pulses in his throat as he follows my actions. "You don't want to do that, not with a man like me."

"You wanted to find me. Didn't you come looking for me at the market?"

His eyes snap back to mine. "What do you mean?"

"Divine intervention. It's as if we were destined to meet."

"You don't believe that, beautiful."

"My husband used to call me beautiful."

He blanches a little. "Look, I--"

When my coat falls open, so does his mouth. The words he was going to say drop off the tip of his tongue and dissolve in the thick air between us. Heat burns hot in his eyes as they settle on my attire--sinful pink and black underwear with thigh high, lace-trimmed stockings and killer heels. The bra makes my breasts spill over the cups, and my nipples are visible through the sheer lace. His hands clench at his sides as he looks me up and down. His chest moves rapidly. His nostrils flare. If his cock could get any harder, it just did. The outline is clearly visible under the fabric of his trousers. He swallows and meets my eyes. His are smoldering with desire. He wants me. Crap, if I'm wrong, I'm going to have sex with a stranger in his kitchen.

Please, don't let me be wrong.

When his hands reach for me, I almost falter, but I have to know, and there's only one, sure way to discover the truth. One thing a man like Gabriel can't alter or fake is the way he fucks my body. Strengthening my resolve, I lift my chin and push out my breasts.

His expression twists with raw agony. Grabbing my arms, he turns me toward the door. "Leave. Now."

I lean back, cushioning his groin with my ass. He offers no resistance when I rub against him. The dip of his knees and the ragged groan that tears from his chest as I drag my ass over his hard-on tells me I won. His reaction makes me confident enough to walk to the island counter and hop onto it. I don't have to say a word. All I have to do is spread my legs.

He charges like a lion. There's a growl on his lips when he twists my hair around his fingers and pulls to the side, exposing my neck. Like a predator, he locks his teeth on the soft spot where my neck and shoulder meet. He doesn't bite down, just holds me in place as he sucks on my skin, marking me. When he lets go, I'm sporting a love bite. Satisfaction washes into his expression when he stares at the mark. Gently, he drags his tongue over it, moaning as he tastes my skin. He runs his nose up the length of my neck to my jaw, inhaling deeply.

Using my hair to keep me in place, he kisses and nips his way down from my ear to my shoulder. Each kiss turns more frantic than the next. He wedges between my legs and lets go of my hair to catch my face. Holding my cheeks between his palms, he plunders my mouth with the pent-up fever of a man who's been denied for too long. Our tongues tangle as he explores the depth of my mouth and the shape of my lips. He eats me as if I'm his last meal.

I can count the times Gabriel kissed me without total control on one hand. His seductions were well thought out and executed. This man is kissing me without an ounce of constraint, like Gabriel kissed me when I told him I didn't want Michael. He's kissing me like Gabriel did the day he married me against my will. I moan into his mouth, my body preparing itself for his possession by growing warm and slick.

He tears his mouth from mine and jerks his shirt from his pants. "Tell me how badly you want this."

My gaze drops to his pants. "I want to taste you."

His fingers reach for the buttons of his shirt. One by one, he pops them with shaky hands. "You can have my cock anywhere you want it."

When the edges of the shirt fall open, he pushes our upper

bodies together, skin against skin. It feels familiar. It feels right. He flips down the cups of my bra, letting the curves spill over, and takes a nipple in his mouth. His tongue is heaven and hell. He sucks on the tip, sending a spasm straight to my clit, and then he follows it up with a white-hot arrow of pain when he bites down. A few repetitions and my core is a melted puddle of arousal. He doesn't let up until he's given the other breast the same treatment. I'm panting and boneless, unable to support my weight when he lifts his broad hand from the small of my back. With his fingers curled around my neck, he pushes me down on the counter. The touch is dominant and possessive, just like I remember.

I gasp when he pushes the elastic of my panties aside and draws a finger over my slit.

He bends over me and hums his approval against my lips. "So wet."

When he parts me with one digit, I cry out harder.

"Is this what you want?" He works his finger inside up to the second joint.

"Yes, oh, God."

"I'm going to give you what you came for."

The promise is more beautiful than erotic, because what I really came for is *him*. He doesn't give me more time to think, because he starts moving his finger at a maddening slow pace. I push up on my elbows to look down at the sight, and he eases the pressure of his palm on my throat to let me. I want to see him claim me. As if sensing my need, he rips off the panties and drops them on the floor, staring intently at the wicked work of his finger.

"God, you're beautiful."

My clit tingles when he presses the pad of his thumb on the bundle of nerves. Gathering my wetness, he starts a slow and gentle massage that has my toes curl.

"Stop." I grab his wrist. "I'm going to come."

His smile is calculated. "That's the idea, beautiful."

"I want you inside me when I come."

His eyes widen a fraction. His jaw flexes the way Gabriel's used to when he fought for control. "You will."

Using the V of his fingers of one hand to open me wider, he adds a second finger to the first. My muscles clench around him.

"Fuck, yes."

His thumb goes back to my clit while his fingers prepares my channel for his cock. Gabriel is long and thick. This is something he'd do. A few hard thrusts combined with the relentless, circular movements of his thumb and I come with a fierce orgasm, crying out my pleasure. I'm still riding the wave when his mouth is on my pussy, his tongue taking over from his fingers. He feels so good. He knows exactly how I like it. He alternates gentle licks and sucks with nips of his teeth. Like Gabriel trained me, I come again quickly, this time in his mouth. He sucks me through the shockwaves until my body is a quivering mess.

"Good girl," he praises, planting a kiss on my mound.

I turn even wetter when his hands go for his belt. At the same time my heart throbs in my throat. This is about more than lust. This is about a gamble. The belt falls away. The button of his slacks pops. Thank God for the hasty way he pulls down the zipper, because my nerves can't handle the suspense. Taking my hands, he pulls me into a sitting position before gripping my hips and lowering me to the ground. He doesn't have to ask. I go down on my knees, like I did countless times with Gabriel, bringing the elastic of his briefs with me. When his cock jumps free, I sit back on my heels. He's thick and long with manly veins, the head broad and smooth. I almost cry with relief and thankfulness. He's exactly like I remember.

He's Gabriel.

Whether he knows that I know isn't clear. The moment is too consumed with his need. His desire is the sole focus of his attention as he drags his fingers through my hair and waits. Knowing my history of abuse, Gabriel never pushed himself into my mouth. My soul soars as I cup his balls and pull him closer. When my lips fold around him, I get back the pieces of myself I left in the debris of the explosion. Flicking my tongue over the slit, I lap up the pre-cum he spilled for me, reveling in the taste that is uniquely Gabriel. My heart flutters with joy too powerful to contain as I take him deep. Sucking Gabriel off has always been one of my biggest turn-ons. I love the way he groans when my tongue swirls around his thickness and traces the vein on the underside to his balls. I revel in the way his knees buckle and his hips jerk, knowing I'm the cause of his pleasure. Having him in my mouth is like a homecoming. It's the truth, the only truth I know. He lets me take him how deep I want, and he doesn't hold back. He comes quickly and hard, spilling his seed down my throat. I savor every drop, feeling the same interconnectedness I felt during oral sex with Gabriel.

He's Gabriel.

I stare at him, my soul bursting in wonder, as he rides his pleasure to the end. When his body goes still, he pulls his cock from the suction of my mouth. Without breaking our frantic chase for each other's pleasure, he grips my arms and drags me to my feet, crushing our mouths together briefly before bending me over the counter.

He positions my arms so I'm stretched out with my fingers touching the edges. "Hold on, beautiful."

Grabbing the cold granite for leverage, I brace myself, knowing when Gabriel takes me from behind it will be hard. Exactly how I want. His fingers play over my folds, gathering moisture and lubricating me. The broad head of his cock nudges at my opening. He's already hard again. One hand is guiding his shaft, the other gripping my hip. Seeing that it's been a while, he enters me slowly, as considerately as only Gabriel can be. After every inch he stops, giving me time to adjust while playing with my clit. By the time he's fully lodged inside, we're both panting. I don't have to tell him I need more. He knows my body inside and out. He knows my needs better than I know them myself.

When he starts moving, it's with the grueling pace I need to push me toward another climax. He slams into me, pivoting our groins together, and shifting my body up and down over the smooth surface. My need climbs high and fierce. When my inner muscles clench around him, he rolls my clit between his deft fingers, taking me over the edge. Coming around his cock, I scream out my pleasure.

He covers my body with his, putting his chest against my back. "Fuck, yes. You're beautiful when you come."

My reprieve only lasts a few seconds. Aftershocks from the orgasm are still rippling through me when he pulls out and flips me over.

"I want to look into your face."

So do I. I want to see his eyes when he comes. There was a time he didn't look at me when we had sex. It was the time he only fucked me from behind, hiding his scarred face and his true person, but I never wanted a different face or another soul. Only him.

He spreads my legs and bends my knees. His expression is tender as he rubs his palms up my inner thighs to the center between my legs. Parting my labia with his thumbs, it's on my eyes he focuses when he pushes inside. I don't hesitate to bare my heart. My feelings are etched on my face for him to read. For his eyes only. I show him my ecstasy as he fills me in the only way that makes me complete--with his body and soul. I show him my reverence as he starts pouring everything he has inside of me. Our desires, emotions, dreams, and essence intertwine as we move together. I take what he gives when his thrusts become more powerful, but I also give back in return. For every shove, I clench down on him, dragging him deeper and holding him tighter. My hands travel over his strong arms and his hard chest, tracing the familiar grooves. I adore every part of him, inside and out, and I'm falling harder than I imagined possible. The sensation is wild and vulnerable, beautiful and frightening in its intensity. I need his arms around me.

"Hold me," I whisper.

He doesn't hesitate. Without breaking his pace, he laces our fingers together and lifts my arms above my head. His chest presses against mine as he claims my lips in an incredibly soft and lingering kiss. I embrace my feelings, letting the love explode and grow inside of me until there's nothing but him. He fills my senses. His kiss tells me what I want to know. He cares. He still cares for me and not just as a possession. I'm pinned under his strong body, a damaged being, but I'm here out of my own free will, and that makes me more than a broken toy. I'm more than a vendetta or a debt, and he's more than The Breaker, because he kisses me like a husband. Right now, he's only a man who loves a woman, and I'm the woman who loves him back. Falling in love––the giddy kind––after deep and eternal loving may be doing things in reverse, but Gabriel and I have never been the norm. Perhaps we weren't meant to be the norm. We're us, and I love us.

"Valentina."

His whisper brings me back to him, to the sensation where our bodies are connected. It's too much and too little. I can't bear more, and I can't stop. My fingers clench around his as a strangled cry of pleasure leaves my mouth.

"I've got you, beautiful."

He does. He always has. He slows his pace a fraction and tilts his hips, changing the angle of his penetration. There. Oh, God. My lips part on a soundless gasp as he hits the right spot.

"Come with me."

It's a plea, not a command, and I obey it more eagerly than I obeyed any of his orders. My vision blurs as my body explodes. He's right there with me, giving me his all. His back arches, and his hips jerk as he holds my gaze. His eyes are open and his soul exposed as he shows me what I do to him. Our connection is perfect. There are no thoughts about the past or the future in my head. What I feel is too intense to leave space for worries and fear. There's only this moment. As his arms come around me to cushion my back and hold me close, I allow myself to fall apart, heal, and for the shattered pieces to come together. I weep in the crook of his neck, unabashedly, for the greatness of this gift, for having him again.

Lightning flashes outside, and the storm erupts in full force.

When he lifts on his arms to look at me, his cock slips free. I moan, not wanting to lose him, yet.

"Cold?" He rubs my arm.

"No."

He kicks his shoes free and removes his pants. I watch with mesmerized fascination as he undresses. There are still scars on his body, but they are different, now. Whatever he did, he underwent severe surgery. I don't care what he looks like, but I miss the marks I got to know, the ones that defined him. No matter. I'll get to know his new scars.

Catching my gaze on him, he says in a low voice, "What are you thinking?"

"That my husband had scars like that."

He doesn't offer an explanation, and I don't push. What I don't want is more lies between us.

"Take this." He helps me to pull on his shirt. I can't help but inhale deeply. The clean, spicy smell is from before Gabriel became Gregor.

Lifting me into his arms, he carries me to the reclining chair, settles down with me in his lap, and covers us with a throw from the chair back. Our cocoon is safe and warm. Together, we listen to the sound of the rain on the roof and watch the sky darken through the window.

He strokes my hip under the throw. "Where's your son?"

"With friends."

He tenses. "Reliable ones?"

"The guys you met at the market."

His tension doesn't ease. "Can they handle a baby?"

"As good as any mom I know."

"You sure?"

I can't resist teasing. "For a first date, you're very concerned about a single mom's baby."

He brushes a stray hair from my face. "He's cute." He says it like it explains his interest in Connor. "You said a *single* mom." He hesitates. "Are you?"

"Would I have been here if I wasn't?"

He doesn't answer.

A part of me wants to dive into this relationship and grab everything with a sweep of my arm, but I remind myself to be patient. I'm not doing this by force or manipulation. This time, it will be out of both our free wills.

I turn his wrist to the light to read the time on his watch. It's past five. "I have to go, soon."

His arm tightens around me. "Already?"

"I said I'd be back to feed Connor before bedtime. His bath is at six."

My heart contracts painfully for the longing that flashes in his eyes. He looks at me for a long time, and when he finally speaks, he pushes the words out, as if they are hard for him to say.

"Valentina, you're a very desirable woman."

"But?"

"But this wasn't a first date."

"What was it?"

His eyes search mine for something I can't name. He takes a breath and licks his lips. "A mistake."

Hurt twists my heart, but I brush it aside. I won't allow him to derail me. "This may not be a conventional date, but it wasn't a mistake."

"You don't know me, and when you do, you'll run. This is every kind of wrong."

"What we just did in your kitchen, did it feel wrong?"

"No. Every bit of it was right, but that's not what I meant, and you know it."

"Then we'll just focus on what feels right."

"No, Valentina." His voice is harsh. "It won't work."

I was so ready to tell him I know the truth, but he's not ready to hear it. I believe he's ready for us, or he wouldn't have come back and looked for me, but if I force things, I may screw this up.

I push on his chest to get up. "I have to go."

He locks me in a tight embrace. "Not while it's raining so hard. Too unsafe on the road."

"Connor--"

"Nothing will happen if you're thirty minutes late. Call your friends and tell them you're waiting out the storm."

Always protective. God knows, I need the extra time with him. "I'll get my phone."

"Stay put." He shifts out from under me and fetches my bag from the kitchen.

I use the opportunity to study him more. If he thought I wouldn't recognize the chiseled perfection of his ass, he really didn't know that each part of his body is forever imprinted in my mind. I don't care what face he wears, scared or handsome, I want the man underneath.

"Here you go." He hands me my bag and gives me space to make the call.

While I speak to Rhett, the smell of freshly brewed coffee fills the space. When I cut the call, he carries a steaming mug to me. Two sugars and milk, just the way I like.

"I would've offered you wine, but I don't want you to drink and drive."

"Thanks." I smile at his protectiveness. "That's very considerate."

"Would you like something to eat?"

"I'm good."

For the remainder of the time, we sip our coffee in comfortable silence while he plays with my hair, almost like in the days when I sat at his feet in his study at night. When only a light mist rain remains, he helps me gather my clothes, but shoves my ripped panties in his pocket. He buttons up my coat and walks me to my car, holding my umbrella for me.

His kiss is passionate and desperate, as if he's saying goodbye. "Be safe."

"You too."

He opens my door but grabs my wrist before I can get in. "Valentina."

I look back at him. "Yes?"

"Thank you for coming."

"I couldn't stay away."

His smile is both sad and tender.

Guilt attacks me on the way home. I feel bad for leaving Connor with the guys so I could have sex with my dead husband. What kind of a mother does that? What if Connor is hungry or feeling cranky? My worries are unfounded. When I get home, I find Connor playing happily in the playpen and Charlie folding the laundry. Rhett and Quincy give me curious looks.

"You look … different," Rhett says. "It went well, then?"

"Yes." I smile, but offer nothing more. Things between Gabriel and I have always been complicated, and it's no less so now. I can't even define what we have, let alone explain it to my caring partners.

"Someone we know?"

"What he means is," Quincy says, "is it someone we'll approve of?"

"I think so."

"Wait a minute." Rhett scrutinizes me. "Is it the guy from the market?"

"Yes. Why? Do you approve?"

"I like him," Quincy says.

"Ditto."

"Good."

They're going to see a lot more of him in the future. I'm determined to make it happen. The question is will Gabriel admit the truth? Will he come back to me as my husband or as a stranger?

21

Gabriel

Damn me to hell and back. How could I give in so easily? Touching Valentina was every jaded shade of wrong. I should've kept my distance. Running into her screwed up everything. I'm not arrogant enough to believe she's attracted to me or my new face. She merely acted on the instinct I trained into her. Valentina needs pain with her pleasure. Dominance in bed. She's drawn to the sadist, the monster. Sensing what I am underneath the polished veneer of a man is what brought her to my door. This is who I am. I can't change it any more than a cat can turn itself into a dog.

After she'd left, I pace the floor. The faint smell of raspberry contracts my chest, reminding me of what I'm missing, and that I'll be utterly alone for the rest of my life. So be it. I don't want anyone else. My purpose is protecting her and my child. That's enough. I'll feel better when I can make up for the financial hardships she suffered after my *death*. Once enough profit from my company rolls in, I'll invest anonymously in her clever company. My heart swells with pride. I always knew she'd survive, and the fact that she's making such a good job of it without me fills me with a pang of sad jealousy. No man wants to be expendable, dispensible, replaceable. All I ever wanted was to take care of her, and look where that got us. It's better that I stay far away from her, even as every cell in my body pulls toward her with a force near impossible to resist. I exchanged her life for freedom. I have to hold onto that oath when I feel weak. Which is all the time.

Of course, I'm tempted to take the golden opportunity she presented me, to claim her as a different man, but that will be just another lie, another manipulation, and I'm not going down that road with her again. Ever. I repeat the mantra, hoping it will sink in and that my dick will eventually get the message. Just being near her makes me hard. Fuck, thinking about her does the job. I clench and unclench my fingers, fighting a sudden urge to go after her and throw the truth at her feet, kneel, and beg her to forgive me and take me back. God, I'm such a selfish bastard. No, I won't blow my cover and her new, hard-earned life to hell. There's only one cure for taming my uncontrollable desire. I pull on my sweatpants and a T-shirt and punish myself with a grueling workout in the gym. With every weight I lift, I try to expel the memory of her taste, her sounds, and how she felt under my hands, but it's futile. The more I push, the deeper she seeps under my skin.

After a shower, I set out to do what I've been putting off since getting back to Johannesburg. I buy a bunch of white roses and drive to the graveyard. Visiting Carly's grave rips me to pieces. I was afraid to come here, and now that the full force of the loss tears the patched-up grief wide open again, I sink down on my knees in the mud and weep over the stone of my beautiful girl I couldn't save. Raw cries tear from my chest. For the first time after her death, I let them out. The violent emotion is far from healing. I'm simply lifting the lid on the simmering pain I carry inside of me. This, too, will always be a part of me, like losing Valentina and Connor. I accept it. This is what I deserve, to be an unhappy man with a whole face and a broken soul. Drying my face on my sleeve, I kiss my fingers and press them on the cold stone.

"I love you, Carly."

I won't fail Connor if it's the last thing I do. He'll never know me, but he won't know need, either. No one will lay a finger on him as long as I live. Allowing the resolve to give me strength, I push to my feet and go back to my house, which feels emptier and colder than ever now that Valentina has marked it with her presence.

ONE WEEK GOES BY. I work myself to a standstill, if not with work, in the gym. I keep a tight watch on the woman and child who give meaning to my existence. I keep my distance, ensuring I don't make the same stupid mistake, so when I come home from the gym on Saturday morning to find Valentina's car parked in front my house, anticipation mixes with trepidation. I'm surprised, and I'm not. I made her physically and emotionally dependent on me when I first took her. It's only natural she'll look for someone to replace that dependency. A darkness rises inside of me when I think of another man fulfilling that role, but the turbulent feeling is quickly squashed when she gets out of the car with Connor on her hip. The sight of them stills me. A deep-sated pain tightens my chest. I press the remote to open the gate, pull into my driveway, and exit my car warily.

"How did you get in?" The words come out more harshly than I intended.

Valentina doesn't bat an eye at my angry voice. "I smooth-talked the guard."

"He's not supposed to let anyone in without permission." I'm pissed off that he disobeyed the rules. It's dangerous. I'll have to speak with him.

"Connor helped," she says with a smile.

I stare at him with barely disguised pride. Yeah, it will be hard to resist that drooling, two-toothed grin. I make a conscious effort to soften my tone. "Why are you here?" Shit, is something wrong? "Is everything all right?"

"I'm taking Connor for a picnic. I thought you might like to come."

"Valentina..." It comes out like the warning I intended, but God, it feels good to say her name. The problem is I want to scream it with her submissive body under me.

Not giving me time to elaborate, she pushes Connor into my arms. "Hold him for a second, will you?"

The lure is too strong to resist. When my arms go around my son, something inside of me snaps. The world tips, and all the wrongs fall into place as I hold his small body against my chest, inhaling his baby smell.

Valentina lifts a diaper bag from the backseat and gives me an apologetic look. "I just need to change him before we go. May I please use your house?"

I'll never deny my son anything. "Go ahead."

Balancing Connor in one arm, I unlock the door and let her in.

She walks over to the only piece of furniture in the lounge. "Do you mind?"

"No."

While she spreads a protective cover out on the reclining chair, I carry Connor to her. For a second I cling to him, reluctant to let go, but she's standing there with the diaper in her hands, so I lay him down. Warmth travels up and down my body as I watch her take care of our child. I devour the intimate moment like a starving man. When he's clean and dry, she turns to me with a smile that holds both friendly warmth and passionate heat, neither of which I deserve.

Her tone is sure. "Ready?"

Despite how I sent her off after our lustful encounter, she doesn't doubt that I'll agree, and she's right. How can I now that

I've had a taste of Connor? I desperately want more. I want more of the self-assured woman standing in front of me, too.

My smile is tight. My weakness burns in me. "Give me a minute to shower and change?"

"Of course."

I rush through a shower and pull on a fitted white shirt and slacks. By the time I return to the lounge, she's sitting on the chair, breastfeeding Connor. I stop in my tracks. Looking down, her expression is nothing but loving. There's no resentment in her features for the child she didn't ask for or planned. My eyes slip to my son. His suckling is surprisingly strong for such a tiny creature.

"Ouch," Valentina says, flinching as he hollows his cheeks.

He fists his little fingers in Valentina's jersey, holding onto his source of food for life. Little sighs, groans, and hums of approval infuse the swallowing noises he makes. He has a cluster of dark hair, not curly like mine, but silky like his mother's. Even at ten months, he looks impossibly tiny. Fragile.

Before I can stop myself, I'm standing in front of them, caressing Connor's hair. Why this particular scene moves me so much I don't understand. Maybe it's because my own mother never took care of me. There were nannies for that.

Valentina stares up at me. "He's almost done."

"Take your time." I mean it. I can stand here and look at them all day. "Isn't he on solids, already?"

"Oh, yes. I still breastfeed because he needs all the natural immunity he can get. He's really only eight months old, if you consider that he was born two months prematurely."

She hands him back to me and adjusts her clothes.

"We'll take my car," she says, "because I have the car seat."

The minx successfully bullied me into an outing without even putting up a fight.

"Do we need to stop for supplies?" I ask.

"I've already packed a basket. It's in my trunk."

I offer a hand to help her to her feet.

She drives us to the zoo, a place I used to visit often when I was little. Not much has changed in thirty-eight years. Connor is too young to appreciate the animals, but we follow the path past the monkeys and birds, walking side by side in a comfortable silence. Under the shade of a willow, she spreads out a blanket and puts Connor on his tummy, leaving plastic toy blocks within his reach.

"He's almost sitting by himself," she says proudly. "He's a little behind on this milestone, but the doctor says its normal with preemies."

She's good with him. She makes a great mom. I shouldn't touch her, but I can't help brushing a strand of hair behind her ear. "How is it?"

"How's what?"

"Motherhood."

"It's tough, sometimes, but I'd never want it any other way."

"I'm sorry it's been hard for you." I mean it with all of my soul.

She shrugs. "It's a matter of finding a routine that works for everyone."

"I'm sure it's not that simple."

"It's not so bad. I have flexibility in my work, and I can take Connor to the office."

"Do you enjoy your job?"

"I appreciate it. It puts a roof over our heads and food on our table. Talking about food..." She reaches for the basket. "Are you hungry?"

"Starving." But not for food. Like a fool I stare into her eyes, getting lost in their murky darkness.

Don't touch her.

Ah, fuck.

I cup her face and push her down on the blanket. It feels natural that my body should cover hers. I ache to taste her, to feel her soft lips, and smell the intoxicating perfume of her skin. Holding her eyes, I bring our mouths closer together. If she wants to back out, I'll give her the opportunity. She closes the last hairbreadth of distance by lifting her head. When our lips touch, the same deep ache as always takes root in my chest. Instead of getting her out of my system, I'm getting more entangled in her than ever. It's all the sweeter when this time she chose me. I didn't kick down her door and drag her here against her will. I'm not seducing her with pleasure to look past my scars. She came to me. I kiss her like a drowning man, so thankful for her free will I can hardly breathe. All the emotions I felt when I was nothing but a cold and empty shell are because of this woman. She taught me the meaning of gratitude. I feel it now, for giving me this moment with her and Connor. There's so much pleasure in having her consent. Not some fucked-up, manipulated version, but the real deal.

I pour my heart into the kiss, and my body responds, going hard and hot everywhere. We're in public, but I don't give a damn. I'm getting deliriously drunk on her and the addictive feeling of happiness.

A gurgle from Connor pulls me back to earth. Reluctantly, I break the kiss. Her face is prettily flushed.

I chuckle. "I think he approves."

She gives me a radiant smile. "Oh, he definitely does."

"Thank you."

"For what?"

"For today." *For allowing me time I don't deserve.*

"You're welcome."

Connor starts to fuss. In less than a second, he goes from happy to crying. My protective instinct goes into overdrive. Perplexed, helpless, I fall over myself to reach him. "What's wrong? What happened? Is he hurt? Is he ill?"

As calm as ever, Valentina takes a bottle from the diaper bag and hands it to me. "Want to feed him?"

Connor wails with a voice that would've lifted the roof had there been one. Pride swells my chest to the point of exploding. When I put the nipple in his mouth, he starts sucking with greedy gulps.

"Again?" I ask. "He just ate."

She smiles at me. "He gets hungry every two hours, more or less."

It's like floating on a cloud. The moment feels surreal. A feeling that matches my joy at just having kissed Valentina surges through me when my son nestles deeper into my arms. He weighs nothing. His body is so small his head fits into the palm of my hand. His mouth latches firmly around the nipple, and his cheeks hollow as he makes hungry little sucking sounds. I swear there's a groan somewhere in the mix and something keen to a growl when I lose my grip on the bottle and break the suction. A deep laugh rumbles in my chest. I cuddle him closer, holding him to my heart.

"You're the man," I say on a chuckle, planting a kiss on his forehead.

As he drains every drop in the bottle, I'm fully in the moment, devouring each second of the precious gift.

"First time giving a baby a bottle?" Valentina asks with a twinkle in her eyes.

"Hell, yeah."

"Not too bad." She winks and plants a kiss on my cheek.

Just like that, my resistance crumbles. All of my supposedly steadfast intentions fall like battle-beaten soldiers. One more kiss, a fleeting moment of weakness, a never-ending memory, and I'm dating Valentina Louw, the woman who knocked my feet from under me, the mother of my child.

IN THE WEEKS THAT FOLLOW, our *dating* becomes official. Regular. We're an item. With the start of winter, we go to indoor playgrounds with Connor. When Kris or Rhett and Quincy can watch Connor, we stay in and make love. I touch Valentina every second I can. Every moment is like borrowed time. Treasured. Whatever we do, I always let her take the lead. She introduces me to her friends as Gregor Malan, and they accept me without question or resistance. Everyone is eager for her to find the happiness she deserves, and I'm flattered that they think I'm the guy for the job. The only issue that spoils this new development is the lie that stands big and ugly between us.

The closer I grow to Valentina in this new relationship, the more torn-up I become. My deceit punishes me in every waking hour and pierces my heart at night. Guilt finds me even in my dreams. She deserves better. She deserves the truth. As my love keeps on overtaking every other emotion and purpose in my life, I know what I have to do.

I have to come clean.

I have to lose her.

Again.

The evening I make the decision, I spend the night on my knees. I kneel on the tiles with my forehead on my fisted hands, wishing for forgiveness and knowing I won't get it. When I face her tomorrow, she'll hate me.

Waiting until a decent hour, I call and ask her to come over after work. Alone. I don't want to do this in front of Connor or my ex-bodyguards. What I have to say is meant for her ears alone. For the rest of the day, I pace around the house, reciting my speech in my head, but no words sound right. Finally, I settle for the simple truth.

"I died to give you freedom. I died because I love you. I'm still dying, a little every day, and I'll keep on doing so if it'll give you the happiness I stole from you."

Too damn dramatic.

I face myself in the bathroom mirror, trying again. "I'm not the man you think I am. I'm…"

Fuck.

I drag a hand through my hair. Who am I? "I'm a ghost of the man who kidnapped and impregnated you." Scrap that. "I'm the man who loves you."

She'll hate me more than before, but it's the right thing to do. Maybe the most honorable thing I've ever done in my life. I give the strange face in the mirror a glance before I head for the shower to get ready. If this is the last time I face Valentina, the least I can do is pay her the courtesy of looking presentable.

Valentina

UNTIL TODAY, things moved slowly between me and Gabriel, or Gregor, as I got used to calling him. We date like two normal people. There have been plenty of opportunities to tell him I know the truth, but I want him to tell me when he's ready. I can't tell him how I feel until he confesses. If he's not ready to listen to me as Gabriel, he's not ready to listen to me as Gregor.

Then came his phone call today. There was something in his tone, a faint tremble in the deep timber of his voice. My hands shake as I fit the new red dress and twist my hair into a bun. What if he doesn't want to see us any longer? No, I have to be positive. Gabriel may not love me like I love him, but he needs me. He wanted me alive, enough to make me pregnant. That counts for something, doesn't it?

Connor coos on the play carpet. I pick him up, burying my nose in his hair. "I love you, baby. So much."

A pang of sadness invades my heart as it always does when I have to leave him, even for a few hours.

"He'll be fine," a voice says from the door.

I turn to take in Kris' soft, compassionate smile. Wonderful Kris who always understands.

She holds out her hands. "Give him here and go have yourself some fun."

I kiss my baby's head before handing him over.

Kris looks me up and down. "You look beautiful."

Absentmindedly, I rub a finger over the stub of my thumb. "You think so?"

"Perfect." She gives me an encouraging nod. "You're running late."

She knows I'm stalling. I'm stalling because I'm nervous. How will this night turn out for us? For me, Gabriel, and Connor? When she leaves with Connor, I slip the gift I kept for Gabriel in my bag. Depending on what he says, I'll offer it to him or bring it home. A part of me wants to put tonight off, but we can't carry on living in our make-believe world.

I say a quick goodbye to the guys. It's pizza and movie night, so Charlie is sorted. Then I drive to Gabriel's house.

He waits outside, dressed in dark slacks and a white shirt. As always, my mouth goes a little dry. He's perfect in every physical sense, but to me he's still the scarred man I fell in love with. On the inside, he's as torn up as I am, and that pain is a bond we share.

Instead of getting the door for me like he usually does, he remains standing on the lawn, drinking me in with a hungry expression as I walk up the path. We don't need words. I know what he's thinking just as he knows what I am, because his eyes drop to the hard points of my nipples under my dress. I stop short of him. My emotions are raw, but so are his. A war rages in his green eyes, the color so wrong and so right. His hands flex as if he's trying not to touch me, but then the fragile cord of his restrain snaps.

Grabbing a fistful of my hair, he jerks me closer. The action makes me stumble into the hard barrier of his chest. He catches me with one arm around my waist, trapping his erection between us.

"Fuck." He buries his nose against my neck and runs it along my jaw. "Just one touch."

That hurts. He says it like a farewell greeting.

"I need you inside the house. Now," he whispers in my ear.

Taking my hand, he leads me to the door. When it's locked behind us, he turns on me, one hundred percent Gabriel. "That's a very pretty dress." For all of one second, he looks indecisive, as if he's fighting an internal battle, but then he takes my face between his hands and kisses me hard.

"Aren't you going to tell me to take it off?" I ask when he sets me free.

"There are things I need to say."

I want to hear, and I don't. I'm afraid of losing him, forever, this time, but I'm not afraid to fight for what I want. I'm not giving up, yet. I push the straps from my shoulders and let the dress fall to the ground. Not wearing underwear, I stand naked in front of him, except for my shoes.

His gaze caresses me with approval, but the battle continues to rage in his eyes. "You came here like this?" He closes the distance, staring down at my mouth. "Why?"

We both know why, but he wants me to say it. "I want you to fuck me."

The taught skin of his cheekbones darkens. "How?"

"Hard. Rough." I deal my trump card. "While you spank me."

The lines of his face turn rigid, and the green of his eyes becomes smoky. "Why?"

"Because it makes me come harder."

His chest deflates with a breath of defeat. "I can't deny you."

"Then don't."

He cups my breast, flicking a thumb over my nipple. "Lie down on your back and spread your legs."

I shake my head. "If you want it, you're going to have to take it."

His body tenses. "I don't want to hurt you, not any--" He bites back the rest of his words, giving me a pained and needy look.

"It's what I need."

His resolve crumbles like a dry piece of bread. His carefully guarded lust unravels, giving me a part of the true man as he folds his fingers around my neck and pushes me to my knees. Holding me in place with one hand, he unzips his slacks with the other, leaving the waist buttoned but freeing his long, heavy cock.

He lets go of my neck to grip my hair. "Touch it."

Our position turns me on beyond anything I've ever experienced with me naked on my knees and him towering over me, fully clothed. Gathering the drop that spills from the slit, I rub the wetness around the crest before dragging my nails along the underside. His skin is hot velvet, his flesh hard granite. I catch his eyes as he stares down at me, reading me like the open book I am, knowing exactly what I need.

"Lick it."

At the permission, I drag my tongue over the head, all the way down and back up. I don't want to play nice, today. With a look of defiance, I suck him deep into my mouth.

His expression is approving even as he gives a small shake of his head. "Naughty, greedy girl. Did I tell you to suck my cock?"

Instead of replying, I gently rake my teeth over him.

He shivers. "We'll take care of your punishment later. If you're going to suck, do it like you mean it."

I do. I curl my tongue around him and touch his length where my mouth doesn't reach. Taking him as deep as I can, I urge him wordlessly to remove the last barrier between us, the point to where he hasn't pushed me, yet. I need this. I want everything from him. I want him to understand he healed me, and that I'm willing to go anywhere for him. He pulls out and shoves back faster. I let him fuck my mouth like I've never done with any man, savoring every stroke he pushes into my mouth. I want to swallow for him. I want to choke and have my eyes water. I want him to take me all the way. Changing the angle of my head, I make him pierce my throat instead of my cheek. My reward is magnificent. His eyes grow large with a heated light, and his erection twitches in my mouth. He pushes harder and deeper, stretching my jaw to the limits.

"Breathe through your nose, baby."

This is all the warning I get before he snips the final cord of self-control he's always maintained while fucking my mouth.

Gripping my head between his large hands, he holds me still and starts fucking my lips in all earnest. When I gag he pulls back, giving me only a brief reprieve before continuing his grueling pace. The way he uses me is so hot. I'm salivating around him, making disgusting noises in the back of my throat, and he loves it. Blinking away the moisture in my eyes, I focus on taking deep breaths through my nose.

"Look at me," he grits out.

I lift my eyes to his, letting him see my smeared mascara and lipstick, laying my vulnerability at his feet.

"You love this, don't you?"

I can only moan around him, feeling him tighten in the way he does before he comes. Instead of giving me his seed, he pulls out. I want his taste in my mouth, but he keeps his cock inches away from my face, taunting me.

Gently, he massages the joints of my jaw until the ache subsides, and then he folds his strong fingers around my throat and pushes my back to the floor, my legs bent under me. Resting his weight on one arm, he stretches out over my body and takes my lips in such a delicious and languorous kiss that my toes curl. While his tongue soothes my brutalized mouth, his hand explores my breast. He kneads the soft flesh between needy fingers, a bit too rough to be comfortable, until moisture coats my folds. Soft kisses land on my cheek, jaw, neck, and collarbone while he grips my nipple and pulls. The sting is delicious. His fingers trail over my stomach to my mound, lightly grazing my clit. We moan into each other's mouths when the pad of his thumb slips through the wetness gathered there for him.

A soft nip on my bottom lip announces the end of the kiss. He pulls away a fraction to look at me. "I'm going to take everything you've got."

I can barely manage a hoarse, "Yes."

He lifts my arms above my head and arranges my hands with my palms showing up. "Keep them there."

He moves down my body, kissing every inch of my skin until I writhe in need. When he finally reaches my pubic bone, he doesn't press his lips on my clit like I crave, but straightens my legs, relieving the pull of my muscles. Taking his time, he massages my thighs and calves. Just when my muscles start to relax, he pushes my legs open, exposing my pussy. He pulls my folds apart with his thumbs and sits back on his heels to study me.

"So pretty," he muses. "So perfect." He thrusts his middle finger inside, burying it up to the knuckle. "So tight." A few hard pumps make my hips lift off the floor. "So wet."

I whimper, needing more of that friction, but he removes his finger. A smile tugs at his lips at my protesting moan. His head lowers slowly until his tongue teases my clit, mercilessly gentle. I lift my hips, trying to make him take more, but am rewarded with a bite that sends a shard of pain through my clit. My cry bounces off the walls, a plea to stop and give more. Then he starts eating me in all earnest. His tongue, teeth, lips, and fingers are everywhere, until I can't tell the nips of pain from the carnal pleasure. A finger eases into my ass, not carefully, but urgently, without holding back. I strain down to claim that feeling, making it mine as he fills me with everything but his cock. A few pumps and my release starts coiling, pulling my lower body tight. He growls with satisfaction as I come in his mouth, my pleasure exploding around his tongue and finger. My arousal coats his lips as he pulls away, giving me a possessive and victorious grin. I'm his, not only in this moment, but always. I want him to drive into me and fill me with the physical knowledge.

"Take me," I manage on a croak.

"I'm the one giving the orders."

To emphasize the statement he flips me on my stomach and lifts my hips. My ass is high in the air, an offering to him, and I already know what's coming before he gathers my moisture and massages it into my asshole. An involuntary moan escapes as he stretches me impatiently with two fingers. I breathe in and out as two becomes three. One hand caresses the globe of my ass cheek as the other punishes me inside.

Bending over me, he kisses my shoulder. "You've been a bad girl, coming here naked under your clothes. The wind could've blown up your dress, and someone could've caught a glimpse." Possession is thick in his tone as his fingers trail over my exposed folds. "And this is mine. All mine."

I revel at the declaration, knowing he'll claim me regardless of what his guarded expression meant when I arrived. No, I don't want to think about that, now. All I want to focus on is him inside of me, around me, fucking me.

The slap that falls on my naked butt comes unexpectedly. My ass clenches, trapping his fingers inside. The heat scorching my skin sets every inch of my body from my waist down on fire. I push up, offering him more, and he takes it, spanking and pumping. My cries are fierce and desperate. I already need to come again.

"My greedy, beautiful girl," he groans. "You want my cock in this tight asshole, don't you?"

The last time he took me like this was on our wedding day. I know it's going to hurt and that I'll love it, but right now I'm craving the sting of his palm too much to focus on anything else. My breasts are heavy, swaying with each slap he delivers to my bottom. The pattern moves from right to left and back again, firing up the skin on my backside and turning my pussy plump and wet. My folds swell and throb. My clit feels overheated. The spanking stops, but not the fingers pumping in and out of my dark entrance.

"You won't walk around without underwear again unless I tell you to."

"No," I whimper. My thighs quiver.

"Good girl. I'm going to take this beautiful, spanked ass." The fullness of his fingers disappears, leaving a burn behind. "Keep still."

Leaning my forehead on my intertwined fingers, I try to oblige, knowing it will be impossible. The broad head of his cock teases the tight ring of muscle.

"I'm going to take you like you asked me," he says in a voice thick with lust. "Fight me."

I know what he means. He doesn't want me to give anything. He wants to take my ass, showing me his true nature without holding back, and he wants me to do the same. Carefully, he stretches me, driving the broad head of his cock past the first barrier of muscle. God, it burns. Perspiration beads on my forehead as he prepares me with shallow strokes, giving me just a taste, and then he spears into me, making my back arch and forcing a choked cry from my throat. He gave me permission to fight, so I try to make my body flat, escaping the harsh pace by lowering my pelvis to the ground, but his arm wraps around my waist, holding me in place. Fueled by my resistance, he slams harder, jamming his cock into my forbidden entrance until my eyes water and my backside burns like the fires of hell. I try to crawl away, but his grip tightens, and his fucking intensifies. His balls are slapping my pussy, and his cock hammers inside of me, driving my need higher with an animalistic mixture of pain and pleasure. The farther I try to move, the harder he fucks me.

"You'll take my cock," he hisses before kissing my shoulder.

I can say stop, and he will, but instead I clench my asshole, pushing him out. The act of defiance triggers the response I want. His hand curls around my throat, cutting my airflow. Oh God, I missed this. I don't care that it's deprived or strange or fucked-up. I want to give him my air, pleasure, pain, and ecstasy. I allow him to half-strangle me while he slides in and out of my ass, feeling nothing but trust and a deep sense of peace, knowing he'll take care of me. As I start seeing white spots, he eases his hold marginally, allowing me to breathe, and then his fingers are on my clit, pinching, rubbing, spanking. A twisted sound escapes my dry throat as I explode in shards of painful pleasure, my pussy contracting around empty air. I reach behind me, trying to find his cock. I need him where I'm empty.

He grabs my wrist and lifts my arm above my head. "Not until I tell you."

He runs a finger around my asshole, making the muscle contract, and then he pulls my globes apart, his fingertips digging into my ass cheeks. Glancing over my shoulder, I see him standing on his knees, his cock rigid and thick. He points it at my pussy and spears my folds. My inner muscles shudder as he drives home, giving me all he's got. Over and over, he takes me, all the while rubbing circles with his palm over my clit. He changes his angle and finds the sweet spot that sends me over the edge every time. It doesn't take long for another orgasm to build. When it breaks, I clench down on his cock, squeezing him until he curses and jerks, but he doesn't come. He thrusts into me, hard and unapologetic, taking because I asked him to. He fucks me bone and senseless, until I lose track of time and place. I'm hardly conscious of my body being used, because I'm drifting in a space of belonging and pure Gabriel. Pure, warped us. I only realize I collapsed flat on my stomach when the force of his fucking shifts me over the tiles. He carries on, pounding into my pussy and palming my breasts until his cock swells and twitches, and warm jets spurt into my channel.

"Fuck." He falls over me, holding his weight on his arms. "Sweet Jesus." Desperately, he pumps twice more, deeper, hitting the barrier of my cervix. "Valentina." He kisses my neck and rests his forehead on my shoulder. "Fuck, Valentina."

My body feels bruised and thoroughly loved in the most delicious way. A lethargic relaxation claims me, turning my muscles to jelly. My lover pulls out of me, causing warm semen to run down my thighs. If I had the strength, I would've pushed up on my arms to look at how he marked me, but I know he's watching.

"Beautiful," he mutters, running his hands through the stickiness gathered on my inner thighs.

Incapable of doing anything but lying on the cool floor, I focus on his hands as they rub over my ass, back, and shoulders. He covers me in gentle kisses and whispers words of praise for how good I've been. Then he gathers me in his arms and shifts me onto his lap, rocking me gently while he strokes my hair and keeps on showering me with compliments. We come down from our high in each other's arms. The aftercare is as much part of Gabriel as the fucking, and I love him for showing me how much he cares. His approval seeps into my skin and past my defenses, making me feel safe and cherished in my own warped way.

When I'm sated on his lingering kisses and soft caresses, he carries me to the shower and washes my body and hair. Afterward, we lie naked on the recliner in the dark, listening to the sounds of our breathing and the crickets outside. The earlier peace is starting to slip, because I have to get back to Connor, soon.

When I stir in his arms, his hold tightens.

"I promised Kris I'd be home before midnight," I say reluctantly, simultaneously eager to see my baby and wishing I could stay the night.

"Valentina..."

The way he says my name is a warning, and somewhere in that tone lies damnation. This is the moment where he either tells me the truth or chooses omission. If he sends me away with a goodbye instead of the truth, my battle of wooing my husband is lost. I shiver, feeling the weight of our future settle on my heart. It makes me feel cold. I turn to face him. I want to look into his eyes, his unreal green eyes, in our moment of truth.

His finger traces my jaw. "Valentina, I have something to tell you."

Despite the gentleness of his touch, his body is tense, his muscles hard and stiff.

I wait silently for him to continue.

He hangs his head for a moment before meeting my eyes again. "I lied to you." When I don't reply, he says, "I deceived you in the most unforgivable way, and I don't want to be that man any longer."

I splay my hands over his hard chest. "Tell me."

He winces, as if in pain. "Just know I acted in your best interest, even if it caused you pain." He takes a deep breath and catches my fingers as if he's afraid I'll pull away. "There's no easy way to say this, and I don't want to hurt you more than you've already suffered."

"Tell me," I repeat.

His brow twists. "Promise me you'll hear me out. Please."

"I promise."

He gives a tight nod. "Valentina, I..." He swallows, his eyes measuring my reaction. "I'm the man who robbed you of your life. I'm Gabriel."

Gabriel

THE NAKED WOMAN in my arms isn't an open book to read. I just told her I'm her dead husband, but her body language tells me nothing. I can deal with a slap, an insult, blame, and anger, but not the level, sober look she gives me. It leaves me defenseless, because I don't know what words she needs next. Do I soothe her? Apologize? Beg? Explain?

My gut knots when she doesn't reply for several long seconds. She can't forgive me. The deceit runs too deep. Her emotionless state can only mean she's finally weaned off from Gabriel. He doesn't matter. Maybe he never did. Only an arrogant asshole would hope differently. I still owe her the truth, so this is what I give her, starting from the day I discovered the evidence of her rape and ending with my plastic surgery.

Not once does she interrupt. She listens quietly as I confess, her attention acute and focused. When I come to the end of my guilty monologue, she finally stirs. My nerves raw and my heart bleeding, I watch her get to her feet and walk to where her bag lies on the floor. She'll gather her clothes, get dressed, and leave. I'll never see her and Connor again, and I can't blame her. I did worse to her than the enemies whose bones I've broken. All I can do is drink in the soft lines of her perfect body. A painful flashback of her hanging from a rope with her underwear around her ankles pierces my mind. She still has those same, gorgeous S-lines, like the ethereal subject in a painter's portrait.

Taking something from her bag, she turns and watches me in the way she listened––with silent concentration. As she walks to me, the strength that makes her the most remarkable women I know shows. Every step is laced with confidence. Does she hold judgment? Will she condemn me? I will take whatever I get, whether it be hate or acceptance, but I don't expect forgiveness. My only hope is that we won't part on ugliness. Nothing to soil this perfect, last moment. A part of me wishes for her to walk away like this, saying nothing, while another part of me screams to know what she feels, what she thinks.

She stops close to me, way too close. "I've been waiting for a long time for you to tell me this, Gabriel."

She says my name softly, purposefully.

My heart starts beating furiously, blood gushing through my veins, burning my skin. "You knew?"

"From the first moment."

If she knew, why did she allow things to go this far? Why didn't she kill me, hurt me, or got one of my ex-bodyguards to take care of me? Where is her revenge? My eyes drop to the object she clutches in her fist. Whatever it is, she waited for my confession before handing it to me. It could be damnation or absolution, but I suspect the first.

I shouldn't touch her, not after what I admitted, but I can't help myself. My hands are drawn to the curve of her hips. I cup them and pull her between my legs, staring up at her huge, brown eyes, afraid of what I'll find there, but there's no anger, blame, or hurt. Only something beautiful I don't deserve. I should plead, beg, explain more, try to put the shambles of feelings twisting and tumbling in my heart into sentences, but the only word I can force from the hollowness in my chest is, "How?"

"I don't need a face to know you."

Hope blooms inside me, but I squash it. "Why didn't you say something?"

"There's only one thing I want to say, and I couldn't do it until you were honest with me."

What can she possibly say after everything I told her, after everything my family did to her? Her gaze is soft and filled with something that makes my heart jerk. I never want to forget how she looks, right now, because for the first time in my life someone stares at me with love and loyalty. She will fight for me like no one ever has.

Her lips part with a featherlike breath. "I love you, Gabriel."

My world and pitiful existence collapse, every defense I cemented into the wall of my life crumbling around me. Regret, joy, hope, disbelief at my incredible, miraculous luck that this amazing feminine creature can love me pour out of me, condensing in big, shameless tears that run over my face.

She leans against me, pressing our skins together. "I tried to tell you, a long time before you left, but you didn't want to listen. Now, with only the truth between us, you have to believe me."

I press my face into her stomach, holding onto her like she's my salvation. "I love you, Valentina. With everything I am. God knows, I tried to stop, to set you free, but I can't."

Where do we go from here? How do we pick up the pieces and build a new life as a family?

She answers the question when she opens her hand and holds her palm out to me. "Gregor Malan, will you marry me?"

The platinum of my wedding band makes a perfect shining

circle on her skin. I stare at it in disbelief, battling to digest her words.

"Where…?" I look from the ring to her face.

"The police found it in the debris."

She hung onto it. She never stopped fighting for me. Overwhelming, bigger-than-life love crashes over me. "You suspected?"

"I knew you weren't dead. I never stopped looking."

I fold my arms around her. I'm a drowning man, and she's my sea. "Don't let me go. I promise I'll never leave you, again."

Her lips tilt into a faint smile. "Is that a yes?"

The burdens of my past lift from my shoulders. For the first time in my life, I feel truly happy. Light. I set my kitten free, and she came back to me.

"Yes." I smother her stomach in kisses. "Yes, fucking yes."

"Give me your hand," she orders.

When I hold out my left hand, she pushes the band that symbolizes our lifelong union over my ring finger, where it belongs. The fit is perfect. We're perfect, like I always knew we'd be. She's my life, my love, my redemption. Not my property, but my wife. Not for nine years, but forever.

EPILOGUE

Gabriel

The day is one of those cooler summer ones with a hint of a brewing thunderstorm on the horizon. The Johannesburg skyline with the Brixton, Ponte, and Auckland Park tower landmarks is visible from the Emmarentia hill, but it's not the view I'm focused on. It's the woman standing in front of the stately old building, her ruby brown hair blowing in the breeze. She's wearing a yellow dress that accentuates the glow of her golden skin. For a moment, her eyes find mine, connecting with me and me alone, and then she's scooped up by the mob of journalists and politicians who all want a piece of her.

I tighten my hand around Connor's, making sure I don't lose him in the crowd, and balance Sophia on my hip. Sophia will be nineteen months tomorrow, and we have a third on the way, although it doesn't yet show in the gentle swell of Valentina's belly. We decided to announce it to the world after today. Today, Valentina didn't want anything to compete with the opening of the center for the disabled.

As much as our children, this is her baby, something she worked hard on during the past year, and even though many families and mentally challenged individuals will profit from her project, she did it for Charlie. The old hospital was turned into a nurse hostel years ago, and when government funds to maintain it ran out, the beautiful three-story building stood empty for almost two decades, the structure dilapidated and its once manicured garden overgrown with weeds. As the city's new mayor, this was one of Valentina's first initiatives. Yup, she came a long way.

The work she did with her company is commendable. After growing it into one of the country's most successful businesses, she started plowing money back into the community to help people who suffer like she used to, people who come from where she does. It came as no surprise that those people came to love and revere her, selecting her onto the local municipal council and now as the Johannesburg mayor. Her connections to Barnard and other clean state officials helped, as did the anti-criminal operation she undertook in Berea. My little pet is a strong, fair, and compassionate leader. It doesn't take a scientist to see she was born for this.

I shift the weight of the diaper bag on my shoulder, staying on the outskirts to give Valentina room to speak to the press as well as to admire her from a distance. Watching her operate, I can never get enough. I'm not the only one. She's a people magnet. Quincy and Rhett, now married with their own families, are crowding close. They're no longer her self-appointed bodyguards, but we remain friends, honoring our standing Saturday poker nights at Kris' place. These days Rhett runs a successful security business while Quincy provides protection for the touring stars of rock concerts. They know me as Gregor. Nobody except for Valentina knows my secret. Kris is here, too, always supporting Valentina in her official and non-official ventures. Her practice in Orange Grove became a benchmark in the industry with such a phenomenal growth that she opened five franchises throughout the city, as well as the biggest animal rescue center in the country. She's also the sponsor of a full bursary for underprivileged veterinary students.

A series of flashes go off as my wife poses for the cameras with the newly appointed president of the Association for the Mentally Disabled. Charlie beams at his sister's side. He comes to the center every day to work as a mail sorting clerk, and the work does him good. He loves dividing the letters into neat destination bundles. The center provides employment opportunities, ranging from filling envelopes to preparing promotional flyers, as well as support and guidance for the members and their families. People like Charlie can find a sense of belonging and purpose here, as well as government sponsored treatment.

Charlie lives with us in the new house we built on an acre of property on the border of Kyalami. It's a family house with toys scattered over the floors, a swing in the garden, and a bicycle on the lawn. We have five dogs, all strays, and an array of cats that come and go, some staying longer than others. Oscar is still with us, but Bruno sadly died of old age last year.

All of our lives revolve around the small woman in the center of the spectators. Another flash goes off as the Minister of Home Affairs shakes her hand. Last month Valentina was on the cover of every magazine and newspaper, and this week she's been invited to a congregation of leaders who hope to vote her into government on a national level, but she already decided to decline. Like any couple with their own business, two young kids, and another on the way, we lead a hectic life, but one I wouldn't exchange for anything. I wish Carly could have known her half-brother and sister and share this incredible moment, but I believe she's here with us.

Since Valentina became busy with city council business, I run her company. My main focus is still protecting her and our children, but I'm happy to have something in which I find purpose, something I enjoy. Something clean. No more breaking. No more violence.

Sophia starts to fuss. I know this particular cry. Soon, she'll be bawling. I lie her down in the stroller to check her diaper and drop the bag to the ground.

"Be a big man and get me your sister's bottle, please," I tell Connor.

He unzips the bag, locates the item, and holds it out proudly. "Here, Daddy."

I ruffle his hair before taking the bottle from the insulation holder and testing a drop of milk on my wrist to ensure it's not too hot.

My little girl takes a greedy gulp when I put the nipple in her mouth, first swallowing air. A soft hand falls on my shoulder, and Valentina's voice washes over me.

"Are you managing?"

I grin at her. "Always."

"You're a good daddy."

I steal a chaste kiss, careful not to tip the bottle and break Sophia's suction. "You're a better mommy."

"Thank you." Her words are soft-spoken.

My gaze rakes over her body. "For what?"

"For doing this," she motions at our baby girl, "so I can do that." She flips a hand at the people enjoying the cocktails and finger food set out on the lawn.

"You're welcome." Truth is, I love daddying my kids, and there's nothing I won't do for my clever, industrious, pretty wife.

"Just a few more minutes and then we can escape."

Connor runs off to Charlie. I keep one eye on him and the other on my daughter. "Go mingle and do whatever mayors are supposed to do. Sophia doesn't need to nap for another hour. I can go home with her and Connor if you'd like to stay longer."

"I was thinking we could put the kids down for their nap and catch up."

My body is immediately interested. "Catch up, huh?" I shift behind the stroller to hide the untimely hardening in my pants.

A pretty flush heats her cheeks. "Um, yeah."

I know exactly how I'm going to catch up with her, and from the way she lowers her lashes and works her lip between her teeth, she knows, too.

"You better get your sexy butt in the car. Now."

I use enough of the assertive tone she loves in the bedroom to make her eyes snap back to mine. Her pupils dilate a fraction, and her nipples turn into two hard points under the soft fabric of her dress.

She clears her throat. "Give me a minute to say my goodbyes and to get Charlie."

"I said now. You disobey me, wife." I lower my lips to hers, not kissing her, but breathing the words over the plump curve of her bottom lip, loud enough for only her to hear. "There will be consequences."

"Promise?" she asks in a breathy whisper.

"You can count on it."

She stares at me with the heated, adoring look that tells me she loves me for who I am, and that no matter what, she'll always be there for me.

"I love you, too," I say as she makes to turn.

"I didn't say I love you," she says with a mischievous smile.

"Yes, you did."

In a few minutes she'll be screaming it, too, in the only language that matters.

A language that surpasses words and time.

A language of love and forever.

Our unique language.

~ THE END ~

ALSO BY CHARMAINE PAULS

Standalone Novels

(Enemies-to-Lovers Dark Romance)

Darker Than Love

(Second Chance Romance)

Catch Me Twice

Diamond Magnate Novels

(Dark Romance)

Standalone Novel

(Dark Forced Marriage Romance)

Beauty in the Broken

Diamonds are Forever Trilogy

(Dark Mafia Romance)

Diamonds in the Dust

Diamonds in the Rough

Diamonds are Forever

Box Set

The Loan Shark Duet

(Dark Mafia Romance)

Dubious

Consent

Box Set

The Age Between Us Duet

(Older Woman Younger Man Romance)

Old Enough

Young Enough

Box Set

Krinar World Novels

(Futuristic Romance)

The Krinar Experiment

The Krinar's Informant

Seven Forbidden Arts Series

(Dark Paranormal Romance)

Pyromancist (Fire)

Aeromancist, The Beginning (Prequel)

Aeromancist (Air)

Audiobooks

Standalone Novels

(Enemies-to-Lovers Dark Romance)

Darker Than Love

Diamond Magnate Novels

Standalone Novel

(Dark Forced Marriage Romance)

Beauty in the Broken

Diamonds are Forever Trilogy

(Dark Mafia Romance)

Diamonds in the Dust

Diamonds in the Rough

Diamonds are Forever

Box Set

The Loan Shark Duet

(Dark Mafia Romance)

Dubious

Consent

Krinar World Novels

(Futuristic Romance)

The Krinar's Informant

ABOUT THE AUTHOR

Charmaine Pauls was born in Bloemfontein, South Africa. She obtained a degree in Communication at the University of Potchefstroom and followed a diverse career path in journalism, public relations, advertising, communication, and brand marketing. Her writing has always been an integral part of her professions.

When she moved to Chile with her French husband, she started writing full-time. She has been publishing novels and short stories since 2011. Charmaine currently lives in Montpellier, France with her family. Their household is a lively mix of Afrikaans, English, French, and Spanish.

Join Charmaine's mailing list
https://charmainepauls.com/subscribe/

Join Charmaine's readers' group on Facebook
http://bit.ly/CPaulsFBGroup

Read more about Charmaine's novels and short stories on
https://charmainepauls.com

Connect with Charmaine

Facebook

http://bit.ly/Charmaine-Pauls-Facebook

Amazon
http://bit.ly/Charmaine-Pauls-Amazon

Goodreads
http://bit.ly/Charmaine-Pauls-Goodreads

Twitter
https://twitter.com/CharmainePauls

Instagram
https://instagram.com/charmainepaulsbooks

BookBub
http://bit.ly/CPaulsBB

Printed in Great Britain
by Amazon